I0822764

Also by the author

The Pond Dwellers

The Emerald Series Vol I

Includes The Karensa Emerald

Emerald Fire Burning Bright

The Emerald Series Vol II

Includes Emerald Earth, Emerald Ice

Emerald Mists

Emerald Rivers

Available separate as ebooks:

The Karensa Emerald

Emerald Fire Burning Bright

Emerald Earth, Emerald Ice

Sequel to The Pond Dwellers

From Common Stream
to Commonwealth:

An American family's journey from
Puritans to Patriots

KELLY SAVAGE

ISBN: 979-8-9886888-2-2
LCCN: 2023913222
Desert Lion Press, McNeal, AZ

Rifle photo: John Spitzer, Wikipedia

Dedication

This book is dedicated to the memory of the brave settlers who fled tyranny in order to establish a new country with liberty and justice for all.

And to my children
Edward Patrick Carroll
Karensa Jo-Agatha Disiena
that they and their children and grandchildren will know about the land once held precious by the Nipmuck tribe as told in The Pond Dwellers and later by
Sons (and Daughters) of Liberty.

CONTENTS

Sequel to The Pond Dwellers

From Common Stream to Commonwealth:

An American family's journey from Puritans to Patriots

KELLY SAVAGE

PREFACE

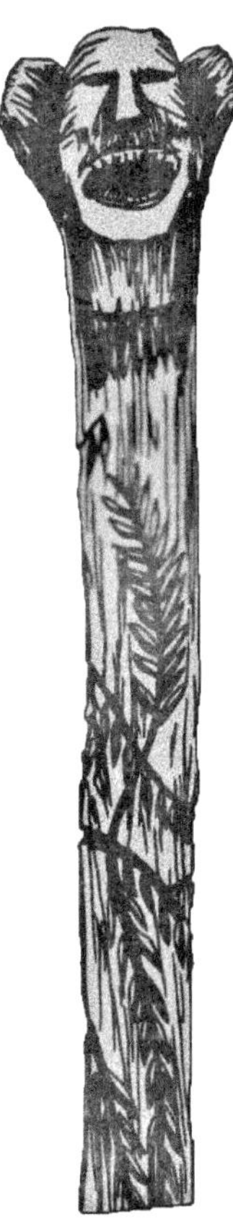

This story is the sequel to *The Pond Dwellers.*

In 1957 my family moved into an old farmhouse on the Massachusetts-Connecticut border and found this Native American war club stuffed into the foundation stones along with a silver hair comb and a silver Liberty dollar.

In an attempt to track down how the club came to be there I researched the original people who lived in that area. and wrote the above-referenced book. In the process I discovered the war club was not from the Central Massachusetts Nipmuc tribe but from a Penobscot tribe in Maine. Further research discovered that the man who built our farmhouse was Tristrum Davis who served as a captain in the French and Indian Wars in Maine and it was probably his war trophy. This story attempts to tell, beginning with his ancestors, how Tristrum Davis from Wales, Great Britain came to settle down in what is now named Wales, Massachusetts.

The Davis family was just one of many who helped settle New England, and I have used artistic license in its genealogy in order to represent how an extended British family might have come across the Atlantic Ocean and dispersed throughout New England and the Southern colonies plus the West Indies.

I attempted to follow the family lineage using the scant information available to me, but there are serious gaps in the data available online and in old New England records, so this work is not to be taken as a literal family genealogy but as a 'Micheneresque' historical family saga work of fiction with characters changed or added to progress the story. The author sincerely apologizes to any who might be offended by any errors and encourage those with missing information to contact me at DesertLion@Duck.com.

AUTHOR'S NOTE

WARNING: This book is not "politically correct" in that I told the tale of the settling of New England as seen through the eyes of the men and women who fled religious persecution but in turn persecuted the Native Americans they found on its shores.

I used the words 'indian' and 'savage' to refer to these people as that is what the people from the British Isles and Europe called them, not because I feel the terms are correct. And I showed their antipathy towards other nationalities, especially the French and Irish. The attitudes in this book are not mine as I have MicMac Native American blood in me and French through my French Canadian father plus Irish on the other side, but are an attempt to accurately reflect how Tristrum Davis and his friends and family would have felt in the 1500s – 1700s in England and New England. Likewise, the word negro was used for African Americans in this time period.

For the tale of the "Contact Era" North America 1620-1676 as seen through the different perspective of Native American eyes I refer the reader to my book *The Pond Dwellers*.

Native American words or names are italicized unless they became adopted by the English, such as *Shawomet*, which became Shawmut.

The men and women who fought to hold onto every square inch of the land they settled is told in these pages and to them the Native Americans were something, like the land, to be conquered and tamed.

Throughout its history Europeans in America, North, South and Central, conquered and drove off or forced Native Americans into 'Praying Villages' or 'Reservations' or to work on Spanish plantations. This is a fact and cannot be changed.

However, the reader needs to realize the tribes were constantly at war with each other even before the White Man came.

Greed knows no race: Lust for Power knows race. War knows no race.

Time changes names and usage of lands and waters but

Mother Earth cannot be owned by any one human race.

IN THE BEGINNING

The great pond saw many forms of life in its waters and on its shores. The river brought bits and pieces of the outside world to it: twigs dropped by beavers upstream, scraps of fish left by hawks or ospreys as they hastily gobbled a meal, ever watchful for foxes or wild cats in the trees or snapping turtles in shallow water near the banks. The rivers brought clumps of deer brains, used by the female humans who lived at the outlet of the ponds as they tanned deer hides. Flakes of stone and slivers of wood bobbed and swirled on the fresh, cold water, washed down from the rocks where boys sat chipping as they practiced making arrow or spear points or helped with canoe construction.

The trees that grew around it, some with roots that sheltered snakes and fish near its banks, were alive with the calls of crows, the songs of blue jays and robins, wrens and finches plus many more day and night birds such as whippoorwills and owls; and at night the bats swooped down over its silvery waves to snatch mosquitoes and flying insects.

The great pond gave life to fish, insects, birds, reptiles and mammals. Without water, life would not exist. Without water, the humans would not be able to live in the structures they built of bent saplings covered with bark shingles near its shores.

For many, many years the Great Pond* and the humans coexisted in the woodlands between the great sea, *Weshakim*, and the Long River, *Quonicticut*. It was one of many ponds, large and small along a path that was used by the deerskin-clad humans as they traveled from the coastal tribal lands to marry, trade with or make war on the river tribes.

The original humans called this area *Quansik.* Fair skinned humans later came and coveted their fertile, lush, resource-rich lands. They warred on the natives and drove them out. (Their story is told in the first book of this series, *The Pond Dwellers.)*

What follows is the story of the men and women who came in 'bird ships' across *Weshakim* to the shores of a land they named New England in honor of the country the first settlers came from. These people would spread inland and re-name the Native American sites after their villages, counties and cities in England. Eventually English cattle would drink the waters of the Great Pond and English men would fish and hunt along its shores. English songs would carry across its quiet waves and the sound of steel axes clearing forests and steel plows pulled by sturdy oxen furrowing the rocky soil would replace the gentle singing of the dark-eyed women with their clam shell hoes and baskets of fish as they planted the 'Three Sisters' while the boys shot crude arrows to drive away the crows trying to steal the corn, bean and squash seeds.

A way of life that lived in harmony with nature ended when 'the knife men' came. The English cut down many trees for building structures or they shipped thick logs of formerly tall, stately oaks, elms, spruces, larches and pines back to England in the holds of their big wooden square masted ships. They tapped the maples for its sugary sap.

Forests of trees were replaced by fields of wheat, rye and corn and the big, docile animals the English called cows or the smaller docile beasts called sheep and goats grazed amongst the stumps. English pigs ran wild, digging up the ground. In addition to hunting the profusion of native fowl, they brought chickens and penned them into yards. They built stone walls and split rail fences and parceled out the rolling fields and forests.

To the English, the land was given to them by their god via their king, for their exclusive use. The forests represented wood to burn for heat and cooking, and fuel for kilns for bricks, pottery and metal smelting. Even the waters would eventually be brought under their control by damming and diverting the streams and rivers for irrigation and for water wheels to power grist and saw mills.

The pond was silent sentinel to the changes around it as its dark surface reflected the full moon above like a giant eye. It continued to provide its life-giving waters and eventually forgot the noises of the Nipmucs as British boys fished in it and British girls picked daisies by its shores. The stone people remembered but they, too, stood in silence as the world around them changed. In time, special humans would who arrive who could appreciate the energies hidden in the stones and they would whisper stories to them of their sisters, giant stone circles across the sea where earth magic still lived.

Many of the people settling around the Great Pond came from the southwestern part of England and Wales where many stone "henges" and tors had been constructed by an ancient race.

The story of how one of these settlers – who had also been a brave soldier – came to live near the Great Pond is told in the following story.

*Lake George, Wales, Massachusetts

CHAPTER ONE

From the Hills of Wales

1400s-1500s

First there was King Arthur and Gawain and the sorcerer Merlin. It is believed that the bones of Queen Guinevere and perhaps Arthur himself, lay near the border of Wales in graves at the Abbey of Glastonbury, west of Stonehenge.

Called Arthur Rhys or Rhiothan by the Welsh, the king was a legend throughout the wild hills and valleys of Wales. From his knight Gawain came the name of Davis (Davies or Davy, Daveys). It was translated as 'dragon' and Arthur's banner depicted a pendragon. Many wars were fought to keep the Celts of Wales free from Roman, Viking, Saxon and Norman invaders. By the sixteenth century the land was peopled with Saxons and Angles, or Anglo-Saxons, the English. Unfortunately, for the ancient Welsh by the seventeenth century the English finally conquered Wales, then Scotland and even their sister island to the west, Ireland., creating what is known as Great Britain.

Descended from Welsh royalty (King Hywel Dda, or Hywel the Good), Sir Griffith Hywel Davis's original territory was north Wales, which, two centuries earlier had been the final bastion against Edward I's conquest until its chief leader, Llwelyn was defeated and then killed in 1282.

During the conquest King Edward I had built a ring of massive castle-forts up and down the coast of Wales beginning with Flint in 1277, followed by Rhuddian, inland on the River Clwyd five years later and Conway in 1283 then Harlech and Caernafon and Beaumaris, which was built after a revolt in 1294. Edward burned the mighty Welsh castle of Powys. Each castle had a town around it and all but one were on the sea. Conway had a cathedral and the last, Beaumaris, was on Anglesey, a strategically important coastal part of Wales as it bordered Scotland and wasn't far from Ireland. This sector of Wales was Davis country.

Sir Griffith Hywel Davis was born in 1450, a descendant of the Prince of Powys. As was the common practice amongst the Welsh they used the title Prince instead of King and their kingdoms were self-governing as Wales, unlike England, consisted of a conglomerate of chieftain kings – as did Scotland and Ireland. Until the Edwards' reigns the border of England and Wales was controlled by "March" or Marcher Lords who acted as a buffer, sometimes siding with the Welsh and at other times with the English, depending on who would benefit them the most.

****

By the late 1400s Sir Griffith Davis and his wife Lady Sage Thomas, (daughter of Rhys ap Thomas, who helped Henry VII at Bosworth come to the throne and was liberally rewarded with land for gaining Welsh support for the Tudors) had two sons that lived to maturity: Sir John, born in 1470 and Sir James Griffen Davis, born in 1487. *This book attempts to approximately follow their progeny into New England, Virginia and the West Indies.*

Daughters took the surnames of their husbands but most marriages at the time were political, to enhance the family's finances and property. Through marriage Sir Griffith came into more lands in southwestern Wales and even southwestern England. *(Although very important, this book doesn't concentrate on marriages of the daughters as, with just two sons there are plenty of sons, grandsons, great-grandsons, cousins, etc. follow.)* Marriages between gentry often involved the husband gaining estates bestowed upon the wives as dowries. Male titles could be passed down through the females to their husbands or skip generations. (In New England titles came to mean nothing after The Revolutionary War.)

As stated, Sir Gufford, (also spelled Griffen or Griffith) Hywel Rhys (Rice) Davis was descended from Welsh royalty. In the last quarter of the fifteenth century he married Lady Sage Thomas, daughter of Sir Rhys ap Thomas (ap meant 'son of' and was used in lieu of a surname in Wales). Thomas was a soldier for King Henry VII and had been knighted after he quelled the Cornish Rebellion in Southwest England in 1497. Because of his service to Henry Tudor in the Battle of Bosworth in 1485 against Richard III he had been rewarded with vast land grants in southern Wales and was appointed Chief Justice of southern Wales in 1505 plus made a knight of the garter. He had a castle at Caeriw (Carew). Through a later marriage (and king) the Davises and Thomases along with other favored families received lands formerly owned by the Catholic church when King Henry VIII dissolved the monasteries and abbeys and gifted or sold their vast holdings to men who wanted titles and status.

Griffith Hywel Davis's brother Thomas ap Griffith was with Good Old Harry at Val d'Or for the peace treaty on the Field of Cloth of Gold with Francis I in 1520. Unfortunately he perished from his battle wounds in 1525, preceded by his son.

Thomas ap Griffith's grandson Rhys ap Griffith got the familial lands but wasn't liked by King Henry VIII as he opposed his anti-Catholicism and adulterous relationship with Anne Boleyn. In 1520 he led an uprising in Wales and was accused by King Henry VIII of plotting with the Scots to become king of Wales after he adopted the title Fitz Urien. He was captured and executed in December, 1530 and most of the familial lands in Glamorgan and Pembroke were given to Walter Devereaux, Earl of Essex, steward of the Princess Mary's household at Warwick Castle.

Rhys ap Griffith had married Catherine St. John, granddaughter of Sir Oliver St. John and Margaret Beauchamp of Wiltshire, grandmother of Henry VII and heiress of vast land tracts in Wiltshire, Dorset and Bedfordshire. She was daughter of Sir John Beauchamp and Edith Stounton. John Boeufort had been titled first duke of Somerset under King Henry VII. The influential Howards were related to the Tudors and Charles, Earl of Somerset, who was second only to Rhys as a chief prince of the Welsh. William Howard First Baron of Effingham was uncle to Lady Catherine Howard and great-uncle to princess Elizabeth. (He had protected the princess and under Queen Elizabeth he held the posts of Lord High Admiral, Lord of the Chamberlain and Lord of the Privy Seal. His son Charles Howard became Lord High Admiral for the Queen against the Spanish Armada.) Howard's mother was heiress of Baron Audley of Walden.

After Griffith's execution his widow Catherine married Henry, Second Baron of Daubney who served at Henry VIII's court. He was the second son of Sir Giles Daubney and Margaret Beauchamp, of Barrington Court. and South Petherton in Somerset.

The Howards were cousins of the Boleyns and Catherine Howard became King Henry VIII's fifth wife (executed as Anne Boleyn had been). Bessie Blount, niece of Lord Mountjoy (Munjoy), had birthed Henry VIII's illegitimate son, Henry Fitzroy.

Fitzroy married Mary Howard and was given multiple titles by Henry VIII: duke of Richmond, earl of Somerset, earl of Worcester and earl of Nottingham.

The First Duke of Somerset, John Boeufort, was father to Margaret Boeufort and through the mother's line Fitzroy inherited Margaret's lands. Margaret Boeufort, daughter of Margaret Beauchamp and mother to Henry VII, loved education and founded two colleges at Cambridge – Christ's and St. John's. Her brother Henry was earl of Surrey and Lord High Admiral. After Henry VIII came to power he was elevated to earl of Bridgwater in Somerset. Because Griffith's widow was a favorite of Edward IV's wife Elizabeth Woodville, she asked of her that lands in Pembrokeshire and Wiltshire be returned to the Davis men and many, but not all, were restored.

The intrigues and jockeying for power went on for years until King Henry VII. The Queen Mother, royal matriarch Margaret Beauchamp/Boeufort/Stanley, lived to an old age and actively oversaw her sons and grandsons upbringing and it was she that arranged young Arthur's marriage to Catherine of Aragon and after his death her remarriage to Henry.

Henry VIII was the last Tudor king but he and his predecessors didn't attain power on their own. The Lancaster line had enjoyed the support of the north of England, south of Wales and the West Country during the War of the Roses. His York ancestors had wrested the throne from Henry VI and had the support of central and eastern dukes and earls. The Tudors were from Wales. In the turbulent years prior to Henry VIII taking the throne of England, the island that contains Scotland, England and Wales and its neighbor, Ireland were in constant battles, amongst themselves and with France and Spain. At any given time, one could suddenly find themselves on the wrong side of the conflict. For peasants in England, Scotland and Wales this could mean soldiers crashing through their fields, confiscating food and drink, raping their women, plundering and often conscripting males for militiary service. In Ireland, the English invaded, conquered and drove the people off their lands, out of their homes, forcing them to flee to the bogs and hills where many died of starvation.

Since Great Britain was comprised of islands, its coastlines were perpetually in danger of invasion from France, Spain or the Dutch. For centuries before New England began, English kings played a never-ending game of diplomacy and fought almost constant wars, winning land across the English Channel in France (Normandy) and even down to the wine-rich Spanish Aquitaine, then losing it. To finance its wars, the crown depended on its richest citizens. Thus, titles of dukes, earls, barons, marquis and others were sold along with vast amounts of land that had once belonged to the church and then the crown. During the Wars of the Roses titles and properties constantly shifted as York kings confiscated Lancaster properties and gave them to their favorites, then the lands and titles were given back when Lancasters regained power.

The War of the Roses finally ended when Henry VII came to power. Henry VIII's sister Margaret married James IV of Scotland, who was a Stuart. Henry VIII had Lancaster, York and Tudor blood so England's internal strife ceased for a while. But beneath the surface many hearts still harbored anger and hatred over the injustices, cruelties, executions and confiscations that had affected their families for decades.

It was during the ascent of the Tudors that the story of New England Davis settlers began with Sir Griffith Hywel Davis''s two sons: Sir John Davis and Sir James Davis. Like the Howards, they were a seafaring family. They helped with the exploration and settlement of what was then called the New World, later New England, Virginia and separate states.

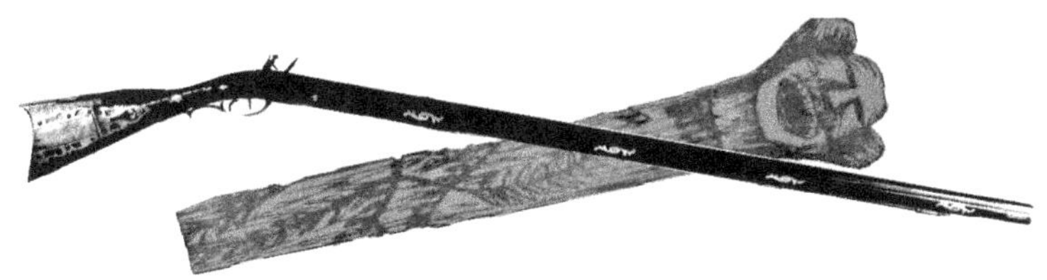

CHAPTER TWO

The Davis Family Rises in England

As New England became settled and then became a new country, separate from Great Britain, titles and royal links became important only in Great Britain and were of little to no importance to the Thirteen Colonies. I present the following to show how influence at Court and with the aristocracy were important for families seeking to take part in discoveries and to lay claim to lands so discovered in the early years of North America.

SIR JOHN DAVIS

Sir John was born in 1470 and settled in Acton-Turville which is 17 miles east of the port of Bristol at the mouth of the Avon and near the Cotswolds.

He had Sir John the Second in 1500.

Sir John the Second had Sir John the Third in 1520 who settled on an estate in Creedy. The Creedy estate would become the main manor for Sir John's line and title. Later, the estate was expanded with a new manor home.

Sir John the Second had a James, who settled on a large farming estate in Stoke Gabriel north of the port of Dartmouth. Sir John's son James had John in 1550 (who became a famous navigator-explorer). John the navigator married Faith Fulford, daughter of the high sheriff of the county. The Fulfords were a very influential southwestern England family. John and Faith had only one son, Philip Francis.

Sir John the Second also had Robert John (called Robert) in 1530, who became a sea captain and fathered William, George and Richard. William married into the Smythe (Smith) family and was a successful ship owner-shipper in the Bristol area. William and George invested heavily in the northern colonies of New England whereas their cousins Captains James and Thomas initially concentrated on Virginia. Smith was also indicative of the sideline the Davis men had: metal smithing.

Sir John the Second had Edmund who fathered Matthew, John and Barnaby. Edmund, like his father was a gentrified farmer. He settled in Tisbury, Wiltshire. He had a dairy, tannery and raised large flocks of sheep for the woolen industry. Edmund's son Matthew became an Inner Temple barrister (lawyer who can present cases before the 'bar') in London and later was the agent for Matthew Craddock. Edmund's son John, born in 1569, was also a barrister and became Chief Justice for Ireland later; Barnaby became a surveyor in the New England.

SIR JAMES

Sir Griffith's son Sir James, born in 1487, was tall, handsome and, as was the case with many Welshmen at the time, married young. He became romantically involved with Lady Maude Verche Morgan when he was only 13 and she was 20. She belonged to the Morgan clan which controlled most of Glamorganshire, in southern Wales.

Their eldest son, Sir David, was born in 1500. He married Lady Elizabeth Stradling of Caernarfonshire, Wales. Her mother was Lady Arundel whose family had owned Wardour Castle in Wiltshire before it went to the Howards. Her family and the Thomases and Howards later received the abbey lands in Tisbury, Wiltshire during the Dissolution of the Monasteries. David's wife was also related to the Talbots, who owned most of Wiltshire. (The wealthy aristocracy were mostly intermarried and many were politically connected at court. or in Parliament.)

David and Elizabeth's son James Thomas ap Griffith (called Thomas,) was born in 1520. He later became treasurer of Wales during Queen Elizabeth's reign from 1550-1601. Thomas became linked to the wealthy Chandler family from Gloucestershire and they lived on an estate in Acton Turville in Wiltshire after he married Lady Agnes Horton Sammons of Chandler. As Clerk of the Exchequer he was in a unique position to get financing for explorations and settlements in the New World, later called New England, Virginia (Elizabeth was considered to be the Virgin Queen) and sugar cane plantations in the West Indies plus helped get his nephew John appointed as Chief Justice of Ireland where the English were scooping up land for vast estates, called plantations.

Sir James and Lady Maud's second and third sons were twins Sir John and David the Younger, born in 1506. Twins ran in the Davis family.

Sir John married Lady Elizabeth Lawrence. He got most of the Dinefwr, Welsh lands. He became a knight of Donnington. She was related to the influential Talbot family.

Sir John's twin David was called David the Younger. (Generally a name was used twice when the first child was sickly and not expected to live to adulthood, or to show respect to an ancestor. David is a very sacred name to the Welsh as they believed Saint David started the first religious houses in Wales.) Unlike the first David who was a gentry farmer in Wiltshire, this David went to college and became the Church of England vicar of St. David's cathedral during the reign of Henry VIII. He had a son Richard who was a vicar and a grandson William who became a priest at Beaumaris in Bulkeley territory. Most of David and Elizabeth's relations lived in Wales.

David the older and Elizabeth had James Thomas in 1530, called Thomas. He married Agnes Chandler (related to Agnes Samone of Chandler) and they had Thomas in 1550; Sir John in 1560 and Robert in 1564. Robert was born near Grimstone, Devon and he sailed with Sir Walter Raleigh. He was a sea captain and married Marie Warren from Dorchester. Thomas junior had James in 1574, who also became a sea captain with interests in Virginia as well as New England. John lived in Easton Royale and married several times. Thomas's son James and his wife Cicely Thayer immigrated to Virginia and New England (as did Capt. James who helped his father Thomas settle their Virginia plantations).

By the mid-1500s the Davises had many estates in Wales and southwestern England including Easton Royale, three miles east of Pewsey and five miles south of Marlborough along an important trade route from London to Wiltshire. The Seymours had gotten Easton Priory with its four farms, manor house and chapel during the Dissolution as William Seymour's wife was a Devereaux. Easton Royale and Creedy were two of the Davis estates Margaret had gotten Queen Elizabeth to restore to the Davis family. They also had one in Kent, obtained as a reward years before when another Davis ancestor served valiantly under King Henry VII.

Sir James's son Sir John became involved in ship owning, captaining and the lucrative sea trade with coastal Europe.

The last son of Sir James Thomas and Lady Maude was James Thomas Rhys (or Rice), born in 1509. He became a vicar in Griffith, near Conway, Wales.

1509 was also the year Henry VIII came to the throne after the death of his father, King Henry VII. Arthur was the heir and had been briefly married to Catherine of Aragon but after his early death the marriage was annulled. King Henry VII was then supposed to marry Catherine but it didn't happen and after his death his son Henry VIII became king and married her. (As was common among the royals, marriage was a political alliance. This one was crucial as it bonded England and Spain.)

Sir James the First's great-grandson John emigrated to the New England. He and his different wives (serial marriages were common as men often lived into their eighties or nineties and outlived the women) had twins John and James in 1584; Samuel in 1587; a second Samuel in 1593 and Thomas in 1601.

In New England Sir James's great grandson Thomas helped found Haverhilll, Massachusetts but later moved to Virginia where he had a huge tobacco plantation. He also had a sugar plantation in the Barbados. He was also involved in ship building, sailing or trading with Europe and the West Indies.

As was the case with the Welsh gentry they often moved between estates in southwestern England or Wales, which was just across the channel. During the height of the summer London and English cities were full of what was called plague: a fever illness that would kill large numbers of people. And smallpox was rife in the cities, too. Most wealthy English escaped to their countryside manors during those outbreaks.

However, the old ways were on the verge of change as Sir John and Sir James's generation passed away. In the first half of the sixteenth century new lands were being discovered and claimed. Wars on the continent were being fought on land and sea but most of the gentry were doing very well in the wool export trade and wine import trade.

New land discoveries and the rise of Puritanism would expand the interests and territories of the old families and eventually shift their power base to the New World and away from England. By the middle of the eighteenth century England would claim most of the land between the St. Lawrence River and Georgia; France those west of the Mississippi River and a small part of Canada and Florida and the Dutch, at their peak in the early years, eventually lost their hold in the New World. At the end of the empirical colonizing phase most of the New World's Central and South America were claimed and colonized by Spain and the West Indies would be divided.

CHAPTER THREE

The Reign of Henry VIII

Henry VIII was crowned in 1509. He had Lancaster blood via John of Gaunt's Henry's IV-VI relatives and Margaret Beauchamp and Welsh Tudor blood through Owain's (Gawain's) son Edmund plus Plantagenet and York blood through his mother Elizabeth, who married Edmund's son Henry VII. Henry VIII married his brother's wife, the widow, Catherine of Aragon.

In 1513 James IV of Scotland led a revolt against England and was killed at the Battle of Flodden. His infant son James V became king, with his mother Margaret Tudor, Henry VIII's sister, his regent. This led to unrest and Margaret had to escape across the border to England.

In 1516 Henry VIII and Catherine of Aragon had a daughter, Mary. Affairs on the Continent were unsettled but Harry signed a treaty with Emperor Charles V at Canterbury and shortly afterwards Charles V was crowned Emperor of the Holy Roman empire in Charlemagne"s magnificent arched throne room of banded stone at Aix-la-Chapelle.

In 1526 Charles V married Princess Isabella of Portugal. Peace was declared between England, Scotland (ruled by the Stuart King James V) and France. However, hostilities continued between the Germans, Spanish and French and in 1527 Rome was sacked and Pope Clement VII was imprisoned in Castel Sant' Angelo. The defeat of the Catholic church in Rome emboldened King Henry VIII to sue for divorce from Catherine who had not produced a male heir to the English throne when his young mistress Anne Boleyn was promising to produce one.

King Henry VIII faced severe backlash from the weavers in Kent in 1528 when he allowed the Cardinal Thomas Wolsey to shift the wool staple town to Calais, replacing Antwerp where many merchants, including the Davis men, had agents. This shift in the wool finishing market seriously affected the English wool trade and the Davis family that had large flocks in Devonshire, Gloucestershire, Denbighshire and Wales.

At the same time King Henry VIII picked a fight, one with an extremely powerful figure, the head of an empire: the Holy Roman Church and its pope. Catholicism was basically the religion of Great Britain, brought over by the Catholic Normans and missionary priests, but following Luther's posting of 95 protests, or his thesis, in Wittenberg in 1517, a new religion was born. By the mid-1500s 'Protestantism' had taken hold in the hearts of many people. Henry VIII capitalized on this to throw off the yoke of Imperial Rome on Great Britain. He declared himself Supreme Head of the Church of England, which also threw off the established Catholic, or popish, masses, transubstantiation, statues, rites, etc. (but replaced them with a very similar Church of England system). He divorced Catherine and married Anne Boleyn, who gave birth to a daughter, Elizabeth (to his great disappointment), in 1533. This began a procession of royal wives and divorces or executions as Henry VIII desperately sought a male heir. Jane Seymour from Wolf Hall, Wiltshire, finally birthed a son in 1537 but she died 11 days after the future king Edward VI's birth.

In 1536 King Henry VIII declared 'Ten Articles of Faith' in order to transfer power from the Church to the King. In rebelling against the papal authority he unleashed a rebellion against Catholic dogma; the Protestants preached that salvation was obtained through faith and not through absolution by priests, or buying intercessions through the Catholic church. Later, a further breach in Protestantism occurred between those who quoted the apostle Paul when he wrote to the Romans and Ephesians, that "The grace of God, life everlasting, in Christ Jesus our Lord is a gift " and "...by Grace you are saved through faith, and that not of yourselves for it is the gift of God." This set up a conflict between Protestants who believed Grace was not obtained through Good Works but given freely by God to His Elect, or

Saints. The Calvinists-Puritans believed only a personal spiritual experience would let a person know they were saved and were guaranteed a place in Heaven after death. People cared very much about the fate of their souls in the afterlife.

After Henry VIII declared himself head of the Church of England the crown ripped vast properties and lands out of the hands of the Catholic church and drove out or executed cardinals, bishops, priests, monks and nuns. Three centuries later King Henry VIII had succeeded where Henry II had failed in 1170 when he tried to take over the power of the church by having Archbishop Thomas Becket executed.

Repeatedly the peasants had to choose: keep their Catholic faith and die or convert and swear an oath of allegiance to Henry VIII as supreme leader of England in all material matters plus in spiritual ones. Most complied. The Catholic Irish fought and were massacred. In the name of religion English lords "planted" new settlements in Ulster after driving away the Irish who had lived there all their lives. These were the first 'plantations'.

In time the anger and resentments engendered by arrogant royal interference with a peoples' religion simmered and would emerge in a bloody civil war led by Oliver Cromwell and his Parliamentarians.

By the late 1500s some of the Protestants felt the new state religion didn't go far enough to separate itself from the Catholic church and they were called Puritans by those who were contented with the new law of the land. Symbols of the Catholic religion such as statues, altar roods, or screens, altar rails and anything that elevated the minister to a priestly status were rejected. To them religion was a personal matter: a covenant between a person and God and a covenant between similarly minded Christians and their community. Some were so extreme that they claimed brothers and sisters in Christ were not answerable to any worldly king but only to God, and refused to pay money to support a Church of England they didn't belong to. This was tantamount to treason and these Separatists were persecuted, arrested, jailed or they escaped to the Netherlands, which was lenient towards religious beliefs.

There were others, though, who were very happy with Henry VIII and his successors as they reaped benefits from the crown. They bought titles and former Catholic lands, then paid "forced loans" to the crown for its extravagant needs and for its wars and militiary expenses. Once the practice of 'villein' was abolished and lords didn't have to provide private armies for the crown, the landlords forced locals off what had been common lands by building fences, or "enclosures" and putting sheep on once fertile fields. They found sheep more profitable than tenant farmers as, in spite of Wolsey, the woolen trade flourished and rich wool merchants such as the Davis men got richer by the day.

In 1536 King Henry VIII also issued an 'Act of Union' between Wales and England that took away the marches and set a permanent boundary line between Wales and its ruler, England. The new boundary didn't follow the traditional one of Offa's Dyke. 'The Act' allowed Wales to have its own justices of the peace (to hold its own courts), and later it added representation for Wales with Members of Parliament, or MPs although their number was scanty compared to those allotted the English boroughs. To emphasize Wales's subjugation, the Act banned the Welsh language at court: No one could hold a position of power unless they used English.

Henry VIII declared himself King of Ireland and head of the Irish Church in 1541. Five years later, at the urging of his council, he founded the English Navy and began a ship building program. Unlike his predecessor Henry VII, this king wasn't keen on exploring. Meanwhile, Spain was mining silver in Peru and loading ships to the brim with gold and silver from the New World.

However after Henry VIII died in 1547, his will which called for a council of 16 men to govern until young Edward attained maturity was altered by Dudley and others to make the rabidly Protestant Edward VI king, ruling without the above mentioned council in order to avoid Henry VIII's daughter, the Catholic Mary from taking power.

During Henry VIII's reign his son had been a fragile child and he died only six years after taking the throne. His two chief counselors were John Dudley, Duke of Northumberland and Earl of Warwick and Edward Seymour, Earl of Somerset. After Edward VI became king. Seymour was Protectorate and King Henry VIII's last queen, Catherine Parr, his step-mother at Court.

King Edward VI didn't live long and just weeks before he died after battling measles and smallpox, and knowing the end was near, Dudley married his son Guilford Dudley to Jane Grey. He had worked it so she would become queen and he would be at the right hand of the throne. (Grey was the granddaughter of Henry VIII's younger sister Mary Tudor.) Court intrigue followed the death of young Edward VI in 1553. Dudley put Lady Jane Grey on the throne but she only lasted nine days and Mary was then crowned as rightful heir. By 1554 Somerset, Dudley and Lady Jane had all been thrown into the Tower and executed as had been Edmund Dudley in 1510. England seemed to be a dangerous place for the Dudleys.

The Davis men were affected as they were linked by marriage to families such as the de Greys, Seymours, Carews and Walsinghams who controlled Norfolk and the West Country. North Wales, especially the counties of Flintshire and Powys, was Davis country, shared with the Dudleys, Bulkeleys of Beaumaris and Denbighyshire, Wynns of Gwydir and Perrots of Pembrokeshire. By the mid-1500s Robert Dudley was earl of Leicester and lord of Denbigh; the Devereaux were earls of Worcester and owned most of the manors in Monmouthshire and Gower. The earl of Somerset was married to a Hebert. The Heberts (or Herberts), were earls of Pembroke and owned most of Glamorganshire. The Rice and Talbot families were married into the mixture.

After young Edward VI's death the Seymours, a very rich and influential Wiltshire/Devonshire family who had served for decades at court, found themselves out as well as their rivals the Dudleys.

Mary took the throne, sending her half-sister Elizabeth to the Tower (under unfounded suspicion that she had conspired to usurp her). Then Mary married Prince Philip of Spain, Emperor Charles V's son.

Queen Mary was barren and, unfortunately, like her Spanish mother, was a fanatical Catholic and the roller coaster ride began again. People had to give up their allegiance to the new Protestant Church of England and become Catholic again or be burned as heretics. Mary was queen for only four years, but she was memorialized as Bloody Mary for her merciless persecution of Protestants.

In 1558 when Queen Mary died childless, the throne passed to her sister, Queen Elizabeth, the daughter of Anne Boleyn, the second of Henry VIII's six wives. Elizabeth's right to the Crown was later challenged by a Stuart cousin, Mary, Queen of Scots, but Elizabeth prevailed in the end.

Shortly after, in an act of defiance or national pride, Richard Davis, Bishop at St. David's (where his father David the Younger was vicar) published a New Testament in the Welsh language and declared every parish church in Wales would receive a copy by 1567. Queen Elizabeth retaliated with the Act of 1563 in which every Welsh church was ordered to have a copy of the Bible written in English.

During Mary's brief reign William Davis, grandson of David the Younger had become a Catholic priest and served in the cathedral next to Beaumaris Castle. He was one of the Welsh priests who refused to change his faith back to the Church of England. In 1593 Queen Elizabeth had him hanged as a traitor in the huge multi-towered cinnamon colored castle by the sea where he had often held services in its lovely vaulted chapel.

By Queen Elizabeth's reign the Davis men had become heavily involved in ship owning and sailing for trade or exploration.

Sir Thomas Davis (now Treasurer of Wales) had Thomas in 1550, John in 1560, Robert in 1564 and James in 1572. All took to the sea to make their fortunes, captaining or owning ships that sailed back and forth from England to the New World and West Indies. His cousins William and George in Bristol were likewise engaged in trade with the New England and his cousin John in exploring. When Elizabeth came to the throne the Davis men added a new dimension to their English, Welsh and Irish interests and shifted away from France and the Levant.

CHAPTER FOUR

Under a King, then a Queen

James Rhyes.(sometimes just called Rhys) was younger than his brother John, the main heir of Sir John of Creedy He had brothers Robert and Edmond as well.

Through ancestors or marriages the Davis fortunes were intertwined with the wealthy Wiltshire Popham, Philps or (Phips or Phillips), Beauchamps, Carews, Raleighs, plus Somerset families such as the Gorges of Wraxall, Pauletts, Sydenhams and Trevelyans plus Nicholas Wadham who later founded Oxford University in 1609. (The Welsh always put a high premium on learning, gauging a man's worth by his mental wealth instead of his material wealth.)

Sir James's uncle Sir David also had a son named James, born in 1530, who settled in Acton Turville.

Sir John lived near Marlborough. There, like his son Edmund he had a prosperous dairy and sheep farm, a large, solid grey stone manor house, and although not a castle, his holdings there and elsewhere were big enough for him to be considered gentry and to enjoy the company of men such as Sir Humphrey Gilbert, Sir Walter Raleigh, Sir Alexander Popham (later Chief Justice of England who built a large manor in Monacute from brown stone quarried in Yeovil), Sir Ferdinando Gorges, Sir George Somers, George Weymouth, the Seymour clan and Sir Richard Grenville. He had enough assets to be a co-owner of trading ships and he put his energies into the East and West Indies trade.

At first, there was a lucrative West Indian pirate business as the Spanish galleons were loaded with silver and gold from central and south America. And later, there was colonizing and the export of items such as tobacco, sugar and rum from south Virginia and the Caribbean (West Indies) islands such as Barbados. From his association with Queen Elizabeth, King James I, Sir Walter Raleigh and Capt. James Smith (who later founded Jamestown), his cousin Sir Thomas Davis was granted large parcels of land in Virginia. He never settled there but his descendants James and Thomas got his grants and one emigrated there with his third wife when he was in his old age. (Blessed with good health, the Davis men who weren't killed in wars or by epidemics lived into their nineties, and, as was common during these years, fathered large families due to successively younger wives. A wife was absolutely essential for a farmer as she looked after the domestic needs, leaving the man to run the estate.)

By the early 1600s his cousins Thomas and Robert Davis captained or were masters of large trading vessels such as the *Mary and John* that sailed from England and up and down the coast of the Virginia.

James's son John, with the help of financing arranged by Adrien Gilbert, led three expeditions to find the Northwest Passage. Additionally, he sailed as a navigator with men such as Hawkins; Lancaster and Cavendish but met his end at the hands of Chinese pirates in the far Pacific where he was overseeing the English trading spice post in Malaysia. Spice became the most important item in the late 1500s and early 1600s as nutmeg was considered to be able to ward off the many epidemics of miasma-born plague that swept through London and the bigger cities. Nutmeg, cinnamon, cloves and black pepper were in demand, both for medicinal and flavoring since the taste of spoiling meat could be masked by heavily peppering and spicing it.

The woolen cloth industry that had made the Davis brothers' fortunes in southwestern England suffered during Queen Elizabeth's constant wars. The importation of French and Spanish wines, a major trade item, had been interrupted due to her quarrels and many merchants went bankrupt during the old queen's reign.

EXPLORERS

Preceded by Portugal, France and Spain, the English Captain John Rut explored from Newfoundland all the way down to where land ended in Florida and continued southeast to the West Indies in 1527.

Captain John Hawkins followed his route in 1565 to the tip of Florida but it wasn't until Sir Humphrey Gilbert in 1583 that a small trading post settlement was attempted on the northern coast of Virginia. Gilbert himself was lost at sea when his ship, the *Dainty,* foundered on rocks off the coast of Sable Island far to the north.

Companies of wealthy men were formed for these explorations as the cost of purchasing ships, repairing and outfitting them for long voyages, with no guarantee of their return, or of their return with valuable goods, was a speculation only men with money to spare could indulge in.

Sir James's brother Edward (Edmund) had no stomach for the sea. He lived on an estate in Tisbury, Wiltshire but was very sickly. He had sons John, Matthew and Barnaby. The first two, like their father, had weak constitutions and did not take to the sea, preferring to manage large estates John and Matthew took to the law.

James lived north of Dartmouth in Devon outside Sandridge Stoke Gabriel in Sandridge Barton. The area had Hathaway House with elaborate arched Doric columns and a two story entry portico built of brick covered by chalk cobble. Other great manors the Davis family visited or resided in included Chesthurst Great Hall near Waltham Abbey, built by Henry VIII for Cardinal Wolsey on the former Shaw estate; Ashyn's Hall and the Seymour's Somerset House in Wiltshire. just outside St. Albans, constructed in 1563 by Sir Nicolas Bacon, Keeper of the Great Seal.

James was a gentry farmer and his son John grew up with the Gilbert family, wealthy mariners, friends of Sir Ferdinando Gorges, Sir Walter Raleigh, Georges Popham, Sir Francis Drake, Henry Cabot and Sir James Cavendish.

Queen Elizabeth favored Sir Gilbert and helped raised funds for his voyages to the East Indies. John Davis was a navigator and he sailed with Sir Francis Drake to explore the Dutch and Spanish monopolized East Indies in 1577 then the northwest seas looking for a Northwest Passage to the Spice Islands.

Queen Elizabeth also helped Thomas Cavendish in his East Indies and Newfoundland/Arctic explorations. and John Davies (as he spelled it) had sailed into the large straight hoping to find the Spice Islands. He was unsuccessful but the waterway was named the Davis Straights after him.

Unfortunately, John got on the bad side of Cavendish when, during a failed attempt on the NW Passage in 1592 during bad weather he turned his ship back to England, forever inciting the ire of Cavendish. John Davis was also the author of *The Secrets of the Sea* and inventor of the backstaff quadrant – a maritime measuring device that enabled navigators to read their positions with the sun at their back instead of glaring into their eyes. He died on a voyage to the East Indies for the East India trading company in 1602.

CAPTAIN ROBERT

While John was exploring, James's son Robert, born in Grimstone, Dorchester, set sail off the docks of Plymouth on an exploration expedition under Captain Martin Frobisher. They left seven months after Francis Drake's fleet of 15 sails loosed their anchors on an historic voyage that would go through the Magellan Straights and then through the South Seas and thence back to England.

Frobisher's fleet of 15 sails set out from Harwich, sailed down the Channel, rounded the south of England and Ireland and then sailed west in search of the Northwest Passage and of precious ores. Because of his famous brother, Robert was the first mate under Vice Admiral Gilbert Yorke in the *Thomas Allen*. Robert worked side by side with the chief pilot, Christopher Hall. Hall had accompanied Frobisher on his two earlier voyages as master of the *Gabriel*, which lost five men to the Eskimos before returning to England, and as master of the *Aid*, the expedition's admiral ship in 1577. Gilbert Yorke captained the bark *Michael* and William Smythe was master of the *Gabriel* during that voyage, which also included wealthy men from the financiers – the Carews, Staffords, Kinnersleys and more. The Carews were a sailing family, related to the Gilberts and Raleighs and even to distant Davises. On the third voyage William Smythe captained the *Gabriel*, which would later be captained by another relative, Samuel Davis.

A furnace was made on the estate of William Winter to smelt any ores found on the voyage and miners form Cornwall were signed on to work ore beds. Iron was a component of steel and also was used in casting cannon and many items used on ships. Also funding the expedition were the Warwicks, Walsingham, Pembrokes and other prominent gentry and noble men of vision.

The *Judith* and *Hopewell*, which was to make many transatlantic voyages over the next decades, along with the *Anne Francis* and Frobisher's admiral flagship *Aid* were in the convoy, which had been well provisioned for eighteen months at sea.

After six weeks with a brief stop at Greenland's shores to claim it for England, the fleet started up what Frobisher thought was Frobisher Bay, but he was wrong as it was at the latitude 62 degrees.10 North. For twenty days the fleet sailed up what Robert and Chris knew was the wrong straight. They and the *Anne Francis* turned back to the open sea, fighting a furious overfall at the bay's entrance. Frobisher and the rest of the fleet, minus the *Gabriel*, rejoined them a short time later and they sailed to the island Frobisher named Anne Warwick in honor of the Warwick matron, where they mined a vein of black rock from the previous voyage that some assayers in England believed contained silver ore. An iceberg hit the *Aid* as she was lowering her anchor, driving it through the bows. Her crew worked like devils to pump out the freezing water and the ship's carpenter was able to bolt a big sheet of lead over the hole once the cargo had been shifted and that side of the ship was angled slightly above the waterline.

The rest of the fleet joined them minus the *Thomas*, as her master had returned to England. Frobisher planned on leaving three ships and 100 men to operate the mine but, though it was early August, the ice was thickening on the seas and the cold was intolerable. The miners, a hardy lot, threatened mutiny and refused to be left on such a desolate, frigid place.

After doing a bit of exploring and naming spots after his sponsors, the tall, thin, finely bearded and mustached aristocratic Frobisher had to capitulate to their demands after the skies became alight with strange flashing lights – considered by all to be an ill omen. Robert and his crew were mining what they thought was gold ore from the Countess of Sussex mine and other captains in pinnaces were busy exploring the coast but they dutifully followed Frobisher as he headed back to England. He dropped anchor off Hall's Island to load more ore but Chris, or Chips, as he was called, said the pinnace they assembled wouldn't withstand the force of the ice and, sure enough, its nailed (and not oaken kneed) sides gave way while they returned from shore.

On the return voyage they stopped wherever they could find anything to re-provision their stores but the *Aid's* main yard cracked and she was swamped and pooped. Frobisher was on the *Gabriel* but the barks were overwhelmed by the *Aid's* crew and a sickness, aided by scurvy, infected the men and they had a sea funeral almost every day. The fleet couldn't stay together due to the stormy seas but The *Emanuel* managed to discover an island and name it the Busse of Bridgewater. It was bittersweet voyage. When they left Frobisher Bay they had high hopes of a great fortune but after arriving in mid-October in Bristol and London they found out they didn't have precious ores: their holds were full of useless black rocks. After his voyage in 1590 didn't find the Northwest Passage Frobisher never received another penny from the wealthy families and died an impoverished man.

Robert learned during those five months that expeditions were risky but he was still in love with the idea of finding a new passage or land mass.

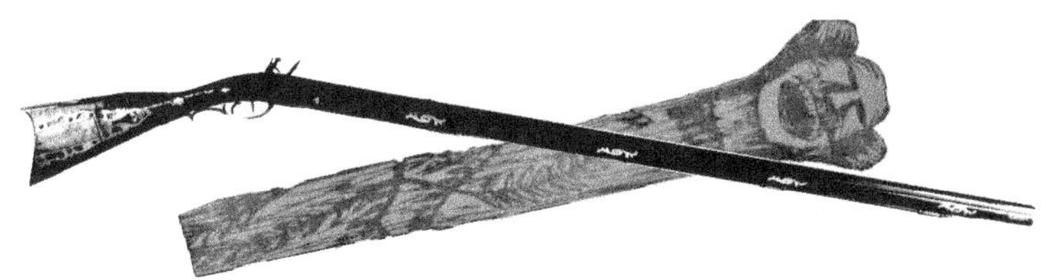

CHAPTER FIVE

England Establishes a New England

1570s

The story of New England actually began with a queen, the daughter of a king who descended from a line of Tudors after the War of the Roses in England and Wales.

But it was under Queen Elizabeth – who reigned for 45 years – that England began to seriously consider planting new colonies in the New World.

But before New England could be settled it had to be explored and the Davis men, who are the protagonists in this book, took an active part in the voyages of exploration.

Spain was fabulously rich at this time as it had 'found' South America and the Caribbean islands and was importing shiploads of Aztec and Inca gold and silver and spices and new foods such as potatoes and yams to Europe. The Azores islands were abundantly fertile and sugar cane, which made molasses, which made rum, was a huge export for any country that claimed land in the New World. But Spain was jealous of her treasure and her fleets hunted down and destroyed non-Spanish vessels in the Atlantic waters.

To a war-torn, resource-stripped land full of displaced tenants (and later persecuted Puritans), the New World with its boundless land and natural bounty beckoned across the sea.

1579

Robert Davis's earliest memories were of the sea. He was the third son of Sir (James) Thomas. His father lived in northern Wiltshire on the Gloucestershire border in the main manor on the large Acton-Turville estate, which was brought to the Davis family through his grandmother, the Lady Arundel.

Robert spent every minute he could with his relatives at the docks in Bristol, Bideford, Plymouth, Weymouth and Dartmouth when his Grandfather James met ships and inspected their cargoes. Occasionally he and his brother Richard, would sail in one of the Davis ships over to France or Spain for shipments of wine. Both countries liked the fat-rich English cheeses and butter that Devonshire produced in quantity.

When he wasn't onboard, Robert would sit in the rope galleries on the brine rich docks and learn how to tie the different knots each sailor needed to know for the yards and yards of rigging on the square sailed three masters that plied the Channel. Every sailor needed to know what blocks, or pulleys to haul up, where to secure the hempen ropes when the sails were hoisted or unfurled and how to move their yardarms or booms to gather wind but not rip the sails. He learned how to sew so he could repair a ripped sail and onboard he loved to climb the ratlines up to the top, sitting in the crow's nest to survey the ports.

Each port had its own character. Plymouth was a very serious port as it guarded the southern coast. Robert met Sir Francis Drake and later Sir Walter Raleigh when they docked there. He sat in the taverns with his cousin William of Bristol as they talked to captains, also called masters, upon return of their voyages and the brightest days of his life were when he visited his cousin John.

John was somewhat the black sheep of the family. He preferred pirating to merchant sailing, although in those days the captains were encouraged to overtake and pillage the ships flying the colors of whatever country England was at war with at the time. Usually it was the Spanish because they were Catholic and England was Protestant so Queen Elizabeth had declared their ships, often laden with gold and silver from South America, as fair game. But John was always talking about the explorers. He looked down on the merchant mariners as tame, whereas the explorers were wild and free to hunt for new lands and new routes.

Like most of the Davis men, John was medium in height. By the time he was 12 Robert was taller than most of his relatives (not a good trait to have onboard with low ceilings between decks). His mother said there was Viking blood in her family, whereas his father's side claimed almost pure Welsh.

The Davis men had estates in Wiltshire bordering the chalk flats where the big ring of standing stones and henge were; in the Pewsy Valley the big estate of Easton Royal; large farms on the River Dart and in Bristol and Somerset near the estates of their relatives the Gilberts and Gorges and in northern Wiltshire, plus an estate in Cheshire and a branch of the family had old monastery lands in Kent. They had large farms in Tisbury that had belonged to Catholic nuns. Most of the estates were rewards for service to their kings or queens as they fought on the Continent or the seas. The Davis men, though not imposing in stature, were big in bravery. The Davis men were men of action.

John was the dreamer of the lot. He wanted to see the whole world. He was friends with John Dee, the navigator, scientist scholar and often had a borrowed book from Dee's huge library in front of him as he sat in the taverns by himself. Robert liked to read, too, and like John he was a mixture of adventurer and scholar. He had the obligatory basic schooling but had no desire to go on to the higher colleges at Oxford or Cambridge, unlike his Welsh relative Richard who had become an Anglican priest in Glamorgan, (a dangerous thing to be under Bloody Mary's short reign) or his cousin William who was a priest and standing up to Queen Elizabeth by refusing to give up his Catholicism.

Robert's cousin John captained or navigated trading ships and from an early age took on Robert as an apprentice navigator. On shipboard he worked with his cousin every day, calling him over at noon to have him help with the daily navigational readings by taking compass readings. Like John, Robert loved mathematics, which were the cornerstone of accurate navigation. John explained to Robert how to use the backstaff, aligning it with the horizon and centering it in his sights, then measuring the angle of the sun behind them. He worked with him at night to take celestial readings, aligning his instruments with the moon, the North Star, the planets, their position in the zodiac signs. He showed him how to work a tide table so he could know if they were entering a harbor at low tide or high tide and explained how the tides were related to the phases of the moon. Using the minute, half hour and hour hourglasses, he showed him how to measure their speed, taking a reading of the sun or an object and then a measured reading at a one minute, half hour or hour interval to track their progress. He had a circle that showed the four directions and all the winds that could be registered so his daily log could record the year, date, longitude, course, leagues, wind and comments such as the compass varied a certain number of degrees in a certain direction. Navigating required the use of an ephemeris to find the Prime year, used to calculate the Epact. Over the years, John, not much older than Robert, taught him that for open sea sailing you had to know how much the planets shifted through their nine year cycle and you had to know where you were in the solar year and the lunar year, as they weren't the same. He showed him how to use a crude globe to measure latitudes and longitudes but the more accurate measurements were always latitudinal on the open seas. He instructed him in the use of the quadrant and astrolabe and how to use sea charts. Robert had a good grammar school education but (as was common amongst men who weren't preparing for the ministry or law) hadn't attended college. Yet his mind was as sharp as John's, able to make instant calculations of degrees, angles, minutes.

"Hey there, Robbie, hold it completely vertical, completely still else ye get a wrong reading!" he often told him as he learned how to use the yard long cross staff. John showed Robert how, by facing away from the noontime sun, his backstaff's shadow could be used on the circle to show their direction. For latitude he had to learn how to measure the height of the North Pole, via the moon, from the equator, which was invaluable in northern voyages.

"On open sea, ye are at the mercy of the wind. If she blows directly at ye, you have to steer either north or south of her a bit to keep yer sails from ripping. This will keep ye off yer true course, which ye have to compensate for and eventually ye try to regain the proper course, referring to your daily log to see how much ye've deviated. Cloudy days are the worst as ye can't get a clear noon reading. However, if ye have to take it during a little break in the clouds, make note of the time of day and ye can work out the math to figure out what it would have been at noon."

A navigator needed to know his maps, where the trade winds were, what direction they blew in different seasons, the tides of the different channels, how to read the sea for shoals or hidden reefs.

Every time he went out with John, Robert learned more and more of navigation and by the age of 17 he was piloting his father's ships over to France or the Levant. He learned how to handle the 60 to 200 tun three masters with square sails, the smaller pinnaces and the newer Dutch fly boats. Once he pulled away from shore it was all port, stern, starboard, aft, foresail, mizzenmast and the other nautical terms he'd been raised on.

It was Robert's dream to one day sail to parts unknown and discover a new path to the South Seas or to even unknown lands.

Even when Robert was at home he was in motion: riding with his father or grandfather to inspect the Grimstone farm near Dorchester or other estates or into Bristol to the ports and woolen manufactures. England basically had two export products: wool and dairy in the form of cheese or butter. The chalk downs were full of Dorset sheep, a hardy lot that could find sustenance in the roughest spots, and others parts of Devonshire were full of cattle and the moors had herds of wild ponies. The sheep produced wool, which had to be sheared in the spring, then it had to be picked, washed, carded, or combed, rolled into roves for spinning and then the yarn was woven into a variety of products. The finishing, or fulling, process determined what the final product would be, from soft flannels to thick felts. Most were in between, suitable for clothing and bedding. Ireland had a lot of flax and produced a nice linen, the strongest was used sail canvas, but a sturdy hemp canvas was used, too. Parts of the west country grew flax, too, but what Europe with its cold winters wanted were woolens. From his father he learned how to inspect a bag of wool and determine its quality from the length of its fibers. From his mother he learned about the quality of cheeses, the most famous being the fat rich Gloucestershire. And his father taught him about the different wines and how to taste a cask and judge if it went to the queen's cellars, the gentry's or to more common folk, who drank mostly home brewed beer, honeyed mead or cider. He had tasted a bit of rum, made from the sugar cane from South America (a favorite of sailors), and a bit of the strong hard, or distilled liquor the Scottish brewed but he mostly sipped whatever was put in front of him just to be polite. His father and his friends often drank port or sherry, but Robert actually preferred beer, or ale as it was called.

At home he would go out hunting and his father showed him and his brothers how to shoot arrows, first with shorter bows and then the longer ones the English excelled in. He learned how to pack a wad of powder and shot into a musket and how to light its touchhole and he had seen cannon fired at sea, which was very exciting. He went to the Raleigh, Seymours, Gilberts and Popham estates for deer hunts but hadn't yet bagged a stag. Everywhere he rode on the hills and dales of Devon he saw rivers and brooks. Small ships traveled the rivers, bringing goods to towns, taking goods out to the seaport towns, mostly for export. (Some were used for smuggling in goods to avoid the duties.) Craft ranged from small shallops with oars and a simple triangular sail to any that didn't ship too much water from deep keels. People fished with lines in the rivers and brooks and off the coasts they also used lines but with larger hooks. Robert loved to fish and it was his favorite pastime, on the estate or on ship. He would never forget the first time he caught a trout in a stream in the Valley. He was chubby then, but his brown eyes were as large as saucers as he saw the fine fish on the end of his line. He pulled it out and ran home, his brown hair matted with sweat as he raced into the courtyard yelling and holding his trophy aloft for all to see.

He fondly remembered his father taking him to Plymouth for the big send off in 1577 of Captain Francis Drake on his voyage to follow Magellan through the straights at the bottom of South America and thence to the Spice Islands and the coasts of India and Africa and then back to England, having sailed around the globe. The whole country was giddy with excitement. Bells rang in all the stone bell towers of the angular parish churches.

Briefly before marriage Robert's father James Thomas had been a sailor on his family's ships, plus those of his father's associates – the Gilberts, Grenvilles, Clarks and Gorges and others. If you were a merchant, you had an interest in a ship, either directly or by hiring it to export and import. He had a relative Neville in Spain, an ambassador, who, before all the troubles between its king and his queen, had been a trading partner and had served as his father's agent in Seville when the wine trade was running strong.

Today, he was sailing a pinnace down the River Dart to visit his cousin John on the farm he had in Sandridge Barton near the village of Stoke Gabriel. John had married Faith, the daughter of the county's High Sheriff Sir Fulford and had sworn off privateering but he told Robert in a letter he had been meeting with the Gilbert brothers – half-brothers to Walter Raleigh – and they were urging him to take to the seas again, to search once more for the elusive Northwest Passage to the Spice Islands as many were convinced a shorter route could be found either over the North Pole, north of Russia or northwest down the huge bay early explorers had found.

Sir Humfry Gilbert whose family lived in Compton Castle near the Davis farm, had gotten permission for a voyage to the coast above Spanish Florida but he dawdled so much he missed his weather window and the voyage was put off for the time being. After the unprofitable Frobisher voyage the wealthy adventurers and merchants were leery of new projects unless they had some guarantee of a profit and the West Indies with tobacco, sassafras and sarsaparilla plus citrus fruits looked more profitable than the barren, arctic north. Drake had yet to return with news of his discoveries so for the time being, there was a lukewarm reception to any explorations.

After traveling through Devon Robert normally approached his father's farm from the coast, sailing between the two tall cliffs with the Corfe Castle ruins overlooking the entrance like soldiers guarding a heavy pillared doorway. But today he had come from Plymouth, hitched a ride with a farmer and then borrowed a small boat to sail down the River Dart from Totnes where every Shrine Tuesday the Adventurer Merchant association met at the town hall to discuss business and then went to the Fox Inn to drink a bit.

John had written to him that he had a new plan in mind so Robert was looking forward to their meeting.

The lush banks of the Dart were heavy with the scent of ripe grass and grain but the harvest was well under way and he could see men scything the tall hay and women following, tying the bundles into sheaves. In the distance there were carts laden with hay pulled by teams of sturdy oxen for transport back to the main farmyards where the ricks would be stacked for winter feed. He could hear singing and occasionally he sailed past a young boy fishing, reminding him of his carefree youth.

After docking he had to climb a steep path to John's somewhat rundown estate. The path was overgrown with hedgerows whose blossoms had faded and dropped but still held most of their leaves.

John was in the courtyard, or dooryard, talking to his blacksmith who was repairing a hay rake.

"Hallo!" he called to the lanky Robert as he saw him crest the hill.

Robert waved and soon was inside the large grey stone house with its thatched roof. John's servant brought them mugs of cool cider as they sat in stiff armchairs in John's study.

"Is that the Mercator map?" Robert asked, rising to examine the parchment on John's desk.

"A copy, but I have other maps on the shelves, too," he said with a broad smile.

Raleigh's half-brother Adrien Gilbert soon joined them and they went over maps and discussed the different books Dee and Humfry Gilbert and others had published about voyages to the Northwest.

Sir Humfry Gilbert had met with the Merchant Adventurers of Southampton and a new voyage, departing from Plymouth, was planned to try to set down a colony above Spanish Florida, between it and the French to the north. Sir Walter Raleigh gave Robert Davis the captaincy of his own ship, the *Raleigh.* However, only four of the five ships made it to the new world and Sir Humfry died at sea.

"Dee is certain he can get Walsingham to pitch this to the Queen," Gilbert said, finishing his glass of wine. "We have merchants lined up to front us the money as everyone knows we have to beat the French and Dutch and get a settlement going on the mainland in order to stake claim for England."

"Cabot already did that," Robert replied as a meal of cold beef and mutton, cheese and bread was laid on the table in the library. During the harvest all hands helped on the farm so meals were kept simple to free up the kitchen staff to help in the fields.

His mouth full of bread and cheese, Adrien replied, "Without a real colony our claims won't stand. Walter knows this and he has influence with the Queen so it won't be long before we get something established. The French are all over the New World like dogs after a bitch in heat. We already lost the best part – the southern lands full of gold and silver – to Spain, but Popham and Gorges are sure there have to be silver mines to the north, too. And they have the money and rich friends to back a colony."

Robert made a rude sound as Frobisher had brought back a cargo of plain black rocks. He said, "Well, I know my people and the Bristol and Dorchester merchants are eager to get a toehold there. We keep losing to the damned London merchants,"

Robert replied. Growing up around sailors he often swore but he had to be careful of offending the new class of people called (in derision) Puritans who strictly forbade swearing, maypole festivities, carousing and events with lots of dancing and music.

"Dee doesn't ever stop in his efforts," John said, slicing almost raw beef off the roast on its silver platter, "the man is amazing. His knowledge of all the voyages, the maps, the newest navigational equipment is just astounding."

"Aye, that I know," Robert replied, "You should have seen all the gear Frobisher had on board. Dee is using him to test some of the newer latitude measuring devices he brought from the continent."

"Tis a pity Martin lost two o' his best ships on that voyage," Robert added, rubbing his jaw.

"I've heard rumors that some captains are double hulling their ships, lining the middle with tar or even felt." Adrien replied.

"Well, a ship's a great thing to own, but it will suck ye dry if you can't make a great profit. And rats will chew though tar and feLt. ye mark my word, plus the snake long termados in the West Indies a eatin' at the wood round the clock." He sighed and added, "Those damned Spaniards with all that gold and silver from the Indians are lording it over all of us."

They all agreed on that and then John took them outdoors to walk off the heavy meal and to show off some of his livestock. Even as Robert listened, he knew John's heart wasn't in farming. He, like Robert and his cousin James and the Gilbert men were men who were wedded to the sea, not bound to the land.

****

Two days later they sailed up the Thames to Dee's plain three-story brick house in Mortlake.

The thin eccentric mathematician/astronomer/scientist/alchemist (and some said warlock) with his thin, long beard and thin, long moustache met them wearing his usual black skull cap and fur-trimmed black robe as they entered his vast, cluttered library. Robert immediately went over to a large painted globe, the first he'd seen in person.

"You like that little toy?" Dee asked with a smile.

"Aye, tis a fine thing to see the entire world laid out like this with the most current maps alaid over it."

"It's highly inaccurate, I'm afraid," Dee replied, "We simply don't have enough maps, but that's where you men can help out. I'm looking forward to Francis's return to see what he's discovered."

For hours the men talked about a voyage, sometimes joined by an interested merchant-adventurer. Towards the end of their visit, Dee gave John a pointed look and Robert saw him pull a book out of his coat pocket.

"I was returning it," he said, his face slightly red.

"My library is open to any serious scholar of the navigational arts," said Dee, "but all I ask is that you ask to borrow and not go a'helping yourself."

Properly chastened, John led them down the steps to their boat as Robert and Adrien chuckled.

"He has to lobby Whitehall and his wealthy friends," said Adrien as they pushed off, "but I think he really has something with this Northwest Passage expedition.

"What about Raleigh's colony above the Spanish one on the mainland?" Robert asked.

John snorted. "I don't want to plant a colony, Robbie, I want to explore and map out new lands. I want to punch through that ice-strewn water and come out in the warm Pacific and stuff me holds with cinnamon, nutmeg – lots of nutmegs – cloves, silks, pearls and exotic fruits."

Robert laughed heartily, "Once a pirate, always a pirate," he chided.

"I have a wife who likes to live on the high side, my friend," he said with a wry smile.

"Aye, and right glad am I to be a free man!"

"That's the curse of being a sailor. Ye loves the sea and its freedom but the ladies want ye because they want the nice houses and goods your sailing funds. And ye do get sick of port tarts," he added with a sigh.

"Especially the ones with that disease Columbus and his men brought back along with silver and gold," said Robert.

"I've heard that the New World is full of sassafras and sarsaparilla," Adrien added, both used for treating syphilis.

"Well, while ye run back to yer farm and faithful wife," Adrien said playing on her name, "Me and Robbie are going to find some nice, buxom hussies!"

Queen Elizabeth believed in a strong Navy. Her Navy under the Howards as Lords High Admirals, and bad weather, twice defeated the Spanish Armada as it attempted to invade England. In between, Admiral Sir Francis Drake sailed to the coast of New England and the merchant adventurers were trading in India and Indonesia. Others turned their attention to the northernmost coast of North America, far away from the southern waters where the Spanish ships patrolled.

In what they would call North Virginia (Maine down through New England) they found great fishing waters, such as Cape Cod, named for the abundance of large, fat codfish. They discovered vast forests at a time when Great Britain was timber poor as the great forests belonged to the crown for hunting and most of the common folk were burning peat and the wealthier folk and industries were burning coal, mined primarily in Wales. In New England there was an abundance of furs, especially beaver, prized by the hat trade. Raleigh had shown that tobacco could be grown in the fertile land of south Virginia. And then they took over the Barbados and Jamaica and Bermuda, where sugar cane grew in vast fields. Sugar cane depletes the soil and new plantations had to be constantly planted in order to keep the world supplied with its sweeteners and distilled rum.

As the Davis brothers were friends of the major captains of the day: Sir Walter Raleigh, Sir Francis Drake, the Gilberts, Greville, Carews, Pophams and others they had turned their attentions to the lucrative, but risky, trade in the West Indies. Most of the trade consisted of ambushing Spanish galleons loaded with gold and silver from South America. It reaped great rewards unless one's own galleon were sunk and the captain and sailors taken prisoner, as had "Sir Water". This was the affectionate nickname Queen Elizabeth called the explorer and knight (when she wasn't punishing him by locking him in The Tower). Sir Walter had discovered a plant called tobacco in what the English called Virginia. He brought it back plus some natives, and he and Sir Thomas Davis had experimented with smoking the strong herb in an ivory pipe while at a neighbor's manor in Somerset.

Sir Walter Raleigh had promised Queen Elizabeth he would find great stores of gold and silver such as the Spanish had found in South and Central America, but instead he found a way to make tobacco profitable. Tobacco grew easily in the moist, fertile soil of Virginia and the Carolinas, which later also grew rice in great quantities.

Dried and rolled, the leaves of tobacco, thanks to Raleigh (who planted a small colony at Roanoke, Virginia), soon became a big fad in Europe and England and the Merchant Adventurers realized it could be as profitable as spices, sugar, molasses and rum. The Crown had granted vast quantities of land to the London Company and the Plymouth Company, from the 34th to the 41st latitudes. This land was deemed the property of the Crown and could be doled out, or granted, to proprietors at the king or queen's whim in exchange for a price and annual quitrents of a shilling per acre. (Later on the grant was expanded from the 38th to the 45th latitudes.)

CHAPTER SIX

To Explore or Defend?

1579-1586

Little did Robert know that not long later – again at Dee's – would be last time he'd see his favorite cousin John.

Sir Thomas Gates had captained a resupply fleet for Sir Walter's settlement at Roanoke, but his flagship became separated from the main fleet and had to dock in Bermuda and be rebuilt. A year later with a ship built of Bermuda cedar he was able to sail north. There he found Sir Walter's original settlement at Roanoke reduced from 500 to 90 men as the result of disease and starvation. He took over as governor of the plantation and sent Sir Percy back to England, then called on Lord De La Warr to take over governorship of the colony called Virginia.

In 1586 Drake and Grenville went to relieve Roanoke but found no one there.

Sir Walter then reestablished a colony, not on an island but a little inland, naming it Raleigh In April 1587 the *Red Lion of Chichester*, named the *Lyon* or *Lion*, owned by George Reynolds and captained by Edward Spicer went to resupply the second colony with John White but found no one there. Lane's governor's manse and the buildings constructed -previously were there but not a soul was to be found.

Into the early 1600s indentured servants who went "voluntarily" had nothing to lose as they had been forced from their lands when the English lords burned their thatch roofs . The gentry found it more profitable to raise sheep for the lucrative wool trade with Europe instead of letting small tenant farmers till the land. These forced evacuations resulted in uprisings and mass starvations throughout England's t of the gentry at the turn of the century William Davis and Edmund were still important woolen merchants in Bristol and Tisbury but they had been hit hard during queen Elizabeth's wars, especially with the prisage charged in their southern and western ports on imported wines. The New World, Virginia, offered unlimited opportunities. Besides fish and timber and tobacco to the south, there was sugar cane which not only yielded a sweet product far superior to honey but could be made into molasses and rum, a rough substitute for French and Spanish wines.

As mentioned previously, Queen Elizabeth had knighted Sir Walter Raleigh and had granted him a patent to found a colony for the English crown on Roanoke Island, off the coast of what was later called Virginia in honor of Elizabeth "the virgin queen". But what the Crown giveth, the Crown can take away, and later on, the Queen literally took away his status and he was imprisoned and almost executed, reprieved, then executed to appease the Spanish by King Charles II – but that is later in this story.

Sir Thomas sent Robert on constant trips to the Barbados and West Indies during these years and he had to take on his brother, James junior, eight years younger. A tutor was hired so the boy could be properly educated but Robert had to train him in navigation, as John had trained him.

On one of his rare visits home, Robert ran into Adrian Gilbert at the Maiden Bradley Fair and they got to talking about Sir Walter's latest voyage to what was being called Virginia.

"I had thought you went with him," Adrien said questioningly.

"Aye, me bitch of a boat lost a lot of caulk when we got caught in a south wind not long after launching. She had to go back to port and the seams were so bad the carpenter said she needed a lot of work. Those damned termados get into the wood and it looks all right but it is nothing but a damned shell and the first buffeting pulls the oak heels out or splits the planks."

Adrian said he felt he could get him a position on John's planned voyage to look for the Northwest Passage but Robert demurred. He said he was getting to like the warmer climes and, unless a fortune in fish was promised, wasn't interested in more ice and seal meat.

In 1586 he got his wish as Queen Elizabeth ordered the English fleet to the fishing grounds around Newfoundland to drive out the Spanish and French fishermen. Little James, nicknamed Jamie, came along. He was an adolescent now but, unlike Robert, he had stopped gaining height and would remain on the medium-short side. Which was an advantage shipboard as he hadn't smacked his skull on the beams as Robert had done a few times, especially when getting off the bottom rung of the stairway between decks. Once, going from light to dark, he hit it so hard he had to sit down and let the dizziness pass. He had a knot the size of a small apple on his forehead for a week or more from that one.

1586

While they were fighting a fish war to the north, Sir Walter led a relief expedition to Virginia. James was taken on as a mariner, or deck hand (but given special privileges) and from him Robert found out all the colonists were gone, murdered by the savages. This was not an uncommon fate for colonists and France and Spain had suffered similar losses to the north and south. Jamie told him he would be accompanying Gov. White by May the next year to bring new colonists as England couldn't hold her claim unless settlers actually occupied the land. He told him about the swamps, the lush inlets and the savages he'd met, lighter skinned than the African negroes and taller than the Eskimos Robert had seen. Always looking for a profit, Sir Thomas was working his influence with the earl of Warwick and lord Say and Sele, etc. in Whitehall to get a grant of land for his family in this new Virginia.

Before they could resupply the new settlement England's ships were drafted by the Queen as part of the Royal Navy to meet the Spanish armada being formed off the coast of Spain. However, Raleigh did not give up on Virginia. After Lane returned with news of the colony's disappearance he realized the problem with the first settlement had been its location. The new one would be further inland on Chesapeake Bay which had ports deep enough to accommodate defensive naval vessels. The land was drier and a new fort could be surrounded by outposts on the numerous islands Lane had charted.

Lane still had the backing of William Sanderson, who owned the *Hope*, and of the explorer's advocate Richard Hackled was sure Spanish silver would be near due to highly inaccurate maps in Antonio de Espejo's account of his expedition. He promoted the Chesapeake plan as Espejo's map showed Mexico almost adjacent to Virginia on the west. The mines would provide a lot of employment once the war with Spain ended, he argued to Sir Popham and, to get his financial support, he promised Sir John Davis of Creedy that his son John would be the next Deputy for rule of Ireland.

In 1586 Sir Walter had incorporated a company to raise money for the establishment of the city of Raleigh and persuaded John White to be its governor. Several coats of arms were drawn up and White had a suit of armor made. Fourteen middle class English and Irish families were among the settlers, which totaled 117 men, women and children. Walsingham forced Raleigh to appoint Simon Fernando to captain the flagship, the 120 tun *Lion*, (also called the *Red Lyon* of Chichester), which had made the first voyage across with Raleigh when he founded Roanoke. Another veteran on the voyage, Edward Stafford, was master of a pinnace and they had a fly boat as part of the fleet, commanded by Edward Spicer.

In late April 1587 the fleet left Portsmouth but had to dock off the Isle of Wight as Gov. White needed to meet with Walter's relative Sir George Carey, captain of the castle fortress there.

However, Sir Walter was not with this fleet as he was already at sea, on a voyage to South America to get silver for his Queen.

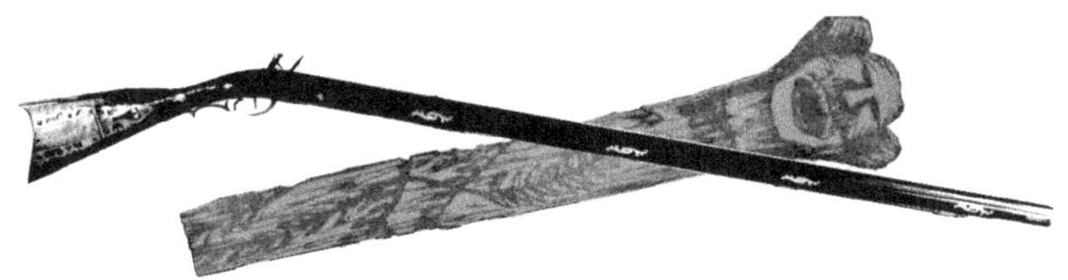

CHAPTER SEVEN

Roanoke's Mysterious Disappearance

1589

William was sitting at a table in the Island Husse inn in the Hoe, in Plymouth.

The atmosphere was boisterous. The English fleet under Drake had defeated the mighty Spanish Armada.

"Aye, ol' Francis was playing at bowls on the green overlooking this harbor when the first ships were sighted sailing up the coast."

William took a swig of his ale and wiped his black moustache. Unlike James, who was fair skinned, and Robert, who was darkly handsome, William was obese and had dark brown eyes. Despite his bulk, he was still active in Channel sailing. His cousins James and Robert had basically taken over the captaincies of the long voyage Davis ships but Will's pride and joy was his cousin John and he never missed an opportunity to brag on him.

"Got 'im a whole bay named after him, did he!"

"I know, cousin," said James, wiping his thin moustache after swigging from the pewter cup, " Robert said he's planning on a voyage to the East Indies next."

William burped loudly, then raised his thigh and farted. The seamen at the next table burst out laughing.

"Well, now that Her Majesty has released some ships from royal service" the last two words said sarcastically, "I am helping Sir Walter get a resupply fleet together for his pathetic colony in Virginia. They've been pretty much abandoned during this war."

James frowned.

"If any are still alive," he said solemnly.

"'Tis a true thing ye say, me boy. Even Columbus, our hero, found his first settlement all a'slaughtered when he was delayed getting back to that land o' gold and heathens."

"So you and my father are going ahead with the Virginia plantation scheme?" James asked, trying to sound neutral although he was nearly bursting with desire to go across the sea again. Open sea sailing was where true skills were tested. Where the strong muscles that roped his arms had been earned as he and the other sailors worked as a team to wind the capstan and pull up the heavy anchors or hoist the massive, heavy sails.

"There's a mass o' land there, boy. Robbie is determined to establish a fishing industry to the north but Tom and I feel Virginia and the West Indies is where the money is. That tobacco is catching on like fire and every gentleman now has to have a pouch and a pipe." He laughed, drawing on his own ivory pipe. The tavern was full of smoke from the sailors' pipes and stunk of spilled ale and body odor. Sailors weren't known for their personal hygiene as months at sea wearing the same clothes tended to make them inured to their own scent. Generally, a hot soaking bath and shave and a fresh set of clothes was the first priority when docking but some preferred their ale first.

"What about the Irish trade, William?"

"Aye, 'tis a profitable one, a way to unload our unwanted woolens, but the real money will be with huge plantations in Virginia."

"Plantations require a large number of unpaid workers to be profitable."

"We'll have plenty of Irish, and if our cousin John becomes Lord Deputy or Attorney General over there, he'll make certain o' that. Munster's been overtaken and Ulster will be ours once we quell O'Neill and his rebels. Plus, ol Popham wants to send all idle English men and women in the cities abroad as unpaid laborers."

James drank, letting his stockinged legs stretch out, closer to the warmth of the tavern's fireplace.

"I'd be wary o' investing in Ireland if I were ol' John," he mused, knowing that a posting there had been disastrous for many, especially the Earl of Essex.

"How do you feel about buying negroes from the coast of Africa?" James asked, watching his cousin's face, red from heavy drinking and burned from sailing. All sailors had a permanent ruddy leather complexion from the saLt. the sea and the sun.

William grunted and farted again. He ate another pickled egg.

"Their own kings capture the brutes and pen them up. If we don't buy them, they just become slaves to the other tribes. 'Tis a sad thing to see, boy, but I think we have enough indigent and insurgent lads here to work our fields without needing the darkies."

James was developing a conscience. He had begun reading the Bible every day, a habit an old sailor instilled in him, and he was full of doubt and questions. He loved the New Testament and found himself reading some of the Puritan tracts that stressed a personal relationship with God instead of getting religion second hand through an Anglican priest. But he kept these traitorous thoughts to himself. As part of his religious awakening he questioned whether one man had the right to own another, even though slavery was common in the Old Testament and the Greeks and Romans kept slaves. It was well known Queen Elizabeth's secretary, Sir Francis Walsingham was a Puritan but he was exempt from punishment and "her beagle" Privy Council member William Cecil"s wife was a Puritan. Cecil, now Lord Burghley, and his son Robert had been recently knighted by the queen. He was immensely influential at court.

William sighed and smoothed back his balding hair.

"So Francis has asked me to see if ye'd accompany him on this resupply trip to the second colony White established at Roanoke. But he can't offer ye a ship o' yer own."

James smiled. He was missing a tooth in his upper jaw, lost to scurvy on a past voyage. He toyed with an earring, the piercing still a bit raw.

"If I can take a pinnace to explore for a Davis grant, I'd be willing to go as a junior officer."

William laughed, spraying egg on the table.

"Tom said ye'd be a' itchin' to get back over there!"

"Do you know who White is planning on sailing with?"

"I heard John Watts would be the general o' the fleet and he's got Abe Cocke with the *Hopewell* lined up. I think the *Moonlight* with Ed Spicer is going and Chris Newport is planning on captaining the *Little John*."

"They are truly good captains to sail with," James said, rubbing his fine beard.

****

It was the 20th of March, 1590 before the fleet was ready to weigh anchor and leave Plymouth. However, Sanderson, the chief financier, ordered Watts to post a 5,000 pound surety to ensure he'd sail straight to Virginia and not take piracy detours. Watts was furious and unloaded the colonists and stores for Roanoke/Raleigh on the docks. White was able to talk him down and told him they could detour, Sanderson just didn't want any seizing and boarding of foreign ships they encountered.

Hopewell, Little John and the pinnace *John Evangelist*, captained by William Lane left but Sanderson's bark *Moonlight* and the pinnace *Conclude* had to be left behind to rejoin the fleet in Haiti.

James was on the watch when the *Hopewell* came to the roadstead in the Tenerife islands where they bought two shallops as theirs had been lost in rough seas. They had been forced to cut them loose as they kept bashing the hull and the crew feared it would be punctured. The master they bought them from was sailing a London ship and illegally buying sugar but they looked the other way as their need for the shallow water ships was critical. In the Canary Islands *Little John* indulged in piracy, capturing a double flyboat and sending her and her crew back to Plymouth as partial recompense to Sanderson.

Watts didn't keep his word on piracy and his fleet took a ten tun frigate and a pinnace before they reached Hispaniola, following Columbus's route. Watts and his crew nosed around Santo Domingo looking for the entrance to the Windward Passage, then went to Havana where they caught the Gulf Stream that would bring them north to Florida and then Virginia. The *Moonlight* and *Conclude* reunited with them and there was great excitement when a sail of 14 ships was sighted. Dreaming of Spanish gold and silver Watts couldn't resist but the fleet had the wind in their sails and he only captured the *Buen Jesus*. Lane took a French 60 tun but it had been spoiled by the crew before capture. They added it to their fleet anyway. Another large Spanish fleet was sighted but they couldn't capture any so all but the *Hopewell* and *Moonlight* went after them, hoping to take treasure home to England from the Azores. So it was that there were only two sails that went north to latitude 30.30, anchoring on an island off Port Ferdinando. It had been five months since the fleet left Plymouth. The lookout in the bosun's chair sighted smoke and the crew felt it was from the settlement of Raleigh (Roanoke).

The two shallops were hoisted out and James was with the group that rowed through the inlet. On the other shallop were the two captains and Governor White. James argued about the wisdom of having all three in one boat but was overruled. They saw smoke coming from Hatarask Island but a day's searching didn't discover any settlers. Wary of hostile savages, the two captains split into separate shallops to go further inland to Roanoke. There was a strong northeast wind pushing the shallops against a bar with the tide ebbing and Capt. Spicer and his shallop capsized. Although Capt. Cocke, Gov. White and James plus the others rowed furiously back to them, the men were all drowned. The shallop was righted and bailed out but the loss was felt deeply. And it was a huge loss for the expedition as Capt. Cocke knew the *Hopewell* like the back of his hand and his skills would be lost on the return voyage.

They set anchor at the north end of the second settlement of Roanoke. To announce their presence, they made music and loud sounds to draw the colonists' attention but as dark fell, none of White's settlers answered. The men, now in two shallops, slept on board, a guard posted to alert for an indian ambush. At daybreak Governor White landed a party to march to the fort.

White cried when he saw the devastation and footprints in the sand. The colonists had buried five chests, one of which contained his precious books. The chests had been unearthed and the contents desecrated. White was sobbing on his knees as he pawed through wet, ruined books and saw his beautiful eight sectioned coat of arms rusting from exposure to rain.

The words *'CRO'* and *'CROTOAN'* were carved into trees and White said that was the village where the friendly sachem *Manteo* lived. The shallops tried to make for that island but a furious storm drove them back and almost ripped the *Hopewell* from its moorings. Despite urging from White to continue, Watts sailed the *Hopewell* for more piracy in the Caribbean and Spicer sailed the *Moonlight* directly back to England. Watts with John White aboard hooked up with the *Conclude* and their prize *Buen Jesus* at Corvo and Flores, where five English Naval vessels lay at anchor.

James was as dejected as the rest of the crew when they anchored in Plymouth later that fall. Some of the fleet went to London with thousands of pounds of plunder but the main mission – to resupply the colony and explore the area – was never accomplished. Blame was laid on White and Simon Ferdinando for locating the colony too close to hostile savages but James knew it was Watts's greed for Spanish treasure that really sabotaged the mission. That and sailing during what the Spanish called the 'hurricane' (after the South American deity of storms) season. Being young and having no real voice in the decisions he was frustrated but resolved he'd get back to Virginia and claim a chunk for the Davis family.

CHAPTER EIGHT

Queen Elizabeth dies, King James I takes the Throne

1603

Born of a dubious and tragic marriage, Queen Elizabeth, who was almost as ruthless as her predecessor, Queen Mary in persecuting those who didn't follow the religion of her choice, had managed to restore stability to England. When she died on March 24, 1603 England truly mourned the passing of a great ruler. But she had never married and had no heir of her own so the crown went to her cousin Mary Stuart's son James, who was King James VI of Scotland.

James I of England was famous for overspending and he abused the system of forced loans and of selling crown lands and titles such as the newly created one of baronet, to any rich enough to pay the price. Baronets were commoners and could serve in the House of Commons but not the House of Lords. Also under James I, all males who weren't engaged in agriculture had to serve an unpaid apprenticeship averaging seven years, and then they had to pay guilds for their licenses to ply their trades. The king sold monopolies on almost every product in the land. The common people got poorer and the rich got very richer. More common lands were enclosed. There were famines and plagues.

After Queen Elizabeth's death Sir Thomas Gilbert, Captain John Smith and his rich friends backed a fleet of nine ships in 1609 to sail once again to Virginia to found a settlement, this time at the mouth of the James River.

King James I also sent Lords to Ireland to rip lands and manors away from the Irish. He persecuted Separatists and declared himself a believer in the 'Divine Right of Kings' to rule on their own without representation of the people via Members of Parliament (MPs) in the House of Commons and the House of Lords. However, he was friendly with the rich peers of Somerset and the West Country in Devonshire and southern Wales who had helped the Tudors retake the throne. And this is where the story of New England really begins as he granted a 20 year patent to a group of merchant adventurers to establish colonies in North Virginia and in South Virginia (Jamestown). Generations on, descendants of these men later came to settle near the Great Pond in a town they first called South Brimfield, then Clinton, and finally Wales.

For men with money, the reign of Queen Elizabeth was golden. She had no love of the Catholic Philip of Spain and no scruples about her mariners capturing and looting Spanish ships on the high seas. The English royalty lived high and were always looking for funds to support their lavish lifestyles in their many castles such as the ring of castles Edward I had built in Wales. The monarchs could sell titles in exchange for lands taken from the Catholic church under Henry VIII and given to the aristocracy, but at their whim, they could revoke their gifts and give them to a new favorite at court. The lords and gentry were always insecure and resented the imperiousness of their monarchs. Oliver Cromwell tapped into this and, under his influence, the role of Parliament was growing in power.

When the queen died, men like Sir (James) Thomas Davis and their sons knew their positions on English soil were tenuous, subject to the whims of her heir, so they sought to establish themselves in the New World where land grants were more secure, out of sight of the greedy crown. Under Elizabeth the Davises had a Welsh relative, William Davison, at court as the queen's secretary but all they had now was Edmund's son John.

But for James Thomas Davis 's son Thomas, the death of Queen Elizabeth ushered in a new age of opportunity.

Under the old queen (and she was very old when she died) England regained naval supremacy but it lost trade with Spain, Portugal and France plus the

Netherlands, depending on the year and her mood. After her flirtation with King Philip of Spain sputtered out – as did any promising marriage for her – trade with the Mediterranean and Levant was severely restricted, both due to royal decrees and to the risk of piracy and imprisonment followed by torture from Catholic Inquisitors.

To compensate, Thomas and his relatives had shares in merchant vessels, or even captained ships, and had turned their attentions to the East Indies, dodging the Dutch.

Sir "Water" had received a patent for a plantation from the old queen but couldn't make it stick. But now, with a new monarch, a king greedy for gold, silver and any other riches the New World could provide for his royal palaces, the chance to try plantations again presented itself and captains were willing to sail to the West Indies.

King James I was so money hungry he eagerly sold titles in exchange for estates, with their manors and tenant farmers. Almost anyone could have a title in these days, unlike the olden days of King Arthur when knighthoods were won in battle by virtue of bravery. Even in Wiltshire and Somerset the locals honored sites such as Glastonbury were where Arthur, Guinevere and Merlin were rumored to be entombed. From the impressive ruins of Stonehenge to lesser burial mounds and circles throughout southwestern England, Wales, Scotland and Ireland there existed evidence of a race of men who created massive religious structures and formations such as the dike separating Wales from England. Little of their history remained, partly due to the Romans and Vikings, but also because the new religion of Catholicism came into England and their priests were diligent in wiping out traces of the Old Religion. Through superstitions and secretive rituals the ancient sites were still revered but some of the new gentry had no regard for their sacredness and had stone circles dug up and replanted on their new estates as 'follies', or ornaments in their gardens.

After the death of the famous mariners Sir Gilbert and John Davies their sons or relatives, also avid captains and seamen, became friends of Elizabeth's successor, King James I. The new King James encouraged the Merchant Adventurers in their plan to found a settlement at what they were to name Jamestown in his honor on the coast of present-day Virginia. In James's times the entire coast of North America from what is now called Maine down to the boundary of present-day Florida was called Virginia. It was believed that only Christians were entitled to own land but a monarch couldn't claim the land unless he or she had planted and maintained a settlement (plantation) on the site.

Throughout 1605 the merchants and adventurers had been busy getting London shippers and merchants to back another Virginia plantation venture and in Southwestern England they cobbled together a group of merchants and ship owners plus the trade unions to back a second plantation further north. A Northwest Passage through to the East Indies Spice Islands hadn't been found but the explorers Mason, Drake, Cavendish and others got the backing of Sir Francis Bacon, Richard Hackled, Sir Francis Walsingham, Sir Robert Cecil plus the Earl of Suffolk and Berkshire Thomas Howard, Lord High Admiral, related to Thomas Lord D'Acres, William Fiennes, First Viscount Saye and Sele and most of the lords of Devon, Somerset, Wiltshire, Berkshire, Dorset and Gloucestershire and southern Wales so England could claim the land from the 34th latitude to the 45th latitude.

The northern plantation site didn't offer gold and silver but had an abundance of fish in its waters plus and abundance of timber in its vast forest lands, a commodity England was running out of as most of the forests were now royal hunting preserves and off limits to commoners, who now had to buy coal from Cornish and Welsh mines to burn for cooking and heating.

In 1603 in a garden ceremony before his official coronation King James knighted Edward Gorges, owner of Longford Manor in Wiltshire, John Davies of Essex, Edward Pynchon of Essex, Edward Pheilps (Phips or Phillips) of Somerset, John Wentworth, Richard Saltonstall, George Grenville and others.

He also made John Davies Solicitor General of Ireland to create a plantation in Ulster. Ireland was a dicey post as the Earl of Essex under Queen Elizabeth had been sent there but was beheaded when he returned without engaging the Irish war captain Tyrone. However, as John Davis was a close friend of King James, he felt he would be supported in his post.

In 1605 Sir Thomas's seafaring heirs were looking forward to the New Year's Parliament as their petition for plantations would be presented to the king by Sir Robert Cecil. The Davis family's entire future hinged on King James's decision. Civil war was coming to England. It was a ways off, but Oliver Cromwell and his friends were not shy in their criticisms of the monarchy. There was an ugly undercurrent and the Davis men wanted to be established in the Virginia, maybe even in the Barbados, before real warfare broke out on English soil. There had been too many wars in the past hundred years. Fighting in France, with Spain, with Italy and the Dutch for territory and rulership. Fighting over religion mostly. Sir Thomas and his friends were tired of it. They wished their sons and grandsons could live in a peaceful time. Thomas remembered the story of how a Welsh relative had been conscripted by English soldiers while he was scything hay in the field. He was taken in his youth and died on a foreign battlefield for a country that had taken his ancestral lands in Wales and given them as favors to the Seymours and others, both in Wales and England. There was a bitterness in his heart, both for the theft of his royal birthright and for the theft of their right in Bristol to trade freely with the Dutch, French, Spanish and Portuguese while London merchants received special favors and trading rights.

Sir Thomas had wanted his family to captain merchant vessels to the West Indies and Virginia due to the political unease in England. Sir Thomas knew King James 1 ruled under a cloud. His mother, Mary Queen of Scots had schemed against her half-sister Elizabeth and was finally executed but her Catholic beliefs were feared to simmer in her son. Everything King James I did was scrutinized for papacy. Even his printing of the Bible was thought to be suspicious. The Church of England was still too papist for many Protestants and the most extreme of these, the Separatists, were either in prison or had fled to the Netherlands to escape persecution. Many, such as the Davis brothers, felt the Church of England could be purified further and hoped that when they got land patents in Virginia they could export their version of Protestantism far away from the prying eyes of the Archbishop of Canterbury and the king. The Seymours and Beauchamps had grabbed most of southwestern England and Cornwall under the Tudors and almost everywhere a man looked he could still see Seymour holdings. The castle of Longleat, the old castle of Wardour, Wraxall Abbey, the forests between Tisbury and Southampton were all held by Seymours and a handful of old families. Marlborough and its forests were held by Seymours and their cohorts the Pophams, all later united against the royal tax called 'ship money' and all united in support for enclosures. To acquire more and more land was the goal of wealthy Englishmen and the Davis men, along with the Pophams and Gilberts, knew the Virginia held vast, unlimited lands: lands they could work with transported prison labor. Because of the constant fighting in Ireland there was no shortage of young men to use.

The Dutch had discovered another source of basically free labor along the Gold Coast in Africa but in 1605 England, Scotland, Wales and Ireland had plenty of young malcontents who could be shipped off to the New World to sweat out their insubordination and – if they survived their three to seven year indenture – would be rewarded with modest land grants.

Besides Merchant Adventurers, the strict Calvinistic Separatists were also looking for a new home in the New World as they wanted to live in religious communes and raise their children to be English, not Dutch.

By the early 1600s explorers had mapped and fished the coasts of the New World for many years. One settlement had already been attempted in Virginia but in 1608 Sir John Popham and Sir Ferdinando Gorges decided to plant a settlement at Sagadahoc on the Maine coast to solidify the crown's claim to the northern lands, rich in forests of lumber and furs, especially for beaver-skin hats and leather plus the coasts were exceptionally rich in fish. (Its history will be told in a later chapter.)

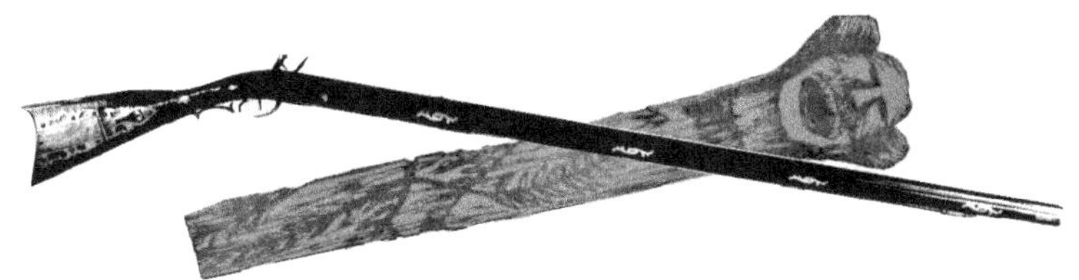

CHAPTER NINE

From the Forests and the Fields

Dolor 1605

Dolor's father William was a grandson of Sir Robert John and brother of Richard. When Richard was young he led a militiary life and spent most of his time in France, Spain and then in Scotland until the Scottish rebels were subdued with the Treaty of Edinburgh in 1560. He then became a partner merchant and shipowner with William. His domain was Kent near Maidstone, a region Henry VIII had given to his Archbishop Cranmer after the dissolution of the monasteries. Kent was famous for Joan 'The Maid of Kent' (daughter of the Earl of Kent Edmund Woodstock, half-brother to King Edward II); Joan was mother of King Richard II; there was also the 'Mad Maid of Kent', a prophetess who was executed by King Henry VIII for publically criticizing his divorce and remarriage to Anne Boleyn and for Wat Tyler and his uprising. It had prime coastline for shipping across the Channel and was close to the outlet of the Thames.

Dolor's brother James Rhys in his early years was also a soldier and went to Ireland to help the settlement of Ulster.

Dolor's grandfather was related to Richard Davis who fought for England in France after the Catholic massacre of Huguenots on St. Bartholomew's Eve in Paris in 1572 and a Catholic soldier's sword almost cut off his right leg. He returned to England as an a invalid and lived the rest of his days in a Wapping Hall manor house in London, supported by an estate in Horsmondon, outside Benefield, near his friend Sir Richard Willard, a fellow Continental soldier (knighted) who went into the fur trade. Always looking for more pelts, the fur skinners' union had backed explorations over the years. Dolor's father had received a share of the estate in Horsmondon but it had been divided so much amongst sons that it was a modest holding by the late 1500s.

Through Rhys, Dolor's father William was friends with Sir Sackville, third Duke of Dorset (in need of a skilled carpenter), and through marriage William was related to the Bristol Clarkes, plus he was close to a fellow Welshman, Griffen Riches (Rice, Rhys),whose son Robert was a member of the first Virginia Company. It was through the Clarkes and Riches that Dolor Davis would later inherit James Clarke's estate in Marden in 1614. Robert Riches was not only involved with James Davis in Virginia, he was involved in the East India Co., the Somers Island Company, the Africa Company, Sir Walter Raleigh's Amazon River Co., then later Providence Island and the Bahamas.

In England towards the end of the seventeenth century a person could hardly turn around without bumping into a merchant adventurer or Puritan or both.

William, married into the Bristol, Dartmouth sailing/mercantile Clarke family, had Rhys in 1590 (who died in early adulthood), then Dolor and two years later Nicholas (who was also a master builder, surveyor, carpenter and finally ship captain) Robert Tobias, Jenkyns, a ship's pilot, plus a daughter, Susan. In Benefield his overseer planted fields of saffron, which, dried and packed into cakes was used by his relatives and other clothiers to dye wool yellow. It was very profitable. The area was bordered by the thick Rockingham forest, which belonged to the crown. The Abbey of Peterborough in the area went to Richard de Engaine then Sir William Hatton. By Dolor's time Hatton and his sons lived there in the manor and old castle.

The fields in the area also grew a large amount of beans (from whence its name Benefield derived), which were dried and baked in pots with a slab of salt pork. Beans, peas, wheat, rye and barley were the staple food crops of southern England.

****

In November, 1605 Dolor (pronounced Dollar) Davis sat on a knoll beneath an oak tree overlooking the gently sloping yellow pastures below that surrounded the small parish town of Benefield. He could hear the church bells tolling to the reapers in the fields to come and learn of the attempt on King James's life by a Catholic plot involving 36 barrels of gunpowder hidden in the cellars of Westminster Palace. Men would be conscripted to help in the search for all the plotters. Luckily, the gunpowder was discovered before it could blow up under the king and his new Parliament. Dolor's cousin Captain James Davis had arrived from London the night before to tell the news. Guy Fawkes and his co-conspirators were in the Tower, and would no doubt be hanged, drawn and quartered for treason and their heads put on pikes on London Bridge. Sir Walter Raleigh was also in the Tower as he supported King James's cousin Arabella Stuart's claim to the throne upon the death of Queen Elizabeth.

Capt. James had just returned from a voyage to the West Indies in the *Swan,* the merchant ship he and his two brothers owned along with George Munjoy. Related to the renowned navigator John Davis, who had recently perished from wounds he received from Asian pirates off the coast of Malaysia, James and his brothers had no interest in the East India Co. and preferred to cast their lots with Sir Walter Raleigh, Drake and the various explorer-trading companies seeking to establish settlements to the west in the Barbados and Jamestown, Virginia. Queen Elizabeth had favored the Merchant Adventurers but her successor had made peace with Spain the year before, putting a stop to the riches they could plunder from the Spanish ships sailing between England and the New World. The Dutch had taken over the East Indies and controlled most of the nutmeg, cloves and cinnamon trade, plus the black pepper that everyone depended heavily on to mask the taste of spoiling meat. Nutmeg was believed to prevent the plague but the good queen had an abundance of it and perished anyway. Virginia had tobacco and needed slaves for its plantations but in the early years of the seventeenth century James and his brothers were not involved with African cargo. Spanish sugar, rum, fish and tobacco were in demand in England and English manufactured goods were in demand in the West Indies. The only human cargo the Davis ships occasionally transported were legally indentured servants or prisoners of war from insurrections in Ireland or Scotland.

But James had not come to Horsmondon, a small hamlet in Benefield parish, just to tell his younger cousin the sad news. Today was Dolor's 15th birthday and he was to leave the estate of Sir Willard, his home since his father became the large estate's manager many years past. James, through his connections at Court (connections now in peril through his friendship with Sir Walter Raleigh), had found a position for Dolor with the Sir Thomas Sackville, Second Earl of Dorset in the major remodeling project he was doing on Knole Manor, the monstrosity owned by past archbishops of Canterbury. The expensive manor had passed through several owners before Sir Sackville including Robert Dudley, Sir William Fiennes, Second Baron of Saye and Sele and Earl of Lincoln plus John Learned. When Sackville was Lord Treasurer in 1603 he got Learned knighted Lord D-Acre. Knole Manor was reputed to be the largest mansion in all of England but it was never finished, each owner adding rooms, courts, ponds, gardens, tearing out and replacing Tudor touches with the new Jacobean fashion.

Dolor was excited about the apprenticeship as, from his earliest years, he had loved working with wood. His uncle had made him a small tool chest and every year new pieces were added until he now had just about every tool a carpenter or housebuilder-joiner would need. He smiled at the memory of little Margery Willard bringing him her broken dolls and how he could carve new arms or legs and affix them to the cloth bodies.

As if sensing his thoughts, Margery appeared through the early morning mist.

"I knew I'd find ye here," she said, gracefully sweeping her long skirts aside so she could sit next to him.

He smiled at her. Margery was the sister of Simon, newly born but already a strong presence in the manor. She and Dolor had grown up together, playing in the fields, running through the forests, wading in the streams and brooks. She knew he often came to this spot to greet the sunrise and to plan out his latest project. His uncle had taught him the rudiments of carpentry but Dolor was a perfectionist and 'good enough' was never in his vocabulary. To be accepted as a workman on England's grandest estate was a high honor and he knew he would make his family proud of his labors.

Margery was the prettiest girl in the region. Dark eyed and dark haired with alabaster skin she was the opposite of Dolor, who was outgrowing his clothes. His limbs were awkward and he had sprouted in the past year so he stood taller than she by a foot. His complexion was fair but he had a tendency to burn in the sun and his hair had turned from the almost white of his youth to a reddish blond. His large hands were hard and calloused from the hard work he did from dawn to dusk. She reached over and took one in her thin, cool hand, running her fingers over his callouses.

"I don't suppose I'll see ye again," she said, softly sighing.

"Oh, Sevenoaks isn't that far away, lass, just west o' us in Kent," he replied lightly. Upon entering adulthood they had become shy with each other. He knew soon she would be married off to a Sir this or that and become a Lady of her own manor. Dolor would always be a laborer and always beneath her class.

She picked a buttercup and held it under her chin, the way they used to do when they roamed the wealds.

"But Knole Manor!" he said, smiling in spite of himself, "Your parents will no doubt be a'visitin the good Earl at some gathering. I shall see you there for sure."

Margery sighed.

"I wish – " she looked away as he picked up an acorn and threw it into the forest.

"I know," he replied stiffly, then rose and brushed grass and dead twigs from his leggings, "'Tis our fates, girl. You were born to the gentry and I to the working class. Maybe someday I will build you and your rich husband a new house, eh? There's an abundance of timber in these parts, unlike the flat chalk downs in Wiltshire where James and the others live. Of course, they have better building stones in their quarries, even huge sarsens such as in the great circles. Did you know they brought stone all the way from the Chilmark quarry in Wiltshire for Canterbury Cathedral? It's the same stone used for Salisbury Cathedral."

Margery laughed, a light sound that was overshadowed by the tolling of the blocky grey stone Norman church. As if reminded of the solemnity of the day, she stood and brushed her skirts then said, "Aye, and the blue stones came all the way from the Presili Mountains in Wales, which you've told me many a time as you are part Welsh royalty, according to your cousin and his stories. And, as you know, the Seymours – of your cousin's part of our island – " she arched her eyebrows in disdain, "tried to get Jane Grey's daughter in as heir under the Tudors but fortunately for us, eventually Elizabeth became queen. When she passed two years ago during the plague season, she named that Scots half-nephew of hers, James the Sixth, to be her heir. I'd heard he was not a true Protestant but had some of the wicked Mary's papist tendencies. I think his recent actions against them set off this plot."

Dolor took her hand as they walked through the tall grasses and wildflowers down to the manor. It occurred to him it would probably be the last time they would meet this way.

"I pray that this plot will show he is not papist and will ensure that all the good reforms our great Queen Elizabeth – God rest her soul – brought to us will not now be snatched away by the pope-loving Catholics again."

Margery stopped and looked into Dolor's grey-blue eyes. Her voice was very serious as she replied,

"Aye, and there are some that aren't done with the reformin'. They seek to further purify the rites besides tearing down altars and rood screens. They want to remove priests, feast days and make the church more of a personal relationship with God like Calvin preached. My father has many friends from the college at Cambridge and they discuss such matters late at night after they think I've gone to bed, but I listen from top the stairs. These 'separatists' as they call themselves are already preaching and practicing in private but there is talk that King James will start rounding them up and punishing them. Did ye know a bunch of ministers resigned after King James said their convocation could only be called with his permission? He believes in something called the Divine Right of Kings, which he interprets as a right for the: king to always be right in what he says and wants. The separatists are talking of taking their followers with them to the Netherlands to escape persecution."

"Ah, Margery," said Dolor, "I find this all so depressing. We had the Catholics and all their rites and rules and cathedrals. They grew so rich and powerful they owned almost all of England. Then King Henry the Eighth because of his wantin' for Anne Boleyn – another Seymour – went and broke with Rome, took over all the monasteries, nunneries and their vast lands and proclaimed himself the highest religious person in England and the Church of England greater than that of the Holy Catholic one in Rome."

Margery smiled ruefully as butterflies flitted around them, "Yes, and if it weren't for them, people like me father and your Davis relatives wouldn't have the grand estates, isn't that so?"

"Well, some as were favored had titles, lands and manors and abbeys bestowed on them in exchange for loans to the crown but for folk such as myself, it hasn't mattered much. Those like me are born to the manor, work for the lord, have few rights and few possessions of our own. What matters to me if I hear a popish priest say a mass in Latin or hear a minister read from the *Book of Common Prayer*? 'Tis of no account. I have one god, Margery, and He made the beautiful land and blue sky and all the animals and vegetation in the air and waters and on the earth. And blessed us with wonderful trees that can be made into items as common as barrels or as magnificent as arches in cathedrals with their flying buttresses – or as fine as this," he said, shyly producing a delicate hair comb he had carved from light chestnut wood and set with small uncut garnets.

"'Tis beautiful, Dolor!" she exclaimed as she ran her fingers over its smooth, oiled lines. He had carved her initials in the top between the garnets.

"It is your early birthday present," he said, sensing that she was going to return it, "as I won't be home again for a long time."

Margery and Dolor walked down the hill in silence. Their hearts were full of sadness for their eminent parting but Dolor's was also filled with the joy of anticipation as a new life was to begin: a life full of work with oak, elm, ash and chestnut, of wood dust and shavings and wood oil and the sound of sawing and hammering and the solid thunk when an adzed timber's pin fell into the precisely cut mortise joint. He would miss his little Margery and his younger brother Nicholas but he knew he'd return for fairs and they'd run into each other in Maidstone or another Kentish village as time went on. He had much hard work ahead of him to become a master builder before he would marry. And Margery's baby brother Simon, born two years to the date of Queen Elizabeth's death in March, and her subsequent siblings would be demanding a lot of her time. Girls were born to help their mothers and boys, such as Dolor, were born to help farm, go soldiering or become skilled tradesmen. Some, such as his Wiltshire relations, took to the sea but Dolor had no sea stomach as a brief ride in a pinnace off the coast of Dover had taught him. The fishermen said they'd never seen a person turn such a shade of green. Even gentry girls such as

Margery had few options but her little brother Simon would find doors open to him that Dolor would never even know existed. He was fortunate to have run into his cousin James on a stay in Twickenham when he had to accompany a local carpenter to the quarries for special stone for repairing the altar of a local church. James knew Sir Sackville and knew he was badly in need of a skilled carpenter such as Dolor so it was a fortunate meeting.

****

"What ho!" James called to him as he entered the workshop next to the manor's stables. James was, like Dolor, broad-chested but he had the ruddy, leathery complexion of a man who spent his days at sea. "Aren't thou ready to start? Sir Sackville wishes to meet you today and we have a ride ahead o' us."

Dolor nodded but said he wanted to say a final farewell to his mother and siblings in their modest cottage on the estate. As usual his father was in their Bristol manor, his residence when shipments were sent or received. It being the harvest season the Benefield estate needed a manager and Dolor's uncle had stepped in to help his sister, Dolor's mother.

James mounted one of the horses and, donning his large-brimmed hat with its fancy feather, smiled down at his young cousin. He was missing a few side teeth on top, victims of scurvy on one of his long voyages.

"Be brief, Dolor. You want to make a good impression so you will get a good master. You don't want to be consigned to grunt work, your skills are much too fine for that!"

Dolor smiled as he mounted the steed. The gold and ruby earring James wore glinted in the sun. But all the gold on the Spanish main and in the countries being looted by their priests and soldiers across the Atlantic Ocean wouldn't hold the appeal for him that wood had. He loved all forms of it and often would play a game with his brothers where, blindfolded, he would try to guess a wood's name from its texture and odor. He'd been fooled when James held a small piece of finegrained wood the night before. When the blindfold was removed he was told it was mahogany, from the jungles of the tropics. The sample was in his chest of tools and he hoped one day to be able to make a piece of furniture for Margery out of larger boards of the fine wood. At the thought of her married to a pompous 'gentleman', he felt a pang of misery, but also a depth of helplessness. A man was born to his station. Few ever rose above unless they were soldiers or were able to go to sea as merchants. But his family owed their good fortune mostly to the Gilberts, Dolor knew. He hoped the Second Earl of Dorset would favor his labors and that someday he would own a bit of land and build his wife – though it would not be Margery – a fine house of timber and stone with real slate tiles and not thatch for roofing.

Such were his thoughts as James and he rode north from Horsmondon to Sevenoaks where the great, great hall of Knole Manor awaited.

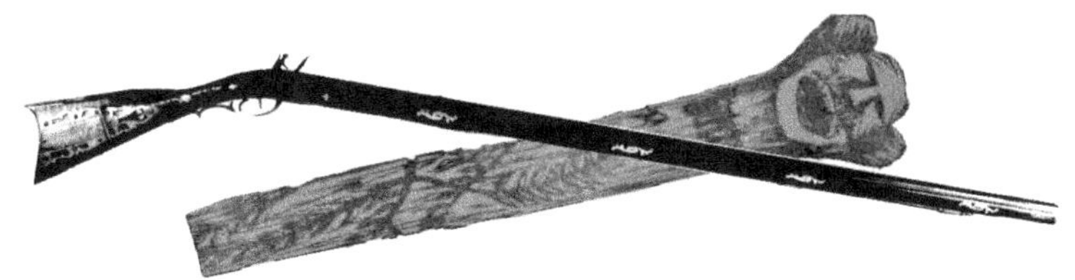

CHAPTER TEN

Planning a Northern Settlement

1580s – 1606

Sir John Popham looked around the study in his newly built Littlecote Manor house. At seventy-four, he was a man well-pleased with himself. He had risen through the ranks under Queen Elizabeth and now under James I was Chief Justice of England, the most powerful man in England besides the king. He owned this newly built Littlecote, a massive Elizabethan mansion full of tall windows and wings, built of grey brick and featuring a walled garden and old Roman villa complete with a beautiful mosaic floor, part of the previous old Tudor-style mansion Henry the VIII courted Jane Seymour in. Sir John was one of the richest men in England with Hemyock Castle and lands in Medford; Wellington House and Hungerford House plus numerous other estates and manors including Publow in Somerset. This particular piece of real estate had been acquired through the murderous actions of a distant cousin, William Darnell who became enamored of Lady Anne Hungerford, wife of his neighbor Sir Walter Hungerford. It ended poorly for both of them and after William murdered his wife's infant by throwing the newborn into a fireplace, he was arrested and sent to the Tower where he died before being executed. He was badly in debt and Sir John saved the manor by acquiring it through 'reversion', thereby keeping it in the family, so to speak. Sir John preferred Wellington House but Littlecote was a magnificent place to entertain King James and his royal retinue when he left London and made his summer country rounds.

He pulled on a pipe full of tobacco and let the smoke fill the air. His neighbor and friend Sir Walter Raleigh had brought the plant back from Roanoke Island in the New World and Sir Ferdinando Gorges was the first to try the aromatic herb with Raleigh at South Wraxall Manor. Popham found it a bit harsh on the throat but stimulating.

He heard a carriage driving up the long tree-lined approach and then the sound of clopping hooves and metal-rimmed wheels thumping over the old Roman cobblestones of the courtyard. His staff met the footman in front of the central wing and a short while later his butler entered and told him Captain Weymouth and two fierce-looking savages were in the front entry hall.

Sir John smiled. He raised his bulky frame out of the brocade-covered chair and told the servant he would receive them here, in his study.

Captain George Weymouth entered, followed by two dark-skinned natives dressed in English clothing. They had thick, straight black hair, worn long and greased back. One had a gorget of silver beads and a large shell hanging down the front of his chemise and both had looped strings of purple and white shell beads hanging over their chests. The other one had earrings made from the handles of English silver spoons. They both wore long coats with silver stripes against a ruby red velvet and their felt hats sported ostrich feathers of the same hue. They wore pantaloons tucked into soft boots that were round toed and laced up the front, the likes of which Popham had never seen. Weymouth was dressed in the more modern fashion with wide sleeves and a split-sleeved doublet of padded, indigo blue satin under his black half-cape. He, too, favored the wider brimmed capotain black hat but his had a silver buckle in its band and the brim wasn't turned up on one side the way the red indians' hats were. He wore bucket-topped high boots and his pantaloons were a bit baggier than the current fashion dictated. His simple pointed collar had just a hint of lace on its edge.

Unlike Weymouth, Popham's narrow sleeved lavender satin doublet jacket was out of style but the lace collar fell full in front, pleated not ruffed. His cuffs were very ornate, unlike Weymouth's which had the minimum amount of lace. Popham wore narrow pantaloons tied to his doublet with satin ribbons topped with arrows of gold and gemstones. His French silk hose was embroidered in an elaborate pattern but because he was indoors, he had favored emerald green velvet house slippers.

"George, my friend! It's been a while. I trust your last voyage was successful?" Sir John said, motioning for the three visitors to be seated in front of the crackling fire in the huge marble mantled fireplace. Outside the window, a sleeting rain blurred the countryside. The butler stood silently behind them as they handed him their wet outer garments. He frowned as he saw wet prints in the deep, rich crimson carpet and noticed some tracks on the black-and-white tiles of the foyer.

The captain smiled, his leathery sea-reddened face creasing deeply over his grey-streaked moustache and Van Dyke beard. He was missing most of his teeth, as many sailors lost teeth from scurvy during their long ocean voyages.

"It was a good voyage indeed, Sir John!" Weymouth beamed, "And I brought back five savages from that wonderful place to tell England all about the great opportunity that awaits men such as yourself who are open to new ventures."

"So I heard from our friend Sir Ferdinando Gorges," Popham said, indicating the drink tray the butler produced, "He was most impressed by your visit to his fort in Plymouth harbor."

Weymouth then introduced the two men as sagamore *Manedo* and *Skidwarres* and then proceeded to detail his voyage and the vast forests full of timber and animals such as the beaver and others that had luxuriant hides and large, deep harbors and capes full of cod, lobster and other fish.

"The forests are vast and full of firs, oak, birch, beech. spruce, larch and the meadows full of gooseberries and strawberries. They much loved our English green peas but they have a wild red pea that is very tart and wild grapes that will make nice wine. I tell you this northern land, unlike Sir Walter's Roanoke Island, has friendly natives and an abundance of fresh water: streams, rivers, ponds, waterfalls and at least four harbors suitable for large vessels. The natives, like these two *Pemmaquid Wabanakis*, have shown themselves very desirous of trading with us, especially for our steel."

Popham smiled and said as he indicated they should help themselves to the drinks tray,

"Our mutual friend and neighbor Henry Wriothesley," he bowed slightly to the sachems, " – that's the Earl of Southampton – and my neighbor in Wardour Castle in Wiltshire the new Baronet Thomas Arundel," he coughed slightly as Weymouth knew Arundel bought his baronetcy from the king just recently (after almost losing his life for accepting an Italian title the deceased Queen Elizabeth disapproved of) "praised the results of your voyage, even if you faced mutiny and didn't find their Northwest Passage," his faded blue eyes flitted briefly to the "magic" sword Weymouth had used to trick the 'indians' onto his ship on Monhegan island. The stories circulating in London said he had magnetized it and picked up metal with it so to the natives, this made him a powwow, or a magician, who had much personal power.

Brandies and wines were sipped. The natives asked the butler for whiskey, which surprised Popham.

As Weymouth went on and on about the bounties England could reap from north and south Virginia, Popham was calculating the costs of funding a voyage.

"It all very well, George, but we both know the king spends more than he takes in, though he tries hard enough, I'll grant him that, with his custom duties, monopoly fees and new baronetcies and other titles. If it's his to sell, he sells it for a high price, to the detriment of his subjects."

"This is why England needs more land, John," said Weymouth, for their friendship was so old they disposed of titles, "We have to expand and plant new colonies before James sells all of the crown lands. He might even start to sell off the royal forests."

"Well, Walter's colony was a bust," Popham replied drily, tapping his pipe on the marble ashtray.

"He picked the wrong spot, that's all," the captain argued, "this area I explored has a lot of fresh water. To the north, the indians are scarce as they've been killed off by a plague and warfare. Now is the time, John! I have it from my friend Captain James Davis that the King would be open to selling a patent for two plantations: one to the north where these fine men come from, and one further south where that tobacco grows so well."

Sir John rose stiffly and walked over to one of the massive, leaded windows that reached almost from floor to ceiling. He sipped his brandy as he looked out at the rain rivuletting down the wavy glass.

"I'll have to arrange a meeting with my Wiltshire, Somerset, Devon, West Country and Welsh peers," said Sir John, "but I can't see financing it without outside stockholders. We've all been hit hard with the King's enforced loans."

Weymouth smiled largely, showing a lot of gum. The indians poured more whiskey and laughed.

"You're right in that. England is sucking you dry. You need new ventures, new products and the Crown only asks for one fifth percentage of your plantation's profits. I've been working on a possible list," he said, reaching inside his doublet and pulling out a parchment with a list of ten names on it, "These are all forward-thinking men such as yourself who want to grab a piece of the New Land for themselves. Being from the same part of England, as owners of the new colonies, you could have your own monopoly on the New World and considerably enrich your regional influence. They are also interested in the West Indies, especially the Barbados and Bermuda but want a piece of the real prize: the continent of North America – before Spain, France and the Netherlands colonize it. France is already setting up fishing and trading outposts in northern Virginia. Now is the time, I'm telling you!"

Sir John took the list and looked it over. Yes, these were rich men whose families had, like his, survived the Wars of the Roses and many had vast Irish estates as payment for their Irish extermination services for Queen Elizabeth and King James. Among them was Sir John Davis, son of Edmund of Tisbury, who, through the death of Sir Humfry Gilbert at sea had become Overseer in Ireland. As he was related to the Gilberts and Grenvilles, John had been the natural candidate and he proved to be very effective in clearing out the savage Irish natives. He'd been richly rewarded with a large tract of land for his services to the Crown. And he got grants in Virginia with Sir Walter but the plantations failed. With his fellow investors he was hoping the new London Company venture would revitalize it.

Sir John Popham was torn between dismissing the visitors as the sky darkened and more rain threatened or of inviting them to overnight. He decided on the latter as he found the two savages with their broken English to be quite amusing and he wanted to ask the educated Weymouth about the marine encyclopedia he gave to the King and he one he was writing based on his twenty years of shipbuilding and mathematics.

Sir John sighed. He only wished he were a younger man as he knew he didn't have the stamina for a long sea voyage and primitive colonizing. But he had a nephew, and he knew a neighbor's oldest son would be interested.

CHAPTER ELEVEN

Early summer, London

1606

Capt. James Davis waited as the barge tied to the steps that lead to Whitehall. It was growing dark and he was bone weary as his ship the *Mary and John* had just docked on the commercial wharves on the Thames. He had been handed a note from Lord Saye and Sele Robert Cecil to come immediately to the palace and was worried. He left the impost duties to his older brother Robert, who co-owned the ship with Raleigh Gilbert. James had sandy colored hair, dark blue eyes and leathery skin. He swayed a little as he mounted the stone steps, not having acquired his land legs. The mosquitoes were vicious and he swatted at them as he made his way to the courtyard of Hampton Court, the massive manor built by Cardinal Thomas Wolsey and gifted to the king. Most of the royal family and landed gentry would be away at their country estates in June as that was when the plagues hit the city the hardest. James was surprised Robert Cecil had stayed on.

King James was planning the construction of a new palace at Pimlico be named Buckingham after his favorite, the Duke of Buckingham but in 1606 only a grove of silk trees had been planted on the site of the future royal palace.

Hampton Court had 13 interior courtyards. James was led through one into

Cecil's antechamber by a servant and left to wait in the deepening gloom. Candles were lit but the buildings of the day relied on massive tall, wide windows full of leaded glass panes to light the cavernous interiors. At night dripping beeswax candlesticks and chandeliers provided only pools of light and, as onboard, it was the time when the rats came out and skittered along the edges of the light. James could hear rustling behind a tapestry and knew the royal ratcatchers would soon be busy with ferrets and traps even through this was a relatively recent building.

As he waited he pondered about how he came to be sitting in a royal palace waiting for the secretary to the king to meet with him. Why was he, a ship's captain, he, raised in a decaying manor near Wiltshire, friends with one of the most powerful men in England?

Some would say it began with Henry VIII. Others would say it went back earlier, to the War of the Roses, the Tudors and Yorks fighting for the throne of England. The Scottish people would say it was a result of England forcing Scotland to come under rule of the English crown. The Irish would also claim that, as would the Welsh. For hundreds of years the kings of England fought to expand their kingdoms to include the lands all around them, even across the Channel to France. The desire for expansion and conquest continued into Queen Elizabeth's reign as she vied with Spain, Portugal, France and the Dutch for the Spice Island trade, and tried to squeeze Spain out of the southern New World, using piracy to enrich her royal treasury.

Whatever the cause of the restlessness, by the mid 1500s it had led to numerous voyages of discovery and attempts to colonize Newfoundland and Virginia plus the islands in the Caribbean, especially the Barbados, Bermuda and Jamaica.

Capt. James Davis was born into a seafaring family. His male relatives had explored with Drake, Hawkins, Raleigh, Pring and Cavendish plus constantly ran trading vessels from ports such as Bristol, Plymouth, Bideford and Southampton to France and Spain and when wars didn't intervene, the Levant and even to Italy for wines and fine silks. He was cousin to the late John Davis, the famous navigator who was killed by pirates in the South Seas. James and his brothers, uncles, grandfather and relatives through marriage of the Davis women were all renown as reliable sea captains, sometimes actual ship owners and ship yard owners. Most of the Davis clan were born to the sea on the shores of Wales but the Tudor wars and subsequent changes of royal kings had forced them across the Severn and into southwestern England, primarily the Cornish and Devonshire port counties where Dartmouth, Bridport, Plymouth and other major ports were.

Since Henry VIII's dissolution of monastic power, the vast estates and lands owned by the aristocracy ,once owned by the Catholic church, were now were in advanced stages of decay and some even uninhabitable. The families so gifted by the Crown became intertwined through marriages until they were one big incestuous mass, some in royal favor at one time, others sent to the Tower. The Davis family of southwestern England had links to the Duke of Somerset's clan through Margaret Beauchamp/Boeufort/Stanley. They had links to the Grenvilles, another seafaring/merchant family in Bideford, to Sir Walter Raleigh and the Gilbert families, all seafarers. And through these connections they knew the more learned cartographers, writers and philosophers such as Sir Francis Bacon and Richard Hakluyt. John Davis the navigator had been obsessed with finding the Northwest Passage making three voyages to the far north past Greenland to Baffin Bay between 1585-7. James Davis was content to use his skills as a captain to bring ships to Newfoundland to trade for fish, furs and timber. But his father wanted land, lots of land, in Virginia and the Barbados to plant tobacco. It was through these connections that James and Robert came to be involved in a new plantation scheme for Northern Virginia.

While he had sailed up the Thames in a barge to Hampton Court's stairs, James had mused that his last trip to London had been on horseback after seeing his cousin Dolor safely from Clark's manor in Kent to Sevenoaks It had been a little over a year past.

The man James was meeting with, along with William Fiennes, Earl of Lincoln, Hakluyt and others had persuaded King James I to grant the Bristol and London Merchant Adventurer organizations patents to establish two plantations in Virginia – one to the south that sprung from Sir Walter Raleigh's settlement of Roanoke, called Jamestown, and the other to the north that would drive the French out of the Hudson Bay. His own cousin John Davis, had accompanied Cavendish in search of the Northwest Passage to the Spice Islands in the Pacific and a straight far north was named for him. Unfortunately this cousin had recently been murdered off the coast of Malaysia but his books and his invention of the backstaff to take daily latitudinal measurements without looking straight into the sun, had lived on.

James and his brother Robert and cousins were actively sailing merchant vessels from England to France or Ireland but the opportunity to be part of an exploration, hopefully a plantation, was exciting. The riches that the New World promised could restore his family's status as large landowners. In the southern plantation tobacco was being grown and demand for its dried leaves, crushed and smoked in pipes, was growing by the day. Off the northern coast the waters teemed with cod and other fish, even whales. The root and bark of the sassafras tree and sarsaparilla shrub were in demand in Europe as a cure for the pox, scrofula or respiratory diseases. The timber, furs and wines plus the new plant, sugarcane, that yielded sugar, molasses and rum had been brought from South America to the Caribbean islands by the Spanish. Sugar could make a man rich beyond his wildest dreams.

As much as James and his family loved England they knew it was depleted. Years of wars with Spain and France had decimated their trade routes, the woolens that English gentry had sold to acquire their vast fortunes were no longer in demand, replaced in many places by lighter textiles, especially the cotton calicoes the slaves wore in the tropical sugar cane and tobacco fields.

Even before the William Cokeyne (sad to say from Bristol) scandal, King James had enacted a law requiring all dressing and dying to be done in London but even without it the West County's wool cloth trade had been in trouble. English textile manufacture had shifted to the Netherlands and Germany. Raw wool was less profitable than finely finished cloth but Capt. James had hauled more than his share of lengths of cloth cross the Channel only to have it rot in his hold. If it hadn't been for John, the Davis family wouldn't have the favorable plantation supply position for the plantations in Ireland.

Sir John had been appointed Lord Lieutenant of Ireland to tame the heathen living there so he determined who got the orders for the cloth to clothe prisoners and forced laborers, plus who shipped butter, wheat, rye and wine to Ireland for the war. King James in 1607 through Cecil, his Secretary of State, had devised a plot to entrap the Irish rebels O'Neill and Tyrconnel. They and leading Irish families fled on a French ship to Rome in what the Irish called the Flight of the Earls. Sir John Davis and Lord Lt. Sir Arthur Chichester declared all northern Irish chiefs traitors and confiscated all their land and that in the rest of the Ulster counties forcing the Irish there to flee or live in the bogs and on the moors.

During the long years when Queen Elizabeth had been at war with Spain, the Davis captains and shipowners had done well importing French wines to Bristol, even after the new rate books dramatically raised import duties but the Bristol merchants were hurt when the prisage on wine was unfairly higher when received at docks in Bristol as opposed to London. In all, it was time for a new frontier to be found, a new land that offered land in abundance, massive timbers for lumber, turpentine, tar or pitch for ship building, crops, pasture for sheep and cattle, furs for hats and hides for leather. There was also iron and slate in the area called Virginia. Sir Popham firmly believed there would be gold and silver to be mined, as well. The Spanish had taken the southern part of the long continent and had filled ship after ship with heathen silver and gold but James felt the northern section held more promise as its climate wasn't the hot, muggy, disease and mosquito infested land south of the equator. Many of the merchant adventurers were calling it New England as it had a similar climate with four seasons and about the same growing season in the north as England so farmers could probably grow the English crops they were familiar with. On the Islands to its southeast the soil was so rich that almost anything planted sprouted but the heat sapped the energy of the laborers so a plantation owner needed many slaves or indentured servants (or prison laborers) to accomplish what a man in a more temperate climate could do in the same time.

And James knew, like most, that a civil war was brewing on England's soil. King James had subdued the Scottish, Welsh and now the Irish. Thanks to the short but bloody reign of Queen Mary, France was a lost cause but there were many non-landowners, that is non-free men, who lived on land owned by the large estate holders, working for the Lord as needed and tending their own small share holds who were angry at the enclosures of common grazing lands, at the exorbitant price a son had to pay to retain his father's right to farm, at monopolies, at the Ship's Money tax that was threatened to be levied on inland towns, at the profligate spending of the royal family: in short, just angry that they had no opportunities left. The apprentice laws had been made stricter, requiring a longer indentured service to a master, the vagrancy laws were harsh as Popham wanted to ship what he termed "dangerous rogue vagabonds and sturdy beggars" off to the plantations as forced labor. With wealthy landowners preferring to graze sheep on their land instead of having small farms occupy it and with the price of wool in decline, the cities were getting overwhelmed by former farm families seeking employment and lodging in non-rural places. The lands that remained after King Henry VIII's appropriations were for the most part marshy (like the fens, some of which were being drained), barren and rocky like the moors, chalky like the lands in Wiltshire, or coastline. Half of England's land was along a coast. But most of the coastline had steep cliffs or had chalky, sloping hills as in eastern England. As a captain and one who had lived at sea from an early age, James knew how treacherous the currents and rocks were along the English coast. Other than the Thames, by the early 1600s there were only a handful of good harbors for the largest ships. And a dock was only good if there were roads or rivers leading out of it for the distribution of imports and supply of exports. Roads in England were poor at best and downright impassable during heavy rains or snows. This was why the London merchants always did better. London merchants had the Thames with its many docks and many Roman cobbled streets leading to many shops and the royal households then out to the countryside. Being near the Throne the Londoners had influence at court but being from Southwestern England James wasn't interested in the city. Maybe it went back to his Welsh origins, but he, like many rural Englishmen, felt a man was only as rich as the amount of land he held. Land equaled freedom and power. Unfortunately, land could be gifted or taken by royal whim. He, and many others like him, felt the best solution was to own a lot of land as far away from the reach of the king or queen as possible. However, land in the far north (Norumbega), New England, in Virginia, in the Barbados and Bermuda would be taken at great cost by a greedy monarch.

Of course, there were other reasons Englishmen wanted to settle across the ocean. There were the extremists, the Separatists, whom King James was persecuting as they disavowed the Divine Right of Kings and the authority of the Crown and Church of England. These people were escaping to the Netherlands but James knew in time they would be sailing across the sea to the new world: a continent that had to be defended from French claims and Spanish incursions. And Dutch. Everyone wanted a piece of this new, rich land. John Speed had published an atlas titled '*Theater of Empire of Great Britain*' which showed an united England, Wales, Scotland and Ireland and King James believed in this vision of an all powerful GREAT Britain.

In Northern Virginia the French had mapped and claimed the mouth of the

St. Croix River and Mt. Desert Island just three years past and the Company sent Capt. George Weymouth to re-map the area and retake the land where they had started a fort on Stage Island. It was urgent that England get a settlement in place. Captains Hanham, Bartholomew Gosnold and Martin Pring had gotten ships together to explore the Sagadahoc River outlet in 1604, even before King James gave the Company a royal charter two years later, in April, 1606. The charter was under dispute as the London merchants wanted the King to secure a settlement with a fort with English troops but the West Country merchants wanted a more independent mercantile settlement scheme. It wasn't resolved but James Davis was determined to be a part of the scouting exploration party.

Gorges was financing the *Richard,* to be captained by Challons, and Lord Chief Justice John Popham backed the *Gift of God,* a Dutch flyboat. A flyboat would come in handy as it had a flatter keel and could explore further along the coastline and into the river. James was an alternate captain of his brother Robert's 60 ton merchant vessel, the *Mary and John,* (co-owned by Raleigh Gilbert, nephew of Sir Francis Raleigh), but would happily captain *The Gift* if it meant going on the expedition. Popham, the Seymours, the Gorges, Gilberts and Raleighs were all practically neighbors of the Davis clan in Wiltshire. Over in Somerset The Company was represented by wealthy merchants of Bristol and Devonshire (with Drake's influence still felt in Plymouth) plus the Grenvilles in Bideford. James knew the men who got there first and explored the new territory could determine the best parcels of land for grants for themselves. Land was power. Land was everything.

Unfortunately, George Weymouth had done a thorough exploration the prior year, financed by Sir Thomas Arundel, son-in-law of Henry Wriothesley, Earl of Southampton, as they were seeking a place to establish a Catholic plantation. Weymouth also took the *Archangel* far north, looking for James's cousin John's obsession: the Northwest Passage to the southern ocean where the spices were. The Gunpowder Plot, as Guy Fawkes's attempted coup was called, squelched any overt pro-Catholic support but Weymouth had kidnaped five natives, gifting two to Sir John Popham and three to Gorges. Through Weymouth's friend Hackled, Rosier had compiled a vocabulary of Indian words so simple trade could be attempted by mariners while they explored for a suitable site for a fort and plantation.

Suddenly the massive arched doorway behind him opened and the small, hunchbacked Robert Cecil emerged.

"Hallo, James! So sorry to have kept you waiting but I was in a meeting of the Privy Council and they are such gasbags it is hard to get away. Actually, I've been fighting with them over the new *Book of Rate*s. It raises the import duties too high and it again favors London for wine, which will really hurt our part of the country. The prisage they are trying to impose will ruin Bristol's docks."

"I appreciate your efforts, Robert," James said, touching the gold and ruby earring he wore. James was aware that he was hot and sweaty and needed a hot bath and strong spirits.

Robert and James shook hands and then went into the spacious private quarters, heavily decorated with French furniture and Moorish rugs. It was hot and stuffy, even with the windows wide open. Sheer gauze cloth had been tacked over the windows to keep the mosquitoes out. That was one thing James loved about the open sea: a virtual absence of flying insects unless one got marooned in the sargasso sea or lost wind at the equator.

They sat on chairs richly upholstered in embossed satin, the brocade dyed a golden color. England was famous for its variety of woolens and some linen (but most of that came from Ireland) and its textile producers could weave almost any yarn. But the finest woven fabrics came from Italy, Spain and France, and even Brussels, as in the case of lace.

Cecil, as aristocracy, could wear lace and silks. Under the law, commoners had to wear plain fabrics. It was one of the things the English people were not happy about. The Church of England's bishops and priests taught that people should be humble and not ostentatious but how many of the common people had ever been in the manors of the landed gentry, of the aristocratic rich? How many had seen the tapestries, carpets, silks and satins and silver and fine china? The Venetian glasses Robert's servant poured Madeira wine into sat on highly polished rosewood that had come from the forests of Brazil. These things Capt. James knew because he had come into a vast estate in Acton-Turville through his marriage to Agnes Chandler. Generations ago Griffen Rhys Davis had been executed and the lands and title went to Sir Thomas's cousin William Davis, who married Anne Pheilps, daughter of Sir Robert Pheilps or Phillips of Montacute, a neighbor of John Popham. Phillips was Popham's chief constable and helped with the arrest and execution of the men, and women – such as another 'neighbor-Arabella Stuart – when James I took the throne. Arabella, who died in the Tower, and Sir Walter Raleigh and their followers felt she had more right to the title than James as she had married the grandson of the Duke of Somerset, Edward Seymour and lived on the grand estate of Longleat House.

This was a another reason James preferred to be at sea. If one stayed in England, one could easily be led into court intrigues and then put in the Tower and lose one's head, and even one's lands.

Robert ordered a supper for them and as they sipped wine from glasses rimmed with old gold, he said he was planning on leaving London for Burghley House with its magnificent silver fireplace surround and patterned ceilings. He had inherited from his father the palatial manor at Theobalds that included some of the old monastery but King James desired it since it was an excellent base for the hunt so Sir Cecil gifted it to him and was planning on making Hatfield House, five miles from St. Albans, his permanent manor, but it needed a lot of repairs.

"I do so miss the fowling and hunting at Theobalds," he said, settling back in his chair. His waistcoat was unbuttoned and James could see the beginnings of a belly. To much fine wining and dining made people soft, he thought. Give him the hard, tough life at sea any day!

"What news of the Bristol demands?" James finally asked as silver platters of cheese and cold meats and bread were set before them.

"I am working on them," Cecil said with a sigh, "But His Majesty is stubborn. He always favors the London merchants. It took all of Sir John Popham's and Sir Walter Cope's and my powers of persuasion to even get two grants from Him as he favored the southern one because of its tobacco trade and wasn't really interested in the northern one but the French threat finally won him over and he saw that if England wanted to claim any of that part of the New World it had better get a fort and settlement going to the north."

"From what I hear there are vast forests full of all types of timber," James said, slicing off a piece of what he knew was rich Wiltshire cheese and popping it into his mouth.

"Yes, and lots of furs and skins and fish," said Cecil with a frown, "But seriously, James, do you really buy Popham's belief in gold and silver?"

James smiled. He was missing a few more teeth due to a bout with scurvy on an extended voyage to the southern coast of the New Land but his face was handsome in a lean, intense way.

"Whatever it takes to get the merchants and king to invest, I will back," he said, refilling his delicate stemmed glass. Holding it in a thick, calloused hand he said, "I heard tales that the East India Company is reaping profits five times what they had just a year or so ago! But they have the trade monopoly down there, thanks in part to our cousin John's navigating." He sighed, drained his glass, refilled it and said, "It is left to us to make the best of this new land, and maybe one day we will find that damned Northwest Passage to the Spice Islands and get our share. John tried hard enough to find it, the good Lord bless his soul!"

"True, but George, Martin and Bart all feel there is great potential in the northern colony. Besides fishing, they feel there is limitless land just waiting for English plows and English cattle and sheep. I have personally met the savages George brought back and they seem to be somewhat civilized. I think we can handle them as we are handling the Irish."

Cecil beamed and continued, "We are getting two sails of ships ready to depart to explore for the best site for our plantation. We can't waste any time. The French and even that dastardly group of radical Separatists are planning on more voyages to its shores. If we don't establish a settlement, we will lose out on whatever treasures are to be discovered."

"So which ship do you want me to captain?" James said with a laugh.

Cecil frowned, "Well, actually, I'm afraid I have a bit of bad news. Gorges wants Henry Challons to captain the *Richard*."

James snorted, "That old fart! He'll be lucky if he finds his own arse with his two hands, let alone the northern coast of the New World. Dammit! My relatives have been on multiple voyages to the area. We regularly fish off Newfoundland. Why Challons?"

Cecil raised a pale hand, adorned with several golden rings, either signets or set with precious gems.

"Don't get all alather, James! Popham is also sending a ship, but he has picked Hanham and Pring to command it. They will have two of George's savages to guide them and Challons will have the other three."

"I'm to be comforted by that?" James exclaimed, his eyes bright with anger.

"No," Cecil said quietly, "But I've been assured that after they find and settle the site your brother's ship the *Mary and John* will be used to bring more settlers." At that James snorted again as he knew John Popham wanted to banish what he called dangerous vagabonds, rogues and beggars to be free labor. Cecil continued, "And the Dutch flyboat, the *Gift of God* will be with it. Popham's nephew John and son George will be with the planting party and he is investing five hundred pounds annually to assure its success. He wants you, Robert and Richard all involved as navigators or pilots. Sir Ferdinando Gorges will also contribute. Sir Humphrey Gilbert is sending his son Raleigh, too."

James stared at the window where a slight breeze was puffing the gauze. His muscled arms were crossed over his chest.

"Your family will be well represented. The *Mary and John* is to be the main supply vessel and I've been assured Robert will be on any shallop that goes inland to explore. I will make sure land grants, when they come, will also go to the Davis men. Like you, I believe the Church needs to be purified of its popish elements but I don't want New England to be settled by those radicals in the Netherlands. Did you know the King is having a new, revised Bible printed in the English language for the people to read instead of the good old Geneva version?"

James let out a long breath.

"All this talk of Bibles is well and good but when can we leave? The southern expedition is already gone."

"The Virginia Company's exploratory ships are leaving in August – from Plymouth, I'll have you know. I am holding my own against the Londoners who wanted the ship to leave from the Thames docks. And the settlement ships to follow will be outfitted in Plymouth while Gorges's and Popham's explorers are abroad. As soon as they return, you will leave to settle and claim a New England."

James relaxed. The mention of the *Mary and John* as a regular transport between the colony and England made him feel better. It was a guaranteed source of income as he knew the land was full of timber and furs, if nothing else. Plus, the settlers in the forts and plantations would need many, many items from the motherland. And a ship could swing south to the Azores or West Indies and pick up goods or sell goods en route either way. As long as the Spanish kept away. (King James had declared war on Spain with disastrous results as Buckingham met a swift defeat). Capt. James felt the southern Virginia plantation had the better land. His father was excited about tobacco, having smoked it with Sir Walter Raleigh in his library on the Wiltshire-Somerset border when Walter, who was now out of favor with the king, first brought it to England. It grew like a weed, he was told, but needed laborers to weed it, cut it, hang it to dry and then put it in barrels to ship. Africa was full of free laborers (after an initial sale) and England, Ireland, Scotland and Wales had an abundance of political prisoners plus indigents that could earn their freedom through an indentured servitude. Robert, he knew, was more enamored of the northern site but James could live with land grants in the southern. "All right, " he said to Cecil, rising and shaking his hand, "I will let the others know and we'll get the *Mary and John* into Plymouth for re-caulking and graving and meet with the Bristol Merchant Adventurers to secure financing of her stores and any needed repairs. "

James whistled a sea chanty all the through the courtyard, down the steps and to his waiting barge. Davis family would grow fat on bounty from the New Land.

CHAPTER TWELVE

Adventure Awaits

Late May, 1607

By 1607 the older generation was on the decline. James Thomas's sons Capt. Thomas, John, Capt. James, and Capt. Robert represented a generation that identified as English instead of Welsh. As did his cousin Sir John's grandsons George, William, Richard, Matthew, John and Barnaby. Since so many in the family had the same names and a James might have a Robert or a Thomas might have James it could be confusing to all but the family, which nicknamed members or used middle names or terms such as 'the younger' to differentiate.

The men of this generation were mostly seamen but there were relatives and sisters who stayed with the land, on the estates in Wiltshire, Somerset, Berkshire, Wales and Devonshire.

Some became smiths as a secondary trade, sail weavers, carpenters (joiners), or land-based merchants in Bristol. But whatever profession they plied they were attached to the seafaring branch since goods produced in England weren't in demand in England as most rural folks had some sheep and the men sheared the sheep, the women boiled the wool in ammonia and hot water, sometimes adding lye soap, then spread the fleeces on sheets on the lawn to dry and whiten. Then they would hand card the wool, combing all the bits of twigs and dirt out. After the wool was carded into rolls, or roves, the ladies would use the big walking wheels to spin it into yarn. The yarn could then be double or triple plied, wound into skeins and the skeins dyed into colors made from common plants, imported woad or minerals. The use of alum, a recent product mined in England, helped set the colors and alum became a profitable export item. Weaving was an art and George and William had big looms for weaving thick canvas sailcloth but it was made from linen from Irish or British flax, not wool. For the sea the women left the natural oil, or lanolin in the wool as it made cloth waterproof. Most rural families had at least one milk cow so they provided their own butter and cheese. The chalk plains of Wiltshire and the surrounding counties of Gloucester and Somerset made the best cheeses in England. The rural tenants would raise pigs for sausage, bacon, ham or pork. The farm wives kept kitchen gardens with some leaf and root vegetables and herbs and a flock of hens for eggs and chicken meat. The Lords of the estates got a share of goods and labor from tenants but the real markets for English goods were the plantations and tropical countries. And from them the captains brought back spices, cotton cloth, indigo, wines and luxury items for the rich merchants in London and their country estates.

William Davis Sr. of Bristol was always on the lookout for new iron sources as his profession of smithing demanded a steady supply. House builders and carpenters wanted timber, which Britain was running out of, except in the royal forests, which were off limits to regular folk. As were the royal deer who roamed the forests. But the New Land, soon to the New England, was lush with timber. Good, sturdy trees such as oak, chestnut, hickory, larch, spruce and elm plus softer woods such as the pines abounded in forests that went on and on and on. If England had been more aggressive she could have had the fine tropical mahoganies, teaks and ebonies but her queen grew old and England grew poor from constant wars with France and Spain so the Dutch and Spanish took over the East Indies and the southern part of the long continent Columbus had discovered over a hundred years past. Though England, Scotland, Wales and Ireland had a lot of fish off their coastal fishing banks, the cod off New England was bigger and fatter and, like the trees, seemingly limitless. And in the West Indies and other sea shores they could harvest a lot of sea saLt. which after it was cleaned and dried was packed around fish for curing in barrels and used inland to preserve, or saLt. beef and pork. Smiths, carpenters, coopers and weavers were always in demand in maritime villages.

In looking towards the New World, Captain Robert Davis wasn't looking for a religious sanctuary. His family observed the Sabbath and didn't care for Catholics but they weren't drawn to churchly professions except for one branch still living in Wales. But like most sailors he had a healthy respect for God, especially in the midst of a hellish storm at sea.

So it was with great anticipation that Robert received his brother James on the wharf in Plymouth in May, 1607.

"James! Ye are a sight for sore eyes!" Robert exclaimed, grasping the shorter man to him as they walked up the gangplank and then to the captain's quarters.

Robert was tall, broad shouldered and broad chested but narrow in the hips and legs. He had thick black hair and devilishly handsome features. His eyes were brown, unlike James's but a dark hue that could almost look black in the dark. He had strong, arched eyebrows and the family joke was that he could pass for a pirate or highwayman due to his cavalier attitude and handsome charm. On the other hand, with the right clothes, James could pass for a member of the House of Lords. All the Davis men were educated through grammar school but none except the Welsh line went to the colleges of Cambridge or Oxford. Cambridge was for the scholarly type: those most interested in becoming ministers or barristers and rising to political power through the ranks of the church or courts. Under Queen Elizabeth new colleges at Cambridge were established to reflect a Puritan radicalism and the prominent ministers of the day had received educations that were more Calvinistic than the Catholic style of Protestantism preached by the Church of England.

Most of the Davis men liked physical work: the hard work at sea or managing estates (which often required hands-on help with harvests or livestock and always included horseback riding. For this meeting with Robert James had ridden across the moors from Bideford to Bristol, spent a few nights there meeting with relatives and merchant adventurers, then a night on his cousin's farm in Tisbury before continuing to Plymouth.

"And ye, too!" James said, stepping back on his fine heeled boots, the tops turned down from the thighs. "The family says hello and wants updates on your progress."

Robert laughed.

"I just bet they do! Are the provisions coming along, then?"

"Sir John is a little slow in paying, but yes, the hogsheads of pork and biscuits will be coming soon. Ale also. And in respect of our dead cousin John's voyages with Cavendish, we will also carry some lime juice as he swore it was the best preventative for the scurvy."

They walked down the stone pier and went out to the 60 ton *Mary and John* moored at the end of one of the wharves. She was typical of the ships of the day: high castles on each end, four masts, including a diagonal mizzen mast, a scrubbed deck full of piles of carefully coiled rigging, extra canvas sails packed against her sides and in chests down below. The first low ceiling level below decks had rooms where privileged passengers could sleep and below them the sailors and a common space for debtor or prison laborers being shipped out from England, then at the very bottom was the deep hold for cargo.

At a neighboring wharf stood the Dutch low-keeled *Gift of God.* The Davis men – generations named George, James, Robert, Richard, William and Nathaniel – had sailed almost all the types of vessels moving goods across the English Channel and Irish Sea. They or relatives had joined Sir Walter Raleigh's great Navy against the Spanish Armada and lost a fine ship, (the first) *Swan,* in the battles. They knew Dutch flyboats could handle the rough Atlantic swells and had the added advantage of being able to get in close to shores as they didn't draw as much water. Since a good part of the business of setting up a plantation would be scouting the rivers emptying into the Atlantic they needed shallops and a flyboat.

"I have some Gloucester cheese for ye," said James as he handed a cheesecloth wrapped bundle to his brother. "From Agnes's father's farm."

The men grabbed the ropes and walked up the gangplank. Sailors were busy scrubbing the decks and loading barrels and crates into the hold. Below decks they could hear the sound of the ship's carpenter and cooper hammering.

"I tried to talk young Dolor to come along as carpenter," James said as they sat at the desk in the captain's quarters, "but he has no stomach for tha sea and got green even at the thought."

The two men laughed at the memory of their cousin on his first attempt to sail.

"I reckon I'll have enou' of that with them Gilberts and Pophams," said Robert.

"Aye, even though they be of seafaring stock they don't have the miles of sea beneath their boots and I wager it will take many days off the Lizard before the pukin stops."

"I don't like the late start," Robert said, his tone serious, "If we leave end of month we be sailing in prime storm season. If we be lucky and don't get into a bad storms or mishaps we'll be arriving too close to winter and there won't be a planting season. T'won't be like sailin' to the southern plantation. The Norumbega land gets a bad winter. This we both know from fishing off its coast."

"I agree. The London Company already got a head start, sending Newport with three ships to the southern plantation in December. I was supposed to go with that fleet, as ye know, but I can't stand that John Smith and knew they'rd be no end of the arguing so begged off. I blame that George Percy for that as with Walter in the Tower he's eager to get ahold of his patents. Even though they can't settle north of the thirty-eight and us north of the forty-first, with storms and drifting off course, who knows where they'll land? And I wasn't happy with the Plymouth's Company's insistence on sending Challons off on an exploratory voyage instead of settling a plantation last August. Then he got himself blown off course due to a storm and is now in a Spanish jail. Cousin Neville and Sir Popham are trying their damndest to get him released but he lost half his crew when the Spaniards boarded the *Richard* and from what I hear the Inquisitors are torturing and hanging his crew in Spain."

"Yeah, they got Hines, too. The duke of Medina is trying through Neville to get them out, but you know as well as I what those papist Inquisitors are like. Bunch of bloodthirsty sadists."

"Aye. But Martin and his crew came back and reported favorably. It seems there's been a war amongst the heathens and their numbers are down. And now we have the royal backing, which they didn't have when they sailed."

James drank down his pewter mug of ale and wiped his reddish-blond bristle of moustache Popham's he. He also sported a small Van Dyke beard.

"Fat lot of good that will do us, eh, Robert? Yeah they will give us some cannon and gunpowder but it's all up to us to get the fort made and defended."

Robert frowned.

"I don't like the idea of Raleigh Gilbert being in charge of the so-called militiary there. He's a damned hothead, loves the fight."

James replied, "Well at least we'll have John Popham, who might be old but has a calm head about him. And his nephew George. Plus the two savages Weymouth brought back will help us with their brethren on shore."

Robert frowned again.

"I think John Popham is too old, although he'd be great on land I don't think he's up to a long voyage.," he sighed and added,"'Tis all in God's hands, me boy. We will do our best for God and country – and do even better for our kin!" he ended with a laugh and raised his newly filled tankard.

"To the Davis boyos," he said and they clanked mugs.

"Aye, we might have lost our lands in Wales but by God we will more than make up for it with what we be a'getting in New England!"

James stood up to his full height. Unlike the area below decks the captain's quarters above the main deck was full height.

"I be off now, Robert. I'm tuckered and me arse is sore from all that horse ridin'. I'd rather ride the waves any old day."

Robert watched him walk down the pier in his rolling sailor's gait and up the dock to the *Gift of God* where James would bunk in its captain's quarters. Once under sail the captain was basically the king of his ship. If high ranking gentry sailed as passengers they would get the first class cabin in the wardroom and even be called admiral but it was the navigators, or pilots, who made the important sailing decisions. Like his cousin John had been. "'Twas a dammed shame he got killed in the South Seas by Asian pirates," thought Robert.

However, once berthed at their destination the 'gentlemen' became the law as governors. Robert and James had agreed to help site and build a fort and oversee its initial operations but he had no desire to stay on as a landlubber. The sea was his home. It was his mother and father and even his god at times. It was so boundless and awesome and terrifying and beautiful that land, even good fertile land, held little appeal for him and James. Many of his relatives were adequate sailors and he'd be happy to have any on board, but they didn't share the youthful passion he and James had for the sailor's life. They saw sailing as a way to make money to buy land to farm, – as he and his younger brother did – but they actually spoke of retiring and living on the land, managing farms like Devonshire gentry. Robert knew this new land would not offer a comfortable, well-planned farm but would be wilderness and would need to be hacked out of forests and defended from the savages. There would be no nice, sturdy grey stone and slate manors but rough timbered huts at first. He preferred life onboard the *Mary and John.*

But he was looking forward to the adventure and the opportunities that would follow.

He and James lived for adventure, for the freedom of the sea, lived to explore like John had. Truth be told, in the breast of the two brothers lived the dream of finding the elusive Northwest Passage and completing John's quest.

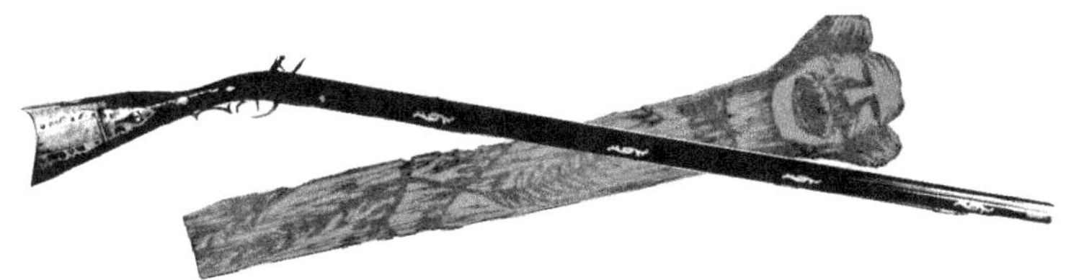

CHAPTER THIRTEEN

The First Voyage

1607

The two ships of sail left Plymouth harbor a little after a year since Weymouth left on Easter Sunday in 1606.

There was a feeling of euphoria on shore and on the decks, lots of shouts of encouragement and a lot of laughter, both from the merchants ashore and the gentlemen and sailors aboard the two settlement ships as the *Mary and John*, with admiral Raleigh Gilbert (eldest son of Sir John Gilbert and named after Sir Walter Raleigh), pilot Robert Davis and First Mate Richard Davis and the *Gift of God* with Capt. George Popham (middle son between Sir John and Francis, both in England) and First Mate James Davis weighed anchor and sailed along the south coast of England on the last day of May, 1607. They left The Lizard, the westernmost point of England, behind them at 6 p.m. the next day.

The two ships sailed southwest. By avoiding storms and under fair trade winds, sailing day and night they made the outer Azores in twenty-four days.

****

On the *Mary and John,* the flagship, land was sited.

"Land ho!" the sailor in the crow's nest called and all hands were immediately on deck.

"'Tis The Island of Corvo!" the titular captain, Raleigh Gilbert, exclaimed.

Robert pulled out his telescope and frowned.

"Nay, we are near Graciosa."

Robert explained that his noon sighting, using his cousin's pear wood backstaff showed them further south than The Islands of Flowers and Corve.

The two men debated and then followed Robert's advice and set course northwest where The Island of Flowers and Corve were supposed to be. Gilbert deferred to Robert as he had more experience in these seas and soon they came to the Island of Flowers and Corve. Finding a good harbor, the ship's boats were lowered and crew went ashore to fill barrels with fresh water: gold to a ship's crew. The oldest man in their party, Popham, wanted to go, too, to explore the island but was discouraged by James. Of the three Davis men Richard was the oldest at 54; Robert the most experienced at 47 and James the youngest, was 35.

They had seen two sails of ships on their southern voyage but sensed no threat from them. However, two days later the two foreign ships appeared on the horizon off the Island of Flowers. The seas were becalmed so the *Gift* and *Mary and John* were drifting apart and couldn't raise sail and escape. One of the foreign ships set its ship's boat down with men to approach the *Mary and John.*

On the *Gift* James ordered men to arms, covering, as their sister ship was hailed. Both ships had weighed anchor and were adrift but from the deck of the *Gift* James could see a sailor named John Gayett on the *Mary and John* yelling down to the foreign boat and a member of the boarding party appeared to wave back in a friendly manner. Robert waved across but he wasn't seen so James and Popham on the *Gift* decided to play it safe and keep their distance. Through the telescope they could see Gilbert welcoming what appeared to be a Dutch captain and crew onboard and into the galley to be entertained. Through the night the sound of feasting and song came in waves across the bay.

The next day Gilbert and crew members left Robert in charge of the *Mary and*

John and boarded the Dutch flagship. Things then turned ugly. The captain ordered crewmembers to grab Gilbert and then he accused him of piracy, a hanging offense. The seas and winds kept pulling the *Gift of God* away from the *Mary and John* as they heard screams from the Dutch ship and saw the top sail of the *Mary and John* struck and hoisted three times, a sign of distress.

James wanted to try to send ships' boats with armed men to rescue his brother and crew.

The old man, Popham replied, "Our mission is to settle the northern Virginia patent. The winds and tides are not in our favor and we will accomplish nothing if we try to rescue the *Mary and John*. Your brother is a master sailor and if they can get away from those scoundrel Flemings, they will. He has Gosnold and Pring's map and will find us if we follow it as planned. I don't know if Raleigh will survive and be released but we have to make a hard decision: stay and possibly perish, be captured and tortured as Challon's crew were or continue on our mission."

It was a hard decision but the winds were carrying them west, away from the *Mary and John* and the two hostile Dutch vessels.

With a heavy heart James set course and they sailed west- northwest for Virginia.

****

Gilbert and his crew were badly beaten, tortured and taunted, some held in the bilges, but after about seven hours the Flemings bored of their sport and released them back to the *Mary and John*. The *Gift of God* was no longer in site but Robert set course west, then northwest, as had his cousin. Gilbert was full of rage that the *Gift* hadn't come to their rescue. He had wounds from the torture and his pride was wounded as well from the contemptuous treatment they had received aboard the Dutch flagship. As gentry, Gilbert had known nothing but respect in England.

Robert was angry, too, but as they put the Dutch ships behind him he became more philosophical.

"We knew the risks when we sailed, Raleigh. We promised the merchant adventurers we would not turn back, no matter what. A tremendous amount of money was invested in this plantation scheme. Since the Pophams are the main investors

I'm sure George made James continue, hoping to salvage at least part of their investment. You know as well as I if we don't plant a fort and settlement we lose our patent and the French will move in like vultures."

Raleigh, nursing his wounds with ale and hot compresses the ship's doctor/cook applied to his head and limbs morosely shrugged.

Robert continued, his eyes scanning the empty, sun-glared seas, "James won't let the *Gift* get captured. Even if he had to leave George he would continue. A captain puts his ship first. A few men can be replaced but a ship, with its cargo and crew is almost a sacred thing. We take these wooden boxes and set them afloat on a vast watery emptiness. 'Tis only through skill, cunning and the blessings of the Lord we actually reach a port, and only through maps and navigational skill do we reach our destined ports. It's all a gamble and don't I know it. How many ships and precious cargo were lost in the Mediterranean and other seas when we warred with France, Spain, Portugal and the Dutch, depending on the year and the whims of the kings and queens involved? How much valuable cargo has been pirated either by us or from us in these West Indian seas?"

Gilbert grunted and drank deeply.

"The tales John told us when he came back from his voyages would be enough to stand yer hair on end! In the East Indies they narrowly escaped from cannibals on one island! At every port they didn't know if the sultan would welcome them or kill them. They would sail into a harbor on one side of an island and find the opposite side occupied by the Dutch East India Company. Yet we English are a stubborn breed and we now have a trading port in Malaysia. It's not a big inroad but one day the Dutch won't be so high and mighty and we shall rule the seas. This voyage to plant a settlement in the north is critical to England's future. James knows this. Don't think less o' im for continuing and leaving us to our fate."

Raleigh grumbled but finally agreed. 'Twas after all an adventure and, although it had been unpleasant, the seven hours of brutality aboard the Dutch ship would make a good story when he returned to England and told his uncle Sir Walter Raleigh about it.

****

On Wednesday, the first day of July, the *Mary and John* was six leagues off Flowers. Robert kept her to a westerly course on the 40th then edged north to the 43rd latitude. A little over three weeks later, on July 27 their sounding hit ground at 18 fathoms. They fished for three hours, taking in 200 cod.

"Will ye look at them cod" Robert exclaimed as they were hauled in, "'Tis the greatest and largest I've ever seen! Why, we could fill our hold wit' them in less'n a month o'fishing off here!"

Later, he and Gilbert studied their copy of Gosnold and Pring's map and they decided they were off the Grand Banks. Robert had fished further north, off Newfoundland, but had never seen such an abundance of huge, fat codfish.

The wind was blowing to the southwest so they set their sails and stood by the wind, running for mainland as they followed the Banks. "Keep her west by north-west," Robert called down to the crewman below who, by the light of a candle and a compass controlled the rudder below the upper deck.

Around ten in the morning on the 30th of July they found deep water, 160 fathoms with black ooze on the bottom.

"Land ho!" yelled the spotter from the crow's nest.

Robert and Gilbert took turns with the telescope and could just make out land to the west but the winds were against them so they struck a hull and fished, waiting until the next day to attempt to get closer to shore.

The excitement filled the ship with a lively energy. Land at last! A chance to go ashore, walk like a normal person and drink fresh water from a stream, eat fresh berries or other fruit, catch deer or rabbits, anything but fish, fish, fish and salted meat for a steady diet.

The following day around 3 p.m. they recovered the shore and came to anchor under an island at 44.1 degrees latitude. From his maps Robert reckoned they were about 30 miles southeast of Cape Le Hevre, putting them within English territory but north of their destination.

After about two hours a shallop with Indians approached the *Mary and John.* Robert and his crew tried to communicate using hand language as the expedition's interpreters *Skidwarres* and *Amant* were with James and Popham on the *Gift of*

God. The galleon's crew threw biscuits down into the shallop and showed knives, glasses and strings of beads to the indians but it took hours before three braves would board. The indians knew many French words but little English. They were entertained and spent the night but the next day, the first day of August, the shallop returned to the *Mary and John* with three females and beaver plus other skins. The indians demanded too much in trade goods so Robert and the crew weren't able to exchange much. Their chief was named Massamett and they pointed to the harbor and called it *Emannett.*

"I think they are trying to tell us they are enemies of the *Sassanoa*, to the west," Gilbert told Robert, "Let's drop the ship's boat and row to shore and see what we can find," he said after the last of the savages had left.

Gilbert and 12 men rowed to shore. Robert was amazed at the forests of high and mighty trees, the gooseberries, strawberries, raspberries and whorts growing in abundance on the land.

"Tis surely God's land," he murmured to Raleigh as they explored.

"Yes, but it also belongs to these fellows!"Raleigh grumbled as he swatted mosquitoes.

"We be best to explore when they are less active," Robert replied as they headed back to the *Mary and John*, the shallop filled with water casks and sacks of berries.

The next day, August second, was the Sabbath. After the service and dinner they went ashore again for more water. Four savages, painted as was their custom with a red ochre to repel the mosquitoes, appeared with bows and arrows but the crew avoided a confrontation and instead rowed out to a point and fished, taking about 50 great lobsters with hooks lashed to staffs. They found they could hitch them off the shoals with ease.

"Look at these 'ere!" a sailor called up as they pulled along the mother ship.

"My lord!" Robert exclaimed, "The fish grow to such gigantic size here!"

He gazed across the harbor at the tall stands of pine, oak and chestnut.

"Yes, 'tis well enough, my man, but we are not where we are supposed to be. I just hope the takings are as good to our south."

"Aye, I agree," Robert said as they helped haul the lobsters and more fresh water onboard and heard the sailors tell them about the aggressive savages on shore.

Around midnight the watch captain woke Robert, "The wind, sir, 'tis coming good and strong from the north east. We can make fine sailing fer ta coast if we cast off."

The ship sailed with coastline in sight on the third of August and then on the fourth at 5 a.m. as the sun was rising they saw white shores that reminded them of white sandy beaches of England. There were three mountains behind the beaches.

"I swear those cliffs yon to the west look just like Dover!" said Robert as he sketched the shapes of the mountains in the distance.

Raleigh agreed but as they skirted the island they saw the white 'sands' were treacherous white rocks, not soft sand.

Robert set course west by north and they came to anchor under an island overhang in 12 fathoms, the water further out only 40 fathoms deep. The tops of the mountains were bare, which puzzled the captain and pilot.

The waves and currents and winds were as wild as the west coast of England with rocky shoals preventing them from sailing due west.

The next day, Friday, the seventh of August they came upon a small island with a cross on it.

"I believe this is the cross Martin put up on his last voyage," Robert said, "Shall we name the island St. Georges?"

"As in slaying the dragon?" Raleigh jested as they walked over the rocky island.

The sun had been up about five hours and was beating down hard on them. Robert mopped his brow and turned to the east. He grabbed his telescope and exclaimed,

"Thanks to God be praised, 'tis the *Gift* in that harbor yon!"

The captain and crew re-boarded the *Mary and John* and with Robert shouting to his brother, they sailed around the point and came abreast of the *Gift of God*, lashing the two boats together so they'd not get separated again.

Robert didn't wait until all the lines were fast to climb the ropes up the side of the *Gift,* an easier task than on the *Mary and John* as it sat lower in the water.

"James!" he exclaimed, clasping his brother tight. Richard also joined and then George Popham hugged the Davis men.

Raleigh had boarded and they saw the apprehensive look in James's eyes.

"'Tis all right, then, James, he not be holding a grudge against 'e."

There was an awkward silence then Raleigh crossed the deck and shook

Popham's hand.

"I shall tell you all about it over some of your fine cognac," he said as they made way for the galley. Dining on deck was out of the question as the heat and mosquitoes made being above deck a torture even with the cool breeze.

On the morn, early so as to avoid the mosquitoes, Capt. Gilbert, Robert, *Skidwarres* and 12 men took the shallop and rowed amongst what Robert referred to as "many gallant islands" until they found the mouth of the Pemiquid River, estimated at four leagues from where the ships were anchored. The cove had a pond of fresh water nearby under the falls from the river. *Skidwarres* said it was where he and the four other braves were tricked onboard Capt. Weymouth's boat and from there taken to England. He remarked that his village was no longer on the banks of the pond.

Gilbert, Robert and *Skidwarres* followed a trail inland and shortly came upon his village of about 100 savages. A loud howling arose at their approach and the savages armed their bows.

Then the chief, *Nahanda*, recognized his kinsman and, after a brief exchange, the savages laid down their bows.

Robert and Gilbert had never been in an indian village before and were amazed at the large longhouse and smaller buildings that they built from bent saplings and shingled with cedar bark.

The chief invited them inside the largest longhouse structure that had curtained partitions made of woven bark fibers and there they saw a large copper kettle over a fire and smelled meat boiling.

Skidwarres was sent back to the shallop and the rest of the crew were invited to join in the feasting.

Steamed clams, boiled duck and venison were served, as well as cornmeal cakes and a porridge of cornmeal. After the salt pork, biscuits, or hard tack, and fish the hearty, greasy, meaty meal was well received. Instead of clay or pewter they used large shells for dishes and drank from wooden cups or hollowed horns.

They had no alcoholic drinks but offered a tea made from sassafras root that the men found very tasty and refreshing.

Gilbert remarked to Robert, "I'm not sure I like all that arguing amongst themselves and *Skidwarres*. They could be planning an ambush."

"Aye, we'd best be getting back to our ships," Robert replied, stiffly rising.

Skidwarres offered their thanks to their hosts and said they had to leave. Many accompanied them back down the little trail and watched as they cast off.

Both Gilbert and Robert had mixed feelings about the encounter.

"Well, they seemed friendly enough," Robert said, seconded by Richard.

"We'll see," Raleigh replied solemnly, "The savages are a treacherous lot. I think the only reason we are being welcomed is that they want us to be allies against the *Sassanoa*. I gathered something about a son of a chief having been kidnaped or killed and the war is about revenge. They have a very strong code of honor and will avenge the killing of kin."

"That's pretty common," Robert replied, making note of the fine, huge trees in the forests as they rowed down river.

"'Tis a shame they have their village near that pond as I think it would make a good place for a settlement."

Raleigh shook his head,

"Nay, we want to get further south. We want no fights with the French about territory. You noticed how French words are interspersed with their own native tongue?"

"Aye, I heard that. And the steel knives and copper pots sure didn't come from us."

"Did you see how some of their arrows had flint tips and some of the others had pieces of steel they had found and sharpened? These fellows would just love to get their hands on our cannon and muskets and if they do, we will be lucky to cast off with our own skins, never mind the furs they like to trade."

The following day being the Sabbath the crew gathered beneath the wooden cross out on the island and their chaplain, Richard Seymour, conducted services.

On Monday, August 10th, Capt. George Popham took a shallop with 30 men and Capt. Gilbert loaded his as before, adding an additional eight men and they rowed up the Pemiquid River to the village, which was on a branch of the main river.

The chief, or sachem, allowed all to come ashore but after a brief visit Raleigh suggested they dock on the opposite shore. *Skidwarres* begged to stay behind with his family, saying he would rejoin them on the morrow.

In their camp across the river, the mood of the English was unsettled.

"I say we weigh anchor and set sails to go further south," Raleigh advised.

"Aye, there is much to be explored and mapped," said Gome Carew, their chief searcher and distant relative of the Davises.

They set up watches and slept on the ground, thick with pine needles and moss but rocky underneath.

The next morning they rowed across the river but Skidwarres refused to come out so they weighed anchors, returned to the main ships and set sails to the coast to find the river the savages called *Sagadahoc*. They sailed in the bay under moonlight until about midnight then struck the sails and laid a hull until morning as they couldn't see the rocks along the shore.

On the next day, Thursday, August the 13th they saw the island the savages said was named *Satquin* but the currents pulled them south and they overshot the river's outlet. The *Gift* dropped her shallop and a crew made it ashore but the rest stayed on board, worried they might lose a shallop if they tried to land both. The wind had picked up and was blowing very hard, pinning the large ships near the shore and it took all of James and Robert's skills to keep the ships from wrecking on the rocks. They were Bristol, Bideford, Plymouth and Dartmouth sailors and knew how to maneuver wild waves around shoals, unlike the captains who just plied the Channel between England and the Continent and sailed up the Thames to the nice, civilized docks near London. Still, the bottoms of the seacoasts of Devon and Cornwall were littered with wrecks from ships being blown into rocks or from wily salvagers setting up false lights on shore to lure ships into dark, rocky coves.

On the following day, despite the winds, Robert and James brought the big ships between two islands, offering a respite from the open sea winds. The *Mary and John* needed immediate repairs in dock and Carew led a party ashore, including Robert, to gather four types of berries and whorts and fresh water and others cut pine for the cook's stove.

The next day, Saturday, August 15th, the storm ended and they were able to sail to the mouth of the *Sagadahoc* River but the winds kept them from sailing into it. Captain Popham sent a fishing party out in a shallop and they caught twenty large cod in no time at all.

The next morning was the Sabbath and after a hurried morning service, the *Gift of God* towed the *Mary and John* into the river so both ships were anchored together and out of the open sea.

On Monday, August 17th, Carew, Popham, Gilbert and Robert plus 15 men took the *Gift of God*'s shallop up the river and sailed 14 leagues up the *Kennebec* River whose the depth was never shallower than three fathoms.

Robert, who was keeping a journal, was much impressed by all the large trees in the forests along it. Although there were many tall pines, he also noted chestnut, hemlock, oak and even spruce, all needed for His Majesty's Navy.

"Even if we only send back timber, this voyage will have been a success," he said to Raleigh.

"George wants silver," Gilbert replied drily, "Although all we've seen is some trace copper and mica. I don't think this granite rock is the type that silver veins appear in. It will be like asking Cornwall to produce gold instead of coal."

"Aye," Robert agreed, "'Tis a shame our ships didn't dominate the south and the Spanish took it. Most of the silver and gold our captains brought back were pirated off Spanish galleons, and the good queen, bless her soul, knew it damned well and even sanctioned it. Walter's family rebuilt Longleat with the silver she let her court favorite keep after one big plunder. " (Sir Walter's brother owned Corsely Manor and Sir Walter's mother-in-law married Sir John Thynnes and got Longleat Castle. The Longs owned South Wraxall and the queen had given Longleat Castle to Sir Thomas Gorges . The manor needed a lot of remodeling and when the money ran out Lady Gorges asked the queen if she could have the wreck of a Spanish vessel from the Armada. The queen agreed, not knowing it was loaded with bars of silver.)

"Piracy is a dirty business," Raleigh said with a sigh, "And I think what bothered me the most on that Fleming ship was to be accused of it!"

"Aye, a man needs his honor," said Robert, lighting a pipe and inhaling deeply, "But from what I'm seeing, we'll have na need to pirate as these woods and these seas plus the furs the savages bring to us will make us all rich men; rich off God's own bounty."

"If the French leave us alone," Popham added, "They are greedy. Champlain already explored inland to a great river south of the Davis Straights and I've heard Henry Hudson is trying to get an exploration going up a big river, backed by the damned Flemings."

None of the men thought about the savages already inhabiting the land. It was their land, given to them by divine patent, from a Christian king. The savages weren't using it as God intended. They built crude homes and moved about often – unlike Christian civilized men who built stone or heavy timber and lathe houses with slate roofs and chimneys and cleared and fenced land for domesticated live-stock and crops. What they were seeing were loose bands of greasy, red-ochered mostly naked savages without any hallmarks of civilization such as a written language. The one Hackled was able to produce wasn't very helpful as they weren't sure of how to pronounce the vocabulary he had written down from Weymouth's captives, but it was the only written one they had.

Around sunset, they began the trip back to the ships in the bay, having decided where they would build their fort.

It was the afternoon of the 18th when they went ashore and began to draw the outline in the soil where the trench around the fort would be – at the western side near the mouth of the *Sagadahoc* river, a site called *Sabino* by the savages.

The plan of the fort featured a tongue sticking out to the dock, then a rectangle with four-sided turrets built into its corners, all to be built of fresh-hewn pine logs. They would immediately build a storehouse and a hut inside for their gunpowder kegs. There was to be a square house for Popham as governor but they knew they probably wouldn't get more than rough shacks thrown up for the others before winter.

As they were planning, a canoe with three savages drifted by but didn't stop.

"Hunting party, most likely," said Richard as he labored with the debtors to dig lines in the sandy, rock-filled soil.

On Wednesday, the 19th, the crew all went ashore to the site and Richard Seymour delivered a sermon and consecrated the site to their Lord God and dedicated the fort to King James I. Then he read the 'Orders and Laws' and said it had been decided that Capt. George Popham would be President of the fort, with Capt. Raleigh Gilbert and Capt. Richard Davies to be Assistants. He also read that Capt. Edward Harlow was to be Master of Ordnance, Capt. Robert Davis would be Sergeant Major at the fort, Capt. Ellis Best, Marshall, Mr. Eamon, Secretary to the President and Capt. James Davies Captain of the fort itself. Mr. Gome Carew would continue in his position as Chief Searcher.

Those who were assigned to the task of cutting and hauling logs (they had no horses or wagons) or digging trenches enjoyed their last day of rest as the work was to be commenced at dawn of the morrow.

The next day, August 21, the ship's chief carpenter or shipwright, Mr. Digby of London, and a crew set about hauling pre-cut timber from the hull of the *Mary and John* so a pinnace could be buiLt. to replace the *Mary and John* after she sailed back to England. Although the days were hot and humid, the early mornings had a nip in the air that told them winter would come early in this new land and no captain liked the thought of having his ship stuck in ice near shore or sailing through a field of icebergs.

Saturday, the 22nd Capt. Popham took a crew in a shallop and sailed up the *Pashipakoke* River. At a village they found out Skidwarres and Nahanda had joined the fight against the Sassanoa and would not be returning to the fort. This was a blow as it left them with no interpreter, just Rossier-Hakluyt's crude vocabulary book as a tool to communicate with the savages. Despite having served on the continent in battles, none of the older men knew much French, which seemed to be the predominant second language there.

The next day Robert and the others concentrated on working on the fort but Raleigh took a shallop out to explore more river inlets. However, a hard east wind blew them back to shore.

The captains and the men worked together on the fort for the next two days but on Friday Raleigh, Carew and Robert plus a crew sailed west to a headland the savages called *Semeanis.*

Robert observed, "'Tis like one o' His Majesty's parks, full of oak, walnuts, pines, hazelnuts with no thicket." Raleigh laughed, "All of this belongs to the King," but he winked, "That is, all His Majesty knows about. There is plenty for ourselves, too and our investors will be delighted to know of the fertility of this place as we fill our holds with much hardwood."

The next day they fought the wind and sailed between many 'goodly islands' and found a great bay between the *Sagadahock* and the mainland full of the above trees plus thick with whorts (berries) and sarsaparilla.

They returned to the fort site and all helped getting a storehouse built inside its rising walls.

On the fifth day of September the savages came to trade, nine canoes of them. Skidwarres and Dehanda were with them, 40 in all. They were fed and entertained and Skidwarres stayed overnight inside the rough fort. On the morrow Gilbert, James Davis and Capt. Elllis Best took him back across the river and they were fed and entertained and spent the night in the indian camp.

The next day Robert began supervising the offloading of the provisions in the *Mary and John*'s hold.

The next day Raleigh, Robert and 21 men sailed up the Penobscot River to trade with the chief sachem, Bashaba, but the winds blew so strongly they couldn't make land and were forced to wait three days before they could retry. However, when they returned, the village on the Pemiquid River was vacant. Running out of victuals, the English returned to the ships and growing fort.

Robert was on deck early in the morning of the 15th when a blazing star shot across the dark sky. He looked over to the *Gift* and saw James on deck, observing it, too. Later, over breakfast on shore, they told the officers what they had seen.

"'Tis an omen, for sure, " said Rev. Seymour.

"Agreed," said Popham, clearing his throat and lighting a pipe, "But a good omen or a bad one?"

Seymour shook his head.

"I'm afraid I'm no prophet. I have studied the Bible and learned its verses and lessons but unlike the prophets of the Old Testament, I have not the gift of foretelling the future. Indeed, it is a thing to be avoided as a tool of witchcraft."

The men laughed lightly.

"Richard, you are too prudish! God sends his portents. Isn't it said that He put the sun, moon and stars in the sky to serve as such?"

"I don't know, George. If a dream comes unsolicited and is determined to be from God and not Satan, then I would take it seriously. However, to be reading good or ill future from shooting stars isn't something I'm comfortable with. I know of men who have been hanged for discerning."

"Especially by those Spanish Inquisitors!" James exclaimed, regaling them with the horrors Challons and his crew recently went through.

'Tis best a thing not to be spoken of," Popham summed up, exhaling and then coughing.

The building of the fort, transferring cannon and provisions took up the most of the following week. They saw geese flying south from time to time in great arrow formations. This, more than a shooting star, was an omen. It foretold of the coming winter and all men intensified their efforts.

On Wednesday, the 23rd of September Raleigh, Robert, Carew and 17 men sailed inland up the Sagadahoc River. Robert declared it exceedingly fertile, "champion" land as they set up camp for the night. The next day's voyaging brought them to an island the savages called *Cushoe* with great falls spilling down its sides. They docked and hiked up and found hops and sweet dark red berries and bright red grapes on the island, wonderful for the making of wine and ale. They also dug up garlic and native onions, smaller than the English ones but pungent. Both would come in handy to cover the taste of salt pork or dried meat that was going rancid later that winter. As sailing men they knew there were times you just had to hold your nose and swallow, hoping you wouldn't be puking your guts out off the poop deck later on.

The next day a large canoe joined them beneath the falls. In it was a savage called Sabenor who said he was lord of the river S*agadahoc*. Sixteen savages in three canoes joined them and then there was some ugliness between him and Raleigh as the skins they offered had little value and Gilbert told them so. The savages then grabbed one of the men and Raleigh ordered two men to stay with the shallop and he and the rest ran after the chief and his savages to his village. There, they wanted to trade harsh tobacco and scrawny, ill tanned hides for fine English copper and knives and Italian beads.

Raleigh refused and made them release the frightened crewman. They went back to the shallop and were followed by a savage who boarded, pretending to bend down to light his pipe from their firebrand but instead he grabbed it and threw it into the water so they couldn't light their cannon powder and fire on them but the guards' muskets scared them off. After a while the lord of the river came out and called for peace and the two parties camped onshore overnight. It was tense but a peace of sorts was gained.

As they sailed out at dawn the next day Robert observed spruce trees along the riverbanks that could serve well as masts in His Majesty's royal navy plus cotton, apple trees and mussels that contained small grey pearls attached to rocks along the shore.

The weather turned foggy and rainy. To return, they followed a river the sachem told them would bring them back to the bay and arrived at the fort on the 29th of September, planting a cross in front of it on the shore.

Building the fort occupied the men for days, then *Skidwarres*, *Nahanda* and the brother of *Bashaba*, the sagamore *Amenquin*, arrived to trade. However, it was the Sabbath so they didn't conduct business. The savages attended the services and appeared to be respectful of the English God, even bowing their shaved, painted, feather-trimmed heads.

Over the next two days they traded and Popham sent beads, small knives or cloth as gifts back for them to give to their wives. *Amenquin* remained a while longer and said he would bring a large company to the mouth of the *Penobscot* River to trade.

That night Robert and Raleigh had it out in the captain's quarters of the *Mary and John*.

"I'm not tarrying to trade with the heathen!" Robert exploded, banging his large fist on his desk.

"We need more products to bring back to the Merchant Adventurers," Raleigh protested.

"Nay! I will do better to get me off, swing south to Jamestown, get a load of tobacco and get back before the ice comes to the Thames and the oceans. I think they are playing with you, Ral. I think they are building up a force and plan to overtake us before the fort is finished. You must speed up its construction and get it secured!"

Raleigh's face reddened and he pulled on his small beard.

"I knew you'd desert us," he fumed, "just as John deserted Cavendish on the northern expedition."

Robert lunged at Gilbert, shoving his fist but stopping before impact.

"That's a damned lie and ye know it! The seas were all wrong. He had no choice but to turn back. He was absolved and ye know it!"

Raleigh pulled his vest down and straightened up.

"For me, this was all about settlement, Robert. Setting down roots. I plan to remain here, probably for the rest of my life. For you, it was a grand adventure, a voyage of discovery. You think like a merchantman captain, always looking for trade goods, always thinking about how much you can stuff in your holds before returning to your home: England. For me, this is now home."

"I know the north Atlantic, Ral. She'll be full of ice floes within a month or two and I plan to be back in a safe English harbor afore then. It's an eight week voyage. Do the arithmetic."

Popham heard them quarreling and entered the small cabin.

"He's right, Raleigh," the older man said sternly, "We knew when the *Gift* sailed back to England in early October that the *Mary and John* would soon follow. You are welcome to share my house – it actually has a fireplace – so you can be warm and secure onshore. It's time to cut the umbilical cord."

Gilbert fumed and stormed, challenging Popham's authority. And Robert took note. This would have to be reported to the Merchant-Adventurers. A plantation couldn't have two presidents. Raleigh would have to be put in his place or be recalled.

Within days the *Mary and John* was full of barrels of fresh water, dried and salted squirrel, raccoon, rabbit and fowl plus sacks of dried berries, one of which was tart but tasty. They'd stop and fish before heading south, catching more of the giant cod and lobster. In the Barbados, claimed by the Crown just two years prior, they would resupply their water and take on figs, fresh fruits, sugar, molasses and rum to supplement their scanty fur and timber cargo. Unfortunately for Robert, most of the timber felled were soft pine, used for the fort and its buildings. They had embarked too late for the plantation to plant fields so the men left behind had dried berries, barrels of slightly rancid wheat and corn flour and salt pork. But the woods were full of deer including a very large deer the savages called moose plus bears so they would have a better food supply than the sailors. No precious ores were found, which was sure to dismay Chief Justice John Popham, but at least if Robert took the southern route it would be summer below the equator and they'd make it back to England before deep freezing of the harbors began. He hoped James had been able to get the *Gift of God* loaded with tobacco in Virginia so the merchants would be pleased with the venture. Captains such as the Davis brothers put the Latin 'ad' into venture. They took the risks and Robert hoped they would be richly rewarded with land grants within the year. He pitied the small fort left behind. It would take every ounce of courage and fortitude to survive the winter and the savages.

CHAPTER FOURTEEN

Robert Returns to Sagadahoc

1609

The return voyage was free from the drama of the Dutch encounter. Robert and the crew of the *Mary and John* ran into fierce winds that blew them away from the continent so they weren't able to check on the southern Virginia colony. The snows came early and their rigging iced up after they sailed northeast from the Barbados, which had a crude fort but was mostly native. They filled up their water barrels, got some fresh fruit and bulky, raw sugar canes that they had to inspect cane by cane to make sure the rats that had chewed on them in the storage shed weren't being brought onboard, too. The Trade Winds were squirrelly so the *Mary and John* didn't attempt a Plymouth docking but went to the east and entered the quieter Thames. By the time Robert's ship arrived, England was having a severe winter and the docks were slippery with ice and the Thames was starting to freeze in spots.

Capt. James met the ship as he was between trips.

"Robert! Ye ol' sea dog!"

"That I be!" he replied, giving his younger brother a clap on the shoulder. In just a few minutes their capes were covered with a layer of snow.

"You need some good, strong spirits in you to get this chill out," James said, leading the way down the narrow streets past a favorite seaman's tavern to a more genteel one where captains and gentlemen mingled.

After filling their glasses with fine French wine the men got down to business.

"Well, did you bring much back?" James asked, looking into his brother's tired eyes.

"Aye and nay." Robert said, but then he smiled, "But by God! The timber! The land! The cod and lobster! Everything is huge over there!"

James laughed.

"Yes. I've already apprised the Plymouth men. But I have very bad news for you. Sir John Popham died just after we cleared England. His son Francis is taking over and is still interested in the colony but he's having difficulties settling the estate. He wants George to come back."

Robert scratched his beard. He couldn't wait to get into a hot bath and have a pretty little maid shave it off. He couldn't wait to have a pretty little maid, too!

"Were you able to check on the southern colony?" they asked each other at the same time and then laughed. They were so alike they often read the other's thoughts.

"No," James replied, "I had to get the *Gift* back as her owners had given me strict orders to return as soon as possible. She's too valuable as a Channel trader to be stuck in port."

"Aye, don't I know! That bastard Raleigh kept coming up with excuses to try to keep me over! I finally had to tell him to be a man and stand on his own two feet in their fort. He was livin' aboard until the day we loosed anchor!"

James shook his head.

"I have a report for the directors," Robert said, "and they aren't going to like it. Raleigh and George are in a power struggle. The eager young hound out to take over the pack from the old 'un."

"George is the better leader," James agreed, "He isn't quick to speak and act, considers all angles but that Raleigh! He's like a loaded musket that just longs for a match."

Robert sighed as he saw the steady white curtain of snow outside the leaded mullion window.

"They weren't in the best o' shape when I shoved off," he admitted, "Those laborers were mostly poor for a good reason: laziness. They would work if ye kept yer lash handy but I had to keep on em and keep the grog barrel under guard. I sure hope they got more houses up. When I left they were in tents and brush huts like the ones savages live in. Popham let Raleigh move in wit' him but I can not see how 'twill work when weather like this closes them in."

"The savages will bring meat and fish to trade," James said, draining his glass and pouring a new one.

"We lost our interpreters, ye know, but Skidwarres told me the tribes go inland during the winter as that is where they find that huge deer, the moose. And they have villages deep in the woods where the snow doesn't blow."

"Robert, you have to get re-supplied and get back as soon as possible," James told him, "or we will lose our hope of land grants."

"Is that what 'the little beagle''s son told you?" Robert replied with a smirk. He was on his third glass of the heady, rich wine.

"The court is poor again. Cecil's attempts to get them to give the royal family a set annual fund and stop all the 'emergency' taxation hasn't been very successful with Parliament."

Robert harumphed.

"Like that big, loud uncouth Scots king will ever follow a budget anyways! The royals spend money like it's water."

Robert lowered his voice and moved his head closer to James. Behind their table the innkeeper's boy added new logs to the fire and stoked the old ones. The heat felt good after the cold of the ship. "I can tell ye this: he'd be hanged on any ship for lovin' on his pets," he said referring to Buckingham and the king's alleged homosexual relationship with his court favorite and the punishment at sea for such activity.

James laughed and said conspiratorially, "I heard he's been eying that Robert Carr fellow."

"Well," Robert said, rising and stretching, "I'm for a long, hot soak and shave and then a long, hot fuck – with a bawdy, busty maid!"

The ship was unloaded and repairs were begun. She'd taken a beating on the return in the rough seas and her sails needed many repairs, some had to be replaced entirely. The rigging was rat chewed in spots and as the weather permitted, the ship's carpenters and riggers worked on the deck as barrel after barrel of salt pork, hard tack, flour, water and tools the new fort would need were brought up the gang-plank and stored in the hold.

Francis had spoken with both the London and Plymouth Merchant Adventurers and they were convinced the new land was a treasure trove waiting to be plundered. George Popham had written a letter to the Merchant Adventurers, loaded with false claims of silver ore and all manners of items including spices that abounded there. Robert and James knew better but held their tongues as they wanted the plantation to succeed.

However, it wasn't until May, almost nine months after the first ships sailed for north Virginia, when the *Mary and John* and a sister ship with loads of new supplies and settlers were ready to leave.

The seas weren't kind to Robert and his crew. They encountered a severe blow between Barbados and the northern coast. They were taken aback and the main mast of the *Mary and John* almost cracked.

It was September, 1608 when the Mary and John regained sight of Sagadahoc fort. They saw a beautiful new pinnace in its harbor and felt joy as settlers streamed onshore, waving and yelling to them in welcome.

However, the settlers were actually a sorry lot, Robert observed as they neared. Their clothes were in tatters and they were emaciated. Raleigh slowly walked onto the dock. He had aged terribly in less than a year. Robert didn't see George Popham. Tales about finding Roanoke deserted flitted through his mind. At least this fort wasn't deserted but the graves on the hillside near the fort were numerous.

"Robert!" Raleigh Gilbert croaked as he came aboard. The crew had to restrain the settlers as they wanted to stream over the decks and attack food and clothing supplies.

"What the hell happened?" Robert asked, shaking his head, "And where is George?"

Raleigh sat down on a wooden chair in the captain's quarters and asked if Robert had any wine. After downing a glass and refilling, he began his tale.

"After you left winter came in early and fierce. We weren't ready. I've never seen so much snow and ice! In February George got the ague and he didn't last long.

Then one of the men was fishing in the bay and the savages attacked him and killed him. I had taken over from George and ordered all savages out of the fort. They kept trying to get at us and we heard they were going to join up with a tribe of cannibals to the north that have sharp, pointed teeth to come and attack us so we tried to make peace and invited some in for a feast, but one of them ignited a barrel of gunpowder and they felt we had deliberately tricked them and became very hostile. The explosion ignited our provisions shed. Around that same time, the one good house we had caught fire on its thatch roof and burned down. We've been praying every day for a ship to appear." Raleigh's eyes watered, "You can't know how grateful we are for you and James – I assume that's James waving from yonder deck?"

"Aye, we all came back to resupply ye."

Robert told Raleigh the bad news about Sir John Popham and said his brother had a hard time raising enough money for the resupply but was dedicated to the plantation.

"Oh, here, I has a letter fer ye," he added, pulling a stiff velum envelope out of his waterproof document bag.

Raleigh used Robert's knife to open it. The ship's cook had brought a platter of meat, cheese and bread for the men, now joined by James.

"That's a fine looking vessel you have here!" James exclaimed as his boots tramped on the hard wooden deck.

"Yes, the shipwright and men did a fine job. We've taken it out into the bays and up rivers, exploring. It's very sea-worthy. We christened it the *Virginia*," Raleigh said and then he let out a cry as he read his letter.

"Are you all right, man?" Robert asked, thinking his friend was having a pain.

Raleigh's eyes watered.

"My father is dead," he said, letting the letter fall onto the scarred wooden table.

"As well as Sir John?" James grabbed the arm of the tall, thin red haired man to keep him from falling and then squeezed it to show sympathy.

"'Tis truly sorry we are," Robert said. His broad Devon accent always nagged James as he said they hadn't attended a fine grammar school to speak like peasants. Robert had blithely replied that if it was good enough for Sir Walter, it was good enough for him. (But James, too, sometimes slipped into a lazier form of speech, a bad habit from being around rough sailors.) Raleigh Gilbert gulped his second glass of wine.

"I am going to have to return to England with you," he told them, "as I am the oldest son and have to take over management of the estates."

There was a commotion aboard the decks and they went onto the quarter deck to see what was happening.

Robert ordered muskets fired to disperse the crowd of desperate, ragged men that had managed to get aboard.

"You will immediately take them back to the fort!" Raleigh ordered his 'soldiers'.

"Didn't ye plant any crops?" Robert asked.

"No. The men have been sick. They've had dysentery and scurvy. We lost many from malnutrition, ague and infections. They haven't been well enough to work. If it hadn't been for fish, we'd all be dead. I'm afraid the settlement has been a failure." He sadly shook his head," We must return to England."

"Dammit!" James exclaimed, "I brought fourteen settlers, hogs, young cattle, poultry and even some goats. There's plenty of grazing to be had and the hogs can even eat crabs if there's nothing else. Why give up now?"

Capt. James stormed off to inspect the damaged fort. His orders were to resupply and return but not to stay and govern.

It took a week of inspecting, traveling to nearby villages where they were met with hostility, even by Skidwarres and Nahanta, and of assessing the health of the men, before James and Robert reluctantly agreed with Raleigh.

"Are you up to captaining?" James asked him.

"Yes, I can sail one of the ships home," Raleigh stated. A week of good food, new clothes and bracing wine had restored him to his usual arrogant self.

"Good," James replied, "I will move supplies to the *Virginia* and sail her to our sister plantation to the south. There will be enough onboard the two ships for you and Robert to make it back to England. Our father got land grants near Jamestown and whereas I would like to take everyone and all the supplies down there, I'll settle for the your new fifty footer and see if there's anything left down there. It pains me sore to leave this fort. I know the French are drooling over it and I fear we will lose it once our sails are over the horizon."

It took James longer than he planned to get the *Virginia* to a state where he'd trust her on the open sea. Unfortunately he was blown too far east and had to return to England but almost immediately the *Virginia* joined a resupply fleet headed for the new settlement named Jamestown. They were the third resupply but the fleet encountered major storms and two ships were damaged beyond repair. The *Virginia* was blown so far off course James was two months behind the other ships getting to Jamestown.

Right from the start James Davis and John Smith clashed. James was assigned to take over a fort named Algernon, which was fine with him as he didn't like Smith. By feeding his hogs crabs, his men were able to remain well fed and James explored up and down the Chesapeake bay until he found the best lands for his deceased father's plantation. It would be here, not in Wales, that the Davis family would be restored to its former greatness. Here, with tobacco and the political, indigent or debtor prisoners his vast lands would bring the family fortunes back. He had no desire to retry the settlement to the north. Let Robert try to make something of that rocky wilderness. Here the land was lush, fertile and not just a scab over hard, unyielding granite. And here the savages weren't cannibals and hostile. This Virginia was truly a virgin wilderness just ready to be penetrated by hard English plows.

Capt. James knew his sailing days weren't over but his exploring days were. Here and in the West Indies there was enough to keep him busy and satisfied in the New World. John had Ireland and became wealthy from his position and estate there and Robert would keep fishing off Newfoundland and try to get another settlement going to the north, but here, in the hot, humid flat lands of Virginia on Warwickshire Creek James would make his mark. His cotton, tobacco and sugar, maybe rum from the Barbados would make many wealthy English happy. And make him filthy rich. He would gloat over every shilling he made from the bastards who had stolen his family's lands in Wales.

CHAPTER FIFTEEN

England in Transition

Early 1600s

Robert and the *Mary and John* returned to an England in turmoil. The new *Book of Rates* came out and small shippers were put out of business. His brother James saw which way the wind was blowing and put money in the Virginia plantation project, plus began buying land grants from the king for sugar plantations in the Barbados.

His brother James began courting Cicely Thayer, a childhood sweetheart who lived in the area of Acton-Turville. She had many siblings due to her father's second marriage.

Robert was courting Richard Warren's daughter Marie from Dorchester. Sailors and captains often married late as it was hard on a wife to be left alone most of the time and some, such as John of Dartmouth's Faith, often proved unfaithful. Her adultery had been so blatant John divorced her and was engaged to Judith Harvard at the time of his death in the South Seas.

Robert had been born on a family estate in Grimstone, just north of Dorchester and most of his father's ships set sail from Plymouth or Weymouth so he often frequented the George Inn and stayed with the Spicers, Clarkes or Watts – all seafaring families – or Matthew Chubb, a wealthy Somersetshireman who had married a fine Dorchester woman and became a leader in the town's Merchant Adventurers Corporation, overseeing the outfitting of ships in harbor.

Sir John Popham had gotten laws passed that reinstated the export of convict labor and shipload after shipload took convicts to Virginia and Bermuda to pay for their crimes with their sweat in the fields. A year after Sagadahoc failed Sir George Somers and a group of colonists bound for Virginia were blown off course and shipwrecked off an island and settled a town there he named St. George, claiming the island for England.

In 1612 Robert tried to get signed onto the King's new Northwest Passage expedition, led by Admiral Sir Thomas Button, fourth son of Miles Button of Wilton, Glamorganshire, Wales. He visited Sir Thomas and played upon their mutual Welsh background but was unsuccessful so he either captained ships running goods between England and Ireland or stayed away, fishing off Newfoundland but during 1612 Barbary Spanish pirates attacked the fishing fleet and Robert was barely able to limp his damaged ship into harbor.

Capt. James made out well that year as John Rolfe found a milder form of tobacco in the West Indies and started selling a mixture of the harsher Virginia tobacco with the milder mixed in so the herb gained in popularity in England and abroad, both for pipes and as snuff. Sir John, now Attorney General, did well in Ireland, too, acquiring vast lands around Ulster and exporting large numbers of indentured laborers to Virginia and other places in the West Indies. He received their land plus a price for the contract of each and the Crown was glad to be rid of them. King James also granted 30,000 acres to each 'undertaker' who would settle 48 adult Scottish or English Presbyterians in Ulster to turn the country Protestant. In addition, veterans of the Continental wars who were owed back wages could receive land grants in Virginia in lieu of pay. Thanks to Henry VIII's taking of all the church property and the conquests of Ireland, Wales and Scotland, land – with or without castles or manors – was one thing King James I had in abundance, it seemed. Money was the one thing his government did not have. The ugly specter of Ship Money, an extremely unpopular tax on non-harbor inland towns and cities, hung over the gentry.

During these times of unemployment, high food prices and shortages due to poor harvests King James I married off his daughter Elizabeth to Frederick, a Habsburg, king of Bohemia, setting off fresh hostilities on the Continent as the

Catholic Hapsburgs didn't want their trade routes through northern Italy disrupted by a Protestant coalition in the middle of Europe. The Hapsburgs were kings in Spain and Portugal and had royal ties to almost every country except France, the southern part of the Netherlands and the important Val Telline and northern Italy. Spain had claimed Mexico, Brazil, Chile and Peru and all the gold and silver they could find in the southern part of the New World.

In the northern part of the New World Captain Samuel Argyll, Gov. of the Virginia Co., and his men sailed north from Virginia and ruthlessly expelled the French fisher-traders from the Kennebec, Mt. Desert Island, St. Croix, Pt. Royal and Nova Scotia.

There had been religious revolts by the increasingly militiant Protestants along the Danube and in Bohemia, where the Emperor, breaking with tradition, declared religious freedom for Protestants as well as Catholics. The royal marriage of Elizabeth to the Bohemian ruler of the Palatine, Frederick V, helped break the Hapsburg's lock on Europe but led to more Protestants fighting Catholics. The Turks invaded Hungary and Sweden took the port of Novgorod from Russia.

The following year the king dissolved the Merchant Adventurers and formed the new King's Merchant Adventurers with a monopoly to export cloth. King James I gave the company the sole right to export 'dressed' cloth and he showed favoritism to William Cockeyne and Yorkshire, where alum, used to set dyes, had been discovered, and to the East India Co. that imported the blue indigo dye plant. This move devastated most of Wiltshire and Devon as the merchants couldn't sell dressed, or treated and dyed broadcloths so they stopped buying raw wool or hand-woven textiles. Only weavers in Bradford on Avon and Trowbridge with 45 cloth factories between them survived this terrible blow. The edict was only in effect for a few years but it ruined most of the woolen industry in the county. Robert's cousin William in Bristol and their relatives in the West Country where the Raleighs and their cronies lived were able to sell uncolored cloth to the plantations for their workers in Ireland but the West Indies and Virginia needed a lighter cotton cloth, imported by the newly established English East India Company.

During the early years of King James's reign Lady Arabella Stuart died in the Tower and the English fleet had a victory off Bombay, which helped the English East India Company's importation of cotton and calicoes, obtained from India and the Far East.

The most exciting event for Robert was the release of their family friend and fellow sailor-adventurer, Sir Walter Raleigh, from the Tower in 1617. The King granted old 'Sir Water' the right to lead an expedition up the Orinoco River in the southern part of the New World to look for gold in Guiana. Robert again failed to get a ship in the venture, for which he was grateful as the following year the expedition proved to have been a disaster. Sir Walter's son died and after they looted Spanish ships on the return to England, Spain, (now England's ally), demanded Sir Walter be imprisoned and executed for piracy against Spanish ships in the Caribbean. South America was a source of great wealth that England wanted a part of as Portuguese plantation owners had imported sugar cane from the Madeira Islands to Brazil in 1520 and then its cultivation had spread from South America to the fertile islands of the West Indies.

Robert made another voyage to Virginia, his ship loaded with 100 young boys and girls removed from the streets of London and sent off to labor for the Davis and other large plantation owners. The youths were stored like cargo below in the dark, foul-smelling hold. Robert felt pity for the orphans and waifs and would allow them to come on the upper deck every evening for a spell so they could get some fresh air, wash with seawater, wash clothes and get exercise. The young girls were a pitiful sight, having been forced into prostitution or stealing to survive the hard London streets. Some, barely more than children themselves, had swollen bellies and he wondered if he'd get an extra bonus when he delivered two instead of one. The boys were a hard lot. Most of them were thieves and liars. How the overseers of the plantations would get a good day's work from the convicts and the poor, Robert didn't know. They were insubordinate, surly and lazy. He'd heard there was a new class of laborers the Dutch were taking from the gold coast of Africa, a more docile people used to being out in the hot sun all day. However, these people had no rights at all. Unlike the poor, they couldn't obtain their freedom at the end of their indenture or sentence. The first negroes the Spanish brought had been sold as indentured laborers but now he saw them sold outright, like cattle. This was something Robert didn't like. Never a religious man he questioned how a life, given by God, could then be owned by a mere human. It was man stealing. He knew his Bible and knew the Egyptians bought the Jews as slaves and that slavery was a practice almost as old as mankind but Robert felt that didn't make it right. He didn't like kings owning all the land and all the deer and creatures and trees in the English forests made by God but he felt until a new order could come into being they were stuck with this system. King James believed he had Divine Rights but Parliament under Oliver Cromwell believed no Englishman should be taxed without his Parliamentary representatives consenting to the tax. Every time he remembered the vast forests and seas full of fat fish and lobster in north Virginia he longed to quit the sea and get a large land grant and settle down like James wanted to. But England and France weren't on amicable terms in northern Virginia and so the crown was discouraging any new settlement schemes. King James was a secretive bastard and liked to conduct clandestine negotiations with Spain or France, trading land for money so no one really knew what was going on behind the scenes. The King was so money hungry he was selling off crown lands with abandon and the keeper of the treasury, Sir John Popham, had built a large manor he called Littlecote in northeastern Wiltshire with his profits. The new rich merchant land owners were kicking out the tenant farmers and raising sheep. If one wouldn't go, they raised the cost of the copyhold when the owner died so the son couldn't buy it and continue the tenancy.

Parliament and the King were at odds. They wouldn't vote new taxes unless he declared war on Spain. King James was against the enclosures that shut the tenant farmers off 'common' grazing and crop lands but the rich members of Parliament wanted enclosures.

Robert, with a hold full of young boys and girls who, in earlier times would have stayed on the family farm or the Lord's estate and been hard working farmers and tradesmen, saw the true consequences of the greed of King James I against his country.

He wondered on the long nights at sea as he smoked his pipe and watched the play of the moonlight on the restless waves how many of the poor children would survive forced labor and if any would ever own a small farm of their own one day. He wondered if the religious dissidents in the Netherlands would ever return to England or if, as rumored, emigrate to the New World to begin a New England. He was tempted to become a Separatist if that would be what it would take to return to the land he couldn't stop dreaming about: that land to the north where the rivers ran gallantly through thick woods of old, majestic trees and there was room enough for all the poor children from England and Ireland to have little farmsteads and live free.

His betrothed and her family had fallen under the influence of a new 'Puritan' minister in Dorchester, the Rev. John White. A graduate of Oxford's New College, he preached about salvation through God's Grace, not man's good works but also preached that the Christian community had a duty to help its poor and educate its children and to provide skilled training and work for those in need, in a type of poor workhouse setting. His preaching style was charismatic and Marie and her family were his disciples. Robert's friend Chubb was very much against this militiant type of Puritanism. Dorchester and most of the West Country was divided between the old school Elizabethan Church of England Protestants and these newer 'activist' Puritans. The Puritans in Dorchester were establishing a free school and other civic activities were helping the poor and hungry and there was talk of having a town brewery to help pay for everything.

1619

Robert's ship was getting ready to set sail when the alarm went up. Even from Plymouth the dark smoke was seen to the north. Every available man, woman and child left off harvesting and their work to rush to Dorchester where fire was consuming the area around St. Peter's church on High Street.

Robert rode as fast as his horse would gallop, his heart in his throat as he thought of his beautiful doe-eyed brown-haired fair-skinned lovely Marie. One of the bailiffs, his friend Edward Spicer, flagged him down and yelled they were saving the gunpowder barrels so the whole town wouldn't explode so Robert was diverted to the Shire Hall to help wrap the barrels of gunpowder in wet sheets and roll them into the fields upwind of the fire.

Everywhere people were running around screaming for water and trying to rescue goods from their houses and shops.

"Marie!" Robert yelled, his voice raw and hoarse from the thick smoke. He could hardly see out of watering eyes through the ash falling like rain all around the mobs of panicked citizens.

Pushing and shoving, he reached her family's town house and found them outside, a pile of belongings in front as the back of the house went up in flames.

Marie and her family were blackened from soot. Robert grabbed her to him and held her to stop her shaking. He pulled her down and they sat as the fire was beaten back by the crowd.

"The chandler – " she sobbed brokenly, "he was heating tallow and it got too hot!" People were in shock. Almost half the houses of Dorchester were either completely burned or severely damaged. Miraculously, the churches were scorched but not destroyed. But many shops full of goods and taverns were burned to the ground. The very center of this Assize (judges and court) town, the heart of Dorchestershire, was burned out.

Robert's in-laws from Fordington took Marie and her family in a wagon out to their country home. Everything stank of acrid smoke. Marie had managed to salvage her family's Bible from their town house before it was lost the odor was so bad they had to keep it outside to read.

Robert and the men slept in the haylofts, giving the house and beds to the women and children. But the harvesting had to continue. As Dorchester smouldered, sending foul wafts of smoke with the wind, the farmers had to bring in the hay and crops. The women organized and did tub after tub of laundry trying to wash the smoke from clothes and linens and bedding. Babies cried, dogs barked, sheep baaed for food and cows lowed. Everything was unhappy and out of joint.

Robert stayed a week to help get Marie and her family resettled and to help in town hauling off debris. But he couldn't wait any longer as the ships he was to meet would be full and needed to offload their cargoes onto his ships.

He found her in the barn, milking a cow as a smudged sun rose over the fields and woods.

Marie smiled up at him. He loved her smile. She had the sweetest soft lips and the whitest teeth he'd ever seen. Her hair was pulled up under a white muslin scarf and she wore a stained apron over her singed work dress.

Robert knelt next to her and kissed her neck above her sweaty kerchief.

"I know," she said softly, her large brown eyes filling.

"Ye know I don't want to leave," he said, taking her hands as she finished milking. There was a hard ridge on her right hand, a callus from working the tough udders.

"'Tis true, my Robbie," she said, looking down at the dirt and hay around her scuffed shoes.

"When I return, will ye marry me?" he asked, surprising himself with the sudden question.

Marie put her arms around his wide shoulders and sobbed with joy.

"Truly there is nothing I would like more in this world than to be Mrs. Robert Davis," she said.

"That ye will be, my love," Robert said gruffly. He rose, bringing her with him, "but ye know I'll have to be away at sea for half the year," he added. "A sailor's wife can lead a lonely life. And I'm no longer a young man, lass."

Marie shook her head, "Nay, Robbie. I have my Bible and my God to talk to every day. I'll no be alone. And there will be babes, I'm sure. Between helping me ma and dad rebuild the home, the town and the church's projects to help the poor and those in need, I'll be plenty busy."

Robert hugged her tightly and they kissed.

He would hold the taste of her in his memory for the long months ahead at sea.

CHAPTER SIXTEEN

The Separatists Emigrate to New England

1619-1620

In the spring of 1619 the Virginia Company had obtained two charters: one for a southern plantation and another for the north. The settlements scheme succeeded due to the efforts of Robert Nauton, the king's secretary (and current treasurer) Sir Edwin Sandys, who sold it to King James. Sandys wasn't totally in sympathy with the Separatists but he hated the king's arrogant dictatorial attitude and wanted more individual religious and civil freedoms, not less.

Soon after they got the charter, Mr. Blackwell sailed with 180 Separatists to the southern Virginia land but the voyage was a disaster and only 50 survived the trip; most died en route from scurvy and the flux. Ten more ships brought settlers in 1619 but the mortality rate was extremely high: two-thirds perished from the heat and tropical diseases. Sandys argued that a one crop system of tobacco cultivation wasn't feasible and proposed a five year plan to import and plant grape vines and olive trees and establish different mills so the Jamestown settlers could establish their own economy.

However, the Virginia failures didn't discourage the Separatists in Holland and, even though their titular leader William Brewster was lying low to avoid the king's soldiers, negotiations continued between English Merchant Adventurers and John Carver and Robert Cushman, who, prior to emigrating to the Netherlands had been a wealthy grocer and woolcomber in Canterbury.

In spite of the tepid backing of the government, the wealthy London merchant Thomas Weston, along with William Davis, Sir Edwin Sandys and John Pierce bankrolled a fleet to take pilgrims from England and the Netherlands to the northern New England to land at the mouth of the Hudson River, near where the Dutch were planning to start a settlement. The Dutch offered the site first to the Separatists but they wanted an English-culture and English-language settlement, which was why they wanted to leave the Netherlands in the first place. The Dutch had been kind to them but they wanted to keep their English ways. They wanted to plant a free Christian 'England' in a new place. The *New* England.

Thomas Weston secured the services of the *Mayflower,* an 180 ton square rigged, sturdy merchant wine transport, berthed in London. It joined the *Speedwell* in Southampton. The *Speedwell* had been purchased and refitted by the Separatists in Holland. However, after they sailed from Delfshaven and joined the *Mayflower* Weston changed the terms and demanded six days labor, not four, from the Separatists for seven years indenture plus the addition of non-Separatists, or strangers to the group. There were hostilities when the pilgrims refused to accept non-Separatists and the changed terms that allowed them no time to work on their own farms so Weston withdrew his financing of the *Mayflower*. In desperate need to get away from England, the pilgrims sold casks of rich Dutch butter to buy the rest of their necessities. The *Mayflower* and *Speedwell* sailed in the fall of 1620 but the *Speedwell* quickly returned to Plymouth as it had severe leakage, making it incapable of sailing across the Atlantic. Some of the Separatists were offloaded in England and some made their way back to Leyden.

Blown off course, the *Mayflower* landed on the cape where cod was plentiful and the Separatists went ashore and founded a colony called Plimouth, (which Weston later claimed infringed his grant as the colony was supposed to be near the mouth of the Hudson River).

1621

Robert and Marie rode out north of Dorchester to get away from the children and noise and to enjoy a beautiful summer day. Marie had packed a picnic lunch for them. They found a nice field under the hillside with Abbe Cern engraved on its chalky side.

Marie spread out an old tablecloth and they sat down, looking over the velvety green valleys and hills.

Robert took her hand and they kissed.

Marie giggled.

"Why, Mr. Davis, I do believe ye are showing passion in public."

"Aye, love. 'Tis good thing the good people of yer church aren't up here to see me real passion!"

They embraced and made love to the sound of black-faced sheep bleating in the fields below. Robert stroked his wife's face and she took his hard, rough, calloused hand in hers and smiled.

"I love your hands," she murmured as she kissed them.

"'Tis rough they are," he said self-consciously.

"I love your rough, strong body. I love how you always smell like the sea."

Robert laughed and sat up, tearing a hunk of bread off the loaf she'd put out, "I'm afraid we sailors are a smelly bunch!"

"No, I didn't mean to insult you, dearest. I love how you smell like salt and fresh air and a little like fish, but not old fish. Your clothes are sorely in need of a good scrubbing when ye come ashore, but even your sweat smells good to me."

"Ye're a strange one, my sweet," he said, chucking her chin. He couldn't believe such a delicate, dainty refined lady would have chosen him for a husband and father of her children.

Marie's brown eyes gleamed with mischief.

"I'm going to tell ye a secret," she said with a smile.

"Are ye expecting again then?" he asked, smiling back.

"Nay," she laughed, "But remember when I lost the first babe and couldn't seem to carry one to term?"

"Aye, but ye grew up more and your body got stronger."

Marie covered her mouth with her small, thin hand.

"Ye see the drawing on the hill?"

Robert looked up and nodded.

"Well, my cousin Elizabeth, she that married my brother Doctor Richard Warren and moved north – she and I came up here and I sat down in its – " Marie blushed, "place where the legs join."

Robert laughed loudly.

"Well, it was thought if ye laid down there ye'd get with child," she said, blushing furiously.

Robert laughed but then got serious, "Ye musn't tell anyone ye practiced witchcraft," he said, his brows straight with concern.

"'Twasn't witchcraft, Robert! 'Twas just a lark, a bit of fun. 'Twas an old wive's tale."

"Rev. White won't see it that way. Just be glad ye didn't go off to the New World with those Separatists. Ye'd be in stocks, if not whipped or hanged for such a thing!"

Marie hung her head, "I'm not that strict, Robert!"

She then fumbled in her apron pocket,

"I've had a letter from Elizabeth. She is staying with Uncle John and doesn't know when she will be able to sail with her daughters to rejoin Richard in New England."

She read the news from what was named Plimouth Plantation.

"Dearest sister-in-law,

"News from Richard has finally arrived. I was half-dead with worry! My dear heart Richard is alive, thanks be to our Lord. He told me they didn't settle where they were supposed to as a result of bad weather and bad shoals and currents but they found a suitable site and have built seven houses, a meeting house and storehouse, which will be surrounded by a strong palisade. To the sorrow of all of the brethren, almost half the saints perished during a terrible, terrible, cold winter. They arrived too late to plant and found some buried stores of the savages' corn but the scurvy, catarrh and flux took the weakest away.

"He wishes for me and the girls to be patient and prays we are safe with uncle John."

Marie paused and told Robert, "As you know, Uncle John is a solicitor in London and a close friend of Sir Saltonstall of Halifax in West Riding. Elizabeth and her five daughters were with the Separatists who had to disembark from the *Speedwell*."

Robert winced, "Aye, the master over-masted her in the Netherlands."

Marie tilted her head on one side and asked, "What does that mean?"

Robert gave her a wry smile, "There's a mighty amount of arithmetic involved in building a ship, my dear. The masts have to be in proportion to the ship's height from deck to keel. If ye make the masts too long the sails are too big and can't properly balance it when confronting winds and waves and the joints pull apart, making it take on too much water. Some say Master Reynolds did it on purpose. I can't rightly say if he did or not for I barely know the man."

Marie nodded and continued reading,

Along with Richards' letter Elizabeth had enclosed another from a friend of her's in which she told of the voyage, that there was no bathing or laundering and the men became hairy and everyone stank.

She read, *"The ships carry fleas and lice and it was a constant struggle to keep free of vermin."*

Marie looked over at Robert, who was smiling.

"Ye never told me o' that!" she said, poking at him with the letter.

"Aye, I always got meself decent in port before coming a'courtin'. But why did ye think I told ye of all the cats on board? The rats carry fleas and itch mites. Plus they gnaw the ship's timbers and gnaw into cargo and piss and shit all over. Rats are the bane of shipowners – and wood worms, especially in warm waters."

Marie felt like something was crawling on her as she continued reading from Elizabeth's friend's letter:

"The day after the first Sabbath in port the men went ashore from the Mayflower to explore and find the site for our new safe haven. We women worked liked crazed animals washing everything, and everyone, with the fresh water the men had brought from shore. The ship was a sight with sheets blowing around like sails!

"Then the savages came round. Richard told me they told our Governor Carver a yellow plague had come amongst them the previous year and there were few savages left. Gov. Carver was one of the men who perished during our first winter and

the colony elected William Bradford as our new governor.

"We were grateful for Robert's listing of the trees they could find as our men found ash trees and cut handles for the axe heads they brought, then felled a great number of oak trees, squaring the trunks with adzes into beams for the exterior framing. The younger men split oaks into clapboard shakes or shingles for the exteriors and the boys and girls helped gather thatch from the fields for the roofs. But our small houses were cold and the wood-framed chimneys are a serious fire risk even when lined with the plentiful clay here. A brick works will be needed if we are to make proper fireplaces. And the thatch used was very dry. During the winter so many died we had to hide their graves on Cole's Hill so the savages wouldn't know how vulnerable we are.

"But 35 more of our number were brought on the Fortune, including Mr. Cushman and his son, Edward Winslow's son John and Elder Brewster's son Jonathan plus a Thomas Pence and Phillip de la Noye and some unmarried young men. Mr Cushman preached a sermon on 'The Sin of Pride' and shamed the men into honoring Weston's deceitful indenture document. We all knew the original agreement was for the men to only have to work for the Company four days a weeks, leaving two for our farms and one for the Sabbath. As you recall, Weston changed the contract in Southampton and our men refused to sign it but now they are little more than slaves to the Merchant Adventurers until our transportation debt is paid.

"Mr. Weston also obtained a separate grant and a shallop with seven of his men appeared in our village, seeking food and shelter, which we, as Christians are duty bound to provide, though it doth sore tax our resources.

"We loaded the Fortune, which will carry this letter, with cedar clapboards and beaver skins, hoping to pay half the debt."

Robert frowned. The *Fortune* had been boarded by French pirates and held off the coast of France until its most valuable cargo was offloaded. Elizabeth's friends didn't know it but they still owed The Merchant Adventurers a big debt.

Marie continued reading, this time from a short note from her sister-in-law Elizabeth, added to the end of the other letter;

"*I confess to you, my dear sister in Christ, that I am sore afeared to be walking onto another ship! But my heart is gladdened at the thought of being reunited with dear Richard and the fellowship of Saints bravely pioneering the frontier of the new world. I know not if we should ever meet again in this world, but I know from what ye told me ye are one of the elect and we shall meet again in Heaven. Please pray for me, for us, all of us as we go through these trials and travails for Christ."*

There were tears in Marie's eyes as she finished reading.

Robert reached across and gently brushed them off her cheeks.

"She is so brave," Marie said, her throat sore with emotion as she burst out sobbing, "Oh, Robbie, I don't think I am that brave! Would you think poorly of me if I said I couldn't do it?"

Robert had a deep laugh.

"Marie, life on ship can be hard but the rewards at the end of the journey can make up for it!"

"But what if little Willie fell overboard?" she said, hiccuping.

"Nay, good wife, the boy is smart. I was a young lad meself the first time I went to sea!"

Marie tucked the precious letters back into the slit in her dress as she wore a shift with a pocket in it underneath.

Robert encircled her with his strong arm and they laid back on the cloth, their eyes on the blue sky and cirrus clouds.

"I was thinking we'd not be going to Plimouth, Marie," he said, brushing straw from her hair, "Nay, I want to help get a fishing village going north of there, between the cape of cods and where Gorges and Popham tried to settle on the Kennebec. I've been promised a land grant there, in the Piscataqua River area. 'Tis wonderful fishing there but I'll not bring you and the boys across the sea unless a village is already built and I've built ye a fine, strong, warm house!"

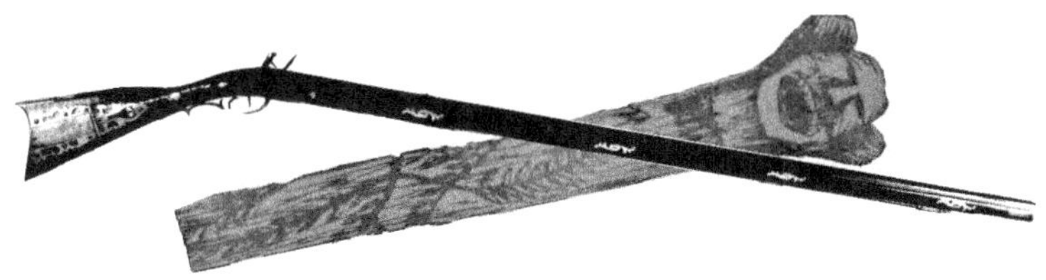

CHAPTER SEVENTEEN

Dolor and Margery

1620s

It was his father's friendship with the Earl of Dorset that got Dolor a job he cherished: supervisor of carpentry on the Archbishop of Canterbury's old estate, Sevenoaks Knole Manor. The manor had been granted to Edward Seymour, Duke of Somerset by Edward IV but when Somerset was executed in 1552 it returned to the Crown. (Peers were vassals of the Crown and all they owned belonged to the Crown and were returned to it if the line didn't have an heir or the vassals became estranged from royal favor.)

Knole Manor had been owned by William Fiennes, Second Baron of Saye and Sele who sold it to the Archbishop of Canterbury who had the lands enclosed and during the reign of King Henry VIII Thomas Bonchier used it as a royal hunting estate. Fiennes lived in Bonchier's old estate in nearby Otford.

In the early 1560s Queen Elizabeth gave it to her favorite, Robert Dudley, but he leased it out as too expensive to maintain. Then Elizabeth granted it to Thomas Sackville, Lord Buckhurst who bought Dudley's lease in 1603. He was Lord Treasurer of England at the time. After his death he was succeeded as Treasurer by Popham, a neighbor of Sir James Thomas Davis in Wiltshire, then by Philips, also of the Wiltshire/Somersetshire region.

Sir Thomas Sackville's son Robert, Second Earl of Dorset, took over the estate, adding a barn, stable, dove house, courts, gardens, orchards and ponds.

From Benefield, Dolor was first hired as a carpenter's apprentice on the estate. His specialty was fine finish work and he soon was moved into more skilled work carving the chestnut ceilings, walls and fireplace surrounds. The Earl was constantly adding onto the huge manor, with a goal of having 365 rooms – one for each day of the year. The great hall had a domed ceiling ringed with carvings of the zodiac. Astrology and astronomy were linked sciences at the time and Hackled was often a guest at the manse. The monstrous manse sprawled over four acres with a large knoll in front of the entry drive. To the north the land sloped down to the Darenth Valley and narrowed to Holmesdale at the foot of the North Downs. There was an 1,000 acre park full of deer southeast of its town. The area had lots of rough pasture and timber and many springs for wells. Because of the sandy soil it was mostly used for pasture land and there were fallows of pigs roaming the forests, fattened on acorns and chestnuts.

In 1618 King James executed Sir Walter Raleigh to appease the Spanish, to whom he allied England and he ordered the English to stop importing goods from the Americas.

In 1621 Parliament voted to facilitate enclosures.

In 1622 Parliament refused to give the king his taxation unless he declared war on Spain. He refused and dissolved Parliament. After three years of confusion and unrest since the Act of 1621 tried to prohibit those now propertyless from moving into towns and cities, making them vagabonds which could then be transported to the colonies as indentured laborers, the Enclosure Act was repealed.

Across the sea in New England, Thomas Morton's trading settlement at Merrymount drew the enmity of the Separatists.

They sent their captain Miles Standish to Merrymount to arrest the heathen-loving merrymaking men. Standish saw the *Swan* lying at hull, unattended. This so incensed him that he and his troops killed any savage they encountered on their way to the blasphemous settlement. Standish charged the drunken men with the crime of going native, ordered his men to seize them and he sent them via the *Swan* north to Monhegan where they could join Weston and the fishing fleet of almost 400 ships off the coast of Newfoundland.

At Monhegan they learned that the settlement in Jamestown had been massacred by the savages.

King James became more tyrannical and in March, 1621 declared himself above mortal laws through the' Divine Right of Kings' and dissolved Parliament six days after he granted the Massachusetts Bay Colony its charter.

In 1624 Parliament imprisoned the Earl of Middlesex, tried to balance England's budget and adopted a 'statute of monopolies' that stated only corporations could obtain monopolies. The next year monopolist Sir Hugh Middleton was authorized to conscript laborers from anywhere in the realm to use in his Cardigan shore coal mines.

Dolor Davis inherited the Tudor half-timber, half white stucco and lattice Marden Manor, eight miles south of Maidstone but Dolor remained in Sevenoaks, renting his estate to a wealthy Londoner by the name of Therry. He continued to work at Sevenoaks but in 1623 there was a terrible fire in the manor and a large portion of the main manse was burned. It took the Earl a couple of years to raise enough money to rebuild so Dolor returned to Benefield, where he and Margery married.

In 1625 King James 1 died. Henry, who had been next in line had died at the age of 18 (many believed he had been poisoned) so the crown went to his brother, Charles.

No one liked King Charles I. He was a small man, weak, vindictive, greedy, duplicitous and overly fond of expensive artwork. He closed off access to the throne by petitioners and went so far as to wall in Richmond Park to keep commoners from seeing it. He was profligate, worse than his father. But worse, he married a Catholic – Henrietta Maria, daughter of the French king. Charles became an ally of the French king to fight against Protestants and he allowed Catholics to practice their religion in England. Parliament tried to stop him from abusing his 'Divine Right of Kings' power and Sir John Eliot of Cornwall, leader of the lower House of Commons called the king's taking of wine import duties (tunnage and poundage) without Parliament's vote an act of treason. Taxation without Representation in Parliament was illegal, claimed Eliot's followers. Charles committed England to war against Spain in league with his sister's husband, a move that was unpopular and Parliament refused to grant more than 140 thousand pounds for the effort.

When tunnage and poundage wasn't granted, Charles took it anyway, dissolved Parliament and raised a forced loan from the wealthy.

The Chief Justice ruled for the king. Eliot and others were imprisoned in the Tower and Archbishop Laud went on the warpath against the Puritans. Preaching or writing of dissension in churches was strictly prohibited. Laud was against the Puritan practice of having a licensed preacher and teacher for each congregation and didn't like them using Lectureships to bring in Puritan speakers such as John Cotton. He decreed his *Book of Common Prayer* was to be used exclusively in all the Church of England's churches.

Amidst this turmoil, Dolor and Margery's second child, John, was born in 1626. They had an older son Nicholas, born less than a year before. He and Margery had become Puritans by then, mostly due to the influence of her brother Simon Willard. They were living in Horsmondon at the time and often traveled a day's distance to hear Cotton, Bradford or others like them including Mr. John White. (Puritans preferred to call their ministers 'Mister' instead of 'Reverend'.)

Returning by cart from one of these meetings Simon said to Dolor,

"There's talk the King is going to revoke the Massachusetts Bay charter."

Margery cried out, "He can't!"

"Aye, he can, my sister," said Simon, "This king is a tyrant. He has declared himself above any mortal laws. He cares not for his subjects and is constantly scheming and conniving behind closed doors to do us evil."

Dolor gave the horses a snap of the whip as Margery comforted their tiny infant.

Dolor said, "My cousin Robert in Dorchester had been involved with settlers on the north shore. They set up a permanent fishing village and families are being encouraged to settle there."

"I thought his wife's brother went to Plymouth?" Margery asked, nursing the hungry babe.

"Aye, but he passed away and that group has become almost as bad as the King. They only want very strict Separatists in their colony. They drove out my brother's and Morton's friends from Merrymount for drinking and having a May pole."

Simon laughed, "And for cavorting with the heathen women!"

Dolor looked back at his wife and the other couple in the back of the wagon, hoping Simon's words hadn't offended anyone.

"Well, that, too. But Robert's widow Marie said John Winthrop is talking about getting a large group of Puritans together to settle north of Plymouth but south of Salem, the fishing village. If Charles revokes the Charter, we will have no where to flee if he comes after the Puritans or makes Catholicism the state religion. The Church of England is hard enough on us, I don't want to go through what Bloody Mary did to our great-grandparents."

The Puritans were reprieved as Charles's attention was pulled away from New England and focused on Scotland. It was rumored that he secretly worked with the Catholic Spanish king to send forces north to quell the Presbyterian Bishops' uprising, further infuriating Parliament and his subjects.

Dolor, Margery and John returned to Sevenoaks and lived in a small cottage on the estate as he worked on the restoration. Everyone was on edge. A civil war, an insurrection, a rebellion, something was coming and all knew it. The King was out of control and Parliament was powerless to stop him. Laud was determined to persecute any who deviated from strict Church of England practices. Margery became pregnant again during these times and she and Dolor worried for the future of their children. In the long winter nights sitting in front of a coal stove they talked about joining Winthrop and leaving their homeland forever. It was sad talk. It was not what either wanted but they felt their backs were against the wall. They were living at the whim of a king and possibly would be plunged into a bloody civil war. Margery miscarried and secretly she and Dolor felt it was a sign from God that they would not bring forth another child on English soil.

CHAPTER EIGHTEEN

James and Cicely

Early 1620s

James made many voyages from Virginia to England, occasionally to other ports, but the Davises, Munjoys, Gilberts and other sailing families built many new ships in the early decades of the seventeenth century near Dartmouth and in other shipyards. James would stay with his cousin William at Twickenham, his brother at Acton-Turville and occasionally with cousins or friends of Lord Stafford, the Thayers in Thornbury in south Gloucestershire, in Tewksbury. The location was convenient as it wasn't far to the merchants and the God-awful port in Bristol that dropped 30 feet between tides, plus it was near the Grenvilles and Bideford.

Sir James Thomas had been friends with Richard Thayer and James often visited when he was a child. James was young when he first met their fourth daughter (three others of seven had not survived birth or infancy). Cecily Thayer was a bit of a tomboy. Four years younger than her brother Thomas and a year younger than Wilfred, they let her tag along on their hikes and romps around the estate. She had no problem pinning up her skirts to climb trees or hop onto rocks to cross a stream. A first James just thought she was amusing, but over time he knew he adored her. She had bright blue eyes, flaming red hair, lots of thick locks that wouldn't stay braided or inside her cap. She had very pale skin with what she called 'fairy dust' or a light sprinkle of freckles over her cheeks and nose. There were many old remnants of stone circles or standing stones, burial cairns or dolmen everywhere in southeastern England and she and her siblings would often play games in and around them, daring the old gods to come out and play.

James had resisted courting her until he had gotten his father's plantation in Virginia started, freeing him to get a land grant and settle in the northern Virginia patent. He had no desire to go as far north as Robert liked, but he was drawn to the Bay Colony, having often sailed along its shores on his trips. Its wild, angry grey sea reminded him of Cornwall, as did the granite cliffs that butted against pounding sea. Yet it had gentle bays with ship-friendly ports, found, as in Virginia, behind dangerous shallow shoals.

In 1618 he and Cicely married and made their first home in one of the manors on her father's estate in Little Buddington, Cheshire. Her step-brother Richard had married Margery Wheeler the same year and James and he talked about emigrating to the Massachusetts Bay once a patent was obtained. James and Richard Davis spent many hours going over what they knew of the land, of its resources, speculating on how close the western sea to the Pacific or Spice Islands was.

"I hear the Indian and Pacific Oceans are just beyond a big river to the west," said Richard. He had taken up that lowly trade of cordwaining, or shoe and book making, unusual for one of his class, but he said in the 'New' England all men would have to have a trade and the land was full of wild animals plus had an abundance of fields for grazing so what better trade than that of cobbler? The skins would be practically free if he raised livestock for meat so every pair of shoes or boots would be pure profit. James agreed as he'd had many conversations with his brother William, and had learned black smithing and weaving in hopes of teaching the trades to his sons or nephews so they would be welcomed on the new shores. Dolor and his brother Jenkins were joiners and housewrights and the other men were sailors and fishermen so they all had important trades to offer the new world.

His cousin Dolor and his family were now living outside Birmingham as James had gotten him a position as master carpenter on First Baronet Sir Thomas Holte's new manor, Aston Hall. Holte wanted lots of carvings and that was Dolor's specialty. He never occupied his house in Kent, much to Margery's dismay, choosing instead to bring his family and his cart full of carpentry tools from Sevenoaks to Aston Hall. After the catastrophic fire at Sevenoaks the work had fallen off as the owner scrambled to try to find extra money for rebuilding. Dolor and Jenkyns had both been hired on at Sir Thomas's huge project. Holte was a very serious man and John Thorpe's building plans were meticulous. There was a massive Great Hall to the right with an archway to the huge fireplace. Holte planned a Saloon, a Best Drawing Room, Library and Great Parlor plus dining rooms, kitchens, bedrooms and so on. Dolor could see himself carving the balustrade and sides of the Great Stairs, made of the finest oak, and the ceilings, moldings and panels of the Long Gallery to Lady's Holte's Drawing Room. Jenkyns liked the more basic mortise and pinion joinery work: shaving down massive tree trunks and securing each finely fitted beam with a wooden pin. The manor 's foundation was made from slag from Holte's iron works and the red and blue bricks used for its exterior came from his brickpits. For Dolor and Jenkyns, used to buildings made from grey Dorsetshire stone, this was a new material and they never cared for its rough appearance. Local sandstone blocks were used for the decorative dresswork. Margery was always fussing over the red stains on Dolor's shirts and his loose work pants that he tucked into his (brick dust stained) socks and held up with garters. The iron oxide was difficult to remove on wash day, but the rewards of living on the Holte estate on a hill overlooking the road to Lichfield and the small village of Aston, near the river Tame more than made up for the inconveniences. Thomas Holte's grandfather had been King's Attorney to the Council in Wales and Justice of Caernarfon, amongst other positions, so he had Welsh connections with the Davis family. He had helped administer Henry VIII's dissolution of the monasteries and was well rewarded. Holte's son William was High Sheriff of Warwickshire and Thomas had attended Magdalen College in Oxford before entering the law in the Inner Temple. Thomas bought the estate of Brushwood from Sir Edward Grenville plus other properties in Warwickshire, was knighted by King James in 1603 and bought a baronetcy nine years later.

But what Margery loved about the estate was the forest nearby. She loved to take walks in it, listening to the birds and smelling the flowers and trees. Margery's brother Simon would tell her of the forests in New England and how they could actually own land with forests there, unlike in England where the lords or the royal family owned most of the chases, or forests. As High Sheriff Holte's father had to hang many a poacher who had taken a deer from the forests. Margery dreamed of a land where the woods and lands were free for a farmer to use as his own. A land of milk and honey, to quote the Bible.

Sir Thomas and his family were living in London and came out to inspect the construction on rare occasions so Dolor and the other supervisors were given a lot of latitude in daily decision-making.

One day Thomas Thayer and his wife, also named Margery, and their children went with Cicely and James and their sons John, James and Samuel and cousin Dolor and Margery and their two young sons John and Nicholas to Lincolnshire to hear a new lecturer by the name of John Cotton talk about how the new land would also be a land where Puritans could practice their religion freely, without persecution by Archbishop Laud.

CHAPTER NINETEEN

Early Virginia

1620s

After the failed Popham-Gorges settlement at Sagadahoc in northern Virginia James concentrated on the southern plantation of Jamestown. The Spanish moved their operations from the West Indies to the mainland of South America and many English took over the sugar, cotton and tobacco plantations on the islands. James and his family invested heavily in Bermuda as James and Richard sailed the *Gift of God* and the *Virginia* of the North Colony as part of the Magazine that criss-crossed the Atlantic to resupply and repopulate the southern Virginia colony. In these busy years Robert, Richard, William, George, and James Davis also owned part of the *Swan* and the *Delight*, the *Charity* (along with Weston) and captained or were officers in the fleet that either crossed from London, Gravesend, Cowes and other ports to fish the northern waters or run goods to and from the southern colony and islands.

By 1620 the French were more of a danger than the Spanish and the English ships made sure to avoid Florida and the St. Lawrence seaway in their voyages. Despite the constant supply of single women recruited by the Virginia Company and sold as wives for 150 pounds of best leaf tobacco each to the indentured laborers and convicts spared execution by transportation, the colony didn't flourish. As a "head right" investors got 50 acres for every man wife and child he sent over. Massive plantation lands were acquired this way. However, after the Jamestown massacre most of the 4,000 people the Davis ships and others had brought over during the subsequent four years had died, many from malaria and tropical fevers and infections. Some had returned to England.

In 1624 King James revoked the southern colony's charter and declared it a Royal Colony. This hurt Sandys and the Merchant Adventurers but the general colonial populace liked it as the Crown would defend them and they received rights due to all Englishmen including the right of representation in the House of Burgesses and the rule of law.

The following year King James granted 1,250 acres to anyone who brought 250 people to the colony to settle on what were called Hundreds or Particular Plantations. This actually saved the southern colony as it was no longer run by Merchant Adventurers who only cared for profit.

Captain James's brother Sir Thomas Davis had immigrated in the *Margaret of Bristol*, in 1618 joining John who had gone over on the *George* with Samuel Argyll in 1617 and his cousin William who had gone over in the *William*, Richard in the *Bona Nova* and Nicholas in the *Mary Gold* the same year. Sir John' son Robert's widow still owned the *Mary and John* with Raleigh Gilbert and it was primarily used to fish the north, run fish down the coast to the southern plantations put into ports along the coast, then take tobacco from the colonies, pick up more and sugar and cotton in the islands and return to either England, Ireland or other ports. On the voyage back across the Atlantic the ships would be carrying manufactured goods from England. Of the Davis clan only Robert had shown no interest in owning plantations on the fertile Bermuda island or English section of the Barbados and in southern Virginia. Robert had received part of Mason and Gorges' patent to the north. He never forgot his expeditions and pioneering of *Sagadahoc* and out of nostalgia, plus a distaste of hot, humid climate, preferred to push for northern settlement, first as fishing villages set up year-round with drying frames and families instead of sailors, then as separate English villages.

Davis ships were in constant contact with the settlers and the captains and officers learned that the *Mayflower* was scarce out of port after returning and taking on some of the *Speedwell*'s passengers when Weston worked a separate deal and got a patent for a settlement north of the Hudson River at the mouth of the Weymouth River – a commercial settlement for trading as opposed to a religious settlement.

A year after the strict, highly religious Pilgrims landed on Cape Cod with their rigid Governor John Winslow, Robert's friend Thomas Weston decided to put his energies further north into fishing villages.

The Separatists had worked hard their first spring to begin repaying their transportation debt and had filled the hold of the *Fortune* with beaver skins, sassafras and split oak clapboards for barrel staves. (Cedar wainscoting clapboards were being supplied by the southern colony.) They felt the cargo would pay off half their debt to the Merchant Adventurers but before it reached England a French ship seized it, with Cushman aboard.

To aggravate them further Weston's shallop full of men were inept at establishing their fishing and fur trading camp at *Wessagusset*. As the pilgrims were bound by Christian duty to help people in distress some of Weston's rough traders ended up living near them as charity cases until they could be sent either back to England or to another settlement. Some went north to what would later be called Boston, others to what would be called Salem and others to Rhode Island.

After his fishing-trading post's fall from grace, Weston generously offered the use of the thirty ton *Swan*, co-owned by George Munjoy and William Davis, to the pilgrims so they could trade with the savages for beans and corn, most of which they used to plant their newly plowed fields.

Robert died in 1622 from an infected wound received when a mast snapped during a hurricane on board the *Mary and John*. Marie, living in northwestern Dorsetshire, was inconsolable and gladly let James take over running the ship she now hated. However, Willie was fascinated by all things maritime and couldn't wait to run out an meet his uncle James whenever he was ashore.

With his mother William visited the quiet grey stone country manor just north of Sherborne Castle near Sir Walter Raleigh's old estate in Maiden Bradley. Marie knew she would never go to New England but she could see the lust for its adventure in her boy's eyes. She still felt connected to the old England: the England of King Arthur and Druid stone circles and fairy magic; the England of the Wars of the Roses, the Tudor kings, the monasteries and church lands taken by Henry VIII, of men gallantly riding off to fight on the Continent for their king or queen. But she could see it changing before her eyes as the younger generation casually broke their bonds with the homeland.

CHAPTER TWENTY

Sir John and the Aristocracy

Late 1500s-Early 1600s

John Davies (he preferred the more elegant Welsh spelling of Davis) grew up on Chisgrove Manor near Tisbury, the southwest corner of Wiltshire. His father Edmund Davis had old Catholic abbey lands and was as a country gentleman who oversaw a highly successful tannery business. His business prospects had been vastly improved through his marriage to a daughter of John Bennett, owner of Pitt House and Fonthill Lake, southeast of the village of Fonthill Gifford where the Audley family had a huge estate. William Pitt was a close friend of the Lord Mayor of London and a major investor in the West Indies. Old Wardour castle was near his father's estate and the Davies often socialized with the Herberts, the Earls of Pembroke, the Talbots, Arundels, Seymours, Cleves, Mountjoys, Blounts, Philips, Gilberts and Raleighs. Audley would later prove very beneficial to John. Francis Bacon, and Richard Hackled were his friends and Hakluyt's father belonged to the Skinners union, as did Edmund Davis. This section of Devon was the nucleus of the movement to expand England's interests in the New World and the islands off its coast.

The famous Chilmark stone quarry that supplied the stones for many a manor was near Tisbury and many local stonemasons worked at Salisbury Cathedral.

Edmund was a gentrified merchant, as was his brother John of Creedy whereas their brother Robert had been mostly involved in shipping, either as a captain or part owner of a ship. This was where the money was in the late sixteenth and early seventeenth century England. If you owned a ship or had an interest in one, the world was your oyster. Most of the merchants had a business home near Parliament and the Court plus their main estate in the countryside. This hearkened back to the days when plague would sweep through London and the only safe haven to be found was in the countryside. Plague, though never as severe as the mid-1300s to mid-1400s when half the population of England had died from the Black Death, still descended on the cities and the poor who flocked there because they were forced off their lands suffered the worst.

The Davis men had switched their interests away from the East Indies following the death of John in the Pacific Ocean. He had helped set up a trading post on Sumatra for the British but the Dutch were monopolizing the trade so the English turned their ships westward.

Like his older brother Matthew, John of Tisbury was not a sailor. He attended Winchester college, then Queen's in Oxford to study law and was accepted to the Middle Temple, following Matthew as a barrister. In the Middle Temple he shared quarters with Sir Robert Cotton, who was appointed mayor of Ireland by King James.

As a young man John became fast friends with the elderly Sir William Cecil, who died five years before Queen Elizabeth, as did many of her advisors. Cecil had been a staunch backer of Sir Walter Raleigh and the New World explorations. John's father's cousin James (Thomas) Davis was one of the more influential founders of the London Company, formed as a share holding organization to set up plantations in the New World to expand the empire and establish trade.

But John wasn't interested in 100 acres in Virginia: he was ambitious. He was a poet and craved acclaim for his poetry and he had the character defect of always wanting more. More money, more status, more power. The key to the above was a royal connection. And John found this in Audley and Mountjoy.

Through the Davis family he had connections to the Lords of Somerset, Wiltshire, Berkshire, Gloucestershire, Devonshire, Cornwall and they still had a vestige of influence in Wales along with the Dudleys and Bulkeleys. His cousin William Davis was an immensely wealthy merchant in Bristol and his uncles John and James had manors along the rivers in southeastern London such as at Twickenham in addition to the beloved farm near Dartmouth. His cousin James had Easton Royale in the Vale of Pewsey, northeast of Salisbury plain and near Malborough (Seymours, Popham and Philips territory) and Richard and Dolor had lands in Kent. The families with the most power around Queen Elizabeth's throne had come from Devonshire, which was where most of the ships were built and, other than the Thames, the sites of the best ports were Bideford (Mountjoy and Grenville territory) on the north, Bristol, then down to Plymouth, Southampton, Dartmouth and Rye.

But John Davies didn't want to be a captain, master or owner of ships. He loved the land: he loved to ride around the countryside and observe nature then ride back and work on his poems. He was a dreamer but also a schemer. He wanted vast tracts of land but didn't want to get grants the way his relatives did, by sailing, exploring and colonizing.

He had met the new king, James VI of Scotland, now James 1 of England in Scotland when the eighth lord Mountjoy had presented him to King James during the christening of James's son Henry and had renewed his acquaintance while accompanying the king en route to London following Queen Elizabeth's death. They spent hours reading their poetry to each other, almost like lovers, drinking and reading, praising each other while Princess Ann entertained herself elsewhere.

Lord Mountjoy was made Lord Lieutenant of Ireland and First Earl of Devonshire, then through his influence, John was appointed Solicitor General of Ireland. As soon as John arrived on the island he became its Attorney General and indicted the earls of Tyrone and Tryconnell for treason and then helped the commission drafting the plan for the confiscation of lands to create Ulster Plantation. He also defended the right of the king to the title of duke of Cornwall.

Ten years after James I took the throne John called an Irish Parliament, going to London to seek permission from the king to be Speaker of the House of Commons for the county of Fermouth.

In 1621 John Davies held a seat for Hindon in Wiltshire and Newcastle under Lymne in Staffordshire, where a brother-in-law related to the Pembroke-Talbots lived. To help matters, he helped Audley, who had coveted Irish land since his soldiering days there under Queen Elizabeth, acquire a grant of 35,000 acres in Ulster Plantation.

The Irish peasants were burned out, massacred and driven into the hills in order to establish the English estates. To John and many of his peers such as Sir John Popham the Irish and Scottish were sub-human heathens, much like the natives found in the islands and New World. They had no rights and could be deported to plantations to be used as indentured servants. The Irish were mostly Catholic, another strike against them.

John did bring English Common Law to Ireland and restored the old inheritance system, cutting the king's take from it. But most of the time he used his position of power to trade land for money while dreaming of the day he could return to the English mainland to build a magnificent manor.

This he did when he bought the old manor and rectory in Pirton in Hertfordshire, then got his main manor of Englefield in Berkshire 14 years later. That same year, 1623, the year when the northern Virginia patentees were establishing a fishing community north of the Separatists, he bestowed a dowry of 6,000 pounds on his daughter Lucy upon he marriage to Ferdinando Hastings, heir to Henry, fifth earl of Huntingdon.

While in Ireland John passed legislation against importing Irish cattle to England and importing foreign (not English) tobacco to Ireland and England.

To his great grief John never had a son to carry on his name but through his influence the Davis family received land grants in the upper north Virginia (Maine),south Virginia and lands in the West Indies. Cousins and their offspring would later capitalize on these grants but John died without seeing the fruits of his labors in the New England. However, his connections and family wealth helped build what would later become an independent nation.

Sir John Davis's brother Matthew was one of the first to capitalize on the West Indies plantations, mostly through his friendship with the Drax family, whose fortunes were linked to the Erles and Craddocks, who had claims via Gorges and Mason in the North Virginia patent.

The Erle family in East Devon claimed its crest of scallop shells derived from the Knights Templars' St. John Hospitalers, a group of Templars who set up hospices for the devoted making the pilgrimage to the Holy Land during the Crusades. In England, after the Dissolution of the Monasteries under King Henry VIII Walter Erle bought Axemouth Manor and solidified the estate by marrying Mary Weeks whose family had the Abbey grounds. Walter was an officer of the Privy Chamber. For his service to Henry's only son, the future King Edward VI, and later to Queens Mary and Elizabeth, he was given Charborough Manor in Colyton, Devon.

Walter Erle's son Thomas married Dorothy de la Pole, niece of John Popham, Chief Justice of England. Dorothy's mother Katherine was a sister of Popham's. Katherine Popham had married William de la Pole, a neighbor who owned Shute House. William de la Pole had been Earl of Suffolk under King Henry VI, whose favored status he shared with the titled Somersets. John de la Pole had been First Earl of Lincoln, son of King Edward IV's sister Elizabeth and John de la Pole, Second Earl of Suffolk. In the Wars of the Roses he sided with Richard and was killed in the battle of Stoke in 1487 fighting against Henry VII. De la Pole's son John was married to Margaret Boeufort briefly but the marriage was annulled and she remarried Duke Henry Stafford when she was 14. When she was twelve she had married and given birth to the future King Henry VII through Edward IV's half brother Edmund Tudor who died when his wife was six months pregnant.

By the early 1600s Dorothy's brother, Sir William Pole, was renown as an historian and antiquarian. He lived in Colcombe House near Colyton, not far from Dorchester to the east and Sir Walter Raleigh's estate to the north. The deer park nearby had been leased to the family by Henry VIII's Queen, Catherine Parr. (The Audleys of Colyton were related to John the navigator on his wife's side.)

Dorothy's first husband, Sir Walter Vaughan of Falstone, Bishopstone was Sheriff of Wiltshire and had been an MP. He had begun building a pier at Axemouth harbor, where their manor was. The Axe River had long been a part of the wine importation business, smuggling wines from small inland ports into Devonshire, thereby avoiding the import duties larger ports had to pay. To the north Bridgwater had been the main export port for militiary expeditions to Ireland and Wales and also brought many goods into the country including coal and paper, the latter a luxury item as late as the sixteenth century.

The Poles shared shipping interests with the Davis and other wealthy shipowners and merchants in Bristol and throughout Devonshire. Although the kings and queens had changed in the past century the old aristocracy still owned most of the large tracts of land that had once been owned by the Catholic church.

While Thomas, James, Robert, Richard, William and George Davis were concentrating on Virginia, North Virginia and Newfoundland and John was in Ireland, his older brother Matthew Davis hooked up with Robert Sanford, Matthew Craddock, Thomas Erle and the Draxes to begin tobacco plantations in Jamaica and the Barbados. Sir James Drax and his brother William favored Jamaica and Henry favored Barbados. Matthew Craddock was also very interested in the northern part of Virginia (later named Maine.

Thomas Drax had married Susanna Fiennes, daughter of William Fiennes, Third Viscount of Saye and Sele.

Lord Say and Sele's Earl of Leicester's daughter Susan Fiennes married John Humphrey, a friend of the Puritan Reverend White in Dorchester (and related to Lord de la Warre and the Pelhams). Another daughter, Arbella, married Isaac Johnson, (related to the Gorges through Sir Fernando's son) and they were friends and shared the Puritan religious convictions of John Winthrop.

In the 1620s the Puritans were gaining ground and would be sending settlers to the New England to establish religious colonies. Others would be sailing supply and trading ships across the Atlantic. And some would be setting up plantations strictly for profit.

1608

Matthew Davis was in the latter category. He had two sons: Barnabas or Barnaby and Theopholis, or Theo.

Barnaby now stood before his father's desk in the large study in Chisgrove Manor.

Matthew took his time reading before he looked up. His expression was stern. He tugged on his Van Dyke moustache and cleared his throat before addressing his son.

"You were sent home from school in Cambridge. This is not the first time you have been expelled from an expensive private school and disappointed your mother and myself, young man. Your prankstering got you into trouble just as it did my brother at Oxford. Only thank the Lord you haven't his overfondness for strong spirits."

Barnaby at age 14 was as tall as he would get: 5'8". He still had what people called baby fat on his face and, despite participating in athletics at school wasn't muscular. His medium brown hair was always a bit messy and his clothes tended to be rumpled. His light brown eyes stared down at the expensive Turkish carpet in front of his father's desk. Outside the tall windows he could see buds forming on the spreading elm trees and sheep grazed on the estate's front lawn. Birds were singing their happy spring songs but Barnaby felt none of their joy.

"I'm sorry, father," he mumbled into his scuffed shoes.

Matthew pinned his steely grey eyes on him. He was in full barrister mode, lacking only the wig as he read his son the charges.

"I got very little sleep last night thanks to your untimely arrival here that called me away from London. I had to file a postponement on a very important case to deal with a son who seems to be bent on taking the path to Hell."

Barnaby blushed to his roots. His whole body felt as if it were on fire.

"Obviously the life of an academic or even a barrister doesn't seem to be in your future," Matthew continued, "you are too young to take over management of any of my estates and I wouldn't trust you to be responsible in any case."

Barnaby shifted from one foot to the other. He noticed his stockings were stained with mud and grass from his early morning walk near the stream and pond.

"I can work in the fields, father," he said, almost in a whisper, "I can prove to you that I am responsible."

Matthew harumphed loudly. He lit his pipe and drew until he got a taste of the sharp tobacco.

"No. I have decided to apprentice you to James Drax."

Barnaby's eyes flew open wide,

"But, father! We are gentry! We don't work for others!"

Matthew's mouth was drawn down into a severe frown,

"It won't be an indenture but you are too young to be your own person. I am sending you to Barbados under his care and tutelage to learn how to run my future tobacco plantation there."

Barnaby's heart leaped for joy. He smiled broadly,

"Oh, thank you, father! I have so wanted to travel to the West Indies and Virginia! It's all the boys at school talk about!"

Matthew stood, towering over the boy, glaring at him.

"You might not be thanking me in a few months, young man. The climate is deadly to many Englishmen. I was so angry with you when I heard you'd been dismissed that I agreed but now I'm not so sure I want to sentence you to a likely death."

Barnaby begged to be allowed to go. It was the adventure he longed for! How he envied his cousins who went to sea at an age even younger than 14. Among the peasantry he was considered an adult but among his class the boys had to go on to Oxford or Cambridge and get a degree before they were accepted into the adult world. Of course, it was a matter of the rich having the luxury of letting their sons and daughters stay at home longer and obtain social graces and the boys would be exposed to the best education available in England. A member of the aristocracy was expected to know French and Latin and, if headed for the ministry, Greek. Often they were taken abroad to visit religious sites in Rome or France, sometimes even Germany or Austria but relations with Spain were strained so that country was avoided. Even though most of the sites were Catholic, the history of the early Church was honored among Protestants, including those like the Davises who gave lip service to the Church of England but secretly leaned towards Puritanism.

"While you are in the employ of Mr. Drax you shall continue your studies. A tutor will be accompanying you and I shall expect your progress reports to be satisfactory, is this clear?"

"Oh, yes, father! I shall study very hard."

"You will also work hard. Mr. Drax intends to plant hundreds of acres of tobacco. He and his brother will also plant on Jamaica but I am interested only in my land in Barbados. My cousin James has hundreds of acres of tobacco under cultivation in Virginia and, if successful, I might expand my operations onto the mainland. Your observations and abilities will make a big difference to the future fortunes of this family. And to yours. Do you understand?"

Barnaby was elated. He eagerly accepted the five year contract and left his father's dusty study feeling as if he were walking on a cloud.

****

The fleet left Falmouth on June 16th. From the minute he boarded the 350 tonne ship Barnaby was ill. His ebullience waned with each blast of frigid air on deck and with every swell of the ocean. Their ship was accompanied by a smaller ship, the 180 ton *Nonesuch,* owned by a planter who remained in London. Both ships had left from there and Falmouth was their final docking on English soil until the West Indies.

The waves were running high and Barnaby caught glimpses of the English coast falling away as they sailed southwest. The two ships would take turns holding the lead, the smaller one pulling ahead in calmer winds and the larger one gaining when the winds blew the worst. Barnaby's seasickness also waxed and waned but rarely went away entirely. His baby fat melted away and his pale skin began to tan from the sun reflecting off the sea and sails. His muscles also began to harden as he helped the sailors pull on the ropes to raise or lower the main sails and he had helped hove the anchor aboard as an extra on the capstan winch when they left Falmouth.

James Drax was voluble and spent hours each day in the captain's quarters or the lounge pouring over crude maps of the Barbados, discussing with other investors of the London Co. the best locations to site their plantations. Barnaby spent an equal amount of time confined to his small quarters or in the saloon with his tutor, a dour faced Puritan named John Smythe, who claimed to be a distant cousin through the Bristol branch. He was dyspeptic and hardly ate, though not due to seasickness. He abhorred the crude hardtack and greasy salted pork that was the main diet of the crew. The London Company members ate better, having salted beef and various pickled vegetables to accompany their meals, as well as port and wine. Barnaby and John Smythe did not drink that or the rum the sailors were allowed in moderation but drank hard cider as the water in the barrels tasted stale and sour.

Off the coast of Spain the ships encountered a 400 ton trader sailing north from Guinney, North Africa. The seas were calm so the captain hailed them and they lowered their sails, floating close together. The captain and a few of his crew boarded Drax's ship and dined with the captain and officers on special fowl pies made from seabirds shot by the crew of the trader.

The captain bragged about the treasure in his hold: gold and elephant tusks of ivory. He gave each officer and even Barnaby a small piece of ivory. The sailors begged for some as they liked to spend idle hours carving, or scratching, pictures into them to give as gifts to their lady loves on shore.

The next day the ships parted and the following day the *Nonesuch* pulled away, heading straight for Barbados whereas Drax's ship had to stop in St. Iago (John) in the Cape Verde islands. Barnaby wanted to be with the *Nonesuch* but was bound to Drax so had to go where his 'master' went. The London Co. had loaded English textiles and goods to trade for horses and cattle in St. Iago. In the lower hold the ship held about 50 Irish men who were under guard. Every night they would be herded on deck, buckets of cold sea water thrown on them and their slop buckets dumped into the sea but the hold retained a nasty, unclean stench and Barnaby avoided it. His stomach was queasy just from the movement of the waves, he didn't need anything else aggravating it.

Barnaby's tutor had studied flora and fauna and he was quick to spot things, pointing out goats, hogs, chickens and geese as they passed small, sparsely settled islands that looked burned to Barnaby.

"Did they burn the tobacco fields?" he asked, wiping sweat from his face.

"Nay, lad. 'Tis this unnatural heat, burning the fields and grasses. I'm afraid their harvests will be poor this season. Look there at the corn stalks all withered and dried up."

Barnaby squinted, leaning so far over the rails he almost fell into the sea.

"Why aren't we docking at any of them?"

"It's not our call, lad. The captain and master make all the decisions on a ship, as ye well know. Our orders are to go to St. Iago then on to Barbados. Every harbor in these islands has dangerous rocks and reefs – a captain takes his chances every time he pulls close to land. We be needing nothing they have to offer and we have to save our stores for trading in St. Iago. I know ye are itching to get off this vessel and get onto dry land, I am, too, but we must be patient. Speaking of which, have you studied your Herodotus lesson?"

Barnaby sighed. Would this wretched voyage ever end?

CHAPTER TWENTY-ONE

Theo in the West Indies

1619

Matthews's eldest son Theo was also sent west, but not because he was to be punished.

He was aboard he *Mary Gold*, captained by his cousin, Richard on the last day of December,1619 when they weighed anchor and left Falmouth. Another relative, Capt. Nicholas Davis, son of William and brother to Dolor, was accompanying them, to rejoin his ship that was at a graving dock near Jamestown. Theo was to become overseer on Sir Thomas's Virginia plantation. (Capt. Sir Thomas had immigrated to that new land in 1618 when he was 68 and on his third marriage.) The *Sampson*, captained by John Ward was the *Mary Gold*'s companion ship. Theo and his cousin Nathaniel, son of Capt. Richard, were onboard it, working as deck hands to earn passage. After setting sail they were joined by a smaller ship.

It took about two months to reach the Barbados, where Drax, again the master, offloaded his copious cargo and his servants. The *Mary Gold* and *Sampson* set anchor off shore and the two youths were able to go ashore together.

Theo was dour. He missed England and his friends and the pretty lasses he'd been flirting with. The ships were full of crude sailors and Nathaniel Davis and

Theo had been the butt of many pranks – and also had to fend off a few unwelcome advances in the middle of the night. His cousin had already decided the life of a sailor wasn't for him. Theo was more sanguine. Since birth he had been shipped off to boarding schools. He had liked staying for a while with his cousin's widow Marie and felt homesick for her tidy, neat grey stone farm in Devon but he was also open to adventure. He had mixed feelings but, unlike Nathaniel, he thought the rocky coast of Barbados was full of exciting pirate treasure. He and his friends often wandered off, looking into every cave they came to.

Two days after they docked they came upon Henry Drax in an inland meadow . He was pacing off a piece of land along a small river.

"This is where I'm staking my new claim," Drax said, his sweaty face wide in smile.

Theo asked what was so special about the spot.

"Well, ye got the river so ye can irrigate from it and also water yer livestock there."

Theo said he'd heard it rained a lot when it wasn't so dry.

"Aye, tis been a dry year, byes, but that's the beauty of having yer land on a river."

"Are you going to grow lots and lots of tobacco?" Nathaniel asked, following the panting, sweating planter.

"Aye, even though the price of it is going down, and I think I'll plant grapes for raisins and try some of the exotic plants from the East Indies, too."

Theo's younger brother Barnaby joined them, hiking through tough grass.

"It sure isn't as fertile as England," Theo remarked.

"Nay, bye!" Drax said, picking up a handful of the black soil, "Lookee here. This soil will grow just about anything. But it does need water. That was the problem last year, a drought. We got some hurricanes but all they do is blow everything down and flood for a bit then it all goes dry again."

"Well, it does look better than the chalky stuff back home," Theo replied, "but will the sheep get enough to eat?"

"I'm not sure this is the best sheep country," Drax replied. His brother James waved and yelled at him upriver so he turned to go.

"Sheep can't take this type of wet heat, sons," he added over his shoulder as he trekked over to his older brother.

Nathaniel asked what the difference was between dry heat and wet heat.

"Well, England has what is called a temperate climate," Barnaby patiently explained, "This is what is called tropical. I've heard our relative the great Captain Sir Walter Raleigh followed the Orinoco River in South America" (he pointed southwest across the sea) "and there were great forests of tropical trees that rained inside all the time."

"'Tis nonsense!" Theo demurred, wiping his face with his handkerchief, "I sure hope Virginia is more temperate! This is just hellish."

"Well, if you hadn't talked me into stealing that ale, I wouldn't have been kicked out of school and wouldn't have been sold to Drax," said Barnaby.

"I don't want to go Virginia!" exclaimed Theo.

"Well, father indentured you to Sir Thomas," Barnaby drily remarked.

Theo shook his head.

"I'll be no man's servant!" he said, anger blazing from his blue eyes, "I was born free and free I'll stay!"

Two days later when the *Mary Gold* left for its northwest journey to Virginia Theo was nowhere to be found. The captains sent out search crews but a storm was moving in so they had to cast off and set sail without him.

Nathaniel cried and said he wanted to stay, too, but was told by Nicholas to act like a man and get to work helping the crew.

"The Drax brothers and their men are on the island," he explained, "they will find Theo and take care of him. I'm not so sure Sir Thomas will be taking this very well. Labor is a valuable thing in the plantations and Theo was sturdy. These Irishers are a measly lot and African slaves cost a lot."

In Virginia Nicholas was proved right. Nathaniel stayed on and, in lieu of Theo, learned how to manage the Davis tobacco plantation but his heart wasn't in it. The next time Richard's ship came into port he begged to be taken on as he preferred a life at sea to the plantation. More muscular and tanned but he had seen a bigger world beyond and gotten the travel hunger. He knew he'd be back to the New England or the West Indies one day soon.

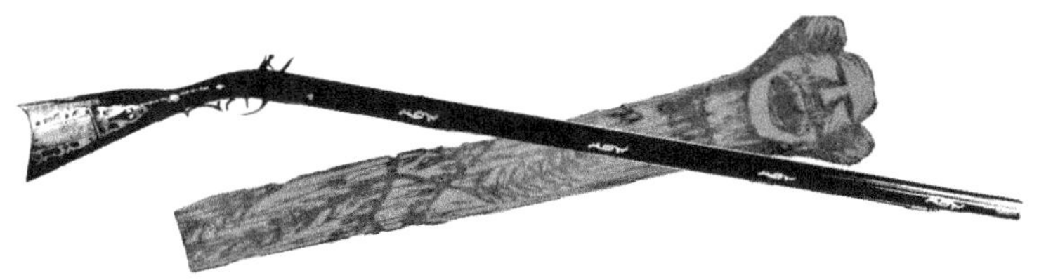

CHAPTER TWENTY-TWO

Early Maine Settlement

1620-1629

After Robert married Marie Warren she had several miscarriages but her prayers were finally answered with the birth of a son in 1620. Unfortunately Robert died not long after, suffering in pain for months from an infected wound.

By then Marie was an ardent devotee of the Rev. John White and never missed a sermon at Holy Trinity church. She usually attended alone as Robert was gone most of the year, sailing back and forth from the fishing lands off Newfoundland and helping his relatives James, Richard, George and even Sir Thomas on occasion as they ran a magazine, or supply ships, back across the Atlantic to provision the small settlements in Virginia and to bring back fish, tobacco and fruits from the West Indies.

In the late autumn of 1622 England was getting a last dose of summer. Marie fanned herself near a window in the women's section of the church, the strong odor of dried, flaked fish wafting in as she listened to her beloved pastor read from a pamphlet Captain John Smith had written praising the fishing along the coasts of Virginia and what was being called New England. The women sat on the long ends and the servants, fosters and non-members sat in the galleries above.

Rev. White had a powerful voice, an hypnotizing voice. He knew how to influence people, to bring forth their charity and desire to help their fellow Englishmen and women to convert others to the simple principles of Puritanism versus the more ritualized, and some feLt. popish or papist Church of England practices. Little William was sleeping in her lap, having suckled deeply on the long ride in from their farm.

"It is our Christian duty to bring the Word of God to the heathen in this new world," Rev. White intoned, "It is not enough to just send our men to fish for a season. I am asking for volunteers to form a share holding company, a Dorchester Company, to establish a Christian, Puritan permanent settlement on those distant shores, much like our brothers and sisters have established in Plymouth Colony."

The Council for New England was begun by Rev. White and Richard Bushrod, a wealthy textile seller and a merchant adventurer. Bushrod was one of the traders who met ships such as the *Mary and John* and accepted fish and furs in exchange for silver. He convinced a fellow MP, Sir Walter Erle to get behind the plan. Since he had a title (from Charborough) he convinced the Privy Council to grant them an indenture to form a new company to settle New England.

Marie frowned. Robert had raved about the land, the trees, the huge lobsters and cod but he had also told about the savagery of the indians and the terrible cold of the winters there. Hadn't her relatives in Plymouth lost most of their people the first winter? Didn't they often live on corn traded from the indians? But she kept silent. She knew Robert would have been one of the first to sign up and offer the *Mary and John* for the venture, but he was dead. His oldest brother, Sir Thomas, had emigrated there in 1618 and he and Robert's brother James were doggedly creating and holding onto an ever growing tobacco plantation. James had even supplanted Captain Smith as a leader in the new town of Jamestown. They also were acquiring parcels in the West Indies, particularly the Barbados as the harsh Virginia tobacco needed to be blended with a milder form grown in the West Indies. But the French and Dutch were all over the West Indies so English traders had to be careful. Plus, there was the constant danger of encountering Spanish ships carrying slaves to the south of Virginia, to their plantations in the lands where Conquistadors had conquered the savages and brought in Catholicism. Piracy, though no longer condoned by England, was still being practiced by the Spanish and French.

Marie sighed. She loved Rev. White but wasn't sure she wanted to immigrate to North Virginia. South Virginia was full of hot, muggy heat and mosquitoes. English settlers died from epidemics, from a variety of fevers from the swamps. Northern Virginia had a lot of mosquitoes, too, but not as much plague. What was more deadly there was the brutal cold. Most English who died there perished from lung disease.

Marie thought to herself that some of that cold would be welcome in Dorchester at the moment. William was waking up and he was fussy as his teeth were coming in. She nursed him, brushing back his dark, sweaty hair while dangling a bracelet out for him to play with.

Sabbath services were long. The entire day was to be given to God and only the strictly necessary jobs such as feeding, watering and milking were done. Even cooking was done the night before and the Sabbath dinner was usually beans baked and held over warm coals and cold meats such as ham, plus bread, butter and cheese with cider.

Monday would start the season's work cycle all over: plowing or harvesting, shearing or slaughtering for the men and boys and laundry for the women. Huge cast iron pots of water would be heated outdoors and everyone's inner clothing washed. Shifts for the women and the long shirts the men wore. Both articles were worn night and day. And there were stockings and soiled baby linens, tablecloths, napkins, handkerchiefs and some of the sheets. The women scrubbed stains out with harsh handmade hard soap and by the end of the day the clotheslines were full of off-white articles, some of heavy linen and others lighter cotton. With winter the laundry was put off if the weather was too cold but the woolens took a long time to dry and often had to be hung over the large, deep fireplaces. The men's long night-shirts were only washed occasionally and the women's flannel petticoats could go the whole winter without a wash. Year round one's best dress or coats and trousers often went months between washing. Marie had two dresses that had a drawstring closing in front allowing her to nurse. She longed for her larger wardrobe of four dresses. She knew many women had only one or two dresses but her father's family was wealthy, as was Robert's. Her finest dress was Italian silk and French satin, trimmed with Spanish lace. But Puritans frowned on ostentatious display so the occasions to wear it were getting fewer and fewer. And with Sir Thomas gone the family gatherings at his big old manse in to the north, on the Creedy River, near Sir John Davis's newer one, had ceased. Even the May Day celebrations were being called too heathenish and dancing around the Maypole was considered to be a sin. She missed the fun and gaiety but often wondered if it were just the carefreeness of youth she was missing. Becoming a wife and the mistress of the manor was a heavy responsibility. Being a mother was, too, but she loved little William so much it frightened her. She knew Robert would have taken him to sea as soon as he was old enough and she didn't want to lose two men to that possessive mistress. Robert had taken in relatives to help his wife and son while he was away (the Davis family was very large and scattered all across Devon and Wales and even into eastern England) and her family had taken in some of her younger relatives to help with the large farms but she didn't feel the same ferocity of love and protectiveness for them as she felt for little Will.

Willie was now struggling, wanting to run free. She quietly carried him outdoors as the service concluded with a hymn, a psalm sung plainly in the style of the Puritans. Some families, like her parents, had bought central pews in the meeting house. However, Robert hadn't wanted to give more than he had for the church's rebuilding after the Great Fire. The whole city had to be rebuilt and every time he came back he was petitioned for donations. In the very back or upper galleries of the church sat servants and the relatives they were fostering.

As the congregation came out into the glare of the hot afternoon they greeted each other and then went their own ways, most of them just walking to homes inside the city. In winter Marie's relatives would invite them to have dinner with them in a town house and stay overnight as the roads were high with snow. Sometimes they had to stay in town because the mud was so bad on the roads, too, but now the harvest was in and people were restless to celebrate a Harvest Home at the next market day. They had given Thanksgiving for the fine harvest earlier in the service and carts were overflowing with wheat sheaves and unstacked hay and the smell of ripe grains and vegetables filled the air.

Marie gathered all her people together and they got on the two wagons that would carry them north to the farm. As she looked back at the town with its three churches and many shops she smiled. Rev. White had helped whip up the energy to rebuild the town. He had convinced them to build a work house for the poor and a grammar school for the children and the brewery was to be used as a source of income for the poor and for students. He ceaselessly preached about their duty to God and their duty to help their fellow Christians. She saw a group of wealthy merchants gathering around the minister on the church steps and knew his sermon had found converts to the cause of a far Northern Virginia plantation that wasn't part of the Separatists in Plymouth. Robert would have been pleased. Ever since he, James and Richard had to leave Sagadahoc he dreamed of returning and, with Gorges, settling their patent. James had grumbled about the French taking over the north, building a fort on the long river that his cousin John had helped explore as he looked for a Northwest Passage.

Now one of the relatives, little John Davis, stood up and pointed out smoke in the distance.

Everyone was alerted. Not another harvest time fire! The previous one had been so bad she could still smell hints of its strong smoke at times.

The carts stopped and the young John jumped down, accompanied by the other children as they ran to a hilltop to get a better look.

"'Tis a'right, Ma'am," he called back, "'Tis only them burning off a shrubby spot near a swamp so's the grass will grow for the sheep!"

The wheels creaked again and the family followed the crude road down gentle slopes, up small hills, across flatter plains. In the distance the fireplaces were damped and the only moving creatures were the sturdy Dorset sheep and a scattering of milk cows, oxen and the big Irish horses or smaller moor ponies they used for farm work.

Marie leaned back a little into the hard wooden seat. One of the girls, little Patience, was holding Willie, playing hide and seek with him. Marie could smell his wet diaper but knew he'd have to be wet until they reached the manor. She had changed him twice since leaving early that morning and the basket was now holding a wet and a soiled nappie.

She loosened the ribbon under her chin and pushed her straw bonnet back. On the far horizon dark clouds were forming. She gave a thanks to the Lord that they had scythed and stacked all the hay the past week. The gleaners had followed and now every little house had at least a small stack of hay for the winter. The livestock would scrounge amongst the stalks in the fields and could be kept fed until the snows when they'd have to be kept in the stone barns.

Winter was when the men slaughtered the hogs and the women made hams, cured in stoneware brine baths down in root cellars: some pork would be chopped, spiced and stuffed into the cleaned intestines then smoked into sausages. Every part of the pig was used, even the tough pighide. Early winter was a time of rest. The men had their outdoor farm chores but women made butter in small churns or helped the men milk in the big dairy farms. Winter was mostly a time of weaving on the looms in the bedrooms, or in the Davis manor, a separate drawing room. The sheep had been dipped, the wool had been sheared, washed, carded, spun and dyed in the spring. In winter they wove and sung psalms or listened while one of them read from the Bible. The children attended Rev. White's grammar school in town, boarding with Marie's relatives. But winter had been a lonely time for Marie as the fishing fleet that left from Weymouth stayed out until the ice got too thick and they had to head home. Before his injury Robert was only home briefly as the southern Atlantic was best sailed then, being full of hurricanes come spring and summer.

Marie had often wondered if she could emigrate if Robert asked. She could see their farm in the distance and was already homesick. She had only been on a ship once as a new bride while it was in Plimouth (Plymouth) harbor. She'd not cared for the small wooden vessel full of coiled ropes and metal tie downs and masts with flapping sails. It was hard to walk on the deck without tripping or catching her skirts on something, It stank of fish and evil rancid things and she found the sailors to be a crude bunch. How her uncle had lived on one for two months as he'd taken his family across the sea, she couldn't fathom. Robert had shown her the 'tween decks' where they bunked and Marie, who was extremely modest, couldn't imagine sharing such a low, cramped space with a hundred other passengers. But she had loved Robert so much she knew she'd go where he asked. Even if it meant leaving her beloved gentle Devonshire valley and taking little Willie over a great ocean to a strange shore.

****

On his own imitative Rev. White wrote to Roger Conant and John Oldham, two refugees from the strict Plymouth Colony now living in Nantasket, asking them to join with the 14 men left on a fishing settlement on Cape Ann to become the agent of The Dorchester Company, 200 shareholders strong. Conant eagerly accepted but felt Cape Ann wasn't the best site, preferring Naumkeag to its south. (A new name, Salem, from the Bible and meaning Peace, was later chosen.) 200 men, women and cattle, Rev. John Lyford, Oldham and the remnant removed to the spot on the north shore. Conant's brother John, a minister in Limington, Somerset, had gone to Oxford with White and it was he who told White that there was a desire for a new plantation, independent of Winslow's gathering group, which was too Separatist in nature. Thomas Weston had also remained independent of the Plymouth Colony and as a trader with ships, he traversed the shores from plymouth to Cape Ann, and east to Nova Scotia and Newfoundland.

To get the new patent for Salem the Dorchester Co. recruited Sir Henry Rosewell, of Ford Abbey, Dorchester's John Humphrey (treasurer for the Dorchester Co.) and Simon Whetcombe of Sherborne. The new patent was called The New England Company. They appointed John Endicott governor of Naumkeag (Salem) and sent him and a cargo of supplies and wine to Conant's settlement in April, 1623 on the *Abigail.*

On that spring day Marie saw the Dorchester sailors leave with great sorrow as her Robert had died the winter before, partly from a festering wound received when a ratline broke free of the mast in a storm and sliced his arm and partly from the ague. He had returned from Virginia, almost sobbing as he told about the massacre by the indians. Sir Edwin Sandys was devastated as he was a prime investor. One third of the settlers the Davis men had managed to ferry across the Atlantic over several years – men and women who had survived the voyage and the climate – were wiped out by the traitorous brother of *Powhatan.* Sandys plans to establish a college and an ironworks were abandoned. The colonists were gathered into one fortified town and their plantations left to the savages. Robert knew King James I, purportedly a syphilitic homosexual and spendthrift and despised by most of the English, would revoke the patent the merchants and adventurers had worked so hard to obtain. On his deathbed he implored Marie to take little Willie to the Northern land, to settle his and Mason's land grants. He told her to work with his cousin John, the heir to Creedy Manor and a close friend of the Gilberts, Raleighs, Gorges, Pophams and the Shipleigh family who owned an estate in Dartmouth near his deceased cousin John, the famous navigator. He signed the ownership of the *Mary and John* over to Marie, to be held in her name until William was old enough to own her, or for her to dispose of if she became desperate for money.

Marie had agreed, hoping against hope that Robert would pull through. He didn't and all that remained of her wonderful hearty, sunburnt captain was a gravestone in the churchyard.

Late the following year Marie, William and his younger cousin John traveled northwest to Creedy Manor to be present at the welcoming home of Sir John's son, Humphrey, named for Humphrey Gilbert, a relative. Earlier in the year she and the boys had gone there for the Christmas-New Year's feasting and had remained for weeks with Robert's relatives as the mud was thick on the roads and little Willie had a bad cold.

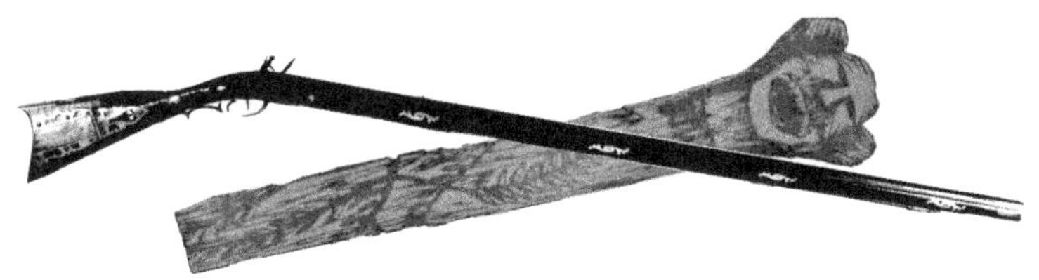

CHAPTER TWENTY-THREE

Salem

1620s

In late 1622 Dolor's son Big John and his wife Katherine were passengers on the *Southampton* which docked near the Kennebec River. Weston had been sending fishing ships such as the *Bona Nova* and resupply ships such as it and the *Charity* and the *Swan* to Plymouth Colony.

In April 1623 Rev. White with Bartlett and the New England Company sent 100 settlers in the *Abigail* to Naumkeag They included the trapper John Oldham.

The *Anne,* captained by William Peirce brought Elizabeth Warren and her five daughters to Plymouth to join her husband.

John Davis made another trip on *God's Gift* and Capt. Richard Davis sailed passengers on the *Jonathan* to a point north of the Plymouth colony on the Piscataqua River, part of the Gorges land grant.

The *Katherine*, under Capt. Stratton brought settlers to Weymouth while the *Samuel* and *Prophet Daniel* went to Virginia. The *Yorke Bonaventure* under Capt. Levitt brought settlers to Casco Bay, to a place they named Kittery. Amongst them was Alexander Shipleigh (Shapleigh), a neighbor of Sir Francis Drake and Sir John Davis in Dartmouth. The Shapleighs were shipbuilders and had iron works. The

Little James brought Theo Davis to Plymouth where he lived with the Warrens while taking measure of the northern settlement. He knew he didn't like Virginia or the Barbados because of the climate and constant danger from savages but he'd heard only good things about the coast from Kittery to Plymouth.

Between 1623 and 1624 the *Return Delaware*, *Unity*, *Charity*, *Elizabeth* and *Zouch Phoenix* brought more and more settlers to the northeastern coast. The *Fellowship* sent three different groups to Naumkeag to join Roger Conant's group, established under the Dorchester Company. The Dutch sent the *De Endracht* and *Niew Nederland* to the south of Plymouth to try to settle New Netherland (New York). In the West Indies the wealthy investors Thomas Warner and Ralph Menifield started a settlement on St. Kitts and the *Olive*, under Captain Powell left Pernambuco, South America to establish a permanent settlement town on the Barbados.

There was a lull between the *Jacob*, captained by Peirce, from Bristol to Plymouth and the *Amity* in February 1626 under Capt, Evans from Weymouth.

But in 1628-9 the *Abigail* brought 50 men and women with (militiary) Capt. John Endecott, Governor, and Capt. Goding from Weymouth to what was now being called Salem. The place had little more than a handful of thatched cottages and the winters were so severe many were talking about leaving for the warmer climate of southern Virginia but Roger Conant persuaded them to stay on. The patent was now under The New England Company for a Plantation in Massachusetts Bay and was governed by a stern Capt. John Endecott who made sure the settlers fulfilled their employment terms by working hard to get a real fishing village established and send sturgeon and other varieties of fish, timber, sassafras, sarsaparilla, silk grass, beaver skins and sumac back to their investors in England. This patent had been obtained by John Humphrey, Treasurer for the old Merchant Adventurer Company plus the High Sheriff of Devon, Sir Henry Rosewell and the former holder of that office, Sir John Yonge. This village was set up along the lines of Jamestown and called London's Plantation in the Massachusetts Bay. Sir Richard Saltonstall and Matthew Craddock were huge investors and motivators in getting the patents and raising money for these primarily commercial ventures. Edmund's son Matthew was the English legal agent for Matthew Craddock.

Gov. Endecott (Endicott, Endicot) was told to treat the old planters with the same courtesy as his newcomers but he started out on the wrong foot by having the frame of the meeting house taken apart and moved west, inland, from Cape Ann to Naumkeag for his own personal use. He then began doling out lots to the newcomers. Roger Conant and the old planters grumbled and griped but finally decided to just pick up and move north to establish a new town they later named Beverly.

Endecott's settlers referred to it as 'Beggerly' as the old planters were a motley group totally focused on making a lot of money for their English investors.

In 1629 Naumkeag's name was formally changed to Salem and the Massachusetts Bay Company sent over 300 new settlers in the *Lion's Whelp,* the *Talbot, George Bonaventure, Lyon, Mayflower #14*, and the *Four Sisters*. The migration to the New England left from Gravesend on the 24th of April,1629 along with the Pilgrim #4, which went to Plymouth.

Rev. Higginson gave a heart wrenching sermon on deck from the *Talbot* as the fleet rounded Land's End saying, "We do not go to New England as Separatists from the Church of England; though we cannot but separate from the corruptions in it, but we go to practice the positive part of church reformation and propagate the gospel in America."

The *Mary and John* went to Nantasket the following spring and the *Swift* with Shipleigh's group. to Casco Bay. There, later John Richards sold half the island he owned (Arrowsick) to John Clarke of Dorchester and Thomas Lake for the establishment of a trading post.

The early fleets would be followed the next year by a mass exodus lead by John Winthrop.

For Puritans in England King James I's son, the new King Charles I's lack of tolerance for their desire to purify and weed out popish practices and to return to a simpler form of Christianity was a real threat. Ministers were being hunted down by Archbishop Laud's men and thrown into prison in Boston. This new church threw out Laud's *Book of Common Prayer* and believed in forming 'covenants' or congregations that were loyal to God first and their fellow covenanters second. They recognized the authority of the King but felt bound by their beliefs to practice Christianity in a simple way without all the gold, statues, fancy music, enormous cathedrals, elevated or screened altars and popish pomp and ceremony. They felt like they were modern day Early Christians in an England that was like pagan Rome.

After he came to power King Charles I didn't like this one bit. Under the Divine Rights of Kings, he felt his people belonged to him, like slaves in a sense, and were duty bound to do exactly as he ordered. For many of the older English men and women who had lived under Queen Elizabeth, a staunch Protestant and abhorrer of Catholicism, this new king's policies and tyranny were too much to take. They overcame what Rev. White called their 'overfondness for their own chimneys' to pull up stakes and risk the two month sea voyage to a raw, undeveloped land.

Marie's own father and her sisters joined her uncle's family in Plymouth but she couldn't leave. She was in constant pain from arthritis and knew from Robert's suffering that the sea would make it worse. Plus she loved her part of England. She loved the way it spoke of the past: the ancient stone circles that drew her to them. She loved to touch the old, weathered stones and walk the circles, wondering about the people who had erected them. She loved the chalk outlines on the high hilltops of horses or people, she loved the ancient wells that rumor said Mary had touched and she loved the dolmen where people even older than the Vikings were buried. To Marie, England was more than just a piece of land where one raised sheep, cattle, horses, pigs and poultry. It was the history of mankind itself: it connected the past to the present. She knew that probably every inch of its soil had seen battle at some point, either from the first invaders, the Celts, the Romans, Vikings, Angles, Saxons, Normans and Gauls or from one faction fighting another. To Marie this King Charles was just a continuation of the long line of kings and queens who used their subjects as cannon fodder, pointing them at an enemy within the British Isles or on the Continent, yet she wasn't willing to leave.

Willie, now nine and eager for adventure, as Humphrey had been at his age, constantly pestered her to emigrate with the many Dorset and Devonshire families that were leaving but Marie didn't listen to him. What bothered her the most was that Robert had left the *Mary and John* to William for when he came of age, but Rev. White had pressured her to sell it to the Company for the Dorchester Puritans to use. Marie knew a ship would just rot in port and had let Capt. James take it out for fishing expeditions to Newfoundland but to actually sell it had been an agonizing decision. What settled the matter was the guarantee that William would be paid handsomely for it and be given a grant of land in addition to the Davis family land grants from Robert's association with Mason and Gorges in Sagadahoc.

When the London solicitor, Matthew Davis, had given her the signed Bill of Sale and the money for William, Marie cried. It was her last link to Robert. She went to his grave and asked him to forgive her for selling his ship, then rode out to her favorite ring of stones and sobbed as if her heart were broken.

She knew William belonged to the future. She and her little Devon farm were part of the past. She had no right to hold Willie back but didn't want him to leave her and cross the sea. She had put on a brave face every time Robert left for port but had prayed for him all the time he was away. She had talked to him in her mind when she did chores, telling herself she must remember this incident or other when writing him next. She knew his passion was for sailing when she met and married him but had never known how lonely it would be during the many months every year when he was gone.

Marie leaned back against a tall, but crooked stone in the field north of her farm. The grass was dry as it was early winter. She could hear sheep bleating in the distance and knew lambing would be upon them soon. The sheep seemed to want to drop their lambs when the weather was the worst: during an icy winter storm or bitter cold snap. Marie smiled softly. She knew deep in her breast this was her world. She wouldn't hold Willie back, and actually couldn't anyway once he reached his majority, but until he left she would take him to every ancient site she knew, both in southeastern England and Wales and tell him the old legends: of King Arthur and Guinevere and his Knights of the Round Table, of Merlin and the magical way he floated the great stone ring from the Presili Mountains in Wales to the chalk downs. She would take him to Glastonbury and show him Arthur and Guinevere's graves. When William left, he would carry a small leather pouch with a piece of the bluestones and some of the chalk earth next to his heart.

Marie sighed, brushing her greying hair back from where it had come loose from under her cap. She hoped she'd get to see her grandchildren, that Willie might have babies before he left, or maybe he'd return with them if he didn't find what he was seeking in the New England.

As she rose she caressed the old, rough stone, wishing it could tell its story. At least Willie wouldn't be sent to France, Germany or Spain or whatever plot of European soil this terrible king would fertilize with the blood of English boys. Marie worried Willie might die fighting savages but the way the men talked about the New England, men were free there and could choose their destinies. William loved working with the blacksmith on her farm who also made items for the ships. He would never go without a trade, she knew, as the occupation of being a country gentleman wasn't recognized in the New England. There, as in Virginia and the West Indies, the planters had to do some of the physical work themselves and a blacksmith was always one of the most important men in any village.

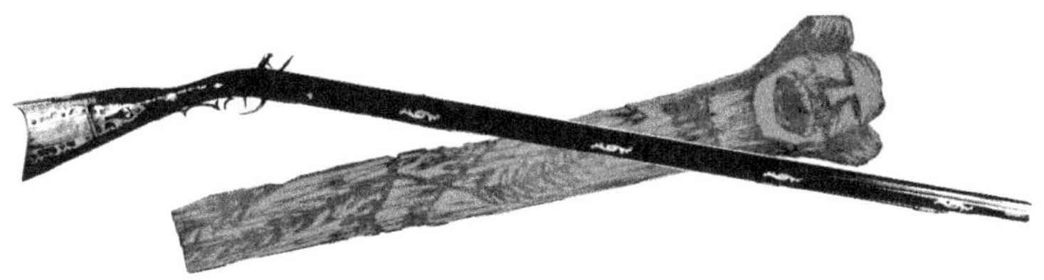

CHAPTER TWENTY-FOUR

New England

1620s – 1630s

Men who came in the first years included Anthony Anabelle on the *Anne* in 1623; Roger and Christoper Conant, one a slater and the other a grocer; the trader John Oldham; the Rev. John Lyford, Matthew and Experience Mitchell on the *Little James*, all friends of the Mathers, Gookins and Cottons.

In 1628 Rev, White published a pamphlet called *The Planter's Plea* and Edward Godfrey and John Endicott came over in the *Abigail* , Endicott to replace Conant as governor . William Sherman brought loads of livestock to Plymouth and Salem, formerly Naumkeag. *The Plea* did a good job and in 1629 Capt. Higginson and a fleet of eight ships brought holds full of Dorchesterites and East Anglia settlers to Salem harbor in mid-July after leaving Gravesend East Anglia in April. From Salem these people and their descendants would slowly spread into Casco Bay, settling York, Yarmouth, Devon and other towns in addition to Saco, Bideford and Kittery. Some would throw in with Winthrop's people and some would eventually go further south to settle the area around the big river *Quoniticut* that ran inland north of the long island (peninsula) the Dutch were trying to settle as New Netherland. Some died and a few returned to England for various reasons. But they were forging a new identity. The wealthier settlers retained an allegiance to the royalty, which would cause many to return to England later on to fight for King Charles. Some were friends or relatives of Oliver Cromwell or his Parliamentarians and would make the journey back to the homeland later on to fight for him but the first two decades of settlement saw very little interference from the mother country, which was embroiled in what later would be called 'The Thirty Years War' on the European continent. The Davis men and other captains or ship owners were affected by it when enemy ships met them in the West Indies or off the northern coast where the French were. Ships battled and the victor got rich cargoes or ships and sometimes both. But the extent of piracy was small compared to the plunder under Queen Elizabeth when she warred with Spain. Most of the voyages from England brought settlers, indentured servants, livestock, tradesmen and precious commodities such as wines that the colonies couldn't produce for themselves.

In March, 1625 when King James died and his son Charles took the throne, his reign began on shaky ground as it was rumored Charles had popish leanings and was going to marry France's Princess Henrietta Marie, the Catholic sister of the King Louis XIII. With a change of kings came a change of attitude regarding New England. The great migration of Puritans was partly due to fear of England reverting to the bloody horror of Queen Mary if Catholicism became the national religion.

1630-35

The *Jonathan*, one of Thomas Weston's ships, was the first to bring a plantation's worth of settlers to *Piscataqua.* From the start the Gorges-inspired colony wanted to be separate from the southern colonies but when the ships began arriving, fleet after fleet beginning in June, 1630 with the *Arbella* and Winthrop's fleet the residents began to feel the long arm of England reaching up towards them. The Bay Colony had a patent that covered north of the Virginia grant to south of Quebec, which did, indeed encroach on Mason and Gorges's patent but involved with the war on the Continent neither could appear at court and plead their case so the northern colonists just tried to be like the fox and stay out of the way of what started as Boston, then spread out with another settlement called Watertown, then Charlestown and Cambridge. West Country people from Dorchester settled a place south of Boston and named it for their home in England. *Naumkeag* was renamed Salem and it, Lynn and Marblehead became prime fishing ports.

In December there was a heavy snow but in spite of it Capt. Walter Neal, Governor of Piscataqua Plantation traveled south and met with Gov. John Winthrop in Boston and told the Council Massachusetts could access the lakes for beaver and use meadowlands along the Merrimac River but they were to keep their settlements away from Gorges's grant.

At this time George, William, Richard and James along with Theo, Humphrey and his brother John were involved in the maritime trade, either sailing as masters or officers or on land as co-owners of ships that sailed up and down the coast from Mt. Desert Island to the Barbados, fishing, selling, buying native goods or imported English goods for resale along the way. Corn was extremely in demand as the newcomers didn't have full store houses and those who arrived had used up most of their provisions en route. Cattle, goats, sheep, swine and horses came into the bay from England or were brought up from the West Indies or caught on northern islands where they roamed free, having been released by French visitors years before. William and George had skills that made them valuable as merchants plus George had a loom and was a weaver of sailcloths and William a blacksmith. William also had a small apothecary for the sailors. Barnaby was a surveyor and Theo was learning the trade from his brother.

James regularly sent ships full of casks of tobacco and corn from his private wharf in Virginia, plus indigo and herbs such as sassafras and sarsaparilla across the sea to England.

New towns sprang up north, south, west of Boston and settlements were begun far south on the Connecticut River; even Plymouth was expanding its settlements. Hundreds of people came in each fleet and there were many fleets arriving every year. The governorship of Massachusetts Bay alternated between John Winthrop and Thomas Dudley with prominent citizens serving as deputies, or assistants, and each town sending two representatives to the monthly General Courts. At the annual General Court the entire population of freemen could vote for governor and assistants but, as in England, there was a core of wealthy, educated men who served as magistrates and another core of educated men who served as leaders of the Puritan church. In general, the settlers were too busy trying to carve out homesteads from the wilderness, digging wells, hauling fieldstones, fencing areas around cornfields, building homes and cutting wood to bother much with the goings on in Boston.

Nathaniel had returned to England but came back in the *Hercules* and settled in the village of Charlestown. Dolor came in the *James* in 1634 and James's son James came over that year. Dolor's son Nicholas came over in the *Planter* and John, brother of Humphreys, left on the *Hopewell* to go to the Barbados.

In 1635 and James's son John and his family came over with a lot of West Country people. Dolor's young son. also named John (as the first one hadn't been expected to live through infancy) came with his mother Margery on the *Elizabeth and Ann*. His sons would also become housewrights and carpenters. Distant Welsh relatives William and John came in the *Increase*, William going on to Connecticut where is skills as a butcher were in high demand.

William Senior himself came over in the *Abigail* to Boston with his son William . Welsh cousins Tobias, Richard, William and Isaac came on the *James* to Roxbury. And a man who was not related to them but was to affect them, John Oldham, was also on the *Elizabeth and Ann* with his wife Margery and young son John. Distant relatives Daniel and Robert came on the *Peter Bonaventure* with Robert from Ireland but went on to the Barbados where John's brother Humphrey was managing the family's plantation. The common last name and similar first names were to cause many a confusion in the early years as the Davis clan was huge in Wales, England and Ireland and many younger Davis men went to New England to seek their fortunes or for religious freedom.

The *Ann and Elizabeth* brought clerk John Davys, a Norfolk relative; Thomas Davies came on the *James* and set up a sawmill in Marlborough and the *William and John* brought young Rowland and William Davies to the island of St. Christopher in the West Indies.

The Davis family was like the others families settling in the New England, After the initial colonists settled, distant relatives came from Ireland, some from Wales, but most from southwestern or East England. They all shared in the dream of religious freedom or freedom to live and trade as they pleased without the onerous taxation and rigid Church of England rules. John Eliot, John Cotton, Thomas Hooker, Roger Williams – all distinguished English ministers – arrived to care for fledgling flocks. Not all agreed on Puritan points of theology or practice, however.

Hooker lived near John Eliot in England and Eliot was Hooker's teaching assistant in Little Budlow. Eliot was related to the MP John Eliot who King Charles imprisoned in the Tower when he dissolved Parliament in 1628. England was to have a tyrant ruling unilaterally with no Parliament for the next 11 years.

Every ship brought rich and poor alike. They brought ministers and merchants. The Winthrops, Dudleys, Oldhams, Saltonstalls, Hitchcocks, Moultons, Allens, Alcocks, Needhams, Warrens, Philips, Sprauges and Stoughtons settled in Boston, Charlestown, Watertown and other new towns around the Bay. To their north, Dorchesterites settled a 'new' Dorchester with Ludlows, Haynes, Phelps, Cookes, Allyns, Clarks, Palmers, Williams, Alvords, Barbers, Marshfields and many more reputable, pious families during these years. And in these years the Goodwins of Bristol sailed back with Big John Davis, who had gone home and fell in love with their daughter Mary and wed her as his second wife in Kittery – setting her up in a 'proper house' built by his father Dolor. The problem was lack of work to the north, though, so he often lived away in the Boston area, leaving his poor wife to fend as best she could with indentured servants sent over by the Crown. Though not of fine English stone, the sharply slanted roof had slate tiles and the sturdy exterior clapboard shingles. It did not have 'fancy' features such as wainscoting as the Puritans in Boston were strict about any show of wealth, whether it be worn on the person as laces and silks or installed in houses as trim. The Puritans in Boston even passed an ordinance against the practice of multiple toasts given at formal dinners.

Boston built its first ship: a fine bark at Mystick, the *Blessing of the Bay,* and launched her on the last day of August in the second year of the colonization of the Bay. A colony having its own ship such as the *Gift of God* enabled its people to freely travel up and down the coast. George and William Davis and the Munjoys and Westons owned most of the local trading ships, such as the *Swan* that would go on to Virginia and the West Indies but a local ship that traversed the Bay and into Long Island and up to the fishing posts, was a real asset to the Boston settlers. The Moulton brothers were shipwrights and set up a ship building site on a point near Charlestown. Men with ship-related building, weaving and smithing skills such as the Davis men had were in high demand. Though the living conditions were crude there was one thing New England had an abundance of and England lacked: opportunity. If a man was willing to work hard he had a chance in this new land. The dream of being a prosperous farmer, trader or tradesman attracted men like flies to honey.

Thus the colony proceeded peacefully until in 1635 the ship that brought Anne Moulton also carried Anne Hutchinson.

CHAPTER TWENTY-FIVE

'A Pitiful Shack' North of the Bay

1622

Sir John's great-grandson Nathaniel (son of Richard, Robert's John's son) spent most of the 1620s as a deckhand running the magazine from England to Virginia. Nathaniel's cousin William joined in but found, like Robert, he preferred the cold, rocky, rugged northern colony better than the hot, humid buggy southern one. Theo and Barnaby were favoring the West Indies for their sailing and trading and in 1630 Thomas's deceased son's Robert's beloved *Mary and John* landed in *Naumkeag* on the northeastern coast of the big bay. To the south lay the plantation called Plymouth where Marie's family was settled.

The *Mary and John* was seven years behind the Dorchester Company's *Fellowship* that made three voyages to *Naumkeag* and eight years behind the *Southampton* and *God's Gift* and the *Jonathan* that brought Nicholas Shapleigh and his friends to the Piscataqua River, from whence they settled further inland at Kittery. Dolor's son Big John and his young wife Katherine were with the last ship and had tried to set down roots in the area but she died in childbirth six months after they arrived.

The *Mary and John* brought Nathaniel to *Naumkeag* as a fur trader, along with some wealthy members of southwestern families such as the Philips, Gilberts, Allens and a minister by the name of Roger Williams.

Nathaniel stood atop a hill near where his cousin John and Katherine had tried to homestead. He took in the thick forests, hilly landscape, scattering of small clapboard and thatch houses and the small herds of cattle, goats and swine, plus some Dorset sheep and Icelandic or East Friesian or milk sheep from Holland. Chickens and a few ducks and geese that came with the settlers ran loose.

Dolor's son Big John spoke first,

"That's my cottage," he said pointing to a very ramshackle building not fit to hold livestock in England.

"Not much of a carpenter, are ye, boyo?" asked Nathaniel.

"Well, 'twas temporary like. We lived in a tent the first winter and it was sore hard on me poor Katherine. I borrowed an orphan lad from the Shipleigh plantation and he helped with the wood splitting and water carrying plus helped me dig a well and line it with rocks. I'm a'used to a crew wit' stones all coming at the ready."

"Aye, no shortage of them, it seems," said Nathaniel with a small laugh.

"Yeah, but they aren't the good ones like we have in Devonshire," John replied, kicking at one, "These are all rough like and don't make good house stones. The fields are just infested wit' em. But they are a'right for making fences with."

Nathaniel shook his head.

"Over there is where I buried me wife Katherine and our unborn son," John said, his voice husky.

Nathaniel puffed on his pipe. He was addicted to the tobacco he and his family grew in Virginia and Barbados.

"The young lasses die at a fearful rate in this New England," Nathaniel said, "Them in Virginia get the fever and are gone in a day. Up here I'm told it's the fearful cold winter as gets them."

John nodded,

"Aye, Katherine never seemed to get over her sickness on the voyage over. Then, living in a tent like a savage she caught a sickness in her chest and the coughing just got worse. Her being with child made her even weaker."

Nathaniel put his arm around his cousin's shoulder.

"Do ye think it's worth it, bye? All this hardship and suffering?"

John shrugged,

"All I know is that I feel there's no future for me and those who think as we Puritans do in England. Do ye know that John Winthrop has a mighty fleet a'comin to the south of us?"

Nathaniel smiled, "Why do ye think we got the *Mary and John* off as quick as we did? Old Gorges and Mason have claims to protect. We aim to get the better land in the area around the bay and aim to have Wiltshire and Devonshire people settle up here in our cousin Robert's land. That Winthrop and his bunch are aiming on encroaching on our patent, ye can be sure."

John laughed.

"I don't think they have the iron in them! 'Tis frightfully hard to live up here. The winter comes early and stays on, not giving a body much time to plant and harvest. But we being of Welsh stock, being hardy sea people, we know how to fish and that is the best way to make a living up here. Them that are coming with Winthrop are mostly from the East country and are used to easier livin'. They won't last up here."

Nathaniel shook his head and stroked his small pointed beard.

"I hope ye are right, bye. This land is ours by cousins Robert and James exploring and settling at *Sagadahoc* with Popham and Gilbert. Mason and Gorges claimed this land and we with them. Even if Capt. Smith sailed the coast and mapped it, part of this land is Davis land. With Cavendish's party our famous John sailed himself almost through the great bay up to tha north that might lead to the East Indies and Spice Islands. Don' ye forget they named the straights after him. If he hadna been killed by pirates in the Chinese sea he might have found it, 'tis certain. We have a lot of blood, sweat and tears invested in this part of the New England."

Nathaniel squeezed John's shoulder and giggled,

"But that little crooked shack ye call a cottage is the pitifulist thing I ever seed!"

They laughed together and Nathaniel added, "But yer father ol' Dolor is planning to come over and when he does, he'll get ye a proper house built!"

"A fearful lot are coming over, cousin. The King and Archbishop Laud are on a rampage, persecuting anyone who doesn't totally accept all their papist rituals and *Book of Common Prayer*. We are on the verge of seeing a true 'New' England arise here. A real place with real villages and real governors and laws. A place where a man can worship the Lord in a proper, simple Christian way without fear."

Nathaniel laughed and spat out tobacco-tinted phlegm.

"I've learned a lot o' history, John. I seed how it was with England, the Irish, the Scottish, not to mention our Welsh ancestors. The men like Winthrop will come over all bright eyed and bushy tailed and then, in time, they will start acting like theys the lords of us all. Why, 'tisn't that what ol' Rhys did in Wilts? There's a pus-like thing in men that festers and festers and makes 'em want to rule over t'others. But if ye live away from their villages ye haves a chance to be yer own boss and live in peace. As we were doin' in Wales a'fore King Edward and King Henry the Eighth and in England a'fore King James and now this King Charles. Ye have ta be sly like a fox, son. Go about yer business but keep hidden in the forest."

John laughed but nodded.

"I think ye've been infected yerself, sir. What is boils down to is that there are men who like to live like tamed sheep and then there are the Davis men who like to be their own masters, nay, also like to be masters of ships and take on the vast sea and nature with open arms, to explore and stretch out, to walk free on the earth."

Nathaniel frowned.

"Aye, and we be always be the enemy of those who would be our masters. Ye'll find yerself a new wife, John, and begin again – in a real house – just ye be careful wit' yer words. I've heard these Winthrop people are very strict and brook no controversy. 'Tis good ye are settling up here for I see another type of Plymouth in what is coming to the great bay."

John groaned, kicking at a rock.

"Aye, theys real strict like down there. Marie's folks and kin write her regular like and she told me it almost appears like they've got a monastery going on there."

Nathaniel started walking down to John's 'house' in the high grass, careful not to stumble on the rocks.

"'Tis a real shame my cousin Robert never lived to settle here wit' Marie. 'Twas his dream, I know. But his William will be coming, that we know. Marie has resigned herself to it."

John brushed back his hair in frustration as he replied,

"Aye, our Robert was robbed of the fullness of his days. But Shipleigh and his bunch are right 'uns and we will slap this wild place into a civilized state that will allow true freedom of worship. The *Piscataqua* bunch are very open minded folk and I think there won't be the strictness that Winthrop and Bradford be a'bringin. I think up here we will be left alone, like we were in Wales before the English invaded."

Nathaniel pointed to an outcropping of granite boulders and said, "Ye know, this place reminds me o' Wales with all them big stone dolmen and circles and mountains."

John shrugged.

"I sorta like the nice softer Wilts and Somerset quarried stone better, but we will find a way to get this tough granite worked. And the trees here will make many a fine ship! Shipleigh's father might live in a fine manor in Kittery Court in Kingswear but his business is ship building and he needs big, stout trees like these."

"Aye, there's one thing this new land offers, boyo: opportunities. It might not have the copper ore Smith wants or the silver ore, but it has iron and many a wonderful product everywhere ye look, just for tha takin' like in Virginia – but without the murderous heathen, swamps and fevers."

Nathaniel pulled the string and opened the rickety door of 'the cabin'. The fireplace had smoked and they waited for the room to air out before entering.

"Well, cousin, don't speak too loud until ye've spent a bitch o' a winter here. We've both been at sea in cold winter fishing ships but there's a meanness to the cold here. It eats at yer bones and dares ye to live. " He cast a sly smile at his kin, "It tests yer mettle to the very end."

Nathaniel laughed and said, "I'll just marry me a pretty young wife, bye! That's the best remedy for long, cold winter days – and nights."

John re-stoked the fireplace and pulled the crane with the cast iron tea kettle over the flames so they could have tea.

John said, "I might be gone sailing and trading to the south and the West Indies this winter. I hope ye find one soon – a good, sturdy Devonshire lass!"

Nathaniel laughed and said he hoped the same for John.

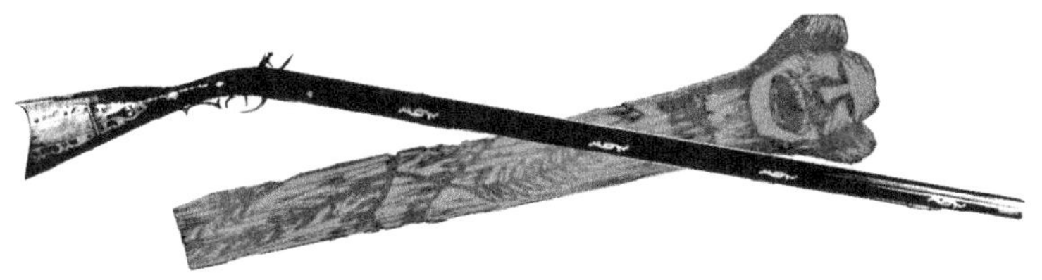

CHAPTER TWENTY-SIX

Of Kings and Commoners

1625

With the death of King James England faced its second Scottish king and longed for the good old days of Old Queen Bess. Under Queen Elizabeth's long reign the kingdom had known a stability, an increase in its standard of living, a sense that the average person could rise above humble origins and attend Cambridge or Oxford and better himself. Queen Elizabeth wasn't perfect – no monarch is – but for the most part she promoted science, exploration and exploitation, even in the form of piracy. She could be capricious and ruthless but there was a fairness, too. The average English citizen didn't feel that under King James I. He was imperial in attitude, he believed in the Divine Right of Kings, felt he didn't have to answer to his subjects. He, like his successor Charles, was duplicitous. Even the innermost circle at the palace and in Winchester never quite knew which way the wind was blowing. King James I had come to be ruled by Lord Buckingham, who, rumors had it, was his latest and last lover. King James I had not been sympathetic to the Separatists and wasn't in sympathy with the Puritans. His Archbishop of Canterbury, William Laud never missed a chance to punish them in devious ways. All King James I really cared for was money and when he spoke of proposing a

Ship Money Tax to build a royal fleet he lost most of the support of the gentry and alienated the inland towns and cities. Unfortunately for England his son was even more profligate. His passion was art and he had galleries full of European masterpieces and commissioned a Sistine like palace to built by the famous architect-designer Indigo Jones with huge family portraits hanging all around. Many subjects whispered, "You can't eat art," meaning that though the paintings and sculptures were beautiful they didn't put bread on the table. The Act of 1621 had prohibited poor rural folks from emigrating into towns or cities. A few years earlier the state, thanks to Popham, had used poor laws to round up indigent boys and girls and ship them off to Virginia to work on the plantations.

King Charles I was getting England deeper into war with Spain and his marriage to Henrietta Marie only seemed to bring a temporary truce with France. Loans forced on the gentry by the king were resented. Sir Thomas Wentworth got enclosure laws passed which drove tenant farmers off the land to the cities and towns that didn't want them so young rural men had few options to survive. Many indentured themselves to the rich plantations in Virginia and many boys and men joined the armies fighting Catholicism in Austria and Germany.

Sir John Eliot from Cornwall and Sir Dudley Digges were openly speaking of impeaching Buckingham and the rumor that King Charles I, like his father, was in favor of an inland ship money tax was rising the ire of inland towns and cities. Eliot, Pym and Digges were part of the 'new' MPs, voted into office in 1614.

To stand up for their rights the Parliament only voted one year's tonnage and poundage to this new king and was stingy with its allocation of money for the army in Spain. King Charles I began to slyly pull the 1614 coalition apart by offering sheriffdoms for some of the members. A sheriff was exceedingly powerful in his district but the position excluded them from serving as MPs.

In 1628 King Charles I dissolved the Parliament and courts after being presented with a *Petition of Rights* and he then ruled by royal dictate, opposed by men like Sir Edward Coke and aided by men like Wentworth, made Earl of Strafford and rewarded with rulership of Ireland plus vast land grants to the west of the Bay Colony.

Religion was a powderkeg. The Scottish Presbyterians seemed too Catholic to the radical Puritans who were grumbling that the state was becoming the enemy of the true Church.

English men and women, from peasants to lords, were unhappy. They longed for peace. The commoners longed for freedom from wars, from heavy taxation and laws that only favored the wealthy. The aristocracy longed for freedom to conquer new lands, to make fortunes across the sea. The Dutch West India Company received a charter from the States General to dominate the African and Northern American trade. They were getting ready to plant a fort on Manhattan Island to take trade away from Virginia: for Capt. James Davis and his kin this was a very threatening prospect.

Sir Capt. Thomas had immigrated to Virginia in 1618 but his sons were too active as merchant seamen to settle down. His son James went back and forth across the Atlantic as he did not care for the hot, muggy, swampy summers in Virginia and preferred England's civilized manors and landscapes.

When Capt. James sailed into the harbor of Thomas Warner's colony at St. Kitts, he narrowly missed the hurricane that destroyed their first tobacco harvest. Warner had recently returned to England with his first successful harvest and, having defending the English mountainous interior (France had the two ends of the island), was seeking the governorship of St Kitts, Nevis, Barbados and Montserrat. Sir William Courteen and the Merrifield syndicates were planting tobacco on the islands but their land grant claims were dubious. The Dutch monopolized the seas in the Caribbean, as they did in the East Indies, but the English were holding on, fighting French and Spanish as the need arose. After Spain banned the importation of tobacco in 1612 Sir Walter Raleigh had tried to get a tobacco plantation started on the Wild Coast between Trinidad and the Orinoco River but had failed.

But by the time King Charles took the throne tobacco was on the wane, partly because King James I had not liked it. In spite of his aversion to it, the people liked it too much and there was an oversupply of it on the markets. King Charles I wasn't anti-tobacco, the way his father had been, but the oversupply was bringing down the price and Capt. James Davis and his father started looking at other crops to plant, such as grapes for wine.

Their relative Sir John Davies had returned from Ireland and bought Englefield House in Berkshire from the moneylender Sir Peter Vanlore who owned the mortgage. He was chomping at the bit for the Chief Justice position of England currently held by Crewes, who had argued with the king against his last forced loan on the gentry.

While serving as Attorney General in Ireland Sir John had helped the Lord Lieutenant Sir Arthur Chichester defeat the Irish and claim the lands in Donegal, Colraine (Derry), Tyrone, Fermanagh, Cavan and Armagh as part of the Ulster Plantation for English and Scottish undertakers. The wealthy London trade guilds got most of Coleraine and the Catholic holdings were given to the Protestant church. Sir John had made a lot of merchants very rich, and helped in the deportation of a lot of defeated Irish men and women to Virginia. He, however, did not care to live in Ireland and had sold his lands in order to buy several estates in England. He had no sons but his daughter had married well. Edmund Davis's' son from Tisbury was a powerful voice for his relatives and the gentry from the West Country in London.

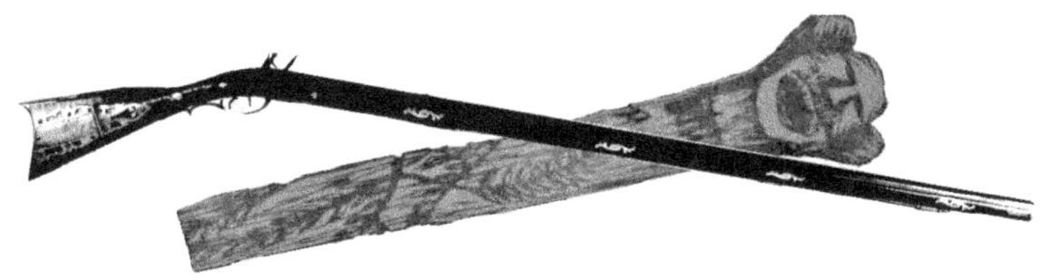

CHAPTER TWENTY-SEVEN

Puritans Receive the Call

Late 1620s-1630

What began with John Calvin and the protester Martin Luther in Geneva in 1536 and spread to England by John Knox of Scotland, was a seed of the idea that the Catholic Church, the Holy Roman Empire, wasn't the true arbiter between Man and God but that Man could directly commune with God. The seed had split into Separatism, Calvinism, Lutheranism and Puritanism in the early seventeenth century. Although under this 'protest'ant religion Woman was still considered the cause of suffering to Mankind through her succumbing to the wiles of the Devil, the Serpent, in the Garden of Eden, she was entitled to Salvation by the Grace of God, the same as Man.

The Puritans believed everyone should read the Bible and be able to use it for daily guidance in their Christian journey through life. The ministers usually went to Cambridge which incubated the rebellious preachers including John White, Thomas Hooker, John Wheelwright and John Cotton. These men spread their preaching throughout the southwestern area of England and the central, or midlands to the eastern villages and counties.

Entire families would travel half a day to hear these inspiring men who spoke of a predestined Grace, or Salvation given by a loving God to the Chosen, who were guaranteed entry to Heaven after death.

Anne Needham, an Alcock by birth, neighbor of the Needhams, came of age as the Puritan fever swept across England. She married Nicholas Needham in 1622 and they moved south from Alvord to Mancetter, a small village with an old Cistercian abbey and a manor house, near the midlands market town of Atherston. Mancetter was purportedly where the brave Celtic Queen Boudica was defeated by the Romans, whose earthworks could still be seen where the old Roman Road (Watling Street) crossed the River Anker. In the 12th century Walter de Mancetter had St. Peter's built there and it had multiple additions over the years. This was the territory the legendary Robin Hood had lived in with his band of merry men in the forests.

Anne and Nicholas often went to hear the Puritan preachers when they led services in nearby towns. They even traveled once across the fens to Boston to hear John Cotton and to Bilby to hear Rev. John Wheelwright. Anne had relatives in Dorset and they wrote to her in 1629 that a group was forming through the efforts of Rev. White to sail to the New England and settle on land Mason, Gorges, the Gilberts, Pophams and Davises had explored and partially settled through fishing, north of the Separatists in Plymouth, who were not overly friendly to the idea of having neighbors who didn't precisely follow their very narrow and strict ideology and practices.

The Reformation that began under Henry VIII radically changed England. The Catholic Church had owned most of the lands, hand massive manors, cathedrals, abbeys and monasteries and basically used the free labor of the monks and communicants to farm its land and feed its coffers. After King Henry VIII took their lands away and gifted it to his favorites the locals were still basically used by the Lords under a feudal system whereby they leased their farms but owed the Lord a percent of their labor, harvest and service in war. Over time the rights guaranteed by the Magna Carta (where feudalism was replaced by tenancy) were eroded as the landlords got greedy and started enclosing the common lands that the farmers used for pasture and crops. This had driven many off their farms and into the larger villages to work as tradesmen or day laborers.

The Alcocks weren't poor but weren't wealthy. They weren't invited to Lord

Cecil Burghley's manor near Stamford or Tattersal, the home of the Third Earl of Lincoln or his son's at Sempringham, nor to the Ludlow's or Warwick's castles. By the early 1600s the men who were rising in wealth were merchant adventurers with homes in or near London or the major ports such as Bristol, Plymouth and Dartmouth.

At the time of Anne's marriage to Nicholas in 1622, her brother George had married a sister of the Puritan minister Thomas Hooker, who moved near William Pynchon outside Springfield. All four families: the Hutchinsons, Alcocks, Needhams and Hookers, though scattered, kept in touch and all stayed strong in their Puritan convictions. All Puritan preachers were considered radical by Archbishop Laud but those who eventually emigrated or fled to the New England were the most radical. Besides eschewing the papist elaborate ceremonies and Saints' Days celebrations they didn't believe in an elevated altar table or formal choirs and preferred small congregations over large masses in cathedrals. Their concept of the church was based in early Christianity when a small group would covenant with each other, giving all their possessions to the one community and living within that sheltered community a simple, Jesus-inspired life based on His new Commandment to do unto others as you would have done to yourself. As Rev. White stressed in Dorchester, charity and a commitment to the common good of one's community through the support of ministers, teachers and schools was paramount. Charity towards the poor was based on the hope that one could be elevated to a godly life if basic needs were met. Greed, avariciousness and laziness were not tolerated and indigent poor who refused to try to become decent members of the community were encouraged to move on. And the Crown under Chief Justice Popham was quick to snatch these souls from the streets and ship them off to an indentured labor sentence in Virginia or the West Indies.

Life was all about what one could do for one's family and community and was to be spent in good, honest, Christian labor from dawn to dusk, six days a week with the Sabbath held out for the Lord.

John Cotton, like many of the enthusiastic young Puritan preachers, preached twice a week; Tuesdays was more of a catechism or teaching sermon, and on Sunday his sermons stretched on for hours.

It was after one of these sermons in 1629 that Nicholas and Ann Needham made the decision to sell their small farm and join with those going to the New England on the *Mary and John*. However, Ann's mother became ill in Coventry so she couldn't go on that ship or with her uncle George (a physician) and his wife Ann in the Winthrop fleet. Nicholas was already there, living to the north of Salem. He was a shipping partner of sorts with the Davis men, his cousin Sir Robert Needham was friends with Edmund's sons Sir John and Matthew Davis, having attended Shrewsbury school and St. John's in Cambridge with them before training in the law in the Inner Temple. He had inherited Shavington Hall in Adderly, Shropshire from his father who had been an MP and High Sheriff plus the Deputy Lieutenant of the county. Sir Robert Needham Senior had been knighted Lord Deputy of Ireland in 1564 but was in failing health and not expected to last out the year. Another cousin was Lord of the manor in Tixhall in Stafford.

Richard, George, William and James and his son "Black Robert" Davis were involved in shipping to and from the northern colonies. They would sail to near where Popham's site had been along the New England coast, acquire furs, fish and corn in exchange for English goods then trade furs, corn and some timber south in Virginia for tobacco and then go further southeast to Jamaica and the Barbados and trade for cones of sugar or casks of molasses or rum to bring to England. The wealthy English in England wanted tobacco, sugar, beaver skins for hats, dried some fish such as Poor John (haddock) and timber. The English in the new world wanted manufactured goods, especially anything made of steel or cast iron, finely woven cloths, wines and spirits. If the ship took a southern route on the return voyage it would bring laborers and the above English and European goods to the West Indies, pick up sugar and some tobacco (for it was smoother than the Virginia type), continue to Virginia, offload indentured servants and English goods for the sprawling plantations and sail north to the Plymouth and Salem colonies, then on to the ones on the northeastern coast for furs and timber.

Anne wanted to be with her husband in New England but he encouraged her to wait until the following year when he hoped to offer her an actual house. He warned her that the houses in New England were built of timber and clapboards and not the fine English stone even the humblest cottage in England was built from. There was slate for roofs, though it was only just being mined but he promised he'd try to put that on her house instead of thatch. A brick works and iron works would be established soon, he hoped, but for the time being she would live in what they, accustomed to great old stone Manors (or Halls) with massive ceiling beams and ornate woodwork and massive arches and fireplaces, fine tapestries and carpets and carved furniture, considered to be little more than a barn. And not a stone barn, either. He wrote to her that there was an abundance of granite in New England and said he hoped masons would soon come over to start quarries. There was a serious shortage of skilled tradesmen and men such as Mr. Winthrop were earnestly recruiting blacksmiths, housewrights, carpenters, coopers, weavers and doctors in addition to ministers and teachers.

Anne prayed every day that her mother would recover and that her father, Humphrey, would consider moving to New England but that winter received a letter from her uncle that his wife Ann had passed away and he was sailing back to England, unsure if he would return to the harsh primitive New England.

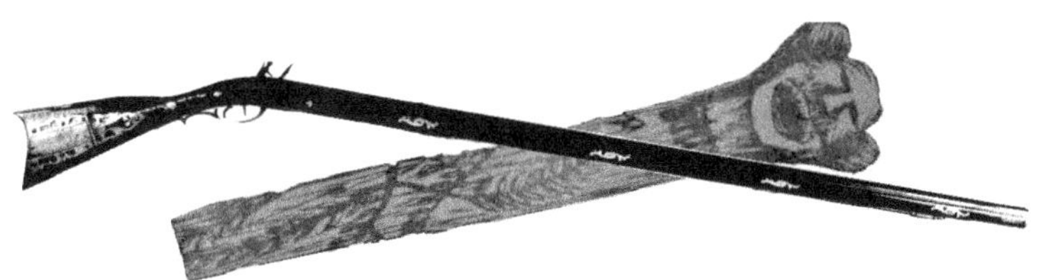

CHAPTER TWENTY-EIGHT

The Great Puritan Migration

1630

Rev. White's people in Dorchester included the wealthy, very pious Sprague families of Fordington and Upwey on the *Lyon's Whelp.* In Salem the immigrants started out as Church of England Puritans but soon turned more Separatist than Puritan. They ordained Rev. Higginson and Samuel Skelton by vote and then, later in a ceremony, by laying on of hands. Thirty members of the new congregation signed a covenant but 100 of the settlers left and were bound for the mouth of the river Capt. James Smith named the Charles. Winthrop later called their settlement Charlestown.

In Salem John and Samuel Browne pushed against the Plymouth-style separatism and gathered a group to a separate Sabbath service where they loudly read from the *Book of Common Prayer*. The majority let them know that they could return to England and weren't welcome in Salem.

In England Rev. White and John Winthrop were organizing a massive migration.

Marie had sold the *Mary and John* to the wealthy Derbyshire Puritan Roger Ludlow.

She and almost 12 year old William (no longer called Willie) accompanied

Roger and his wife Mary to Plymouth to spend a last day with them before they boarded the ship that would take them across the great ocean to a strange, new world to found a new Dorchester. Mr. Warham Maverick and his wife Cecilia were going to Naddock's Island as missionaries to convert the savages. They had heard as many as 30 a day were dying of smallpox.

Some of Samuel Allen's relatives were headed for the West Indies. The surnames of the families going included Gilberts, Philips, Richards and many well to do farm or merchant families from Dorset.

Rev. White preached to the congregation in the New Hospital in Plymouth where they held a day of fasting and prayer. Later in the day the men conferred and elected Mister Maverick as their preacher and Mister Warham as a preacher-teacher as was the custom of the new puritan congregations. It was a grey day in late March when Marie bade tearful farewell to Nathaniel Davis, Robert's cousin, son of Capt. Richard. Newly wed Nathaniel was to be First Mate to Capt. Squibb on the ship of 140 Dorchesterites that included Roger Ludlow, Edward Rossiter, the minister Roger Williams, a godly man named Jonathan Edwards, Roger Clap's family, the families of Joseph Hickock and wealthy gentry Israel Stoughton and militiary Captain Southcote. A distant cousin's family, the Alvords from north of Boston, Lincolnshire, were on board as well as Dyers, and the wealthy Allen (Allyn) family.

Capt. Higgins was in charge of the rest of John Winthrop's fleet which included the *Ambrose, Arbella, Talbot, Charles, Hopewell, Jewel, Mayflower, Success, Trial and Whale.* They left Southampton about the same time but were pushed back to Cowes on the Isle of Wight due to storms that didn't give them a following wind. All were bound for Salem and scheduled to arrive in mid-June and July but the *Mary and John* was headed for a spot up the Charles River that was sheltered but could support large ships for trade. Nathaniel had told Marie and William that he wanted to get in on the lucrative fur trade further north near Sagadahoc and he would partner with his cousin Nicholas, Captain of the *Trader's Increase* to run goods from New England to Virginia and the West Indies and then to England and return to the great Salem bay and north to Piscataqua, Merrimac and the Kennebec harbors to resupply for new runs. Robert's cousin William had a brother George who, with him, had interest in George Mountjoy's ships. Robert's brother Capt. Thomas had a son James who ran ships from Virginia north, south and to and fro

England but his family preferred the southern climes and wanted tobacco plantations instead of small homestead farms.

William begged Marie to let him go with Nathaniel but she said until he was older he had to obey her. She worried until the ship weighed anchor and set tearful sail that he would defy her and be a stowaway. It wouldn't be long before he followed his father to sea, she knew. The call of that mistress was in the hearts of all the Davis men, a call that went back to Wales where their ancestors lived on the coasts.

She would miss the Ludlows and the other families of Rev. White's congregation in Dorchester but all felt they had a mission to spread the true faith and convert the natives and to practice their pure version of Christianity without interference from the Church of England. Every year it got worse as Archbishop Laud and his thugs arrested and persecuted some for the simple act of not kneeling at the altar or of not reading from the *Book of Common Prayer.* Marie felt these acts were minor to a loving Christ who just wanted people to be in communion with Him but the king and his church used the strictness of the church to control people, as had the Catholic church in the past. It made no sense to Marie but she dutifully listened to the ministers as they laid out argument after argument about how Liberty was the most important value for if a man had no Liberty to worship as he pleased (within their own belief system), he wasn't a free human being. Marie, as most women, saw a real contradiction in this as the Church gave women no power or voice and the Government gave them no vote. The ministers harped back to Eve's Original Sin as their rationale but Marie doubted that God would create the female of the species as an inferior being. After all, Adam also ate of the fruit. But the men were in total control so she said nothing. At least she came from the Warren family and had some of her own holdings to the north so she wouldn't be destitute once William came of age and inherited two-thirds of everything.

EAST OF PLYMOUTH, DOCKS OF SOUTHAMPTON

The Rev. John Cotton delivered a rousing sermon on the deck of the *Arbella* to those gathered on the ship and on the docks.

He titled it *'God's Promise to his Plantations'.*

He quoted 2 Samuel 7:10 : *"Morever I will appoint a place for my people Israel and I will plant them, that they may dwell in a place of their own and move no more."*

Mr. Cotton (the Puritans didn't care for elevated titles and used Mister, Pastor, Elder and Deacon for their clergy) liked to use a list of points when he spoke, His first point to the departing emigrants was that David's purpose was to build God a home. He was to 1.) Design it; 2.) put a plantation of worshipers there who would receive a three-fold blessing; 3.) and He promised they should have a peaceful resting place. After hours and many scriptural references he summed up their purpose in New Jerusalem. He told them to keep the weeds of unchurched out of the Plantation, to keep God's ordinances planted firmly in their midst that God's word "be ingrafted into you"; to pray for our Jerusalem at home ; to have a public spirit and put the Community first; to realize how important Christian teaching to children would be and to "offend not the poor natives but try to win them to your love of Christ". To the tearful people leaving behind everything and almost everyone they knew he gave strength with the closing words, "What He hath planted, He will maintain, every plantation His right hand shall prosper and flourish. Go in Peace and Safety. Neglect not wall and barricades and fortifications for your own defense but ever let the Name of the Lord be your Strong Tower and the Word of His Promise the Rock of Refuge. His Word that made Heaven and Earth will not fail til Heaven and Earth be no more. Amen."

The mass exodus was partly due to '*The Planter's Plea*", printed by Rev. White, who exhorted the pious to go to the new land to convert the savages to Christianity and for England to stop trying to put plantations in Ireland, which didn't need an influx of new people, but to send them to the New England, which definitely needed as many colonists as it could get to spread a pure form of Christianity. King Charles I was not liked by the Puritans and he used vindictive means to harass them. Many felt if they didn't emigrate they would end up losing their estates and possibly their freedom or lives in the Tower. Circumstances had become dire. It was leave or be hanged for many.

Sir Robert Rich, Earl of Warwick, and John Pym, Eliot's close friend and former colleague in Parliament, were trying to get settlers to go to Providence Island and the Barbados, arguing that the New England winters were too brutal and the soil poor and the summer mosquitoes too loathsome. They got a new charter signed by the King in 1629 for the Massachusetts Bay Company (MBC) which narrowed and defined the MBC's territory slicing across the southern part of the original patent.

Theo Davis and his cousin Humphrey, now 19, did go back to Barbados where Humphrey took over the management of his uncle's land claims. Theo eventually returned to Salem, later Dorchester, New England, settling down and raising his family in the English tradition. Barnaby was establishing himself as a surveyor.

Humphrey loved the wildness of the West Indies. He loved the hot labor in the fields where tobacco grew like a weed. He helped build a wharf and bridge into a small town and, like the Drax brothers, had a manor built outside the town on his family's plantation. And he kept acquiring more land to enlarge it, using negro slaves bought from the Dutch to tend the fields and cure and pack the tobacco for transport.

The Dutch were experimenting with another crop called sugar, which when processed was better than honey to sweeten the hot, but bitter, East Indian tea some English were drinking as a supplement to their room temperature apple cider, wines and ales. Humphrey and his brother John were eager to try planting some of the shoots but in 1630 sugar cane was only being cultivated on a large scale in South America.

In Salem the arrival of John Winthrop and his people changed the attitude of men like John Oldham and many of the independent Dorchesterites. They knew Winthrop's East Anglian people would eventually overrule them and they looked elsewhere to settle – first what they named Dorchester and eventually south of Plymouth to Hartford on the Connecticut River and the seashore near its mouth.

On board the *Arbella*, which had a somewhat uneventful crossing except a maid fell down the stairs (but was caught by a deckhand) and some severe onboard punishments by the captain of the crew, John Winthrop, Thomas Dudley and Sir Richard Saltonstall spent many hours discussing how they should set up their new government for the Massachusetts Bay Colony. They agreed they weren't happy with the dictatorial style of Plymouth but didn't want the wealthy-only style of the English Parliament and Monarchy. They wrote out tentative drafts and crossed out and replaced phrases or words in the saloon, which was the dining room and one common area, other than the decks, that the passengers used. Their sleeping quarters were crammed into the 'tween decks, separated by sheets hung between the lice-infested straw mattresses on the boards. The women complained amongst themselves of the constant battle to try to keep a bit of cleanliness in the quarters. In nice weather they would drag the mattresses out on deck for airings along with outer clothing dipped in sea water to remove some of the grease and dirt the voyage layered on them. If a rain squall happened they would try to catch fresh rainwater in barrels on deck but it was too precious to be used for laundry and the captain wouldn't even let them hang clothes over the sides to dry. The decks belonged to the crew and passengers were not welcome amongst the lines and sails. They felt dirty. They stank. The babies developed terrible rashes from diapers rinsed in sea water. But they kept the complaints amongst themselves as their men were united in unity. The mothers worried constantly that their children would chase each other on deck and fall overboard or get injured in the rigging. Especially the boys. More than one had tried to climb to the crow's nest and been scolded down. A servant boy was stripped and whipped at the capstan with a cat o nine tails for stealing lemons from the ship's surgeon and there were some other punishments meted out during the voyage by the Puritans and the Captain's officers. A few fights broke out, the culprits laid in the bolts overnight or tied and forced to walk the deck out over the sea. The stress of close quarters and hours of idleness and the taking of too much strong spirits was blamed on most of the misbehavior. But the settlers had agreed there was to be no infighting in their new plantation. They were a covenant of brothers and sisters in God. The women on the ships silently prayed or sung simple hymns as they searched seams for lice and fleas spread by the ship cats or the many rats on board. Some never got over seasickness and spent the entire eight weeks full of nausea and dry heaves. Any little broth, gravy or cider the women could coax down them came right back up. The stench in the quarters was enough to cause nausea unless they sailed through heavy winds and the openings in the decks could flush out some of the rancid smell of unwashed humans who were wearing the same clothes for two months.

The twice daily meetings on the decks to pray and hear the word of God were their manna. "Be of good cheer! Goodman or Goodwoman so and so was the greeting, the smile sometimes forced.

The sailors were of two types: the rough, crude sort who only thought of rum, women and malicious sport and the ones with some education and manners who respected the convictions of the passengers but didn't share in their desire to be landlubbers. The mariners had crossed the ocean many times and encountered hurricanes and storms, scurvy, pirates and accidents. They were a tough breed. For them, this was another voyage, another transport of humans from England, Wales, Scotland or Ireland to the raw lands the king wanted settled so he could rape it for whatever treasure was to be found. They already knew there was no gold or silver, the Spanish got all that down south, but timber was in high demand and certain herbs such as sassafras and sarsaparilla were needed to treat fevers and the terrible syphilis disease the Spaniards had brought back from South America. It would show up on the genitals as sores and later the sores went away but it could work its way to the brain and cause insanity and cause birth defects on to a child in the womb. And some of the sailors had seen negroes trussed up on the docks in Africa, to be transported in chains on shelves like sardines between decks.

Unlike the passengers the sailors had a new sleeping device: the hammock, made from knotted rope. They hung it between rafters at bedtime and stored them along the walls when not in use. In nice weather the sailors even hung them on deck and enjoyed the pleasant sea breezes. This was one positive thing the Spaniards brought back with them from their pillaging and looting in the South, they thought.

THE *MARY AND JOHN* ARRIVES

The 400 ton ship encountered its share of storms and had to navigate around shoals near the coast but finally on the last day of May, 1630 the *Mary and John* came to drop anchor off Nantasket Point. The original plan was to sail into the bay and up the Charles River but the captain was exhausted and had lost his pilot to scurvy. Without a good navigator he had no desire to try to weave in amongst sandbanks, small islands and shoals. He told Nathaniel Davis to call the passengers on deck early on the Sabbath.

Roger Ludlow was furious when the captain said they and their goods and livestock were to be offloaded on the Point but it, being the Lord's Day, he held his temper and waited until after their morning service to visit the captain's quarters on the half foredeck.

"Ye aren't keepin' yer word, Captain!" he said. The cabin was crowded as he was accompanied by Samuel and Matthew Allen, Company Assistant Edward Rossiter, Henry Wolcott, George Dyes, Josiah Wolcott, Roger Williams and Nathaniel Davis.

"I have poor charts, sir," Captain Squibb said, "And me pilot is on his death bed with the scurvy. He never came into these waters anyway."

Nathaniel raised his voice, "All ye had to do was get a good pilot in Plymouth!"

Capt. Squibb shook his head.

"Capt. Higgins had the best one, Nate. We was supposed to be a'sailing with the main fleet but never caught sight of it on the whole voyage. He was on the flagship *Arbella* with Mr. Winthrop."

Roger Williams spoke up, "Brethren, let us not be of bad temper. The Lord has brought us all across the great sea to the shores of New England. What matter if we have to disembark here and walk the rest of the way to our new Jerusalem?"

Ludlow scowled.

"We are weak and don't have steady legs from being on ship. We will have to rest for days before we can attempt the journey up the river. And there are savages all around in the woods. Our livestock are also weak. I am not happy with this, sir, and will write to the Company to let them know you have not dealt with us honorably!"

He stormed out of the cabin, followed by the others but Nate stayed behind.

"Tom, I sympathize but, dammit, man, my family has ships and could've hired ye a better pilot!"

The captain gave Nathaniel a stern look.

"This is my ship, Nate, not yours. Ye are just the First Mate here. When ye are Master ye can call the shots. We are fully loaded down and have a deep draught. I know not that bay but know from what other captains have said that it has a lot of dangerous spots. I'll not risk my ship and passengers and cargo, plus crew because ye are all anxious to get to your precious Charlestown."

Nathaniel sighed and withdrew.

Most of the passengers were elated that they were to get off their wooden prison on the morrow and were busy getting their belongings sorted out for unloading at dawn's first light. The mood at the afternoon service was full of smiles and laughter. The hymns were sung with a little too much joy but Mr. Maverick didn't mind for he, too, wanted off the ship.

The Point had nothing to offer. It was quickly decided by the men that they should send ten of their number led by Continental war veteran Capt. Richard Southcott, who along with Rossiter was an Assistant, inland in search for a more suitable place to set up. Those staying behind moved out the next day. However, they sent others after the Southcott group to call them back from the river a couple of days later as they found a spot that had good salt water marshes for grazing on a neck of land the savages called Mattapan. Southcott told them they'd found a boat belonging to an old planter and met Thomas Walfourd who could speak the native tongue near a small village of wigwams, At his home Walfourd gave them some boiled bass without any bread or cider but they had biscuit left over from the ship, some of which they had offered to the savages when they first spotted them. There were a lot of savages about but they rowed up the Charles River unmolested and found a nice spot they later named Watertown. Capt. Southcott and his men had built a small shelter for supplies when they were recalled to the coast. The men were disappointed as they felt they'd found a better spot but within a week were heartened as John Winthrop's exploring party found them and told them they would lead them back to Salem. Winthrop went to the Point and sent word for Capt. Squibb to come ashore. The plantation's governor dressed him down over his treatment of the 'West Country immigrants and so chastened him that the captain gave Winthrop a five gun salute when he left.

CHAPTER TWENTY-NINE

Watertown

1629

A year before Winthrop and his fleet left England, in April 1629 a fleet of six ships, inspired by Rev. White, sailed from Gravesend to Salem, New England. Marie's uncle Thomas and his family from Fordington were on the *Lyon's Whelp*, captained by John Gibbs. The other ships were the T*albot*, captained by Thomas Beecher, the *George Bonaventure*, captained by Edward Cox, (with Davis co-owners), the *Mayflower #14,* captained by William Peirce; the *Four Sisters,* captained by Francis Harman plus the *Pilgrim #4*, which was bound for Plymouth.

After Marie and William had seen Rev. White's fleet off in London. she felt alone, as if she might be the only one left to carry on the Warren line in England if this emigration continued. She totally felt committed to simplifying the Church of England but felt loyal to the king. The Separatists in Plymouth were challenging his authority and the authority of the established church, which made Marie very nervous. In England there was talk of Oliver Cromwell kicking the king out of power and establishing a 'Common'wealth where the members of Parliament would rule without royal oversight. She could not imagine an England without a king or queen at its helm. France, Spain, Germany, Denmark – indeed, all the civilized countries had a royal leader. Yet no one could turn a blind eye to how these royals embroiled their countries in wars that impoverished the commoners and gentry with taxation and forced loans and spent vast sums on royal banquets and parties and luxuries while children starved in the streets of the cities.

Months after she bade the *Mary and John* a tearful farewell she received a letter on a return ship from her cousin Joanna (Warren) Converse.

"To Marie, my Dear Sister in Christ," it began, *"As you know, your brother-in-law Thomas brought us over last April on the Lyon's Whelp under Capt. Peirce. We arrived in the middle of July, which was hot, humid and filled with mosquitoes. Yet this hard place is one full of wondrous things.*

"The strange sea creatures we saw on our voyage were unlike any thing we could have dreamed. The size of the lobsters and cod our men catch in the harbor are gigantic. God surely has provided well for his pilgrims in a strange land!

"I admit it was very hard to arrive on a distant shore with no warm stone manor to receive us and provide a well-laid table but our minister, Mr. Higginson, has encouraged us with the Lord's words and our men wasted no time in clearing spots and cutting trees to build homes with.

"Uncle Richard sailed in a pinnace from Plymouth and invited us to join their community which is already taking on the appearance of a small town with cottages, fenced gardens, streets and a strong palisade around it. My father went back with him but returned within a fortnight as he said they were very strict about who they would accept into their commune, as they call it. Once has to completely agree to everything Mr. Bradford and the ministers and elders say or they are punished or expelled. Father didn't like it at all so we threw our lots in with the Salem folk.

"We recently rejoiced to be joined by people who arrived on your dearly departed Robert's Mary and John. Its captain, Mr. Squibb was to bring them to a nice spot previously chosen on the Charles River but he set them ashore on Nantasket Point, a rocky, miserable place. Some of their young men found and old boat and sailed up the Charles and we heard about them. By the time we could send men to greet them they had moved down the coast and settled in the southern part of the great bay. They intend to stay there and name it after our own Dorchester but some said they liked the place the young men first found and called Watertown on the river they named Charles in honor of our king Many ships have arrived this summer

and the land is getting crowded and fresh water near the shore is scarce.

"There are some in our party that are planning on going to that other spot to the south and checking it out as the leaders in Salem are starting to sound more like those in Plymouth than the type of tolerant, moderate planters Mr. White wanted to settle on these shores.

"I do not relish the thought of uprooting yet again and having a new home built in this Watertown but have to admit with the arrival of Mr. Winthrop and Mr. Dudley and the large number of immigrants with them Salem is feeling a bit crowded and we, who came here first, seem to be getting pushed aside by Mr. Winthrop and his group. He is very bossy. Although our family was called gentry we tried not to be overbearing in the treatment of our tenants. These new leaders in Boston have a dictatorial streak in them, I fear.

"I have prayed and prayed that the restlessness some of our people felt in England will cease now that we are on these shores but there are men who, I'm afraid, will always be contentious and unsettled.

"I sorely miss dear old England with its stone cottages, cobblestoned streets, rolling green meadows, shops and markets and tamed lands but as a woman I am owned by my father and then my husband so, as Ruth said in the Old Testament, 'Whither thou go, I shall follow.'

"So many people die within months or a year of coming over, here and in the southern plantations in Virginia! We pray every day for the safety of our planters. Some perish from illnesses, others from accidents, such as the tragic drowning of Mr. Winthrop's son Hugh upon arrival in the place that is being called New Boston in the middle of the great bay. And we are always on the lookout for the savages who appear like ghosts on the edges of our fields or even in our homes! Mr. Higginson says we must pray for these heathens and that missionaries will come soon who be try to teach them about our True Lord but they are a frightening sight. I've heard the men talk late at night about how they need to be driven out but can't see how the two things are compatible: either you love, accept and convert them or you drive them out and kill them. I pray daily for guidance to understand the correct Christian path we must needs follow to establish a Christian plantation in this new world. I've heard Mr. Maverick and his wife are going to live on Noddle's Island to minister to them and try to treat them as they are suffering greatly with a plague that doesn't

seem to make our people ill.

"*Dear Sister in the Lord, I pray you are safe in your manor in Dorset and that your son William is well. If he arrives on these shores you can be assured he will be given a true Christian welcome in my home, wherever it might be. I miss you and our church but must stay strong and make the best of every small blessing we receive in what is now my new home.*

"*Please give my love to Mr. White and our congregation.*

"*Joanna*"

CHAPTER THIRTY

Joanna and Ralph

1629-30

Thomas Warren's daughter Joanna was courted by Lt. Ralph Sprague in England and came with him and their two young sons in the Higginson fleet to Salem in 1629.

Salem was in between the new Winthrop colony in Boston and the older colony of Piscataqua and the fishing villages to the north. Theologically Salem's planters had more in common with the Winthrop group than the Plymouth people, who operated trading posts near them and further north. There was a strong streak of superstitiousness amongst the settlers, probably due to their small English village heritage. If your cow died it was because old woman so-and-so put the evil eye on it after it ate her cabbage. If you had a bad spell of luck you blamed someone placing a malevolent spell upon you. And there were some folk who bragged they had the ability to do such things, possibly people with gypsy blood in them. Severe religiousness and a constant belief in the intervention of God in daily lives and in one's salvation went hand in hand with an equal belief in evil and sorcery and witchcraft.

For most people it was always in the back of their minds. If they did good deeds and didn't go out of their way to harm another they felt they were likely to be under

Divine Protection.

Joanna kept pots of rosemary near the front and back doors and a small cloth bag of herbs hanging over the mantle to ward off witches but never spoke about such matters to Ralph or the children. She made sure the family sat down to study the Bible every morning and every evening before it got too dark to read without candles, which were precious in the New England. They attended the Sabbath meetings and the mid week prayer meetings and always shared what they could spare with those in need – as most of the Puritans did.

The coming of Winthrop's large body of worshipers didn't immediately affect Salem.

But before their first Boston Christmas a group of Winthrop's men started scouting to the north for a new town site. Earlier in the year Captain Walter Neal, representative for Sir Fernandino Gorges and Governor of Piscataqua had sailed south in the bark *Warwick* and met with Gov. Winthrop. Neal told Winthrop his people were free to fish and trap beaver from the inland lake to the mouth of the Merrimac River but that their settlements would have to be made in and around the Great Bay and not to the north as it was granted to Sir Fernandino Gorges, John Mason and others.

The Boston General Assembly met on the 21st of December and agreed Watertown would be the next planted site.

The next weeks were extremely cold with ice and frigid air. Three of the servants of the governor tried to sail to Plymouth in a shallop from Boston with Mr. Garrard and his daughter and a maid but an ice storm stranded it on the shoals near Noddle's Island and the next day savages went out in their canoes and rescued them but Mr. Garrard died from frostbite. The Charlestown congregation was in great distress over this and the fact that the heavy snow and ice prevented them from traveling to their meeting house for prayers and to give thanks for God's gift of the baby Jesus in a manger in Bethlehem. For many of the people accustomed to somewhat mild Dorset southeastern English winters this was an entirely new experience. Most were living in huts fashioned after the savage's sapling and bark wetus and the English woolens were no match for the bitter cold nights. The savages wore heavy fur capes and slept together on little benches around their fires but the English had bedding suited to stone houses with fireplaces and that could be closed tight with well-fitted oak doors and shutters on windows.

Joanna and other women had learned herbcraft in England and, at great personal peril, brought remedies to the Bay. Often the remedies were just 'simples' they'd learned such as to wrap onions on the feet to pull fevers down and out or boiling horehound tea for lung congestion.

The Rev. Maverick and his wife had gone out to Noodle's Island to convert the dying savages and learned from them some of the plants they used for coughs and fevers, the illness that took many English. The savages fell to a pox that covered them from head to toe with ugly bleeding blisters. Many English seemed to be immune to this, perhaps from a childhood exposure to a milder form, cowpox. But the early winters in New England were a dying time for the Puritans as many were weakened by scurvy. Capt. Peirce and the *Lyon* were greeted with great joy in February in Boston harbor as he brought jugs of lemon juice. He also brought another 20 passengers from the port of Bristol and 200 tons of English goods plus a new minister, Mr. Roger Williams. The Gov. declared a day of Thanksgiving for their arrival as they had experienced a very harsh crossing. Luckily, Boston's harbor rarely iced in, as did the others along the coast to the north.

Joanna was reunited with many of her Dorchester friends that winter. They settled south of Boston and named their new town Dorchester.

The hardships were terrible for the Puritans and every day they searched the grey skies for signs of coming spring.

In late March Sir Richard Saltonstall lost a prized calf and men were called out to search for it. So many wasted shot firing muskets to keep wolves away that it was subsequently ordered no piece should be fired after dark unless a general alarm for indian attack was raised.

As spring arrived, Winthrop's Council were advised that Sir Christopher Gardiner, supposedly a knight of the (papist) golden melice and who was an agent for Sir Ferdinando Gorges was living with a buxom maid he called his 'cousin' on the outskirts of Boston in what was judged to be the offense of bigamy as he had a wife in England. The General Court summoned him but he took off and moved up and down the coast until savages seeking favors from Winthrop caught him and brought him to Boston.

In protest of how Boston's oligarchy was overstepping its authority, Gov. Neal forwarded letters from Gorges to Gardiner to forward to England but Winthrop seized them and opened them. Not only was Gorges reasserting his patent rights in the letter but had included a letter to be sent to Thomas Morton in England, banished from Merrymount by the Plymouth folks for his heathen, immoral activities in Weymouth. Needless to say, Winthrop was not pleased with Neal and Neal was not pleased with Winthrop for intercepting his mail.

The summer finally arrived and held a very joyful event, as, under the direction of shipwright Robert Moulton, a new ship for the colony was built and formally launched at Mystic on the fourth day of July. It was named the *Blessing of the Bay*.

That summer a strange event occurred when Mr. Ludlow came upon French coins while digging his foundation hole (which he would line with huge stones to support the house he was building in Dorchester).

The last Massachusetts Bay Colony General Court of the year was held in September and a servant man John Dawe, was accused of having intercourse with a savage maiden and publically whipped. Henry Linne was also whipped for writing letters criticizing the new plantation and he was banished to England.

In October a fierce storm came and Gov. Winthrop's fine stone house fell down as it was mortared with clay and not lime and the rains melted the clay. Many other residences were damaged by the storm, which lasted a full day and night.

In early November Joanna and Ralph went out to greet the *Lion* and its master William Peirce when it docked at Nanatasket. Mr. Winthrop's wife and four children, his oldest son by his first wife, a new minister, Mr Eliot and 60 passengers were on board but Mrs. Winthrop wouldn't disembark as she was in deep mourning for her youngest, a girl named Anne, had perished at sea about a week out of England. The Governor sailed in a pinnace and boarded the ship and stayed with her the night before the captain sailed the *Lion* south into Boston harbor's dock the next day.

When the Winthrop family arrived in Boston word went out and planters brought a feast of partridge, geese, ducks, venison, pork and chickens plus corn, peas and other foods and a large outdoor feast was held, followed the next week by a day of Thanksgiving. The next week Gov. Bradford of Plymouth arrived and stayed in the *Lion* while paying his respects to the Boston Governor and his family.

However, the celebratory mood was disrupted when an elder of the Watertown church, Mr. Richard Brown, publically questioned certain beliefs and it took most of the month for Mr. Brown and the people he had stirred up to be reconciled with the Boston church.

Joanna and Ralph were used to such disruptions and she heard private grumblings when she visited her Dorchester friends. The planters had dissented from the Church of England and were used to being able to question Puritan clerical authority but under Winthrop a hammer of almost papal fundamentalism had come down and Mr. Pynchon was already scouting out a site for a new settlement to the south that wouldn't be under Winthrop's iron thumb.

Joanna and Ralph were just getting settled with a real house and planted fields, a kitchen garden and some outbuildings and were not anxious to pick up and start again but there were many who were looking for greener pastures and more freedom to worship as they pleased.

CHAPTER THIRTY-ONE

Early Boston, Plymouth

1630s

Whereas Thomas Warren settled in Watertown, then later Charlestown, his brother Richard had been one of the first Separatists to settle Plymouth Plantation. He passed away in 1628 and his widow Mary remarried Robert Bartlett, who had come over in the *Ann* in 1623. Mary had given birth to several daughters but by the time the large Winthrop fleet settled in the Bay had yet to give Robert a son.

From the outset the elders in Plymouth had conflicted feelings about Winthrop and his group.

As the plantation was not where it was supposed to be based on its original charter and trespassed on Sir Fernandino Gorge's patent, in early January 1630 Isaac Allerton (a land speculator in the Eastward who later lost his trading house at *Machias* due to an indian uprising in 1633) moved south to a place named New Haven. (He also later sheltered regicides who fled England.) Allerton obtained a new patent from the Committee of Council of Trade for New England signed by Robert Rich, Earl of Warwick. It gave the Plymouth planters the lands from the Cohasset River to the north (very close to where Winthrop's 2,000 planters were settling) and south to Narragansett Bay plus all of Cape Cod, Buzzards Bay on the southeast plus expanded their trading post patent to the north on the Kennebec River.

Rev. Higginson's people had settled north of the great Bay so Plymouth felt little threat from them except when they infringed on their fishing and trading posts. The north shore fishing posts under Gov. Endicott were settling into towns based on Plymouth's system and were evolving from wild frontier trading posts to civilized Puritan villages.

However, Mr. Winthrop and those settling in what they referred to as Newtown, Charlestown, Watertown and New Boston were too close for comfort to Plymouth's boundaries. Travelers between the two settlement areas told the Pilgrims that more and more ships kept arriving, most for settlements inland up the Mystik or Charles Rivers and to Salem but the new town of Boston was just across from Allerton Point in the Bay.

They heard of the drowning of Winthrop's young son shortly after his arrival and prayed for the family but kept their distance. Gov. Winthrop and his council held a first General Court in late August, just two months after their arrival. It was followed by a Fast Day. The Plymouth planters heard that wolves were ravaging the livestock and later that the Lady Arbella Johnson died, followed by Mr. Isaac Johnson a month later. Johnson had been a major investor in the Massachusetts Bay Colony plantation

In late October the *Handmaid* docked in Plymouth, captained by John Grant. It had been a rough voyage, taking twelve weeks. Its masts were all in terrible shape and of 28 cows, ten were lost. The 60 passengers arrived well, however, and the Pilgrims gave many thanks to God for that mercy.

In mid-November Capt. Miles Standish and two others sailed up the coast to Boston on the *Handmaid*, where it was to be repaired. They went ashore with the captain to ask if they could plant a settlement close to the Winthrop group but because they had no letters of recommendation from the minister and elders in Plymouth they were refused.

It had been early November 1631 when the *Lyon*, with Captain Peirce, John Eliot, minister, and Charles Glover, a shipwright, arrived in Boston with 123 people, half of their number children. At that time Governor John Winthrop's third wife, Margaret, was on board but unfortunately his 18 month old infant daughter

Anne had perished a week out at sea. The grieving parents stayed on board the ship the whole night in the harbor before coming ashore, coaxed by John Winthrop Jr.

At that time some of the Boston planters explored south of Boston looking to settle a new town to be called Roxbury. The Boston Puritans sent shallops out in the frigid bay to explore its islands and it was then in Mid-December that the bark *Warwick* brought Capt. Neal and three gentlemen from Piscataqua to visit Gov. Winthrop and his associates. Capt. Neal had been appointed by the king as Governor of the land Sir Ferdinand Gorges and John Mason claimed to the north.

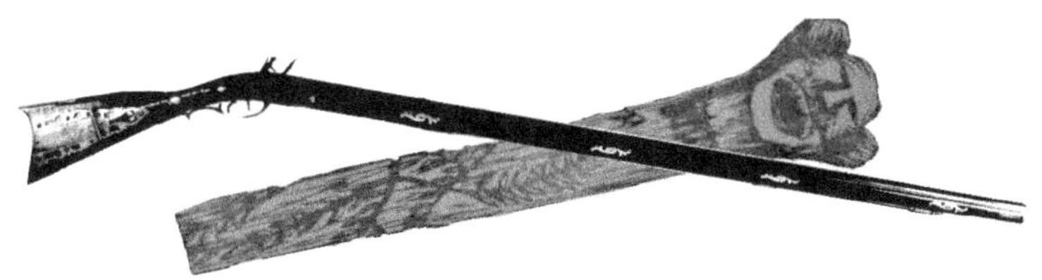

CHAPTER THIRTY-TWO

Boston

1630

Tom Walfourd found a small group of men wandering around off Nantasket Point in early June, 1630. They had used a boat they found and were trying to sail up the Charles River, telling him Capt. Squibb had dumped their group on the Point but they were supposed to have been transported up the river to a site previous planters had deemed habitable. Old Tom, one of Weston's men from Wessagusset, introduced them to some local natives and fed them some sea bass, apologizing that there was nothing to go with it.

After he had shown them around, he took his own small boat and rowed over to a point where his fellow Weston friend William Blackstone was living all by himself.

William had heard that a large fleet was heading for the Bay but didn't know any had arrived. His small cabin was stuffed with books and pages of writing. Blackstone had settled there after the Merrymount rout. Other Morton men had gone to Strawberry Banks and Cape Ann. None liked the stiff necked pilgrims in Plymouth but Tom told William these newcomers weren't in with Winslow, Bradford and his bunch but were mostly West Country folks. The group stranded on the Point were actually from the Dorchester area.

William took his cast iron pot of clams and fish off his fire and offered Tom a wooden bowl.

"So it looks like our little Bay is soon going to be a'crawlin' with a new bunch of these religious refugees," he said, slurping the salty broth.

William had been a minister and was highly educated. However, he liked to live like a recluse and treasured his privacy. This news did not please him.

"If they go up the Charles we won't be too greatly impacted," he said, scooping rubbery meat from a clamshell.

"The Dorchester folks are already heading south," Tom said, lighting a pipe and inhaling, then coughing.

The men were seated outside as William cooked over a fire pit during the summer months.

"There's a nice neck of land south of us," William said, referring to the place where the new planters would find pasture for their livestock.

"The big problem," Tom said, drawing again from his pipe, "is that the pilots don't know how to get their great ships up the Charles, Mystik or Merrimac. No one has done a chart and we both know these rivers have squirrely currents and shifting sandbars."

"Why didn't they go south towards Plymouth?" William replied, likewise smoking, "Or up the coast to Piscataqua?"

"It was that Allerton who went and got them a new patent between the two places," Tom replied, repeating what the *Mary and John* fellows had told him.

William groaned.

"Well, if they leave me alone, I'll just try to ignore them. God knows we've had a lot of ships in and out of our waters these past seven years. Mostly English, but some French and Dutch."

"Like dogs sniffing around a bitch in heat!" Tom said and William, who was more cultured, winced at the common phrase.

"My cabin is near the best fresh water source on this neck," Blackstone said, "They would be better off finding land up the freshwater rivers where water is abundant."

"Aye but ye have something they are sore wanting," Tom said, squinting as smoke from the fire blew into his eyes.

"What?" Blackstone snorted.

"A place to dock their large ships."

Blackstone mused on this.

"Aye, and they might put in a ferry to the Charles." He sighed and scratched mosquito bites.

"Captain Dick Southcott was the leader of their expeditionary group," Tom continued, "He said the leader of the big fleet is a feller named John Winthrop. He and Tom Dudley are more like the Plymouth folk, very big on rules and laws, religious and civil."

Blackstone sighed again.

"I was really lovin' this free living here. Trading with the savages and some of the ships like Jamie or Dick Davis's that would set anchor for a few days to trade on their way south from the north shore en route to Virginia. No one was botherin' me. I could just sit out in the sun and read all day, do a little fishing, write when the spirit moves me. It's been the type of life I craved ever since coming over on one of Weston's ships."

Tom stood up.

"Well, I got to be getting back before dark. Tide will be going out soon and I'm too tired to be fightin' it."

Blackstone walked with him to the beach.

"Well, old friend, it seems that we moved away from England but it is following us here."

"Aye," Tom agreed, pushing his skiff into the waves, "We thought we were good in Wegagusset and them Separatists drove us out, now we will see what new gift or burden God will be a'bringin to our dooryards."

****

Within a week Blackstone found out that Tom's prediction was to come true. His little neck of land was the spot Winthrop preferred for a plantation he was to call Boston. Ship after ship set anchor in the Bay and hundreds of newcomers spilled out of them like ants out of an anthill, bringing along belongings, poultry, cattle, sheep and pigs.

Governor Winthrop and Dept. Gov. Thomas Dudley and Rev .John White paid a visit to Blackstone and informed him that his homestead was actually part of the new grant, even though Blackstone had an Indian deed to the whole area.

William didn't like conflict. The Pilgrims had driven him and Weston's group out of Wegagusset and he left Plymouth Colony before getting deported to England. He just wanted to live in peace and quiet. He helped the Puritans by showing them where the freshwater springs were and the best places for forts or wharves, then signed his deed over, only holding six acres out for future descendants.

He then set out in his small pinnace for Narragansett territory, southwest of the Plymouth folks but not as far as Block Island or Long Island. He and his books sailed up Narragansett Bay and set down away from the Separatists in what he called his New Providence. Blackstone let it be known before he left that his settlement would be open to all English who were tolerant of other people's religious views as he, though an ordained Church of England minister, had embraced a new type of religion where one's conscience and one's personal relationship with God came first before any formal, established church, even the Puritan church. As such, he would be called a heretic if he stayed in Boston.

CHAPTER THIRTY-THREE

Moultons and Needhams in New England

1630s

In Salem, Nicholas Needham became friends with Robert and John Moulton, from Yarmouth. Robert was a shipwright and came in the Higginson fleet a year before Winthrop and his group. His brother Thomas settled up the Charles in a place to be called Charlestown and talked Robert into joining him. Nicholas and the Davis men had dealings with Robert as ships were always in need of repair. Ocean voyages wreaked havoc on the hulls, waves pulling at the beams and winds beating on the masts. William Davis, brother of George and Richard, set up in Boston weaving sailcloth for the ships but any sailor good with a needle was always in demand as a ship docking from a ten or eight week journey needed repairs before she could unload and reload cargo and continue to her next port. Blacksmiths, ropemakers and carpenters were in high demand in New England.

William Davis, son of Richard's son Abraham Isaacs was born in Wales in 1618-19 and took up his father's trade of black smithing.

The Moulton brothers talked in private about how the newcomers – Winthrop, Dudley and Johnson – were stiff necked, priggish Puritans, set in their beliefs.

"Aye, arrogance and ignorance 'tis a bad combination in some o' them," Robert told Nicholas as he surveyed damage to the hull of Glover's ship. They were in the cramped, damp, stinking hold going over the planks of the bow by lantern light. Nicholas had wanted to hire the ship but was told it had a leak and wanted it boarded over and caulked before he'd hire it for his associates. Many of these families traced their roots back to Wales and then later to Ireland as landlords. The Crown had robbed them and displaced them but, as is the case with men of deep pockets, hadn't broken them. However, some such as the Moultons weren't happy with the long arm of England trying to dictate to the planters in New England. The fishing villages on the north coast were mostly independent of the Crown, giving it lip service, but Winthrop's group felt too much like King Charles I's puppets : quick to tattle to the King, quick to judge and act harshly against fellow religious refugees.

"I personally like several of the fellows," Needham said, flicking a roach off his shoulder as he ducked under a beam, "but they don't seem to respect the fact that we came to Salem to get away from heavy handed government. Our people got a real taste of liberty these past years. Like oxen left free to roam and graze and enjoy freedom, we are now feeling like the yoke is being put back upon our necks."

Robert laughed.

"Aye, Nick, always seems to be the way, 'tis true. Ye give some men a bit o' authority and it goes to their head. All of a sudden they think they are kings and start looking down their long noses at others and start ordering them all about."

Nicholas nodded, almost dropping the lantern, which sputtered in the damp.

"I've been to Virginia," he said as he pointed to a spot where there was a sheen of water seeping through rotted boards, "The planters there are basically left alone. They seem to each have their own bit o' kingdom with their tobacco plantations, even have their own private docks."

Robert snorted, "And their own private supply o' labor thanks to the Crown!"

"Well, yes," Nicholas admitted, "but the men and women who come over – who survive their indenture – "

"Not many!" Robert interjected.

Nicholas continued, "Be that as it may for the fevers take many gentry as well as laborers – the point I'm getting at is that at the end of their servitude, they can buy a bit o' land and set up their own farms. If it weren't for that damnable soggy air and the incessant mosquitoes and snakes I would be tempted to settle down there meself."

Robert shook his head.

"Nay, friend. We have better climate here and a bounty of natural resources to hand. Our waters are full of fat fish and shellfish and so far the savages haven't turned on us like they did in Jamestown. Perhaps Gov. Winthrop and his Deputy Dudley will mellow in time."

Nathaniel frowned as his lantern spotted another leak.

"Do ye think she needs to be dry docked and completely graved and caulked?"

"Nah," Robert replied, "She's a good ship, is she. I'll have me head carpenter and his apprentice and me boys down here with the hot pitch and within the week ye can be loading her full for yer voyage to that paradise in the south!"

Nathaniel laughed.

"I've promised Anne I'd have a real house ready for her in the Bay. She loves the fellowship of the church and wouldn't be happy living in an isolated manor down there." He sighed, " She'll be one of Mr. Winthrop's dutiful followers and I her dutiful husband."

"Aye, and I plan to get in good with these new fellows so I can start a shipyard out in the Bay. I've chosen the perfect spot to start a'building a New England fleet and me and me boys have been cutting and stripping oaks and larches, not just for transporting across to the King's Navy, but for our own Navy so we can fend off the Frenchies and the Dutch who keep nosing around. And them pirates that are a'botherin the fishing fleet way north!"

They climbed the ladder-stairs to between decks and then up through the square hole to the top deck.

The spring air still held the chill of winter.

"I hope Dr. Alcock decides to return," he said, looking out over the green-grey waters, ruffled by a stiff, icy breeze.

Robert was heading towards the stern and replied over his shoulder. The wool was wet from the hold and stank. "He'll come back. Losin' yer wife like that is a shock, specially when ye are a doctor and have medicines, but I think most of the people who come over here stay, unless they inherit a nice manor back there," like the others he was starting to think of England as 'back there' and no longer 'home', "He's tasted this freedom, Nick. It's like yer first pipe of tobacco, tastes so good ye want more, or yer first mug o' ale. There's something addicting about being so free. Ye're not a'steppin on the Lord's manor or afraid ye're hunting in his chase or woods. All this land – " he spread his arms towards the shore – " all this land is ours for the takin'. It's ours, Nick!"

Nicholas smiled but added, his finger pushing a loose tooth, "Aye. But will the savages let us just take it or are we going to have to fight 'em for it?"

Robert shrugged. As long as his men could go into the woods and fell and haul the trees he needed for his ships he didn't care. He wasn't a farmer. A small lot and the use of common grazing lands suited him just fine. He traded his shipwright's skills for the corn and wheat the farmers sowed and harvested. As long as his family had a good milk cow and a few pigs for hams and bacon he was content. He basically wanted to be left alone and was already resenting the demands of the new governor for church attendance and the governor's constant calling for bloody days of fasting and prayer. Robert believed in God and the Bible but just felt a man wasn't meant to live his life on his knees unless he wanted to be a monk. Some of the Puritans, such as those in Plymouth, took it to extremes, he felt. He liked to be able to question anything that didn't quite make sense to him but that got most of them in trouble in England and now he was starting to feel it might get them in trouble in the New England.

Nicholas pulled out a bloody tooth.

"'Tis a bit o' the scurvy. We need lemons and fresh green food."

"Aye. I'll get this ship afixed by the end o' the week and it can go and bring us some from the West Indies!" Robert called back from the poop deck. He was looking over the side and beckoning a ship hand to climb down on a rope to inspect a spot he felt might need exterior reinforcing.

Nicholas threw the tooth into the cold waters and carefully walked down the gang plank, holding the rope as the boards had a sheen of ice on them.

He missed Anne terribly and prayed inside the house he was building every night for God to send her across the seas and back to him.

The winter had been brutally cold and many of the newcomers died. The savages on Noodles Island were dying of the pox in alarming numbers.

And the damned Dutch and French were threatening to take lands to the south on the Long Island and to the north where the French had a fort at the mouth of the

St. Lawrence River that they called Quebec.

His felt his cargo would make it to Virginia without much peril but a captain never knew what he might encounter once he sailed southeast away from the land named Florida.

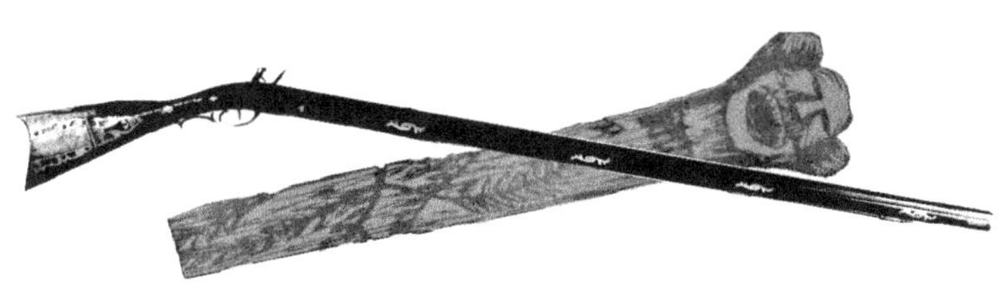

CHAPTER THIRTY-FOUR

Early years

1630-34

The Davis men were friends with the Dudley family, their intertwined fates going back to the European battles and sea battles fought for Queen Elizabeth plus through the Bulkeleys in northern Wales and Dolor's employment at Sevenoaks Manor. The queen's paramour, Robert Dudley, was created Earl of Leicester in order for him to woo and marry her rival Mary Queen of Scots but she deliberately sabotaged it by putting pretty boy Henry Stuart, Lord Darcy before Mary with the understanding that if she married him she would relinquish her claim to the English throne. Robert Dudley's first wife, Amy Robsart, had died after falling down a staircase and he had been banned from court until he was cleared of suspicion in the death, which many thought was his convenient way to clear himself to become the Queen's husband, or consort. Following a brief stay in Scotland, the ever ambitious Robert Dudley had returned to court and resumed his post as Master of the Queen's horse. Robert was uncle of Sir Philip Sidney, married to a daughter of Sir Francis Walsingham (the queen's privy counselor and senior secretary until his death who was a close friend of Sir William Cecil and his successor to the post under King James 1, Sir Robert Cecil, Lord Saye and Sele). The Dudleys were close friends of the wealthy Buckingham Bucks County Fulke Grenvilles. Robert fought in Europe and was wounded. However, in secret Robert Dudley bedded Douglas (the Lady Sheffield) and had a son by her, named Robert. Lady Sheffield was close to Hakluyt and helped him publish his collection of voyages of discovery (an early atlas of sorts). As the questionable "marriage" had not been sanctioned by the Queen it was kept quiet and young Robert was sent off to be raised as a step-son by Robert Sr.'s father, John.

Robert's brother Roger Dudley was a captain and served with him abroad, both receiving gratitude from Queen Elizabeth. Roger's son Thomas was two years younger than Robert Dudley Jr. and they grew up together like brothers. Robert Jr. took an early interest in geography at Oxford and later set up an exploration of the southern part of the New World with Sir Walter Raleigh in 1594. Sir Walter Raleigh couldn't get his ships ready in time and Robert Dudley's fleet left without him, incurring his unending wrath. Robert's fleet made it to South America and explored the mouth of the Orinoco River and the island of Trinidad north of the mainland, claiming that place in Spanish territory for Queen Elizabeth.

The Dudleys were never far from the royal ear and Ambrose Dudley, Earl of Warwick at Essex Manor was the person who pushed Frobisher's third voyage looking for the Northwest Passage in 1578 in which Sir Thomas Davis's brother Robert was the First Mate of the *Thomas Allen*. The relationships between the Davises, Grenvilles, Dudleys, Raleighs and Gilberts were close and it was Admiral Sir Richard Grenville who brought the first natives back to England from Virginia in the *Tiger,* which had offloaded Gov. Ralph Lane and the first settlers at Roanoke island in 1584.

Robert's father (nicknamed Robin by Queen Elizabeth) had married, with Queen Elizabeth's consent, Lettice Knollys the widow of the First Earl of Essex. The Knolly family was related to Queen Elizabeth. Robin served his queen in the Netherlands and was made Earl of Leicester. He replaced Sir Walter as her favorite at court after Sir Walter married Mary Boleyn, first cousin to the queen. (The family estate was Knoles Manor that Dolor worked on.)

Basically, in the last decades of the sixteenth century southwest England felt like one big family between Sir Richard Grenville, who sold Buckland Abbey to Sir Walter Raleigh and Carew Raleigh who bought South Wraxell Manor in Wiltshire near Monkton Farley, home of James Clark, who married into the Seymour family and was a business partner of William Davis in Bristol. One big, wealthy family that owned and captained ships for trading and colonizing.

So it was no surprise when Thomas Dudley was a fellow passenger on the *Arbella,* with John Winthrop, Sir Richard Saltonstall and George Alcock in 1630; Dudley, the primary landowner in Denbighshire County, Wales came over as representative of the Earl of Lincoln. Dudley's cousin Robert Jr. was working on a set of atlases titled *Del 'Arcana del Mare,* or *Secrets of the Sea* while licking his wounds over ill treatment by the court when King James I not only denied his legal paternity but also gave his father's lands and titles to Sir Philip Sidney. Robert helped Duke Ferdinando build an Italian Navy, using his knowledge of shipbuilding and navigation to develop the port of Livorno. Around this same time King James I was "gifted" Theobald Manor from Sir Robert Cecil, who moved to and rebuilt Hatfield Manor as his primary residence. It was the price one paid to remain in the royal good graces and Thomas Dudley had moved into position as steward to the Earl of Lincoln, whose daughter Susan was sister to Lady Arbella, wife of Isaac Johnson, related to the Gorges and Humphrey families and in with the Del la Warr and Pelhams who were trying to get Virginia colonies settled.

To plan the settlement of what would be the Massachusetts Bay Colony Thomas was in attendance at the Earl of Lincoln's second organizational meeting at his estate in Sempringham along with Sir Richard Saltonstall, John Winthrop, Sir William Pynchon and John Humphrey (related to Lord de la Warre and the Pelhams). Humphrey had married Lady Susan Fiennes, daughter of the Earl of Lincoln and sister to Arbella Johnson. Also in attendance were other prominent investors in the Massachusetts Bay Colony plantation. The shareholders of the Company chose John Winthrop as its plantation's first governor, but, distrusting King James I to leave them in peace, he only accepted on the condition that the charter be physically carried to America with the settlers. He sold his manor at Groton to help finance the plantation and ten other wealthy Puritan gentlemen also pledged to migrate with him.

Once on New England soil, Thomas Dudley wasted little time moving up the rungs of power beginning with being named executor of Isaac Johnson's will after Sir Johnson died in September, 1630, preceded a month earlier by his wife. Around the same time Gov. John Winthrop flexed his magisterial muscles and persuaded the court of Assistants to have Thomas Morton expelled from Merry Mount as the Pilgrims had done with Weston's men at Wessagusset as he was of a lewd and unruly character and a bad influence on the colony, cavorting around a Maypole and selling liquor to the savages. He was one of the first prisoners in the new jail in Boston, held there until he could be deported back to England.

William Pynchon, a gentleman from Writtle, just east of London, near Springfield, Chelmsford, was one of the Puritans who became alarmed at the state of England after King Charles I dissolved the Parliament in the spring of 1629 after resolutions were passed against illegal levying of tonnage and poundage (taxation without representation) and 'innovations' in the High Church. The king imprisoned the Puritan leaders and did not call another Parliament but went back to forced loans (and later 'ship money' taxes). Like other Puritans he had disliked the new king and supported those in Parliament who spoke against Buckingham and were against the billeting of soldiers in private estates, and his imprisonment of subjects without cause and the constant waste of money by the crown.

On July 28, 1629 the Massachusetts Bay Company held their annual meeting at the house of its Governor, Matthew Craddock in London. He and Richard Bellingham had obtained the first royal charter for the company with Saltonstall and Johnson three months before. John Winthrop and Emmanuel Downing (married to a sister of Winthrop's) left Groton and rode north to the family manor in Tattershall to meet with Isaac Johnson, John Humphrey and Thomas Dudley. Edmund Davis's elderly son Matthew Davis was present as Craddock's legal advisor. Winthrop and the three he met rode with him south to Cambridge and in Emmanuel College met with Saltonstall and William Vassall, Increase Nowell and William Pynchon. The College was familiar to many of these men as they had attended, were graduates and/or had sons enrolled at the time.

It took a month to hash out the wording but by late August of 1629 the six men signed a compact at Cambridge stating they would sell their lands and goods and enter into a joint venture to plant a colony in New England by the following March. The Company's Deputy Governor, Goffe took it the next day to the General Court, which voted in favor of the plantation. The clock began ticking on that date and seven months later the fleet was assembled at Southampton, led by the flagship

Arbella, with Winthrop and the Johnsons aboard. The Dorchesterite *Mary and John* had left from Plymouth about the same time, headed for Salem. Capt. William Peirce sailed the *Lyon* about the same date from Bristol. He had been crossing the sea in other ships to resupply the Plymouth and Salem Plantations but was feeling that if Winthrop's group was successful it might be time to bring his wife over and settle down in the Bay.

William Pynchon sold the manor and lands in Springfield and Writtle, inherited through Sir Richard Weston's marriage to his mother, and increased as the result of the wool trade with the Netherlands (which by 1630 was in decline in England). The Dutch influence was all around him in Essex as windmills dotted the landscape. They would later power machines that converted raw, carded wool into rolls for spinning and then weaving and finally fulling and dying. A lot of the textile work was still being done by hand on the farms but grist mills needed wind power to turn the huge, heavy granite wheels. Pynchon's fortunes had also increased when he married a neighboring gentleman's daughter, Agnes Andrews, and he obtained more lands through her dowry.

Pynchon's grandfather was friends with Rev. White's grandfather, having gone to college with him. It was through Rev. White in Dorchester that Pynchon became an advocate of the new plantation. His neighbor, Rev. Thomas Hooker, had tried to talk him into it but Pynchon disliked the man and never attended his church services. He called him the "Son of Thunder" behind his back.

Pynchon, his wife and four small children (including Margaret, who would later marry William Davis in Boston) boarded the *Ambrose*, bound for New England as other Puritans boarded the *Arbella*, the *Mayflower* (not the Plymouth one), the *Whale*, *William and Francis*, the *Hopewell* the Success, the *Jewel,* the *Trial*, he *Talbot* and the *Charles*. Bad weather kept the fleet off the Isle of Wight for a week while the *Mary and John* and the *Lyon* were already at sea.

Pynchon lost his wife during the sickness that carried off the Johnsons. He left his children to the care of a servant in Dorchester, then removed to Rocksbuy (Roxbury). Over the next years he coped with his grief by running a pinnace back and forth from the Plymouth settler's trading post on the Sagadahoc (now called Kennebec) down to Boston and Plymouth and even further south, around Cape Cod to the trading posts on the *Quonicticut* (Connecticut) River and towards New

Netherland and Block Island. As Boston grew, he became the largest beaver and fur trader on the coast, trading English steel items for corn and furs. He and Thomas Mayhew ran afoul of Winthrop's government when they lent arms to the savages to shoot animals for furs and they were fined. Pynchon was also annoyed with Winthrop because he had been sold a monopoly on the fur trade (even though he disliked the practice of granting monopolies) and then the government let others trade in furs. He felt they had reneged on their agreement and as Treasurer of the Massachusetts Bay Colony, he held back five pounds of his assessment. The General Court then 'fined' him five pounds for not paying his latest assessment in Roxbury so Winthrop got his money and earned Pynchon's antipathy. Winthrop was also gaining antipathy from the northeastern settlements as he fought with Craddock's man and resisted Mason and Gorges's claims to the land north of the Merrimack River.

For the first four to five years Winthrop, Dudley and the elite basically ruled with an iron fist. The elections were a sham as the deputies, appointed by the governor, elected the next governor. This was something Dudley didn't like as it smacked of the old cronyism of the English gentry and he felt they were trying for a more egalitarian state in this 'New' England.

The biggest problem the plantation faced was its too rapid growth. It became obvious at an early stage that the small neck of land wouldn't be enough for hundreds and hundreds of immigrants so parties were sent out to find suitable sites for new villages. To the north they met the antagonism of the Mason-Gorges coalition and to the south the Plymouth folks were claiming all the land west and south of their colony. The patent makers in London hadn't accounted for the Puritans having a large number of non-adherents such as fishermen and people who were anti Church of England but not necessarily followers of the Winthrop-Boston brand of Puritanism plus Antinominists, Baptists, Scotch-Irish Presbyterians, Quakers – the list was long of people who sought relief from King Charles I's religious persecution in Britain. But Winthrop and his inner circle had only one concept, shaped by the Rev. John Cotton, which stressed obedience to the body politic as a religious duty.

By April of 1632 Thomas Dudley was so frustrated with Gov. Winthrop's dictatorial attitude that he put in his resignation as Deputy Governor but it was refused.

Winthrop had his new house in Newtown torn down and accused him of being ostentatious since he'd installed wainscoting (even though the paneling was plain pine clapboards) in his first home. After Mrs. Winthrop had arrived on the *Lyon* in November of the previous year Winthrop became more hard nosed about how the colony was to think and be managed. At first people were tolerant feeling he was dealing with the death of a son and daughter but as time went by they realized he'd always been that way.

By the colony's second year there were settlements at Boston, Dorchester, Roxbury, Watertown, Charleston and Medford, in addition to Salem. Most of these new towns were provincial, settled by West Country or Essex folk who came from common areas in England. In 1631 Marblehead, Newton, Lynn and Cambridge were added. Because of the difficulty of either obtaining and financing a minister for each town, the worshipers had to travel miles to meeting houses every Sabbath and mid-week for prayers.

In May, 1632 the governor and his assistants were dining at Winthrop's house and Winthrop accused Dudley of usury when he sold seven bushels of corn at prices the governor and his court felt took advantage of the corn scarcity to make an excess profit. Dudley hotly argued with him but was appeased after the dinner was cleared away and Winthrop said he was open to Dudley's suggestion of having the governorship elected by the whole court and not just the assistants at the next General Court, scheduled be held in little over a week. However, Roger Ludlow was outraged. He rose up and, banging his fist on the oak trestle table shouted, "Then we should have no government but an interim where every man might do what he pleased!" Ludlow was so angry he threatened to return to England and take all his money with him and to use his influence at court against the Bay colony.

The minister tried to calm everyone down and enjoined them to bow in prayer to restore their fellowship but as the men left Winthrop's house there were plenty of frowns and black scowls.

By the time of the General Court on May 8th tempers had settled down and Winthrop through a series of private meetings had backed off on a General Election by the Court and instead the Court passed a term limit law whereby a new governor should be chosen every year from the Assistants. In absentia John Humpfrey and William Coddington were chosen as Assistants as they were expected to return to

Boston in the near future. John Winthrop, Jr. was also chosen as an Assistant.

Residents had petitioned the Court asking that each company of trained militia could be free to choose their own captain but Gov. Winthrop talked them out of it.

The Court decreed that every town should choose two men (representatives) to attend the next Court to help decide how to deal with the question of how public stock should be managed.

Acting as a beneficent ruler, Winthrop then told those gathered that he would no longer accept gifts except from Assistants or special friends as his was not a paid position and therefore gifts were a form of salary.

The next few months were busy ones as fortifications were begun at Corne Hill, Roxbury and Dorchester. In July, all the talk was about a great battle between a mouse and a snake in which the mouse won. The Puritan ministers saw this as a battle between the Evil Serpent (Satan) and God's meek Puritans in New England and from their pulpits proclaimed it showed the Puritans would prevail against factors trying to tear the New Canaan apart. He didn't come out and say it but they knew the little mouse was them against the all-devouring snake (the king). And, regarding snakes, there was an abundance of rattlesnakes that summer and everyone was very cautious when clearing brush and around outhouses, where they often lay in ambush for rats.

While the politicians and ministers were proclaiming this and that, the common people were going about the laborious work of starting out with practically nothing in a foreign land. Trees had to be felled and squared off with adzes, houses had to be buiLt. fences erected, outbuildings (crude thatch and sapling affairs), had to be made and crude meeting houses built. Plus the new fortifications. Every man and young boy was engaged in this labor, plus in planting and driving crows and deer from fields. Wolves were a constant menace at night and bounties were paid for their pelts. Besides the natural dangers of a heavy rain washing away young plants or flooding a pasture, there were dangers of fire from sparks on thatch roofs or poorly clayed chimneys and the women had the extra worry of keeping little children safe from fires, drowning and from wandering into the forests where wild animals and the savages lurked.

Ann Moulton and Anne Needham wrote to Marie Davis and others about the challenges but tried to end each letter with a praise to God and a Thanksgiving for

His Mercy in sending them to a place safe from royal persecution.

However, in August, the antagonisms between Dudley and Winthrop flared again. Dudley complained to Rev. Thomas Weld, the new pastor at Roxbury and to Mr. Wilson about Winthrop's mistreatment of him. He was especially aggrieved at having the frame of his Newton home disassembled and carted away by order of Winthrop.

Hoping to salve Dudley's wounds, the men arranged a meeting between them, Deputy Gov. Dudley, Gov. Winthrop and a deputy, Mr. Nowell, the Rev. Maverick and the Rev. John Warwick, pastor of the Dorchester church in Charlestown. Dudley spoke his peace but Winthrop argued that he'd had the house removed as none of the others had started building that far away from town and Dudley wouldn't be safe without a village around him. Dudley asserted that Winthrop had overstepped his authority. The ministers removed themselves and returned with the decision that Winthrop was at fault for not giving Dudley prior notice. The group then dined and after dinner Dudley demanded to know where Winthrop thought he got his authority to be a dictator. Dudley said the patent gave him as Deputy Governor the same authority as the Assistants with the added ability to call a Court into session. Winthrop said no, he had sole authority to govern as he saw fit, granted under English Common Law. They both rose and shouted 'roundly' at each other over the table, neither mollified by the ministers trying to bring calm to the situation until a lot of angry words were exchanged.

Two days later men from the congregations of Boston and Charlestown began constructing the first church, sited adjacent to Winthrop's land, between Fort field and Bendell's Cove on State Street. Roxbury also began a house for Rev. Wilson, the money for which was raised from the Boston and Charlestown congregations.

August was very chilly and wet and the mosquitoes were vicious that year but the people turned out in early September when Hopkins of Watertown was convicted of selling a musket and shot to the indian Sagamore James. As he was publically whipped and then branded on his face savages from the Narragansett tribe were whispering amongst themselves and Boston was under alert for a possible attack. Captain John Underhill set up a night watch and decided to test the readiness of the militia by sounding the alarm. The speed with which the men grabbed pieces and shot and assembled pleased the captain but there was a lot of grumbling about unnecessarily panicking exhausted people who needed their sleep.

A week and a half later three sachems appeared at Winthrop's house and assured him there were no plans to wage war on Boston but the populace was anxious, looking into the forests as they diligently worked on erecting structures and storage sheds or pits before winter set in.

Dudley's re-assembled house then caught fire and almost burned down as he had stored musket powder too close to his hearth.

Word arrived by ship that First Viscount Lord Saye and Sele William Fiennes in Broughton Castle, Oxfordshire and Sir Basil Brooke in Ireland had taken over management of Piscataqua Plantation.

(In England The Earl of Warwick held with the Earl of Brooke the arms of Greville. In 1630 Robert Greville Second Baron Brooke, John Pym and others bought Providence Island off the coast between New England and Virginia. Robert Rich was the Third Earl of Warwick. Henry Richard Grenville and Sir Fulke Grenville descended from the old Earl of Warwick, who had owned the ruins of Warwick Castle but died of wounds received while fighting the Spanish on Lord Admiral Thomas Howard's ship the *Revenge* in the Azores.) Sir Fulke was created Baron of Beauchamps and lived in Beauchamps Court in Worcester County, England and was related to Richard Neville, High Sheriff of Worcestershire, Leicestershire and Warwickshire. Warwickshire was the heart of the English manufacturing industry producing iron items including buttons, anvils, nails, pistols and many other products for domestic and foreign markets. Its city Birmingham occupied a crucial location on inland rivers with a ready supply of coal and wood to fuel forges. Lord Saye and Sele along with John Hampden was a staunch opponent of King Charles I's forced loan in 1626 and met with fellow opponents John Digby, first Earl of Bristol, Thomas Howard, Earl of Suffolk and Dudley Diggs in his castle on the river southwest of Banbury to plan resistance. Howard had been Lord High Treasurer but was charged with peculation in 1619 and had been imprisoned by King James I and forced to pay a heavy fine for his freedom. Diggs was charged with treason and imprisoned in the Tower.

In late Oct. 1632 Gov. Winthrop and Rev. Wilson sailed in a shallop south to *Wessaguscus* (later Weymouth) and then walked south to Plymouth to meet with its Governor John William Bradford and his elder, Mr. Brewster. They observed the

Sabbath together and afterwards Roger Williams (a former pastor in Salem who had been blocked from preaching the first spring after Winthrop's fleet arrived because he felt church and state should be separate in the matter of laws and who also had criticized the Bay Puritans for not officially separating from the Church of England), prophesied at the urging of Rev. Ralph Smith.

In late November a Fast Day was observed and Mr. Wilson was ordained as the minister for the Boston church and Thomas Oliver, who with his sons were clearing the trees between Boston Neck and Roxbury, appointed an Elder.

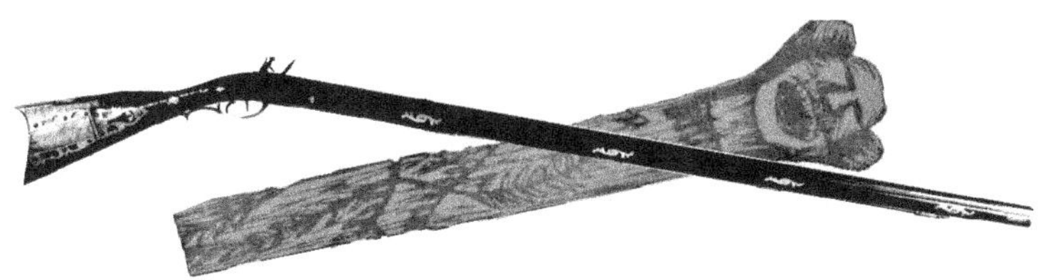

CHAPTER THIRTY-FIVE

Down East

1633

The year began quietly. Pirates were terrorizing traders and fishermen to the north and the leaders of the Massachusetts Bay Colony (MBC) in Boston sent men and pinnaces to catch them but they returned after only hanging an indian, Black William, because it got too ice-bound to further pursue the rogues who had murdered Walter Bagnall in his trading post.

In Plymouth Edward Winslow was elected governor, finally freeing William Bradford of the duty.

The French bought the Scottish plantation near Cape Sable. The Puritans were alarmed as that was bringing the Catholics too close to their territory. It was decided to construct a fort and a plantation at Nantasket for defense, plus to finish the fort in Boston harbor and to settle a plantation on the north shore at a place named *Agawam* (not to be confused with *Agawam* on the Connecticut River). John Winthrop Jr. was in charge of these matters and left with 12 men to begin the projects.

In England, Fiennes, First Viscount of Saye and Sele and Lord Brooke got a patent to begin a "real" plantation at Piscataqua for Gorges and Mason. According to Mr. Trevore, master of the *William*, which docked at Plymouth at this time

Christopher Gardiner, Thomas Morton and Phillip Radcliffe were punished for badmouthing Boston leaders over their disputation of Mason and Gorges's claims to the Bay territory. Morton carried a long petition of complaint to London about their mistreatment. The *William* also carried passengers to set up a trading post at *Scituate* and was bound from there to trade at the mouth of the Hudson River.

In late February the governor and four assistants and three ministers plus others, totaling 26 in all, sailed to Nantasket to check on the progress of the fort. The seas forced them to drop anchor and seek shelter inside an old, dilapidated shack from which they had to pull straw roof thatching for bedding between themselves and the frozen ground. The trip was not productive and the men, though jubilant at the adventure, decided it would be impractical to set a plantation and fort there so John Winthrop Jr. was relieved of the duty to proceed any further at that site (later settled in 1647 as Hull). John junior however, with another 12 men did begin *Agawam*, later named Ipswich, in March.

In April Mr. Hodges arrived in a shallop from Virginia bringing news that Capt. Peirce lost a ship in November on the shoals of Feake's Isle. Some of the sailors, passengers and the goods from Plymouth and Boston bound for England were lost but Capt. Peirce survived. A packet of letters was also salvaged.

By mid June three large ships from England – the *Mary and Jane*, the *William and James*, owned by Sir Thomas Davis, and the *Elizabeth Bonaventure* – brought more settlers, goods and livestock including 34 Friesian milk sheep from the Netherlands. Unfortunately, they lost 40 sheep en route but all three ships made very good time on the trip over and Rev. Coddington and his wife arrived, a precious asset to the burgeoning colony in need of ministers.

About this time Plymouth's Governor Winslow and William Bradford visited Boston and beseeched the colony to help them build a trading post at the mouth of the Connecticut River but after much discussion the MBC governor and assistants said they felt the large sandbar there would make a port dangerous and impractical.

A letter told the governor and his council that Sir Richard Saltonstall, John Humfrey and Matthew Craddock had to appear at court to answer the charges from Gardiner and his men but if Winthrop and his council could satisfactorily answer the charges they would probably be dropped as the king indicated he wouldn't be forcing the ceremonies of the Church of England upon the colony as its value in cordage, timber and furs was too valuable to be lost over a question of religious practice (Gardiner's bigamy). Gardiner, who had been Gorges's agent, had left the colony in March.

The Piscataqua plantation felt Capt. Neal was the rightful governor of the patent, down into the Bay, but Winthrop and his men adamantly asserted their patent rights and refused to be subordinate.

A day of Thanksgiving was called for the safe passage of the new colonists coming over and in late June a ship arrived from Weymouth with 80 passengers, bound for New Dorchester. They had a horrendous crossing, twice as long as the six weeks of earlier ships that month, as, due to a severe leak in the hull they had to sail south to the West Indies and while waiting there many on board died from fever in the searing, humid heat. Then, after arriving in Plymouth, many of them died of summer fever. There was much mourning and praying throughout the colony as many of the deceased immigrants were related by blood or marriage to others in New England

A Court session was called in early July and monies were agreed upon for the governor to pay bills and expenses that occurred in the commission of his duties. Also in July, Capt. Graves, carrying a cargo of fish from Plymouth, docked briefly in Boston harbor and the governor and council sent their answer via letter with him to London regarding Gorges, Mason and Morton's charges.

The Bay colony sent out another pinnace full of men after Dixie Bull and his pirates but they returned, empty-handed as he'd gone over to the French.

The harbor was quiet in early August except for the drowning of two disreputable oyster men from Roxbury.

Capt. Graves returned from Piscataqua carrying Capt. Neal and eight Northmen. Capt. Neal refused to come ashore and sent word to Gov. Winthrop that he was upset as letters he had carried when he was last in port had been illegally opened and read by the governor's spies. He said he wasn't offered proper hospitality, either.

Feasting wasn't offered to him this time as the colony was low on corn stores. Corn had become the staple food and its meal was cooked in various ways and used as a thickener in stews. The hogs had either gotten into the corn fields or been fed from the corn cribs during the winter when there were no acorns for them to forage due to the deep snow cover.

Then an event happened on September the 4th that was to permanently change the colony.

The *Griffen* arrived from the Downs with about 200 passengers, including the ministers Cotton, Hooker, the Hutchinsons and Wheelwrights.

CHAPTER THIRTY-SIX

The Dutch Threat

1633

The September day was one of the rare "Indian Summer" days New England gets as a gift from Nature after she has begun to show her white winter teeth during cold nights. Tender crops were being harvested yet the corn could take a few more weeks on the stalk before it was cut with scythes and the cobs put in a bin to be husked later on. The stalks would be gathered in the fields, tied into sheaves that the farmers would let stand until they could bring them in to be chopped or fed whole as winter silage for the livestock. The settlers had known this summer the corn crop would be poor as corn seed had been fed to the hogs and, after planting many stalks were damaged in the fields by rooting hogs. A farmer's hogs provided multiple needs: lots of lard for cooking; pork meat for hams or roasts, fatty sections with meat for bacon and sausages and the hide could be tanned into a tough leather for farm aprons and other items that cow hides normally were used for. Even the pig bristles were used for brushes. The hogs ate mostly acorns and roots and any inedible or spoiled food thrown to them as swill. In England the settlers were spoiled by having plenty of lush meadow for cattle and sheep but they had to adjust to New England's harsher, raw environment by getting their milk from goats and even sheep and by eating more pork than beef as their cattle herds were still small.

During Indian Summer the *Bird*, captained by Mr. Yates sailed into Boston harbor, later followed by Captain John Gallop as he sailed the 300 ton *Griffin* into the Massachusetts Bay Colony, cutting through the calm waters to dock at Bendell's Cove, near Gov. Winthrop's land and house.

The passengers were overjoyed to be at the end of the voyage. One had drowned off the north coast two days before as he leaned out too far casting a line for mackerel.

The passengers included Rev. John Cotton and Rev. Thomas Hooker, both wanted by the Crown for their Puritan preaching. The two ministers had boarded under cover of darkness from the Downs off the Kent coast after the royal warrant officers boarded and searched the *Griffin* on the Isle of Wight. Their 'escape' from the English crown reminded many of how the first Separatists had fled at night over the Downs to board a ship for the Netherlands a couple of decades earlier.

During the voyage Rev. Cotton's wife Sarah had given birth to a boy with the assistance of Anne Hutchinson, a midwife. Mrs. Hutchinson, from Alvord, was a fellow immigrant along with her husband, brother and family. The illustrious list of predominantly Lincolnshire passengers included William Pynchon's neighbor, the Rev. Thomas Hooker, related to the Alcocks, Moultons and Needhams; John Haynes, Thomas Mayhew, Thomas Leverett, Rev. Samuel Stone, Atherton Hough, a wealthy Lincolnshire merchant, Captain Gallop's wife and young son John and William Peirce – a cousin of the shipmaster William Peirce who made numerous trans-Atlantic voyages – plus William Brenton, a wealthy, educated man who was friends of the widow Francis Sanford, having attended Oxford with her deceased husband, Tobiah, who had been a physician in Dorchester. He'd also been friendly with her first husband (Smith) and was a member of Rev. White's congregation. Hearing of his arrival the widow, her son Henry Smith and daughter Elizabeth traveled from Roxbury to Boston to invite him to stay with them. Revs. Hooker and Stone went to Newbury to stay with friends or relatives and only the Rev. Cotton stayed in Boston.

Rev. Cotton was the guest speaker on the following Saturday night 'exercise', using the *Canticles Sixth* to describe how some churches were queens, others concubines and others of lesser status to the Mother Church. Rev. Cotton always used the question and answer format in his sermons, awing his audience with his prodigious knowledge of the Bible. The Boston elders voted to immediately admit Rev. Cotton and the next day his newborn son Seaborne was baptized. Rev. Cotton said he had not baptized his firstborn at sea as he felt seawater was not pure enough and he and his wife were not members of an established congregation while on board plus he felt a minister didn't have the power to give the seals (of the covenant) to himself. Prior to the baptism Sarah was questioned in private (by request of her husband) and admitted as a member to the small congregation.

Throughout the service Mrs. Anne Hutchinson, a member of Cotton's congregation, who had often traveled by sea from Alvord to hear him preach at St, Botolph's in Boston, kept frowning at certain phrases but no one knew that she was already starting her own church in her mind. The *Griffin* brought more than the much needed ordained pastors: it brought people who were thinking for themselves and would eventually stand up to the Boston Puritan oligarchy.

John Oldham and the three men who had gone overland from Boston to the Connecticut River to trade returned with many beaver skins and sacks full of hemp and black lead from a place the savages called *Tantiesques*.

In October Oldham's house near the weir at Watertown burned down as he tried to make a fire inside it without a chimney.

The *Blessing of the Bay,* now called the *Blessing*, made a trip to Long Island and returned with a cargo of high quality black and white wampum to use as a trade good with the indians. Captain Gallop had shown the Dutch there a letter from King Charles I that said England owned the Hudson River and the Connecticut but the Dutch said the West Indies Company owned them. Gallop was eyeing an island off Long Island for his farm but after the hostile encounter with the Dutch decided to there stay close to the Boston settlements for the time as savage tribes surrounded the English to the south.

In retaliation the Boston leaders sent a bark to the Connecticut River to erect a trading house down river from the Dutch one, provoking more ire from that quarter. In England Lords Saye and Sele and Brooke were working on getting a colony started to the southwest of Boston and Plymouth and on October 10th the *James* with Captain Wiggen docked at Salem and brought a letter showing the Lords Saye and Brooke had bought the land there from the Bristol merchants. Rev. Leveridge went north to *Piscatawqua* and the ship continued south to Virginia with 30 men, 60 cattle and news that the *Richard,* which had started with the *Griffin,* had to run back at Weymouth due to leaks. The ship also unloaded four Irish wolf hounds, sent from Gov. Winthrop's brother-in-law in Downing for the colonists to use to hunt down the wolves that were terrorizing their livestock.

The following day Rev. Hooker was elected minister of Newton and Mr. Stone elected Teacher.

Around this time a plague killed many savages and Puritan families took in the orphaned children, hoping for free servants, but they learned that indian children were not raised to do chores but were allowed to run and play. Most of the children, however, died of the smallpox plague and the missionary Rev. Maverick was burying over 30 a day in *Winnesmesent.*

In November, the *Rebecca,* a 60 ton bark was built and launched at Medford and a watermill was built at Roxbury by Mr. Dummer.

The New England economy was struggling. Wages were raised as skilled labor was scarce and in high demand. Workers grew fat on the wages but slacked off on hours worked and spent more on tobacco and strong spirits, much to the dismay of the church leaders. The Court ordered wages lowered yet prices on English commodities increased, hurting most the newest immigrants who had arrived in 1633 on the *James, Bird, Clement and Job, Elizabeth Bonaventure, Elizabeth and Dorcas, Jonas, Mary and Jane, Neptune, Seaflower, Griffin, Truelove, William and Jane, William* and two other ships bound for the northern colonies and one for St. Christophers. Very short of corn and cattle they were vastly overcharged when buying them from the settlers who had arrived before them.

News was received that the French had killed two Plymouth traders at their fort at *Machias*, claiming the territory belonged to France.

The Boston congregation voted to raise money to cover Rev. Cotton's voyage costs and to fund the building of his house and to provide him and Rev. Wilson with a maintenance wage.

Sagamores John and James died of the plague and James left his son to be raised by Rev. Wilson. The plague killed all but two savages at Piscataqua. To the south, the Narragansetts and Pequots were also dying of a disease the English were little affected by. The Puritan ministers said this was because the Puritans were

Christians and that God was punishing the heathen who were slow to convert to the true religion.

In late November the Rev. Wilson went to *Agawam* to teach, arriving a week before a terrible blizzard of snow and ice forced people and animals indoors.

Rev. Cotton's preaching brought many converts into the Boston church, increasing it by fifty percent. He quoted scripture to show that his maintenance, as well as that of Rev. Wilson, should be paid from a treasury built by weekly offerings. However, the Boston church was met with a challenge when Rev. Roger Williams in Salem wrote a treatise based on the book of *Revelation* questioning the right of the English to claim lands settled by the savages, stating they were acting like the Beast, like devils going forth into the kings of the earth. It took many hours of writing and conferring between the Boston and Plymouth councils before Rev. Williams relented and said he had been in error. He said it had been written for a private reading of the governor of Plymouth but would gladly burn it as it offended the clergy and elders of both churches.

CHAPTER THIRTY-SEVEN

The Savages Attack the English

1634

In late January William Stone and men were discovered murdered on Block Island off the mouth of the Connecticut River. Stone, a trader and member of the Virginia plantation, judged to be a bad influence for his heathenish ways, had been evicted from the Bay the past summer. His corpse and that of his companions had been found at a spot where they had apparently camped during fowling and visitors from the Plymouth colony alerted Boston, saying the Pequots had done it. Because the Puritans felt little connection or responsibility for Stone, they agreed it was a matter for the governor of Virginia and wrote a letter to him detailing the attack upon his citizens.

However, in the northern area Mr. Jenkyns from Dorchester was murdered in his sleep and his goods were stolen when he went in to trade at the mouth of the Saco River.

Also north, Matthew Craddock's house at Marblehead burned down. Mr. Allerton and fishermen were inside and said about midnight sparks from an oven lit the thatch on the roof. Allerton had eight ships fishing off Richman's Isle and the Isle of Shoals that winter and spring.

In *Saugus* the settlers planted many fields of barley, oats and corn using new metal ploughs.

On the fourth of March the Massachusetts General Court ordered a public market be erected with a public house to be operated by Samuel Cole on the common near where William Blackstone's hut had been. The day for the monthly market would be the fifth day, a Lecture Day. John Cogan set up the first shop on the square. Robert Cole over imbibed and was arrested for drunkenness and forced by the Court to wear a ribbon hanging from his neck with a small square of cloth embroidered with a 'Scarlet D' on it for a year.

In April a census was taken of all homes and all men 20 years and older were required to take a loyalty oath, if they were not already on the rolls as free men. Originally all freemen were able to attend and speak in the annual General Assembly when laws were voted on but by May of 1633 there were so many new immigrants that the Court decided each 'town' would select men (selectmen) to attend it instead. This was based on the English Common Law where counties sent MPs, or Members of Parliament to London. But in New England these representatives weren't just self-appointed 'Scot and Lot' wealthy gentry and merchants but any freeman could be elected to be a selectman.

Around Boston all was not peaceful and happy. Two ministers – the Rev. James of Charlestown and the Rev. Nowell – were at odds and wanted to break with the Boston congregation. Through the intervention of Rev. Cotton and the Assistants the quarrel was resolved but Mr. Morris, ensign to Capt. Underhill, became disgruntled and wanted to quit; he was placated with a promotion to lieutenant.

That spring Kenneth Hockins arrived in Piscataqua to trade in a pinnace owned by Lords Saye ad Sele and Brook. There he met Plymouth traders who refused to let him dock. Undeterred, the 30 men with him sailed upriver and set out trap lines. The Plymouth men followed in canoes to cut their lines and Hockins and his men shot at the Plymouth men, who returned fire and killed Hockins. John Alden, from Plymouth, a relative of Hockins, witnessed the event and a half dozen men involved in the violence were condemned to death for murder by the Court. This caused a lot of grumbling amongst the Plymouth people and the Piscataqua people and Rev. Cotton preached a long sermon on the sanctity of magistrates.

At the April General Assembly Thomas Dudley was elected governor and

Roger Ludlow his deputy. John Haynes, a recent arrival, was elected as an Assistant and it was decided that four General Courts would be held every year with three selectmen from each town to deal with the issues but at the annual General Assembly *all* freemen could cast a vote for the governor and other officials.

The *Hercules* from London arrived with Capt. Richard's son Nathaniel Davis.

In all, 14 ships would arrive by the end of July, most bound for Boston but some for St. Christophers, the Barbados and a Dutch ship, the *de Endract* set anchor off New Netherlands. The *James* from Hampton had mostly tradesmen from Marlboro, Amesbury and Longford. It was with this group of laborers, weavers, servants, carpenters, shoemakers, surveyors and surgeons that Dolor Davis and his wife Margery Willard and their son Little John arrived. They met the *Bonaventure* later when it docked, carrying John Davis, son of Capt. James, and his wife Cicely and their son James, a tailor and mariner who settled first in Plymouth then in Boston and Haverhilll.

The *Francis* carried mostly laborers as did as the *Elizabeth*, also sailing from Ipswich but the *Francis* carried Thomas King, Mr. Stebbing (Stebbins), Newell, Holden, Lindsey and Suffolk, all bound for Watertown.

At the March Court it was decided that all swamp land over 100 acres would be public, or common land, for grazing and harvesting of the small sour berries(cranberries) that helped fight scurvy.

Nathaniel's relative Nicholas followed on the *Planter*, captained by Nicholas Triece from Stepney. Nathaniel didn't stay in Boston but sailed north to Kittery.

Another new Davis passenger was Barnaby Davis, youngest son of Matthew, son of Edmund from Tisbury. Barnaby wasn't interested in the law as his two older brothers John and Matthew were but loved surveying, a trade highly in demand. He'd been in the Barbados with Theo but had returned to England. After arriving in New England he became close friends of William Pynchon and accompanied him often on his trips to the Connecticut River and the trading posts along its shore. His cousins were also asking for his help in the Mason and Gorges territory to the north.

At this time there were basically four main English settlements in New England: Piscataqua and Kittery and the fishing posts to the north; the Boston Bay area with many settlements springing up around it almost daily; the Plymouth colony which had a couple of outlying settlements and small trading posts at the mouth and lower part of the Connecticut River. Each area had its own characteristics with the northern posts more interested in fishing and fur trading than religion, the Boston and Plymouth towns highly religious and the southern settlements major fur trading posts. Only Plymouth and Boston had courts and governors although Matthew Craddock insisted that his northern settlement was as civilized as the two main Puritan colonies and deserved its own.

In Boston Dolor was immediately hired to build a house for Simon Willard, his brother-in-law. A relative through marriage to one of the Davis clan, Henry Pease, also hired him to build a house near the one Dolor was constructing off what was being called Court Street, north east of the small causeway that led to mill field and not far from Bendell's cove. John Glover, north of the Davis lands, was also in need of Dolor's construction team. Dolor wrote to his older son Big John, back in England after a stay in the Barbados, that he must come back over as there was such a shortage of skilled laborers that experienced housewrights such as they could basically name their own rate. (The Pease clan later settled Enfield, Connecticut.,)

At this time Nicholas, later captain of the *Trader's Increase*, came over in the *Planter.* He was cousin to Sir Thomas, James, Richard, Robert the Black and Robert Tobias, all in the shipping trade, owning or co-owning ships, captaining the same or hiring them out in constant trade between England, the West Indies, Virginia and the New England coast from the Long Island bay around the neck called Cape Cod, up the coast from Plymouth to Boston to Salem to Cape Ann, Dover, Piscataqua, Kittery and as far north as Newfoundland. The seasons determined the paths their ships took plus the seasonal availability of cargo from New England, Virginia, the Islands and passengers from England. Being mariners was in the Davis blood but a ship could be lost at sea or forced to be in drydock for extensive repairs or even get taken by pirates. This was one reason the Davis men wanted land: lots of land. The sea could make a man or break a man in an instant but land was constant. It was one commodity England was now short of. Once in a family, estates, which could consist of many manors in many different parts of England, Wales, Ireland and even Scotland, were partitioned and handed down to in a prescribed order with the firstborn son receiving the family seat and his brothers getting others. When there were no sons the eldest daughter married and her husband took the family seat but often an uncle would lay claim so daughters usually were married off to wealthy gentry who had their own family estates. As it was common for a man to remarry if his wife died, families in England and New England were large. Sometimes a man had children by three wives, such as Sir Thomas, who left England and set up a plantation in Virginia, and a woman sometimes had multiple husbands though less prodigy as females were limited to their childbearing years. In New England there was plenty of land for the original children and the step children of these marriages but England, Ireland and Wales had been parceled out into ever smaller estates long ago. Not only did the New England lands have actual land, they were wealthy in natural resources and Dolor found no want for good, strong timbers for the Dutch-styled steep roofed 'saltbox' style houses (with only one story in back) he was building. What was wanting was the labor to fell, haul and square the trunks for solid beams and to split shingles for siding. In England he was used to building in stone but quarries weren't in full operation and it was too much work to haul blocks of granite on sleds so the settlers used the materials that were closest and easiest to haul. The largest stones worked out of the virgin fields were used to line the cellars but from snow level up the houses were of wood. Clay lined chimneys were originally used for fireplaces but replaced by stones as more were unearthed and piled in rows and as soon as brick kilns were built the chimneys and fireplaces were made of these fire-resistant materials and once slate quarries were established the steep thatch roofs were replaced with slate, tiled row upon row beginning with the bottom first.

In May Rev. Parker and 150 members of his congregation arrived and settled north in *Agawam*, later renamed Ipswich. They had had a short voyage and were well blessed with many provisions left unused onboard. The captain of their ship, the *Dover*, continued east to cut masts for English ships.

Six men from Newtown went south to explore the Connecticut River for possible town sites. These men, followers of Rev. Hooker, had gone north to the *Merrimack* River a few months earlier as they wanted to move their settlements away from the tyrannical Boston council.

The *Thunder*, piloted by Jenkyns Davis (brother of Dolor, Robert Tobias and Nicholas) arrived from Bermuda with corn and goats from Virginia. Jenkyns had a propensity to drink too much but stayed sober when piloting the coastlines. Most of the corn from Bermuda had been destroyed by weevils but he had molasses and rum from the new crop being started there: sugar cane. He also told men in the Boston common public house that a convoy of large ships under Lord Baltimore had arrived to the south. This was causing a lot of aggravation in Virginia as the king wrote to Sir John Harvy, governor of Virginia that Baltimore was granted a new plantation on the *Potomoc* River to be called Maryland after Charles's queen. Like the queen, the settlement was Catholic. James Davis went into a panic at the news and immediately sailed his father James Sr.'s merchant vessel the *James* for Virginia to protect his plantation. James (co-owner of The *James*) had a heavy investment in the Red (or Reed) Creek plantation in Virginia and was originally only staying in Boston before leaving for St. Domingo. His son John was only five years old and was living with his mother and siblings in Acton-Turville in Marlborough as Virginia's climate bred yellow fever and other fevers that could take a person within a day.

The Bay Colony received a much needed influx of capital when John Humphrey (Humfrey) arrived in the *Planter.* Humphrey had been a major financial backer of the Company and served as its deputy governor and treasurer in England, Hie was brother-in-law to the deceased Lady Arbella Johnson and upon arrival was immediately voted in as an Assistant. He brought his wife and children and 16 heifers – one for each minister – or to be given to an official of the minister's choice. He brought more ordnance and provisions and had a letter from Mr. Levinston in Northern Ireland stating a lot of the Irish were good Christians and wished to immigrate, plus letters of support from churches and gentry in the Mother country. These people argued against Archbishop Laud's desire to stop the flow of England's best and brightest to New England by reiterating that the colonies were a treasure trove for England. There was one letter that caused a lot of consternation, though. Matthew Craddock sent a letter to Winthrop, who was no longer governor, demanding the patent for the Massachusetts Bay Colony be sent back to England. Winthrop, Dudley, Ludlow and the others were adamant that it would not leave their hands for they knew the king would like nothing more than to tear it up and impose a restrictive leash on them. They decided to leave it for the General Assembly in September to discuss. In counterpoint to Craddock's letter Lord Cecil, Earl of Warwick wrote a private letter to Winthrop stating he would help the plantation with their grant if it were challenged at Court.

In July, feeling the pinch of over crowdedness the *Blessing* was sent to New Netherlands with a mission to explore east of the Connecticut River for new town sites. Bradford and Winslow plus the Rev. Smith arrived in Boston to confer with Dudley and the Assistants about the Kennebec murder to the north and the rights of the Plymouth colony to land there. It was agreed that Plymouth had the right to sentence men to death for the murder of Hockins but that England should mediate in the matter so a letter was drafted and signed by the leaders of both colonies.

To the north, the holders of the Gorges and Mason patent in *Pisquataqua* established two saw mills on the *Pasquataqua* and *Agamenticus* Rivers and Roger Ludlow was put in charge of a team to plan a fort on Castle Island in Boston Harbor. Every minister's congregation and official involved was taxed five pounds to cover the expense of two platforms and one fortification. on the little island, located strategically in the heart of Boston's bay.

With the heat of August pounding down upon the Bay the council granted town status to *Agawam* but renamed it Ipswich, preferring a good English town name to that of a savage one (which was also used for a village on the Connecticut River).

The *Bonaventure*, arriving via St. Domingo and Virginia, and the *Elizabeth* and the *Francis* arrived. A letter to Winthrop from Mr. William Jeffreye, an old planter from Wessaguset, included one from Thomas Morton, who said he had won his lawsuit (written by him in the Clifford's Inn in London) and the patent was to be returned immediately to King Charles I, who was ordering the Plantation Commission for the MBC to oversee the Massachusetts Bay plantation more closely and they were to send over their own governing body. This issue was one that the Council would passively resist for many years. One thing Winthrop and the others knew beyond any doubt was that the patent wouldn't leave their hands freely. The Plantation Commission had been established in April 1625 by King Charles I shortly after his father's death. It was given broad powers to govern the colonies beyond matters of trade. Its members included the Earls of Dorset, Holland and Carlisle and Sir Edward Coke as secretary.

The summer was extremely hot but the beaver harvest from the Connecticut River was the largest yet. The Plymouth colony was freely trading with the Dutch and brought corn, sack, sugar, sheep and cloth to Boston as well as beaver skins.

At the end of the hot and humid month of August the *Dove*, a 50 ton pinnace, arrived from Maryland with corn to trade for fish and other commodities. Its governor, Leonard Calvert, related to Lord Baltimore had letters of support from his assistants and the governor of Virginia for the colonists that were due to come over that winter. Most of the men on board the *Dove* were severely ill and the merchant who delivered the letter died within a week in Boston. The colony had been planted six months before and in granting the patent King Charles gave the governor absolute power to rule it. Calvert had originally had a huge grant in Newfoundland but traded it for Maryland (which contained part of the Virginia patent). Maryland even issued its own coinage and had permission to create peers, both rights exclusive to the monarchy under the Divine Rights of Kings doctrine.

At the annual General Assembly in early September the government decided on whether to let Rev. Hooker and his followers from Newton, Dorchester and other towns leave Boston to settle a major town on the Connecticut River. Many arguments were made pro and con as sweat trickled down the men's starched cravats, (mostly plain cotton but some with a little lace). The MBC government wanted to tax tobacco, spirits and fancy clothing in order to raise money for the Castle Island fort.

During the session the *Griffen* arrived again, carrying two new ministers: Rev. Lothrop and Rev. Simmes, along with 200 passengers, among them the rest of the Hutchinson family from Alvord. Revs. Lothrop and Simmes told the council that the Archbishop had persuaded the king to send over a new council from England to govern the colony. Rev. Lothrop went to *Scituate* to be their minister. He was very frail as he had been imprisoned in England's Boston for a long time for refusing to take the oath ex officio, in which he denied non-conformity.

There was a letter from the Lords Saye and Sele and Brooke about Kennebec in which they threatened to send a man of war over to see justice done about the murders.

Most of October was quiet except for the drowning of five men in a ketch off Kettle Island and the fire at Rev. Wilson's place where his servants set an improperly piled, undried haystack afire to prevent spontaneous combustion.

In November, Salem brought an issue to the council as the red cross had been cut out of its ensign, the perpetrator claiming the cross was 'papist'.

The *Rebecca*, Oldham's trading bark built in New England, arrived in port from Narragansett territory with 500 bushels of corn. He had been promised another 1,000 bushels and was deeded the island of *Chippacusett*. (Prudence Isle). Capt. Peirce said he had explored it previously and it was full of savages but had good views of Narragansett Bay, which could be useful for a fort.

Around the same time a Pequot messenger arrived with two bundles of sticks saying the tribe would provide as much beaver, otter and wampum in exchange for English friendship and protection from the Narragansetts. Dudley sent a fine moose hair coat in return but said until the murderers of Stone and his men were delivered the English would not parley with them. They begged, offering land on the Connecticut if the English would settle there. While the Pequot ambassador were in Boston about 200 Narragansett warriors sailed canoes upriver and docked at Taunton, west of Plymouth. A mediation party was sent out to settle a temporary truce in which the Pequots promised to hand over to the English the two men who had killed Stone.

The following week Rev. Eliot in Roxbury preached a sermon that said the English had no right to the treaty without putting the matter before the people. Rev. Williams of Salem spoke out against the patent and they, along with Rev. Hooker were sent notice to appear at the next court.

Barnaby Davis was then chosen with other surveyors to lay out the division of lands under seven proprietors on the peninsula of Boston. Isaac Johnson's land north of Winthrop's had been bequeathed upon his death to the town for the construction of a jail, meetinghouse, school and cemetery. Atherton Haugh (Hough), a wealthy merchant who had arrived recently on the *Griffin*, was to receive a nice lot on the eastern shore of the bay and that area was later called Haugh's Point.

The year ended with news that the Dutch had tried to force the Plymouth English out of their trading post-fort on the Connecticut River but had been repelled, emphasizing the need for the Bay to let Rev. Hooker and his followers go down there and establish a large, permanent settlement.

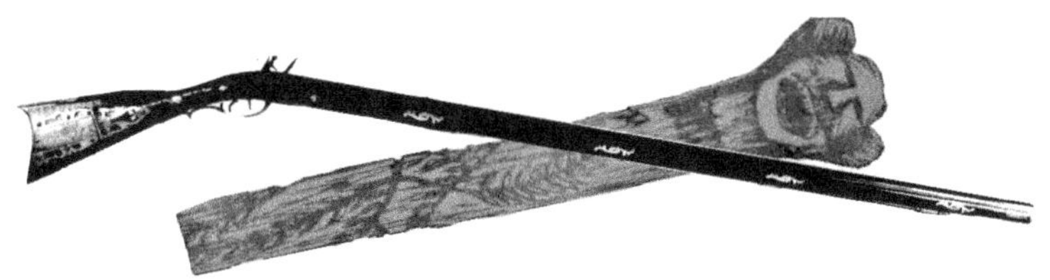

CHAPTER THIRTY-EIGHT

Ship Money

1634-5

The phrase and the onerous taxation the two words represented further alienated King Charles I's subjects in what was now called Great Britain as the crown had subjugated Ireland, Wales and (sometimes) Scotland. John Hampden, a gentleman from Buckinghamshire openly defied the writ and was arrested and thrown into the Tower awaiting trial. Previously Sir John Eliot and Sir Dudley Digges had been imprisoned during King Charles's second Parliament for speaking against the king's policies. Eliot had perished in the Tower but the others submitted in order to regain their freedom (such as it was under this dictatorial king). The king tried to retake the church lands in Scotland from their Tudor owners, another very unpopular move to the north of his kingdom. In 1630 he'd signed a peace treaty with France, giving them all the northern territory of the New World, a move that gave Gorges, Mason, Popham and others who had explored and were trying to settle the coast of northern New England fits. He also signed a peace treaty with Spain but any English sailor who veered into Spanish waters south of Virginia or northern waters near the Saint Lawrence seaway knew these treaties meant little outside of

Europe.

Oliver Cromwell was ruling in the name of King Charles I without any Parliamentary input as the Parliament had been dissolved by the king in 1629 and not recalled. Archbishop Laud opposed enclosures for sheep grazing but Cromwell said the Church was encroaching by claiming land that belonged to some of his fellow MPs. Cromwell then began prosecuting estate owners who practiced enclosure while ordering forests cleared in Warwickshire, Wiltshire, Devon, the Severn Valley in Chilerne and the Cotswolds for fuel and he turned the magnificent deer-laden woods into land for crops. The king asserted he had all rights to the forests and the villagers' protests fell on deaf ears. To create more land for crops the king ordered the draining of fens beginning with Hatfield Chase and Axeholm. Cromwell opposed the draining the fens in Essex and Sedgemoor. For this he was called 'Lord of the Fens' behind his back.

Sir Thomas Wentworth, Earl of Strafford, was now Lieutenant Deputy of Ireland, where he ruled with an iron fist. King Charles I loved him and was planning to grant him a patent for all the lands north and west of the Massachusetts Bay (New Hampshire). Lord Treasurer Weston, a Catholic like the queen (and many suspected the king) had a huge amount of influence in the court but Lords Saye and Sele and Brooke were able to get a large grant for a plantation at the mouth of the Connecticut River.

When the 'Ship Money' tax was declared, England almost had a civil war (it was perhaps the reason for what was to come five years later). Instead of port towns and cities paying taxes to support a royal Navy, it was dictated that every village, town and city in England had to pay these duties. The phrase 'no taxation without representation' was heard in every public house throughout the land. Wealthy landowners who were Puritan at heart but had not been dedicated enough to pull up roots and resettle now began to sell off their estates or hand them to a young son and board ships bound for New England, Virginia and the West Indies where their lands and money would be beyond the greedy grasp of Cromwell and the king.

Sir George Calvert, created Baron of Baltimore in Ireland by King James I, related to the Earl of Warwick and Sir Nathaniel Riche through marriages, past secretary of state and a shareholder of the Virginia Company, left England for Virginia in 1628. When he refused to take the Oath of Supremacy in Virginia he went back to England to obtain a separate patent, granted by King Charles I in 1632, originally from the Roanoke River extending west into the mountainous countryside. He'd been a member of the Council for New England, a position obtained though his daughter's marriage to Cecilius Arundel. He'd purchased part of the southeastern section of Newfoundland but his attempt to colonize it had failed in 1620. He, like Sir John Davis, had extensive lands in Ireland (although after leaving Ireland Davis sold his in order to buy and build manors in England). After bitter controversy and opposition from the Virginia planters in late February, 1634 his son Cecilius obtained funding for the transport of 200 settlers in the *Ark* and the *Dove*. The Second Lord Baltimore organized the expedition, which arrived in the Virginia Capes after sailing through the West Indies. Virginia's Governor John Harvey, although opposed to a Catholic settlement so close to his territory, was cordial and helped the new settlers, even sending word to Plymouth and Boston to accept what the king had granted.

By 1635 Sir William Courteen's colony on Barbados, begun in 1627, had over 1,600 residents growing tobacco, indigo and ginger. The main town of Bridgetown had neat rows of steep red-tile roofed Dutch-style whitewashed wood or brick houses and was very pleasant but sailors didn't like how the only navigable harbor had to be approached from the west due to constant eastern breezes that could founder ships on the shoals offshore. Although Courteen was originally from the Netherlands he was made an English Lord by King James I and was experimenting with sugar cane cultivation in the West Indies. (The cane was being grown by other Dutchmen in South America.) At this time Sir Thomas Warner was the Governor of Barbados, St Kitts, Nevis, Montserrat and Antigua.

It would be another two decades before sugar cane production in Jamaica and the Barbados plus other West Indian islands came into full swing but the Crown granted charters to wealthy Puritans of the Providence Company and granted them the right to settle Providence, Henrietta and the Tortugas, over which Anthony Hilton was appointed governor. Hilton had been living on St. Kitts but the Spanish had forced him off the island. On Providence Island Governor Hilton sent word that he planned to run the settlements like the Massachusetts Bay Colony but the ever present hostile Spanish spelled disaster for Tortuga where they raided the town, hanged the men, deported the women and children then burned the settlement to the ground. In response, King Charles I granted Providence Company the right to fight back with privateers, or government commissioned, sanctioned pirates. This part of the Caribbean was a dangerous, lawless place that most merchant ships avoided.

Capt. James Davis and his cousin Nicholas were two fearless captains sailing the Caribbean. James, preceded by his father Thomas, was an early Virginia merchant marine, expanding to Providence Island and, when sailing and political conditions were right, the Barbados and West Indies. William and George Davis preferred to manage ships from their onshore offices and rarely sailed below the Connecticut River in the New England. Captains Richard and Robert Tobias Davis preferred the northern waters and concentrated on the fishing industry and ship building or mast hauling from the vast forests below the French settlements on the St. Lawrence Seaway.

In the 1630s tobacco prices dipped so fur and timber trading took precedence. The trading companies knew that goods came into favor and demand, such as wool or wine, and faded, perhaps resurging but usually replaced by a different commodity so a good captain was always keeping a finger on the pulse of the consumer. The Davis men realized early on that New England would one day be mostly self-sufficient as it had an endless supply of natural resources and an almost endless supply of hard-working men to labor in its fields and woods. The main problem was the Savage. Until the tribes could be subdued, exterminated or driven west they posed a constant threat to settlement and trade. Even in the West Indies the Carib could suddenly appear and in one day destroy what had taken years of backbreaking work to build.

Every ship that weighed anchor and left England was a risky venture. However, the Puritan immigrants paid very well so most ships carried human cargo as well as livestock and manufactured goods from England or the Continent. As New England expanded so did the number of ports dotting the coast.

When the *Griffen* docked in Boston there was talk of a new settlement to be founded on the Connecticut River, a prime, rich fur trading area. Rev. Thomas Hooker and his Dorchesterites had requested permission from the Assembly to start a plantation there. By a vote of 15 to 10 it was approved, with many Assistants against it but Gov. Dudley in favor. The Assembly also voted against allowing England to send its own government officials over to rule them.

In 1635 a small party of men led by Rev. Hooker went overland to the Connecticut to decide on a settlement site during a winter that was bitterly cold. The harbors iced up and Richard Bellingham's servant fell through the ice and drowned.

Captain Wiggins, Governor of *Passaquatick* sent a case of sodomy before the Assembly to try but Dudley and Boston refused to handle it.

In March, 1635 at the General Court at Newtown Rev. Hooker preached on three great evils.

At the same Court there was discussion on Mr. Endicott's objection to the red cross on the flag. The issue was put off.

The Court ordered that brass farthings were outlawed and decreed that musket balls were to be used in lieu of them. The Commission for Militiary Affairs was created. In the General Election John Hayes (Haynes) was elected new governor. The Dorchesterites petitioned that charges against Israel Stoughton for circulating a treatise against the MBC's magisterial powers be dropped but the Court refused. It was decided that a body of common laws for the colony would be drafted. Ipswich members petitioned for a new settlement at *Quasacunquen* and the Court approved it, naming it Newberry. Roxbury and Watertown were also granted persmission to expand as long as they were still under Boston's governance. The rapidly growing population brought with it a rapidly growing livestock population and the grazing lands around Boston couldn't handle more cows and sheep.

In Saugus that spring a rift occurred amongst the brethren but it was smoothed over. A whale beached on Cape Cod and many people from Boston sailed across the bay to cut off some of the precious fat, which would be melted down to lamp oil.

The northern colonies sent an alarm about a French fleet off the fishing banks but nothing came of it.

In late April an 160 ton Dutch ship arrived from the small island of St. Christopher, which was encompassed with the Lesser Antilles into the French king's creation of the 'Compagnie des Isles d'Amerique'. The Earl of Carlisle immediately put forth an objection as some of the territory was within his 1627 English grant but the Spanish had forced the English and French off the island in 1629. Carlisle was sending a settlement of 150 men to the island to counteract the French landing of 500 men on it. The island was known for its superior tobacco but Capt. Huddleston brought 140 tons of salt and only 10,000 pounds of tobacco to Boston.

In early June two Dutch ships, one named the *Teasel*, arrived in Boston with 26 Flanders mares, three mixed breed horses and 88 sheep.

Over a dozen ships from England docked in the Bay in the summer of 1635. Many more went to Virginia, the Barbados, St. Domingo, the Somer Islands, St,. Christoper's and Newfoundland. Some shipwrecked and some settlers were drowned off the coast and there was a hurricane that summer. Nicholas Davis and his nephew, Dolor Davis's son John, came over in The *Planter.* Sir Richard Saltonstall and his wife and child sailed in the *Susan and Ellin* with a patent to start a colony at the mouth of the Connecticut River. William Fiennes, Viscount Saye and Sele. was active in obtaining it. A proposal to divide the land into 12 provinces, each with a governor in England, was not accepted by the king.

There was general pandemonium when a ship or fleet arrived with the settlers swarming the docks to obtain precious goods. The Assembly tried to prevent this by declaring each town should send only one delegate each to the docks but the order was ignored.

The Boston theocrats were focused on Salem, which supported its minister, Roger Williams in his apostasy. The town petitioned for a settlement at Marblehead but the Assembly refused as it was still interrogating Mr. Williams who had become estranged from his congregation.

In mid-October over 60 men, women and children from Newtown either walked or sailed to the Connecticut River to settle a town upriver they would name Hartford after Hertford in Hertfordshire, England. Winter came early and the *Rebecca* was icebound at the mouth of the river, its cargo unloaded by small ships from shore when.rain temporarily softened the ice. It tried to break free but was stuck on shoals.

The snow began early that winter and was very deep but it didn't stop the Dutch from trying to take back the river. Two English cannon on shore drove them back to Long Island.

Gov. Hayes and his assistants felt as if they were trying to hold sand in their hands. Everywhere people were spreading out, moving further and further away from Boston harbor and further and further away from the primary church there. Rev. Williams in Salem and Mrs. Hutchinson were two thorns in their sides and they knew they would have to resort to drastic measures to rein in these Antinomian factions.

England kept demanding the original patent, which they would not part with as they knew the despotic king would destroy it. King Charles I was threatening to take over control of the colonies and John Winslow went to England but was snubbed when he asked for help to fight off the French and Dutch (and savages). The only help came when Lyon Gardiner was sent over by Viscount Saye and Sele and Lord Brooke to take command of a fort he was to build at the mouth of the Connecticut, at a place to be called Saybrook.

Rev. John Wilson and John Winthrop, Jr. went to England to straighten out issues but were separated on their return and had to travel through Ireland and northern England to reach Barnstaple once again. Everywhere they went they spread word about the munificence of New England, which further encouraged more immigration.

The year 1635 was full of birthing pains for New England and to the south Maryland and Virginia. The constant threat from the French to the north and Spanish and Dutch to the south in the islands kept settlers on edge as they labored to clear forests, dig wells, plant fields and put up split rail fences or stone walls near their little saltbox houses. It was all work and no play, for any time not spent in the arduous toil of homesteading or hunting was spent in prayer and meditation, either at home or in the meeting houses. Yet the immigrants didn't complain. They had something here, in this new land that they hadn't had in England: freedom. Freedom from the Crown's tyranny. Even the gentry that gave lip service to King Charles didn't like him and new immigrants told of an undercurrent of pending civil war as Oliver Cromwell and the Parliamentarians were getting ready to move against the king. New Englanders thanked God they were far, far away from the reach of his conscripting armies and greedy taxes.

CHAPTER THIRTY-NINE

Of Homes and Forts

1635

Dolor was summoned to the 'shack' of the Houghtons soon after the *Abigail* brought them from Easton Bray, Dunstable. The Houghtons wanted a fine house built north of Boston but inland.

Leaving Margery behind in their rough-framed cottage in the new town of Concord, Dolor walked down a rough trail to meet with the three older Houghton brothers, one a butcher and one only four years old. A letter with certification of two justices accompanied the family that lived in Bedfordshire, Devonshire not far from Lord Cecil's manor, Woburn Abbey on the Dunstable Downs and the ancient Roman town of Cirencester. A brother, Robert Houghton, was a brewer in Southwark, part of London, and he and William Hiccok (Hitchcock) had sent ten barrels of gunpowder to Captain Underhill for Boston's Castle Fort on the *Abigail* so the Houghtons were given the choicest spot in Concord for their home. Dolor had been recommended to them in England as his ancestors were, like the Houghtons, displaced aristocracy from Wales. The Houghtons had originally occupied the little town of Brimpsfield, (Brimfield) which had a castle atop a grassy mound, but that was ancient history. The area was known for sturdy homes built of Cotswold stone.

There was an old Roman spa in Cheltenham but mostly the area had profited from sheep and woolen textiles and its line of public or ordinary houses since it was on the old Roman road leading north from London. Robert Houghton, being a brewer, along with a distant relative of Sir John Davis, operated pubs that men such as Lord Cecil and the Lord Saye and Sele often frequented in their travels between the king's court and their manors, giving them the ear of influential men.

The wealthy Rev. Peter Bulkeley (related to the northern Wales/Northwestern England family) and friends of the Willards, had come over on the *Susan and Ellin* the year before along with Simon Willard, Dolor's brother-in-law. Dolor and Margery had arrived a few weeks earlier on the *James*. His oldest son John had just arrived in New England, to help build the many homes the new immigrants needed.

Rounding a bend in the path that had crossed the *Muskataquid* River where Bulkeley had obtained six miles along its shore for his new town, Dolor sighed as he saw the rough assemblage of branches and thatch that was serving as little more than a tent for the Houghtons. But this was a big commission and if he could get a crew together quickly he and Margery could finish their own home before winter.

John Houghton greeted Dolor outdoors and poured him a large tankard of ale.

"I am grateful for your speedy reply," he said, his little brother standing next to him in the rough clearing.

"My pleasure," replied Dolor. He wiped his mouth on his sweaty sleeve and pulled drawings from his leather pack.

"I haven't been to yer family's place in Bedford," he said as way of apology, "but I've a'heard of the Earl Batshurst's manor. I always wanted to go to the Duntisborne Rous and see the herringbone work in the old Saxon church there." He paused then added, "You do realize that whereas we have an abundance of boulders, we have very little cut or dressed stone here."

John Houghton laughed, swigging his ale.

"Aye, my good man, we felt it was better to have a rough roof over our heads than no head to put a slate roof over."

Dolor, still recovering from six weeks of constant seasickness, sat down, soaking in the warm spring sunshine. He removed his hat and wiped his hair off his forehead.

"I have several commissions already in the Boston and Dorchester area," Dolor continued, “with full crews cutting, hewing and stacking timbers. But these are all just basic one and a half story saltboxes. I’d like to show you some drawings of what we might be able to do on your home with the materials available. Of course, the interior can be finished with more exotic woods, as long as the Boston council doesn’t take offense, but you are looking at a full two-story home with two fireplaces, a parlor and sitting room downstairs, two large bedrooms upstairs with a kitchen to the back on the ground level with its own fireplace and two servants’ rooms over. By English standards this is not fitting for a man of your status but you must realize we are just getting a brick kiln and ironworks in New England. If you will notice, I designed a small portico with two fluted columns at the entry to make it more classical.”

John nodded appreciatively.

The little boy looked at the drawings and pointed to the little trees Dolor had drawn on the lawn.

“I wike to ride horsies in the woods,” he said, sucking his thumb bashfully.

“Well,” Dolor said, kneeling to be at eye level with the little lord,”over here the forests come with the house and don’t belong to the Crown.”

John laughed again.

They discussed a price and Dolor apologized for having to charge extra for putting Houghton’s home at the top of his list. He then added, “In time I can return and build you a finer manor with quarried stone and leaded glass, even some stained glass windows.”

Another Houghton brother or cousin came out of the woods where he had been laying out their lot.

“Well, we’ll see if we stay here,” he said, wiping his hands on his breechclouts, “there is a lot of land to choose from and I’m actually bent towards the southern plantation on the Connecticut River. From what I hear the meadows there are lush and look more like England than this tree-filled wilderness.”

“Aye,” Dolor replied, “but ye must know you are safest building near the towns. The savages in these woods can be yer friend one day and shoot an arrow into yer heart the next. They have no religion other than wild caterwalling and jumping around a fire. They seem to worship the devil, is what I hear.”

The men laughed. Dolor didn’t. He’d heard plenty from his relatives about how they seemed to appear out of thin air from the trees, laden with bows, arrows, knives and clubs. It was against the law to sell firearms to them but the French fur traders sometimes did so a person had to be constantly searching the forests for signs of hostile natives. Dolor didn't feel comfortable working out here so far away from the settled towns.

"If I can get a crew pulled together, I will return with men and tools within a fortnight. Being a ways from the Concord common, we will have to have some type of lodging," he looked mournfully at the wigwam "and food and drink. It should take us less than a month to get something habitable with roof and walls but I might have to leave off and return after winter to work on interior plastering and moldings. We aren't allowed to put in wainscoting but if we say it is just pine paneling to stop the drafts the governor and his council might leave you alone. Although they tore down ol'Dudley's place over it," he said with a slight smirk.

The men shook hands. Dolor had known Houghtons in the south of England and he inquired about their relationship.

"Aye, we have family all over. You can thank Good King Henry the Eighth for that. He was like Robin Hood for us: he robbed from the church and gave to his loyal soldiers and supporters – and I know of no family that turned down a nice Catholic manor, abbey or estate," he added, giving Dolor a stern, challenging stare.

"'Tis true," Dolor said, pulling his leather satchel over his well-muscled shoulder, "but here we will make our own fortunes and not be living in the king's handouts."

He felt their Royalist eyes boring into his back as he began a the long walk back towards Lynn, where he was to stay with another client in a better, wooden shack. He hoped to gather his crew from there but skilled carpenters were as rare as hen's teeth. Worst case, he would have to go back to Boston and see if the ships had deposited any new skilled tradesmen in his absence. The ships arrived almost daily now. The *Rebecca* had freed itself from the Connecticut River outlet and sailed to Bermuda. It had docked in March with exotic goods such as potatoes, oranges and limes. Tragically there was a letter to a bondsman in the Colony from his father saying he had purchased his freedom but the young man had hanged himself just before it arrived. However, it was learned the young man had stolen from his master and was known to be of disreputable character so there was no widespread mourning for him.

Earlier, Dolor had gone to Dorchester to check on a home his crew was building there and he heard Mr. Mather had petitioned the Court to start a new church (congregation) in the settlement as most of the original had moved south to Windsor, on the Connecticut River. That winter they had lost a lot of cattle on the western side of the river but those on the eastern shore had thrived.

Dolor knew there were two factions in Boston: the Winthrop supporters and the Dudley men. Henry Vane, son and heir to Sir Henry Vane, King Charles I's comptroller of the Treasury had come over as a sort of ambassador to the colony. He'd been immediately admitted to the Boston church and from the start there was talk of making him governor at the next General Election, which the freemen did.

Sir Richard Saltonstall through Lords Saye and Sele and Brooke had sent supplies and an engineer, Lyon Gardiner, to build a fort at the mouth of the Connecticut River.

In the spring/late winter of 1636 the Rev. John Maverick died in Dorchester.

The Plymouth leaders sent a delegation to the Dorchesterites' new settlement near Windsor and demanded one-sixteenth of the profits from trade as they declared the plantation was within their patent. Windsor said no.

Captain John Mason, grantee of the northern coast, also died that spring – to the relief of the MBC as he and the Gorges were thorns in their side. Then in May Rev. Hooker took his congregation to Hartford on the Connecticut River.

Dolor avoided Boston as much as possible because there was constant religious contentiousness, one minister preaching something and the Bostonians taking offense, one merchant saying something the council or court thought blasphemous or heretical. In Concord there was an attitude of acceptance of differences, more of a *laissez- faire* attitude but Rev. Bulkeley had to be careful to tow the official line or he, like Roger Williams, would be called to Boston and banished.

The settlers had just recently heard that their friend, the trader John Oldham, had been murdered on an island in Narragansett territory and Roger Williams, who had settled west of the Plymouth plantation in Narragansett Bay acted as a mediator to try to broker a peace between the Pequots, Narragansetts and the English.

While negotiations were going on two pinnaces returned to Boston, one carrying Samuel Maverick, the Rev. John's son. Maverick, who with William

Blackstone, had settled in Massachusetts Bay – Blackstone on the Boston peninsula and Maverick, on Noddle's Island – after being dispersed from Mount Wollaston (Merry Mount as the Plymouth people called it). He'd helped Winthrop and his fleet and the early Salem settlers but under the increasingly strict, fundamental governance in Boston, he'd been forced to leave the colony. He sailed his pinnaces south to Virginia and the Barbados and had come back, only to find his father had died. But one pinnace, made of cedar in the Barbados, with another brought 14 heifers and 80 goats to Boston. Their corn had been sold to the Virginians who were starving, living on the weed-like purslane plant, he said. He had encouraged them to eat clams and mussels and to take their corn meal dry, as he had shown the early Bay settlers. But for the English, any meal without beef or mutton and bread and butter was considered inadequate. He told the that Captain Powell was one of the almost 2,000 Virginians who had died that winter.

As Dolor made his way over the causeway to Boston, Lt. Edward Gibbons, John Higginson and *Cutshamekin* were meeting to the south with *Canonicus* to find a way to resolve Oldham's murder. *Mianatomah* sent one of the murderers to Boston but claimed the other escaped. The mood was ugly in the town, lifted briefly by the launching of the 120 ton *Desire*, built by shipwrights in Marblehead.

Dolor arrived in time for the General Court session, in which the governor and assistants voted to raise 120 pounds to fund an army, commanded by Capt. John Endicott. Four companies under Capt. John Underhill, Captain Nathaniel Turner, Ensign Jenyson and Ensign Davenport were to travel with 90 men south to Block Island to enforce the fact that the English had the legal, God-given right to the lands and would not tolerate any savages killing English from Long Island bay to the Connecticut River. The MBC was under heavy pressure from its wealthy English financiers to lay down the law to the savages.

In Boston Dolor stayed in the crude house his oldest son Big John had erected as his crew was building a home for the Hutchinson family, located across from Gov. Winthrop's house.

"Taking good, strong lads off to fight savages is a waste of precious manpower," John told his father as he handed him a pewter tankard of warm ale.

"Right ye may be, son," Dolor replied, draining his drink in one long swallow. Ten-year old Little John, who was apprenticed to Jenkyns, refilled his mug.

"However, if we don't drive them out now we'll never get them to go away." Dolor continued, scratching his head. Ever since leaving England he'd never felt clean. Three carpenters, feeling equally grungy, had recently drowned bathing in the sea near Mt. Wollaston. The women did the laundry once a week, on Mondays following the Sabbath, but it was a laborious affair with water being hauled from common wells and requiring massive amounts of kindling to stoke the outdoor fires heating huge cast iron cauldrons of water. Subsequently, each person had only one undergarment to wear for the entire week (put on after their weekly bath on Saturday night) and outer garments were worn until they stunk so badly they had to be washed. Baby clothes and diapers took up most of the hot water. Other articles such as sheets were only done as needed so the entire colony had to adjust their concept of what constituted cleanliness. Lice and sand or animal fleas constantly infested their clothing and bedding and men such as John and Dolor and those operating the new windmill or water powered grinding mills also got "the itch" from grain or sawdust. Dolor's hair was greasy and he hated to put on his hat as it absorbed the stench and oils.

"'Tis all we need," John said, nodding. They were both sitting on log stumps, "We've got the likes of Craddock wanting to have us ruled by new men from England and now we've got troubles with savages to our south. We have enou' on our platter to keep us busy, what with trying to build meeting houses, schools, jails and homes."

"Aye, them houses don't just grow on trees," said Dolor, then realizing he'd made a joke, he laughed and John joined in.

"'Tis a good thing we've plenty o' them!" he replied, hoisting his tankard, "but I sure miss working with the nice honey colored stone we have in England."

Dolor agreed and they reminisced about how house building over there was so much more organized and civil than in the rough and ready towns they were erecting.

"I feel sometimes like I'm in England before the Romans came in with their roads and stone buildings and bridges. Now, them were real engineers!"

"Aye, and the Normans, even though they weren't very original, built good, solid, geometrically perfect perpendicular churches and manors."

Both father and son sighed.

Dolor then mischievously eyed John, “Do ye regret it, then?”

“By the Blood, No!” John heartily replied. He quickly looked around, making sure no one heard his blasphemous papist oath.

They stood up, going back to work. A tradesman took only small breaks. Work began right after breakfast (if you didn’t count livestock feeding) and continued to noon when the full dinner was laid out. After dinner they worked with one or two small breaks until sundown. During harvests the women would bring field laborers switchel, an apple cider, honey and salt mixture in special clay rings to slake their thirst but most drank beer or wine, the cheapest being sack, unless they were near a brook or stream with fresh, cold water.

Tea, which came to be the English’s favorite hot drink, hadn’t reached England or New England yet. For years the East India Dutch Company had been importing it from China to Europe and the bitter brew was being tried in Paris but only in the homes of the very wealthy – the same men who had first tried tobacco in England. The French king had recently decreed that tobacco could only be obtained in France under a prescriptions at apothecaries. Tea and sugar from the West Indies would be another full decade in getting to New England. The bitter tea needed sweetening so the two items arrived almost simultaneously, each needing the other like alum and dyes.

“Well, ‘tis back to a’buildin’ this house for the Hutchinsons,” John said to his father under his breath, “That Mrs. Hutchinson is a right one. Ye should hear her go on about the scriptures! I swear she was born to be a preacher but we both know women can’t be in the pulpit.”

Dolor clapped his hard, full hand on John’s sweaty shoulder, “Don’ go a’listening to all these preachers, boy. Just do yer work, put on yer Sabbath clothes and sit in the pews, standing when ye are told, nodding when ye are told to, singing a bit when told to. Just take no truck of their fancy words. They can run on at the mouth like a river, babbling on and on about words in the Bible, using them any which way they please to make their point. I’ve a’heard Rev. Cotton – and does he ever go on and on – but I can’t say as I think he has a monopoly on God. Just make no waves and we’ll keep getting commissions to build their meeting houses and homes. Once ye get on the bad side of Winthrop and his group ye’ll find no more work, this I can tell ye.”

With that, they picked up their tools and returned to building the non-spiritual things the Puritans needed. Across the way they heard William Davis blacksmith at his smithy, banging metal on metal, whiffs of smoke from his furnace carried on the sea breeze. Scents of horses and cattle wafted over and the cackling of hens could be heard as the sun sunk lower over the Bay accompanied by the annoying high-pitched sound of mosquitoes looking for their daily blood meal.

To the south, the first real battle between the English and the savages was just beginning.

In England Sir Ferdinando Gorges had a huge ship built but when it was launched it broke its supports and sank into the sea. Later Gorges sent many settlers over on ships to Yarmouth Point, some from Wales but he never made the voyage himself. Capt. John Mason (who had been funded by Sir Ferdinando) had submitted a petition to the Council for New England to divide the country into 12 provinces but King Charles I turned it down after Gorges's huge ship sunk.

CHAPTER FORTY

Enemies Without and Within

1636-7

Captain James Davis had been staying in a small house in Boston in between trips to England, Virginia and the West Indies. At the time of the muster to fight the savages in the south, he volunteered to go along and pilot one of the ships bringing the soldiers to Narragansett-Pequot territory. There, the savages tried to board their vessels but were driven off by musket shot as the soldiers climbed the embankment and went on the offensive. By the time it was all over the sky was cloudy with smoke and the men who came back a week or so later were blackened by soot but they were whooping and celebrating.

"We showed them good!" one of the fellows said as he lifted a tankard of ale. The men had bathed in the sea but their clothes were in sad shape.

"Right ye are, son!" another toasted back as they told the sailors about how they had chased down savages and penned them in their fort and then set fire to the whole thing, killing every man, woman, child in the place.

"I thought I smelled meat cooking," one of the sailors joked.

Capt. James was not amused. It was not the first encounter he'd had with murdering savages as he'd seen what happened in Virginia. He knew today's victory would fester and they would be seeking revenge, as it was their code.

As soon as they offloaded the men in Boston harbor James sailed north to meet with the Bristol ships that had brought people, livestock and goods to *Pasamaquash* for Sir Ferdinando Gorges's plantation at *Agamenticus.*

He met with John and his second wife Sarah and stayed a couple of nights before taking a load of timber, sassafras and sarsaparilla south as the herbs helped fight the fevers that plagued Virginia and the islands.

From the Bay new towns could be seen springing up at Saugus, Marblehead and all around the original peninsula of Boston. The sounds of trees being chopped down and two-man saws cutting them into lengths, of oxen dragging loads of logs to the new towns, of hammering of iron nails into wood and of iron on iron rang out across the grey-blue waters of the Bay.

Fields of corn and rye waved in the late summer breezes and James smiled as he set sail for the warmer climes of Virginia. His father Sir Thomas had a large tobacco plantation in an inlet with his own wharf, as was customary down there. His third wife was very attractive, years younger than the elderly Thomas, and James knew he would be well entertained with good wines, fine hams, corn meal pudding and sweet cakes. James vacillated between wanting to bring Cicely over or keeping the estate in Little Budsworth. In a sense, he felt he had the best of all worlds: a nice, well established manor in England to retire to during the hurricane season in the Atlantic, a small dwelling in Boston where he could conduct business and touch base with his relatives, plus his relatives in Virginia where he had a small plantation, and the Barbados.

His route didn't take him near Roger William's bay or the Connecticut River as, with the ongoing hostilities he felt it better to give the entire area wide berth. His first mate was his cousin George's son Samuel, who had captained the *Gabriel* until it shipwrecked off Sable Island while returning to England.

They were sailing their cousin Nicholas's ship the *Trader's Increase* and James's almost elderly cousin Richard was still captaining the *Gift of God,* which he, George and William ran along with the *Swan.* Thomas also owned the ship named for his firstborn son: the *James*. Sir Thomas Rys Davis had four sons: Captain Thomas, Captain Robert, Captain James, and John. Most were seagoing but some preferred to be landlubbers. Between English and Irish estates, plantations in the

Barbados and Jamaica plus Virginia and the Sagadahoc territory north of Boston the Davis men had their fingers in many pies. They had relatives that had settled on land such as Dolor and his son John plus Barnaby, William, Humphrey in the islands and a Robert Tobias in Yarmouth who captained a fishing ship. Richard's son Nathaniel was in the Kittery area, as was Joseph, Daniel and Theo, who had been made Constable in Saco, where Thomas lived. Because of the Irish intermarriages, the pure Welsh line of Davies or Davises was changing. The older Welsh sons had married into English gentry or merchant families so the only David left was in the Old Country. He was the Church of England minister in Conway and the last time James had docked in Glamorgan he had a hard time understanding his ancestors' Gaelic tongue. By 1635 the older generation was giving way to the next and there were lots of Roberts, Thomases, Jameses, Johns and William Davises from Maine to Virginia.

Unbeknownst to Captain James, Boston was facing a different enemy: an enemy within as Rev. Wheelwright and his sister Anne Hutchinson began speaking against the Puritan theocracy, against Rev. Cotton's preaching, and indeed, against the entire concept of attaining Divine Salvation through good works. Like Rev. Williams who had been banished the previous year the Wheelwrights and Hutchinson insisted that Grace was something the Lord gave. It could not be earned through good works alone, although they were to be encouraged, but that God considered one a Saint, or Elected, from birth and no amount of charity and philanthropy and kindness could buy one's way into Heaven. These teachings found fertile soil in the Puritans as the concept of Salvation through Good Words smacked to them of the Catholic practice of selling indulgences for deceased relatives in purgatory. They felt one could not buy Salvation and that anyone with a Bible could read the Scriptures and understand the Word of God and didn't need to sit for hours and hours as a minister debated with an unseen questioner about the meaning of the verses and books in the Old and New Testament.

Dolor's son Big John, like many of the Kentish men, began to question if he wanted to remain in Boston or to move back north, further away as Dolor had. Rev. Wheelwright had begun exploring north of the Merrimac River in hopes of taking a non-Winthrop congregation there.

Capt. James was getting long in the teeth and knew his active sailing days would be ending soon, as had William and George's. James's sons favored New England so he wasn't sure who would inherit the manor in Little Budsworth upon his death. Sir John, son of Sir John, had stayed in Creedy, England and he had the family coat of arms hanging in a new manor in Twickenham. Such things as titles and coats of arms were not fully appreciated in New England where a man's moral pedigree was worth more than a suit of armor and shield hanging on a decrepit manor wall.

Looking at the endless miles of coastline off starboard he couldn't blame those who left England. Unlike England which was all settled, each village connecting to another similar village with a grey stone church and square tower and market square and houses all lumped close together, this land had no limits. It went on and on and on and the only obstacle to taking it was the Savage and the French to the north. Once they were cleared out Englishmen such as the Davis men could take their fill of fertile fields with running streams or rivers and acres and acres of big, thick hardwood trees and pines. King Charles could try to wrest the land back but the men who had trod its soil knew how precious this place was and would fight to the death to keep it.

CHAPTER FORTY-ONE

A Time of War, A Time of Healing

1637

In January 1637 Nathaniel Turner's house in Saugus, a new settlement between Boston and Salem, caught fire during the night from an oven that hadn't been properly banked. His neighbor in Southwark, John Houghton heard of the disaster and sent word that he would help him rebuild. Unfortunately most of Nathaniel's possessions burned down with his house. The man was totally distraught at losing everything he had brought from England.

Dolor was sent over to talk to him about getting a new house built in Saugus, which had a lot of bog iron. John Winthrop Jr. was looking to get a group of English investors to back an ironworks there with a forge at the site.

Capt. Turner's son William was helping him snuff out small fires that kept springing up around the ruins.

Dolor straightened his cravat and smoothed his light brown hair which was getting thin.

"I'm sorry for yer loss, that I am," he said, squinting through the acrid smoke as snow flakes floated down.

"'Tis God's judgement on me," Nathaniel said mournfully.

Dolor cocked his head to one side, waiting for an explanation.

"'Twas my order that burned out a village in Ireland. God has passed His judgement on my actions."

Dolor sat down on a rough bench. The snow was starting to come down a littler harder.

"John says ye are to come and stay with him in Concord in his house there that I'm almost done a'building."

As he said this Dolor's son Simon came down the path with a team of oxen and cart.

Nathaniel snorted angrily.

"Ye'll have no need for that!"

Simon surveyed the total destruction but then said, "Well, we can bag up yer hens and rooster and put your smaller livestock in the cart. Everyone in Concord is taking up a collection of goods and my father will be out here as soon as the weather clears to begin a new home for ye."

Nathaniel held back tears. He was a soldier; a fighter. He wasn't used to the pity and charity of others. His voice was gruff as he led the way to his ramshackle barn.

Dolor walked beside him, their thick leather shoes making wet prints in the snow.

"I was going to start on another house next week but John asked me to put your's first so that I will. As for it being the wrath of the Lord, I saw what happened in Dorchester twenty years or so ago and I can't believe God would do such a thing to good people. 'Tis just a natural thing, fire a'getting out o' hand. Happens all the time, Captain."

As they loaded the cart the Turner family roused from their trance and William Turner spoke up,

"Father, the savages would've burnt us all alive in this house and never have felt a drop of remorse. Ye know this o' them: they are absolutely cruel, that they are. Cruel and Godless."

Nathaniel tried to smile but he was broken.

"Thank ye my friend, Dolor," he said as they began the walk west to Concord, "But I'm no certain I'll be staying in Lynn or Saugus or even Boston. We might be a'moving south to one of those new villages on the upper Connecticut River or down to the coast after the savages settle down."

Dolor cast him a questioning look.

"Aye? Aren't ye afraid of them taking revenge on ye for being an English soldier?"

"Nay, we all look alike to them. Didn't they say that after they killed Oldham? They said they didn't know the difference between Stone, who was Dutch, and the English."

Dolor scratched his neck.

"Well, all this eye for an eye stuff from the Bible is well and good, I suppose, but for meself, I'd just like to live and let live. Turn the other cheek, like Jesus said."

Nathaniel stopped and gave Dolor a hard look, his eyes flinty.

"There'll be no living and let living with these savages! Ye didn't see what they did to poor old John Oldham – cut off his hands and feet while he was still alive, one at a time. Probably cooked them and were going to eat them, too if John Gallop hadn't arrived when he did!"

Dolor shivered, pulling his heavy woolen cloak tighter.

The group was watching the woods on the long trek inland as winter was the season when the savages liked to wage war. He'd heard about the Tarrantines to the north, about how they were cannibals.

"At least ye'll be safe in Concord," he told him, the snow now completely coating their capes and hats.

Nathaniel sighed.

It was a long, somber walk with the women and children, bundled in neighbor's quilts as all they had were the night shifts and night shirts on their backs, riding in the cart, the boys herding the livestock behind. One of the little girls clutched a tattered, smoke smelling cloth doll as she sobbed into her mother's breast. In each man and woman's heart there was an unspoken longing for the peace and quiet of England.

Nathaniel spat into the snow, "If that Mr. Cotton dares to say we are blessed for not losing a life, I swear I'll strike him!"

"Aye," Dolor muttered. They had a lot of things to be thankful for but this wasn't one of them.

It was a stormy January and towards the end of the month the Boston church called a Fast Day to pray for the Protestants in Germany and Puritans in England, to pray for peace within the churches and for the young settlements in Connecticut.

The *George* from Bristol barely limped into Plymouth with a spent main mast.

In February a group of the settlers had had enough and boarded a vessel to sail back to England. The Rev. Cotton and Rev. Wilson went aboard and with many exhortations and pleadings, talked some out of leaving. The argument over Works vs Grace was tearing the unity of the Boston church apart. Winthrop and Dudley, although at odds personally, both put on an united front to try to keep everyone in harmony. At all costs dissension was not to be known in England where there were many at Court, including the King, who wanted to revoke the Massachusetts Bay Colony's charter and redistribute the lands to the current favorites.

The March General Court was contentious. Many were calling for a separation of church and state in the legislature and Rev. Wheelwright caused a scandal by writing an essay in which he called those who preached Justification by Good Works the Antichrist. He was charged with sedition and ordered to Boston to address the Assembly's next meeting.

In Connecticut *Mianatonah* sent a Pequot hand and 40 fathoms of wampum in reparations to Boston and Captain Underhill enlisted 20 men to man the Saybrook fort as the savages (and Dutch) were still restless.

In Concord the congregation held a Day of Humiliation as they prepared to ordain Mr. Bulkeley as teacher and Rev. James as their pastor. Both ministers had been Church of England preachers and they spent the day praying for forgiveness for their sins of following it and not being ardent Puritans in England.

As spring arrived Mr. Haynes moved to the Connecticut River valley. He reported back that the savages had killed six Englishmen as they toiled in their fields in Wethersfield and killed three women, kidnaped two maids and killed at least 20 cows.

And the leaders in Plymouth kept harassing the settlers and Boston court, claiming the land belonged to their patent and not the Massachusetts Bay Colony and that Boston was of no help to them against the French in respecting their rights to their northern trading villages. Winslow told the Boston court that Haynes's settlement along the river and its mouth had incited the Pequots and their actions had been defensive.

The May General Court was held in Newtown and Winthrop was elected governor with Dudley as his deputy governor. Endicott, Stoughton and Saltonstall were among the Assistants they chose. A Day of Humiliation was held as ministers and teachers prayed together and tried to reconcile their differences about Justification by Works or Grace or even both.

Stoughton and Rev. Wilson raised 160 men and 16 of *Mianatonah's* Narragansett braves in response to the sachem's desperate plea for English help against the Pequots. In addition, Capt. John Mason and a small company slew eight Pequots and took seven squaws and the Dutch began negotiating a hostage exchange of the squaws for the two captured English maids. A day after the Fast Day word was received from Rev. Williams that Mason and an army of volunteer soldiers had burned the Pequot fort at Mystic to the ground in late May and all the savages in the area were driven out.

CHAPTER FORTY-TWO

The War with the Pequots

1637

Sir Ferdinando Gorges suffered a setback when the large ship he was going to load with Welsh and English settlers bound for New Somersetshire (his father's grant between the Piscataqua and Sagadahoc) broke as it was launched off its cradle. However, his nephew William Gorges went over to govern the settlements (holding court at Saco in 1635). In June, 1637 the *Hector* brought a commission from King Charles I stating Gorges could appoint commissioners to govern his province but Boston ignored it. George Cleves also brought a commission giving him the right to settle from Saco west to the great lake of *Iacoyuce* (Iroquois or Lake Champlain). The Cleves and Gorges families had been fighting over land grants for years and with Richard Tucker were constantly land speculating. In spite of their internal battles, none of the down-easter settlers felt a strong bond to Boston.

The King let it be known that for 3,000 'merks' a man could buy the title of Baronet and get 30,000 acres of land in Nova Scotia.

In 1621 King James I had given a charter to Sir William Alexander to the area but it was now under French control. In 1635 Charles La Tour was running a profitable fish and fur trading operation in Acadia. His rival Charles d'Aulnay with Cardinal Richelieu's settlers were on the St. John River on lands the Virginia Company's Samuel Argyll had wrested from the French many years before, demolishing the fort at Pt. Royal. The Scottish Alexander had tried via his royal baronetcy to begin settlements in Acadia on what he called New Scotland (Nova Scotia). Due to English and French politics the area was claimed by both and the Scottish had been routed and sent packing back to England on a French ship after King James I gave the territory back to the French.

On board the *Abigail,* captained by Capt. Richard Davenport and his son and the *Hector* were four more ministers including Rev. Samuel Eaton and his brother Theopholis and merchants Edward Hopkins and Humphrey Davenport. Hopkins was a friend of John Haynes, who had moved to Connecticut. With the exception of Nicholas Easton, a tanner, the prominent families that went to the Connecticut settlements were wealthy. Nicholas, from Wales, settled in Newbury but, like his friend John Davis, got involved with the Wheelwrights and Hutchinsons and later went to Rhode Island.

In Gorges's *Agamenticus* ship the *Abigail* more Davis men came over: Theopholis, or Theo, who, with Humphrey and John and William would keep a hand in on the New England and West Indies, Philip, the 12 year old runaway son of Philip Francis Davies (who indentured himself to William Ilsley as a shoemaker), plus William and Isaac from Wales and another John, who unfortunately drowned not long after landing as the pinnace he was hauling goods in shipwrecked on the shoals. Robert Tobias, a Welsh relative and owner of the *Tristrum and Jane* and a close friend of Sir Needham, and his grandson Robert Davis, brought more people over including his infant son Tristrum.

****

Philip Francis Davies was in Hartford searching for his illegally indentured son at the time the English decided to war with the Pequots and he joined up as a sergeant in the campaign against the Pequots. He, with Captain John Mason, Miles Standish, Lyon Gardiner and Captain John Underhill had been professional soldiers, trained under Sir Horace Vere and Sir Thomas Fairfax, Cromwell's lead general, in the Netherlands in a lingering war that would last thirty years.

Miles stayed in Plymouth to defend it but his son went out with Lt. William Holmes's troops, joining Lt. Seely's contingent from Hartford, Windsor and Wethersfield. John Gallop, Jr, enlisted as an interpreter as he had been sailing the area with his father for years and John Pynchon volunteered to sail the men to the fort at Saybrook. Simon Willard (made lieutenant) had also served on the Continent with Vere but, like Miles, he had to stay behind to defend his town (Concord).

The Pequots weren't in the north and in spite of the territorial spats the land was getting settled beginning in the mid 1620s with *Agamenticus*, a half day walk from the port of York. Its heavily forested mount was a great lookout point with a view from Cape Ann to Cape Elizabeth and a landmark for sailors. Further north was Piscataqua, Shapleigh's plantation at Kittery Point, the next was Black Point, basically owned by Capt. Thomas Commock and Henry Josselyn and farmed by their tenants, many of them indentured poor from Ireland. Then there was the Lygonian Plantation, mostly a trading and fishing post and a scattering of outlanders along the *Androscroggin* River. Near its falls on either side was the *Pemaquid* Plantation.

The passenger Nathaniel Davenport on the *Hector* was later to be a captain of the *Gabriel,* which he and Samuel Davis would take turns captaining. (Samuel Davis of Haverhilll later married Nathaniel's widow, but that is another story.) As with most 'ancestral' families, sons were given the same names in honor of brothers, uncles, etc. which sometimes caused confusion in New England when a man identified himself. Amongst themselves they would give nicknames such as 'Black Tom' for Capt. Thomas Davis who sailed the *James* back and forth to Virginia. Like Thomas Fairfield he got his name from his jet black hair and eyes and Moorish complexion. Captain Black Robert Davis had come about his name through the same features.

To the north of Massachusetts Bay Gorges gave a grant of 8,000 acres just below Sheepscott on the Kennebec River to Sir Richard Edgecomb who owned Mount Edgecomb in Devon in hopes that men of wealth would settle to supplement the fishermen, farmers and trappers living in the territory. The Gilmans, Allens, Mavericks, Algers, Aldworths, Elbridges, Dyers, Godfreys, Humphreys (John Humphrey was the treasurer for the New England Company until its dissolution), Pepperells, Spencers, Symonds, Hiscocks, Mountjoys and other families of worth were entrenching themselves along the north coast and inland along the rivers but most of the wealthy from England, Ireland and Wales were going to Boston and the new Connecticut settlements.

Capt. Robert Tobias Davis from Ireland and Wales, Nicholas Davis and his nephew Daniel (son of George) were early settlers of the northern lands. Captains Richard and Nicholas Davis owned the *Trader's Increase* that sailed from New England to Barbados and on one trip transported their family friend, Humphrey Davenport to Hartford from the island.

Although New England was evolving as a separate country people from every town had links to new arrivals who founded new towns through in-laws or neighbors. Someone like Fulkes Davis, from Glamorgan, who settled in Hartford but was banished as being of immoral character, tainted their relatives as far away as Sagadahoc. It was vitally important to be accepted by a town as every community was dependent on its members for survival.

During the Pequot War the Massachusetts and Connecticut governors ordered all men 18 and over to carry arms when traveling to or from public meetings. This was easy as the young men began militia training with their elders as soon as they could carry a musket.

As was common amongst the southwestern families in England and Wales, a son would become a captain, others part owners or outright owners of ships, others took to weaving sailcloth or trained in trades important for sailing: black smithing, carpentry, coopering or rope making. And some learned knitting as well as sewing for warm sweaters, scarves, caps and mittens needed mending or replacing on long voyages. Another one or two would serve as agents on land, obtaining cargo to be shipped and buyers for incoming cargo. New England needed all these tradesmen, too, and a shipbuilder was especially welcome. Whether or not in the maritime trade, boys in New England, apprenticed themselves to learn trades from fathers or friends in their towns.

While sharing a pint in a Hartford ordinary after the short swamp fort battle with the Pequots, an enlisted relative, Fulkes Davis, told Lt. Philip Francis Davis the whereabouts of his son Philip. He immediately boarded the *Swan* and sailed north to Saco where a cousin Thomas was living.

News of who he was preceded him and as he entered a public house near the harbor he was immediately accosted by locals eager to hear about the great English victory in Connecticut.

"I heerd ye saved Capt'n Mason's life!" a farmer yelled, raising his tankard of ale in salute.

Cries of "Tell us then!" sounded round the small room and Philip recalled how he'd arrived behind a savage just in time to cut his bowstring as he aimed for Capt. Mason. He told how a couple of citizen soldiers survived arrows shot at their throats because of the thick knots of their handkerchiefs and how Lt. Seely pulled an arrow out of his eyebrow but kept on fighting.

"When we got them cornered like foxes in the swamp, the battle became ours. They couldn't get out and we had them surrounded. Their forts were set afire and we began rounding up any women, children and old people who escaped into the frozen swamp and sent them under guard by foot to Boston. After the fort was fired and all the indians inside burned up the indians were finished and I'm glad to tell ye the savages learned what happens when they war with Englishmen!"

"Now," he lowered his voice, "I'm looking for a young Davis – "

The public house keeper held up his hand.

"I'm terrible sorry, sir. He drowned with his small ship just t'other day."

Philip felt the blood drain from his head to his feet.

"My boy Philip drowned?"

The innkeeper exhaled and smiled, "Nay, I got the wrong Davis! 'Twas an Irish John Davis as wrecked on the shoals carrying cargo south. We get wicked winds and squirrely undertows up here. Men and small ships go down all the time but usually we sound the alarm and the men are saved and sometimes the cargo, too."

One of the sunburned farmers with very light blond hair pushed forward and said,

"The shoemaker, Bill'm Iseley and his son have a young apprentice by the name o' Philip. Be he yer young pup?"

Philip set his face, smoothing his thin moustache and goatee. He was the son of Sir John, the famous navigator. His son would not be called a 'pup'!

He set his pewter tankard down on the rough bar and asked the whereabouts of the shoemakers.

"Down tha road a ways and take a left. He's set up in a little shed sort of place."

"Much obliged," Philip said with a nod. He had the money to buy back his son's indenture but wondered if he should send him to the Barbados to work in the fields to teach him a lesson. Or perhaps Bermuda if he was truly repentant. Looking around at the lush woods, craggy cliffs, wild sea and total abundance of this land Philip could see the attraction, especially if one were a die hard Puritan and a target of Laud and the King.

He inhaled the cool sea air, watching the gulls on the wharves.

As he walked down the dirt path he realized he was facing a battle with young Philip that would stress him more than the rough and ready combat with the Pequots. He straightened his doublet and cravat, took his large beaver hat off and smoothed his hair before knocking on the door of the small cordwainer's shop where he could hear soft 'tap tap tap'.

Philip looked up from his bench and dropped the thick leather shoe he was affixing a buckle to,

"Father!"

Bill Ilsley looked up too and sucked in his teeth.

"It's time to go home, son," Philip said as he pulled the boy up by one arm.

After he'd settled his son's debt to the shoemaker and shoved him aboard the *James* in the harbor he sat on the wooden bunk next to him.

"You have two choices, young man."

Philip dodged what he thought was a blow as his father raised his lace strewn sleeve.

"You will immediately go to Somerset school and train for Cambridge and the ministry, which is what your 'aunt Judith' Harvard wants – "

Philip groaned as his father referred to his deceased grandfather's overbearing, book loving fiancé.

"Or ye will go to Bermuda or Jamaica and work for the Beckfords for a couple of years to pay me back for your debt to Mr. Ilsely by planting, weeding and picking tobacco or cotton – or that new crop people are talking about: sugar." The Beckfords owned land in Tisbury near Edward's estate and were building the new, huge manor, Fonthill Splendors.

Philip almost fainted with relief and happiness.

"Could I go to Bermuda, Father? Please?"

"Ye know ye'd never know ye are a grandson of a man known for his love o' learning and books."

"I think I got his adventuring spirit instead, Father," Philip replied, trying very hard not to smile.

The big ship rocked heavily at anchor and father and son caught up on news while waiting for the captain order the anchor weighed. Young Philip was full of stories about his voyage over, how he helped the deck hands and climbed the rat lines and sat in the crow's nest and what the Irish laborers told him about the cruelty of their imprisonment.

Philip senior sighed as he listened. It was always the same: England conquers, England imprisons, England deports to lands it conquered. But he knew the other countries were doing the same thing around the globe. A couple of years under the blistering sun in Bermuda would sweat the eagerness out of the boy. And gain his father a foothold in the West Indies, the profits from which could fund the building of a new manor near Dartmouth.

But first he'd track down the recruiting agent (thief) who had spirited away his son, selling him to a disreputable captain in Bristol. There would be a few scores to settle on that account. Philip felt man stealing and selling people as slaves were the lowest things a human could do to another human. When he served in the army under Gen. Vere he'd seen some atrocities but the selling of a human to another, even for a period of "indenture" was wrong. The slave owners worked their servants 14 hour days in the summer and grudgingly paid off those who survived the suit of clothes and new shoes and whatever money or land was due at the end. Philip Francis had learned enough about his father's adventures in foreign countries to know that Englishmen should be held to a higher standard than the un-Christian savages. Judith was always talking about raising men up through education instead of lowering people down to the meanest denominator. Every time Philip ventured into a sailors' bar in ports he saw sleazy recruiters talking to young men and women about how they'd be better off selling themselves as laborers to English masters. Captain Matthew Craddock of the *Abraham* was one of the worst offenders, announcing his arrival in port with drums and fanfare as he gathered up poor, ignorant souls to be shipped to Virginia. It made him sick and angry. He would get definite payback plus interest from the men who tricked his young, impressionable son into being a servant to a lowly shoemaker!

****

In August Revs. Hooker and Stone, coming from Roger Williams's village of Providence arrived in Boston, joined by John Pynchon, Roger Ludlow and a dozen other men who came by the Bay Path trail. They presented to the Assembly a lock of hair and scalp from *Sassacus*, his brother and five other prominent Pequot sachems who hadn't been killed in the swamp but were captured fleeing north to the Mohawks. Pequot heads were also dropped at the feet of Governor Winthrop and Lt. Governor Dudley along with wampum and scavenged goods from the villages.

Late in August the hands of the three Pequots who had slain Captain Stone were also brought to Boston and put on public display.

James Davis in Virginia had a lot at stake for he received some of the Pequot slaves from the swamp fight for his tobacco plantation; others were sent to Bermuda but Capt. Peirce was blown off course and delivered them to Province Island instead.

The *Abigail* brought Revs. Eaton and Davenport to *Quinepack* (New London) to establish a plantation there.

Gov. Winthrop had printed a leaflet listing 82 Antinomian "errors" and a synod was called to address these. In the meantime Revs. Cotton and Wheelwright had pasted over their differences and were attempting to present an united front but eventually they all agreed on three "errors" to charge against Wheelwright. The Boston synod said there could be no union with Christ without a person's profession of faith; that the Justification couldn't be called Sanctification without the church member receiving evidence of that Sanctification; that Christ works through a saved person but isn't dwelling within; that God does not Justify a man or woman before they are 'called' by their conversion experience and a man might do good works to show his conversion but only good works cannot make a believer a Christian. Wheelwright took exception to most of the above.

On the last day of the synod it was further declared that if a woman held a meeting (specifically Anne Hutchinson who met weekly with 60 women to give prophecy and interpretation of the Scriptures) she was a disorderly person; that only Elders could answer questions after a sermon; that if a person was called to appear at the Assembly because they had criticized the elders and ministers that person could be forcibly brought by the magistrate to stand trial; that if a person requested leave from a congregation because he disagreed with its teachings another congregation should not accept him or her as they were heretics.

Dudley and those who wanted less religious rule and more freedom to worship were almost apoplectic at these new 'laws'.

In October a Day of Thanksgiving for the victory over the Pequots and for the new laws was called. John and Nicholas Davis and many of the Connecticut soldiers including Benedict Alvord, John's carpenter friend from Windsor. did not attend, not because they weren't happy the Pequot menace was eliminated but because of Winthrop's dictatorial rulership. To them, the last election had been a major step backwards for their new country.

In November *Mianatonah*, the chief Narragansett sachem went to Boston with a delegation pledging peace and was given permission by the Assembly to avenge the insult of *Ninigret* who refused to surrender his Pequots. In all, about 800 Pequots had been captured and either enslaved by other tribes or delivered to the English.

The minister John Eliot was moving amongst the tribes, converting sachems and their followers and there was talk of putting converted savages into 'praying villages' where they could learn the Bible and the English God yet be free from threats by their fellow savages and English settlers who lived in fear of attack.

Virginia and the West Indies took some of the male captives for field laborers and some of the women for domestics but in general there was vast distrust and many of the Pequots slipped away, aided and abetted by the inland Nipmuck tribes as they made their way north to the Mohawks or other northern tribes in unsettled French territory.

With them in their breasts they carried the fire of revenge.

CHAPTER FORTY-THREE

Banished!

1637-8

The year ended with a victory for Winthrop and Cotton but a defeat for religious freedom as Rev. John Wheelwright, Anne Hutchinson and others were disarmed (a severe hardship) and banished from the Massachusetts Bay Colony. Wheelwright knew this was going to happen and went with his wife and two children to the falls at Swampscott while seeking a permanent place far away from Boston.

Ten families of his followers from Mt. Wollaston and the Boston area went there. John Humphrey, disgusted with the intolerance of the Boston church, housed the Wheelwright family in his large Tudor-style house with its overhanging second story.

Wheelwright's early supporters included the families of Big John Davis ,Augustine Storre (Story), Darby Field, John Compton, Edward Calcord, Nicholas Needham, Samuel Hutchinson, William Wentworth, Richard Morris, Thomas Wright, Henry Elkins, George Walton, Samuel Walker, William Coddington, Henry Vane, Richard Dummer, Richard Bulgar, Philomon Purmort, Isaac Gross, Christoper Marshall, George Bates, Thomas Wardell and William Wardell, Thomas Wilson, George Rusbone and the shipwright Robert Moulton and his brother Thomas of

Newbury.

Not all were able to leave immediately and some, like Anne Hutchinson, who was examined by the Boston church and banished in March, traveled further north to *Piscatatqua* plantation. She ended up going from there south to settle across the Narragansett Bay from Roger Williams in Rhode Island as Boston told her she couldn't settle near Plymouth where the new settlement of Sandwich on Cape Cod was being planted by families from Saugus and Lynn. Rev. Batchellor of Saugus also settled a new town on the Cape named Yarmouth but he was too old and feeble to be the minister so a younger man was chosen to lead the congregation.

However, winter was a poor time for traveling and this New England winter was harsher than previous ones so the band of exiled Antinomians felt as isolated and persecuted as the original Separatists had two decades earlier in England. From Swampscott Wheelwright planned to go north to Hampton but Winthrop let it be known that it was claimed by the MBC which set up a settlement there so Wentworth and Needham with James Cole, James Wall and Lawrence Copland were sent to scout out the Exeter region where the sachem *Wehancowit* and his son were eager for Englishmen to defend them from the aggressive northern tribes. A deed was witnessed by them in that winter for land in that territory to found what would have been Hampton. The governor of New Somersetshire was petitioned to accept the dissident group on the *Ogonquit* River and there were rumors he might be willing to let them start a plantation north of Kittery at a place to be called Wells. Winthrop wrote to the governor of New Somersetshire and to Lords Saye and Sele and Brooke and to Gov. Underhill in Dover urging them not to accept these vipers into their Christian homes. Among the settlers in Dover was Robert Bartlett who had married Richard Warren's daughter from Plymouth as his second wife. He'd gone to England after his first wife died and had ties to families in both Piscataqua and Rhode Island.

Big John Davis tearfully parted from his father after he was disarmed.

"I'm on my way north, father," he told Dolor that winter, "The church has banished me and my family."

Dolor put down his chisel and sat heavily on a mortar and tendon joint he was finessing.

"Dammit, John! I told ye not to get into this religion fight. 'Tis what drove most of us out of England! I've heard there are at least four ships getting ready to sail this spring to get away from King Charles and Archbishop Laud's army."

John sighed, sitting next to his father on the beam.

"I tried to ignore it, father. I tried to tune out the wrongs being preached every week from the pulpit but I could not take the hypocrisy and sanctimony of the elites who feel they have the only one true path to God."

"Aye, as many said the Pope hasn't," Dolor replied, wiping his brow.

"I'm sorry father. I really tried to turn a deaf ear but Rev. Wheelwright was right to call those who feel you can buy your way to Heaven by Good Works alone the AntiChrist."

"Ye know, don't ye that Mrs. Hutchinson's real crime is Antinominism, that is, she is standing up to the authority of those in power in Boston. She says people in a true state of Grace are answerable only to God, not man. She said Winthrop and his men are agents of the Evil One, putting their faith on laws and ordinances and good works instead of being humble and just trying to serve the Lord." Dolor rubbed his lower back. He was feeling his age and spring was slow in giving warmth to his bones. He added,

"I heerd the *Desire* with Capt. Peirce just got in from the West Indies. He'd been at sea seven months and visited Tortuga and Providence Island plus Bermuda and the Barbados and has a hold full of cotton, saLt. spices and some negro slaves, like the one Hutchinson has. He said the seas there are lousy with Spanish ships selling the slaves."

Big John shrugged.

"I don't really care about that stuff. I will be very busy building houses up north. I don't know when I will see you again, father."

Dolor rose. Sitting too long stiffened his muscles.

"Well, son, I can't be a'preachin' at ye as it was me own religious foolishness that brought us away from England. I've been told Gov. Winthrop and Dudley are coming to Concord next month to divvie up the lots of land. Margery and I might be moving on because o' my work so if ye want to send word to me do it through your cousins William or George in Boston or Robert Tobias, now in Yarmouth in Barnstable but he might be a'goin to Sudbury."

The two families parted with tears and prayers and Dolor sent a handsome teak carpenter's box full of sharp, oiled tools and nails of different sizes with his eldest son.

That year summer was slow in arriving and the corn had to be planted several times before there was enough heat to get it to grow.

New England was full of signs from God that summer: a big earthquake was felt from Piscataqua down to Connecticut in June, sending aftershocks throughout the region for almost three weeks afterwards and a big hurricane that devastated *Aquidneck* occurred two months later. This was the place Anne Hutchinson and her followers such as the Big John Davis and the Peasle family from Kingston had fled to so the Puritans in Boston interpreted it as a sign of Divine Wrath and didn't mourn the losses from it other than voicing frustration with Roger Williams for letting escaped servants seek refuge in the region.

Many Scottish prisoners and immigrants arrived that summer. King Charles I was determined to subdue Scotland the way he had Ireland and, because of the defiance of the covenant published by the Presbyterian Edinburgh ministers in resistance of English episcopacy he was preparing another attack. In the wings Oliver Cromwell was waiting, taking the temperature of the country that had risen with Ship Money and the increasing persecutions. A civil war was brewing between the Parliamentarians and the Crown, this everyone knew on a subliminal level. King Charles I's imperial reign was chafing the necks of many of his people and if they couldn't escape through immigration they knew they would only have one choice: rebellion.

One ship that crossed the ocean that summer was the *Diligent,* Captained by Mr. Martin. It carried Edward Gilman who would marry a daughter of Antipas Maverick in Kittery. (A grand daughter of his would later marry Stephen Dudley, son of the deputy governor Dudley and after Steven Dudley's death would marry John Davis's grandson in Concord in the intertwining streams that combined the immigrant families, rich and poor, in New England and the New World.)

In November the Assembly had two important matters to attend to: England wanted the Massachusetts Bay Colony's original charter as they wanted to send over their own governors and council. Gov. Winthrop and the men of Boston argued that the request was invalid as no one particular person was summoned to England to answer to charges of improper governing. With King Charles I in a precarious political position they decided to delay taking action.

The second matter was divisive. Capt. John Underhill had sailed to England after the Pequot War and, upon his return voyage had seduced a woman on board. He told her he shared Rev. Wheelwright's religious beliefs. She told a member of the Council and Underhill, who was petitioning for the 300 acres of land he had been promised as reward for his services in Connecticut, was severely questioned about his allegiance to the Boston church. Although Capt. Underhill denied the charges made by just one woman, he was admonished for dallying with the wife of the cooper, Joseph Faber. The matter concluded harshly with Capt. Underhill banished and not receiving his due.

A month later Dr. John Clarke, a Hutchinson supporter, sent a letter replying to Gov. Winthrop that it was true Mrs. Hutchinson had been delivered of a monstrosity with multiple lumps and no real human form. The Boston theocracy felt vindicated in banishing her after this news, and the hurricane.

December of 1638 was very cold and stormy. Some said that was what pushed goodwife Talby to murder her youngest child, a daughter approaching her three year birthday. Dolor had done some carpentry work for John Talby in Salem in the past and knew his wife Dorothy was prone to sudden, violent fits in which she claimed the Devil was in her husband or her seven children and she would attack them with whatever she had at hand including a dipper, knife or an iron skillet. He noted that her house was always dirty and the children unwashed and there were dirty dishes, laundry including dirty diapers in piles inside and outside the disheveled home. The older children did their best to feed and clothe the younger ones but it was always an unpleasant urine-scented chore to do any work there. The Assembly had admonished her and even whipped her but she soon returned to her malicious ways and in early December she broke the neck of her youngest, a little pitiful scrawny girl with matted blond hair named Difficulty.

Mrs. Talby was arrested and tried but refused to speak in her defense. She was told she'd be pressed to death unless she answered the charges and she finally confessed to the infanticide. She begged to be beheaded and not hanged as it was quick and she'd heard painless, but the court sentenced her to be hanged. At the public execution she tore the hood off her head and tried to put it between her neck and the rope but the hanging proceeded. She swung and grabbed at the ladder as she was pushed off and many turned away, aghast at her suffering but not feeling a lot of sympathy for a woman who had killed her little girl. Soon afterwards Mr. Talby was excommunicated as neighbors said his wife had been driven to her insanity because he forced her to perform unnatural acts, the nature of which were not made public.

On the Connecticut River William Pynchon's group at Agawam separated from Hartford due to a quarrel between Pynchon and Rev. Hooker. The Connecticut towns were trying to establish a separate ruling entity, like Plymouth, that didn't answer to Boston's authority but Pynchon was loyal to the Dudleys and by private letter he told Deputy Gov. Dudley his goal was to form a new town named after his English home of Springfield.

Gov. Dudley communicated by letter with John Haynes and apologized for grievances the Connecticut towns held regarding their treaty with the Narragansetts, etc. Haynes had come over on the *Griffin* with Revs. Thomas Hooker and John Cotton and he and his wife's family had many connections to wealthy families in England. During that winter John Haynes's brother-in-law Roger Herlakendon (who often bragged to deaf ears about his Plantagenet ancestors), caught the small-pox and died. Boston at this time was desperate to maintain its outlying settlements as problems in Salem (this time with a defiant Mrs. Oliver) and further north with the Wheelwright followers, the Mason and Gorges's settlements and to the south with the Williams and Hutchinson groups were tearing at the fabric of the common-wealth. The prominent men in Boston knew if the Puritans didn't present an united front to England everything they had fought to establish would be ripped apart and new lords would come across the sea; a handful of rich landowners would take it over as England did to Wales and Ireland. This desire to maintain an independent identity, to be a country that ruled itself while being loyal to the mother country, was felt in every small village up and down the coast but whether that loyalty would be to Cromwell or King was a question the people ignored as they struggled to build and just survive in an often hostile environment.

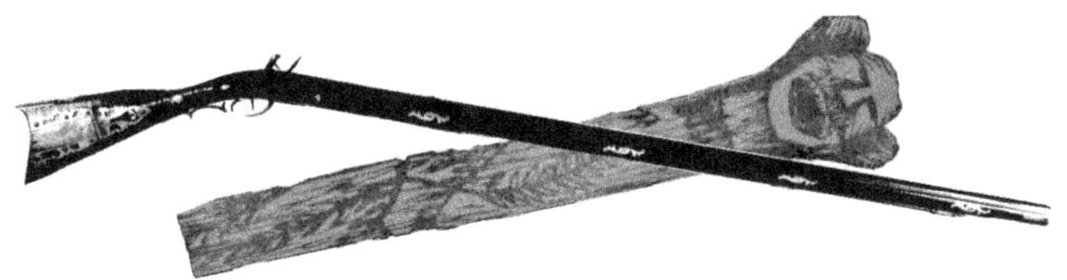

CHAPTER FORTY-FOUR

Of Herbs and Humans

1639

In late summer of 1638 a momentous event occurred, which would prove to have an even greater influence on the lives of those in the new colonies than the hurricane and earthquake for on the *John* came a large iron machine that could mass print pamphlets, booklets and books. The Rev. Josse Glover, who unfortunately perished en route, had sent it on with Stephen Day, a locksmith living in Cambridge.

Robert Day had first come over in the *Elizabeth* in 1634. He was one of the men who went with Rev. Hooker to Hartford. The Days came from Warminster in Wiltshire, northeast of Cadbury Castle, the alleged site of King Arthur's Camelot. Warminster was near Glastonbury. The entire district had sites pertaining to the legend of Arturus (said to have been a Roman soldier who unified Briton against the invading Anglo Saxons) or Riothamus (Rio from the Welsh Rhys) and made famous in William Caxton's book on King Arthur, one of the earliest books printed in England.

In 1476 Edward IV patronized the establishment of a printing press by Caxton. He printed Malory's *Morte d'Arthur* in 1485. Welshmen love literature. They believed in Talisen, a Merlin-like figure, a bard, a traveling teller of wondrous stories.

Bridwater (possibly named after St. Bridgit, who with St. Patrick, was believed to have consecrated monastic or churches in Glastonbury during the early years of Christianity when the Church of St. Michael stood upon the tor) was just across the sea from Wales, and Wales was just across the sea from Ireland. Many Britons believed Joseph of Aramithea had brought the Holy Grail from Jerusalem to the Druids at Glastonbury and that the Catholic church had continued the Old Ways but with different idols and names. The Mother of Christ replaced the Great Mother and the Transfiguration was the blending of the white waters and red, the white male and red female, in a holy 'grail' – a bowl, cauldron or cup.

Glastonbury, a marshy place reached through causeways made of raised wooden walkways, was adjacent to Sir Walter Raleigh's place in Wiltshire, as well as the Gorges's and Pophams' lands near Monacute. Sir Francis Drake was also from this area, as were the Davises, or Davys or Daveys, however they spelled their surname. Western Wiltshire and Somerset were full of ancient tombs called dolmen and standing stones, sacred wells and hills or carvings that all had an ancient history, most not written down but carried in the hearts of the residents of Dorset.

Richard Davies was bishop of St. David's in on the southwest coast of Wales and he helped translate the New Testament into the Welsh language. So popular was this, that by 1567 every parish church in Wales and Hereford were required to have a copy of his translation available to their ministers and parishioners. Just prior to the Separatist immigration to the New World William Morgan used his translation when a Bible, adapted by John Davies, of Mallwyd, whose sister was married to Richard Parry, bishop of St, Asaph, was printed in 1620 then reprinted in a smaller form in 1629 and called the '*Little Bible'*. The first Richard Davies of Conway had fled with the Pilgrims to the continent during the reign of Bloody Mary and returned under Protestant Queen Elizabeth.

Not all priests accepted the Church of England's ban of Papists and William Davies, a priest trained at Reims in France, who refused to submit was one of the first priests to be hanged at Beaumaris, accused of treason against Queen Elizabeth and the Crown in 1593.

With the coming of a printing press to Boston the Davis men and their Somersetshire relatives felt a renewed pride in their past. The Glovers – mariners and shipwrights – were friends and colleagues of the Davises plus they shared much with the wealthy and/or educated Days, Haynes, Dunsters and Stebbinses. Many of these families were drawn south to the Connecticut towns and later to the land west of Boston to settle the plantation of Lancaster.

William Davis Sr. of Bristol moved to New Haven, having followed Revs. Prudden, Eaton and Davenport south as many of the people in their congregations were from Hertfordshire in the Welsh marches that separated England from Wales. Hertfordshire was adjacent to Worcester, where Leominster and Ludlow were and Warwickshire and Gloucestershire, where Sir James Davis had a manor. These people shared a semi-Welsh background and idioms and customs different from the Boston Puritans that mostly came from Lincolnshire and Kent and the Dorchesterites that came from Devonshire. However, once in New Haven the followers of Prudden separated into their own village that they called Milford. The one thing all the immigrants shared was a contentiousness. Although few went as far as Williams, Hutchinson and Wheelwright, they had strong beliefs and felt an allegiance first to their part of England and its ministers before feeling subordinate to Boston.

The Irish were totally displaced in New England but began to form small groupings in the area south of Boston in Roxbury, Dorchester, Braintree and Weymouth, the latter, founded by people from the new village of Lynn. They had no separate voice as most were servants and many families had been separated, some sold to Virginia and West Indies planters, but their Catholicism, although not publically practiced, kept them from joining the congregations of the Puritan villages. Amongst themselves they talked of Maryland and dreamt of going there once their indentures were up.

After Stephen Day set up his printing press the first thing he printed at the bequest of the Governor was a *Freeman's Oath.* The next job was commissioned by Capt. William Peirce who had brought the first negro slaves in February of 1638 in the *Desire.* He brought the normal cargo of wine, cotton, tobacco and salt but his ship held something new: the first negroes to be sold on New England soil. (Mrs. Hutchinson and a few wealthy families had brought negro servants over with them but they weren't chattel. Upon their master or mistress's death they were free to go wherever they wanted and to live as freemen.)

Capt. Peirce was a learned man, much like John Davies, and he put together an almanac that the farmers and mariners could use and Day printed it. The press was next devoted to printing a psalter with translations from the Hebrew by the Revs. Mather and Cotton with input from other Bay area ministers. Day was rewarded with a grant of 300 acres for his contribution to the colony.

The Almanac was to be found on many a farmer's mantlepiece but the *Freeman's Oath* was received with resentment by those who felt Boston was overstepping its authority as it made a man pledge fealty to their local church – as an offshoot of the mother Church of Boston and its anti-Antinomian, strict Puritan teachings – in order to be an accepted citizen with the right to vote, own land and join his town's church. Even as the ink was still wet on the paper Dudley and Winthrop were at each other's throat over *The Oath* and it would be a point of contention amongst many settlers, including men such as Dolor who had to live in various towns to practice his trade. Dolor had a lot of company as this *Oath* would make only one fifth of the male population able to vote and own land.

In this year William Davis left his mother and began to sail with his cousin John, only a year older but with three years on William as a veteran of the sea. England was fraying apart. King Charles I was an unpopular, weak king and Oliver Cromwell and John Pym led Parliament in its loss of support for Charles's wars with Scotland. The King's authority was constantly under challenge and his inclination to be lenient, if not encouraging of Catholics fed the fires of dissent at home.

Just before William left for the sea Marie took him on a trip from the port of Bridport straight north through Crewkerne, where they stayed with William Phelps Bissell, a former classmate at Cambridge and a year older than John Davis. "WP", as he was nicknamed by William and John, told them that the legends said Joseph and 11 men landed in Bridport and traveled in a straight line to Glastonbury, each striking a staff into a mound along the route. As they approached Glastonbury Joseph was the only one left with a staff, and he struck it into Wearyall Hill, the site where the weary party stopped and the thorn tree immediately blossomed. This Holy Thorn (hawthorne) bloomed every Christmas at the site, which was where Marie and William were bound, the trip taking them through Yeovil and Ilchester. Along the way they noted the old trade route that ran through Chard wasn't as prosperous as it had been some years before. King Charles I's overspending and overtaxing and the emigration of many to the New England, Virginia and West Indies had depleted the once thriving countryside, which was now full of enclosures, a sight that made Marie almost weep.

"Will," she told the tall, dark eyed, dark haired handsome young man at her side, "when I was a girl this countryside wasn't all divided up by stands of elms. It was lush with field after field of corn, beans and sheep grazing all over. Ye see these enclosed pastures are a reflection of what is going on in London. Instead of sharing their wealth, the gentry are closing themselves off from the villagers. 'Tis what Mr. Pym and Mr. Cromwell are saying: we need to give more power to the people, to support a common wealth of mankind, not a rich royalty and gentry with the rest of the people living in poverty."

William stood next to his horse, his hair coming loose from the ribbon at the back of his neck. He looked so much like Robert that it gave Marie a pain in her heart when she looked at him.

"Aye, Mother. 'Tis why I must go on with John and find a place for ye in the New England. There are dark days ahead for England, I fear. 'Tis why I am choosing to go on and learn about herbs and curatives to be found in the West Indies so I can open an apothecary shop in Boston. Our cousins Dolor and his son John can build ye a grand house there and our relatives will be 'abringing new herbs and medicinals to me all the time."

Marie shook her head. Her hair was totally grey now and she wore it under a cap and, as now in spring when a cold wind blew, tucked beneath a woolen bonnet under the hood of her dark green woolen cape.

"My dearest son," she said, touching his arm, "I want you near my hearth but know it is a man's fate to follow his dreams. Your father loved the sea and you inherited this from him. Before ye leave, though, we will take the walk up the tor at Glastonbury, walking round and round that sacred mound. Do ye know that in olden times the land all around there was wet, flooded from the sea this time of year? This is why it was called the Isle of Avalon and once there stood a large church on its mount. Ye'll see now only a tower of the church of St. Michael's. I've shown ye the old Cadbury Castle, some say Arthur's Camelot, and taken ye out to the St. Michael's Mount off the tip of Cornwall. 'Tis said the old ones, the Druids, aligned all their sites in such a way as to harmonize the earth's powers flowing beneath our feet."

"Mother, to speak so is heresy," William said with a frown.

"Nay, son, I am free to speak of the Old Religion as long as I don't practice it. 'Tis said now that the Druids were in league with the Devil but in my heart I think Joseph wouldn't have brought the two chalices to Glastonbury if he felt it was antiChrist."

When they got to Glastonbury Marie brought him to the two sacred wells: one with reddish water and the other appearing white.

"These are the two earth energies, Will: the male and female. 'Tis why Arthur had two rampant dragons as his crest: a red dragon and a white dragon."

William took her arm as they began the long walk up the wide terraces ringing Glastonbury Tor. They had stopped at the Holy Thorn and walked up Chalice Tor but Marie saved the highest tor for last. At the top they could see the gentle, rolling green English lands and waters as far as the eye could see.

Marie couldn't help but weep at the beauty.

"Ye see what the Fisher King story was all about, Will? The King and the Land are one. If one is ailing or out of harmony the other withers away, too. I felt a real sense of suffocation when we went through the countryside and saw each neighbor's field cut off from t'other from the enclosures. It is as if this country isn't one entity anymore. It is little pieces all a' fighting with t'other. The King is not in harmony with his people and ye can see it reflected in the villages."

Marie sighed, "Forgive an old woman, son. I get sentimental seeing so much beauty. From this site ye can see the bigger picture, not the everyday stone walls and fireplaces and dirt paths. Ye can see why our Lord Jesus was approached by the Devil on top of a mount and tempted there. This 'tis truly a holy site, for certain. Even the air feels holy," she smiled a bit at her imagination. She drew herself up and said, "I just wanted ye to see this a'fore ye leave from Bristol. I don't know if ye'll ever return to England but ye need to remember it is a beautiful, sacred land. Its people knew God before Joseph brought the Holy Grail as it knew God lives in everything, in all creatures great and small, in every blade of grass and grain of sand and drop o' water."

William was torn between criticizing her for her 'naturalistic' religious views and finding a middle ground between the strict, lecture-like Puritan teachings and her semi-pagan wanderings. Instead, he put his strong arm around her and held her tight to his side as they turned and took in the scene, slowly turning 360 degrees.

"Ye're shiverin' Mother," he said, "pulling off his dark grey cape and placing it over hers.

"I'm afraid I caught a chill and am a bit feverish," she said softly, "but 'tis nothing, son. I will be fine when we get to the tavern and I sit 'afore a fire and drink a hot toddy."

As they descended a light rain settled in, hiding the countryside in fog.

"See, Will: 'tis why they said Avalon can only be reached by a fairy boat. It appears and disappears."

William shook his head.

"WP said he plans on starting a real ferry service across the Connecticut River when he gets to New England," he said, bringing her back to the present.

"Aye and I'm certain he will be successful there, as ye will be," Marie replied softly, "for our England is plagued by fighting dragons once again and I don't know which will win."

Marie never made it to Bristol. That night her fever rose and within two days she was dead from pneumonia (the ague). William had left all his medicinals with friends and the housekeeper at the farm outside Dorchester as he knew he'd be getting a new supply in the West Indies. He tried in vain to find sassafras root or sarsaparilla or mullein but Glastonbury wasn't a port town and the one apothecary was away in London on a family matter. An inconsolable William buried her in the Abbey cemetery where she said King Arthur and Guinevere were laid to rest. 'Twas holy ground, she'd said as she begged him to bury her there.

A very sad William met his cousin John at the pier in Bristol. He was a very sad young man who looked a lot older than 18, a young man who had said goodbye to his mother for the last time and in all probability goodbye to the England of his youth.

The months at sea crossing first south to Bermuda and the Barbados where John's brothers Humphrey and Theo were, then to Virginia where Sir Thomas and his family had a huge plantation, then finally north to the Connecticut River where he stayed with his Uncle William and was entertained by the Pynchon family (especially the young Margaret), then on to Boston, were months of mourning and of healing. The young man who stepped off the gangway in Boston harbor was harder, tanner and full of the one thing America promised: hope for a bright future created by his ingenuity and the sweat of his brow.

He was looking forward to working with his older cousin William in his apothecary shop and would board with another William, his cousin a year younger, over his blacksmith shop. There would be three William Davises in Boston and it would be confusing until they each established nicknames. William's true love was healing and he began acquiring his "store" of herbs and medicinals for the shop he dreamed of. He had not yet received his father's money from the sale of the *Mary and John* as Marie had sent it over to Robert's relatives in Virginia, fearing England was on the brink of bankruptcy and its banks might fail. Just knowing he had it waiting helped him as his Davis relatives let him ship aboard any family or friends' ship at his pleasure in order to acquire healing herbs up and down the coast and even in South America, although travel there was perilous due to the Spanish. William's father Capt. Bissell took him under his wing and over the next few years William grew into manhood and grew in knowledge of the nature of herbs and humans.

****

The Boston William arrived in was suffering from overpopulation. Ship after ship arrived in its harbor with new Puritan immigrants. In the summer of 1638 20 ships arrived, carrying over 3,000 passengers including one from Barnstaple that carried 80 congregants of Rev. Matthews. He went to found Yarmouth on the Cape. Most Puritans settled in the towns in and around Boston, some went north like Robert Tobias Davis, some went south, some even went to Connecticut. A group from England had formed a church of Essex people under Ezekial Rogers from Rowley, Wethersfield, England and they called the town Rowley in his honor.

Shortly upon William's arrival he witnessed a festive, rowdy occasion when a Muster Day was called. Over1,000 men and older boys showed up on the Boston common to drill under two regiments, one headed by Gov. Winthrop and the other by Dep. Gov. Dudley. A lot of drinking and celebrating in tents followed the event, which was declared a success.

Newton (renamed Cambridge) received the Rev. John Harvard's sizable bequest so a college could be built there, named in honor after him. Judith Harvard sent

John Davies's huge collection of books via James Davis to be donated to the new college by to a relative of hers – one of the 50 or so learned men in New England who had either attended or graduated from a college at Cambridge, England. There were some Oxford men, too, but they were talking about founding a second college to the south (Yale).

To the north in *Passamaquadick* Rev. George Burdett had removed Capt. Wiggin, agent for Lords Saye and Sele and Brooke as governor and replaced him with Capt. Underhill, a foe of Boston's elite. (Burdett left his wife and children in Salem to go north and the Boston theocracy severely criticized him for abandoning his family.) A new church and village sprung up at Dover under Rev. Hanserd Knollys of Lincolnshire. Also in the Eastward, *Pennecook* was found to be outside the Massachusetts Bay Colony and part of Gorges's Sagadahoc patent but Boston took no action on the new Gorges patent that had been granted that March. Boston wanted escaped prisoners returned from the north but the new Gov. Underhill wasn't subservient to Boston. Gov. Winthrop had written to Edward Hilton to bring Underhill to Boston the year before for contempt but no action was taken.

To the south Roger Williams and his wife were becoming cultish and some of his followers left. He insisted on being re-baptized by a Baptist minister, Ezekiel Holiman. At A*quidneck* Rev. Coddington and three other ministers were sent away by Anne and her husband Rev. William Hutchinson. Mary Dyer had birthed a monster similar to Anne's and there were rumors Dyer was a witch who consorted with the Devil and gave oil of mandrake to women to conceive. During the birth of Dyer's child the bed and floor shook violently and women and children in the room went into convulsions. These statements presaged a shadow that would spread across the colony, a shadow that would take the form of witch trials in other places beginning ten years later and ending in hysteria in Salem.

For the time being, in 1639 the church leaders chose to banish heretics and to pray that they would disappear, much as an ostrich buries its head in the sand when faced with danger. For the time being there was plenty of land all around Boston in which new towns could form. Boston was content for the time to push out the nonconformists, sending them back to England when possible, and to deny men the right to vote unless they were members in good standing in churches that met the standards of the mother church in Boston. The newly printed *'Freeman's*

Oath' was administered only to men who could show they were true, upright Congregationalists.

Plymouth Colony worked with the Massachusetts Bay Colony to figure out the boundaries around Hingham so everyone had their share of grazing lands. Plymouth was feeling pushed out, having lost its northern trading post and western edge with Roger Williams, the Hutchinson cult and new settlements on the Connecticut. Its original settlers were clannish and preferred to live amongst themselves but all around them they saw new villages erupting and ships were constantly seen off its coast. What the Separatists feared in Holland seemed to be coming true in New England as their children were drifting away, moving further out and even joining the Boston or Connecticut River churches. They knew they would either have to adapt or be smothered by the hordes of immigrants coming across the Atlantic.

Along the Connecticut River plantations quarreled amongst themselves and Wethersfield split off. New Haven was solidified into a settlement under Rev. Theopholis Eaton.

A church gathered at the infamous Mount Wollaston under Rev. Tomson and Mr. Flint.

In Boston Nathaniel Eaton, brother of Theo, was covented and censured as he severely beat a scholar boarding with him and other scholars came forward and said he'd abused them and that the proper meals and beer their parents had paid for were instead watery mush and the portions scanty. Eaton escaped by ship, leaving a 1,000 pound debt behind.

Robert Keynes was one of the many Boston merchants accused of overcharging for goods that summer. He had a daughter married to a son of Dudley's so there was little punishment but Rev. Cotton preached a sermon in which he laid down rules for fair Christian trading in the Bible commonwealth.

The only religious matter Dolor cared about was the construction of a new, bigger meetinghouse, to be built at the head of State Street. Because his son was a Wheelwright follower Dolor was not considered for the project even though Margery was a member of the respected Willard family. In like manner, Dover and Salem's petition to be accepted as part of the Boston church were rejected as they had sheltered Wheelwright followers.

Under pressure from men such as Dudley, the Assembly was considering a

Body of Laws or Liberties, drafted by Nathaniel Ward of Ipswich. Each session of the Assembly had become contentious as some felt positions granted for life or governors repeatedly re-elected to office were in direct conflict with the spirit of the Bible commonwealth. The leaders knew their patent was based on English Common Law and on obedience to the Crown and they could make no laws that conflicted with those in England. With King Charles I fighting with his Parliament – when he even called one – the situation across the sea made matters tenuous in New England. Already in private Parliamentarians were speaking in favor of John Pym and Oliver Cromwell or as Royalists in favor of King Charles I. Many Puritans sided in spirit with Cromwell as he was for rule By and For the People and against the Divine Rights of Kings but the wealthy families owed their fortunes to the Crown and many had estates or relatives with political power back in England or Ireland and didn't want to commit to open rebellion against King Charles I. Even the Scottish were involved as the English king was trying to impose his Church of England rites and rules on them and abolish their Presbyterianism.

But for William, who was writing loving letters to Margaret Pynchon in his free time, the New England summer and fall of 1639 was a magical time. He'd gone exploring north with James and John and found vast stores of sassafras, sarsaparilla, willow root, cranberries, all sorts of old and new 'native' curatives mentioned in his dog eared Culpepper's herbal and given to him by Rev. Maverick's wife and the apostle to the Indians, John Eliot. Every trip away from Boston was an adventure, a treasure hunt for items such as sulphur spring waters for sore eyes or mugwort to induce sleepiness in patients suffering from insomnia. William wasn't a doctor but was friends of Doctor Child in Boston and Dr. Clark in Newbury. They were enthusiastic about his arrival and he had already chosen a spot for his planned apothecary shop in the heart of the merchant section of Boston.

His New England travels were interrupted by an urgent letter from his cousin Humphrey in the Barbados that arrived with Capt. Jackson who had taken a Spanish bark full of money, silver plate, indigo, sugar and silver for the English crown. They were losing their negro slaves at an alarming rate due to fevers and he begged William to come south for a season to see if he could bring sassafras and sarsaparilla and any other curative with him to help the plantation owners. The Davis men were experimenting with the new crop, sugar, and it absolutely required large numbers of slaves to work the fields. The Bostonians went mad over sugar and fought over it at the docks plus bought all the indigo for blue dyestuff Capt. Jackson had onboard. He was under obligation to take all coins and silver back to King Charles I after he sailed south to get more brown sugar for England.

William had a taste of the West Indies en route to New England and he found it pleasant but when he traveled south on Nicholas's *Trader's Increase* the following year he went during the hurricane season and the voyage was brutal. Sails ripped, masts cracked, the ocean did its best to crush and swamp, or poop, the ship and when he got there the weather was unbearably hot and humid.

He told Theo and Humphrey he would only stay until fall. The conditions in the slave huts were deplorable: cockroaches crawled over the negroes sleeping in hammocks, biting them at night. William used many salves to treat infected bites and begged the owners to show more humanity: to at least give the poor slaves more clothing and blankets but William saw that they had no regard for the slaves other than as investments they would work until they died. John, Humphrey and Theo were the exception but they said it was a given than a plantation could only expect three years' work from their slaves before they died. William was appalled. He'd seen how indentured servants were mistreated by English owners in New England but hadn't experienced this accepted callousness towards fellow human beings.

"The sugar plant gets boiled and ground then shaped into cones and wrapped in paper or the syrup is bottled," Humphrey told him with a shrug as they toured a sugar mill, "The mills are costly to erect and require constant cooking of the plant, constant drying and granulating and some even mix white clay with the grains to make it more appealing to the housewives in England."

William asked how the cones were used.

"Oh, the blacksmiths make nippers and the women can nip off a lump and then drop in into hot liquid or grind it in a mortal and pestle."

"The sugar cane fields need constant weeding and new plants need to be put in. We don't have a cold winter down here so we can work almost every day unless it gets too wet from the seasonal rains," John added.

William worked with a local plantation owner who had some training in medicine and spent months drying herbs and either sewing them into paper bags or bottling them so when he caught the *Trader's Increase* on its last northward voyage in 1640 he left with the satisfaction of having contributed a little to the comfort of the slaves in what he saw as a very nasty business, even worse than on the tobacco plantations in Virginia.

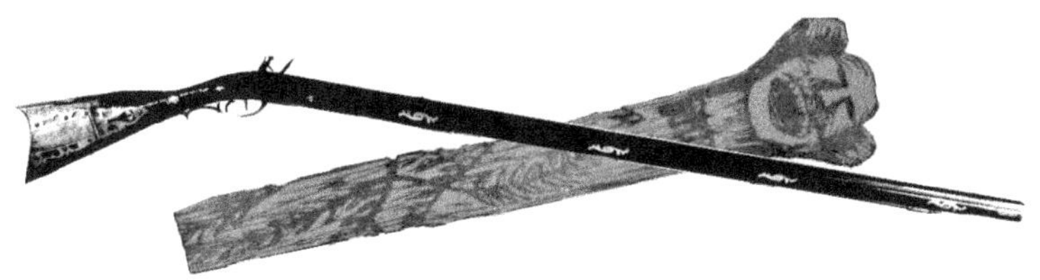

CHAPTER FORTY-FIVE

Growing Pains

1640

William didn't know that his friendships with Dr. Child and Dr. Clark would plunge him into ongoing controversy and conflict with Gov. John Winthrop and the Assembly as time went on.

Dr. John Clark was married to a sister of Sir Richard Saltonstall, gentry from Halifax, West Riding, Yorkshire. When William Davis visited relatives in Connecticut he met the Saltonstalls and his son, Robert, who had introduced John to his aunt Martha in Holland, Richard, who moved to Haverhilll and was friends of James Davis's sons there, Samuel and the youngest son Henry Saltonstall who was enrolled in the first class at the brand new Harvard College.

Henry was interested in medicine and though younger than William Davis, had many long, insightful walking talks with him as they strolled around Dr. Clark's farm in Newbury. William had originally met Dr. Clark through Dolor, who was friends of Matthew Chaffee, a ship's carpenter, and who was building a Boston home for Dr. Clark's family. Dolor had sold the Kent estate he'd inherited from James Weston Clark in order to fund his family's voyage to New England. A cousin of theirs, a William Clark, was a wealthy Bristol merchant. His widow remarried a

Davis but he was a step-cousin and not a direct relative of Dolor's and Sir Thomas's descendants. Capt. James's son Ephraim, a cousin of William's and Dolor's had settled in Newbury. James's son Samuel was captaining the *Gabriel* but had a home in Haverhilll, as did Thomas and James jr., who was born in Thornbury, England in 1619, around the time William was born to Robert and Marie in Dorchester.

William had tremendous respect for Dr. Clark, who kept a stable of magnificent, purebred horses and who was an inventor on the side. In one of his sheds he had a cast iron box with a metal pipe that he was tinkering with as an alternative to the wood wasting fireplaces with inefficient, often dangerous, chimneys, in common use. His first experiment had been a disaster and a shed had burned down, taking with it some of the firewood and trees he was hoping to conserve by bringing heat into the middle of a room instead of having it on an end and mostly going up the chimney with rain and drafts coming down it. Fireplaces had to be meticulously banked (the coals covered with ashes) at night and sparks from them onto rough wooden floors or an item too close to the flame caused most house fires in that time period. Housewives were always watching the hems on their long skirts and made sure to wear long, lindsey woolsy aprons that pulled their skirts in, but little children weren't always careful if they were playing and all it took was one hot coal or one popping spark and non-wool or waterproof wool with the oils in it and natural fabrics caught instantly. Hot water from the cauldron hanging from the crane was also a danger. The womenfolk were very interested in Dr. Clark's new invention as it would contain cooking fire and give them a nice, solid surface to place pots on instead of having to pile coals on the hearth and cook in Dutch ovens with coals over trivets or fry on pans that again, had to be pulled out by their hanging handle.

Dr. Clark wasn't directly involved with controversy but Richard Saltonstall and his brothers had to be involved in the administrations of Boston or Connecticut as their father was either a close friend or related to the Earl of Delaware and Lords Brooke and Say and Sele plus others still in England. The Saltonstalls were always serving as assistants to the governor and Sir Richard, blond with a blond moustache and a perpetually questioning expression on his very Saxon face had come over with Gov. Winthrop. He, with Dudley, Pynchon and others had been one of the men to sell his main estate in England and throw in his lot in Cambridge when the Massachusetts Bay Company was planning the mass emigration to New England.

Sir Richard was very involved in Connecticut politics but Richard was more interested in the legal, or magistrarial side as he had been briefly, like John and Edward Davis, an Inner Temple barrister in London before coming to New England. He bragged that his newborn son Nathaniel would one day be a Supreme Court judge in New England.

When William met Dr. Clark the doctor (not a true licensed profession at the time) was in the process of renting his Newbury farm to Matthew Chaffee and having a house built by him in Boston. Dr. Clark loved his horses but wanted to keep them in Newbury where he could ride them as he desired. A physician needed a good horse as the colonists were spread out far from the center of Boston and if a doctor were called it was an emergency as the herbalists and housewives knew a lot of home remedies and only called if major surgery were required, say from an infected scythe cut on a leg that would require amputation or a difficult birth that the midwife couldn't handle.

Dr. Clark's cousin (also named John and also a physician), had gotten involved with the Hutchinsons and had moved with them to their village they called Portsmouth at the tip of Aquidneck Island. He was in contact with powerful men at court in England and was trying to obtain a separate charter for the area that the Hutchinsons and Roger Williams were "exiled' to. He knew Big John, Dolor's son, a Wheelwright "heretic" but wasn't close to his cousin in Boston. The Boston Clark was very careful to let those in Boston know he wasn't the "Hutchinson" Dr. Clark.

Dr. Robert Childs was involved with the settlers to the north and friends of Richard Vines of Saco, whom he had first met in the Barbados. He had studied medicine in Padua, Italy, and was trying to talk Henry Saltonstall into going there after Harvard. He wasn't a religious dissenter, as was Vines, who had been a witness to the Wheelwright deed from the indians, but had serious differences with the Puritan oligarchy's clannish attitude in Boston. He wanted more diversity in rulership and more input from the populace and felt a free Englishman should be a free New Englishman with full rights under English common law without having to take *'The Freeman's Oath'* and be a member in good standing of a church body. He felt it wouldn't be long before he'd be banished, too, and with that in mind was looking to land west of Boston for a future settlement. However, in 1640 there were too many savages in that area and a doctor's services were in high demand when ships docked in Boston. The old enemy of sailors, scurvy, was still prevalent, and lice and fleas carried diseases amongst unwashed passengers closely packed in the 'passenger' hold of the ships. Some passengers actually died of seasickness as they vomited anything they swallowed and perished from dehydration and malnutrition.

William liked talking to Dr. Childs as he had brought knowledge of some of the simples, or herbal remedies, from the Barbados. One thing they all knew, dating from the great explorer Cavendish, was that lemon juice seemed to be the best remedy for scurvy and that other citrus fruits from the West Indies and green vegetables brought about cures to patients who were carried off the ships looking like they were bound for the cemetery.

In England one could hardly move in a county without meeting a relative or friend of a friend and William was observing that in New England the same was holding true, but instead of it being just limited to a county, it was throughout the entire settled areas. Some were primarily from just one area, such as the Dorchesterites, but by 1640 the original settlers had spread out through their children and New England was becoming a mixture of Lincolnshirites, Devonshirites, Kentish men, West Countrymen and Welshmen, Irishmen and even the Scottish. Every ship brought something new to the mixture, even the negroes that Capt. Jackson brought from Africa. However, the French weren't welcome and they went north. The Spanish likewise weren't welcome and went south to Florida and Central and South America. In the West Indies the French or Spanish often shared islands with the English, one country occupying one side and the other the opposite. These weren't happy marriages but for the sake of trading tobacco, sugar, rum, molasses, indigo and cotton they tried to avoid open hostilities. What Capt. Jackson had recently done, seizing a Spanish ship with silver plate and coins, was sure to bring trouble and the New England colonies weren't endorsing piracy. There had been too much under Queen Elizabeth. Too many ships lost, too much valuable cargo sunk to the bottom of the sea.

But with King Charles's reign on the brink of collapse men such as Sir Richard Saltonstall knew one day news would arrive in port that would splash England's Civil War blood onto New England's shores.

It is not easy to remain neutral. New England had its own internal religious struggles and was trying very hard to remain an united colony. However, England was splitting apart. Before 1619 the Separatists had fled King James I, staying in Holland until they could get a patent to start Plymouth Plantation. The second Scottish king, James's son Charles I was harsh against the Puritans and also the Scottish. He, like his father, felt the king had Divine Rights in the matter of religion and also had the right to tax indirectly without Parliament's approval. By 1640 the situation in England had become so dire that almost every family was on one side or the other: one, supporting the king because the royal families had been generous to them *vis a vis* lands and titles and the other supported Oliver Cromwell, John Pym, and men such as John Hampden that stood up strongly for the rights guaranteed under the Magna Carta for free Englishmen to be free in their persons and property and to have a say in the taxes the government desired to impose on them.

.John Hampden had briefly visited the Plymouth Plantation in 1622, staying with Edward Winslow's family. He returned to England and chose to fight the king through Parliament instead of fleeing to the wilderness of New England. He opposed the forced loan of 1626 along with Sir John Eliot, Sir Thomas Wentworth (recalled from Ireland), John Pym and Sir Edward Coke. These men had attended Oxford or Cambridge and were contemporaries of ministers such as John Cotton and Richard Hooker, the Winslows and Bradfords, doctors Clarks and legal men such as Winthrop, Dudley and John and Edward Davis's sons.

John Hampden was a friend of the Warrens in Plymouth, John Pym and Thomas Wentworth, First Earl of Strafford. Archbishop Laud arrested and charged them with high treason against the people of England, and in Strafford's case, also against Ireland, which was in revolt. (In 1641 the Catholic Irish would massacre over 4,000 English Protestants in Ulster.) The king had lost his battles against the Scottish Presbyterians and was being forced to pay 850 pounds a day to room and board the Scottish soldiers who were occupying the northern border towns of Newcastle and Durham on the English side. The MacGregors and Stuarts who had had lands and titles taken away, and who hadn't fled to Ireland, had signed on with James Graham, First Marquis of Montrose's army but they had been badly defeated and the Bishops' War, as it was called, was draining the Royal treasury dry. King Charles I had taken the gold bullion the London goldsmiths had deposited in the English mint plus seized the black pepper stored in the English East India Company's warehouse but was still desperate for money to continue his war against the Scottish uprising. And his war on the Continent.

To live in New England meant one had ties to former classmates or neighbors in England and when King Charles I out of sheer desperation finally called a new Parliament in early November, 1640 the Cromwell Parliamentarians came loaded for bear.

In Plymouth a new minister, Rev. Charles Chauncy was baptizing infants using full immersion or dipping and sprinkling with holy water. Boston disapproved. Gov. Bradford said he didn't feel it violated Puritan practices but felt immersion was impractical during the cold New England months and others felt it was too Anabaptist so Chauncy wasn't ordained to be a minister in or around Plymouth.

To the north Capt. Underhill and the new minister at Dover, Rev. Hanserd Knolles, fell out of favor with Boston. Underhill for his adulteries with married women and Knolles because he was an opinionated familistic. Both had also openly criticized the Boston church either by writing or in person in England. They appeared under a flag of truce in Boston but ultimately Underhill was excommunicated and Knolles was not accepted.

Boston tried to reach out to Rev. Coddington at *Aquidnay* but the church there was still under the influence of the Antinomian Hutchinsons.

That summer, helped by strong winds or currents, two ships, one from Bristol, the *White Angel,* and another built at Marblehead, the *Desire*, made it across the Atlantic in under three weeks, a vast improvement over the two months previous voyages averaged.

In May at the General Elections Thomas Dudley was chosen governor with Richard Bellingham elected deputy governor. Winthrop was still in the Assembly as one of the eight assistants. Winthrop was under scrutiny as his bailiff of his farm was caught selling corn below market value to his neighbors and of incurring debts of 2,500 pounds without Winthrop's approval. Richard Dummer, an Antinomian who had been turned out of his office and disarmed, helped by paying 100 pounds towards the debts. The bailiff, James Luxford was tied to the whipping post on the common and his ears were cut off, the punishment for thieves.

Lord Saye and Sele and Sir John Humfrey began a campaign to encourage New Englanders to move south to Virginia and Providence Island and the West Indies where Humfrey ruled under direct English governors. Winthrop and the Boston men put forth arguments against New Englanders emigrating south but many ships left that summer for greener, warmer pastures.

The village of Lynn was overcrowded and approximately 40 families sailed south and set down on Long Island, west of the Dutch settlement. They tore down the Prince of Orange's arms from a tree and drew a crude face there instead. The Dutch complained to Boston and the Lynnites pulled up and went east, settling down in a place to be called Southampton in Shout's Bay. Their minister and most of his congregation later migrated to Branford in New Haven's colony. A lot of West Country folk ended up moving from Roxbury to New Haven. Minister John Davenport led families there in 1638 along with minister John Eaton. New Haven was to be the southern shore's trade competition to Boston. John and Humphrey Davis settled there, also. Another minister, Peter Prudden, split his congregation off to form Milford. Then Branford and Stratford (which Roger Ludlow favored) split off from Wethersfield. In time many of the families including the Smiths, Burts, Shermans, Blisses, Williamses and Stiles (Thomas Stiles from Ampthill, Bedford, England, had served with Philip Francis Davis during the Pequot War and was shot but the arrow went into his neckerchief and not his throat), worked their way up the Connecticut River to found Northampton, Deerfield, Springfield and other towns along the river.

The Rev. Roger Williams, from Wales, an in-law of the Dudleys and friend of Oliver Cromwell, split from the Boston Puritans and went to Narragansett Bay to establish a village he named Providence in what became Rhode Island. His relative John was an early Windsor settler and his son John became a minister in Deerfield. He married a daughter of Rev,. Ebenezer Moulton. Roxbury settlers went with John Pynchon to settle Springfield where Tobias Davis set up corn and wool fulling mills on the river.

In Roxbury the Rev. John Eliot established the first Latin school for boys in 1645. That year a great fire burned down a lot of the young town. Many thought it started in the great iron furnace on John Johnson's place as he was smelting bog iron for wrought iron rods for blacksmiths to use to turn into farm and household goods. His house was full of gunpowder and when it burned down all the records of the town went with it. Besides the Pynchon and the Curtis brothers, Stebbinses, Parsons and Chapins moved from Roxbury to the Springfield and Brookfield Plantations.

The news of the new Parliament and the arrests of Strafford and Laud arrived in December with the last fishing vessel of the season off the Isle of Shoals. Ships with provisions and immigrants from England ceased at that time, also. While the Massachusetts Bay Colony tried to hold its outlying communities together through persuasion or coercive means the wealthier residents were feeling torn between their duties to the King or Cromwell's Puritans in the mother country and their pledge to help establish and grow New England, Virginia and the West Indies.

James Davis was one of those so torn. He finally decided to move permanently to Virginia but several of his sons stayed in New England and helped form the new town of Haverhilll. The older generation felt English. The newer generations felt English in name only but identified as citizens of a separate, quasi-independent country. Those living without a king breathing down their necks were getting used to the idea of Liberty and self-rule. For most the first loyalty was to their congregation, their village of covenanted saints. They gave the 'governor his due' out of respect and in hopes of protection against enemies but a new spirit was spreading in the colonies: a spirit that in seven generations would rise up and throw off the royal yoke.

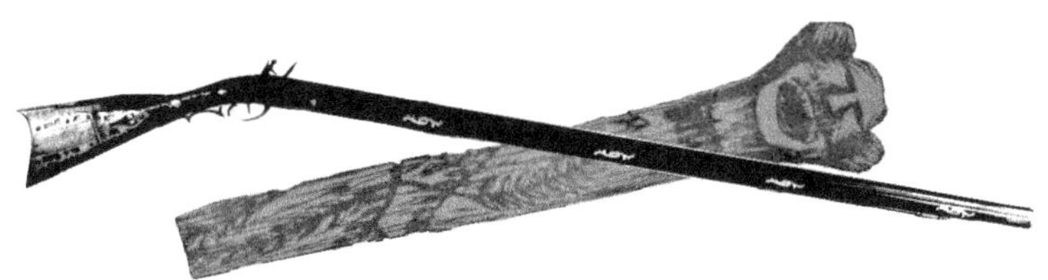

CHAPTER FORTY-SIX

Civil War Begins in England

1641

In 1641 while England was in the throes of a takedown of the royal form of government and Parliament was busy attempting to take all power away from King Charles I beginning with the execution of Wentworth and imprisonment of Archbishop Laud, New England had its own sufferings.

Because of the civil unrest the ships coming to America ceased. New Englanders had become dependent on a steady supply of English goods and suddenly the goods and the immigrants ceased. To meet the need two ships were built so the colonists could trade with the southern plantations and West Indies but very few would sail to England for fear of being captured or their crews impressed.

A few years earlier Sir John Humphreys (also written as Humfrey or Humphreys) had come over with his third wife and two daughters from a second marriage. Humphreys was a friend of the Tisbury Davises, having attended Trinity College and then served at the bar in Lincoln Inn. Like them, he hobnobbed with the powerful men in Wiltshire, Somersetshire, Dorset and Devonshire plus he socialized with the Winthrops, Dudleys (who were close to the Davis shipping concerns) and other prominent men who financed the Massachusetts Bay Colony. Humphreys served as its treasurer and was to be the deputy governor but had to cancel his original plans to emigrate with Winthrop in 1630. His first wife died in 1621 and he remarried Elizabeth Pelham in Wiltshire and they lived in Fordingham near the Warrens. Marie was friends with them and Humphrey's children John Jr., Elizabeth and Anne often played with her William. Unfortunately Humphrey's wife Elizabeth died in 1628. The Humfreys had belonged with Marie to Rev. White's congregation in Dorchester.

John Humphreys immediately began courting the daughter of Thomas Clinton Fiennes, Third Earl of Lincoln, a prime investor in the Massachusetts Bay Company. Through marriage he was related to Isaac-Johnson (the wealthiest investor in the plantation) who was on the *Arbella* with John Winthrop and other wealthy investors when the colonizing fleet sailed from Plymouth in 1630 for Boston harbor.

At the time of the departure Humphrey's third wife Susan was with child and couldn't travel so reluctantly Thomas Dudley was chosen as deputy governor. Even though Susan miscarried the pregnancy, John and Lady Susan lagged behind in Fordingham. However, so convinced were his friends that he would join them in Boston they kept electing him an assistant in absentia. Humphreys was useful in England as he successfully argued the patent claims of the MBC against Gorges's claims at court and in London. Humphreys had a knack for fund-raising and served the early colony well in England. He and Lady Susan (Clinton-Fiennes) finally came over in 1634 with their infant daughter Dorcas and his two daughters from his first marriage. John Jr. remained in England as he was still in school and headed for Cambridge.

William Davis senior had many dealings with John Humphries as he and his brother George sent shiploads of cargo for him over to New England in his ships, based out of Bristol. William's sons William Jr., Dolor and Jenkyns had settled in New England and when John Humphreys came over he hired Dolor and Jenkyns to build him a sturdy stone house on his 900 acres of land northeast of Boston. As was the custom with gentry he named his 'manor', calling it 'Swampscott' since the land was marshy plus Lady Susan Humphreys felt it was more of a 'cottage' than a real house. Barnaby Davis had also gotten a land grant there in payment for surveying work.

Although Humphreys was warmly welcomed by the other Boston Puritan elites and was granted a judgeship immediately, he was soon plagued by a contentious neighbor.

Lady Deborah Moody, widow of Sir Henry Moody from Avebury, Wiltshire, immigrated on the *James* in 1639 and the Mass. General Court granted her 400 acres of land adjoining Swampscott. This granting of land to a female without a male was unheard of and made her controversial right from the start.

Lady Humphreys and Lady Moody did not like each other. Lady Moody had been forced to leave England as she had befriended Anabaptists and Quakers. Regardless, she was accepted into the church at Salem. She moved to her 400 acres adjoining the Humphreys in Lynn in 1640. By then, Lady Susan had given John three daughters and three sons, (birthing a son and a daughter within the same year). Lady Susan was, in the eyes of the Puritans, overly fond of fine linens and laces and extravagant English goods.

Humphreys was extremely busy with his Boston duties, having served on the tribunal that banished the Hutchinsons and also working with Lord Say and Sele and mariners such as the Davis men to get a patent to establish a new plantation between New England and the West Indies. Named Providence Isle it was to serve as a trading post for New England, Virginia and the islands of the Bahamas.

Lord Saye and Sele granted Humphreys the governorship of Providence Island and he spent most of his time in and around Boston talking to prominent men about emigrating from New England down to the island. This, and his undisguised contempt for Winthrop and Rev. Cotton's strict fundamentalism and lack of tolerance for those who practiced Christianity a little differently from the Boston church was making him less than popular and between these domestic frictions and troubles in England which were bankrupting his financial interests there, he sold his estate to Lady Moody in the fall of 1640 and with his wife and youngest daughter and sons left for England.

In June ships full of reinforcements from New England bound for the church in Providence Island docked at St. Christopher's Island. They heard a large Spanish fleet had attacked and taken possession of Providence. Despite Capt. Peirce's sage advice the settlers did not want to turn back and Capt. William Peirce and the cotton merchant Samuel Wakeman from Hartford were killed off Providence when the Spanish ships turned their fire on them in port. The mission was aborted and the ships – minus their main captain – returned to New England.

John Humphreys was also involved with Lord Saye and Sele to the north in Piscataqua and before their representative left for England he had gotten Dover and Portsmouth to agree to join with the Boston government instead of the Gorges plantations. Maine at the time was plagued by packs of wolves that attacked the settlements and these towns hoped for more protection if they aligned with the MBC.

The Humpheys, as was the way of the wealthier colonists, had servants. Jenkyns Davis, Dolor's younger brother, a skilled joiner, or carpenter, was living near Swampscott and he, along with John Hudson, looked after the farm in John Humphrey's absences. Another neighbor, Daniel Fairfield, also worked on the Humphrey's place.

Lady Susan did not seem to care about her little girls. She let them run wild and unlike Anne, who was a strict Puritan and engaged to William Palmes, eight year old Dorcas and six year old Sarah fraternized with the servants and the neighboring Fairfields at the time. Fairfield often made lewd comments to the girls when they visited. The attention-starved girls enjoyed the attentions of Fairfield and Hudson and sat in their laps and let them touch them in inappropriate ways behind the barns.

This was how the oldest lost her virginity to Fairfield and was worried about becoming pregnant.

After her step-sister Anne married and her parents had left for England Dorcas confessed what Fairfield had done to her and her younger sister. Dorcas said she had slept with Hudson after she and her sister and brothers were left alone on the farm. Humphreys had left the girls with Jenkyns Davis and his wife, who was very pregnant at the time and, like Fairfield and Hudson, he had taken advantage of the young girls, who were very flirtatious and hungry for male attention.

She told Anne her older brothers had also taken her to bed.

Anne was shocked and immediately told her pastor, who then contacted the sheriff who arrested all of the men involved.

Intense interrogation revealed that Sarah had only been touched but Dorcas had been violated. The boys were judged to be too young to have had serious intercourse with their sisters and went sent to live on the Humphries's plantation in the Barbados or with stern farmers in villages far away from their sisters.

Around this time another scandal involving an adult male occurred as 17 year old Jonathan Thing (Tyng) was charged with raping a seven year old girl in Piscataqua.

Dolor, William, John and the other Davis men refused to have anything to do with Jenkyns and didn't even visit him in the Boston jail. They tried very hard not to be touched by the stench of the scandal. James left for Virginia and others spent time sailing to the Barbados and Bahamas, redeeming their family name by bringing desperately needed goods from the south to New England and goods from the New England ports to the southern plantations.

In England the Parliament demanded a 'Bill of Rights' be signed by King Charles I and in Boston a 'Bill of Rights' was finally voted on in the MBC Assembly.

England was on the brink of a bloody civil war. New England had its own problems and Lady Moody was gathering, like Anne Hutchinson, a group of followers to defy the theocracy in Boston. She had gloated over the troubles the Humfreys children had caused but her glee was short lived as it wasn't long before the Puritan arrow of intolerance would be pointed at her breast.

There had been an hurricane and a very wet summer that year. The corn rotted in the fields and people who ate it developed worms, so William's small apothecary in Boston sold many vermifuges that fall and winter. Although his shop was not far from the jail he, like his cousins, avoided Jenkyns like the plague. He continued to socialize with Dr. Clark, now white haired and very respected. William also had a dark horse relative (to the south with the Hutchinsons) and knew how a family name could be ruined in the small, provincial colony.

Stroking his very full white moustache, Dr. Clark gave William this advice, "You can stay and stand tall, William, or ye can slink off like a dog with its tail between its legs. I, for one, will stand up and let my personal character and my Christian actions speak for me. I happen to agree with Mr. Cotton that good works are important as well as a personal bond with God. We might not know who is saved and who is not but I believe bad works won't buy a man a ticket into Heaven."

William looked up from his mortar and pestle and replied as he fiddled with a pair of spectacles on his nose (William had trouble seeing things up close), "Well, JC, I think God is in everything from lowly weeds that cure disease to the mysteries of hurricanes and lunar eclipses. I don't think He is to be worshiped as the savage powwows do with lots of shrieks and screams but I believe He is in everything, the way they do. They say prayers to their heathen god every time they kill a deer, did you know that? John Eliot told me that in their own way they are very spiritual but they are like ships lost at sea that need to be guided by our Christian church into a good harbor. I am ashamed of Jenkyns's weakness of the flesh and feel that whatever punishment the courts eventually declare he will never be accepted into Heaven. I cannot in my heart ever feel, even if he is forgiven by his pastor and accepted back into his church, that he is saved. A saved man would not do what he did: betray the friendship and trust of Mr. Humphreys and his vows to his goodwife and prey on the innocence of those young girls. 'Tis truly was the Devil's doing, certain o' that am I."

Dr. Clark agreed and they changed the subject to speculate on when they'd see a new ship from England. They both agreed that this interruption of trade helped make the colony stronger as they had been overly dependent on the mother country.

"Aye, and the women are all busy spinning the flax grown in their own fields," said William, "and carding and spinning their own wool and weaving it on their own farms. 'Tis a lot like Devonshire, seeing them now on their own two feet, raising their own sheep, cattle, pigs and chickens and growing wheat, rye, peas, the indian corn, beans and squash and not be mobbing the ports for English goods like hungry piglets on a sow's tits every time a ship docks."

Dr. Clark harumphed and sternly corrected, "Well, if Mr. Humphreys doesn't get funding for an iron works in Saugus, I won't be able to make my new stoves. We still need English money, William, don't ever forget that."

In December the General Court held a three week session and passed 100 laws, called *The Body of Liberties.* A copy of the proposed laws had been delivered to the selectmen in every town in the colony during the summer and returned with corrections or suggestions. It was to be agreed that once the laws were passed they would be in effect for only three years during which time they could be revised, revoked or amended. However, after the three years if there was no opposition, the laws would be accepted as the law of the land. Primarily this code was based on English Common Law but with a Puritan slant. Morality, obedience and respect for the law and the leaders was uppermost yet the rights given by God to every free English man were stressed. The long bill basically boiled town to the assertion that a man had a right to own property and conduct business as long as it wasn't injurious to the public good (in other words promoting blasphemy, prostitution, idleness or drunkenness) and to seek redress for wrongs and have the right to be told his crime and have the opportunity to be heard before a judge and punishments were to be based on the facts and not automatically determined. Matters of religion were relegated to the Church leaders. Through these means, though not official, crimes were divided into types: Civil and subject to civil judgments and punishments and Clerical and under the jurisdiction of the synod. This was meant to separate Church and State.

Many saw the *Body of Liberties* as Cromwellian/Parliamentarian and almost a declaration of independence from the crown of England but others said all it did was codify what everyone already had been abiding by.

To the north, James's sons and other Davis men had followed Rev. John Ward to establish a village on the Merrimac River that was named Haverhilll after the English village. Rev. Ward had preached in Hadleigh, England and when he came over first preached to the north in Kittery. The Haverhilll in England was in Suffolk near Kersey, a town known for its coarse ribbed cloth (which the Dorchester women dyed red and attached strings to for their petticoats) and Orford, where the Orford Castle, built by Henry II sat on a spit of shingle, guardian of East Anglia. It was also near the town of Adlebourgh (Attleboro). The fishing was rich with oysters and the ports had many taverns and public houses for the sailors who fished the Channel or crossed over to whatever country England wasn't warring with. Rev. Ward was an Emmanuel College graduate, a Cambridge man as were most of the Puritan preachers at the time. He had only 12 congregants when they planted the new town on the muddy shores of the Merrimac. It was inland from the coast and surrounded by dense forests of oaks and pines that sawmills on its tributaries sawed into planks for the ships being built downstream and for housing. Samuel Davis, captain of the new *Gabriel* along with Thomas Davis capitalized on this location, which was also a great place for the townsmen to trade for furs from the north. Samuel, Ephraim, Jamie's son James, and Dolor's son John (leaving the Wheelwrights) built farmhouses on the hills amongst its plentiful streams. Although the frontier town was along a path used by the savages the tribes around them were not hostile and beaver skins for hat making were a prime trading good.

Haverhilll was established as an offshoot of Newbury, a ship building town near the coast and on the opposite bank of the Merrimac River. As would happen over and over new towns sprung up as congregants found it too hard to travel (especially in winter or rainy periods) overland to a distant church for the Sabbath and weekly Bible classes. Roads were scarcely more than rutted paths and travel by boat was a faster way to move up and down the coast.

For James Davis the land reminded him of the Pewsey Valley in Wiltshire with its gentle sloping hills and many streams and lush forests. This land, though, would be filled with honest farmhouses built by Davis men and not full of old, ruined castles and stone manors confiscated by the crown from the Catholic church and handed out to a favored few families. It exemplified the new spirit in this New England but he felt torn between his plantations in Virginia and the Barbados and loyalty to King Charles I.

As 1642 began with a bitter cold winter his sons in Haverhilll waited for word from him about affairs in England and how they might affect their fortunes in this God gifted fertile land.

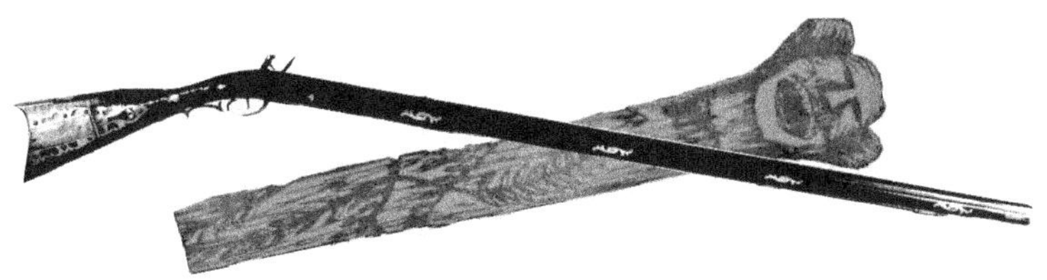

CHAPTER FORTY-SEVEN

Civil War in England

1642

January, 1642 began in England with King Charles I accompanying 400 swordsmen to the House of Commons to arrest Pym, Hampden and three other Parliamentarians. The House was warned and the men escaped. King Charles I was furious and left spitting, "The birds are flown." The leader of the House refused to say where they'd gone but King Charles I declared he would return as "Master of my Kingdom." He sent his wife back to France and began to build an army. When Parliament members later suggested they send a militia to quell the riots in Ireland it was voted down as the distrust of King Charles I was so great that many felt he'd turn the militia on his own countrymen. A Militia Bill was passed taking control of the militia away from the tyrannical King. Parliament issued an ordinance whereby only they could appoint militia commanders for each county. King Charles I wouldn't sign the bill and declared anyone obeying it "violators of the laws and disturbers of the peace of this kingdom". Parliament had gone even further with its .'Nineteen Propositions' by demanding the king put all castles and forts under their command, demanding they have the authority to appoint the royal tutors, denying the vote to Papists and dismissing the militiary.

King Charles I replied in August when on the 22nd day he raised his standard on a green hilltop in Nottingham. As the King's flag unfurled the Civil War began officially in England.

In January in New England Rev. Samuel Gorton had been whipped and banished by Rev. Coddington from Aquiday, Rhode Island but he continued to cause problems to the religious communities in Narragansett territory.

The winter was so cold that sleds were used to traverse areas normally covered with water and much lumber was carted this way to Boston and the growing towns around it.

Another upsetting event occurred in New Haven where it was discovered that a man had had sexual intercourse with a sow and it birthed a half-human monster. For his crime of bestiality George Spencer was sentenced to death.

At the May court Winthrop was again elected governor and Endecott deputy. Thomas Dudley was so upset he refused to attend the court. He, and many others, felt Winthrop was setting up a life tenancy as governor and not abiding by the will of most of the people in that they wanted their government officers to serve a term or two and then let others have a chance. Richard Saltonstall was also upset at this court as his small book that criticized Winthrop for hogging political power was called to account. Above all, the court wanted its assistants to be in accord and harmony to present an united front to England so Dudley and Saltonstall were appeased before the session adjourned.

That summer a mother attempted to drown her young son and she was whipped and imprisoned. At the May Court session Jenkyns Davis, Hudson and Fairfield were sentenced for their crimes against the Humphreys's daughters. Fairfield was severely whipped, his nostrils slit and seared with a hot iron – one nostril at Boston and one at Salem – and he was confined to reside on Boston neck only. Jenkyns Davis was whipped publically with 40 stripes both in Boston and Lynn, as was Hudson and Jenkyns and Fairfield had to wear a hangman's noose around their necks (Jenkyns was allowed to remove his the following year) and pay fines to John Humphries. Following the case the court decreed that in the future rape of a child by any male over 17 years old would carry a death sentence.

Five ships were built in New England and the lake beyond the White Mountains was discovered. In July Edward Bendall, owner of Bendall's Cove on Boston neck, devised an ingenious tub that could be lowered with a man inside so towing chains could be affixed to a wreck, the *Mary Rose* from Bristol, that had been sabotaged, blown up and sunk in Boston harbor two years earlier. The Puritans responsible for destroying the 'heretic' ship and killing its captain and the nine or ten sailors who had refused to go into town to attend Sabbath meeting were never caught or charged. It was considered to be an Act of God.

A ship from England brought a book of Rev. Cotton's sermons about the seven vials of the Apocalypse and another brought linen, woolens and other English goods that three merchants had managed to ship to New England the previous year. Israel Stoughton, previously commander of the Massachusetts troops against the Pequots, was chosen to carry the profits from the sales back to England but he never returned to Boston as he was caught up in the Civil War and killed in battle in Lincoln two years later.

Leaders of the New England churches were asked to attend a synod in England but by then were informed of the Civil War and prudently decided to stay in New England until the war ended as they were needed at home more than at a religious meeting in the motherland. The colony sent two ministers to Virginia to answer their pleas for men of God to help them in their settlements.

Roger Ludlow and John Haynes appealed to Boston to help with rumors of an uprising of the savages but all Boston did was call in local natives and disarm them. The Narragansett sachem *Mianatomah* and his councillors were invited to dine with the court and by the end of September it was decided that the rumors were propaganda by the Mohegans and Narragansetts to try to pull the English into their feuds. The September court also decided to return arms to the savages as they needed them for fowling and hunting but the settlers were on edge and a false alarm called out the militias in Dorchester, Watertown and Salem when a man shot his musket at night at wolves and the townspeople panicked, fearing it was an indian attack.

That fall people such as Lady Moody sold land and moved to Long Island near the Dutch or to the West Indies as ships with goods from England were scarce. To the north the French Catholics and Protestants were feuding over Acadia but Boston backed off after a ship going to trade with the Protestant Charles de la Tour's fort in the Bay of Fundy was warned off by his opponent, Monsieur D'Aulnay, who also had a fort in the bay. With civil war in England the Boston leaders had no desire to get involved in any French wars to the north.

In England professional soldiers such as Lord Thomas Fairfax led Cromwell's new Model Army under fellow generals including Philip Skippon and Henry Ireton and Cromwell's Army of common men had the backing of the people.

Harvard College in Cambridge matriculated nine young men that fall but lost all but two to England where the new students went to fight for the Cromwell Puritan cause.

In Boston Marie and Robert's William was courting Margaret Pynchon from Springfield. His cousin William moved to Roxbury and his wife Elizabeth was pregnant with their first child (a son named John.).

While the English farmers, working lands laid out and cleared long ago and recently enclosed, were fighting against royal tyranny, the New England farmers were fighting nature, felling trees, clearing fields, using steel plows to turn over lands and plant crops and use the many field stones they found to make fences to keep the livestock away from their crops. Every day it was man against nature as acre after acre was surveyed, fenced and tamed. The stoppage of ships affected the farmers as new livestock wasn't arriving but they weren't worried that King Charles I's soldiers would trample their corn or conscript their sons from the fields.

Mariners such as the Davis men enjoyed the suspension of English import and export duties at this time but with many ships sitting at port and not traveling across the Atlantic it was cold comfort.

As the year ended there was a lot of correspondence passing between the leaders in the northern, Boston, Plymouth and Connecticut settlements about forming a union to defend against the Dutch, French and Indians – all a more immediate threat to their peace than the Royalists and Roundheads.

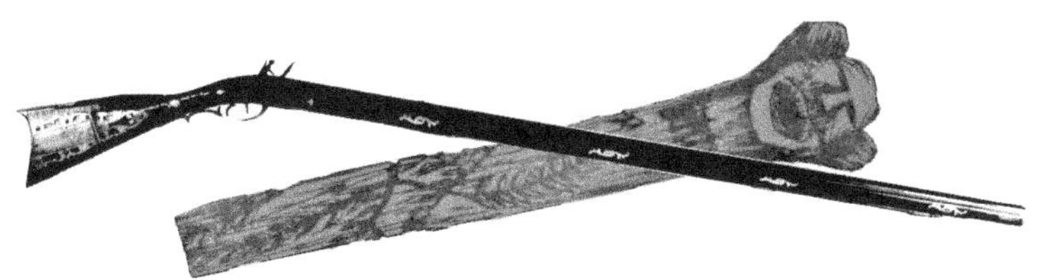

CHAPTER FORTY-EIGHT

The Natives are Restless

1643

Narragansett became the focus for the first half of the year. Roger Williams sailed to England to obtain a patent or charter for Aquidneck and Providence. While he was away the leaders of Connecticut, Boston, Plymouth and New Haven met at the Court of Elections to create the United Colonies of New England, which territory included Rhode Island. Williams did obtain the charter for what was called Narragansett Bay, which bordered Massachusetts on the north and north east and Plymouth on the east and south. The patent was vague and Massachusetts disputed it for several years.

In June Gov. Winthrop and his family were staying on Governor's Island in Boston harbor which he had planted with vineyards and orchards when the French Lieutenant General Charles LaTour sailed into the harbor in a 140 ton warship, the *Saint-Clement.* LaTour told Winthrop his enemy d'Auldenay had blockaded the St. John's River so he couldn't sail this new ship made in Rochelle to his fort. Winthrop brought LaTour and his entourage by LaTour's shallop to Boston and sent word for the Assembly to meet to discuss whether the United Colonies of New England would give militiary aid to LaTour. The presence of a French warship in the harbor was unsettling and many colonists objected when Winthrop allowed 40 French soldiers to come ashore and practice drilling and firing at the annual muster the following week. LaTour represented himself as the governor of Acadia but the Boston commissioners later found out d'Auldenay was the true governor. There was considerable debate as the French were entertained for a couple of weeks but one of the ministers quoted Proverbs 26:17, *"He that meddleth with a strife which belongs not to him, takes a dog by the ear, which is very dangerous."* No official aid was given to La Tour but Thomas Hawkins and Edward Gibbons were allowed to lease four ships and a pinnace for two months for La Tour to use to break the blockade to the north. Rev. Nathaniel Ward and the townspeople of Ispwich and Rowley soundly protested Winthrop's almost unilateral handling of the affair, feeling that all of the commissioners from all of the United Confederation of New England should have been summoned into session to make a decision that might have far reaching political consequences (the memory of how the Crown embroiled England in constant wars in Europe fresh in their minds).

In August *Uncas*, sachem of the Mohegan tribe, went to war against *Sequasson*, a relative of the Narragansett sachem *Minanatomo*, killing 30 Narragansetts and wounding many. *Minanatono* was taken captive and Rev. Samuel Gorton (who had purchased land in *Shawomut* from *Minanatomo* after Gorton had been cast out of *Aquidneck*. The sachem *Punham* had challenged Gorton's deed, going to Boston to say *misawomet* (Warwick) belonged to him and because he was an ally of the English, to them and not the man they banished). Boston wrote a letter to *Uncas* stating he had better turn over *Minantomo*, who was now in Hartford or the English Army would war with *Uncas*'s people. Gorton had the audacity to infer that Gov. Winthrop actually endorsed his position. The United Colonies of New England, called the New England Confederation sent word to Hartford to hand *Minanatono* over to *Uncas* for the Mohegans to kill as Winthrop and others were angry with him for selling land to Gorton and they also felt *Minantono* was plotting against the English behind their backs.

Gorton had also earned Boston's disfavor after an altercation with Benedict Arnold of *Pawtuxet*, who had petitioned the Massachusetts general court in 1641 for relief of the Gortonists. The Massachusetts leaders had told Arnold if Pawtucket submitted to the jurisdiction of the Bay they might intervene.

After the *Uncas-Minantomo* war, Boston summoned Gorton and his followers to appear in court. Gorton sent an arrogant letter to Winthrop calling him "the Great and honored Idol General now set up in the Massachusetts". Winthrop sent 40 soldiers to arrest Gorton. He and nine of his Gortonists were barricaded in a house with two flankers, or defensive towers, on its side, but the Gortonists were captured, put on trial and extensively examined about their heretical religious beliefs. The Court sentenced Rev. Gorton to hard labor in iron chains at the jail in Charlestown. Randall Holden, his second in command was sent to Salem and five of the other Gortonists were spread out amongst the villages and put to hard labor, their movements monitored and severely restricted. Captain Cook then returned to Warwick and herded all the Gortonists' cattle, bringing them to Boston to sell to pay for the costs of Gorton and his followers' imprisonment. All their muskets and arms were given to *Pumham* and *Sacononoco*.

During the Narragansett-Mohegan war savages near the Dutch attacked Anne Hutchinson and her six children where they had settled in Pelham Bay on Long Island. Her son-in-law, William Collins (the main male defending them as William Hutchinson had died in 1642), was also killed along with 14 other English settlers. In revenge for the Pequot Fort massacre the English were herded along with their cattle into their homes and their houses set afire. The savages then turned on the Dutch settlers, likewise burning any they could capture and driving the rest west to *Monhaton* (Manhattan).

In December ministers from Cambridge, Dorchester, Charlestown, Boston, Roxbury and Watertown were appointed by the Court and the magistrates were appointed for life terms as governors of Harvard College.

While the six men were being sworn in three of the five ships recently built in New England set sail for England, taking many of the wealthier families with them (to support King Charles I and his Cavaliers) with a hold full of beaver skins. As with the parting in England of Puritans heading to New England, there was a lot of sorrow to see friends and relatives sail away, possibly never to return. Long prayers for their safe passage and safety once on English soil were heard in churches in the little towns up and down the coast of New England.

William Davis had gone south to Springfield to be with the Pynchons on the Connecticut River. William Pynchon had received permission from the sachem

Wrutha for a site initially named Agawam in order to establish a trading post for the furs and black lead mine he'd discovered on the overland trail from Boston to the Connecticut River and William was courting Margaret. Sewn into busking bags with a board between them he slept next to her on the long, cold winter nights that year. Physically hampered from intercourse they never the less cuddled and kissed and whispered secrets in the cold dark of Pynchon's crude house as his saltbox was being built. All the settlements were on full alert because of the recent tribal wars and of the atrocities done to the Dutch and English on Long Island but for William and Margaret their world was one of bliss and hope and they were impatient for the day when they would marry and live in a nice house in Boston, built by Dolor Davis.

CHAPTER FORTY-NINE

Massachusetts Government Grows

1644

A year before William married Margaret Pynchon in Springfield his cousin William in New Haven had a son, whom he named John. As Marie's and Robert's son William was celebrating the beginning of life in marriage, William was mourning the loss of his wife to one of the many chest sicknesses that so afflicted the New Englanders during the bitterly cold winters. In deep mourning he had moved down to New Haven, hoping to heal from the loss by moving to a completely different location. In this, he was fortunate as his father, William from Bristol, was a very wealthy man and William Jr. was not hindered by lack of funds. In 1639 the new settlement of New Haven had eagerly welcomed the influx of his money and his shipping connections plus his skills as a blacksmith.

William Jr. immediately became involved with the Pelhams, Clintons, Fiennes (all related to the marquis of Newcastle in Nottingham and Derbyshire where the family owned extensive manorial spreads of fields and rare, precious stands of forest). He remarried Martha Wakeman, sister of Samuel Wakeman who was killed along with Capt. Peirce off Providence Isle. Samuel Wakeman had come over with the Talcotts on the *Lion* in 1632 and the families remained close, settling in

Connecticut towns. John Talcott served in the first assemblies in Connecticut, having moved to Hartford with Rev. Hooker. The *Lion* or *Lyon* was owned by one of the Lyons of Somerset, Marquis of Southwold. The Lyons were related to the Heaths, who settled in the north. (William Lyon from Harrow on Hill, Heston moved near the Davises in Roxbury in 1646. He later got a land grant in Woodstock, Connecticut but his grandson was the one to settle it.)

In June, 1643 William Cavendish, the Marquis of Newcastle, led an army for King Charles I against the Roundheads (Cromwellians) in a battle on Adwalton Moor in southern Yorkshire. The king's forces had a victory but Cromwell's New Model Army under Fairfax and others, joined by Scottish Parliamentarians, squeezed the royal army at the battle of Marston Moor in June, 1644. From then on, King Charles I, personally leading his Army of Cavaliers, suffered defeat after defeat, vastly outnumbered by the Roundheads.

The Civil War in England touched almost every family in New England as many men, feeling a loyalty to the English crown, sailed across the sea to help King Charles I, and others, feeling a loyalty to the Cromwellians, likewise left off clearing, plowing or trading to sail over and assist the Puritans in England.

Thus William Davis of Boston was surprised to see William Jr. when he visited Springfield in the summer of 1644.

(There were multiple William Davises in New England at the time, some there to increase their wealth, others for land and still others had come due to religious persecution by King Charles I. There were many Johns and Jameses, too, including a William Davis whose ancestors had sold Twickenham Manor in with its three smaller manors to Thomas York, who sold it as York Manor to Edward Seymour, Earl of Hertford, Duke of Somerset in exchange for other lands. Twickenham, conveniently located on the Thames only ten miles from Charing Cross in London was a desirable suburb within commuting distance for the wealthy politicians and merchants. Besides James Davis, residents included the Thayers related to Lord Stafford, at Bungey Hall, and Edward Bacon in Twickenham Park House and a relative of Lucy Russell, Countess of Bedford. James 's son James born in 1619 was a strict Puritan and eventually with his wife Cicely Thayer immigrated to New England.)

"What ho, cousin!" William Jr. hailed as he entered the newly married (Marie and Robert's) William's Boston apothecary shop.

"Cousin Will!" he replied, shaking his hand and offering him a seat in front of one of Dr. Clark's prototype stoves in the middle of his shop.

"I've come to see about getting a cargo to send to England to help King Charles's troops," he replied, sitting heavily on an upended casket of wine.

William frowned.

"Ye might not want to be saying that too loudly here, cousin. 'Tis Cromwell country, to be sure."

"How can ye say that, young man when ye yerself have what ye have by yer cousin's explorin' with Cavendish?"

William returned to his mortar and pestle, powdering herbs to be mixed with lard for ointment.

"I can't say I feel my father or his cousin were much helped by Cavendish – after all he turned viciously on John when he turned back from that disastrous North Passage voyage."

"Aye," William Jr. said, pulling on his pipe to get the tobacco burning. He drank the wine William offered him and asked questions about the safety of the stove.

"Ye know it's a lost cause," William told his cousin in what would be called New Haven, "Oliver Cromwell has the backing of the majority of the people, plus now the Scottish. King Charles is a tyrant and even worse than his father. He is arrogant, greedy and dictatorial. How he has treated people elected by their towns and villages to represent them in the commons is inexcusable. He will be defeated and those that side with him will feel the wrath of the Roundheads, this I can assure you."

William Jr. shifted his bulk on the cask top whose iron rings were biting into his buttocks.

"Ye are a young fool, Willie," he used their childhood nicknames, "the history of England shows that the Crown always triumphs in the end. And it dispenses lands and manors and privileges to those who remained loyal."

"I have to heartily disagree with ye," the younger William said seriously, mixing his ointment in a red clay bowl, "The whole Puritan movement, this whole New England movement, has shifted the balance of power. Who would have thought common people could have upset the authority of the Archbishop of the Church of

England?"

William Jr. harumphed, stood, took his wide brimmed beaver hat off a peg near the door and buttoned his jacket, which stretched tightly over his large stomach.

"Well, I guess we will see, young Will," he pronounced as he opened the door, "just because ye came into a nice inheritance from yer father's *Mary and John* doesn't mean it will get you very far in this wilderness. Ye are but a flaming arrow away from losing everything to the savages, and don't ye forget that!"

"Margaret and I are very much aware of our perilous environment, cousin," William said, adjusting his crude spectacles, "But when I lived outside Dorchester in England I saw a land of haves and have nots. Rev. White was always preaching about how those who had more should help those who weren't so blessed. He opened schools for all the boys, not just the rich, he started a brewery that the town could operate in order to feed and house the poor and he opened work houses where orphans could do an honest day's work and learn an honorable trade such as weaving. England is changing, William, it is no longer feudal. No longer do people have to live on manors under the thumb of the Lord who can pluck them out of their fields and send them off to fight for England in France or Europe or wherever the people in their ivory tower in London feel can be conquered and enrich the few while further impoverishing the poor. I get indentured servants in my shop every day who have terrible maladies that their English owners won't treat. The Irish are a pitiful sight and I've seen how the fieldhands are treated in Virginia and the West Indies. Don't preach to me of how the King is always all wise and always has England's best interest in mind when he declares war. Rev. Eliot, who often stops in when he travels between the villages of the savages, said we are doing to them what England did to the Welsh, Irish and Scottish. It is something to be ashamed of, cousin, not something to be supported. Margaret and I pray every day, on our knees in front of the fireplace, for Jesus to come and take the saved to Heaven so the great Restoration of His kingdom on Earth will come."

William snorted and then laughed heartily, then coughing from his tobacco smoke,

"Aye ye be one o' them thinking the End of Days is near!"

"Nay, dear cousin, I just feel there is so much evil and greed in the world that we are in need of a giant cleansing. I pray that we, here in New England, will be the instrument the Lord uses to accomplish it. If it means I have to die for Christ, I am willing to go today. But I am not willing to die for that Scottish tyrant and his court of fools!"

William slammed the oak plank door behind him as he went in search of William Pynchon, hoping he'd appeal to his business side as the troops needed many goods Pynchon's trading post could sell.

Later that spring in Boston a young wife and her lover were accused of adultery and put to death, the crime a capitol offense under the new *Body of Liberties'*

In late May a ship arrived from Virginia reporting that the savages had massacred 300 settlers. The Boston elite said it was Divine Justice as the communities had driven out the ministers they had recently sent to them as Sir William Berkeley, royal governor of Virginia was antagonistic towards Puritans. The Davis families immediately sent letters to their relatives there to inquire of their safety.

That summer the Boston elite tried to circumvent the Assembly by trying to establish a Commission that granted seven magistrates and three deputies and John Ward, son of Rev. Nathaniel Ward, to determine matters in between sessions. Ward's younger brother James had recently committed theft while a student at Harvard and along with Rev. Weld's son John was publically whipped for burglary. (Unlike with adultery, there was no set punishment established for burglary.) With anti-royalist sympathies raging, the magistrates' Commission idea was immediately shut down by the June Court as contrary to the foundation of New England's government and the Freemans' liberty.

The deputies and magistrates were not appeased but the General Court said it would not rule on the matter until the October session. One of the magistrates stated that if an occasion occurred in the meantime the justices would take over and William Hawthorne, the speaker of the Assembly from Salem who had come over in the *Arbella* with Winthrop stood up and loudly shouted, "You will not be obeyed!" In New England the English civil war had made many feel Winthrop, Endecott was acting like King Charles I and the common People like the Cromwellians.

However, the magistrates's declaration that they alone had executive authority during adjournment of the general court sessions was formalized when Gov. Endecott, Deputy Gov. Winthrop and seven Assistants drew up a writ declaring their authority if new hostilities between *Punham* and *Uncas* were brought to Boston that might need immediate militiary action by the New England confederacy. Richard Saltonstall and Richard Bellingham abstained from voting on the dictate as they felt the only power given to govern was by the People through annual elections.

In June the English Civil War came to Boston Harbor when Capt. Thomas Stagg from Virginia blocked, boarded and seized a merchant ship from Bristol with fish bound for Balboa, claiming authority from Robert Rich, Earl of Warwick, Lord High Admiral of England , He stated he was authorized to take any vessel outward bound or from Bristol, Barnstaple, Dartmouth and other ports as their areas were against the King.

The following arguments by those in power pitted those who felt New England had a right to self-government against those who quoted the royal charter that made the Massachusetts Bay Colony a territory of the East Greenwich, Kent Parliament representation. Stagg said he had authority from the English Parliament so he was acting in its interests and had to be honored. The founders of the MBC had agreed to this proviso for English oversight as it allowed them to rule themselves in local matters and to have lands allotted to citizens plus to be free from compulsory militiary service. William Davis Sr. was one of the merchants who then wanted to sue Capt. Stagg for taking their goods but the magistrates in Boston said they would write to the Earl of Warwick to seek redress. The incident caused a lot of unrest in the harbor towns but in Stamford, Connecticut, an English village on the border of New Netherland, a mother was attacked in her house by a savage who violently bashed her head while she bent down to pick up her infant out of its cradle. The mother eventually recovered and identified the savage and the New Haven court sentenced him to death by a falchion, or Middle Eastern curved sword. It took eight blows before he was beheaded but the mother suffered permanent brain damage and was never the same afterwards.

In the fall Thomas Morton was arrested in Plymouth after returning from England where he had published a book speaking against the New England Puritans. He was old and judged to be of no threat so the court fined him 100 pounds and he went north to *Acomenticus*.

Charles La Tour and/or his wife made appearances in Boston during the summer and fall as did d'Aulnay to plead their separate cases and Elias Pilgrim, master of the *Gillyflower* had contracted with Captain Bayley under charge of William

Berkeley of London to bring meal and peas to La Tour's fort but the ship was impounded in Boston harbor. Pilgrim appealed to the court in Boston for his share of the cargo's worth and for his crew's wages.

To the south the Narragansetts agreed to a cease fire so the southern towns felt a reprieve in the intertribal warfare that spilled out into English settlements such as Stamford. The savages claimed they were weren't at war with the English but with the Dutch settlers.

Roger Williams and his family returned from England with a patent from Parliament creating the colony of Providence Plantations. He appeared in Boston with a letter of safe conduct signed by 12 prominent members of Parliament including members of the Commission for Plantations in the West Indies and the Lord Mayor of London. Williams had published a book about the language of the savages titled *A Key into the Language of America* in London in 1643 and the New England missionaries such as Eliot and Gookin were all eager to obtain copies to help them in their work amongst the tribes.

After setting up an apothecary shop in New Haven William Davis returned to Springfield where he was contacted by Dr. Clark that fall to help prepare plasters for the skull of little Abigail Eliot, daughter of the older brother of Rev. John Eliot in Roxbury. While playing hide and seek she had overturned a cart and a piece of iron had punctured her skull. Dr. Thomas Oliver of Boston performed a trepanning then inserted a small silver plate to cover the wound but drawing plasters were needed to prevent infection. It was experimental surgery but, with the help of William's herbs, little Abigail survived what most people felt would be a fatal wound as brain tissue was actually leaking out of her little skull. Unlike the mother in Stamford, Abigail never suffered from brain damage and physicians up and down the coast marveled at Dr. Oliver's daring and his surgical skills while congregations attributed her healing to their many prayers.

The magistrate-commission issue was again considered at the October General Court. Many wanted the input of the clergy, but the members who drew up their Commission that summer resented and refused to consider it so the matter, although approved by the deputies, the judicial and clerical authorities, went back and forth all winter and spring as they debated the roles of the governmental branches of the legislative, judicial and consultative (or directive of the public affairs, i.e., 'elected freemen') in the New England confederacy.

In December, 1644 in England Cromwell and members of Parliament passed a 'Self Denying Ordinance' that forced sitting members to resign their militiary commissions. The King's Army had suffered a massive defeat in the battle of Marston Moor in June and the Marquis of Newcastle fled the country. Fairfax and the New Model Army led by Essex, Manchester and Waller had lost almost a third of its original 30,000 men but had 11 regiments of horse, one of dragoons and 12 regiments of foot soldiers with muskets and pikes. Under Fairfax the Army was taught to hold fire until they could see the whites of the enemy's eyes to conserve powder and improve efficiency. The Roundheads wore red coats with different colors of 'facing' to identify the regiments. In battle formation the musketeers were deployed with pikemen to their rear. Unlike conscripted armies with set terms, the Parliament established England's first standing Army and the men were heavily drilled and disciplined and received regular pay from the government. Within a year their ranks would swell to 80,000 men and meet King Charles I's Cavaliers at Naseby.

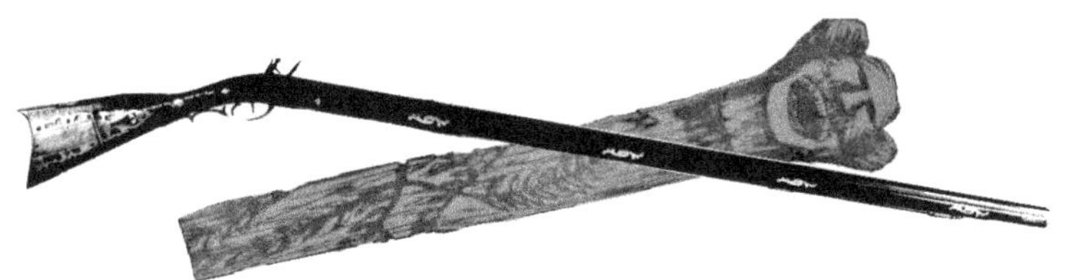

CHAPTER FIFTY

William and his Little Shops of Healing

1645

The Battle of Marston Moor in Yorkshire was a big victory for Cromwell and his Ironsides. With help from the Scottish Parliamentarians the field was won and Sir David Leslie went back to Scotland. During the battle Prince Rupert, Charles's nephew, hid in a bean field. In early 1645 the Parliament had enacted the 'Self-Denying Ordinance' whereby members of Parliament couldn't be involved in the fighting and the New Model Army was now run by professional soldiers such as Fairfax, Edward Manchester, Sir William Waller and Henry Ireton, son-in-law of Cromwell.

In New England, William and Margaret (nee Pynchon) moved north to the frontier village of Haverhilll, north of Boston and inland on the Merrimac River.

Besides being a safter environment, the move occurred because Giles Firman married Rev. Nathaniel Ward's daughter in that new village and he, being the son of an apothecary in Sudbury, England knew William and asked him to move his business there. Firman and William had attended Cambridge where each had studied anatomy and physiology but William dropped out after one semester as he wanted to work with herbs and plant remedies and discover medicines to help doctors, who were still relying on leeches and bleeding as their main curatives. In addition, William's relative James had received a large lot on the river and his sons had settled there. Tristrum Coffin, a friend of the Davis family from Devonshire, set up an 'ordinary' or tavern near the ferry dock where George Carr's raft crossed from the island he named after himself. Rev. Ward, who was a lawyer as well as a minister there, had drawn up the *Code of Liberties* for the federation a short while before.

Two years prior James had sailed the *Trial* down the coast buy wine, sugar and cotton in the Barbados for the Federation. The New England women were expert flax spinners and weavers, especially of sailcloth and a lot of hemp was twisted into strong ropes for ships but the fine cotton from Barbados was highly prized. The Merrimac River had a lot of small tributaries that were perfect for water-powered mills and Job Clement set up a tannery off the river near the mouth of the Plug Pond.

To the south of Boston In 1645 the Rev. Peter Hobart was summoned to the federation's General Court as he, along with his brothers Thomas, Joshua and Edmund had sided with Anthony Eames, from Fordington Dorset, near Dorchester, against Bozoan Allen from King's Lynn in the militia fracas in the new village of Hingham the previous year. Most of the Hingham folks had sided with Allen. Rev. Hobart eluded the authorities initially but when brought to Boston he defiantly questioned the authority of the governor and Council and demanded to know where they had authority to charge him with sedition and contempt of authority as they had no royal warrant. The Court fined him and deferred on a final judgment until the next court.

In Boston William was working in his first apothecary shop, now run by his cousin William, who had set up the first pharmacy in that town, when Firman came storming in, furious with the Council.

"He were a good friend o' mine!" he spat as he had William's assistant wrap sarsaparilla in a paper packet.

William agreed that he knew Eames as he was from Fordington and his family were friends of the Warrens.

"I feel 'tisn't really about who is to captain the militia in Hingham," William said, "but what seems to be occurring is that if anyone speaks against any authority the Winthrop group will punish or expel them. It's tyranny. Dudley is the better governor, for sure, but that Winthrop is acting like King Charles and the Allen group comes from a part o' England that has long challenged royal authority. Remember, 'twas in one o'their towns the people made King John sign the Magna Carta which reined in royal power. It's only been violated since King James declared this whole Divine Rights of Kings nonsense. Me mother said under Queen Elizabeth England was a happier country."

The wooden door blew open, gusting in cold March wind.

William's eyes opened wide as he saw the young doctor in front of him.

"Jacob!" he hailed, embracing his friend from Cambridge, "Ye have left the islands?"

Jacob laughed, "Only for a bit, my friend. I was asked to come by our friend Josh Hobie to attend the plague of Venus in Roxbury."

The four men fell silent. William blushed.

"Aye, word got that far abroad?"

Jacob laughed, "Nay, I just heard about it in harbor when Josh came to greet me. I'm only here a'visitin' for a spell to get away from the relentless heat and humidity in the islands."

"Do ye have word from me cousins?"

"Nay but I heerd John might be going back to England to fight for the king. Samuel comes round regular like in the *Trader's Increase* and occasionally I see yer cousin William in port as master of a ship but trade with England is severely restricted now and we are forbidden to trade with any but the English."

William looked at Giles sternly, "Ye aren't a'buyin' that sarsaparilla for the lues veneria are ye?'

"Nay, 'tis for a sore caused from a burn me wife got at the fireplace," he said sheepishly tucking the packet into a pocket of his calf-length woolen coat.

Jacob handed a bag of herbs over to William.

William told Giles to liberally apply butter to the burn before putting the powdered herb on, wrapping the burn afterwards with a strip of clean cotton.

Jacob then said to William, "I hoped to find ye here," and gave him instructions on how he wanted an herbal preparation made. "I have new herbs that have proved effective in the islands for the curse of sailors," he said, alluding to the rumor that a ship's cooper had spread the venereal disease amongst nursing mothers and others through copulations in Roxbury.

Just then Dolor Davis walked in, exchanging greetings with his fellow townsman as Firman left with his secreted packet.

William made the introductions and Dolor talked with Jacob about where he'd come from in Suffolk.

"Aye, I once traveled a bit in that neck of the woods. Crossed the bridge to Houghton's Mill on the Ouse and visited Hemmingford Abbots church with its yellow brickwork on one wall. Saw St. Albans and Woburn Abbey back a'fore I married and was free to travel a bit and look at the old architecture. Ye have Colchester castle up there, one of the oldest in all of England."

"So are ye living in Boston, then?" Jacob asked them.

Both men shook their heads. "Nay," said William, "We be north in Haverhilll – ye'd love the place. It is like Haverhilll in Suffolk, full of small brooks and streams, nice gentle hills and a lot 'o marsh land. It doesn't have that rich black soil of Suffolk and Essex but has an abundance of big, tall trees, both hardwoods and pines."

Jacob sighed. He was tired of island vegetation, warm salt air and the strength-sapping humidity of the West Indies but he had taken on doctoring to the plantations as a sort of sacred mission.

"Tell ye what, Jacob," said William, clapping his hand on the other's shoulder, "When ye be done in Roxbury, find a Davis ship in port and she'll bring ye up the Merrimac to us for yer vistin'!"

"But ye can't stay for more than two weeks per 'King John' and his Royal Council," Dolor added with a frown.

Jacob raised an eyebrow but Dolor left.

"Aye, the rules be a bit harsh here," he mumbled, "but this is a good, God-fearing Protestant land, be assured of that."

William told him he'd been done with the physick the next day as the herbs had to be boiled into liquid. He gave him directions to Richard Bellingham's house with a slip of paper identifying him as a friend in need of a room for a night.

"So ye don't have to stay at the publick house," William said, indicating the presence of lice in the bedding by scratching.

"Aye, just like at college!" Jacob laughed as he went out to explore Boston.

CHAPTER FIFTY-ONE

News from England

1646

In June 1646 the King and his troops were solidly defeated at Naseby, a small town west of Cromwell's Huntington and southwest of Lord Cecil's manor at Burghley. Prince Rupert was then sent to hold Bristol. The three most important battles had been fought in the area and James Davis had many friends whose houses were destroyed in the fighting.

James Davis had been master on a ship that docked in Jamestown when he saw his old friend and fellow mariner Arthur Cartwright. A ship from England had brought news of the victory for the Roundheads but Cartwright was in tears.

"Me manor, me beautiful, new manor, all burnt up!" he lamented over his pint of ale in a dockside ordinary.

Capt. James was stiff from arthritis. He eased himself into a chair across from Arthur and sipped from his mug.

"Aye, I just aheard. 'Twas a terrible blow for King Charles and Prince Rupert. I fear Cromwell and his thugs have now got the upper hand."

Arthur shook his head. Like James, he was greying and getting too old for the rigors of sailing.

"I put all me eggs in that basket," Arthur moaned, "built me a beautiful manor to spend the end of me days in, did I. And your," he looked at James sternly," King Charles's Royalists burnt it out of spite. I never supported Cromwell and always paid up when the Crown asked – and now I have nothing."

James patted the man's large arm.

"Me family saw this a'comin', Art. 'Tis been brewing a long time, ever since Charles put the crown on his small head. We knew when his father took the throne after Queen Elizabeth that England was entering stormy waters. That's why me and my kin invested on this side o' the Atlantic – here in the Boston areas and Virginia, and in the Islands and up north in Mason's land and on the Merrimac River. Some 's gone south of Boston to avoid Gov. Winthrop's tyranny but I hear his son now has a new plantation at *Pequod*, which is being referred to as New London. One thing I can say is even though we have our own tyrants a'rulin' using the Bible, we don't have soldiers a'fighting outside our homes."

Arthur shook his head, "Dammit, James! It just seems ye can't win in England these days. 'Twas time when ye could curry royal favor by bringing spices or dainties from foreign shores – "

James laughed and interrupted, " – Or by pirating Spanish ships!"

"Aye, and ye know where that got good old Sir Walter."

They both drained their mugs and got refills from the tap room.

"As I was saying, we had it good under Queen Elizabeth. She 'twere vain, 'tis true, and could be vindictive but she put many things aside as long as ye were a good Protestant and brought her nice cargo."

James rubbed his jaw, rough with stubble as he hadn't been to a barber since arriving in port. He wore the ruby and gold earring but it no longer set off a virile, strong, young face. Both men at the battered wooden table had sagging chins and were heavily tanned and wrinkled from many years squinting over the vast sea.

Arthur wiped his eyes with a stained handkerchief. He sighed deeply.

James spoke, "Ye know, if ye want to come over, I'll bring ye and yer family as a goodness and we have friends, the Vassels, near the Plymouth plantation who are looking for more settlers of any religion to come and build up a village. We don't have Roundheads and Cavaliers over here but we have plenty o' savages that get all riled up and fight each other and if ye be in the middle ye can get killed or yer place burned out."

Arthur sighed raggedly. His pewter mug was empty and James fetched him a refill.

"Me family had that land for years, James. 'Twas so pleasant – ye should've seen the apricot trees a'bloomin' every spring! My father would accept apricots for rent, ye see, so the tenants would pick them and then we'd make apricot brandy and preserves."

"We have a lot of small green wild apples in this New World," James replied, "but we could sure use more fruit trees. If ye decide to come over, get a gardener to uproot and wrap as many young apple and fruit trees as ye can. Ye might be able to buy a piece of land to plant 'em in as people are hungry for new produce over here and love cider. Ye get mighty sick of corn, barley, wheat and native apples and every time I bring cargo up from the West Indies ye should see the throng a'wantin' to buy any lemons, limes or fruit that survives the voyage. O' course New England is colder than England so citrus doesn't do well but if ye bring good sturdy English apple stock, pears or apricots we'd sure love to add them to our larders!"

Arthur nodded, half-listening.

"Aye, if them troops haven't burnt down me orchards or cut all me trees down. I'm sorry ye have to see me so broken, James," he said softly, sipping his ale.

"Well 'tis not as bad as yer ship getting swamped in the sea," James said, wiping his mouth with the back of his hand, "I've seen ships make it through storms that sunk others. Ye never know if ye'll make it or not."

"Aye, and at least I didn't get a'thrown in the Tower like Pym and Eliot and them others."

"Back under ol' Henry the Eighth my family lost most of its lands in Wales," James said reflectively, "yet we rose up again. It just takes time, Art. If ye can hang in long enoug' ye can pull yer ship into safe harbor."

"Unlike that unfortunate ship what got a'frozen in the sea off *Pequod* in January," replied Arthur, "We heerd o' it all the way to King's Lynn."

"Aye, she were crank sided being new. Before she could be cut free o' the ice she keeled over in a tempest about three miles offshore. We lost Captain Turner and about seventy people plus peas, wheat, many West Indian hides, beaver and plate. 'Twas a terrible loss." He added, "As ye know, Art, ye can lose all ye got at sea as well as on land."

Cartwright agreed, saying he had lost some ships over the years but he had hung all his retirement dreams on the manor he'd built. He now had to form a new picture of his future and it was causing him a lot of grief.

"Like ye said, ye put all yer eggs in that basket," James agreed sadly, "Me – I put a few here and a few there. This Virginia venture is very risky but if we can get some of those black Africans to work our fields we won't be a'losin' so many laborers to the fevers. O' course, me being a fine Christian man, I am against man stealing so for the time being we Davis men must run our plantations with the scruffy lot scraped off the bottom of England and Ireland's barrel. And now the Scottish who fled to Ireland are starting to come over! They may be Protestants but I think they lived in Ireland too long and have Papist tendencies."

****

When Capt. James returned to Boston later that summer he wished he'd brought more corn as a plague of black caterpillars had arrived in a thunderstorm and were decimating the corn crops.

Religious problems were festering to the south of Boston in response to Winthrop's rigidity in not allowing any other religions other than Boston Puritanism into the United Colonies. A few years previously Parliament had set up a 12 man commission to oversee the plantations in New England. The Earl of Warwick headed it and he was very tolerant, granting Roger Williams a patent of land and Samuel Gorton had just received permission to remain in Shawomut.

The West Indies, especially Barbados where William Vassall (friend of the Hobarts in Hingham), who moved there after he left New England in protest of the anti-tolerant Boston Puritanism, was becoming more important economically with the export of sugar. There were sugar plantations on the Barbados, Bermuda and Jamaica plus in the middle of Guiana, which the British shared with the French.

Rev. Hobart continued to be a thorn in the side of the Boston theocracy but another challenge arose when a petition was presented to Plymouth and then Boston for the right of freedom of religion from what were called the Remonstrators – Dr. Child, Thomas Fowle, Samuel Maverick, Thomas Burton, John Smith, David Yale and John Dand. It wasn't a priority as the clergy were more interested in gathering in a synod in Cambridge to establish a uniform system of clerical government and punishments.

The synod was seen to be pushing "Presbyterianism" onto the United Colonies – a Scottish system whereby the church ruled the state instead of the state ruling the church. This difference in how a state was to be ruled first erupted under King James I and was made worse by King Charles I's actions. Thomas Goodwin, Philip Nye and Jeremiah Burroughs spoke fervently for religious Independence when the Boston theocracy persecuted Anabaptists in 1645.

By the end of 1646 after lengthy debates over royal authority versus the authority of the United Colonies, Dr. Child and others boarded a ship bound for England to plead their case. On another ship John Winthrop left to defend the colonies against the Remonstrators' charges against the MBC to the earl of Warwick.

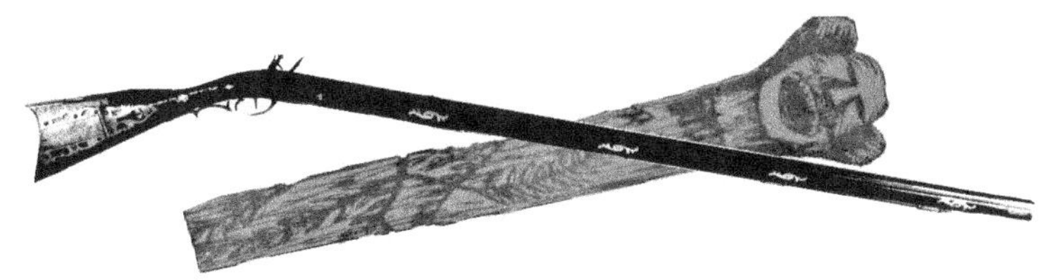

CHAPTER FIFTY-TWO

Witches and War

1647

William Davis Sr. of Bristol had married the widow Mrs. Clark and had raised her son, William Clark. William Clark emigrated to New England and opened an ordinary in Salem. He was a militia officer and a church member and citizen in good standing until 1646 when he quarreled with the town's constable who, under the influence of the Boston Puritans, wanted him charged and fined for keeping a shuffle board in his house. Winthrop and the church elders felt such an object encouraged citizens to idle games instead of hard, Puritan labor.

He, along with Samuel Maverick and Dr. Child, Thomas Fowle, David Yale, Thomas Joye, Thomas Burton, John Smith and John Dand were to appear in the March 1647 General Court regarding the petition 'The Remonstrators' had signed. They were planning to send a copy of their petition to the Commission of Plantations in England protesting the intolerance in the New England Federation towards religious practices and their feeling that the colony was acting too independently and not seeking advice or counsel from England's Parliament. The petition was seized from the ship that was to take it along with Dr. Childs and Dand and the three ringleaders Child, Dand and Smith were arrested and held under a casual house arrest under the supervision of George Munnings, the Boston Prison Keeper until the March 1647 General Court session.

However, that winter William Clark took sick with a respiratory ailment and despite his cousin William Davis's best tinctures and poultices passed away before the court was held. Fines were levied and Smith and Dand paid for their bail but Dr. Child refused and was held at Munnings until he could raise the money to pay his high fines and then sail for England.

Robert Tobias Davis of Yarmouth was friends of John Young and the Davis family shared his grief when in late May his wife Alice Young was accused of witchcraft and hanged in Windsor , Connecticut on the same day the General Court of Elections was held in Boston. John Young was a respected soldier and representative of Windsor who was helping the Connecticut colony drive out the Dutch on Long Island. After the hanging, in deep grief and humiliation, he sold his lands in Windsor and moved away. (In later years Sarah Davis, daughter of Robert Davis of Barnstable/Yarmouth would marry his son Joseph Young in Eastham.) Both Yarmouth and Eastham were far out on Cape Cod and the men were fishermen who occasionally dragged a dead whale to shore for the Wampanoags and locals to harvest fat and bones from. Joseph Davis was one of the men on the committee that surveyed the boundary lines between Ipswich and Salem.

John Young remarried Elizabeth, widow of Joseph Isaacs in Cambridge, and moved to York. Issacs had been talking to the Connecticut men about the possibility of founding a college in New Haven to be named Yale. He came from a highly educated family in England and his relatives continued supporting the endeavor after his death.

It seemed to the colonists that every year the same old men were reelected to power, which made those in sympathy with the Remonstrators grumble but the Court did allow one of the demands (a critical one) of the Remonstrators' petition to stand: they allowed non-freemen the right to serve on juries and to vote for their local town officers and tax assessors.

At the spring General Court George Denison (Dennison) of Roxbury was chosen as a captain of their militia as he had recently served in England on Parliament's side in battles against the crown. Denison was very popular with the young men who insisted he be chosen even though he was not yet a freeman. To keep the peace his opponent for the position, Lt. Isaac Johnson, through the efforts of Sgt. William Pritchard (who later helped settle Brookfield, or *Quaboag* Plantation), conceded and Boston was spared another dispute such as the one in Hingham. George Denison had a pretty and amusing wealthy wife from Ireland where she had inherited the Borrodell family estate in Cork but she chose to live in primitive New England with the man she loved.

Dolor was in Roxbury when Dennison got back from Court. He bought him a pint of ale at the ordinary.

"So ye been a'soldieren against the Dorset and Devonshire men?" Dolor asked, wiping foam from his lips.

Denison said he had but he had terrible news.

"I enlisted to fight under Charles, Prince of Wales. He was only fourteen when his father appointed him to take charge o' the fighting in the southwest. He set up headquarters in Bristol. Lord Hopton the governor of Bristol and a brilliant general, was his chief advisor. Lord Capel and the Earl of Bentford plus the Master of the Rolls, Lord Culpepper and Sir Edward Hyde, Chancellor of the Exchequer, were to be his War Council. The Prince was to be the King's man over the fight in Cornwall Dorset, Somerset and Devon and the Corporation of Bristol lodged the officers in a manor and provided a pile o' coal and hogsheads of wine."

Dennison took a swing of his warm ale and then continued, "It all began well with Sir Richard Grenville in charge of the sea blockade of Plymouth."

Dolor groaned. "Aye. We've been sore short o' ships from England these last few years."

"Sir John Berkeley, governor of Exeter assisted Grenville. George Goring was in charge of rousting the Roundheads from the West Country. The Parliamentarians had garrisons in Taunton, Plymouth, Lyme, Weymouth and Poole. Their main general in the West was Sir William Waller. Goring managed to get him and his troops a'fleeing back towards London that March."

Other men gathered around to hear of the Civil War. News had been as rare as English ships.

"A couple of months later the plague hit Bristol. Prince Charles and his entourage moved west. He was a sight, was he. His armor was all gold and he rode on a pure white stallion. In spite of his darkish complexion he was like one o' the knights of King Arthur. He sat tall in the saddle, strong and brave. The problem wasn't wit' young Charles, it was with the bickering and infighting between his councillors."

"Aye," a farmer said, raising his tankard, "'tis always they nobles that get to fighting for the royal ear."

Dennison nodded.

"'Twarnt a real honor to be shunted West," he said," and I don't think the men liked being away from the King's Court where the real influence is."

The keeper of the ordinary refilled their tankards. He, too, was listening intently.

"In May ol' Goring routed the Parliamentarians from Taunton, which was under siege. But he was severely wounded and 'twas thought he would die. His army didn't want to serve under Grenville, who was truly cruel to the Devon and Cornwall men. And they were truly loyal to Goring, not Grenvillle. There was a mass desertion, I tell ya.

"Grenville was given the task o' blockading Lyme and he was offended that they didn't just give him Goring's command so he resigned and tried to resume his post as High Sheriff of Devon but reluctantly took the task of goin' after Goring's deserters after a royal dressing down from the Prince hisself."

"I meself wasn't in Goring's army at the time but I was with him when he recovered and renewed the siege of Taunton. The Roundhead governor there declared he'd rather eat his boots than surrender!"

The crowd laughed and cheered.

"By this time the countryside was completely sick o' this war. The King's troops had razed their fields, had forced the farmers to provision them and to billet, or feed and lodge his soldiers. Some began to meet in private to get a petition together to present to King Charles. But the Roundheads had a big victory at Naseby and were coming after Goring and our Army."

"Aye, I aheard about the constant attacks on Bridgewater, Sherbourne Castle and Bristol," one of the men said, "Me family's from there. Said they brought in siege cannons and all."

Dennison continued, "Well, the money ran out to feed and supply the troops. Prince Charles moved to Exeter. He then tried to assemble a new army in Cornwall, as by title he was their duke and all. But ol' Grenville had been there afore him and had raised up so much rancor that he was lucky he wasn't knocked off his 'orse and beaten, I tell ye true. The people had had enoug' o' the constant fighting.

"General Goring marched into Devon in early October but there just wasn't the heart or the money for the effort. He sent us back to west Devon and he set sail for France to recover his health, which had never returned after his wounding in Taunton."

The farmers made sounds of sympathy or derision, depending on their personal feelings for the war. Most New Englanders were Puritans and favored the fight of the Parliamentarians as they'd never liked King Charles I and his Catholic queen. But most of the Davis men had been staunch supporters of the Royalists, knowing they owed their lands, manors and shipping concerns to royal favor.

"Prince Charles tried to regroup an army from west Devon in order to relieve the King's men in Exeter but I tell ye true: the roads were a real bastard that winter. It rained and rained and ye could hardly take a step with'out a'getting mired in mud. And the horses couldn't hack it, either. We was mud bound for certain. And the cavalry took its orders from Lord Wentworth while we foot soldiers were under Grenville. It 'twas a mess. The Cornishmen got fed up and went home while the officers argued amongst themselves. In tha middle of the coldest month, February, the mud froze and ol' Hopton led us towards Torrington. It 'twas a massacre. Cromwell's New Model Army overwhelmed us. I was lucky to escape wit' me hide! They managed to get Prince Charles on board a ship and set sail for the Scilly Isles in early March. A month later Gen. Hopton surrendered the western army. Prince Charles was surrounded by ships on his island and 'escorted' to the island of Jersey. In the meantime the Catholic Queen was sent on to the Netherlands and on to Paris and King Charles went north and joined the Scottish Army."

Dennison sighed deeply. "And they Scots turned traitor and gave him up."

"Aye and the Irish were devious, too!" an old farmer exclaimed, slapping his thigh.

"Well, do ye blame them?" another replied.

There was grumbling and the innkeeper distracted the group by refilling tankards.

"The terrible news lads, is that the Prince is in exile and the Parliament is aholding the king in the Tower."

This news struck fear into the hearts of those loyal to the crown and made those who backed Cromwell and the Parliamentarians crow with glee.

However, in England the Parliament was becoming unpopular as it refused to pay the soldiers their back pay and then passed legislation extremely intolerant of Anglicans and Independents.

The men who left the public house that afternoon felt a heavy weight on their shoulders. More than anything else they wanted to be left alone, to be free to clear their lands and farms or ply their trades. It seemed to them that England was always at war with her neighbors. They were alternatively friends or enemies of Spain, France, Germany and the Dutch. Wars in Europe affected trade and affected travel and New England had enough of its own problems to deal with having to fend off the French and Dutch as well as the savages.

For the New England, Virginia and West Indies men the Civil War in England was a giant, looming cloud that could rain disaster down on their new colonies and plantations. The captains of ships made in New England had taken advantage of the lack of English ships to run a profitable trade up and down the coast and into the Caribbean but knew that any ship that was not registered in England was in violation of the 'Navigation Act'. And to trade with the Dutch was forbidden yet so desperate were the islanders that they took the risk.

To the south of Boston John Davis sold his lot on Heartbreak Hill near Plymouth to Daniel Rindge and moved his herd to the north side of the river.

At this time there were Davis men in lower Connecticut, on the Cape and near Plymouth, in Boston, north of Boston in Salem and Haverhilll and even farther north in York and Dover.

By 1647 the population of New England had exploded and new towns were springing up as people arrived and settled further away from the already divided and populated towns. Embroilment in a civil war in a country that had been their home but was fast just becoming the motherland was the last thing they wanted.

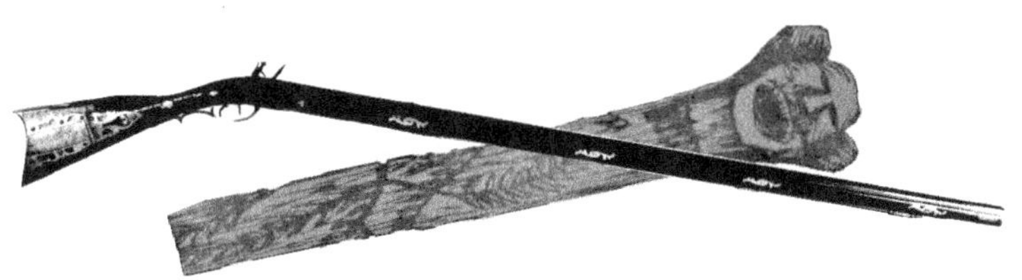

CHAPTER FIFTY-THREE

War for Sugar in the Islands

1648-49

In 1647 the trade with Barbados opened, partly due to Richard Saltonstall, who was friends of Lord Saye and Sele, nephew of Sir Richard who had been mayor of London when Queen Elizabeth was on the throne and had so much money and influence he was the first Assistant Gov. John Winthrop appointed on the voyage of the Massachusetts Bay Colony's founding fleet.

Saltonstall received a large land grant northwest of Bridgetown on Barbados as Lords Pembroke and Carlisle got the choicest port in what they named Carlisle Bay. Inland and northeast on the river James Drax and his Wiltshire neighbor John Davis (Humphrey Davis's son John was brother-in-law to Richards's brother the Rev. Gordon Saltonstall in New London, Connecticut), had gotten nice grants bordering the London Company's 10,000 acres. All up and down the western coast were small holdings granted to indentured servants. The main crops were tobacco, which was depleting the soil and which had been supplanted in popularity by the milder Virginia tobacco; ginger, indigo and cotton, which also depleted the soil.

In 1647 Richard Ligon undertook a voyage to Barbados via St. Igenio in the *Achilles* to report back to Humphrey Moseley about the new crop being raised:

sugar. Moseley was related to Samuel Moseley of Boston, purported to have made his fortune pirating with the Dutch off Jamaica and the other islands in the West Indies.

Sugar cane plants were first imported from South America by the Spanish but the first processing mills came from Brazil, South America via the Dutch. James Drax built the first sugar mill and built a two-gabled, two story manor on his grant. The rich soil of Barbados and the West Indian islands was perfect for sugarcane cultivation and many English gentlemen invested in plantations. Ligon sent information back which would later be compiled and printed in a book in London. Meanwhile Saltonstall, Davis, their relatives the Bristol Clarks and Smyths and Drax, to name a few, warred with the William Hebert (earl of Pembroke) and James Hay (earl of Carlisle) factions, burning each others' crops.

A severe plague killed many in the years 1647-50 but with the introduction of slaves from Africa sugar became the new gold from the Americas. The *Trader's Increase* was often seen on the island's leeward side, docking up and down the coast, which had treacherous, sharp rocks that could cut thick anchor ropes. Captain James Davis preferred to run the *Swan* up and down to Virginia but his son Samuel captained the *Trader's Increase*, jointly owned by Nicholas Davis. Captain Nathaniel Davis preferred to run furs from the Connecticut River and northern coast of New England. The end of the long war with Spain had ended but the English Civil War created a whole new set of trade impediments. The Dutch were not welcome on Barbados but unofficially were welcomed by the plantation owners who would alert any Dutch ship to the presence of English war ships via lights burned on the eastern slopes. Islanders are always desperate for goods they cannot grow or raise and any manufactured goods or metalware were always welcome in port, regardless of country of origin.

With trade from England on pause New England ships had no choice but to turn southward and trade with the islanders. On Barbados the settlement around Bridgetown looked almost like a little Dutch village with neat white houses and (illegal) Spanish red tiles on their roofs. Inland the plantations were coarser, more agricultural and the landscape rough and hilly. But the soil was rich and the windmill-driven sugar mills never stopped unless a hurricane blew in from the east. The winds were always bad on the eastern coast so very few planters settled there and the ones who did often packed their sugar down to the western ports via camels. Sugarcane, once boiled and the grains separated from the molasses syrup, was sold in two forms: hard loaves of brown or white. The white was sugar mixed with fine white clay and it was preferred by wealthy consumers. The molasses was the cheapest form of sugar and was used mostly by the poorest families and the slave owners to ration out to their slaves. It wasn't very sweet but added a bit of flavor to plain breads or griddle cakes. Barbados slaves especially welcomed molasses as there were no bees on the island to make honey. Or wax. One of the most prized goods a ship could bring was wax candles and only the wealthy plantation owners could afford them.

Drax became one of the *nouveau riche* in England and had bought Fonthill Abbey in Wiltshire, making him neighbors of the Raleighs, Gilberts and other wealthy Devonshire families. He saved money in crocks buried under his dirt floor for the new, huge manor he was building near Sir John Davis's childhood estate and Warwick Castle where Lady Arundel and her tenants had bravely fought off the Roundheads.

While John Winthrop and Roger Dudley were taking turns governing the New England Confederacy and fighting the Gordonites and other religious dissenters and busy mediating between them and their alliances with the Narragansetts and other tribes the Davis men who had ships or interests in ships were raking in lots of money, the war in England be damned. However, Drax was a Parliamentarian and many of the other gentry on Barbados were Royalists so the war touched the little island.

In 1651 Cromwell's Parliament issued a Navigation Act that prohibited trade with the Dutch. As Barbados was primarily Royalist, The Act affected all shipping as only ships buiLt. owned and captained by British owners could trade between England and its colonies. To reinforce this they sent a new governor, Sir George Ayacue, with a fleet to Barbados. The negative impact of this Act reached across Roundhead-Royalist lines and Lord Francis Willoughby, the governor and lessee of Carlisle's grants, built a fort so Cromwell's fleet couldn't land and it blockaded the main port for months.

Even before the Act the situation was tense. The planters had a terrible dilemma: All that sugar and no way to get it off the island other than to portage it in canoe or by camel to a harbor not under English guard.

In New England matters of religion, personal squabbles and witchcraft, omens read into drownings and apparitions in clouds, of the wreck of a new ship launched from New London that drowned 71 passengers and crew, and relations with the French to the north took up most of the daily attention but when news arrived that the Parliamentarians had beheaded King Charles on the last day of January, 1649 Governor John Winthrop took to bed. He succumbed in the spring after a lengthy fight with his illness.

In Connecticut the Assembly banned the public smoking of tobacco.

With the death of the king and surrender of Prince Rupert every man and woman in the colonies knew a point had been passed that would alter the very heart of their homeland and their identity as royal subjects. What was England now? A Common Wealth led by men who couldn't even agree with each other. The ship of state had lost its captain and was adrift in a sea of uncertainty. And its historic enemies France, Spain and the Netherlands were waiting for the opportunity to sink it in the New World.

On land the Davis men put one foot in front of the other, clearing lands in places such as Haverhilll, Roxbury, along the Connecticut River and to the north in and around Dover and Piscataqua and on the Merrimac River. And their sons and daughters, some born on New England soil, grew tall and strong as the torch was being passed to the next generation: a generation that felt little loyalty to a country that had persecuted their parents and one they had never seen across a cold, dark sea.

William remembered the Old Country and told his children of Stonehenge, of Cadbury Hill, showed them the bits of bluestone he'd chipped off the massive stone ring in the middle of Wiltshire and had saved, wrapped in a linen napkin his mother had woven and stitched her initials into with pink and green threads. He told of the miles and miles of rolling green hills and stone churches and villages and the enormous sprawl of London but his children were more concerned with seeing savages or bears in the woods or looking at the black rocks John Pynchon brought back from *Tantiesques.*

A new land was taking shape. A land of small, wooden houses with steep saltbox roofs covered with local slate tiles and sheathed in local wooden shingles nailed with local iron nails. A land of small farms with crops enclosed by walls made from the many stones their plows turned up. A land that their ministers said was the New Jerusalem: full of milk and honey and a stern piety.

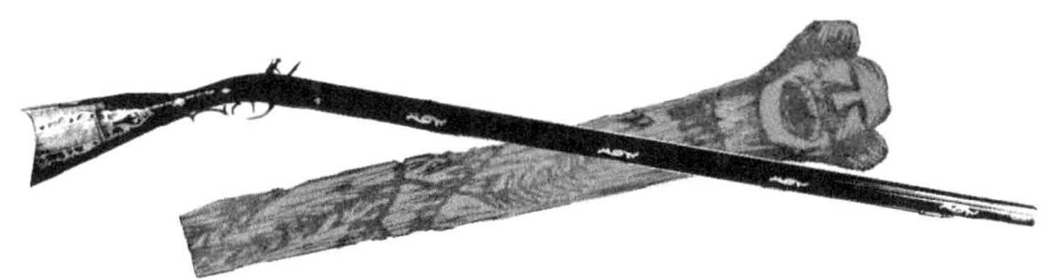

CHAPTER FIFTY-FOUR

No Turning Back

1649-50

Lincolnshire, England had three regions: the coast, which had Boston harbor and other eastern ports that were important in the wool trade with the Netherlands and France, just across the English Channel; the lower section which had many marshy areas, or fens, that, in the less boggy areas grew wheat, rye and Dutch tulips and were often drained by windmills that pumped excess water back out to sea; and the western section that was a long north-to-south cliff of limestone.

The Romans set up the beginnings of the no-nonsense brick towns in Lincolnshire and magnificent manors such as the Bolingbroke castle the Roundheads demolished in the Civil War and the Lincoln Cathedral and Heckingham church with many beautiful stained glass windows and the church of St. Helen full of intricate iron works, stained glass and precious metal ceremonial objects forged by generations of the Faheyes, renowned blacksmiths. Many of the manors there such as Brant Boufhton were built over the centuries but many of the county's ancient buildings were in decline or had been demolished by 1630 when the Great Migration of Puritans assembled their congregations for the long voyage across the sea to what they would name Boston in the New England.

Simon Bradstreet, a highly educated man and son of a minister from Horbling in the fens, was one of the emigrants that threw his fortune and religion into the Winthrop Fleet. He married Anne, a daughter of Roger Dudley. and after first settling in Cambridge moved north to Andover, established in 1646 two years after the village of Reading on an inland trading path from Boston to Malden which continued north to Haverhilll on the Merrimac River. The ordinary in town was known for always having a big pot of beans warming on its hearth to refresh travelers along the route. For Bradstreet, who, through his education at Emanuel College was friends with the William Phelps family in England, the location was where he visualized establishing a seminary and a preparatory school for New England's young men who would later attend Harvard or other colleges such as the one proposed to be built in New Haven. Phelps had settled in Dorchester but his brother George had settled in Windsor, Connecticut.

Through his relationship to Dudley and his interests in New Haven and Windsor, Simon Bradstreet and Thomas Prence, who like Bradstreet was a Wiltshireman and had served as an Assistant to the Court before moving to the farthest eastern land settlement on Cape Cod and established the town of Eastham, were appointed in 1650 as representatives of the Confederation to parlay with the Dutch to try to bring about an end to the hostilities between the Dutch on Long Island and the settlers along the Connecticut River and its shore.

The Dutch claimed they owned all the territory from the northern shore of Cape Cod up through Massachusetts, skirting the great lake that the French claimed as Lake Champlain and along the river and then back down to the coast via the Hudson River. Through the efforts of Bradstreet and Prence the Dutch, sapped by the long war in Europe and negotiating from a position of weakness, agreed in the Treaty of Hartford to relinquish their claims to the lands of the Connecticut Valley. Gov. Stuyvesant and Governor Endicott were satisfied with the deal but the English settlers in New Haven felt they had the rights to the territory all the way over to the Hudson as it was a major waterway for the transportation of furs and timber from the north.

Prence had marine interests and it was not a coincidence he moved to Eastham as it freed him to trade with any ship, English, Dutch, French that sailed past away from English eyes in Boston and Plymouth. Some of these ships were Davis-owned or captained and news from England arrived along with goods and fish. It was learned that Cromwell's New Model Army had victories against the Royalists in Worcester and Dunbar and had destroyed the deceased king's nephew Prince Rupert's fleet. However, what was to be called the' Navigation Act' was being discussed in Parliament and the New Englanders knew it would be fatal to their trade unless they ran illegal ships up and down the coast. Eastham was to become a major harbor for smuggling non-English goods or goods shipped in non-English ships up and down New England, to and from Virginia and the West Indies. One of the goods now being shipped was rum, made from the molasses by-product of the sugar plantations. Sugar became like gold. Ship owners had to supply a daily grog ration for their sailors and if they could buy cheaper American distilled rum instead of having to buy spirits imported from Europe it was to their advantage. Likewise, casks of American salt pork and salt beef were cheaper to use as provisions onboard instead of any meat imported from England. The 'Navigation Act' so embittered the mariners and merchants in the New World that many were turning against the Cromwellians but the king's teenage son was in exile and most waffled and were hesitant to throw their support whole-heartedly into one side or the other. To the Puritans and planters their farms and plantations came first. England was in chaos and despite the Treaty of Hartford the feeling ran deep that as soon as they licked their wounds the Dutch would rise again to challenge the English in the New Land and West Indies.

Besides Eastham few villages were settled in these troubling years. The mass immigration had petered out so towns were now filling out with the second and third generations. In Haverhilll James's son James was now 30, Ephraim 26 and Samuel in his twenties with almost a decade of sailing behind him. His son Thomas had moved his family down to his grandfather's land grant in Virginia with his own James, now 14 years old.

William Davis and Margaret had a son born in Springfield, Benjamin, now five years old. Some of the first settlers were dying, either due to the plague that had hit New England hard in the late 1640s or due to illnesses from aging or, for women, childbirth. The primitive living conditions were hard on people who were used to living simply but weren't used to the severe winters and food scarcities that sometimes occurred due to insects such as the ones that came out of the ground and buzzed loudly all night or the crows that ate their corn in the fields. And then there were the savages that came out at night and raided fields or stole livestock. And packs of wolves that took cattle, sheep or pigs while they were out grazing.

Dolor and Margery were in Barnstable in 1648 when their three year old daughter Ruth was baptized. They had two younger sons living with them: twins Simon and Samuel. As with most of the English the first names were often the same as parents, aunts, uncles and grandparents so many of the same name were found in the Federation, their distant roots going back to far flung villages and market towns across Wales, England, Ireland and even Scotland. And every few years certain names became the most popular so there would be a lot of Nathaniels or Sarahs then a lot of Jonathans and Elizabeths, for instance. New Englanders became very provincial, as they had been in Britain. One's family and one's church family were centers of their universes. To move away to another village was a big event, usually precipitated by a dispute with a relative or a difference of opinion with one's minister or elder.

Much to the chagrin of the Boston theocracy there were many versions of Protestantism in New England and with the coming of more Scotch-Irish the divisions were growing. The Winthrop-led government had opted for peace whenever possible, sending the dissidents away to found new colonies in Rhode Island or up north near the Piscataqua River but in the involuted society during the Civil War in England there was little room for dissension. Most of the Puritan folks went along and kept quiet, even when a friend or relative was accused of witchcraft.

As happened with Margaret Jones. Many a goodwife had traded with her for her medicines yet was loathe to speak up in her defense for fear of being painted with the same stick. Many a man had dallied with a young maid behind the barn but wouldn't speak up when a friend or relative was accused of adultery or incest. It was a secretive society, one in which people prayed for forgiveness twice a week in long services and during the daily home Bible readings or Fast Days. Almost all carried a secret sin inside and were very superstitious of unusual meteorological events or eclipses or strange deaths or accidents. The Devil was very real to them, always near by to tempt them from the path of goodness and piety.

The Bible was used to teach children how to read and stories from it were used to illustrate how God punished humans for bad behavior. The weekly Bible reading classes were long and the weekly sermon services even longer. Activities that the English had enjoyed such as the singing and dancing around the MayPole and harvest festivals with songs and dances were no longer practiced. Life was to be devoted to God. The settlers were to work, pray, give thanks for His blessings, be afraid when He punished people and live very straight laced lives. This would later be called the Puritan Work Ethic. In the late 1640s and early 1650s it served the small and growing towns well as survival had to be a communal effort, especially since the option of returning to England became dimmer with each setting sun over the New England bays and hills.

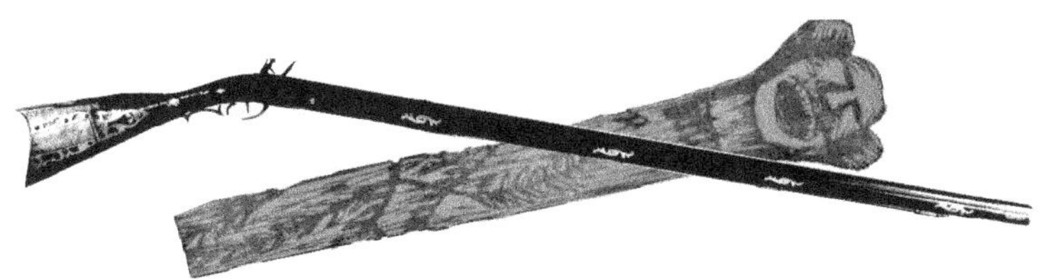

CHAPTER FIFTY-FIVE

Trouble with the Dutch

1650s

The wealthy men who helped found New England: the Earl Brooke, Sir Nathaniel and Robert Rich, the Earl of Warwick, the Grenville-Fulke family; the Earl of Lincoln, the Saye and Seles Fienne family, linked to the Pelham-Clintons, the Earl of Manchester, the Arundels, Smythes, members of the Vane, Pym, Warner, Wharton and Cromwell families – and others who formed the corporations that funded the settlements in New England, Virginia and the West Indies found war in England to be profitable before the 'Navigation Act'. Many of these men sat on the Commission of Foreign Plantations by the late 1640s.

Cromwell's army defeated upwards of 14,000 Scottish at Dunbar on September 3, 1650 and with the blessings of the Chief Justice and Cromwell's Parliament shipped the prisoners, mostly male, off to the West Indies and Virginia. Cromwell's army had massacred thousands of Royalist Irish at Drogheda on October 11, 1649, using children and women as human shields, and in later battles defeated the remnant of Owen Roe's resisters. Huge shipments of Irish were sent to Virginia where Charles Rich bought most and sent others on to Barbados, Jamaica, St. Kitts and other West Indian colonies. The prisoners were slaves but some of the Scottish prisoners of war from Dunbar that arrived in Boston in the summer of 1652 on the *John and Sara* were in such bad shape after imprisonment and a voyage spent in dark, dank holds that Rev. Cotton wrote to the Commission that their agent, Thomas Kemble (Kimble), a wealthy Charlestown merchant with ties to shipping and related to a prominent Boston blacksmith, had taken pity on them and not sent them on to Charles Rich in the Barbados but retained them in Boston as indentured servants for a six to eight year service and built small houses, each providing shelter for four men, for them during their indentures.

The transport ship was under the captaincy of John Greene, related to William Greene in London and the mariner Richard Greene in Boston. In the Barbados Charles Rich was to release the ill men after their indentures and expenses he laid out for them were reimbursed. He was to require only three days on with three days off of labor on the sugar plantations. Rev. Cotton wrote that he felt Rich was showing much magnanimosity in this gesture. At the time many Cromwellian soldiers declared they had seen Devil's tails on many of the Irish and Scottish soldiers and it was felt that shipping them off to labor was a way of ridding the British Isles from these Catholic and Royalist 'demons'.

During this time five-sixths of the Irish population perished from war, famine and plague. Wealthy Parliamentarians and soldiers received women and children as slaves to work on their Irish plantations. In September, 1653 the Irish people were declared to be the property of the British soldiers who had won them by the sword as Parliament encouraged its soldiers to resettle Ireland as an English possession. After May, 1654 the Irish were relegated under penalty of death to live west of the River Shannon.

Sugar was becoming such an important commodity that in 1651 merchant-shippers in Dover, the Isle of Wight, Barnstaple, Bideford, Southampton and Appledore petitioned the Parliament to be allowed to trade with the West Indies as "free landing places" not subject to the 'Navigation Act' but the London ship owners protested and refused to grant them special treatment.

While northern colonies were trying to avoid the 'Navigation Act' (especially the merchants in Connecticut who had the *Tyrell* built in 1649 for trade with the West Indies), the southern colonies were flourishing.

In 1655 the English fleet arrived in Jamaica and fought the Spanish for control of the sugar-rich lands.

In 1656 Cromwell appointed a standing council to handle Jamaican affairs and the West Indies that included one of his admirals, one of his major generals and other supporters including Capt. Limbrey, a merchant in London who had a plantation in Jamaica and who had often sailed back and forth from the West Indies to England.

Oliver Cromwell disposed of the Rump Parliament in 1653 and introduced a new system of government with a constitution and elected body in 1654. It was replaced in 1657 after he had declined the Crown and the system of two houses was reinstated. He died in 1658 and his son Richard took over as Lord Protectorate but the militiary refused to accept him and instead England brought back the monarchy, but Charles II was to have only limited powers.

The decade of the 1650s was a turbulent time for England and her colonies as it threw out the old system of government and, after considerable strife and accumulation of government debt, tried a Parliamentary system but then reverted to a revised version of the old monarchy. Family fortunes see sawed back and forth as Royalists had their estates and titles and money taken by the Parliamentarians and masses of Scottish and Irish were ripped from their ancestral lands and shipped to the West Indies. With the Restoration of the monarchy many who had been loyal to Charles II's father had titles and lands reinstated and Cromwellians found themselves in between, no longer holding sole power but not totally left out in the cold, either.

During this time the Saltonstalls and Davises in New England expanded their plantations in the Barbados and the pattern of profitable trade shifted from England and the Continent to New England, Virginia and the West Indies and Ireland and England. During this time the main commodity being shipped from East to West changed too, becoming human cargo: prisoners of war and negroes from Africa.

The northern colonies pulled further away from the southern ones as fishing and lumber without slaves were their main products, not the southern slave labor crops of tobacco and sugar.

Daniel Davis of Kittery and most of James Davis's sons in Haverhilll became land lubbers as, unlike in England, the new world had a lot of land so a man didn't have to turn to the sea to make his fortune. Nicholas Davis, owner of the *Trader's Increase* received 2,100 acres of land in Windsor, Connecticut in 1657.

Others received land grants in other ways.

New Haven wanted to become a part of Connecticut but with affairs so unsettled in England couldn't get the right people to sign any new patents regarding the American colonies. However, it was part of the United Colonies of Massachusetts, Plymouth, Connecticut (based in Hartford-Windsor) and had two representatives in each biannual session of the UC which was held sometimes in Boston and sometimes in Hartford. As in Boston, the governor and deputy governors merely kept getting re-elected, changing places occasionally. Assistants or magistrates might change, one here or there, but the governments of the United Colonies pretty much remained the same, alternating between John Winthrop Sr. (until his death in 1649, some said brought on by shock of the news of the execution of King Charles I), and Thomas Dudley in Boston; in Plymouth by John Brown and William Bradford, who occasionally gave way to Edward Winslow or Thomas Prince; in Connecticut by Edward Hopkins and George Fenwick or John Haynes and New Haven by Theopholis Eaton and Thomas Gregson. As most colonists were too busy building their homes and farms they were happy to leave the business of government to men they were familiar with. There was too much political strife in England for the New Englanders to want to start trouble on their shores. After the English Civil War some Royalist captives were also sent as prisoner of war laborers to the Barbados.

In New Haven William Davis, cousin of Robert's William, became fast friends of Richard Berkeley, who was related to Sir John Berkeley in England who tried to mediate between King Charles I and Cromwell's Army. The war had begun with Parliament angry with the king for his imperial attitude and excessive taxation and had evolved into a war between Presbyterians and Puritans and then, after Cromwell had purged the Parliament of Presbyterians, between the army and anyone who still spoke in favor of a monarchy. Cromwell had led expeditions to Scotland, uniting through battle and blood the two countries into a Presbyterian-Puritan conglomerate with their common enemy King Charles I and the monarchy, then he sailed and marched through Ireland along with Ireton and Cromwell's son Henry as his chief soldiers, utterly massacring and devastating the Royalists in that country.

As thousands and thousands of Scottish and Irish prisoners were sent off to Virginia and the West Indies, Royalist families also took off for those parts to get away from Cromwell's avenging New Model Army, hastily selling their lands and goods before his government seized them.

Richard Berkeley received a rare letter that had slipped through the net of the English Navy and he spoke with William many afternoons in his general store about the horrors the war was bringing upon England.

"When Cromwell and his Army come to town they take over and force people to take in the soldiers, feeding and sheltering them. They take farmers' horses if they need them and promise to pay later, when they can't even pay their soldiers the wages a'owed to them! People are so sick and tired o' this constant fightin'. Most are longing for the old days and would prefer the stability they had under King Charles to the chaos and slaughter they are living through under King Cromwell."

William stopped rocking near his Clark stove and gave his friend a level stare.

"'Tis a good thing we've stayed neutral in this whole affair," he finally said, tapping out his pipe. Smoking with others had been banned in 1647 but William knew he and Richard were safe as the May weather, which had been nice and springlike had suddenly turned foul, sleety and freezing and most people weren't traveling to town or the shops. The severe winters had been something the English, used to milder weather, had to adapt to but the Scots were used to it and withstood it better, even though most were sent off as unpaid laborers to the hot, muggy southern plantations.

Both men were worried about how their crops would do in their in their raw fields come May. In New England a farmer couldn't plant until almost June and the crops had to be harvested before the first frost which could be as early as late September.

"Aye, but me son John is planning on going to England along with other scholars soon to finish his education at Cambridge," William said, pulling on his pipe.

Richard shook his head.

"If ye ask me, he'd be best to avoid going there," he coughed and spat into a cotton handkerchief, "Even though the king's head was chopped off and his son has fled to Paris, the whole situation over there is very unsettled. Cromwell still hasn't reinstated the House of Lords and he only has a skeleton Parliament running the country."

Storekeeper William grunted, "Ye try a'talkin' him out o' it! He says it's safter there than here wit' them savages always attacking our towns."

"We never should have gotten involved with that Uncas fellow," Richard replied, scratching his beard, "it has caused us no end of grief with the Narragansetts and Niantics."

"Aye and their Mohawk and Pocumtuck allies," William added.

"Ye and yer young cousin – the one there in Boston by yer same name who married Will Pynchon's young lass – at least ye got a toe in with ol' Pynchon on this Connecticut business and a'learned some of their language so ye can trade with them."

William opened the door to the stove, added a log and spat into the fire.

"Does me no good, friend. All we seem to do is fight with the Dutch, who egg on the Narragansetts and their friends, then Uncas and his Mohegans show up again and the fighting begins all over again. They savages can't get along wit' each other and now they gang up on the English, the Dutch, the French and even the Swedes are getting involved over near the Dutch."

Richard nodded and added, "And the Dutch are fightin' over our claims in Delaware Bay, now! I tell ye, William, England and her neighbors got their squabbles but I am agreein' with your boy John than it's not really a lot safter on these shores."

"Did ye hear young Winthrop – the one as went to England a bit afore – he's gotten the right to any mines and three miles around them to mine ores for England?"

"Nay, I don't read all the news from the Assemblies," said Richard, "I'm sometimes at sea for months, ye know."

"Well, ol' Will Pynchon found all that black lead north, on the path to Boston, and he's steamin'! He says first Saybrook had tried to charge impost on the beaver skins and goods he ships downriver and then Massachusetts and now Connecticut claim Springfield fer themselves. He's pretty upset at the whole mess. He says he found the lead, he should have rights to it."

"Will isn't in with the right people," Richard replied, taking a sip of his ale, "Ye know how it goes here, as in the old country: ye need to hang aroun' the throne, that is in the United Colonies the statehouses, to have any real influence in these matters."

"Like working men have the time to play at being courtesans!" huffed William, "It takes all o' me labors just to keep this shop a'runnin' and tend to me farm." He smoked and added, "I do have some influence here, 'tis true, but we Davis men have our fingers in lots of pies from the Kennebec River all the way to Barbados. We got most of our lands from the king, though, not from Cromwell's Parliament!"

"And from Good Queen Bess," added Richard, referring the earliest settlements to the north and in Virginia.

"Aye, but our friends at the royal court are long gone – court is long gone – and now we are in a state o' waiting to see when t'other other shoe will drop."

The door suddenly blew open and both men hid their pipes. A gust of icy sleet blew in and a man in a soaked cape stood in the doorway blowing on his frozen hands.

"Well, shut the door, will ye?" yelled William, rising to meet the customer.

"I've ridden from Boston," he said, warming himself near the stove, his cloak dripping and creating a puddle on the wooden floor.

"Aye?" William replied as he poured him a tankard of ale.

"There's more of the indian troubles a'brewin'" said the messenger.

"Aye?"

"And there's talk that the Narragansetts are getting ready to gather a huge force and attack the assembly next month!"

"Aye?"

"Some o' the settlements are calling in their folks and there's talk of sending them to Fort Saybrook, which is getting reinforced."

"If I had a penny fer every time there's an alarm – " Richard said but was cut off by the messenger,

"Nay, this time 'tis truly serious. Ye know they haven't honored their treaty in years, putting off sending the wampum and coming up with all sorts o' excuses and diversions to avoid having to make real peace with the Mohegans. They say Pessagus has taken in the Pequot remnant that Uncas was supposed to take care of and is adding them to his army."

This got both men's attention. The visitor continued, "The Pequots say Uncas and his people are terrible cruel to them."

William stretched and then sighed.

"Aye, 'tisn't been a real truce and them Dutch haint helped any, either!"

Richard added, "And the French sailed down to Boston, remember, and asked for our help up north but they were told we had our own hands full o' trouble."

The frozen rain started to subside outside and the sun made a feeble attempt to shine through the dirty windowpanes of the shop's front.

Dripping could be heard at the back of the store and William almost cursed. There was a fine to be paid for cussing and with the imposts and costs of raising armies to stave off the savages and the saving he was doing for John's voyage and schooling in England he was barely making a profit.

"Thank ye fer the news," he told the stranger, "but I've got more pressing problems right now. I will be sure to spread it in town, though."

The Dutch were causing the English who owned lands in the Delaware Bay no end of trouble. William's friend Jasper Crane complained to the Connecticut General Court when his and William Tuttle's ships were seized by the Dutch as they were docked and ready to unload settlers and goods on their plantation lands.

The Governor of New York, Peter Stuyvesant, denied the charges and Gov. Eaton of New Haven replied that he was prepared to send 150 men to defend the English claims against the Dutch and Swedes in the bay. Capt. John Mason of Saybrook, who had distinguished himself in battle against pirates and in the Pequot War of 1637, offered to go to Delaware with men to defend the planters but the Connecticut assembly said they couldn't do without his services as the savages were being aggressive and only seven of the towns in Connecticut were paying taxes towards the upkeep of protection at the fort.

A month later at the late June Assembly the elected officials decided it was a priority to bring Fort Saybrook up to fighting status as the Dutch were selling arms, ammunition, powder, swords, coats and waistcoats to the Narragansetts and Niantics in exchange for wampum.

A committee of Francis Newman, one the current New Haven Assistants, Marie and Robert's William Davis and John Leverett of Boston, who had come over in 1633 with Rev. Cotton and Governor Haynes, were assigned to go to New Netherland and speak with Gov. Stuyvesant and to arrange for the return of English settlers captured by the Dutch and indians. William was asked to go as he knew some of the native sachems and languages, learned while working with William Pynchon. Through his cousin James he had been friends of Virginia's governor Samuel (Argyll), friend of the Earl of Warwick and Sir Edwin Sandys but there had been differences and Argyll, who saw the New World as a plunder paradise, was to be replaced by Lord de La Warr, ex-governor of Jamestown who had been in England for many years.

Argyll had gotten the governor of New Netherlands to swear an oath of allegiance to the King of England when he first sailed over to rout the French from Mt. Desert Island before heading south. Now with the king dead and Cromwell in charge, the Dutch felt no compunction to be friendly towards the English. Instead of returning with his tail between his legs, Argyll , foreseeing possible disgrace, had years before shipped out his booty before the ship with De la Warre was supposed to land. De La Warre died on the voyage as he had gone to England because the climate of Virginia had made him permanently ill with fevers. (Argyll left but received command of a fleet and defeated the French fleet in the English Channel – for which he was knighted in 1625 – and had then been named one of the commissioners to oversee the colonies. and set up a system of government for them. He and his Scottish relatives played an important role in the Stuart monarchies.)

Another commissioner was a relative of William's: Sir Thomas Smith. The officials in New Haven felt William, through his family connections, could talk to the one-legged Stuyvesant and remind him of the Dutch oath towards England. However, because of William Kieft and the greed of Van Renesselaer and his nephew Wouter Van Twiller, William saw that New Netherlands was just as bad as Jamestown had been under Argyll in that a handful of very rich Dutch owned most of the prime land along the peninsula and bay and felt no allegiance to anything other than lining their own coffers.

At this time *Ninigret* was a guest of Gov. Stuyvesant in Manhattos. Stuyvesant had a large, sturdy wall erected along the main street (Wall Street) to keep the English or unfriendly indians out. The talks between the Colonies and New Netherland were useless and the party returned during the time of the General Court but a special session was called in Boston and the men told them the Dutch were belligerent and were demanding the English living amongst them take an oath of fidelity to the Netherlands and that the oath Argyll had obtained was negated as there was no English king anymore.

It was decided that the English should raise an army but the United Colonies' commissioners demurred. Many in Connecticut and New Haven were all for war with the Dutch, who they felt were conspiring to overthrow the English but most in Massachusetts were saying the latest injury was only one instance and not justification for an all-out war.

The Connecticut General Court and New Haven Court had convened separately – one in October and the other in November – and, receiving no satisfaction from Massachusetts, decided to send a letter to England. Captain Atherwood was to go to England with the letter and to give it to Gov. Hopkins. who had been in England for a while.

Stamford and Fairfield and the settlements near Long Island lived in fear of attack. They posted sentries and demanded a James I of war. Two men, a Mr. Basset and Mr. Chapman, were arrested and charged with trying to incite an insurrection. They were fined and, partly thanks to New Haven William Davis's intervention, their fines went to support a fellowship at Cambridge College.

On September 11, 1653 the meeting of the United Colonies was so contentious that the union was almost dissolved. The courts of Connecticut and New Haven wanted a declaration of war and said that the United Colonies were obligated to join in but Massachusetts (with the exception of Rev. Edward Norris of Salem, who supported war with the indians), the northern settlements, said they didn't feel it was a just cause.

In March, 1654 Governor Haynes died. His family had chosen to fight during the Civil War, but were on opposite sides. His son Robert had died on a ship bound to England as he was going over to fight for King Charles I but the younger one was promoted by Cromwell, thereby preserving the family estate of Copford Hall in Essex. Knowing that Gov. Haynes was terminally ill, the freemen in Hartford convened in February to elect Thomas Welles Moderator for the General Court, and as governor until Dep. Gov. Hopkins returned or until the next general election.

That spring *Uncas* and the residents of New London had a terrible falling out regarding their boundaries.

While this was happening a ship from England brought an order from Parliament stating the Dutch were now declared enemies of the English and the colonists were to seize any Dutch lands and property at Hartford and elsewhere without compensating the Dutch. Roger Ludlow of Fairfield had tried to go to war with the Dutch without official sanction and, disgusted with the way the Massachusetts members of the United Colonies had defaulted on their obligation to join in the protection of their southern settlements, sold his lands and left for Virginia in late April. Captain Richard Manning of Salem and Kennebec had his ship impounded in Milford Harbor while he was being tried, charged with attempting to trade with the Dutch. His crew set the ship free and set sail for Manhatos but the local citizens took to sea in a small ship and overtook the ten gun ship and its goods as a lawful prize to help offset the terrible costs incurred during these times to defend their town.

In late May the General Election chose Hopkins as governor of Connecticut, even though he was still in England, and Welles as Deputy governor. Amongst incumbents or prior magistrates, John Talcott was elected as a magistrate and his wife was elected as the treasurer. In New Haven Samuel Eaton joined the magistrates along with Benjamin Fenn.

In Boston Major Sedgwick and Captain Leverett arrived with a fleet of several ships and some troops, sent by Oliver Cromwell to assist the colonies in fighting the Dutch. Governor Eaton read the letter from Lord Protector Cromwell and certified the ships, men and ammunition were indeed sent by England. On June 13th the General Court of Connecticut assembled in Hartford and sent Captain Mason and John Culick to Boston to enlist 200 to 500 men. The General Court in Massachusetts had been in session a week by then but had not raised an army. After Major Leverett and Major Sedgewick arrived they agreed to raise 300 volunteers from Connecticut and New Haven to accompany the 200 men on board the ships.

Before the army could leave a letter arrived via ship that the Dutch had agreed to a peace as their Navy had been virtually destroyed in April by the English and so the two countries were no longer at war. However, the fleet was sent north to drive the French out of Penobscot, St. John's and the coastal area north of Kennebec. This expedition had been a sub-order in Cromwell's letter regarding 'cleansing New England of foreign claimants'.

Connecticut and New Haven were not in the mood to meet with Boston and Plymouth as they felt they had reneged on their covenant by refusing to war on *Ninigret* and his alliance of savages so a General Session was not called in June but in July a letter was received from the Assembly in Boston and the two colonies set their differences aside in the name of peace.

Peace was not coming from *Ninigret* and his alliance of Pocumtucks, Mohawks and Wampanoags who were raiding and attacking the Connecticut and Long Island tribes who were under the protection of the English.

Deputy Governor Welles and Clark let Gov. Eaton know the Connecticut assembly was going to send Capt. Mason with men and ammunition and asked for Lt. Seeley and men plus ammunition from New Haven to join Mason at Fort Saybrook to defend the Montauks from *Ninigret's* men. Their orders were to try to get *Ninigret* to agree to peace but if he wouldn't, to withdraw to defend Long Island. Johnathan Gilbert was sent to *Ninigret* to demand he come to Hartford and pay the tribute that he never paid for the Pequot War.

Gilbert returned and said Ninigret claimed the savages on Long Island had attacked *his* people and killed a sachem's son and 60 braves. Ninigret said his allies were with him to avenge these deaths and it was not for the English to interfere.

In mid-October 1653 Connecticut and New Haven raised 40 horsemen and 153 soldiers from Massachusetts, 45 men from Connecticut and 35 from New Haven, 20 horsemen from Massachusetts with an additional 24 men from Connecticut and 16 from New Haven to immediately march into Niantics territory under Major Gibbons, Major Denison and Captain Atherton to reply to *Ninigret's* insolence. But Massachusetts demanded Major Simon Willard be given chief command. His order was to march directly to *Ninigret* and demand he hand over the Pequot captives and wampum he owed the United Colonies and to take them by force if not delivered upon demand. Massachusetts and Connecticut's troops were to meet up at Thomas Stanton's farm.

When the army arrived at *Ninigret's* village they were told he'd fled into the swamp, leaving his people and their crops undefended. Major Willard didn't pursue but did take the hundred or so Pequots who wanted English protection back with him. Upon his return he was rebuked for neglect of duty. The Connecticut and New Haven Commissioners felt that Willard was secretly following orders from Massachusetts to avoid direct conflict with the Narragansetts.

Ninigret resumed his hostilities on Long Island and Rev. Thomas James of Easthampton, Captain Tappin of Southampton and Captain Underhill wrote to the commissioners that their communities were under imminent danger of attack. The Commissioners sent Captain John Young with a ship to cruise the sound to observe and intercede if the savages attempted to cross Long Island sound by canoe to raid the mainland. Capt. Young was authorized to raise local men if needed for the defense of the communities.

In the meantime, Gov. Eaton compiled a list of laws, based on Rev. Cotton's discourse on the nature of colonial government and in keeping with the list Massachusetts had compiled earlier. Copies were printed and distributed and a copy sent to England for Governor Hopkins to inspect.

In New Haven it was decided an army needed to be raised for defense and a 16 man troop of horse was authorized, to be housed and fed and be in a state of constant readiness. These men were exempted from taxation and were considered to be professional soldiers.

To the southeast in the West Indies England had driven the French out of Jamaica and Cromwell was pushing for New Englanders to settle on the island, which he liberally furnished with prisoners of war for labor. Captain Gookins was one of his promoters in New Haven, saying there was dire need for good Christian people to settle the island and ensure its moral character was in line with the Puritan ideology. However, the commissioners didn't want to lose Gookin and wrote a letter to Cromwell thanking him for all he had done but saying they couldn't spare missionaries at the present time. Rev. Gookin was too valuable as he was setting up praying villages away from the English villages and working to convert natives with the help of Rev. John Eliot. At this time the Long Island Pequots Major Willard had brought back were settled along the Mystic and *Pawcatuck* Rivers in two of these strictly regulated 'praying villages'.

The United Colonies met at Plymouth in June and read a letter from Gov. Stuyvesant saying he was happy the two countries had reached a treaty and were no longer at war. Their reply was pleasant but reminded him he hadn't paid for the damages he'd done and that Oyster Bay and Greenwich were considered to be English, not Dutch, territories and that the immoral actions of certain persons in Greenwich and its practice of giving refuge to adults and children who were banished under Puritan law was not acceptable and that the worst offenders were to report to Connecticut for reproof. This lack of a moral compass in a territory so close to the Puritan settlements truly rankled and upset the people who had risked a perilous voyage and sold everything they owned to come to a new land where the people could form communities based on a common covenant with their church and faith. If there was one glue that held the United Colonies together it was this strong sense of religious righteousness, of their desire for peaceful coexistence with their Puritan neighbors, their desire to be humble and to put God above all else in their lives. Their mornings began with a family prayer and ended with one and on the Sabbath they attended two services, either returning home for a cold dinner or, if they were outliers, bringing bread, meat and cheese in baskets and jugs of cider to dine on the common or in friends or fellow congregants' homes. The ultra strict Boston Puritanism of the early 1630s had dimmed a little but church attendance was still a requirement to be considered to be a member in good standing in the community.

The spring of 1656 Henry Wolcott died. He'd been a wealthy estate owner in Somersetshire and had emigrated first to Dorchester, then to Windsor where he helped found the town.

At the 1656 annual election in Hartford John Webster was elected governor and Welles deputy governor. The rest of the officials remained the same.

In April 1657 the savages murdered indians in Farmington and harried farmers in Southampton. Major Mason and a contingent were sent to demand the surrender of the murderers and the Norowattucks and Pocumtucks who had committed atrocities.

William Davis and his kin began looking inward for farmlands and his northern cousin Robert Tobias Davis's widow Bridget married Thomas King in Sudbury. Thomas later was one of the men who moved west of Concord and began a town at a site named Lancaster that the Nashaway sachem *Sholan* had promoted as good for farming. Of course *Sholan* was looking for English protection from marauding Mohawks or *Passaconnaway's* warriors but distance from the Puritan oligarchy/theocracy in Boston and the strict merchant/Puritans on the south coast of Connecticut was preferred by discontented men such as Thomas King and his cousin, also named Thomas, who had been, along with Dolor's son Big John, one of the men disarmed by Boston in 1637 for siding with Wheelwright. John Prescott, a blacksmith from West Riding, Yorkshire (Cromwell's home turf) had originally settled in Watertown but he, too, was looking westward by the mid 1650s. As was Simon Willard and his family.

The western section of Massachusetts was seeing small, unincorporated settlements such as Haverhilll, founded from Ipswich families. During the late 1650s and into the mid-1660s Ipswich families later settled Quaboag Plantation, which became Brookfield. The western inland towns of Deerfield, Hatfield, Hadley (settled by Wethersfield families) were getting tentative starts and John Pynchon purchased land from the indians for Springfield, Longmeadow, Northampton and Westfield, the latter the westernmost settlement of the colony along the Connecticut River.

The biggest deterrence in the 1650s was the presence of indians who might be friendly one day and hostile the next. *Ninigret* had been temporarily quieted by *Massasoit.* But his oldest son Alexander and his younger son Philip were making noises that the coastal English hadn't heard, grumbling about English land purchases and the encroachment of English farms into their hunting grounds. *Massasoit* was aged and it was merely a matter of time before the old Wampanoag chief sachem passed away and his son took his place as chief of the peaceful confederation his father had woven along the coast when the English first arrived and set up Plymouth Plantation in 1620.

By now the colonies were taking on separate identities. Boston was associated with Harvard, with education, religion, government and as a main trading harbor for ships from England. Plymouth was relatively insular and provincial. It had a cultish appeal but was dominating the bay's fishing industry to the south whereas the settlements along the Merrimac and Kennebec were dominating trade to the north. Connecticut was primarily theocratic and mercantile with many of its wealthier citizens also owning plantations in Virginia, Delaware, Barbados and Jamaica. It, too, was becoming known for its scholarly bent and a new college, to be named Yale, was being planned. Rhode Island was insular, shunned for its religious tolerances, but it, too, traded via its ports with the rest of the coast.

Away from the big trading coastal towns of Hartford, New Haven, Boston and Salem the smaller towns felt a sense of independence. The Connecticut River united traders from the far north all the way to the sea and the Merrimac River hosted settlements that fed into Boston and Salem. In this way New England was similar to England as the inland villages settled along rivers that fed into the Severn or Thames or Dart and other main waterways. Mills that could use waterpower began springing up along the inland rivers and massive timbers were floated downstream to be used in shipbuilding or sent to England for manor houses. This inland independence was fragile – as the settlers in Connecticut well knew when *Ninigret* began his hostilities. The local militia was a rag tag collection of farmers with an assortment of arms from muskets, flintlocks (some in disrepair or without ammunition) to rakes, homemade spears, old swords and scythes. The outliers were constantly losing crops when fences were damaged by deer or indians and even lost livestock to hungry indians but such thefts were always hard to prove as they usually occurred in the dead of night when the only creatures stirring on English farms were owls, wolves and foxes.

James's sons in Haverhilll were prospering and Davis men in and around Springfield, such as William, were also feeling their communities taking on the shape of English villages with meeting houses, taverns (also called public houses or ordinaries), shops, smiths, liveries for travelers on the Bay Path and other industries such as grist mills, brick works, potash works or ironworks. Ropemaking, sailcloth weaving and lumbering were in constant demand and the women worked tirelessly to card, spin and weave cloth and sew household items and clothes. Men who worked with leather were in high demand as it was used for many items including straps and shoes plus cut into thin strips and used as lacing. The tanneries were located downstream from the villages as there was a terrible stench from the scraped and tanned hides. The indians provided a steady supply of baskets and simple fired clay bowls or pots, which they traded for better English iron and steel items. The outliers furnished many raw goods such as cattle for leather, potash for fertilizer and soap making, hemp for rope and flax for linen. They also grew a lot of wheat and corn for city dwellers and to ship south. From the southern plantations the cities received tobacco, cotton, indigo and a variety of fruits that couldn't grow in New England. English apple trees such as the new, sweet Dr. Harvey variety from East Anglia began to be planted in orchards using varieties that were better than the native small apples but hardy enough to survive the harsh winter. Berries grew everywhere in marshy soil and were picked by the indians, English children, and eaten by birds, foxes and bears.

What the Davis men and women loved was the openness of New England. Back in the old country the land had been cut up, parceled off, divided, fenced, enclosed, ringed with royal forests and dominated by local manors. Here, they felt they were creating a new type of England. An England that was For the People and By the People, not for the Lords of the manors and owned by the aristocracy and landed gentry. Here, if a family was willing to suffer the hardships of starting out with nothing, within a generation they could look around and see a nice farmstead with a modest wood frame house, a barn full of livestock, sheds, fields and kitchen garden. In England, all was owned by the Lord of the manor and could be taken away in a heartbeat if a tenant fell afoul of him. Without a farm to live on in England a person or family had to move into a town and survive by doing the lowest jobs and living in poverty, which often led to petty crime and possibly deportation as forced labor or even execution.

The 1650s and half of the 1660s were the calm before the storm. Families said prayers in the morning and evening, went to morning and evening services on the Sabbath, built roads and common buildings, neighbors helped neighbors raising barns or building homes and the sounds of hammering, sawing, cattle lowing, chickens clucking or roosters crowing intermingled with the sounds of nature: brooks burbling, bees buzzing, birds chirping and crows cawing.

Thomas King, James, Ephraim, John and William Davis were living hard, but pleasant lives in this new land.

Until *Massasoit* died in 1662.

CHAPTER FIFTY-SIX

Westward Expansion

1660s

Dolor was a son of William, who was brother to Richard and George, sons of Robert John.

Richard owned the *Gift of God* but Dolor didn't want the seafaring life and became a housewright and carpenter.

Dolor's brother Nicholas began sailing on the *Increase* in the 1630s, later called the *Trader's Increase* when he and Dolor's cousin Captain Nathaniel Ambrose Robert Davis (Richard's son) bought it and it began trading between Virginia and Delaware, the West Indies and New England. Robert's mother was the daughter of fellow Welshman Captain John Rice (Rhys) Trader Hughes. Robert's cousin, called Robert the Black, basically ran the Virginia route and Nicholas took over the northern route. Robert had a tobacco plantation in on the *Pumunkey* River in Virginia.

Dolor's son Big John, who came over on the *Increase* in 1635 along with lifelong friends William Warner and William Houghton, a butcher, had been banished with Rev. Wheelwright and lived in Exeter for a while then settled in Newbury, which was a large trading port to the north of Salem and Boston, near Kittery where Daniel Davis was settled and not far from James and his sons in Haverhilll. Like his father, John preferred working in wood to a life at sea. Dolor's cousin Thomas came over in the *James* (owned by his father James Davis) in that same year and began his life as a sawyer, an occupation very much in demand and one that complimented his relatives' business interests as they could obtain lumber at a cheaper rate and their houses could therefore be more affordable plus lumber was in demand as an export good to England and for use in shipbuilding. In house building in New England Dolor mourned the loss of the beautiful English stone that had been so plentiful in Devonshire but north of the Merrimac a hard granite stone was now being quarried and in the Newbury area limestone could also be quarried, but most of that went to the West Indies as a trading good. Marble was being found, too, but the simple dwellings being constructed had little need of great polished marble floors, fireplace surrounds, mantlepieces and pillars.

Through his connection to Matthew Craddock as agent for the Mason/Gorges grant, Nicholas was banished: his crime: tolerating the Quakers. It concerned him little, for as was common of mariners, he kept two residences: his main one on Barbados and a family home in Charlestown. He had earlier obtained by grants the entire Nahant area north of Charleston and 2,100 acres of land near Windsor on both sides of the Connecticut River. James Davis got 2,100 acres of land in the area near the hot springs, later to be called Stafford Springs, after the Woodward and Saffrey survey determined it was part of Connecticut and not Massachusetts.

Dolor, due to the nature of house building, moved often at first: from Cambridge to Duxbury, then Barnstable and Concord. He had helped found Groton in 1645, a settlement just north between Concord and Lancaster, but he left the settling of it to his youngest sons Simon and Samuel, both born in New England. Dolor loved Barnstable the best and returned there to live out his final years. (In 1663 Dolor's daughter Ruth married Stephen Hall in Concord.)

The Coffin family were fellow mariners and good friends of the Davis family and Tristrum Coffin lived in Barnstable and later his relatives went out to Nantucket and set up a trading post there. The sailing families who weren't keen on Boston-style puritanism preferred trading to the north and on the cape and then in New Haven and followed the coast down to Virginia then put out to sea for the Barbados and Jamaica and the rest of the small islands of the West Indies where sugar was hugely profitable.

Dolor's cousin William, son of Robert and Marie, had apothecary/general stores in Springfield, Haverhilll, Boston and New Haven, the latter two shared with a cousin William Davis. William's cousins supplied him with goods from the West Indies for his formulations and his former wife's family, the Pynchons, kept them well supplied with furs and graphite from the black lead mill to add to the items traded in his New Haven and Springfield stores. William's wife Margery died in 1654 and he remarried Huldah, daughter of Rev. Zechariah Symmes of New Haven. William of New Haven's oldest son John had been a teacher and one of the young men lost at sea in 1657 on Robert Garret's ship along with Jonathan Ince, Nathaniel Pelham and Thomas Mayhew (who had come over with Rev, Hooker and Rev. Wheelwright on the *Griffen)*. They had been en route to England to continue their religious studies at Cambridge.

Marie and Robert's William's former father-in-law William Pynchon had run afoul of the Boston Puritan clique when he published a small book about his religious views. His book was publically burned on the Boston common and to avoid being charged with heresy he had fled back to England during the Civil War in the spring of 1652.

William Pynchon left his business dealings to his 25 year old son John, who was a close friend of William Davis and had been a friend to William's cousin's deceased son, the scholar lost at sea. Families were large in the 1600s and it wasn't unusual for a man to have 12 children or even more by one to three or even four wives. The women didn't live as long as the men in general for they not only had the hard labor of daily chores but the added physical stress of childbearing and nursing without servants to help, as would have been the case in England. Their bodies simply wore out. Families were not only large but also very spread out, from the far northern trading posts near the French all the way down to Virginia and the West Indies. With each generation the ties to England became a bit vaguer and the ties to their local communities grew stronger. In time a family would have relatives it didn't even know existed but in the 1660s there were still threads connecting brothers, sisters, nephews, nieces, first and second cousins.

James and his brood had settled around Haverhilll for the most part but Daniel settled in Kittery, not far from Newbury where Little John was and Newbury wasn't far from the North Shore, which then connected to Salem and so on. Sailors such as Nicholas kept families connected via letters and news when his ship docked in Newburyport. John and his family would join the other members of the community that eagerly assembled on the lower green to meet ships as they sailed into the harbor.

John Winthrop, Jr. had obtained a large land grant from the Nipmuc sachem Black James for the land around the lead mine on the overland path between Springfield and Boston but it never produced much silver ore and it closed in 1658. Originally Thomas King was the agent for John Pynchon in the provisioning and overseeing of the mine but under a 14 year lease to William Paine and wealthy Boston merchant Thomas Clarke in 1658 William Deins oversaw the extracting and shipping of barrels of black lead to England for two years via the Connecticut river along with beaver, moose, muskrat, fox and other skins. The Pynchons were the biggest, richest fur traders in all of New England at this time and the largest merchants west of the Massachusetts Bay area. John Pynchon was a magistrate and treasurer of Hampshire County and dealt with the indians all the time either in Springfield or in their villages.

In 1657 residents of Ipswich petitioned for a plantation and in 1660 the Massachusetts General Court granted a petition for an area six miles square to be called Quaboag Plantation. But the situation in England prevented movement in the colony as King Charles II had been brought back and enthroned and he intended to have royal commissioners rule New England. This, plus the insecure relations with the indians in Connecticut prevented settlement. However, in November 1665 John sent an agent, Lt. Thomas Cooper, to obtain from *Shatookquis*, the chief sachem of Quaboag, a deed for the six miles that began north of *Wickquaboag* pond on the north west, ran east to hills and skirted *Quaboag* Pond on the southeast, then west to a small pond. The *Quaboag* River ran diagonally through the land. The tract wasn't a perfect square as important indian sites were skirted, but it included the formerly important village of *Asquoash* on the eastern slope of 'Indian Hill' and the western shore of *Quaboag* Pond. Elizer Holyoke, Samuel and Japhett Chapin witnessed the deed. Humphrey Davis in Boston registered a deed obtained from *Wascomo* for the mine area, witnessed by Joseph Crowfoot, James Warner, William Diens, and John Pettibone. This backed up one obtained from *Wascomos's* father *Nadawahunt* (a Christian indian) and his son *Nommorshot* in 1644 by Thomas King and Stephen

Day. These deeds helped the Massachusetts Bay Colony grant land for a plantation as they felt there were Christian indians in the area (although there were only ten families left at *Asquoash*) and that the savages weren't going to war on the English the way the ones under *Uncas* had in Connecticut and Long Island. However, their neutral status put them under constant attacks from the Narragansetts and Mohegans and some Pequot bands.

The English had Royal land grants from their original patent which ran from sea to sea but to make sure they stayed in the good graces of the savages they went through the formality of obtaining deeds and paying for lands. This purchasing of large tracts of land was later to be a big point of contention with *Massasoit's* sons and Alexander's wife *Weetamo*. The way the indians thought of land was radically different from the European way in which a person owned a parcel and everything on it. The Native Americans used the land and fought over the rights to hunt and fish on it but never felt they owned it outright so deeds meant little to them other than the receipt of gifts.

William Davis had moved to Springfield and was in contact with his cousin (Dolor's son) John in Concord. John's fellow passenger on the *Increase* William Warner, became interested in settling to the east of Springfield on the large tract of land Pynchon had bought. This place was to be named *Quaboag* Plantation, then Brookfield Plantation by the English.

This plantation began with families including John Warner from Ipswich, John Younglove, William Pritchard and Thomas Wilson. An unmarried man, Thomas Parsons, the ferry keeper in Windsor, came partly to oversee the burgeoning plantation for Pynchon. Some came from England, others, like Parsons, from Virginia and Wilson from the West Indies. These families were shortly followed by the Coys and Ayres. Only seven families were settled on the tract in the first years but nearby towns such as Hadley, Lancaster, Northampton, etc. were being plotted, cleared, fenced, plowed and planted. The English loved the hills of inland New England as, once cleared, they reminded the settlers of the gentle hills and valleys of their former homeland with brooks, streams and ponds and rivers adding to the area's charm. But, unlike England which had been domesticated over thousands of years, New England settlements were mostly isolated. Only very self-reliant folk took up the challenge to live far away from the main towns. So it was also in Kittery and inland along the northern rivers and for those who chose to live south on Long Island. There was no one to call on for help other than one's neighbors so these plantations were very close knit with sons and daughters intermarrying.

For the planters in western Massachusetts Springfield was the main trading center. They would travel along what was called the Bay Path to the large village to obtain tools and seeds, later to trade corn, apples or cider or furs for English goods such as fine metal pots and steel knives – items the indians also desired.

In 1655 the missionary John Eliot was given 1,000 acres of land near Quaboag by the sachems *Wetoleshem* and *Nakin.* It ran to the shore of *Pookookapaug* pond, south along the Bay Path and west where a gravestone-like marker was set by Eliot and the sachems just above a swamp.

A few years before the first planters settled, the great sachem *Massasoit,* who was now called *Ousemequin*, or White Feather, died near *Quaboag*. His eldest son Alexander had been handling the federation's affairs for several years and formally inherited his father's confederacy. Alexander was hunting on a hot summer day when Winslow sent men to him demanding he come to Plymouth to answer charges he was forming an anti-English treaty with the Narragansetts. While in Plymouth he became ill and died and his younger brother Philip, amidst *Weetamoo's* cries that her husband Alexander had been poisoned, came to power as an angry chief set out for revenge against the English.

The settlers in western Massachusetts and Connecticut felt a change in relations when the Massachusetts tribe went to war against the Mohawks. The Connecticut River flowed from Pocumtuck territory to the north down to the Atlantic Ocean and intersected the *Chicopee* east-west river that ran into Nashaway territory where the Lancaster Plantation was and north through Hoosac territory on the eastern edge of the Mohawk territory. In Pocasset near the Plymouth Plantation Alexander's widow remarried twice, once to an unsuitable man, then to Ben Petonowet, a good friend with the English.

Lands up and down the coast and inland were being sold to the English at a fast rate during this time. Some of the deeds were challenged by Philip who was demanding English silver in payment for the land. He then went to the French and Dutch and bought guns with it. Smallpox raged through the savages' villag-es for several years and during the Mohawk battles on the Piscataqua River the

Pennecooks killed an Englishman. The Pigwacket sachem and Nashoba sachem *Monoco* immediately held a trial and executed the guilty warrior, avoiding war with the English on the north shore. Basically they let the English know this was an intertribal affair and no concern of the settlers. But Boston punished the wife of the sachem *William Ahaughton* for adultery by making her stand on the gallows for an hour after the child of her affair was born, then brought her to the praying village in Natick where she was whipped in public. This imposition of English laws on the Christian indians raised their ire. It ran contrary to their system of justice and helped turn many savages against the English.

That summer near Kennebunk one of Gorges's descendants was digging a well and found what looked like thousands of clay bullets buried there. The savages said Mother Earth was making ammunition for them but most English ignored the threat and felt they had been created by an act of nature.

Rev. Eliot established more praying villages during this time, settled mostly by grandchildren or daughters of the old sachems. It was in one of these villages, the one called *packachoog* where *Matoonas* was chief constable that the coming war with the English began. *Matoonas*'s oldest son had worked as a laborer for the English but he got into an argument and killed one of settlers. He was arrested, tried and executed in Boston. First they hanged him, then they cut off his head and stuck it on a pole outside the town as a warning to the other indians. *Matoonas* vowed revenge and the Assembly in Boston summoned him to swear an oath of loyalty. They also ordered Philip to take the pledge. Instead Philip gathered warriors and built a fire outside Taunton, around which they held a war dance. War would have begun then and there but Roger Williams interceded, going to Philip and persuading him to do as Boston wished.

Then the United Colonies demanded the indians give up their arms. This was a common English demand against any person or faction (such as Wheelwright) that threatened the Puritan establishment. Philip turned in only old, broken guns and Boston sent a delegation to forcibly take the arms in the Sackonet territory and around Middleborough. Philip was told by Roger Williams and two other Englishmen that he had to report to Plymouth but he refused, going to Boston instead. He signed a treaty of submission and they turned in weapons but immediately the savages began bringing in more skins to Pynchon to trade for silver, which they used to buy the new flintlock guns instead of using the silver to pay off their debt to Boston of 100 pounds of silver. The flintlocks were better than the old matchlock guns and the savages replaced their outdated stock with newer weapons. Philip sent out word out that the sachems could sell as much land as they wanted – for silver – as after the war when the English were driven out it would be returned to them. Between 1620 and 1675 the indians realized that they were being pushed out and under King Philip began to push back, hoping to retake their ancestral lands. Like ticks on a dog, the English were dug in and felt the lands belonged to them as they had royal grants or patents and had signed deeds with the indians for the lands they occupied. What had happened was one style of government, the Native American one where oral treaties were made that allowed non-aggressive travel and limited hunting and fishing within another's territory, sealed with wampum belts, had been replaced with a codified English legal system of proprietary land ownership that excluded hunting and fishing rights. The two cultures literally weren't speaking the same language and the French and Dutch played on their confusion to turn them against their competition.

Rev. Eliot and Gookin held a large prayer meeting at the bottom of the great falls where the Merrimac and Concord Rivers meet. Eliot and Gookin claimed that converting the savages was the best way to avoid future hostilities but the settlers in the outlying villages saw bands of armed warriors moving furtively along the paths and through the woods and lived in constant vigilance.

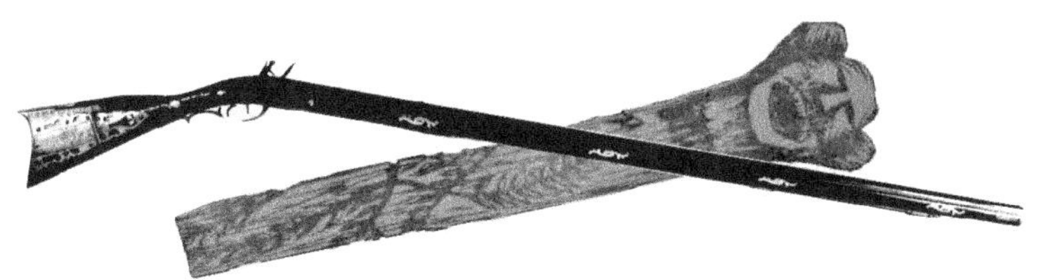

CHAPTER FIFTY-SEVEN

King Philip's War

1670s

In 1674 John *Sassasamon,* a Wampanoag married to a Pequot woman was murdered at *assowompsett* pond. He had been killed by Philip's warriors as he was en route to the English to warn them that Philip had amassed a federation of warriors and was ready to make war against the settlers. The two savages guilty of the crime were captured and held for about six months for the murder, angering the savages as they felt they had the sole right to punish their own people in their own manner. The leaders of Boston and Plymouth then sent delegations to the praying villages to find out if the Narragansetts were in league with the Wampanoags and other tribes.

During Cromwell's war in the 1670s several young Davis men who had been born in Ireland had been sent to New England as prisoners of war sentenced to forced labor. Thomas went to James Davis's plantation for a term of four years and William and Edward both went to William Merick's plantation in the Barbados for four years each. A cousin, John, sent to the Kennebec area to work in the ironworks, went to Scotland to fight for King Charles II.

Louis XIV of France invaded Holland in 1672 and England was his ally. King Charles II declared an 'Act of Indulgence' in which the Catholics were to be treated the same as the Protestants and the Protestants became furious with him. Fearing he'd meet the same fate as his father, he withdrew the Declaration even though his commander of the English fleet (his son James, the Duke of York) was an avowed Catholic. Parliament then passed a 'Test Act' which excluded any man for militiary service if he didn't take an oath of allegiance and supremacy, deny the Catholic belief of transubstantiation during communion and only follow the sacraments of the Anglican church. The duke of York resigned as did the royal Treasurer and Lord Chancellor, the earl of Shaftsbury; other outraged Catholics also resigned their offices in protest.

In 1674 Charles II was forced by Parliament to make peace with Holland. Now England was an enemy of the French, not the Dutch. Charles's son James had a daughter named Mary and she was wedded to William, Prince of Orange to consolidate the Dutch alliance. The politicians who followed the king were now being called Tories. Shaftsbury had been imprisoned in the Tower, but upon his release he organized anti-Catholics (mostly rural people) into a party called the Whigs – not a particularly complimentary name as it referred to Scottish Presbyters who had murdered Catholic bishops. The Parliament was primarily comprised of Tories (previously called Cavaliers). It had been sitting for more than a decade and the Whigs were agitating to have the King dissolve it and call for a new election.

In New England these affairs affected their relations to the Dutch on Long Island and the French, north of Kennebec and the coastal trading ports. The French were selling arms to the savages and, even though England and Holland were officially now allies, the English suspected they were also trading arms with the savages.

The winter of 1674-5 was a hard one, especially for the outlying villagers as it had become very dangerous to venture into the woods to cut firewood so men had been called from late hay harvesting and slaughtering just to stand guard while others cut and stacked long logs on the wood sleds. The governors of the United Colonies had obtained a French weapon, the bayonet, and the 73 militia companies in New England had mustered and were issued the weapon and trained in how to use it. The old standby, the pike, was also issued as the flintlocks had to be primed and loaded before firing. Now, when the ammunition ran out the rifles could be used as spears. Every community had guards. Even though the indians in the praying village and villages near Springfield and along the Connecticut River said they weren't in league with *Massasoit*'s son, now calling himself *Metacomet* or *Pometacomet.*

In 1670 Quaboag Plantation's James Hovey married Priscella Warner. In 1672 John Ayres married Abigail Hovey and Judah Trumble, son of John of Rowley, married Mary Pritchard and in 1674 Richard Coy, from Salisbury, married a second wife, Sarah Kent, daughter of Samuel who, along with his brother had brought their families there from Gloucester. The Coys were well known as prosperous traders near Kennebec, having purchased half of Arrowsick Island and Richard had training in the law. He served as constable for the plantation and was also Pynchon's agent, bringing furs, including many wolf pelts from there to Springfield. He was trained in surveying and helped in the layout out of the Hadley Path in 1674. Using the eminent domain law, he received compensation for the land he lost to the section of the road that circled his pond. The Coys and Davis men had intermarriages also as Nicholas Davis's widow married Richard Kent in Newbury in January, 1675.

All the Quabaog marriages were civil ceremonies as the Puritans did not consider marriage a sacrament. They were performed in Springfield by John Pynchon, the magistrate for the district.

Samuel Moseley of Dorchester had a tavern in Springfield at this time. He had been a sailor and pirate in the vein of Sir Henry Morgan and had brought two ships to Boston full of booty. His take of the loot helped him set up his business on the Connecticut River. His relative John was one of the people who went from Dorchester to settle Windsor, then further out, to Westfield. Samuel's fortunes were further enhanced when he married Ann, eldest daughter of Boston's wealthy merchant Samuel Addington. Her brother knew William Davis well as he was trained to be a surgeon and often used William's medicines for his patients.

About the time Quaboag Plantation was started, a group of men from Stratford, a port between New Haven and Bridgeport, got deeds and permission to start a plantation to the west of Waterbury, to be called Woodbury. Roger Ludlow had first noticed the area during the brief Narragansett Swamp fight in 1653. Thomas Fairchild had the most assets and became the chief planter of the town. He was joined by William and John Curtis, both traders, like the Pynchons. They had come over on the *Lion* in 1632 with the Rev. John Eliot and had been instrumental in the conversion of the Quaboag Old Fort indians near Brookfield. Also settling Woodbury were the wealthy families of Samuel Hawley, Joseph Judson, Timothy Wilcoxson, the Rev. John Birdsey, and Samuel Welles (a son of the Connecticut Governor Thomas Welles). Later Rev. Adam Blackman of Leicester and Derbyshire brought a lot of his congregation from England with him to the outlying town.

Western Massachusetts and Connecticut were full of beaver and the fur trade was a major money maker for traders, as it had been in England through the Skinners Guild that helped fund explorations and colonizing efforts in the late 1500s. Skinners and Shippers (either ship owners, ship builders or captains) were the wealthiest men whose ancestors had often inherited large estates under Henry VIII or by royal gifting. In New England traders tended to settle in port cities but by the early 1670s many were cutting their ties with the sea and moving inland along the new trading posts of the major rivers. Many, such as the Welles, had properties to the north (the North Shore and into Maine where Clarke and Lake had a trading post at Arrowsick) and then acquired new properties to the south in Connecticut , covering many bases.

It was at Moseley's tavern that many learned the indians had attacked Swansea and Dartmouth in June, 1675. Dartmouth was practically annihilated.

While the United Colonies were mustering their militias, such as the one that would be under Captain Samuel Moseley in Springfield, the towns of Menden, Rehobeth, Dorchester, Middlesborough and Taunton were attacked by '*King Philip*' and his warriors.

In mid June, Army Scout Ephraim Curtis had just returned from Quaboag where the sachem *Konkawasco* signed a paper pledging friendship with the English and the promise to remain neutral in any hostilities. Ephraim Curtis was a close friend of Joseph and his nephew Cornelius. Joseph was brother to Cornelius's father John in Haverhilll. Ephraim Curtis had lived in Topsfield, originally settled to provide iron ore to the Boxfield Iron Works. Plus, Ephraim's uncle lived in Pemaquid and was friends of the Kittery Davis clan there.

Philip Davis, having been sent back to England by his father, soon returned to New England and was living near his cousin William Jr. in Boston.

At this time there were three William Davises in Boston: Robert and Marie's William whose wife Margaret Pynchon had died. He had interests in Connecticut and Springfield as well so was a part-time resident. William and Margaret had three sons: Thomas, Benjamin and William. And there was William, brother of Humphrey and John, both more involved with Connecticut than Boston but with shipping offices in Boston for their Barbados, Jamaica and Virginia trading. In England John often resided at the family estate in Creedy. There was another William, William Jr.,, brother of Dolor and Jenkyns and cousin to Richard's sons Captains Samuel and Nathaniel, both mostly involved in settlements outside Boston and the Mason and Gorges lands to the north. Richard's grandson John had been banished from Boston and lived near Saco with his son Sylvanus and near his brother Daniel in Kittery.

A fourth William, son of Richard, briefly lived in Boston before going to Roxbury. He had many children, his two oldest born in Wales, where he had been born. Richard's son Abraham-Isaacs had William, who was father to John, Samuel and Joseph, who was father to Tristrum. The Welsh Davises considered themselves the true family as the others had moved to Bristol, Gloucestershire, Wiltshire, Devonshire, etc. and there was even a branch, Dolor's grandfather, who had settled in Kent.

Dolor had four sons – Big John, born in England (and father of John, born in 1645, Zachary and Cornelius, born in 1653); Little John and late sons, the twins Simon and Samuel, both born in the 1650s, after Little John in New England.

In May, 1675 Marie and Robert's William in Boston caught a vicious cold and despite all his remedies he died. Philip sailed from Hartford for his funeral, along with Capt. Edward Palmes, husband of Connecticut Governor John Winthrop's daughter Lucy. She and William's (second) wife Sarah had been close friends but Lucy was in poor health and couldn't make the trip. Plus, her husband had just returned from England where he had been asking for help to counter the actions of New York's Governor Andros who was suspected of allowing the Dutch to sell muskets, shot and powder to the indians so he needed to report his findings to the Boston officials.

After the funeral Philip Davis decided to return to Connecticut overland, at least as far as Smith's Landing in Rhode Island as his two daughters had married Plymouth men and were living there. He'd heard that the indians under *'King' Philip* were burning barns and killing cattle in anger over Winslow's execution there of *Sassamon*'s three murderers. Portents of comets with blazing arrow trails and strange northern lights were seen all up and down the coast.

By the time Philip Davis got to Plymouth Gov. John Easton of Rhode Island and Samuel Gorton had met with King Philip (he insisted he was equal to King Charles II) and instead of obtaining a peace, obtained a long litany of complaints, mostly about the two justice systems - one for the English and another for the indians; the unfairness of fining the indians when cattle got into their corn and they shot them and of taking their land in lieu of fines. About this time Capt. Benjamin Church returned to Plymouth from Sackonet where he had been at a dance held by the squaw sachem *Awashonks*. He was alarmed to find out the dance was in honor of ambassadors from Philip.

Benjamin Church entered the house where Philip Davis was staying, removed his large brimmed black hat and sat heavily in the high backed chair in front of the fire. It was hot outside but the fire always had to burn as it was the source for cooking and heating water.

"Beg pardon, Missus," he said to Philip's barely adult daughter as he removed bandoliers and his jacket, "but 'tis fair warm this morning."

Church had stopped in to see if any indians had been spotted in the area.

Philip took over the conversation,

"I've just come from Boston, sir," he said, "and me relatives to the north and west – ye know we Davises are a large clan – are all saying the indians are burning outhouses, stealing cattle, even entering and robbing the houses when they are at church. There's fear arisin'. What say ye?"

Church sighed deeply, taking a long swallow of ale.

"Aye, 'tis true. I'm very sorry to hear about Capt. Davis Aden. He was a fine horseman and led a well trained troop of horse. Suppose Tom Prentice will take over now – or Will's son Benjamin – but he's probably a bit young for command. I've been to see Winslow to get patrol boats out along the shores and I'm a riding throughout the area to see if any houses have yet been burned. Me men are out scoutin. Ye see or hear of anything here?"

"There's rumor two houses were burned in *Mattapoiset* and a farmer shot at some indians trying to break in Job Winslow's door while the family was at meeting in Swansea."

"Aye. Our governor at the request of Gov. Leverett is sending out Capt. Hutchinson, Seth Perry and William Powers and some of his three-county troopers to scout and meet with the chiefs in Narragansett to see what is going on. They've been friendly but after what I saw at *Awashonk*'s camp, I fear even our praying indians are falling under Philip's spell. I've never seen them so afire with hatred for every English man, woman and child. 'King' Philip's got them convinced if they all band together they can drive us clear back to England and reclaim all the land they legally deeded to us!" Church harumphed at the thought.

"What does Roger say?"

"Hutchinson is going to pick Williams up in Providence and take him with him to meet the Narragansetts. I tell ye, the biggest mistake England made was to allow that rotten seat of heresy in our midst! And between the two o' us, I don't believe Gookin and Williams about how their praying villagers are all Christians, peaceful and English lovers. Although Roger's book on their language has been a big help."

Philip took a swig of ale and ate some bread and cheese from the platter his daughter had set down.

"That Andros isn't a sweetheart, either, Ben. He seems to be our enemy more than our friend."

"Aye, and ye're in the middle o' it all in Connecticut and New Haven!"

"Well, at least the Mohegans under Uncas haven't shown any hostilities," Philip said, adding, "I was going to go down to Smith's Landing and sail over to Hartford but I'd be happy to ride with ye, as a favor, into Narragansett as I know many of the chiefs through me family's vast trading network."

"I'm a'headin to Bridgewater to check Miles's and Bourne's garrisons. Bourne's place is made of stone so it should be a good fortress. Even though Miles is a Baptist, we are thankful he built a strong defensive house. Ye're welcome to ride with me. I hope to get some fresh troopers there and bring Major James Cudworth and William Bradford, John Fuller and John Gorham to go into the villages and see what is going on." (The Gorhams were from Benefield and knew the Willards and Dolor's family.)

A few days later Philip Davis and Capt. Church arrived in Bridgewater, About 70 settlers had fled to Bourne's garrison for protection. Church warned any settlers they saw in the farms in the area to get inside and stay inside but six farmers went out to gather corn in the fields and were killed in an ambush. Most of the outliers abandoned their farms and fled to garrisons in Rhode Island for safety.

Boston dispatched Major Thomas Savage and Capt. Thomas Brattle, a wealthy Boston merchant and iron works owner, to see if they could effect a treaty but when they found men slaughtered and left to rot in the heat along the way they sent word the indians were in no mood for negotiations and the militias needed to be called out immediately.

Towards the end of June William Davis Jr. of Northampton, who had been in Boston for his father's funeral and estate settlement, was enlisted under Captain Daniel Henchman as one of his three-county troop, the 5th Massachusetts Company. Samuel Davis and his friend Joseph Fiske also enlisted along with Joseph Belcher who served as quartermaster. A messenger was sent west to Captain Hutchinson (a relative of Anne Hutchinson) to alert him to the dangers. He had a large land holding in *Quinsigamond,* between Marlborough and Brookfield (Quaboag). Ephraim Curtis, the trader, also lived there with his son John and knew the local indians very well. He'd been visiting, scouting and getting neutrality agreements throughout the Nipmuck territory for the past month.

At Swansea settlers were fired on as they returned from a Day of Humiliation at church. Captain Prentice's troopers then joined the United Colonies' force and he and his troopers rode to Plymouth. The foot soldiers were all given a knapsack, six feet of fuse, a pound of powder and across their chests had bandoliers containing over 12 cartridges of powder already measured, a belt with a pouch holding three pounds of bullets, a horn of priming powder for their muskets or flintlocks plus a pound of tobacco and a day's food. There were teamsters driving oxen carts of provisions including food, water and extra clothes or shoes as some of the farm boys were used to going barefoot. The troopers mostly came from more well to do families but they received provisions for their horses as well as themselves plus carried swords and a carbine or a pistol on each hip. The foot soldiers had knives that could be attached to the barrels of their long guns in case they ran out of ammunition (the newly invented bayonet) and had to fight in close quarters. The spirits were high in the men as they left Boston for Plymouth, many singing, and there was a lot of talk about how they'd put those heathen Devil worshiping savages down like dogs.

Thirty miles out of Boston the sky suddenly turned full dark as a full eclipse of the sun occurred. All movement ceased as the men marveled at the sight, some seeing signs in shapes on the moon. As soon as sunlight came back they continued from Dedham to Attleboro where the footsore men and horses were given a well-deserved rest.

At Attleboro Captain Moseley and men from Dorchester joined the force. He had several pirates, or privateers, in his company, men used to fighting hand-to-hand that had been recruited from the taverns on the docks.

The foot soldiers and troopers, totaling over 250 with teamsters, then marched to Swansea, arriving near Cudworth's and Miles's garrisons at sunset. Eager for engagement, a group of Prentice's troopers crossed the bridge below Miles's house and were ambushed. William Hammond, a guide, was killed and Capt. Joseph Belcher and Corporal John Gill were wounded. Major Savage sent a troop out to kill or capture the indians and his son, Ensign Savage was wounded by friendly fire from the riverbank.

It began raining and wouldn't stop but the men were so fired up they chased after the indians who were burning houses, barns and killing settlers, putting their heads and hands on poles as an act of defiance. It was grisly and for the first time many of the men knew this was not going to be a simple shoot and go home type of action.

Major Cudworth with Major Thomas Savage, now Commander-in-Chief of the Massachusetts forces, along with Captain Noah Paige's troopers which included William of Wales's son John Davis and his grandson Hopewell Davis, set out in a force of 500 to take King Philip at his fort on Mount Hope. In the pouring rain and mud they didn't find indians but found torn Bible pages, heads and hands on poles and a path of ruin so the troops retreated and marched back to Swansea after burying any bodies or parts they found.

Captain Prentice had been joined by Capt. Oakes and at this point Simon Davis, Dolor's young son (twin of Samuel) had enlisted from Groton and was with the troopers. They were able to drive off or kill some indians but were then ordered to Pocasset where it was rumored King Philip had been seen. Major Savage left a contingent at Mount Hope to build a fort so the English could have a garrison there. Henchman, Prentice, Capt. Isaac Johnson, with Simon's twin Samuel and his cousin Robert of Sudbury, plus Cudworth and the Plymouth men met up in Swansea.

Major Gookin under Captain Johnson brought a company of Christian indians to join the Plymouth and Massachusetts men at Swansea. The United Colonies Commissioners then ordered Captain Edwards Hutchinson and his three-county Massachusetts troopers along with Joseph Dudley into Narragansett to force a treaty with the chiefs there. As Major Savage marched to Providence, Moseley, Williams and Dudley went by ship to Smith's Landing.

It was at Smith's Landing in the beginning of July that Philip Davis parted ways as he felt he should go back to Connecticut and warn them of the seriousness of the uprising and help raise a force under Major Robert Treat to come to Plymouth to help the English hunt down and kill King Philip. He had begged his daughters and their families to return to Connecticut with him but their husbands were in the Plymouth militias and chose to stay and fight so it was with a heavy heart that Philip set sail for Hartford, forsaking any plans to take the Bay Path or lower exposed trails to the Connecticut River. The acrid odor of wet, charred wood from burned fields, outbuildings and slaughtered livestock filled the air. Philip had heard stories about the Pequot War but he, like most of the English settlers, had grown up in an era of relative peace between the English and the indians. Outlying settlements had sprung up all over, many along the northern Connecticut River, and the English had taken it for granted that the indians would be their aboriginal neighbors, a nuisance at times, thieves, dirty, lice-infested, but mostly they lived as the wild animals in primitive villages on the outskirts, bringing corn or furs to trade at the trading posts or wanting to trade with the farmers for iron implements or steel knives for hunting. Earlier all arms sales to indians had been forbidden but many had muskets they'd gotten from the French or Dutch to the north and west and whereas they had favored the bow and arrow for hunting before the white settlers arrived, now they were dependent on their muskets to fell deer, moose and bears and didn't want to part with them.

The ship met troops under Wait Winthrop from Connecticut who had marched cross country to Smith's Landing. Winthrop brandished a parchment with the old Narragansett sachem *Ninigret*'s signature, or mark, stating they would be neutral. Other old sachems were signing what would prove to be useless pieces of parchment as 'King Philip' was already attacking Middleboro and heading to Dartmouth and Taunton.

Cudworth, ignoring Church's advice to be offensive, not defensive, had marched with a full force to Taunton. He sent Fuller with 36 men to Pocasset but Philip's warriors, warned by the odor of burning tobacco as the men took a smoke break, retreated. Cudworth was joined by Church and they split the two companies, Church and 19 men taking the swamp route and Fuller's near the water's edge. Fuller was able to hail a passing sloop and move his men to the island of Rhode Island for the night. Church, however, marched on, the men complaining of mosquitoes and then, after encountering a nest of rattlesnakes, refusing to continue. Church agreed and split the men into two forces, marching through a pea field towards the shore. The indians fired on them from an abandoned stone house, pinning them between the swamp and shore until almost sunset. Seeing that they were trapped Capt. Roger Golding of Newport (related to the Gouldings in the West Indies), set anchor in his sloop and sent a canoe over to remove the men two at a time to his sloop. Golding was one of the merchant mariners who helped by sending provisions by sea to the various troops throughout the war.

While Church and Fuller were retreating the Massachusetts troops that had been in Narragansett marched from Rehobeth to Taunton where Cudworth's Plymouth troop joined them. They marched 18 miles into the *Pocasset* swamp in search of Philip but, after an ambush, they found only deserted wetus in the area.

The commanders ordered a halt and it was decided to have Capt. Henchman build a fort to keep the indians from getting out of the Mount Hope peninsula. Captain Prentice took his troopers back to Menden and there found a half dozen settlers had been massacred while gathering crops in their fields. Meanwhile, Philip and his people had escaped during the night, crossing the Taunton River. Lt. Nathaniel Thomas was stationed at the Mount Hope garrison with a dozen men. Alerted that local volunteers were pursuing Philip, he brought his men out to join them and, with the help of Mohegan scouts, they found *Weetamo*'s camp near dawn. Silently tying their horses, they approached on foot and a heated battle ensued with the surviving indians fleeing into the swamp. The Mohegan scouts refused to give chase as they were engrossed in acquiring the wealth of plunder from the camp. Henchman was called off the fort construction and rode north near Menden where he joined Captain Moseley, who was bringing supplies for the army.

Church and Captain Eels managed to get 160 indians to surrender after

Weetamo fled. They were sent to Boston to be sold as slaves in the West Indies or Spain. Early experience had shown the English the indians made poor field workers and had insolent attitudes so most of the planters didn't want them but estates on the Continent that would use them in a different way welcomed the chance to buy cheap light labor.

The towns in the United Colonies were ordered to go to full alert and Connecticut was sending troops to New London, Stonington and Saybrook under the command of Capts. Wait Winthrop and Thomas Bull. Bull was a veteran of the Pequot War and had commanded Fort Saybrook. He had recently fought off Gov. Andros's attempt to take the fort for the Duke of York and wasn't afraid of battle. Winthrop joined Capt. Hutchinson in his scouting of the Narragansett territory.

By the time of the indian attacks in Plymouth John Pynchon had been promoted from Captain to Major in the Hampshire County troop of horse under the command of Lt. Thomas Cooper. John Ayres in Brookfield was appointed First Sergeant of the company. William Prichard was Second Sergeant and Richard Coy was Corporeal. During the eight musters of the militia per year on Pritchard's Hill the Massachusetts flag of red with a white canton in the upper left hand corner was flown (as the English St. George cross flag had been banned following protests of its popish cross in Boston some years before). As per an Act passed by the United Colonies in 1667 every town had to have a garrison house in which the women and children could gather during attack. In Brookfield it was Ayres's tavern, which had been reinforced after it was built. Acres and Moseley knew each other well as they often met the ships from England to bid on wines and liquors they couldn't provide in their mostly cider and ale-serving taverns.

During July, 1675 the militias were mobilized. They knew the indians were going for outlying towns and settlements such as Lancaster, Halley and Brookfield were the most vulnerable. Dolor's young son Simon joined Capt. Thomas Wheeler's regiment. His cousin Cornelius, son of Dolor's son John in Newbury, and cousin of Thomas Davis, a sawyer, joined militia companies. Cornelius, 25-years old, was in the one led by Captain Samuel Appleton of Ipswich, who was a year younger than he. They were close friends. They were New England born, as were most of the men who fought in 1675-6. Their fathers had been immigrants and some had fought in the Pequot War but most had settled into the life of farming, fishing or skilled trades. The country now belonged to Cornelius's generation and they were the men who volunteered to fight for it. The older men also fought but as with any army, men were needed to defend the women and children and only the strongest could endure the hard marches on rough trails. However, men such as Major Simon Willard had actual experience fighting for the English army on the continent or in Cromwell's New Model Army so they were naturally chosen as the major generals and majors. Of course, the form of combat they were used to was European with a field of battle and mutual protocols. The indians they would encounter were used to ambushing and then disappearing into the woods. The friendly indian scouts tried to warn the commanders they needed to change their tactics but were ignored for almost a year, much to the detriment of the English Army. Most of the company captains were from the wealthier families or had proven themselves exceptionally virtuous in their communities. To be a trooper a man had to have his own horse. He received a small stipend per year towards its upkeep but the foot soldiers were mostly poor farm sons, some descended from fathers who had fought in the Pequot War thirty years prior.

On August 1, 1675 Army Scout Ephraim Curtis led a troop of soldiers under Capt. Edward Hutchinson and Capt. Thomas Wheeler and 20 mounted men to Brookfield, their mission to discern the intentions of the neutral band of indians there. Curtis and his son had already secured a treaty but Boston wanted it renewed in light of the vicious attacks in Plymouth. Curtis found the indians in Quaboag Old Fort hostile and sent word via a messenger to the troops in Marlboro en route to Springfield. He waited for the indians to come out and treat but they wouldn't so the Council sent Captains Hutchinson and Wheeler with 20 troopers, including Simon Davis, to Brookfield to find out why the supposedly friendly indians had turned hostile.

They had to search for the village as it had moved to an island in a swamp. No one would come off the island and meet with them at first but finally Curtis was told they would meet the English on a plain three miles out of the plantation near a tree at 8 o'clock the following morning.

No one showed up. Hutchinson and some Brookfield settlers talked to a friendly indian by the name of David, and ascertaining the indians camp, decided to proceed and meet them there. Ephraim estimated there were 200 warriors gathered on the island. As they rode in single file with a wooded hill on one side and swamp thick with sumacs and grass on the other, they were ambushed. The indians fired upon the English, wounding five including Captain Wheeler's son Thomas and Capt. Hutchinson and killing five men from Concord and the Boston area plus Brookfield's Corporal Coy and Sergeants Acres and Prichard. Prichard's daughter Mary (now Trumball), had just given birth to his grandson and the whole town had been celebrating the birth when Hutchinson's troop arrived in the settlement on Sunday morning.

In the ambush outside town five horses were killed. Troopers rode back to the town to warn its 14 families comprised of 35 adults and 43 children to get to the garrison but James Hovey, whose land was furthest from the center of town, was ambushed and slaughtered. Two women: Sarah Coy and Joan Kent, large with child at the time went into premature labor and both delivered twins in Acres Tavern during the ensuing siege.

Once safely inside the garrison Capt. Hutchinson, severely wounded, called Simon Davis to his side.

"I fear I'm not going to make it," he whispered to the man who was like a son to his friend Simon Willard, "I give you the command, Simon. Get word to Marlboro and Springfield to relieve us."

Ephraim Curtis and Henry Young were then dispatched to ride as fast as they could towards Boston to bring help but the exit was blocked by the indians sacking the deserted homes. After several hours Curtis was finally able to sneak past to get help from Marlborough while the Brookfield garrison was attacked. Travelers on the Bay Path had seen smoke from the fires the indians set and heard the gunfire so reinforcements from Marlborough and Pynchon both arrived, but not for three days.

In the meantime Samuel Pritchard tried to get supplies for the people inside the tavern from his father's house but was captured and decapitated. The savages used his bloody head like a football, kicking it around the front of the house before setting it on a pole in front. Witnessing this sacrilege Henry Young was mortally wounded as he fired from his post at a window in the attic of the tavern.

Alerted by Judah Trumble, a new father, couriers rode to Hartford and Boston. Springfield sent a troop under Lt. Thomas Cooper a carpenter, surveyor, farmer, sometimes attorney and bonesetter, from Windsor who had friendly Mohegans with his troopers and Capt. Thomas Watts from Hartford came up the Connecticut Path to the rescue. Capt. Moseley and most of Henchman's company from Menden brought the total of men under Major Willard to 350 plus the Mohegans. Major Simon Willard had been heading for Lancaster but immediately re-routed for Brookfield. Judah Trumble, father of a newborn boy, who left for Springfield during the siege alerted that town as he bought rum for the injured,. John Pynchon immediately sent a letter to the Governor of Connecticut requesting help. Pynchon sent the surgeon Dr. Daniel Denton back with Trumball to tend to the wounded and the two women who had gone into labor, each prematurely delivering a set of twins amidst the chaos and confusion of the attack.

On the fourth day of the siege Major Willard and Captain Parker arrived after sunset with 46 men and five indian scouts. Their army was followed by a large herd of cattle that had been left out in the pastures and were in need of milking and water. The indians were preparing a second attempt to burn the settlers out by lighting a wagon full of wood and hay and shoving it towards the house. They had attempted it earlier that day but a rainstorm put their fire out. With the arrival of English troops the indians set fire to the homes and the mill outside town and left, screaming their hideous war cries into the night. Capt. Beers from Watertown and Capt. Lathrop from Beverly-Salem arrived with Dolor's son John and his son Cornelius as troopers from Newbury. His grandson Zachary was in the company of foot.

Simon Davis and Wheeler's company then went to Marlborough where Capt, Hutchinson, suffering and in much pain, died.

Simon's company returned to their base in Concord three weeks after Brookfield was leveled by indians who had supposedly been friendly with the English and accepted the Christian god through the work of Rev. John Eliot. The attacks stunned and shocked western Massachusetts. The Quaboag-Brookfield survivors abandoned the plantation, returning east to the towns from whence they had come or west to settle in Suffield, Springfield or Windsor. During the rest of the war the town was only used as a garrison for troops. Settlers would not return to the area for many years.

Moseley, Beers, Watts and Lathrop burned any villages they could find, then Watts marched his men from Halley down to Springfield and the others scouted the Bay Path with Moseley. Everywhere they went the indian villages were deserted and no warriors were found.

Halley had the best defenses so was chosen for their headquarters although the other towns were put on high alert. The attacks had come so suddenly it was hard for the settlers to believe the indians who had lived alongside them had suddenly turned into murdering enemies.

In Springfield Major Pynchon wrote to the Connecticut Council and told them his town was all alone and needed reinforcements. They sent Major Talcott and a company but suggested he send Curtis or another trader to Albany in New York to see if they could get the Mohawks on the side of the English. Word came back via Gov. Andros that the Mohawks preferred to be neutral. Pynchon urgently requested Massachusetts allow him to enlist friendly Naticks in his area as scouts.

In the meantime Capt. Moseley had headed northeast to Lancaster as he heard seven settlers had been murdered there. The English settlers in that plantation had never liked the praying village (and wanted its land) told him the Christian indians had been behind the attack so Moseley invaded their village, which had been disarmed by Capt. John Ruddock, one of the founders of Marlborough and a close friend of Dolor as both were housewrights. Moseley sent 11 captives to Boston, yoked together at the neck for the march. Everywhere he went he set fire to the wetus, burning stores of corn and supplies. As a result of his naked hatred of all indians, the friendly ones in the area sneaked away and joined King Philip's fort at the Nonotuck village on a bluff north of Northampton. They, too, had turned against the English who were demanding disarmament and then seizing indians and selling them into slavery. King Philip's ambassadors to the villages told them they would have two choices: fight and regain their lands and freedom or be captured and sold as slaves. He said they had nothing left if they didn't drive the English out.

On August 24th the commanders held a council of war at Hatfield and it was decided Beers and Lathrop, who had arrived from Brookfield on the 22nnd, would lead a party before dawn, collecting Northampton soldiers across the river and march into the indian village and physically disarm each and every Nonotuck man. The village was deserted so they sent half the troops back to Northampton and Halley and the rest found many indians in a swamp. There was heavy fighting but after several hours the English prevailed and drove the remnant out of the swamp to the north.

In early September one of the Connecticut troopers went out from the Deerfield garrison to find his horse as it had strayed. He was shot by indians who were hiding in the woods near the river. The garrison was immediately secured but sheer panic created a chaos amongst the settlers, who had been in church service in the meetinghouse at the time.

The next day Northfield was attacked. Farmers gathering corn in the fields were murdered and the alarm was raised as settlers fled for the garrison, manned only by Capt. Watts and ten men. The settlement was unfortunately set at the foot of a mountain, which made it vulnerable to attack from above. As the settlers mourned the loss of eight of their men flames and smoke told the 17 families of settlers all their goods, their cattle, their hard work as pioneers in this isolated outpost had been in vain. They didn't know that Capt. Beers had been sent with 46 troopers and a team of oxen to reinforce and resupply the garrison. As Beers and his men worked their way up the river they followed a plateau but where it dropped and crossed Sawmill Brook the army was ambushed. Fighting valiantly and bravely they managed to regain high ground but Beers and most of the men were slaughtered. The few remaining soldiers straggled into Halley. Some of the men were taken captive, including Robert Pepper, a friend of Dolor's son John who had moved from Roxbury to the new settlement of Northampton not long before the hostilities began.

That day before, being Sunday, settlers in Halley were in the meetinghouse when the alarm was sounded and sheer panic seized the settlement. It was a false alarm but the subsequent one in Northfield wasn't.

Connecticut sent Maj. Treat and 90 troopers via Westfield up the river to use their own judgment and reinforce where needed in the river settlements. His company arrived in Northampton as reports from Northfield and Halley poured in about the massacre of Beers's company. Early Sunday morning, September 6th, Treat and his men plus ten from Northampton, began marching north. They had to set camp in the woods that night but the morning revealed a grisly path of heads of settlers on poles. Treat ordered his men to gather the bodies and heads and bury all but the indians sniped from the woods and Treat was wounded before all of the bodies could be buried. That night the settlers from Northfield accepted Treat's escort and abandoned their settlement. Capt. Appleton met them en route and tried to talk the settlers into going back and defending their garrison but no one would listen. The settlers and troops that returned to Halley were very depressed and exhausted.

The commanders held a council of war at Halley on September 8th. Acting upon the advice of the indian scouts and settlers, it was decided that the best course was to reinforce the garrisons and stop trying to track down the indians. The settlers were distraught at the thought of all their hard labors wasting in the fields but the commanders insisted anyone who went out to harvest had to be escorted by soldiers.

Henchman and Brattle were sent from Boston to scout and guard Chelmsford, Groton and Lancaster. Appleton went to Deerfield but Connecticut briefly recalled Treat and his troops, leaving only a handful of men at Westfield and Springfield, where Pynchon was appointed Commander-in-Chief for the western front with Treat as Second in Command. Treat and his troops then immediately returned to Northampton.

Word was received that the northern settlements were being attacked and Dolor sent a letter to his sons Simon and Samuel telling him their cousin to the north, Captain Sylvanus, said outbuildings were being burned around Saco and between the Kennebec and Merrimac rivers.

The settlement of Deerfield was exposed. On September 12th 20 men ran from one garrison to another and were ambushed but able to fend off the attackers. The indians took over the north fort and plundered it, talking its guard Nathaniel Cornbury. Two homes were burned and a lot of salted pork and beef stolen. The settlement at Halley was hit twice, once in August and again in October when Springfield was attacked. The following night, Sept. 13, John Davis got some settlers from Northampton and others got men from Halley and the volunteers joined Capt. Appleton who marched them to Pine Hill. The indian village was deserted.

Capt. Moseley arrived at Deerfield and Maj. Treat at Northampton with *Uncas*'s Mohegan guides. So many troops were arriving that Maj. Pynchon realized the corn in the fields needed to be brought in so he sent Capt. Lathrop to load the corn that was already stacked in sacks in the fields near Deerfield to bring it into the garrisons. Moseley reported no sightings or activity so it was felt that if a group of Deerfield farmers were escorted by Lathorp and his men the corn could be put on carts and safely brought in.

The road out to the fields was rutted and the oxen slow. The soldiers, tempted by the lush grapes growing along the way put their muskets on the carts and gathered bunches as they progressed. Six miles south of the main settlement the group had to go through a marsh and cross what was called the Muddy River. It was there the indians ambushed them. John Davis's friend John Tappan from Newbury was wounded but managed to hide in the tall grass. The indians massacred Lathrop and the 17 farmers. Only Tappan and a few who had straggled behind the main convoy escaped.

Capt. Moseley and his 60 troopers were scouting when they heard the gunfire and they rode as fast as the swampy land would allow. When they got to the scene of the massacre the indians taunted the captain, yelling, "Come on, Moseley, come on! You want Indians. Here are enough indians for you!" Moseley kept his troops together and charged at them as they were ripping open the bags of corn and feather mattresses the men had salvaged from a farmhouse, scattering corn and feathers all over. The indians fought back and Moseley would have suffered the same fate as Lathrop if Treat hadn't heard the noise and come rushing to the rescue with 100 Connecticut men and 60 Mohegans.

It was dark by the time the survivors reached Deerfield's garrisons. The next day, a Sunday, the troops returned to bury 71 men and boys; many of the Deerfield farmers had been in their teens.

Deerfield, like Northfield, was then evacuated. The commanders decided they couldn't defend the outlying settlements and Deerfield settlers had to go to the garrisons of Halley and Hatfield on opposite sides of the Connecticut River.

Maj. Pynchon, who was knowledgeable in the thinking process used by the indians, told Boston the English needed to take the offensive and drive the indians out of the river valley all the way up to Canada and northern New York or heavily fortify the garrisons but Boston wouldn't listen to him. Pynchon, in a series of heated letters, said the only thing the indians would respect was offense, that defense made the English look weak in the eyes of the enemy, whose numbers were growing daily as more and more tribes and bands joined King Philip's Army. He added they shouldn't take any men from the garrisons but should reinforce them. His words weren't heeded and in late September Pynchon's mill on the west side of the river was burned and two days later, on Sept. 26th two Northampton settlers were killed while trying to cut wood for the increased demands the garrisoned troops put on the towns. The indians scalped them and cut off their arms.

On October 4th Maj. Pynchon and a large force set out from Springfield to Halley. Pynchon intended to take Agawam captives at Longmeadow to use to ransom the hostages the indians had. Pynchon left Lt. Cooper in charge. The next day he took Thomas Miller, who was constable and surveyor of highways, with him to see if he could get the Agawams to sign a treaty. Miller was shot dead before they crossed the Mill River and Cooper was mortally wounded, dying in the saddle as his horse galloped into the nearest garrison. Then the settlement of Springfield was attacked. The settlers had been warned by a friendly indian, Toto, so the loss of human life wasn't as great as it would have been if they hadn't gone to the garrisons but 32 houses and 25 barns were burned and the Rev. Grover's precious library burned. Maj. Treat came from Westfield but couldn't cross the river due to heavy enemy fire. It wasn't until the late afternoon that Pynchon and Captains Sill and Appleton arrived, having ridden hard with 200 men from Halley. By the time they reached Springfield the indians had retreated to Indian Orchard. Moseley only found an old squaw and in an act of pure rage, had her torn to pieces by dogs.

Boston reaffirmed its orders" "Pursue and destroy." Pynchon's suggestions had been ignored and in frustration he requested for the third time that he be replaced. On October 4th Appleton was given command of the western frontier and arrived at Halley on October 12th. He found only Massachusetts men in the garrisons as Treat had been recalled south to Wethersfield where a group of indians had been sited.

Finally, the United Colonies mobilized on November 3, 1675, authorizing Captain Joseph Gardiner to raise two large Armies in Salem and the adjoining towns to go to the Narragansett territory. His recruiters went out to the Boston-Salem area towns with the authority to impress, or draft men such as Hopewell (Howell), Davis who didn't want to volunteer after hearing of the massacres of Beers and Lathrop's forces and the mutilations the indians practiced on the young men who weren't trained soldiers but had played at soldiering on muster days, mostly clowning around and drinking. Appleton was given command of the entire Connecticut River area.

Cornelius Davis rejoined Appleton's company nine days later after burying his father Big John who died on the day the armies were mustered. Thomas Davis of Dedham joined General Josias Winslow's company to the south in Plymouth around the same time. In Lynn their previously shunned relative John Davis joined and Vincent Davis joined in Gloucester. Captains Davenport, Ting and Houghton were in command of some of the companies who were either charged with defending the eastern towns or would be sent west to Narragansett territory for the united offensive planned against the indians.

CHAPTER FIFTY-EIGHT

The Narragansett Swamp Fight

1675

As winter moved in Maj. Walderne thought he had a reprieve to the north, where winter came early and hard. But in Massachusetts the United Colonies issued an official Declaration of War against the Narragansetts on November 2, 1675. They had refused to surrender the hostile Wampanoags that sought refuge in their villages despite empty promises to the English to do so. Josiah Winslow was appointed Commander-in-Chief and Connecticut was told to appoint his second. An allotment of men from each colony was set and a week's provision was ordered for each man impressed.

On December 2, 1675 The United Colonies declared a Day of Prayer and Fasting throughout the colonies. Quaker meetings, profanities and idleness were preached against or, in the case of Quaker meetings, actually forbidden.

Rhode Island wasn't included in anything the United Colonies did even though the Narragansetts were in their territory. Neutral indians were rounded up and sent to Deer Island and other empty, basically unlivable islands in Boston harbor. Companies were organized and captains appointed.

Connecticut raised an army of 315 men, mostly from Norwich, Stoningham and New London. Maj. Treat was appointed Second in Command to Winslow with Captains Watts, Marshall, Mason and Lts. Avery, Seeley, and Miles to serve under them. Rev Fitch of Norwich was ordered to assemble a company of friendly Pequots and Mohegans.

On December 8th, after conferring with Governor Leverett in Boston, Winslow with Church, Dudley, surgeons, ministers and a volunteer Massachusetts Army marched to Dedham where the Connecticut valley troops were to meet them. Appleton and Moseley were there with their men, many left over from the fall battles. Johnson brought Roxbury, Dorchester, Weymouth and Hull area troops, Davenport brought Cambridge and Watertown area men, Oliver brought Boston area; Gardiner troops from Essex County and Prentice a company of troopers, including Benjamin Davis. Altogether 465 foot soldiers, 275 troopers with horses, volunteers, teamsters and servants were assembled on the plain in Dedham. There, Maj, General Denison spoke and promised that every man who fought in the upcoming campaign would be allotted a grant of land, and if they perished, their land grant would be given to their heirs. A great "Hurrah!" was shouted as the men heard this. None of the men shivering on that cold field that morning had any idea of the hell they were about to enter.

Denison, not feeling well, then gave field command to Capt. Winslow and he gave the command to march out. The march took all day and the exhausted men didn't reach Woodcock's garrison outside Attleboro until dark. Tents were pitched and peas boiled with ham and the men dined on bread or biscuits and a thick, hot soup filled with chunks of salty ham. Rations of rum were drunk, songs were sung around campfires and sore feet were massaged and rubbed with homemade ointments the women had sent with their men. They rose early the next day and another long march brought them to Seekonk. Richard Smith's sloop was in the harbor, loaded with fresh supplies. Leaving the foot soldiers to march overland, Moseley, Church and Dudley and some of their men went aboard and Smith sailed them around to the head of the bay in Providence. There, the commanders were joined by Maj. William Bradford and Capt. Gorsham with 158 men from Plymouth. It was bitter cold and so dark many of the divisions got lost, staggering around swamps and hills. The entire army didn't join up until well into the night. After setting up camp Moseley and Church rested their men while Bradford and Gorham took men out to search for *Punham*, a former ally of the English but now in league with King Philip.

On the 13th of December all the commanders met up at Wickford, at Smith's garrison and Landing. The men there had rounded up and killed indians and captured a good 20 prisoners, who Capt. Nathaniel Davenport bought as plantation slaves for 80 pounds. Nathaniel was the son of Richard who had commanded Castle William until struck dead by lightning on the fort (considered a Divine punishment by the Wheelwrights for his persecution of their group). Nathaniel was a friend of Capt. Samuel Davis whose ship the *Gabriel* often docked at the fort to deliver supplies. He was a friend of Endecott, who had cut the red cross out of the flag, and he married one of his daughters. His relative Francis was a ship captain and another cousin Humphrey, had a sugar plantations in the Barbados. (This was for whom he bought the slaves.) His relative John was one of New Haven's founders.

Winslow's troops had been approached by an indian named Peter Freeman who had fallen out with Philip. Even though his daughter was thrown in with the slaves he agreed to help the English and guide them to the fort where the bulk of the Narragansetts were holed up for the winter.

The commanders were tired of waiting for the Connecticut troops that always seemed to show up a day late and a pound short and decided to attack the village of squaw sachem *Matanatuck*, called Queen Magnus. Her fort was on top of a hill and surrounded by large boulders. The troops burned over 150 wetus but the Queen and most of her people escaped. They captured nine, killed seven while Capt. Oliver's company, left behind to guard the stores, killed a warrior and his squaw and captured several others with them. These skirmishes only whetted the soldiers' lust for blood and revenge. Almost to a man they were either related to or friends of families that had lost houses, barns, livestock and precious English furniture and silver goods. Many lost relatives to brutal indian deaths and every man knew with the loss of the corn in the fields that this was going to be a long, hungry winter – and all because the indians decided to start a war with the settlers.

On the 15th of December an old former indian friend approached the army. He was recognized immediately by Dolor's grandsons and son Little John as Stonewall John for his father had helped the indians learn how to build sturdy houses with cut stone. He had helped build many English garrisons, or forts over the years but also built some for the indians. He said he had authority to act as a peace negotiator but the men who knew the ways of the indians dismissed him and said they would only treat with the chiefs, or sachems. His suspected duplicity was proven as indians hiding in the woods fired on Gardiner's company as he left the encampment. Others fired from a stone wall on Moseley and Gardiner's men as they rode out along with Oliver to bring in Appleton's companies. Eight miles away was Jirah Bull's place, the rendezvous garrison. Made of stone with a nice stone wall in front it was chosen for the safest place for the Plymouth and Massachusetts armies to rendezvous with Capt. Treat's Connecticut force. However, during the night the indians broke down the door of the garrison and massacred 15 of the 17 men inside.

****

"Sir!" Trooper Benjamin Davis yelled, pointing to the smoke rising from the direction of Bull's garrison. Like his father he loved horses and loved to ride. Marie and Robert's William had been one of the first men to bring good stock over and William's sons had ridden since they were toddlers. Most farmers preferred oxen to horses as they were stronger and didn't require oats or supplements, surviving on just the hay in the pastures. A horse was somewhat of a luxury to the farmers but the more well-to-do outliers had at least one. By 1675 the colonies were full of horses as the older men and women preferred to ride in carts instead of walking to the meetinghouse, which in scattered settlements could be miles away.

Prentice and his men saw the burned out fort, buried the dead and returned with the two wounded soldiers by afternoon. It being December the sun set early and the cold was very intense. The men in camp became despondent at the tale the survivors and Prentice's men told. Many questioned if they would, indeed, survive the big fight to come live to see their grant of land. Men who had left pregnant wives behind worried that their garrisons would be attacked during their absence and many wondered if they'd ever see their families again. But men such as Simon and Samuel and John and Cornelius Davis came from a sturdy stock and knew their fathers or grandfathers had faced such an unknown crossing the dark, grey Atlantic ocean and, once arriving, found themselves in a place with no shelters, no towns, no goods other than those they brought with them on the ships. These desolate places were now bustling towns filled with goods from around the world. Their farms had acres and acres of nice cleared pastures and field after field of peas, corn, wheat, rye and hops for ale plus the kitchen gardens the womenfolk planted and tended. They knew if they lost to the indians that everything they had worked so hard for would be forever gone. A house or barn could be rebuiLt. a cow or pig replaced, but there was really nowhere for them to return to if they didn't make it in New England. The place the older generations came from was closed to them, either from the Civil War or because it was overcrowded to begin with as gentry bought up lands and enclosed them for sheep or cattle and shoved the peasantry into towns that didn't want more mouths to feed.

The Irish were being deported en masse to the West Indies and Virginia but wealthy landlords with holdings in the southern colonies preferred the more English-like climate of New England to the humid, buggy, disease filled subtropics.

"Hey Simon," Samuel whispered to his twin as they tried to sleep in the canvas tent outside Bull's garrison.

"Yes?"

"You scared?"

Simon laughed but it sounded hollow.

"I plan on taking out plenty of indians, brother, not on dying. Ye hear?"

"Aye, I plan on fightin' to the death, too. But did ye hear what they do to a fellow after – I hope after – he's a'murdered?"

"Dead is dead. We will all meet in Heaven. I truly believe God is on our side. The indians are heathens. We will be spared. They will be eliminated. Remember the story of Constantine and how he saw a cross in the sky?"

"Aye. I thought I saw what looked like a scalp on the moon when that eclipse happened a while ago."

"It was an indian scalp, brother. Not an English one. Remember that. Be like Constantine and have faith. Pray with me, brother."

The brothers said quiet prayers, joined by the muffled voices of the other men in their cramped tent. Outside a snowstorm began and gusts blew snow onto their blankets. The wind howled through the trees and it sounded like the Devil laughing. That was a long, cold, lonely night for the armies of the United Colonies.

However, the next morning scouts rode into camp with news that the Connecticut men were nearby. Three hundred and fifteen Englishmen and 150 Mohegans were at *Pettaquamseut* with Maj. Treat. The Massachusetts troops broke camp and marched out to meet them, joining them as the short winter day was coming to a close.

Sunday morning at 5 a.m. the troops were ordered to begin the march west to where they were told 5,000 Narragansetts and their allies were holed up in a fort deep in a swamp. It was snowing and cold. The men marched with their blankets wrapped over their woolen coats and the brims on their hats pulled low as the Massachusetts men and troopers went on ahead and the indian scouts flanked them. The Connecticut troops pulled up the rear and Plymouth was in the middle. Capts. Moseley and Davenport led the way. For seven hours the men marched, in and out of swampy areas, up and down hills, skirting higher hills. The viability was poor due to the driving snow but shortly after noon the fort was sighted. It seemed to be on an island whose only entrance was over a fallen log, right in the gunsights of the indians. However, Moseley and Davenport found another way in where the fort hadn't been completely finished. They urged their men forward. The indians instantly began firing and Capt. Johnson fell dead, followed by Capt. Davenport, an easy target in his light-colored coat. The indians seemed to have an endless supply of ammunition: bullets were landing everywhere. The men were called back and had to fall onto their faces in mud and snow to avoid being shot. Moseley and Gardiner sent in reinforcements and Capt. Appleton yelled to his men to brave the log bridge and advance, to gain entrance at the blockhouse. Many fell dead or wounded into the half-frozen swamp but enough breached the perimeter so the fort was taken. Capts. Gallop, Marshall and Seeley were killed but their men, joined by the Plymouth soldiers, got inside and after firing just a single bark-shingled wetu, the whole fort went up in flames and smoke. The indians fled into the swamp but Capt. Church and his Plymouth company were able to kill many before Church was wounded.

As darkness fell the leaders met in the smoky, deserted fort and Church argued that the troops should hold the fort and stay there for the night. Six captains had been killed. Over 20 men were killed and over 150 were wounded. As much as they all wanted to stay and nurse their wounded and exhausted troops Church was outvoted and the men – hurt, tired, and cold – stripped saplings and took muskets from those who fell and with rope made rude litters to carry their wounded back through the dark and deep snow towards their garrison, 18 long miles to the east. For three miles the firelight of the inferno that had been a fort gave them some light but then men stumbled and got lost and it wasn't until 2 o'clock in the morning that the first group staggered into Wickford, 21 hours after leaving. Winslow and his men didn't reach camp until 7 a.m.

The English Army lost seven captains and 75 men in the battle. The army was starving and the arrival of Capt. Richard Goodale and Capt. Andrew Belcher's sloops with provisions at Smith's Landing was such a welcome sight some of the men cried with relief. Ships took the wounded Massachusetts and Plymouth men to Rhode Island but Connecticut's forces were so weakened Maj. Treat had to withdraw back to their territory.

After the snowstorm there was a thaw and the snow melted, turning the roads into muck.

Prentice and his troopers found *Pumham*'s village and burned it but the indians had fled beforehand.

Following the English victory over the Narragansetts in the swamp the United Colonies Commissioners in Boston raised a new levy of men and on January 6, 1676 Capt. Samuel Brocklebank set out with men from Rowley.

CHAPTER FIFTY-NINE

The Hungry March

1676

Capt. Brocklebank had been one of the prime recruiters of men from the Rowley, Haverhilll, Newbury, Ipswich and Topsfield areas. It was due to his efforts that John, Cornelius and William's son Thomas had enlisted and Hopewell had been drafted against his will. Knowing Hopewell might be a problem to control in the field he was generally assigned garrison duties during the war. Simon and Samuel eagerly enlisted early as did Simon Willard's son Simon. His father, Maj. Simon Willard Sr., like William Davis, had a chest complaint and was often laid up in bed with weakness, fever and coughing. Willard senior had serious experience fighting the Catholics on the Continent in the Thirty Years War but his son had only known peace in New England. He had been tempted to go and fight in the Civil War but his father had talked him out of it saying there would be no real victor for the Roundheads would eventually yield the power back to the Royalists, that is, the king, who, as events showed, did indeed get restored to the throne. The only good that came from the war, his father said, was that the common people got more power and the crown had to answer to Parliament. The restored king, Charles II wasn't well liked and was too Catholic for most of the people but they were weary of war and wanted a semblance of normalcy now that the Dutch wars had ended. Thomas Osborne, Earl of Danby, was Charles II's primary councillor. The Whigs and Torys played a back-and-forth exchange of power and it was rumored that King Charles II's brother, James VII of Scotland, was very Catholic but his daughter Mary very Protestant so a marriage between Mary and the Protestant Dutch Prince William of Orange was brokered to unite the countries and hopefully have a Protestant queen should James II die before taking the throne. Just before King Philip's War King Charles II had dissolved Parliament and there had been plots to murder both Charles and James to prevent Catholics from openly regaining the throne.

In New England these Catholic-Protestant battles had been set aside as every Englishman was a target of the indians, regardless of his religious beliefs. The dissidents in Rhode Island had been attacked, the more independent settlers to the north had been attacked. Only New York, which still had a lot of Dutch settlers up the Hudson to Albany and was friendly to French traders, seemed to be spared. Captain William Turner's son, along with patriotic planters, had sailed back to New England from the West Indies to assist in the fight. Many mariners such as Stephen Hascot, captain of the *Swan*, now owned with Capt. Savage, assembled a fleet of ships such as Peter Traby's *Primrose* and Anthony Law's sturdy freighter. Additionally Andrew Belcher, Richard and Nehemiah Godell, Ezekial Gardiner, and the Woodburys were all helping, as were Capt. Sylvanus Davis and his Davis relatives, with their ships to the north.

By 1676 most of the old men were dead or retired so a new generation was sailing the seas, involved heavily with trade to the West Indies and Maryland and Virginia. These ships kept provisions flowing from port to port from the far northern trading posts down the coast, around the Cape, down Rhode Island's bays and along Connecticut's coast, then to Manhattan and on to Virginia. During King Philip's war they brought badly needed food to the United Colonies as their harvests were either ungathered and rotted in the fields or were burned by the indians. They brought cotton cloth and wines and leathers as so many cattle had been killed or taken by the indians that shoes and padded armor were becoming scarce. The indians also suffered as they and their corn had been burned out of their winter villages where sacks of corn served as insulation stacked against the bark walls. Church and other commanders rued the burning of the Narragansetts'swamp fort but after that great battle a lull in fighting had occurred.

It was during one of the coldest Januarys the settlers had known that Capt. Brocklebank with Lt. Swett and Cap. Daniel Fiske marched a large number of the 1,000 soldiers the Commissioners had called up south from Boston to Wickford. The four day march in ice and snow took its toll and several men died from the cold and others had frostbite. After they reached Wickford Canochet and sachems sent a request to Winslow asking for a month's ceasefire. This was when they said "not a pairing of a nail or a nail" of the Wampanoags they harbored would be turned over to the English. Winslow was indignant and replied in a solid negative. Winslow got word from Connecticut's Gov. John Winthrop Jr. that Gov. Andros of New York had received news that King Philip and about 500 warriors were encamped 40 to 50 miles northeast of Albany and Philip was sick. Instead of sending troops north it was decided the army would pull out and abandon the garrisons of Chelmsford where Hopewell and Walter Davis were stationed, Billerica where Joseph Davis, the Fiskes and Welches and many others were stationed, Groton with Simon Willard Jr., Lancaster where Walter Davis had been stationed and Sudbury and to instead reinforce Marlborogh, making it the main headquarters in the east.

About this time Capt. Arthur Fenner and his men from Providence captured indians marauding and raiding the Warwick area and they captured Joshua Tift, an Englishman who had been helping the indians. Tift was tried as a traitor, hanged, drawn and quartered as a message to any whose loyalties were not solidly on the side of the English.

Towards the end of January the Connecticut troops joined the others and the combined forces now totaled about 1,400. In what was later referred to as 'The Hungry March' the men were sent in deep snow and bitter cold with poor provisions into Narragansett to search for any villages or indians. The tents were pitched in deep snow and the men were so hungry they killed and ate horses that weren't going to survive without oats and hay. They dug up ground nuts (Jerusalem artichokes) yet didn't find the enemy. When they completed their circle of Narragansett territory and reached the garrison at Marlborough the Plymouth and Connecticut men were sent home and Capt. Wadsworth was left at the garrison with the men who were in no shape for marching. Capt. Brocklebank was bringing them much needed supplies.

The United Colonies' Army, now reduced to 600 horse and foot, was ordered to the indian "old fort" at Quaboag. While they were there Lancaster's five garrison houses were attacked. The Rev. Rowlandson was in Boston begging the Council not to abandon the garrisons. Forty-two people including his wife and infant daughter in his garrison were shot as they fled the burning building. Most of the men were killed and the women and children taken as hostages. Capt. Gookin sent an urgent message to Capt. Wadsworth in Marlborough but by the time they arrived any survivors in Lancaster were already packed and ready to leave.

Concord's settlement was then attacked. A teenaged girl, Mary Shepherd, was one of the captives but during the night she stole a horse and rode for help. Lts. Oakes and Jacobs with troopers were ordered to scout the area, but found no indians.

Twelve days later Medfield was attacked. Lt. Adams was killed and Captains Jacobs and Oakes rushed to the garrison where witnesses said One Eyed Sam was leading an assault. Lt. Adams's wife was in deep grief in the bedroom above the parlor and Lt. Jacobs accidentally shot and killed her as his loaded musket, carried upright as he walked to the door discharged and the shot went through the floor and killed her in bed. Jacobs was inconsolable as he had tried to save his captain, Isaac Johnson, at the Narragansett Swamp Fight and had been promoted from Captain to Lieutenant. as a result of his bravery.

Before the troops could organize a party to respond to the attack the indians had retreated across a bridge to a neighboring hill. They burned the bridge but left a note tacked to the end, *"Know by this paper, that the Indians thou hast provoked to wrath and anger will war this 21 years if you will. There are many Indians yet. We come 300 at this time. You must consider the Indians lose nothing but their life. You must lose your fair houses and cattle"*.

While Medfield was attacked the Council voted to raise another 100 foot and 75 troops under Maj. Savage with Capt. Whipple taking command of the troopers and Capt. Turner the foot. Moseley and Gillam added foot soldiers and John Curtis led a scouting unit of six friendly indians. This new force was immediately sent to Brookfield but found it deserted so marched on up to Halley.

At this time the indians attacked Weymouth and then Groton, where they stole a large number of hogs and cattle. Maj. Willard and Capt. Sill found no indians in the burning settlement but some hid in the outhouses and attacked four farmers who went out to their meadows the following morning. A few days later Capt. James Parker's company gave chase to indians spotted on a hillside and many of his men were ambushed and killed.

The settlers packed up and, under guard of Lt. Oakes, set out for Boston along frozen roads. Willard, who had moved his family to Charlestown earlier, had gone on ahead as he was needed at the spring meeting at the Court of Assistants. He was old and very, very sick. He was doubled over in his saddle, coughing all the way. The destruction of his beloved settlement seemed to be the final straw and he barely made it back east before he had to take to bed. Simon Davis was given leave to visit him but was then sent back to the western front.

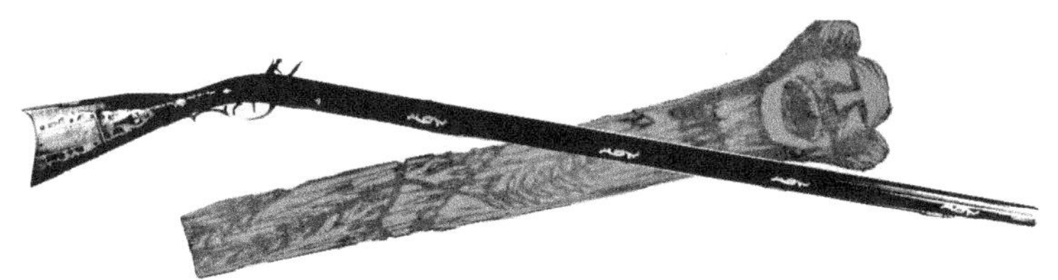

CHAPTER SIXTY

The War Continues

1676

March in New England is cold. There is ice on the rivers and it makes stalagmite-like formations on the waterfalls. There usually is snow on the ground but an occasional thaw will melt everything into mud. The trees are denuded and the sunlight is poor although the days are longer and humans and animals are beginning to feel the hope of spring when a day turns sunny.

It was in the early hours of March 14th that the indians attacked the garrison at Northampton. They broke through the stockade at the lower end of the town on Pleasant Street but were surprised to find that the garrison was full of soldiers as Maj. Treat had arrived during the night with 200 new Connecticut troops. The army there was now close to 300 armed soldiers plus armed civilians in the fort and the indians were driven off. They skulked around the area and the garrisons at Halley and Hatfield were on full alert. Inside the garrison the local settlers were afraid to go to their homes that day. It was already crowded from the outliers who had abandoned their farms earlier in the war. The men were hungry. These were hard working farmers used to having a light breakfast of eggs and side meat with bread then a heavy dinner of beans or peas, roasted meat, potatoes, maybe mashed with turnips, relishes, vegetables from the kitchen garden, lots of bread and homemade butter, perhaps mixed with dried cheese and mustard or fresh cheese served on the side, all washed down with homemade cider. In a normal March provisions were getting low and the pigs slaughtered in the winter were hanging as sausages in the smoke houses or curing in crocks as hams. Salt beef and salted pork were supplemented by freshly slaughtered chickens and on the farms with sheep, male lambs were slaughtered for spring meat.

This March wasn't normal. The corn which was a staple for the three grain bread the women made, using wheat, rye and corn, hadn't been brought in. The root cellars couldn't be accessed and it was supposed that when the houses were burned the timbers fell into the cellar holes and the indians had probably scavenged in the burnt timbers for foodstuffs and anything that hadn't burned. Even corn meal for flat fried patties or pups and boiled mush was scarce and the children were all hungry. Many cattle had been lost so milk was scarce. The people were getting sick of peas porridge flavored with lard and little else and tough hard tack biscuits. There was a hungry stare in the faces of the people and the mid-March attack dispirited even the ministers who were trying to rally their congregations with the hope of Easter, of how a murdered Jesus had risen so that all who believed in Him would be saved.

Capt. Savage and his troops left off pursuing indians in Quaboag and brought his men to Halley. Capt. Turner and his men likewise left off looking for Nipmucks and joined the garrison at Northampton.

Moseley and his men reinforced Hatfield. The northern settlements were abandoned and the indian scouts said there were rumors many sachems were traveling to the area around Northfield to hold a huge war council with King Philip. The sachems weren't in their normal territories so the English had to wonder where they were. The Northfield location was a prime agricultural area and full of deer and fish from the river. While the English hunkered down in their garrisons and their farms burned the indian war parties were on the move.

Weymouth had been attacked in late February and just before Northampton was attacked a war party attacked the garrison house of William Clark outside Plymouth. Not only did the indians kill 11 settlers but they were able to make off with a good supply of guns and powder. Roger Williams tried to meet with Narragansetts who had been friendly but he was rebuffed. They told him he would be spared as he had dealt fairly and honestly with the indians but others were slaughtered. An old man who believed he wouldn't be killed as long as he held a Bible was killed, his abdomen split open and his Bible stuffed inside. The contempt for the Christian God seethed inside the indians. They blamed Him for the Puritans' strict laws and their concept that anyone who wasn't Christian was a heathen and not a person of value in English eyes.

Two days after Northampton was attacked the indians attacked Warwick, burning everything down to the shore except a stone house. The Narragansetts and others then hit Pine Meadow (Windsor Locks) and Simsbury and crossed the hills to Hartford on Sunday, March 26th. Maj. Treat and his troops were immediately withdrawn back to defend Connecticut.

Another war party struck to the east that day, attacking the settlement of Marlborough while its people were in church. They were alerted and fled to safety, losing only one of their number but 13 houses and 11 barns were burned. That evening Lt. Jacob went out and was able to surprise and kill the war party. Capt. Peirce, related to the maritime Peirces, had been sent from Scituate with 15 men and a contingent of friendly indians under Capt. Amos but the next day they were drawn into an ambush. The men formed a circle and fought bravely, waiting for Capt. Edmunds of Providence, a mere eight miles away, to arrive and help them. The messenger hesitated to disturb Edmunds at service and in the meantime most of Peirce's company was killed with nine men captured to be taken away and tortured.

The same Sabbath the indians attacked Longmeadow where Capt. Whipple was escorting a party of worshipers to church in Springfield. As they slowed to carefully cross *Pecowsic* Brook the indians attacked. Two people were killed and two women captured but the rest were able to run to Springfield for safety. Capt. Whipple was blamed for the losses as his troops outnumbered the indians yet didn't kill them. Early the following day Maj. Pynchon led a party from Springfield and managed to kill most of them and retrieve the two women but Sarah Keep died from her wounds, The other told them it was 'friendly' indians who led the attack and she learned two Dutch traders, Jacob and Jared had sold four bushels of powder to the indians and there were some French and Mohawks with them. She said she learned there was a large gathering of indians to the north and two camps of over

300 warriors were on the river near Deerfield.

Two days later the indians attacked Seekonk, destroying all but the garrison and one house. The same day the indians attacked in the west.

Boston sent out the order for all settlers in the west to gather in two garrisons: Halley and Springfield as they could not be defended otherwise. But the settlers didn't want to abandon everything they had toiled so hard for and, with spring coming, knew they had to get back on their lands and get the ground tilled and planted. Maj. Savage didn't respond to Boston immediately and instead spread his 150 men amongst the garrisons so the settlers could go out in the daytime and gather any livestock still surviving and try to plow and plant.

Boston again tried to get Gov. Andros to enlist the Mohawks but he wasn't cooperative. sent ambassadors to the Northfield area to try to seek a peace treaty but the answer was that the indians were going to fight to the death as they had nothing to lose. However, the Mohawks did drive King Philip's warriors out of their territory as they reaffirmed their neutral status.

John received a letter from Sylvanus Davis that spring telling him the northern territories were on fire and settlers were abandoning their farms and fleeing to islands off shore. Seen from the sea it looked like the whole land was on fire, he wrote.

New Haven sent out Maj. Palmes, son-in-law of Gov. Winthrop with 79 soldiers under Capts. George Denison, James Avery and John Stanton plus friendly indians scouts to Narragansett. They arrived at William Blackstone's place in early April and discovered *Canochet*'s camp. The war chief was captured and Palmes, victorious, marched him towards Stonington.

Unfortunately the Halley settlers weren't so lucky as a party going under escort to till fields in Hockanum were ambushed. Deacon Goodman was killed and Thomas Reed taken captive as he attempted to climb Mount Holyoke to get a sighting of the indians.

News of these depredations reached Boston and they told Savage he could leave 150 men with Capt. Turner to protect the remaining settlements and scout in the area. Savage waited to see if Treat would return and when he didn't he marched his men eastwards on April 7th. The army stopped in Quaboag and a war council was held. Savage wanted to go to Mt. Wachusett and kill any indians gathered there but Capts. Moseley, Gillam and Whipple, plus Lt. Drinker, a Baptist potter from Boston, outvoted him as the men were hungry, war weary and needed to get back to their farms for spring planting.

The only hopeful news they received was that *Canochet* was executed outside Stonington. Palmes had indians help in the quartering of his body. He was first shot by a Pequot, then beheaded by a Mohegan, whose fellow Mohegans cut up his body and the Niantics burned it, sending the head to Hartford.

But the English victory was short lived.

Bridgewater was attacked on April 9th and to the north the indians coming down Mt. Wachusett where King Philip's headquarters were, attacked Billerica. Chelmsford then fell, followed simultaneously by Marlboro, Hingham, Weymouth and Wenham. The only settlement left to the north was Sudbury, which was a hub with supply routes to all directions passing through it. The principle garrisons now were Marlborough and Quaboag (Brookfield). Capt. Wadsworth and the 70 men he was able to impress marched from Boston to Marlboro to relieve the garrison soldiers there. Marching from west to east was Capt. Edward Cowell, a cordwainer by trade, with 18 mounted troopers from Quaboag. Before he could reach Deacon Haynes's garrison his party was attacked and, though they were able to fight off the indians and lost only four men, the houses and barns of Sudbury were set afire by the indians. Concord saw the smoke and sent 11 men down to Haynes's garrison but they were ambushed and all but one massacred. Capt. Hugh Mason reached the east bank of the river, running high with melted snow and marshy along its banks. They crossed a bridge but weren't able to reach Haynes's garrison, instead had to take refuge in Goodnow's garrison to the northeast. Wadsworth received news of the attack and turned his men back, arriving that evening from Marlborough with Capt. Brocklebank. Wadsworth and Brocklebank were drawn into an ambush and their men fought bravely but only a few men managed to escape to Noyes's mill where Mason, reinforced by Cowell and volunteers from the area found Capt. Hunting with indian scouts and some of Prentice's troopers. The next morning Mason's men found and buried six of the 11 hapless Concord men and the desecrated corpses of Wadsworth, Brocklebank and their soldiers on Green Hill.

The following day the war party appeared outside Marlborough and defiantly fired their guns 74 times to signify how many they had killed. Lt. Jacob and his few garrison soldiers including Vincent and Hopewell Davis watched as the remaining structures in the settlement were burned and the surviving cattle rounded up and driven off with the indians.

In Boston, Gookin, Eliot, Savage, Henchman and Prentice met with the Commissioners and told them the only way the United Colonies would win the war was if they followed Connecticut's example and included a lot of indian scouts. They could not afford another ambush, they said. The army needed indian warriors who knew the territories and how the indians fought. The Council overcame its and distrust of all indians and finally relented.

And thus, with this decision, the tide turned.

CHAPTER SIXTY-ONE

King Philip is Captured

1676

On April 3rd, 1676 the Massachusetts Council sent one of Gookin's Christian indians, Tom Nepanet, to Mt. Wachusett to try to negotiate the release of Mrs. Rowlandson and the other captives.

On the day Haverhilll and Bradford (part of Rowley) were attacked, almost a month after Nepanet made his first trip to Wachusett, John Hoar met with sachems at a large boulder west of Lancaster and payment was made for the release of prisoners but only Mrs. Rowlandson was handed over. She had a poorly healed wound in her hand where she had been shot when Lancaster was attacked. The bullet had passed through her hand and mortally wounded her infant daughter who suffered greatly before she finally died. As Hoar, Seth Perry, Rev. Rowlandson and Peter Gardiner (whose son Samuel was killed in early April) continued negotiations, John Woodcock and his son Nathaniel and laborers in the fields were attacked. Bridgewater was attacked, followed by an attack on Halifax, on the outskirts of Plymouth.

While Middlesborough was again attacked, followed by Scituate, more hostages were ransomed until almost all the early captives were returned.

Boston sent a large force under Henchman as Commander-in-Chief over Capts. Sills, Cutler and Holbrook's foot companies and his and Brattle and Prentice's troopers and Capt. Denison reported killing 76 indians in Narragansett territory but by late May the rains had come and the mud made travel almost impossible so he brought his troops back to Connecticut.

On the 5th of May a hunting party of indians was ambushed as they chased a bear and 16 indians were killed but there wasn't much action as a large number of the men were laid up with severe colds and were granted temporary leave to recuperate at their homes.

Capt. Turner still had most of his 51 men at the Halley garrison. He also deployed nine to Springfield and 46 were stationed in Northampton. Poorly clothed and shoed they were suffering from the cold that was afflicting most of the people that May.

John Gilbert from Springfield escaped from the indians' village of *Peskompskut* at the falls and gave report that they were planting corn in the settlers' fields between Deerfield and Northfield and Thomas Reed also escaped and made his way to a garrison. He said Thomas Eames's wife and children were with the indians in the village above the falls, having come down from Hatfield.

The settlers had brought their emaciated cows down to a meadow to try to fatten them up. The indians attacked from *Peskompskut*, driving the entire herd of 70 cattle and horses off to their village. This completely enraged the settlers. It was bad enough the indians were using the fields they had spent years clearing, had burned houses and barns that would need rebuilding, but to take all their meat, too, was the final straw.

Against Boston's orders Capt. Turner, still sick with the cold, gathered an army of 180 men at Hatfield – many locals – and, using horses that hadn't been stolen by the indians on the 18th of May they marched out of the stockaded garrison shortly after sunset with a thunderstorm coming down the valley. For hours they rode, crossing swollen brooks and the Pocumtuck River and seeing, in flashes of lightning, the blackened skeletons of former houses and barns. Shortly after crossing the Green River they tied their horses and climbed up the hill, gaining the high ground above the indian village.

Full of fury that matched the driving rain and thunder raging all around, the

English descended upon the sleeping village, killing men, women and children and setting fire to wetus from the fires where their cattle had been roasted. No mercy was shown. The indians fought fiercely and many of the men were pushed back to the river or the falls. Capt. Samuel Holyoke found old people and children hiding in rocks beneath the falls and slew them all. Turner led the men back downriver to where their horses were, with Capt. Holyoke holding off fire from the rear. As the men reached their horses and began to gallop away Holyoke's horse was shot out from under him but he wasn't injured. Capt. Turner, however, was shot in the back and the thigh and fell dead on the riverbank of the Green River. The indians pursued the men all the way back to Hatfield and only 46 returned that night. Over the next few days six more found their way back to safety but in the end the English lost 38 men. The loss to the indians was far greater. Not only had they lost a lot of warriors but they lost women and children, tribe members who would do the planting, cultivating and harvesting of the precious Three Sisters of corn, beans and squash.

Hearing of the battle Capt. Newberry left only three troopers at Westfield and with 80 men came to Northampton. He sent an urgent communication to Boston asking that Maj. Talcott be sent with 50 men to Quaboag along with Samuel Cross and his hunting dogs to aid in the search for any indians hiding there.

At the same time Capt. Brattle and his troopers killed a party of indians in Seekonk. The English were now definitely on the offensive and Capt. Densison and Talcott were raiding Narragansett. Brattle wrote to Boston saying 500 men should go to Quaboag, Wachusett and Squakeag and Denison should leave 70 men in Norwich and join them there along with Henchman's troops.

On the 2nd of June Mgr. Talcott lead an army of 250 Englishmen and 200 Mohegans from Norwich to Quaboag. When he reached the pond of *Chabonakongomung* Henchman hadn't caught up with him but after forcefully interrogating 19 indians fishing on the pond, his men slew them all. An indian scout told him there was a party near Wachusett but Talcott wasn't going to attack without Henchman's men so he pushed on to Brookfield, then Halley. His men were badly in need of supplies and Capt. Denison brought powder and provisions from Hartford a few days later. Henchman had been diverted to *Washakim* Ponds near Lancaster where his men killed seven warriors and captured 29 women and children. He had to return to Marlborough to resupply so he was delayed in getting back to Halley.

On the night of June 11th the indians attacked Hatfield but were met by a force of 500 soldiers, who drove them back up the valley. Then Talcott and Henchman led the men up the river, one army on each side, but no indians were sighted. The rains made riding a slog but they found the bodies of Turner and the other men and gave them a Christian funeral. All the villages they came upon were deserted. The constant damp turned their bread moldy and the men wanted to get back to their farms to plant what they could and fell trees to rebuild homes and barns so by late June the remaining troops consisted of only Capt. Swaine and 30 men, who were to clean out *Peskomquacot*, then head back towards Marlborough or Connecticut. Henchmen had been told by a captured indian that King Philip had returned to his original territory of Mount Hope and that the other indians had fled to the far north where the French were.

Brattle immediately set out for the Mount Hope area, joined by Moseley and 70 men. They found the indian fort abandoned. But Philip and his warriors had attacked a farm outside Swansea, shooting Hekeziah Willet in the fields and then beheading him as his father screamed for them to stop. They left the headless boy's body lying there as they carried the young man's head off as a trophy. The Willets were related to the wealthy, influential New York Willets. Throughout the war New York had not sent one company of soldiers to help its northern neighbors – likewise England hadn't sent troops and very few had sailed up from Virginia or the West Indies to help their English neighbors in New England. The Quakers refused to fight as they were pacifists but for the men in the United Colonies New York's lack of help would not be forgotten and much of the later anger against Gov. Andros was taking root as settlers lost everything they had worked so hard for during a year of terror when the only fertilizer in their fields was their own blood.

Capt. Thomas Davis, who ran ships up and down the Hudson River from New York to Albany, was torn between wanting to help his relatives near Saco and the necessity of keeping peace with the Mohawks, his main fur supplier. He sent a couple of wheat shipments to help those between the Kennebec and Merrimac Rivers but he was constrained by the laws of New York and couldn't send arms or take up arms, other than the defensive ones every trading vessel carried on deck.

Many ships had been attacked on the north shore but the indians burned them as they didn't know how to sail sloops or anything that wasn't powered by oars.

Luckily the fires didn't do much damage and most of the ships were towed back to shore for repairs.

The massing of troops, both English and indian, sent the message to the indians that the English would not walk away this time. Every acre of land would be defended. Nevermore would the indians hold the river valley, or the coast.

It took the English a year to realize that this war would only end when the last hostile indian was killed or surrendered. Many even felt the praying indians should be sold off as slaves to the Spanish but Gookin and Eliot were still advocating for the ones who had helped the English and not joined King Philip's Army.

In the middle of June a comet was seen in the sky. To many it looked like a bow and they were afraid it meant the indians would be the victors but the ministers interpreted it like the rainbow in Genesis: a sign that God would never forsake them.

The English living in Ireland raised a large sum of money and sent it to Boston and Connecticut to be distributed by the ministers to families who had lost all their possessions. New York, Maryland and Virginia sent very little even though at least 14 'summer ships' arrived from England. Boston was talking about levying a force to send to the fort at Black Point in order to keep the French from swooping down and reclaiming the English settlements and trading posts that stretched north of Salem well up to Canada, some on shore and some on islands in the north Atlantic.

On June 21st the United Colonies declared a Day of Humiliation and Prayer. June 29th was declared a Day of Thanksgiving as the raids in the western frontier appeared to have ceased and farmers were back in their fields, working unmolested.

Maj. Talcott spent the next week reorganizing his troops and left Norwich, Connecticut on July 1st with Capts. Denison and Newberry and a force of 300 English and indian soldiers to reconnoiter Narragansett and kill and capture any indians found in the territory. On Sunday, July 2nd, his scouts sighted a camp in a cedar swamp on the south bank of the Pawtucket River. The troopers split up to encircle the camp and the indians rushed downhill. Stonewall John and *Pesacuss* and *Magnus* were killed. One of the survivors told the indians Philip was at Mount Hope but Talcott couldn't get the indians to leave off grabbing the rich plunder to take up pursuit.

Capt. Church had moved his family to Duxbury. While riding from Plymouth to Narragansett Bay he discovered two indians fishing near Falmouth. He personally knew the two and one of them, George, said Squaw Sachem *Awashonks* of the Sakonets was tired of fighting and wanted to surrender. He set up a rendezvous at Richmonds' Farm and, with permission from the governor of Plymouth, began negotiations as part of a three-man team consisting of Church, Lt. Jabez Howland and Nathaniel Southworth, Church's brother-in-law.

Awashonks and her tribe surrendered and offered their services to Church and the English against Philip. As was their custom they then held a feast and dance that night to celebrate the treaty. Gov. Bradford wasn't completely won over but the English, like the Sackonets, were tired of fighting. Sightings of Philip were being received almost daily in and around the swamps and on July 11, a week and half after his master Hekeziah Willet had been murdered, Willet's servant escaped and found the English to warn them that Philip intended to attack Taunton so the town was prepared when the strike came and easily drove off the indians.

On July 14th Bridgewater was attacked but finding it defended by resolute young men who had refused to abandon their community, the war party only succeeded in killing a few cattle.

Meanwhile Bradford set up guard at the fording places along the Taunton River, which Philip would have to cross to leave Mount Hope and Moseley and Brattle heavily scouted the swamps, using the indian method of smearing red clay on their exposed faces to prevent being eaten alive by the mosquitoes. The indians at the time of contact with the white man, wore only loincloths in summer and slathered themselves copiously with iron ore red mud that stained their skin. They were called 'redskins' at first because they appeared to be red whereas their natural complexion ranged from mahogany to almost olive in color.

In mid-July Moseley and Brattle almost captured Philip, surprising his camp while food was simmering in the kettles. Wounded warriors left behind told them they were very close but Boston called the Massachusetts troops back on the 22nd as the northern settlements were in great distress and they needed to send men there. At the same time Massachusetts and Plymouth sent out notices that any indian surrendering within 14 days would be given amnesty. Over 300 Cape and Plymouth area indians surrendered within a week. Sagamore Sam also asked for mercy as he had helped ransom Rowlandson and the others but the English in Boston wouldn't listen to him and he took his tribe up north to join the Tarrantines.

On July 27th Capt. Hunting with English and indian troops near Dedham surprised and captured *Punham*, who, though unable to stand due to wounds, fought bravely and 15 of his band and 34 were taken captive, including his son. That same day Sagamore John of Nipmuck surrendered with 180 men.

With Bradford guarding the fords, Maj. Bradford and Capt. Church combed the Pocasset swamps and Connecticut's men the Narragansett territory for any and all 'rabid animals', which is what the English now called the indians.

Talcott and his men went to the Connecticut River where they captured and killed indians trying to flee west to Pocumtuck and Nonotuck. Amongst those at the river was *Konkowasco*, a sachem from Quaboag.

On July 25th Church was put in command of a hand-picked special force of 18 men and 22 indians and sent to Middleboro. There they learned Philip and *Quinapin* were a mere two miles off, camped in a big cedar swamp. Church split up his troopers, sending some to the east and the others to the west to entrap Philip. He rode to Plymouth to enlist aid and reached *Monposet* Pond by nightfall. Twenty men from Bridgewater were to meet him but they encountered Philip first. The English losses were light but when the men joined Church they said they'd killed Philip's uncle *Akompoin* and that the indians were trying to fell a great tree in order to cross the Taunton River.

Early the next morning, the first day of August, Church with 30 English and 20 indian scouts set out. Church saw an indian sitting on the stump of the felled tree and went to shoot him but a scout held back his arm saying he thought it was one of their men. He then recognized the indian as Philip and shot but the leader of the revolt against the English had been alerted and escaped. Church's troops crossed the river using the tree trunk and the next day, with Lt. Howland's men managed to capture or kill 180 of Philip's men. The sturdy warrior *Totoson*, recognized by a great rattlesnake skin tied to his two locks, fled into the swamp.

The English withdrew and a settler in *Metapoiset* killed a squaw, beheading her and placing her head on a pole. Church's indian scouts recognized it as *Weetamo*, Alexander's widow, a notorious squaw sachem who had allied with Philip. Her head on a pole in Taunton set up a piteous wailing from the captives who had been her subjects. Church in the meantime had caught up with *Tatoson*'s band. They scattered but he captured Sam Barrow, who was summarily executed by one of the indians with Church. *Tatoson* escaped, heading north.

Church went back to Plymouth for supplies but was back on the trail on August 9th where he met Maj. Sanford of Newport, R.I. and Capt. Goulding, of Newport but also the new owner of 100 acres of land on the north side of the Sackonet, granted to him when he had used his ship to evacuate the soldiers the year before. Excitedly, they told them an indian they had come upon had offered to lead them to Philip's camp. They split up to surround Philip and Goulding and his men tied up their horses and crawled on their bellies to the spot in the marshy swamp where Philip was still sleeping. Philip was alarmed as a gun fired and he jumped up, clad in his small breeches and moccasins and, clutching his tobacco bag, ran into the swamp. One of the indians with Church, by the name of Alderman, shot Philip directly in his heart and then fired again, hitting him above it.

The indians beheaded and quartered Philip and Church vehemently refused burial of the muddy remains. He said, "As much as he has caused many English to lie unburied and rot above ground, not one of his bones shall be buried." His head, however, was taken to Plymouth where it slowly rotted on a pole and didn't come down for 25 years.

By the end of summer the resistance in the United Colonies had been put down but it intensified to the north.

CHAPTER SIXTY-TWO

Sylvanus Davis, the War in the North

1670s

Sylvanus Davis of Sheepscot was the son of John, brother to William in Roxbury. Both had been ship owners or merchants operating out of Bristol before coming to the New England. They were blacksmiths and gunsmiths.

Sylvanus was also cousin to Dolor's son John who had been banished from the Massachusetts Bay Colony as he wasn't a strict orthodox Puritan. Sylvanus had become the agent for Messieurs Maj. Thomas Clark (related to William Clark, the trader in Bristol partnered with George and William) and Capt. Thomas Lake in their stockaded trading house/fort on the island of Arrowsick.

Two large guns were on the fort, which was in the northeast corner of the property. Since its original beginnings with John Richards in 1649 it had sprouted a sawmill, warehouse, gristmill, bake house and blacksmith shop plus a cooperage and shipyard.

The island was located opposite Bath on the Black River and referred to as Black Point. From September 1675 on settlements had been attacked and settlers murdered including in *Pepyscot* where the wealthy London merchant Thomas Purchase's manor house was on the *Androscoggin* River; settlements at Oyster

River, Exeter and Salem Falls were all burned and abandoned also. If they could, the indians killed the men and took the women and children into captivity in Canada. On the Saco River Capt. Boyntons' house was attacked and across from him Maj. Phillips watched helplessly as the indians burned everything, taunting him to row over and put out the flames. Winter Harbor was attacked and burned and the settlers fled up the Saco River, some killed in the boats. (Samuel Acres from Brookfield moved there after the attack on Quaboag Plantation and was killed in 1710 from an indian attack.) Capt. Wincoll, originally of Kittery and now a settler at *Newichawonock* (South Berwick) got 16 of the militia to go to the rescue but they were ambushed as soon as they landed at Winter Harbor. Eleven men of Saco came to their aid but were massacred as the English fought off the attackers from behind a pile of shingle bolts.

At the same time another band of indians attacked Black Point, burned seven houses and killed many of the settlers.

At Salmon Falls Richard Taylor's house was attacked but luckily most of the inhabitants were able to flee to the nearby garrison at Plaisted. Richard Tozer's farm was burned and Lt. Richard Plaisted, coming to the rescue, was ambushed. The next day while bringing a cart out to the fields to retrieve the dead English for burial Plaisted, two of his sons and others were ambushed and killed.

Within a month of the start of the hostilities 150 men, women and children between the Kennebec and Piscataqua Rivers had been killed or captured.

Maj. Walderne, governor of the colony and a trader with a post at Dover was able to get some of the friendly indian sachems to sit at a peace table. However, the English killed any indians they found around Saco so the process was not going well but the hard, cold northern winter intervened and both sides hunkered down in winter camps, pausing the hostilities.

Capt. Davis went to the fort at *Totonnock* where the *Kennebec* and *Sebasticok* Rivers met to get the powder and shot stored in the trading post there. While there he sent a messenger over to the winter camp of the Penobscots to see if he could broker a peace. The man he sent was arrogant and demanded the indians surrender their arms, at which point he was rudely sent away. This bothered Sylvanus as his relations with the Penobscots, which he considered moderately civilized, had always been good. He, as many in the north, blamed the settlers in Plymouth for starting the hostilities.

After the attempt at negotiations failed, Davis returned to the Clark and Lake mansion on the cove with the shot and powder and Maj. Walderne was informed the indians at *Totonnock* were moving camp to 'the Eastward' in order to join the other hostile bands there.

John Earthy of *Pemaquid* had an ordinary and was on good terms with the natives but they were sullen and told him the English drove them away from their corn harvests and kept powder and shot from them so they couldn't kill deer or fowl and had forced them into a state of starvation. He and Sylvanus made one last attempt to bring peace in August, 1676 when they met with the chief sachems *Madockawando, Mugg* and others.

Sylvanus, who, in the fashion of many of the traders, wore buckskin coats and leggings and a heavy beaver hat, sat down with the sachems but only heard contempt and anger as they said Capt. Laughton, on the pretense of holding a treaty, received 14 indians on board his vessel then seized them for sale as slaves.

The sachems told Sylvanus, "It is not our custom when messengers come to treat of peace to seize upon their persons."

Sylvanus and John both smoked the pipe offered as they sat cross legged in front of one of the fires in the sachem's longhouse.

"It is not our custom, either," Sylvanus replied, "For we allow messages to come between warring parties under the flag of truce. Captain Laughton must have felt threatened to have acted in such a manner."

The sachems angrily replied that they were facing another winter without corn or ammunition and asked what the English would do to help them.

"I will personally go to Gov. Walderne and find out where your tribesmen are," Sylvanus said, his long blond hair falling across his face as he bent forward to receive the wooden bowl of soup, "The men will be returned to you and any wrongs we will try to right. We have always been brothers," he added, his eyes sad, "I would hope we can walk the path of peace together in the future."

The Commissioners wouldn't meet with Sylvanus and John Davis but they discovered Capt. Laughton had acted under orders from Walderne to seize any indians he encountered. While Sylvanus and John were going back and forth to try to affect a peace, Squando attacked Falmouth on August 11th. He had been harboring hatred for the murder of his infant when some Englishmen, in jest, had tipped over the canoe his wife and baby were in to see if it were true indians babies knew how to swim from birth. His wife had dived down and rescued the babe but it soon died from the waters it had inhaled.

The first house attacked in Falmouth belonged to Anthony Brackett, related to Sylvanus through Nathaniel Mitton, related to Jane Mitton Andrews Alger, married to her second husband Andrew Alger, a friend of Robert Davis. Nathaniel Mitton was slain but the rest of the family taken captive.

While the indians were busy burning and killing or capturing their neighbors, the Bracketts escaped and, using a sailor's knowledge of sewing, Anthony was able to sew a ripped seam in an abandoned canoe and row his family to safety across Casco Bay to Black Point. From there they got on a ship bound for *Piscataqua.* The captives from Falmouth were carried to the Eastward.

The indians next attacked William Hammond's trading fort on a point near the Kennebec. Although Hammond had been a friend of the indians he and his family were slain. A young girl of the household said the indians had approached as friends but she hadn't trusted them and had hidden in the corn field. When she heard the awful shrieks coming from the fort she ran ten miles, barefoot, to Sheepscot.

As Sylvanus Davis sent out the alarm the indians moved upriver to Francis Card's place, captured him and his family and then moved down the Kennebec and crossed it to Arrowsick Island.

Panic spread throughout the area. Families abandoned their homes and, led by George FeLt. who vowed vengeance, brought them safely across the bay to James Andrews's garrison on an island and then went back to join with others to chase the bloody savages. Felt owned several small islands in the bay and vowed he would die defending the English rights to live there. Before he could get a party of men together to row over to Arrowsick Island a squaw in distress appeared at the Clark and Lake garrison's door towards evening and, feeling pity for her, they let her come in. They didn't know it but she was a saboteur. During the night she opened the iron bolts and before dawn her tribesmen invaded the fort, killing most of the inhabitants.

Sylvanus escaped from the garrison along with Capt. Thomas Lake, a wealthy merchant who years before had married New Haven's deputy governor Goodyear's daughter. He and Clark had bought half of Arrowsick Island and had been running a very profitable trading house there.

"Jump in!" shouted Sylvanus as he untied a canoe banked in the rocks.

The two paddled furiously but musket balls were like mosquitos around them. Lake was shot in the canoe and Sylvanus grabbed him and jumped from the canoe, swimming with him to the rocky shore of Mill Island. As he pulled Lake to shore he was shot. He saw Lake was dead and ran inland, finding a place in the rocks in which to hide as he ripped his shirt and bound his bleeding wound. By the time the dozen survivors of the garrison gathered in Bath the toll of killed or captured was 53 settlers.

About two weeks later George Felt led a party of men to Munjoy's (Mountjoy's) Island to retrieve the sheep stranded there as the refugees were in dire need of food. He was warned not to go but hunger drove the men on and they brought a small boat across the narrow channel between Andrews's place and Munjoy's. As soon as they pulled the boat ashore they were attacked and fled to an old stone house that John Palmer had lived in until he and his family were burned out the previous year. It was a sad day for the settlers as they heard the gunfire across the water yet no man returned after it ceased.

Sheepscot and Pemaquid were attacked around the same time.

Gov. Walderne was sending urgent messages to the United Colonies and on September 3rd Boston sent Capt. William Hathorne who had assumed command of Capt. Gardiner's company after he was killed in the Narragansett Swamp Fight. Sylvanus joined his troops as a guide. Also with the army were Capt. Samuel Hunting, who had been active in the Sudbury fight and Capt. Sill with 30 English men and 40 Naticks as they marched to the Eastward with orders to enlist volunteers along the way from Dover to Black Point. There they boarded ships and went as far east as Casco Bay to discover that the settlements at Wells and Cape Neddeck were smoldering ruins. No indians were found along the way.

Walderne had been meeting with the Pennacooks and *Wamsetta* in Dover. In bad faith Capt. Frost of Kittery disarmed and seized the old Nipmuck chiefs and sent them to Boston where *Monoco*, Old Jethro and *Muttawump* were haltered together like oxen and paraded in the streets before they were hanged on the Boston Common.

Mugg, the sachem who had sold a large tract of land between the Kennebunk and Saco Rivers to Maj, William Phillips brought a war party and attacked the garrison of Capt. Henry Joceyln of Kent, a close friend of Sir Ferdinando Gorges and a prominent early settler in the area. While the inhabitants fled the burning garrison and gathered on shore Jocelyn, still thinking a peace could be brokered, tried to negotiate with *Mugg*. Instead he and his family were taken captive. Like Mrs. Rowlandson, they were treated kindly during their captivity as the indians had a code of conduct regarding captives which survivors later wrote about.

The northern winter, which was normally regarded as an enemy, came early that year and was a blessing as the indians retired to their forts in *Ossipee.*

To the south the hostilities had ceased with the death of Philip and his war chiefs.

In the north, however, there was to be another season of terror, death, burning and fleeing.

CHAPTER SIXTY-THREE

Samuel and Sylvanus

1677

At the beginning of King Philp's War William of Wales had sons John, Samuel and Joseph old enough to fight in the battles. James of Newbury-Haverhilll had sons John, Samuel and Joseph and grandsons Zachery, Daniel, Hopewell and Vincent. George had Robert of Maine and sons John of Oyster Bay, Daniel of Kittery and others in and around the area north of Newbury and south of the far northern fishing villages. Marie and Robert's William of Boston was a trooper but died early on, as did Maj. Simon Willard. Samuel and Simon, youngest sons of Dolor, served in Western Massachusetts. A Davis or two was found in almost every regiment with John and his son Cornelius at the Narragansett Swamp Fight.

Samuel, born in 1663 had been living on a farm outside Northampton. He fought with Capts. Turner and Moseley and Henchman's troopers. His brother John and cousin Vincent went to the Eastward with Capt. Gardiner's replacement, Capt. Hathorne, and his cousin Hopewell was with Capt. Sill when he and Hathorne were ordered to attack *Ossipee* in October, 1676.

Sylvanus, now recovered from his wound, was with them. Throughout the war men from all over the United Colonies were thrown together in the marches and camps and Samuel, John and Joseph discovered relatives to the north that they hadn't known well and they heard about Irish relatives from Albany. Addresses were exchanged but the men knew that some of them wouldn't be returning to their burned out farms for many years so generally a common relative's address was given as well, someone in a large town such as Boston or New Haven or Salem as those towns hadn't been attacked.

The march to *Ossipee* was in deep snow across rivers, swamps and streams that were not yet frozen. The indian fort was deserted so all the men could do was burn and destroy the empty wetus and longhouse before heading back to South Berwick.

An expedition under young Fryer of Richmond Island had been sent from *Piscataqua* to Black Point by boats to retrieve any goods not ruined or taken following the battle there earlier. As they were loading their boats at Black Point they were ambushed and Fryer was wounded and captured, along with his men.

On the first of November the sachem *Mugg* appeared at Maj. Gen. Denison's place in Piscataqua Plantation, the wounded Fryer in tow, to seek a treaty. *Mugg* was seized and sent by ship to Boston whre he signed a treaty between the Massachusetts governor and the United Colonies council on November 6th.

Boston immmediately dispatched an expedition with *Mugg* as a hostage on board to find the rest of the men that *Madockawando* had promised to return to the English. He had only returned two settlers and *Mugg* convinced the leader of the expedition that he could go out and bring them in. They let him go but after waiting in the harbor for a week realized they had been duped so pointed their ships south. At Pemaquid they found Thomas Cobbett and a few other settlers who had been captives but no other men from Piscataqua were found.

The Council in Boston voted in early February 1677 to send an army of 200 English and Naticks under Maj. Walderne to the Eastward. The troops took a route via Falmouth and skirmished with *Squando* and a war party there. Walderne sent a small force to Arrowsick to hold the blocky, octagonal two-story garrison there while he took the main force to Pemaquid. Before negotiations could begin for the release of the Piscataqua captives and others Maj. Walderne noticed signs of impending ambush at Shurt's Fort and immediately called his men ashore. Seven indians were killed, including the old chief *Mattahando*, one of *Madockawando*'s war chiefs.

The weather turned bitterly cold and the snow and ice made travel by land or ship impossible in March but in April the indian Simon attacked Wells and then tried to lay seige to the garrison at Black Point. Lt. Bartholemew Tippen was in charge, recently commissioned to re-establish the settlement of Scarborough but pulled off for this operation. Tippen's men fought off the attack for three days, succeeding in killing *Mugg* and driving off the other warriors, who hit York once more before disappearing.

In late June, 1677 an army under Capt. Benjamin Swett and Lt. James Richardson of 200 friendly indians and 40 English soldiers set ashore at Black Point. Swett led the English soldiers and the friendly indians after a band of indians, and at the top of a hill they were ambushed all around, with 180 friendly indians surviving but all the English dead.

Thomas Davis of Albany tried to sail up to the area with bushels of New York wheat but the waters had become so dangerous he had to dock in Salem and offload it there, hoping Boston would send it north. Ships were wrecked all over the shoreline as the indians would attack, kill sailors and set the large ships adrift to be smashed on the rocks. Luckily most of the large sail-powered ships were saved. While the lands were burned and pillaged in what would be called Maine and New Hampshire, their harbors and piers were also desecrated.

It wasn't until August when the fires burned out. Andros, spurred on by Charles II's brother James (II), the Duke of York (who considered Sagadahock his personal province) led a large armed expedition accompanied by Mohawks to Penobscot to build a fort and try to negotiate a peace. During King Philip's War the Connecticut Assembly had repeatedly refused to ask for New York's help as it felt Andros would use his soldiers on Connecticut soil to turn on the people and take the contested southern Connecticut River land and Long Island tip as New York's own territory. The lack of New York support and the way Connecticut kept calling its troops home had angered Massachusetts but the leaders in Hartford and New Haven regarded New York as a wolf that was licking its chops every time the troops were sent north or east.

Over the winter Andros worked with the governor and council in Massachusetts to set up a peace commission at Casco consisting of Maj. Nicholas Shapleigh of Kittery, Capt, Francis Champerson, also of Kittery and a nephew of Gorges, and

Capt. Nathaniel Fryer of Portsmouth.

On April 12, 1677 the indians including *Squando* signed articles of peace in which captives were to be returned and each settler's family would pay an annual quit rent of one peck of corn to the indians with Maj. Phllips of Saco to pay one bushel. Both sides were tired of fighting. The land was laid waste for both the English and the indians. Peace was temporarily declared but forts were being rebuilt. Sylvanus was given command of the new one being constructed at Falmouth but for many of the settlers starting over was too much and they moved to more civilized towns to the south.

In Massachusetts the farthest western and northern settlements were left to the elements as settlers either moved to bigger towns or started new ones closer to the bigger towns in Massachusetts or Connecticut. Any farmer who chose to return to their outlying farm had no official protection and no neighbors. Some, like John of Northampton, felt all was not lost as at least fields had been cleared and stone and log fences were in place for cattle but most of the brave pioneers were too traumatized by the brutal killings and burnings to return.

The land grants Denison promised before the Narragansett Swamp Fight weren't forthcoming as men with families were not eager to expose them to danger and the Assembly wasn't eager to sanction new settlements it couldn't protect. Any indians found in Massachusetts after the war were forced onto Eliot's praying villages and strictly monitored. If they strayed from the villages they were arrested and shipped out or even executed. Many had slipped away to join the northern or western tribes. They lost their 'fine homes' and fields, too.

The time of peaceful cohabitation between the English and the natives had ended. Even King Philip's son was sold into slavery. No quarter was given. The hacking, shooting, scalping, beheading and mutilating had convinced the English that the indians were not their friends and that when they put their marks on parchment they meant nothing.

For men such as John Pynchon in Springfield the war had been a disaster on more than one front. He no longer had the friendly trade of the indians.

In Albany a new fort was built to replace Fort Orange and Andros imported Irish, and some Scottish men to guard it as they, unlike the Dutch, were always eager for a battle and were hard fighters.

Capt. John Needham and Mathias Nicolls, a relative of James Davis of Malden, were given prime property in New York city and plied trade with relatives in Boston, Springfield and Exeter as the Hudson River was still trading heavily with the Mohawks and French in Quebec.

But the peace in Massachusetts didn't extend to the northern lands close to the French territory in the Eastward and islands off the coast.

Some settlers never returned to the western towns but instead settled with relatives or friends in "safter" towns near Boston, Plymouth, New Haven and Hartford. Some left and returned to England, Wales or Ireland where relatives waited with open arms. Some left and went to Virginia and the West Indies.

The years 1677-1763 were filled with uncertainty. The Massachusetts government lost its charter and an English governor was chosen (Andros), which led to an insurrection and the arrest and deportation of Andros.

The Massachusetts Council didn't honor its promise of land grants to the Narragansett Swamp Fort soldiers until 1723. By then most of the original soldiers were dead so the grants went to sons, son-in-laws or even grandsons, many of whom weren't eager to try frontier life until all the savages were driven out or killed.

The following chapters follow a few of the Davis men during these uncertain times. Their lives were typical of what many of the New Englanders endured for almost a century due to England's wars with France and other countries in Europe. Co-Regents William and Mary were succeeded by Queen Anne and then later by the Kings George I, II and III. The Stuart dynasty was over but the Hanoverian one had begun and would lead to the colonists finally cutting the cord with their mother country under King George III (but that comes much later).

The late 1660s and 1700s up to 1763 when England finally won Canada from the French were hard years for frontier settlers. Their persistence and love of the land they had claimed with blood, sweat and tears kept them plowing, planting, harvesting, fishing and building ships that sailed up and down the coast as far as Virginia, then later the Carolinas and eastward to the profitable West Indian islands.

Relations with England were strained. The Civil War under Cromwell had divided the people into Royalists and Parliamentarians and had given the 'common wealth' more power and taken lands and some power from the landed gentry and the royalty.

In New England people began to identify themselves as being from their townships and by the end of King Philip's War only a handful were polishing coats of arms and claiming lineage to knights and duke and earls.

As Andros was to find out, one's status in the royal court was no guarantee of power to rule over the independent and now war-hardened New Englanders.

For many New Englanders in the late 1600s the Devil replaced the Savage as the main threat to the peace and security of their Puritan lives.

CHAPTER SIXTY-FOUR

Bacon's Rebellion

1677

As King Philip's War was winding down in Massachusetts another militiary event was happening in Virginia.

This event affected Sir Thomas Davis, who had a large land grant and tobacco plantation outside Jamestown. It also affected the Maine traders Robert, Nicholas, George, William Jr. and James Davis of Newbury as these men were involved in shipping timber and horses to the southern colonies and bringing tobacco, sugar, molasses and rum north to New England and Virginia.

The' Navigation Act' forced all ships coming or going from England to be either English owned or manned by a majority of English officers and sailors. New England was able to circumvent this by sailing its New England made ships just up and down the coast but trade across the sea with England and Ireland was getting more challenging, as was trade between Ireland and England with restrictions on wool but an exemption on Irish linen.

In November 1677 Mary, Protestant daughter of the Prince of York (later James II) married William of Orange in Holland. In 1679 the Parliament passed the Habeus Corpus Act whereby prisoners had the right to know why they were being imprisoned, to be indicted within the first term of their imprisonment, to be sentenced no later than the second term of the Parliament and if found innocent and released, and couldn't be double jeopardized, that is re-arrested and tried for the same crime.

This rising tide of rights for the 'common people' reached a tsunami in Virginia where Nathaniel Bacon, wealthy cousin of the Governor William Bulkeley, fomented a rebellion as the elites were grabbing all the good agricultural lands such as those associated with Jamestown's Green House and forcing freed indentures – which included Africans bought by Gov. Sir George Yeardley in 1619 off a Dutch ship that had been forced off course, and their descendants – to settle on land that wasn't close to docks or as fertile as the riverbank plantations. Bacon published the *Declaration of the People of Virginia* in late July 1676. It charged Bulkeley with eight counts of violating the rights of the less wealthy to own productive land that they had helped win from the Powhawten confederacy. He also called Bulkeley a traitor.

As with Massachusetts, the savages (the common term the English used for the Native Americans) had been attacking outlying farms for years, burning and looting, killing, scalping and then retreating. Bacon and his fellow settlers had had enough. They wanted the government of Virginia to act as the United Colonies had and declare war on the savages, driving them all out of the colony. Bacon with about 500 men marched on Jamestown, burning and looting the plantations. Gov. Bulkeley fled.

However, while occupying the city Bacon came down with fever and a fatal case of dysentery and died by October. John Ingram took over but he was captured and hanged as a traitor along with 22 other 'insurrectionists'.

King Charles II wasn't happy and Bulkeley was recalled to London. Sir Herbert Jeffreys was sent to Jamestown with 200 soldiers to restore order and become the colony's new governor.

Thomas Davis's plantation wasn't spared the fire but as he was in Newbury and not living in Virginia at the time so he had been in little physical danger.

Shipping to Virginia was interrupted and fur monopolies were in abeyance since the furs came down from Canada via inland riverways that ran into Powhawtan territory and unrest amongst the English and river tribes in Virginia spread to a disruption in the well-oiled machine of trade.

After the Rebellion the Davis ships sent a lot of good, big timber from north of the Merrimack down for rebuilding Jamestown and also a lot of indian corn as storehouses were burned.

The Bacon family was in with many prominent families in New England but Nathaniel's revolt wasn't held against them. He had been sent to Virginia to avoid a scandal in England in the first place. What incubated from these events was the spirit of independence that would erupt 20 years later in Massachusetts against the tyranny of Andros.

At the next meeting of the Virginia House of Burgesses in a move to prevent future uprisings a bill was passed banning the importation of any new indentured servants and it required future imported labor to consist only of purchased African slaves with no voting or civil rights.

The poll tax was increased so poor freemen couldn't vote and the "head right" system was reinstated whereby any man who wrested (outlying) land from the savages would receive 50 acres. To placate the *Powhawtons* a Treaty of the Middle Plantation was signed whereby they gave them back some of their lands but the treaty wasn't implemented.

(The indians of Virginia were in a confederacy with the tribes to their north. A Virginia uprising later led by the Susquehannas was to affect New York, Maryland and New Jersey.)

The English were shortly to learn that the savages to their north and south weren't going to be conquered as easily as the Massachusetts and Connecticut tribes.

CHAPTER SIXTY-FIVE

Witches

1682

William of Wales's son John Davis was a blacksmith and he followed the Pynchons to the new settlement of Springfield. While there he made friends with Hugh Parsons and his wife Mary Lewis, (like John from Wales). In 1668 John married Mary Devotion from Muddy River near Roxbury and they moved to the Connecticut River as John's skills were in high demand for the ship building and repairing going on in Connecticut.

John's younger brother Samuel Davis had been working with the Lymans and Parsons in Northampton to develop a lead mine.

In Springfield Mary and Hugh Parsons (who had a tavern) had both been accused of practicing witchcraft in 1651. Hugh was also a sawyer (like Thomas Davis to the north they were regarded as a necessary evil as the settlers needed their logs sawed and planed but resented having to pay for it) and his wife Mary had a bad temper which often resulted in violent outbursts of mean speech towards her neighbors or others in the town. Hugh had quarreled with the town's minister, Rev. Moxon, over the cost of building a brick chimney in the parsonage. Hugh was the son of a parson in northwest Devonshire. When John Stebbins of Northampton mysteriously became covered with small spots it was speculated (but never charged) that Hugh Parsons had cast a curse on him as Stebbins had been working in Parson's saw mill at the time.

After the birth of her second child Mary was accused of casting a spell on it to cause its death. Hugh was accused of being a Devil worshipper and working against the child's birth as he cut boiled puddings longways during her pregnancy in the manner of slicing open the gut of a pregnant animal instead of cutting them sideways.

Mary was one of those women who was always overwhelmed by her household tasks. There were piles of soiled laundry, stacks of dirty pans and dishes and unswept floors. Chickens were allowed to walk into the house and pecked on crumbs left on the rough wooden table, often leaving droppings behind. She was slovenly in appearance after the birth of her daughter and often ignored its cries from its cradle. She was an angry woman and longed for her nice quiet old village life in Wales, detesting the cheerfulness her Puritan neighbors wore in public.

The neighbors said she cast the evil eye on livestock and the Parsons began to be shunned in church.

When the second infant, a boy named Joshua, died soon after birth the next year (1651) the rumors began. It was said Mary had told the nursemaid to leave her first child, Sarah, out in the cold to freeze to death while she was pregnant with the second. Neighbors said they heard the sound of demonic sawing coming from the Parson's house in the middle of the night.

Hugh and Mary Parsons were called before the magistrates and charged with covenanting with the Devil. Two years earlier Mary and Hugh had been forced to pay Widow Marshfield 24 bushels of indian corn and 20 shillings because Mary had accused the widow of lying and saying Mary had bewitched the minister's children. Hugh told the widow the money would be to her like moths in her clothes; would never profit her anything. Another settler accused Hugh of causing his leg to be deeply cut when a group of them were in the woods sawing timber as he had quarreled with Hugh earlier and said Hugh used witchcraft to cause the injury.

After the alleged infanticide trial Mary was sent to prison in Boston but Hugh was acquitted.

Witches began to appear everywhere. John's cousin John Davis from Kittery had a wife named Mary who in 1688 was accused of witchcraft. (Mary Goodwin Davis was the daughter of Thomas Goodwin of Hartford who later moved to Halley.)

Around the same time John Bradstreet of Rowley was whipped in public because Francis Parat and his wife said he was cavorting with the Devil in his dreams, which he shared with them afterwards. They said he was told to build a bridge across the bay and a ladder up to Heaven. He was condemned for lying and fined 20 shillings.

In Fairfield, Connecticut Mrs. Thomas Staples was accused of witchcraft. Roger Ludlow was one of the magistrates at the trial. Mrs. Staples was condemned to hang but Ludlow also fined her accuser Elizabeth Knapp who said she had heard her confess on the ladder before stepping off and also said when she looked at her corpse it had witch's teats. After fining Knapp 25 pounds for defamation of character Roger left for Virginia in disgust.

In New Haven Elizabeth Goodman was accused by the Hookers who claimed she bewitched their son with the Evil Eye to become sick. Elizabeth had lived in the Bishops' house and they said she had bewitched their children. Goodman was charged, jailed and tried but let off with a fine.

Accusations flew more than the supposed witches on broomsticks causing the Rev. John Cotton to have witchcraft added as a capital crime to the abstract of laws of New England in 1655.

The second Parsons accused of witchcraft was Mary Parsons. Born Mary Bliss. in Wales she married Joseph Parsons and lived in Northampton. Mary was the sister of Elizabeth Bliss, married to Miles Morgan of Wales and the daughter of Thomas Bliss, whose widow moved the entire family by herself to Springfield after his death in Hartford. Mary had first been accused in 1656. Her second accusation came in September, 1675. By then Joseph Parsons was the wealthiest man in Northampton, Mary was often haughty and arrogant and for this crime she was accused of casting a spell on Mrs. Mary Bartlett, wife of Samuel, who had died of mysterious causes in July of that year. The trial and bond were both heavy weights on the couple, whose son John was also accused. However, absorbed by King Philip's War, Gov. John Leverett, Assistants Gookin and Denison downplayed the case and the jury acquitted all in May, 1676.

After the War Newbury became the scene for witchcraft accusations. James

Davis and his family were affected indirectly as Newbury settlers in 1679 accused Mrs. Elizabeth Morse of using a white cat familiar to work evil against residents (the cat later found bludgeoned to death in a neighbor's field against a tree trunk) and her bewitching of a neighbor's sheep causing them to die while he was driving them on a very hot summer day and bewitching a heifer so it would not go to its calf. There were other charges as pretty much anything unusual that happened anywhere near her was attributed to her bewitching or if she looked at anything she cursed it with the Evil Eye. Caleb Powell, a sailor, was accused by Mr. Morse of causing most of the mischief by causing chimney bricks to fall and pots and pans to fly about the kitchen. However, Elizabeth Morse was found guilty and sentenced to be hanged on May 27th in Boston. Three days later Governor Bradstreet reprieved her until the October session. She remained jailed for two years and was finally allowed to return to her house opposite St. Paul's church, although her sentence was never fully repealed.

In 1680 three women were charged of witchcraft in Hampton. Eunice Cole, who had previously been accused in 1673 plus Rachel Fuller and Isabelle Towle were charged with going out at night and cavorting in a coven that worshiped the Devil and Rachel was accused of causing the death of John Godfrey's child through witchcraft. According to testimony Rachel had come in with molasses on her face, tried to take the sick child's hand but it was withdrawn by Mrs. Godfrey. Rachel then clapped her hands and said the child would be healed. She spat into the fire then went into the yard and smote herself on the arms while facing the house. Rachel had told the Godfrey children that bay leaves spread at doorways would keep witches out so they put some down and next time she visited she was unable to enter the house, instead sitting down, rubbing against the post like a cat until her hat fell off, all the while making ugly faces at the children. The charges were eventually dropped due to lack of evidence but apparently the villagers felt the Devil was still at work as a century later Jonathon Moulton's mansion and two store houses would mysteriously burn to the ground; a house and estate the locals said he obtained by being in League with the Devil. (The Moultons and Davises were among the first settlers to found the Springfield-Brimfield area.)

The Puritans brought all their old superstitions with them from England, Wales, Scotland and Ireland and fear of witches was one of them. To them any unusual occurence such as a comet or sudden storm was caused by supernatural forces. For instance, a damaging hail storm would cause the settlers to search their hearts to see if they had brought evil upon them. In like manner, a person whom they believed to be evil would be blamed for anything that happened. Often the accused were old, ugly women with sharp tongues or men who had treated others in a harsh manner. To say the people deliberately lied about those they accused wouldn't be true as they sincerely believed that a person in concert with the Devil could work mischief upon people, especially children, animals and weather.

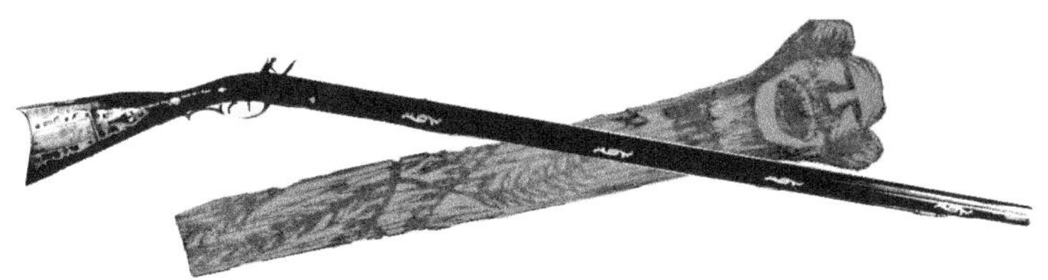

CHAPTER SIXTY-SIX

William from Wales

1683

In 1617 William was born in Radnorshire to Richard's son Abraham Isaac in Wales. William was brother of Nathaniel and Abraham Isaac, called Abiss. His family became known as the Bristol branch. Although born in the family manor in Carmarthenshire William was sent to sea at a young age. He was of medium height with sandy colored hair and had eyes that could change from a greenish-brown to a brownish-green.

Before being sent to Bristol to sail with uncles William and George, the young boy spent hours and hours roaming the valleys and hills and mountains of southern Wales before being sent off to boarding school. He and his brothers and friends knew every castle, castle ruin, abbey and abbey ruin, stone burial (dolman) and every stone ring nestled in the ancient valleys and knew where to find the best shale deposits, the soil richest in iron. They fished in the numerous brooks and sailed in small boats on the rivers. They went to the shore and harvested oysters and shellfish and loved the endless vista of hilltops and vales in every hue of green, blue and purple that Wales, like a tapestry woven by fairy hands, had to offer. The land was rich with ancient tales, especially of Merlin and Arthur and William had sailed up the coast and visited the isle of Anglesey where young men had been sent in the old days to learn the magic of the Druids. The Welsh loved storytelling and singing and William's carefree youth was spent in song and story. The Welsh were touched by English politics, it was true, mostly in the realm of religion as a spirit of independence made them, like the Scottish, unhappy with the rigid Anglican Church of England.

After moving to the busy port city of Bristol William was exposed to the persecution of the Puritans and his family became torn between loyalty to the Crown and loyalty to one's own conscience in religious matters.

During school breaks William made many short voyages between Bristol and Irish ports and came to know the entire English coastline and most of the western coast of the Continent, depending on the shifting state of peace or war between England, France, Holland and Spain. He later accompanied his brothers, uncles or cousins on ships to Virginia, the West Indies and the coastal ports from Maryland to New York to New Haven, Providence, Plymouth, Boston, Salem and then on to the most northern harbors of the Merrimack, Piscataqua and Kennebec Rivers. He'd visited Mt. Desert Isle and sailed the northern fishing route back to England by the time he was eighteen.

William's family was linked to the Gorges and Mason families through commerce and to the Royal Court through Cecil and other ties mentioned elsewhere. What exact motive made him board the *Planter* to emigrate to Boston in 1635 at the age of 18 is hard to define. Most of his relations were moving there so there was peer pressure. Plus the young lady Elizabeth he'd met while at school in Oxford was going over with her family so they wed and he went along with them to set up in Roxbury.

Relatives came and moved from the Boston-Cambridge area north to the new towns of Haverhilll and Newbury and others went south to Springfield and Connecticut, even out to Long Island and far north to Albany and the coastal towns in the Eastward, later called 'Down East'.

His brother Abiss, just called Isaac at the time, had committed one of the many Puritan crimes and, after being fined and forced to make his own stocks, stood in them bravely then, to avoid deportation, went north to Casco Bay and never returned to the Massachusetts Bay Colony and his Welsh wife Elizabeth Stringer had John in

1643 followed by Samuel in 1646 and Joseph in 1649. There were two other wives and other sons as well. His son Samuel married the Welsh Hannah Edwards. His son Joseph had Joseph Jr., Tristrum and others. New England was full of opportunities and he spent the first years of their marriage mostly at sea in the ships his family partly owned: the *Swan, Charity* and the *Increase,* then called the *Trader's Increase* owned by Nicholas. His cousin Sir Thomas was a prosperous captain and had a large plantation in Virginia although he preferred northern New England when not at sea as the climate to the south was not healthy for Englishmen. There were too many fevers and too many surprise attacks by the savages there for him to want to raise his family in the swampy, yet fertile, lowlands that tobacco thrived in. New England was colder than England but during the spring through fall it approximated the English climate and the landscape was similar with gentle hills, valleys, rivers, ponds and a lot of coastline. There were some different species of trees but many familiar ones such as oak and ash, and wheat and Indian corn grew fast and hardy in the soil. The English and other Europeans had brought the livestock familiar to them so by the mid to late 1600s a person looking out over salt marsh at grazing cattle or seeing the pigs rooting in the woods might feel they were back in England.

What was radically different was the lack of good, solid, old stone houses and buildings. Most of the one room homes were built of rough-hewn timber and the slate and stones William had seen everywhere in Wales were replaced with rough clapboard shingles. The houses were drafty and the winters could be severe. Many people died in the early days from respiratory infections, made worse by breathing the imperfect, clay-lined fireplaces' smoky air as it clouded the rooms. Infants perished the quickest from being exposed to drafts, followed by elderly who already had illnesses making them feeble. So it was when William and Elizabeth's youngest child was only nine years old Elizabeth succumbed during an epidemic of "cold" that swept through the towns.

William and Elizabeth had spent every hour of every day since arriving in Roxbury building up a homestead. They had a two-room saltbox home with a half-loft for the boys upstairs; a large barn; a shed for corn, a brick smoke house, pens for pigs and cleaned, plowed and planted fields plus Elizabeth had brought flower seeds and had a precious flower bed in front and the kitchen garden on the side that the chickens helped keep free of insects. He had a small smithy as most of the Davis men were trained in black smithing as a trade to enable them to fix iron objects for the ships they sailed. A small orchard of apple trees was growing in a lower field near a pond and the well next to the house had been dug out by hand by William and his brothers the first year he and Elizabeth had set down their roots.

Everything on their rustic farm had Elizabeth in it and it pained William severely to look at it after her death. He left his sons when the youngest was 11 and the oldest was 17 to go back to sea for a while, sailing along the coast down to Virginia and back. In Duxbury when he docked to unload a cargo from the West Indies, brought from Jamestown, Virginia, he stayed with his cousin Phillip and during the course of his visit met the widow Alice Thorpe. In 1661 William-met her again while he was visiting relatives in Wales and they married, returning to his Roxbury farm.

Alice knew the sorrow of losing her spouse (eight years past) and hadn't pressed William to return to a place laden with memories but, as a widow, she had nothing of her own to offer. Her brother and brother-in-law Bullard had received most of her father's estate and she had sold her "widow's third" and sailed back to Wales. Her deceased husband John had been a carpenter and knew Dolor and Dolor's sons John so Alice was immediately accepted into the Davis clan. William's oldest son, John was now old enough to go out on his own and he and Samuel went to help settle towns forming on the northwest frontier along the Connecticut River and to help with the lead mine in Northampton. Joseph was 16 and invaluable as a helper on the farm. He was soon half-brother to William, born in 1663, Matthew was born the next year and Jonathan in 1665. The last two were born at sea as Alice loved sailing and accompanied William on voyages between New England and Great Britain whenever possible. However, she had been towards the end of her childbearing years when she had Jonathan and her next two pregnancies ended in miscarriages, the last taking her along with her stillborn child in 1667.

Again William took to sea, this time leaving Joseph to care for the farm and relatives to look after Alice's young sons.

The next year William was visiting John in Hatfield and met and married his third wife: Jane Adams, a 17 year old widow, daughter of William Heath, whom he knew as they were both from Roxbury and related to the Mittons in the Eastward.

Jane was totally at home in William's farm as it was close to her family. She bore him a daughter that they named Mary in 1669. Mary was followed by Jane two years later then Rachel and a son Benjamin, born in 1674. He was followed by Ichabod, Ebeneezer, William, Sarah and Isaac, the last and final child born in 1683.

As Jane was giving William children his sons were marrying and having children of their own. Samuel was settled in Northampton where he was helping Robert Lyon, William Clarke, John King, Samuel Bartlett, the Parsons, Preserved Clap and Meded Powery establish a lead mine. Lead was a valuable commodity as shot for muskets and cannons were made of it and it also had other uses as a heavy metal used in weights such as plumb lines or mixed with other metals. The mine at *Tantiesquies* hadn't played out well for the Pynchons but Samuel felt very optimistic about the Northampton vein.

William's sons John married Mary, daughter of John Devotion and Samuel married Hannah Edwards, a good Welsh girl.

William, only 60 but with the rheumatism too old to sail, retired from the sea and, like everyone, was preoccupied with King Philip's War and the northern attacks by the savages. His sons were the most vulnerable as they had settled in the outlying towns, the prime targets for the indians in 1675 and 1676 and they were enlisted to fight with the army along the Connecticut River and down into Narragansett territory.

William died in 1683, spared the horrors of what John and his family would endure in Deerfield. As was the custom, the youngest son inherited the Roxbury farm William and Elizabeth had created from love and the sweat of their toil in a foreign land surrounded by hostile savages.

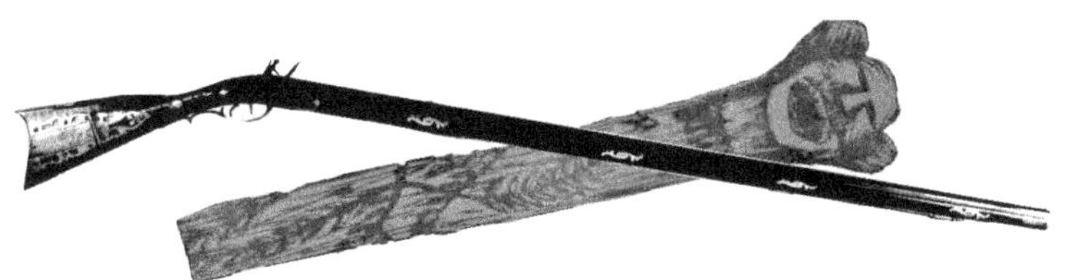

CHAPTER SIXTY-SEVEN

The Brief Reign of Gov. Andros

1685-89

As King Philip's War ended in Massachusetts, Connecticut and Rhode Island King Charles II decided to act to take the Massachusetts Bay's charter away. Fueled by reports that the New Englanders weren't following the 'Navigation Act' and depriving the Crown of income, he sent a letter to Boston to surrender the charter.

The Massachusetts General Court met and decided it would be better to send two men in person to speak with the King and Lords of Trade and Plantations. They drafted a reply regarding Mason and Gorges's claims and voted to send William Stoughton and Peter Bulkeley with the letter to London.

Edward Randolph had been sent by the Crown to New England some years earlier to make sure the Navigation Acts were followed but he had returned to England with a negative report.

In July 1677 the Lords argued with Stoughton and Bulkeley that the Puritan oligarchy had persecuted Quakers, dissenters and violated Royal and Parliamentary Acts, even coining their own money and holding that the only legal marriages were to be performed by magistrates, not ministers.

In October, 1677 the Lords declared the charter void. They told Stoughton and

Bulkeley they had mountains of proof that tobacco from North Carolina was being shipped to Ireland, Scotland, Holland, France and Spain under the label of "fish" and then hidden behind legal casks of Madeira wine and didn't appear on doctored manifests in the Canaries.

The colony received a temporary reprieve when England had to deal with a failed Catholic uprising by Titus Oates in London. The Massachusetts men sailed back to Boston and there they were rebuked for having yielded on too many points and even brought with them a stern letter from the King appointing Edward Randolph as the royal Collector of Customs. Randolph tried to seize the *James* in Londonderry (in which two hogsheads of tobacco were secreted). He said he was going to write to every port in England and the West Indies to refuse dockage of any vessel that wasn't cleared by the king.

In 1681 a new election brought in a Whig majority to Parliament but King Charles II refused to seat it and dismissed the Parliament in violation of his promise to rule under their authority. The King and his son and heir, James, went after Virginia and every colony, trying to dissolve their governments and set up councils answerable only to the Crown. As Massachusetts had refused to surrender its charter King Charles II nullified it via a *quo warranto* issued by England's Attorney General and replaced it with Royal Colony status with a governor chosen by the King and not elected by the people. Massachusetts hired Robert Humphreys to defend their charter and he appealed this imperial decree. He was joined by Joseph Dudley and John Richards in February 1682 as per the King's statement that they had three months to send representatives to defend it. In Boston Deputy Governor Thomas Danforth replied to Randolph's letter by saying no one had the right to seize any ships in New England's ports except colonial officers. The General Court appointed James Russell as the colony's Chief Naval officer but Gov. Bradstreet wouldn't swear him in due to the quit rent controversy and his claim to Casco Bay so Danforth swore him in. (Russell's son William Russell married William Davis's daughter Sarah. He settled in Wethersfield and didn't support James II's later claim to the throne.) At the next election Dudley was voted out and Bulkleley and Stoughton resigned in protest as they felt the only way to deal with the King was to yield on some points. The majority of voters in Massachusetts Bay agreed with them but the Puritan leadership wasn't about to give up any of its power.

A second Civil War was brewing after King Charles II died suddenly in February 1685. His successor, his brother James, the Duke of York was a papist. Many relatives of the New Englanders rallied around a different James, the illegitimate eldest son of King Charles II, the Duke of Monmouth. Monmouth landed in Dorset with a conquering force but James II's army overpowered them and Monmouth and his ally, the duke of Argyle were executed in the middle of July. Jonathon Gardiner brought this sad news with him when his ship docked in Boston. News then came across the sea that the new King James II was going to appoint Colonel Percy Kirke as the new royal governor of MBC. Randolph knew that Kirke would spark a revolt in the colonies and suggested Edmund Andros since had was known there, having been governor of New York.

In the interim an unelected Council headed by Joseph Dudley was chosen to rule with Pynchon, Dr. Bartholemew Gedney, John Mason, Captain John Winthrop, Richard Wharton (Richar'ds son-in-law was a Tyng and had 500,000 acres in Penobscot) and Randolph, despite protests from magistrates and Bradstreet, Nathaniel Saltonstall and Dudley. Bradstreet refused to take a seat on the Council. The sense of betrayal was smarting in the hearts of the people. They had fought bravely and fiercely against the savages for survival and to hold claim to the lands they had cleared and settled for England and now their independence, freedoms and rights as freeborn Englishmen were being given away and they were regarded as no better than the Irish, subject to direct rule from London.

Some of the colonists welcomed the arrival of Gov. Andros and his councillors as they had been refused the right to vote since they didn't belong to the orthodox church (which they had to attend or be fined) and they felt civil and militiary offices should be open to them and not based on membership in the Congregational church.

Gov. Andros held a training day for eight companies and the Loyalists celebrated with cheers and red paper crosses pinned to their hats. They felt the days of the Puritan tyranny were over and they would have their proper English rights restored, rights not based on church membership.

The cheering was short lived. Andros ruled dictatorially with his Council. He made laws and levied taxes and withdrew the right of Habeas Corpus. As time went on a tax of a penny per pound of worth was levied on homesteads and a 20 pence poll tax was instituted plus another on liquors and a 'stamp act' fee imposed on all legal papers. Across New England men formed groups to protest and fight back. The Rev. Cotton Mather preached that the land had been taken over by insatiable land-eating "crocodiles". Increase Mather slipped away on a ship bound for England and there he joined Samuel Nowell and Elisha Hutchinson to petition the Lords of Trade.

For over two years New England was in turmoil with daily rumors of a Catholic invasion from Ireland, or new indian attacks – rumors encouraged by Andros. Many men were arrested and charged with insubordination, even treason, for their resistance to the tyrannical Andros.

In April 1689 word came via ship from Virginia that William, Prince of Orange had landed on English soil to retake the throne through royal lineage of his wife Mary (James II's oldest daughter). Both were staunch Protestants. James II fled and William and Mary were co-crowned with William taking the title of William III.

Upon hearing this a crowd gathered in the Boston Town House to read a 'Declaration of Condemnation' of Andros. The governor and over a dozen men surrendered and were imprisoned in the garrison on Castle Island.

Increase Mather sent almost daily letters home to keep the people current of the situation in England, during what they called 'The Glorious Revolution'. However, he said that since the original MBC charter had been declared invalid via the *quo warranto* and *scire facias* rulings Massachusetts had to write a new charter and find a sponsor. King William III was in favor of home rule but insisted it be non-secular, kneecapping the Puritan oligarchy. All freeholders' titles were restored and they could vote if they had a minimum income of 40 pounds a year or owned property of at least 100 pounds in value. Although not a perfect solution the New Englanders grasped it and elected Sir William Phips as the first governor in 1692.

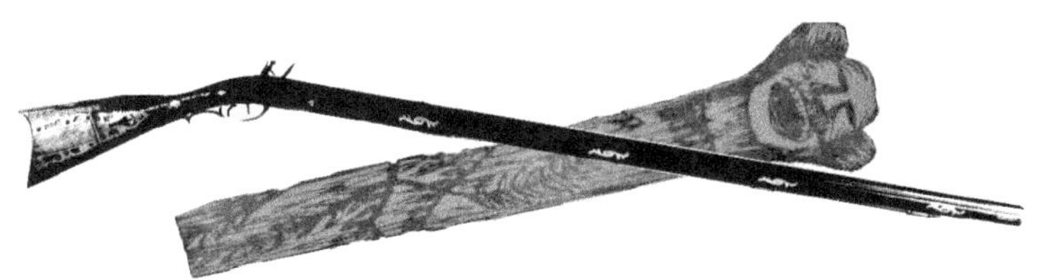

CHAPTER SIXTY-EIGHT

Sylvanus, John and Northern Davises

1690s

After Gov. Andros brokered a peace at the end of King Philip's War he returned to England but later was back in New England as the king's colonial governor. Following a prolonged tour of Maine he had forts built from Piscataqua to Penobscot and had existing ones reinforced. The largest was Fort Loyal in Casco Bay, but the string of forts up the coast were manned to show the savages and French the English meant business about defending its settlements.

This set off a series of indian attacks on farms and cattle and the savages captured English, who in turn captured natives.

Andros had also appropriated between 6-10,000 acres of land each for his favorites while they toured what the locals in the Pemaquid area called the County of Cornwall. This area had been settled early and had an octagonal fort at North Edgecombe with a narrow tower on top. One of these grants, a new 'proprietor' Col. Thomas Dungan, had the *Swallow* seized offshore for nonpayment of excise tax and its cargo of wine confiscated as the captain was unaware that the harbor he was docked in was now Dungan's and therefore English territory, where it had been formerly considered French.

Andros, who was overly fond of Maine, finally left in 1688 after appointing Nicholas Manning magistrate in the Duke of York's Province called Sagadahoc, or the County of Cornwall.

Like other ship owners-captains Robert, Richard and William, had been plying the ports, shipping "fish" to England or behind casks of Madeira wine and then sailing back to the Barbados and West Indies and Virginia to load up with more "fish" to be sent to British men to smoke in their pipes. The royalty had despised tobacco from an early time although it was a very profitable crop. In spite of royal disapproval, its use was widespread both in England, Europe and the New World. In New England its use was confined to one's own home but even women were smoking it in their sitting rooms. In addition, the Davis men were associated with iron ore workings in Saugus and Saco as their black smithing skills could turn the red ore into ornamental and functional items for land and sea.

Sugar was the second most profitable cargo and some of the Davis men had tobacco plantations in Virginia and (later) sugar plantations in the West Indies in addition to their English estates and farms and shops from Virginia up to what was being called Maine.

James and Cicely Thayer's son John moved up to Dover in Oyster Bay. Sylvanus, son of a different John, owned 500 acres of farmland between the Darimiscotta River and Kennebec on Casco Bay and he worked with his maritime relatives as a land speculator and trader, acquiring lumber and furs and (genuine) salted fish to put in their cargo holds as they sailed down the coast and further south, then to England, Ireland and Spain. He also had a gristmill and sawmill in addition to his trading post.

William Phips, born in Arrowsick, Woolrich, above the Sheepscott River, Maine, was a ship's carpenter turned treasure hunter. He had persuaded some of the Davis men in Boston (in residence there after being forced to leave Maine during the attacks of King Philip's War) to help him find a wrecked Spanish galleon off the coast of one of the islands in the Bahamas. William Hilton, married to Francis Davis from Kittery Point, rented a house from Nicholas Shapleigh in Kittery and kept a ferry to Great Island. His son was in with Phips and the Davises in the Barbados shipwreck venture. During Andros's reign as royal governor Sir Thomas Davis and Sir John worked on the Duke of Abermarle in England to fund an expedition and from the wreck Phips and his divers raised 34 tons of silver bars, mined in South America, gold, pearls, precious gems and jewels. King James II had richly rewarded Phips plus gave him a knighthood and he was appointed High Sheriff of all of New England.

Sylvanus had served as a captain in King Philip's War and after the new Fort Loyal was completed he was put in command of it until a full time British officer could arrive to take over.

Maine hadn't known true peace in the 14 years following the death of King Philip as many of the savages who hated the English had escaped to the north and joined the tribes between Massachusetts and the French territory along the St. Lawrence seaway. The French felt they owned the far northern trading posts and called that part of the coast 'Acadia'. Tensions were always just under the surface as a tribe, egged on by the French or their militiaristic Catholic priests, would attack an outlying farm; burn, kill and destroy and then slink back into the endless forest that was their refuge. The savages resented the dams and fishing weirs that disrupted their rivers (their water highways) and their hunting.

In 1688 Capt. Gendall and the soldiers who were building forts on opposite banks of the Royall River near North Yarmouth were attacked. Gendell was killed and John Royall taken captive, later ransomed by Baron Castine. In response Gov. Andros sent over 700 English soldiers to Pemaquid. The troops marched north in November, a cold month in Maine. They spent the winter in the different garrisons along the coast, under supplied and cold, but the indians had retreated back to their snug winter villages and didn't engage the enemy.

In April 1689 Andros, upon the fleeing of King James II and the subsequent arrival of William and Mary on English soil, was seized and sent to the prison on Castle Island with about ten of his despotic underlings. When word of his overthrow reached the forts the British soldiers rebelled and left their posts, returning south. The French and indians immediately occupied the forts, leaving 11 settlements at the mercy of the enemy. The fort at Saco repelled them but Dover fell to an ambush and there was a resulting slaughter at Major Richard Caldron's garrison. Caldron had a bad reputation amongst the natives as he was a blatant cheat. The indians tortured him in front of family and settlers then took 29 captive up to Canada. Caldron was killed in retribution for seizing about 400 indians in 1677 at Dover and as the

English learned, English laws and punishments meant nothing to the indians for they had their own system of justice: retribution or restitution.

To attempt to end the hostilities *Madockawando*, chief sachem of the Pemaquid area, whose daughter had married Baron Castine, who lived with the indians, went to Boston with a party to parley for peace. The provisional government in Boston assured *Madockawando* they didn't approve of Andros's actions and sent him home with gifts and a letter apologizing to Baron Castine for the encroachment of the forts upon his territory. However, on May 7, 1689 war broke out between England and France as James II had fled there and the Catholic French king sided with him against William and Mary. In retaliation William III immediately authorized an expedition to retake Nova Scotia and Quebec from the French.

In mid-May 1690 Sylvanus took over temporary command of Fort Loyal as its commander Edward Tyng (married to Capt. Thadeus Clarke's daughter Elizabeth) went to Boston. From Boston Sir William Phips sailed with seven ships and approximately 500 men to retake Fort Royal and the northern forts along the Bay of Fundy as the area was the center of French trade and Fort Royal was its most important port. The expedition was a great success and an English governor was installed at the fort.

However, while Phips and his ships were sailing to Boston with news of victory and cargo holds full of loot, the savages attacked the southern forts.

During Tyng's absence a large force of French and indians attacked Fort Loyal, under the command of Monsieur Burneffe and Lt. Capt. Monsieur de Portneuf. Sylvanus had always tried to maintain good relations with the savages, learning their customs and many words of their languages as he traded English steel knives, hardtack and iron and steel items for precious beaver furs. Occasionally he'd get wolf pelts or a large bear pelt but beaver was still the fur most in demand as it made excellent waterproof hats. When news arrived of indians sighted nearby he wasn't alarmed, feeling they were coming to trade.

The attack took them totally by surprise on the morning of May 16, 1690. It was merciless. The settlers and soldiers within the wooden fort were attacked on all sides for days. Dodging English fire the French and indians dug a trench near the fort and threw hand grenades over its walls then rolled barrels of tar and put brush around it ready for firing. For four days Sylvanus and the soldiers bravely held the fort but after they ran out of food and water and ammunition and knew their fate was to burn to death or surrender Sylvanus flew a flag of truce and parleyed with the French commander Portneuf. Portneuf took a solemn oath that the Articles of Capitulation would be sacredly honored which stated the English would be given their freedom once they surrendered the fort. He promised Sylvanus that the occupants wouldn't be harmed if he surrendered. But the next day as the fort's doors were opened and the 70 men marched out the indian troops swarmed around them and massacred most of the men. Sylvanus was in shock at the unexpected brutal killings. He and others, mostly women and children, were spared by the intervention of French soldiers and taken north to Canada.

The bitterness Sylvanus felt over the betrayal stayed with him the rest of his life.

Phips learned of the fall of Fort Loyal and the fate of his friend Sylvanus when his fleet arrived back in Boston. A fleet was being readied to sail north to take Quebec from the French and an overland army of 4,000 men was being mobilized to march north to Montreal under Major General John Winthrop Jr. Phips was promoted to the rank of Commodore and he sailed on the flagship the *Six Friends* in a fleet of 32 ships with 2,000 militiamen from the port of Hull on October 16,1690. The fleet had been delayed due to an outbreak of smallpox in Boston harbor and in the meantime Gov. de Frontenac had reinforced the Quebec fort with 3,000 soldiers.

When the English arrived in the St. Lawrence seaway they were met with heavy resistance and after being battered by the heavy guns at Ft. Quebec they retreated. Phips was able to redeem his friend Sylvanus and a few other prisoners but France preferred to send captives they felt they could ransom for large amounts to France so not all the prominent people were released.

On board the *Six Friends* Phips met his old friend Sylvanus with a hug, which he promptly broke off.

"Good Lord, you stink!" he exclaimed, pushing his diving buddy away. Sylvanus was still wearing the buckskins he'd been captured in and hadn't bathed in months and his dirty blond hair and beard were matted and full of lice.

"Aye, the savages aren't much for bathin', certainly not at this time o' the year," Sylvanus replied with a smile that wrinkled his sun-burnt face.

Phips called for a hot bath to be prepared at once in his quarters and led his friend, now stooped and aged beyond his years to the captain's' quarters.

"I be told ye are a Commodore, no less!" Sylvanus said, his smile showing yellowed, decayed teeth.

"Aye, we got the northern forts," Phips replied, removing and handing his dark haired wig to his valet who immediately began checking it for lice.

His broad face with even features suddenly screwed up as he burst out, "By God, I'd have given up all o' that Nova Scotia business if I'd known ye were in such peril!"

The servants held out the leathers at arms' length as the filth-caked Sylvanus lowered himself into a tub of hot water and grabbed a cake of perfumed soap and a wash linen. He dunked his head and scrubbed his hair and beard, which were still itchy from lice, and scrubbed as Phips sipped wine from the gold cup King James II had given to his mother (Andros's second wife) as her share of the salvage. She had given it to Phips when he was promoted to Commodore as she felt it was only fitting that a knight and Commodore should drink only from a vessel of gold.

Sylvanus accepted a silver cup of wine and drank greedily as he dunked and soaped, scrubbed and scrubbed some more. The water was foamy with dirt and dead lice.

The servants held out towels for Sylvanus and he stepped out, dripping on the polished oak floors of the swank cabin. The tub was immediately whisked away and the contents dumped overboard and a fresh tub was set out for Sylvanus to rinse off in.

"Ye know," said the now rinsed and freshly clad Sylvanus as he sat across from William, "The only thing that saved me skin was a'knowin' the ways o' the savages. A lot o' that dirt was bear grease. They slather it on to help keep them warm. Many o' the women and children with me refused and suffered greatly from the cold."

Phips snorted angrily, "We'll drive all them bastards out!"

Sylvanus, whose hair and beard were being clipped and cleaned with a fine-toothed ivory comb by William's servants, smiled sadly.

"Nay, friend. Ye are a'fightin' a proud people. The French gave as good as they got on the Continent and they aren't a'goin' to hand England one acre of land if they can help it. They got them indians on their side, all roused up with talk of how they'll get their lands back and drive the English back to England. They, too, are proud people."

Phips was turning the intricately carved goblet in his wide, calloused hands. Having worked on ships as a carpenter he was still taking the hammer and saw to lend a hand on repairs. The sea was now his master but his heart, like Dolor's son John's was wedded to wood.

"Syl," he said, pulling the cover over his friend as he had him placed in the captain's bed, "I know ye've had a bad time of it. Ye look like death warmed over. But I promise ye I'll get ye settled nicely in Hull and no one will ever place an ounce of blame on ye for that bastard's treachery."

Sylvanus closed his eyes, all the pain and exhaustion of the past months closing in on perfumed Irish linen and English wool.

"'Twont ever erase what I feel in me heart," he whispered, "to me dying day there will burn a fire o' hatred for the French and the savages in it. I saw all them brave men be sliced to pieces a'fore me eyes, their scalps ripped off while they were still screamin'. More than anything else I wanted to die, too, but me arms were held back by soldiers. I screamed, the women and children screamed and the whole world was one big, endless scream. Nay, Will, nothing ye can say or do will ever, ever erase that blood bath from me head."

Before he slept, Sylvanus held out a hand,

"Promise me, Will, that ye'll get them prisoners out. I don't care if ye have to burn the whole of Canada and chase the last savage into the sea as long as ye can bring all those poor women and children back."

Phips smiled. He'd be in charge soon if things went his way – and not just on the sea – and the French and indians would know what a real English fighting force could do!

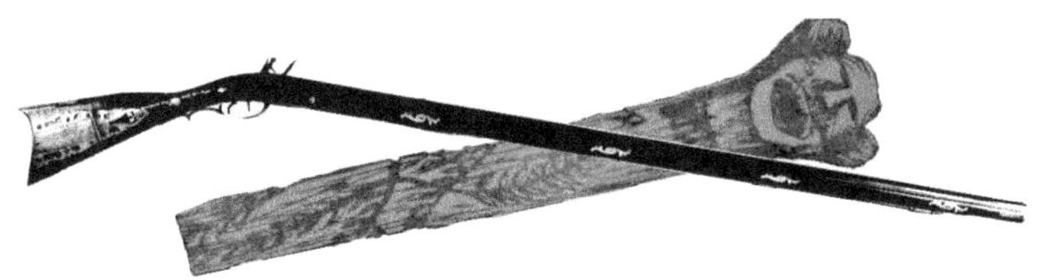

CHAPTER SIXTY-NINE

Isaac Davis

1688 -early 1700s

In early August 1689 about 200 French and Indians attacked Fort Charles in Pemaquid. They hid in abandoned cellar holes from homes that had been burned out and behind boulders and ambushed settlers in fields around the garrison. Lt. Weems, commander of the fort, sent out troops but most of the settlers didn't make it to safety and over 50 were carried off to Canada as captives. After a fierce battle Weems accepted the terms of surrender wherein the settlers inside the fort could board a ship for Boston, taking whatever possessions they could carry.

In the west during that summer Capt. Jonathan Bull sent 90 Connecticut and Massachusetts soldiers to Albany, 24 of whom were from Hampshire County. In 1690 Capt. David Burt, son of one of the founders of Northampton was captured. Joseph Marks from Brookfield was captured, Samuel Beam from Hatfield was captured and escaped; Robert Alexander and Jonathan Clark of Deerfield were killed. Sixty settlers from Schenectady fled, some to Connecticut, others to Albany. In May, 1690 as Fort Loyal was taken and Sylvanus and Phip's fleet was sailing northeast the newly created Hampshire County in Western Massachusetts began building fortifications in its outlying towns.

The Massachusetts General Court conscripted 160 men for defense, some sent to Albany. Major Pynchon was ordered to impress 60 men from Hampshire County's pool of 450 adult men but he could only raise 40 as smallpox was raging and sending more would leave the towns under defended. Twelve full time soldiers had to be stationed at Deerfield as they sent scouting parties of four soldiers out every day to patrol the area in all directions. Nine of the new conscripts went to Northampton; eight to Springfield; four to Westfield; six to Hatfield; five to Halley; five to Suffield and three to Enfield.

So many indians were prowling around Western Massachusetts that no soldiers could be spared for Church's Quebec expedition to *Maquoit* (Brunswick, Casco Bay) in September, 1690. He had 300 soldiers and immediately upon landing they marched to Fort Andros on the *Androscogggin* River. They surprised the indians there, killed 21 and captured wives of important sachems before firing the village and sailing to Winter Harbor (Saco). The wives of two of the chief sachems were used to redeem 80 English captives later in Wells. Church had taken the offensive and destroyed indian villages up the *Androscoggin.*

Phips's expedition took Port Royal and in August launched another expedition against Quebec. Commodore Sir William Phips returned to Boston that October with some indian captives including Sylvanus Davis after failing to capture Quebec and Major Church returned with most of his army from Casco and Pejepscot.

The indians promised Church they would return and sign a peace treaty at Storer's garrison in Wells the following May and Maine's president Thomas Danforth (formerly deputy governor of Massachusetts, appointed by its Council to be president of the separate territories including Richard Wharton's recent and contentious purchase of 500,000 acres that would include the Brunswicks, Topsham, Harpswell and all land east to the Kennebec River) let the sachems return home and he returned to York but ordered 35 more soldiers into the Wells garrison, already manned by 15 troopers under Capt. Converse.

A six month truce was signed on November 29, 1690 at Wells, Wheelwright's garrisoned village. (Wheelwright and his followers had been forced to relocate from Exeter to Wells when Massachusetts 'acquired' that territory.)

After returning to Hull and Boston, Commodore Phips then sailed to London to get support from King William III and Mary for another attempt at Quebec but while he was there Increase Mather convinced the King and Queen to appoint Phips as royal governor of MBC.

Phips was married to Mary Hull, widow of John, but in his wild youth had been involved with an Irish colleen and the Lord Chancellor of Ireland, Sir Constantine Phips, was allegedly his illegitimate son. As Phips, like his male relatives on the west bank of the Kennebec River, was a carouser, heavy drinker and fond of the ladies, the rumor was believed but the Puritans kept closed mouth about it.

Phips's father James had sired 21 children and William, born in 1651, was the youngest. George Davis was William Phips's friend and a fellow gunsmith (originally from Bristol). James's son William Phips became a ship's carpenter. Through English contacts at court, the Davises and Phips were able to hire the king's ship the *Algier Rose* for a treasure salvage in the Bahamas. William had captained ships on voyages to India and was used to the rough life of a sailor. He, however, was a bit too rowdy for the stern Puritans in Boston and his wild parties were casting aspersion on his wife, rumored to be a witch.

With the return of (now royally-appointed Governor) Sir William Phips to Boston from England a sort of peace was worked out with the northern tribes and, with fear of witches replacing fear of indian attack, John Davis returned to Northampton, then moved even further north to the settlement of Deerfield.

John's brother Joseph, minus his brother Samuel who settled in Northampton to work the lead mine, went back to the ancestral lands in Denbighyshire, Wales. John went to Enfield where James's son John was living with his in-laws the Peasles.

James and his sons were in Haverhilll, Newbury and Amesbury and doing well as ships were being built and West Indian ships docked regularly at Newburyport. Trade was basically uninterrupted during what would be called King William's War and then Queen Anne's War.

Dolor's sons and grandsons were returning to the Quinsigamond area and settling in and around what would be named Worcester and Rutland. Joseph Ayres went to Brookfield along with the Symonds and Warner to attempt to resettle the town. William of Roxbury was related to the Warners through marriage of a son and a daughter. John Warner and Mary Davis resided in the new Brookfield plantation for a brief period before moving on.

Sylvanus stayed in Hull, joined by Robert, who had several children, one named

Tristrum, a good West Country name. The Davises were friends of the Tyngs and Coffins and had a trading post at a docking point on Nantucket Island. Wherever a prominent Welsh family such as the Morgans, Dudleys and Bulkeleys were, there were some Davis men. Friendships that had been forged in Elizabethan England continued over to New England and many towns were settled by families who emigrated from a common area in England or Wales.

By the turn of the century there were Scotch-Irish and Irish and Scottish laborers in iron works or in mills or large farms. The ones in Virginia had been 'liberated' but lived in terrible poverty as, after Bacon's Rebellion, African slaves came in to take over the labor on the tobacco plantations and they were forced out to scratch an existence on small farms in indian territory.

In late 1691 a large group of indians from Albany camped near Deerfield. Samuel Partridge of Hatfield and John King of Northampton wrote to the Massachusetts Council about the problem. The indians had a letter from the governor of New York giving them permission to camp there so they could hunt. In early February Capt. Whiting with 50 men from Hartford reinforced the Deerfield garrison and a few months later the indians left.

In late July of the same year 26 of these indians attacked Brookfield and carried off a man, woman and child after killing six settlers. Major Pynchon immediately sent a county force of 58 troopers there under Capt. Thomas Colton (from Springfield), with Capt. Prescott Clapp, Lt. John King and Ensign Edward Baker, all of Northampton. (His son Timothy Baker was a friend of Sylvanus of Dover.) They pursued the indians into a thick wooded swamp and as they fled, they dropped the goods they'd stolen and then left the captives behind. The distribution of the recaptured plunder became a sore subject when the government wanted to give it all to Colton's troops. One of the hatchets recovered was identified as having been made by blacksmith John Davis's forge in Northampton.

In 1689 Timothy Baker's three month old son was captured in Dover and not redeemed until 1714 when Baker accompanied Col. Stoddard to bring home the captives taken during the French and Indian Wars that raged for almost 20 years.

In February, 1692, an army of about 300 French traveling on snowshoes in the dark attacked York's two-story garrison houses in the early hours before dawn. Within a couple of hours half the settlers were either killed or captured. Rev.

Dummer was slain and his tomahawked body was left to bleed out on the snow. His wife was taken, screaming and fighting, into captivity. Some old people and children were later released as they had shown kindness to certain indians in the past.

Two sloops and a shallop with 14 sailors were sent to aid the settlers at Wells where 500 French and indians were attacking the fort, held bravely by Capt. James Converse. The attacking army set fire to a raft to take out the sloops in the rivers and the fort on its shore but the wind shifted and carried it to the opposite shore. They tried to take the fort or force it to surrender but Converse wouldn't yield. After a couple of days the indians withdrew. For his victory and bravery Converse was promoted to Commander-in-Chief of all the troops in Maine.

To bolster the defense of the territory Gov. Phips sent a force of 400 men to begin construction of a stone fort named Fort William Henry (not the later one in Western New York). Located about three miles above Pemaquid Point it had 29-foot high walls and 18 cannon, each capable of firing an 18 pound ball. The indians tried to attack while it was being constructed but were repelled by an English man of war ship.

At this time Major Church was roaming the Eastward with troops to rout out any savages they could find. On August 12, 1692 18 sachems, including the five chief sachems who were held as hostages to the truce, came to the fort at Pemaquid and sued for peace. They renounced all ties to France and said they would resolve differences in English courts in the future, instead of on the battlefield.

To the west, in June 1693 Whiting and men were sent to Northampton as three daughters of the widow Hepizeibah Wells had been tomahawked and scalped. Only one survived. Around that time Thomas Broughton, an early Northampton settler, and his wife and children were killed by marauding Canadian bands of indians.

In August, 1694 an army of 250 Canadian indians and French soldiers under Claude Sebastian de Villieu (goaded by "the fighting priest" Fr. Louis Pierre Thery and Fr. Rale of Norridgewock) attacked 12 garrison houses including that of Ensign John Davis in Oyster Bay (Dover) on the Piscataqua River. John had died before the attack but his family were either killed or carried off into Canada. One hundred settlers in all were killed or captured and 13 houses burned to the cellarholes. As sport the indians made a nine year old boy run a gauntlet in which hatchets were thrown at him until he was mortally wounded.

The peace was broken a second time as in mid-September, 1994 Deerfield was attacked again. Five men were bringing wheat to the mill to be ground and were ambushed. Joseph Barnard was wounded, picked up and put on a horse. It was shot out from under him and he was wounded again. His comrades brought him into a garrison house but he died later. Lt. Hollister from Connecticut with troops came a few weeks later and the area was searched as it was rumored 600 indian were en route to Albany but none were discovered. Major Pynchon reinforced Deerfield with Northampton soldiers including Kings, Wrights, John Parsons and Benjamin Stebbins.

Hope for peace was once again kindled in May, 1695 when William Phillips, John Hawthorne and Commander Converse met with sachems at Fort William Henry. The English demanded the return of all captives before they would hand over the indians they had captured. The sachems were offended and left in a huff. William was related to Samuel Phillips of Salem (a goldsmith, as were John Hull (not the mint master) and Robert Sanderson who made gold and silver spoons in Maine during this time). John Hull's widow had married Sir William Phips in 1674.

In the late spring and summer of 1696 the French began an offensive campaign along the Maine coast. The prize they were after was Fort William Henry as it held a critical defensive position on the coast. It was the pride of New England and Benjamin Church had personally overseen its construction.

Pasco Chubb from Crewkerne County, on the border of Devon and Somerset, was the British commander of this new fort in Pemaquid. With ten to 22-foot high walls and a 29-foot round bastion, all made of local stone, defended by 20 cannon and 60 soldiers the fort seemed impregnable. (Pasco' brother William had served with the Davis men in King Philip's War in Halley.)

In mid-July, 1696 Baron Castine and Pierre Le Mayne d'Iberville led an assault on the fort. Their army had three French men o' war ships, canoes and 500 men. They surrounded the fort and began a cannonade. The fort had been constructed hastily and its stonework wasn't solid. Chubb refused to surrender and continued fighting back but as the walls crumbled so did his resolve. Castine sent a messenger over with the offer that if the English gave up the men would be allowed safe conveyance to Boston where they would be exchanged for French and indian captives. Chubb surrendered but when the indian soldiers entered the fort they found an indian in chains and in revenge for the unfair way Chubb had enticed and then captured some of them earlier that year, began killing English soldiers, in a repeat of what they'd done at Ft. Loyal. Three were mortally wounded but Castine stopped the impending massacre and sent 92 English, including Chubb, via ship south. The men on deck cried as they saw their once beautiful fort being reduced by the French and indians to rubble with the French flag flying insolently above in the bright summer sun. Chubb became a pariah. Church went on a rampage, and led a fleet up the coast from Monhegan Island to Penobscot Bay and then by foot up the western bank of the Penobscot River then again by ship to the Bay of Fundy where he razed and burned a small French fishing post. Five hundred troops were sent under Major March to reinforce the remaining Maine forts as 1,500 French and indian troops retook Nova Scotia and whatever they could up and down the coast. Maj. March had a victory at Damariscotta on September 9, 1697, unaware that across the ocean peace talks were concluding that in two days would, with the 'Treaty of Ryswick', end King William III's War against the French.

The news reached Boston on December 10, 1697 and in January, 1698 the French signed a treaty in Brunswick. Without their French soldiers and arms the indians also ceased their hostilities. The English wanted all French missionaries to be removed from Canada but the indians refused, only agreeing to an exchange of prisoners. To the war-weary northern New Englanders a compromise peace was better than no peace at all and they prayed the raids and carrying off to Canada (about 500 English over a ten year period) would finally cease. Some captives, especially if taken as small children, didn't want to return and it took many years for children such as Eunice Mather Williams of Deerfield, adopted by the Mohawks, to leave their indian homes and return to English life. Some captives, victims of torture, never re-integrated and preferred to live in solitude in the wilderness.

It was during these times that John's and Joseph's brother Samuel died. When Samuel first married he had sailed across the sea to Wales with his Denbighshire wife. The English civil war had ended many years prior and the lush, quiet, civilized hills and valleys of an England at peace called men who had lost everything to the flaming arrows of the indians to go back to where their grandparents or great-grandparents had fled to escape religious persecution. The landlubber Davis men had a big advantage on their side: they were smiths and knew how to work iron ore into functional tools and fancy ornaments for the gentry who were building manors with the profits they were making from the sugar trade in the West Indies. Their skills were always in demand wherever they went and Samuel Davis had heard the new gentry were generous.

Samuel's son had married Jemima Easton. Her grandfather William Tilton had died in 1696, the same year as Samuel Davis Sr., and she was to inherit his large estate in Windsor, Hadley and England when her imbecile brother Peter died.

TRISTRUM COMES INTO THE WORLD

In the meantime Joseph expanded his father's farm in Amesbury and went on a visit to Wales to see the old country. They were accompanied for a short while by their sons William, Nathaniel and Joseph, born in Amesbury, and in early 1702 Sarah gave birth to Tristrum in Wales and later Samuel and Isaac. Joseph Sr. wasn't eager to return to New England as too many lives and homes had been lost due to the French and Indian attacks. Humphrey Davis's grandson Pegge, who owned the *Pegge,* doing a steady trade between Newburyport in the north and Virginia and the Barbados, was mastered by his brother John Davis and they needed an agent in the Bristol and to the west in Wales as the Severn River had been dredged and was now providing good inland ports. Duties had been lifted and the Welsh woolen trade was flourishing. The sugar plantations in the West Indies were desperate for any English manufactured goods and, with Joseph being a good blacksmith, as were most of the Davis men, plus a weaver, he could see opportunity on his wife's English lands where there was a lot of iron ore plus a weaver's union was being organized in Devon that would guarantee a steady supply of finishing mills to convert the wool from his estate in Wales, where he had large herds of sheep, into finished cloth. He decided that until things settled in New England he would work and save enough to rebuild what had been lost. What he hadn't factored on was that the English would once again go to war with France, this time under Queen Anne.

His cousin John in Oyster Bay died before the French and Indians attacked the garrisons there, killing or capturing most of John's family and the families of the other residents. In Deerfield his other cousin John's family were taken north to Canada along with the Williams family to be held for ransom. In every northern village the French were leading their savage partners to attack in pre-dawn raids, laying waste to the carefully built and much beloved farms as men were killed and women and children forced to march north under horrendous conditions.

And, if the indian savageries weren't enough, men and women were being accused of witchcraft and hanged by the English in Salem on the basis of a vengeful or jealous neighbor's pointing of the finger.

On his family's ancestral lands in Wales Joseph had found peace. His brother John had returned to New England from his stay in Wales only to be drafted to march to Canada in what was called 'The Snowshoe Expedition' to recapture as many English as possible and bring them home.

Joseph Jr. had gone back to New England but returned to Wales after marrying Sarah Colby.

By the mid 1720s in New England his brother Tristrum bought land north of his cousin John's in Enfield and was busy cutting and clearing, building stone walls and planting. John had married Mary Pease and her relatives were settling the area east of Windsor and south of Springfield. Other relatives of hers were Quakers and, along with Big John Davis had been banished for supporting Anne Hutchinson in Kingston, 18 miles from Dover.

John's brother William Davis was also settling along the Connecticut in the Windsor-Enfield area where in 1723 Cornelius had obtained 2,100 acres for his grandfather John's and his father Cornelius's service in the Narragansett Swamp Fight. (The land was considered to be in Massachusetts but would later be assigned to Connecticut when the boundary lines were redrawn in 1642 that gave Connecticut more land south of Massachusetts' boundary.)

In Wales, Joseph and Jemima, whose brother from Deerfield had been taken captive and held in Canada a long time, and his family of six children and wife lived on a nice estate but they worked the land themselves. Unlike the hard labor of farming in New England where pastures had to be created by cutting forest and digging out tons of rocks from the poor soil, Wales was old. The farms and villages were old. The work had been done by many generations past and as it was now part of Great Britain, the constant warring with the English had ceased so every day it was a joy to go out in the fields and breathe in the clean air, plant, weed, harvest and watch lambs play in the gentle rolling valleys between ancient hills.

CHAPTER SEVENTY

Queen Anne's War, England and France

1690s to early 1700s

King William III was always in poor health. He was thin and had asthma and a perpetual cough. However, he personally joined his generals to go on the attack to bring Ireland into submission.

James II had fled to France but returned to Ireland where he amassed a great army under the promise of Home Rule (freedom from direct rule by England) and Catholic dominance. During his brief reign he had appointed Richard Talbot, Duke of Tyronconell Lord Lt. of Ireland and Talbot replaced Protestants in all the high offices with Catholics. James II had the support of his uncle, Louis XIV of France and his army, like the army of the indians in Canada, were enhanced with French solders and armaments. During his brief tenure Talbot called an Irish Parliament and they passed 35 Acts , including the 'Act for the Repeal of the Act of Settlement' whereby English Protestants sent over by Oliver Cromwell had to give up the rights to the lands they had confiscated from the Irish. The native Irish loved Talbot; the English hated him. One of the ministers in the new Parliament, Thomas Davis, publically stated that he felt the Talbot/James II Irish government had shown great restraint in establishing a taxation program that equally divided the burden and didn't persecute the (mostly) wealthy English settlers.

The Irish fought fiercely and had victories or stand-offs under General Philip Sarsfield against the well-trained and well-equipped English soldiers as their independence was at stake but by 1691 the tide turned. William III had John Churchill, created as the First Earl and later Duke of Marlborough, and the men he had encouraged to desert James II after the defeat of Monmouth, plus a seasoned Dutch general, Duke Frederick Herman Schomberg. The English troops were trained in the manner of Cromwell's New Model Army. When James II retreated to France the Irish lost their French troops and William III with his generals took the last bastion of Limerick. After repeated offers, the Irish finally surrendered in late September, 1691. King William III was very generous in his terms of surrender, offering amnesty and peaceful transportation of the soldiers inside the town's walls either to England or France and promised there would be no reprisals against the Catholics, who were free to practice their religion without persecution. Unlike what happened with William III's victory over Scotland, where England's envelopment of the country under the flag of England offered it the same trade privileges as English harbors under the 'Navigation Acts', the trade laws that prohibited export of the fine Irish cloth and Irish cattle were not repealed and hurt the Protestant merchants as much as the Irish.

However, the Protestant Irish Parliament in 1694 passed onerous anti-Catholic laws, disarmed and depowered the Catholics and enslaved them so severely that many commoners and Ulster Scots boarded ships bound for the territories interior to Maryland and the Carolinas (the Appalachias) where they could live as freemen, own land, vote and practice their religion without penalty.

In 1694 Sir William Phips was recalled to London, where he died. He was replaced by Joseph Dudley as royal governor. Phips had died childless but his widow Mary, daughter of Capt. Roger Spencer, a mariner from Saco was sister-in-law to David Bennet of Rowley. (Mary was Hull's widow at the time of the marriage in 1674.) Spencer was a friend and colleague of Thomas Davis, also a sea captain at the time, who had a simple residence in Saco as early as 1636. Mary's sister Rebecca and David had a son named Spencer and after Sir William's death he took the last name of Phips. Unlike his rakish uncle, he was studious and graduated from Harvard in 1703 with high hopes for the governorship one day.

King William III was not only a great militiary strategist, he was shrewd when it came to foreign commerce. During his reign he expanded England's trade in India and the Far East and the English East India Company surpassed the Dutch East India Company. Spices, cotton cloth, tea, coffee, saltpeter for gunpowder, fancy embroidered shawls and other luxuries continued to make it to London in spite of French privateers. One of the men who made a fortune in India was Thomas Pitt, who then built an impressive manor in Devonshire. A Bank of England was established in 1694 that covered the country's debts with private investors who collected interest on the debt. This replaced the 'forced loan' policy of previous regents.

His war with King Louis XIV of France over the French insistence that James II was the legitimate heir to the English throne was called' King William's War' and raged in France, on the seas and in Canada and northern New England from 1689-1697.

In 1698 King Charles of Spain died without an heir. He named Philip of France, Louis XIV's grandson, as king of all Spanish territory. A contender to the throne, Emperor Leopold of Austria challenged the succession. England was against the uniting of France and Spain via Philip and it put forth a compromise where Leopold would get the Austrian territories and Philip the country of Spain. An united Spain and France poised a direct threat to England's naval trade as a blockade by the two offshore of the Spanish Netherlands would close a critical channel for commerce between England and Europe. England, the Netherlands and Emperor Leopold signed a Grand Alliance. In their determination that an united France and Spain would not be acceptable to the balance of power in Europe they were also adamant that the French shouldn't have Spain's South American colonies. The status of the Spanish Netherlands and disposition of the colonies weren't finalized in the Grand Alliance.

Then James II died and King Louis XIV proclaimed the young James III the legal, rightful heir of the English throne, in violation of the Treaty of Ryswick.

Shortly after, in March 1702, William III died after being wounded while hunting and Tristrum Davis was born in Wales to Samuel and Hannah Edwards. Samuel and Hannah moved back to Wales for a time but then returned to New England. Queen Mary had died previously and there was no accepted male royal heir so her niece, Queen Anne, daughter of James II and Anne Hyde was declared ruler of

England. As she was a devout Protestant no one in the halls of power in England had quarrels with the choice but they definitely had quarrels with Louis XIV and a potential James III and King Philip.

Thus began the European 'War of Spanish Succession'.

In the New World colonies it would be called Queen Anne's War. It raged on the Continent under General Churchill and in Canada the French resumed their assaults upon the English settlers and ships along the northeastern coast.

CHAPTER SEVENTY-ONE

Tristrum

1722

When he'd left Wales Tristrum had first moved in with his uncle Robert in Maine. Robert had married a wealthy widow – she'd been an Adams, Andrews and Alger before she married Robert – as the indians had killed her husbands but left her with a lot of land and money. Robert had been in love with Jane even when she was married to Arthur Andrews whom he and Sylvanus tried to save when the indians ambushed Arrowsick. One of her sons, 30 years older than Tristrum, was named Tristrum Alger Davis in honor of her last husband so they called him Tristrum Alger when Samuel's Tristrum visited in order to avoid confusion.

Tristrum knew from John's surviving relatives at Oyster Bay how the indians could appear just before dawn and, with hideous screams and painted bodies descend like demons from hell upon innocent, peaceful British settlers. When Massachusetts Governor Samuel Shute formally declared war on the Eastern indians in November, 1722, Tristrum had signed up along with John's son John and other Davis kin in south and western Maine.

In June, 1724 he'd been with Captain John Lovewell's company when they came upon his cousin Moses and his son Moses's corpses outside of Dover. Tristrum had always been a bit stoic but he found he couldn't stop crying for two days as the company respectfully buried the brave settlers. The youngest son, Ebenezer, just a year younger than Tristrum, joined their company seeking revenge for the murderers of his family. Capt. Lovewell tried to talk Ebenezer into staying behind to help his mother and Norfolkshire grandmother but Ebenzer was full of anger. He said he'd ran as fast as he could when he saw the war party emerge from the woods and ran, screaming, waving at his father and grandfather as they were planting in the upper field. The desecration of the bodies was beyond comprehension. Blood was everywhere. Ebenezer had gotten off a few shots but none of the savages had been wounded. However, he'd been able to save the others before the house was burned.

After Dover, for the rest of his life Tristrum would associate the smell of burning wood with the smell of blood. These had been his flesh and blood relatives. Suddenly the war had turned very personal, not just for Ebenezer, but for Tristrum, too.

He continued to re-enlist every six months and served in the Colonial Army in Maine under Captain Johnson Harmon and was one of the 208 soldiers in the whale boats that sailed up the Kennebec to the Norridgewock's territory where the English-hating French priest Father Rale was inciting the savages to murder the English settlers. They were there to capture Father Rale but he was killed. Previously Captain Westbook had tried to capture Rale but had only gotten his strongbox – which had letters in it that showed the French were in active war against the English despite saying they weren't.

After killing Father Rale the four colonial companies returned to Fort Richmond triumphantly brandishing 28 scalps, some very small. Tristrum also served under Captains Jermiah Moulton and Kittery's Joseph Heath, one of Mary's relatives. During what he called his 'black years' he'd seen how the savages loved to rip the bloody scalp from their dying victims and even roast some captives alive in torture. Some of the tribes were cannibals and some only ate the liver or heart of their victims.

While his cousins Nathaniel and Isaac were in Wales peacefully farming with Joseph, Tristrum was fighting an enemy he hoped the others would never have to face.

Tristrum knew the old European way of fighting: forming lines, firing in unison, advancing in unison, didn't work with indians. To fight indians one had to hide behind something and fire and if they burned a settlement the British soldiers were to track them down and burn them alive in their wigwams in revenge. All the rules of Continental warfare did not apply to frontier warfare.

After Governor Dummer got the Penobscots to sign a peace treaty in mid December 1725 under which terms they swore allegiance to the British crown and promised to fight on the side of the English in future hostilities, Tristrum headed south, first to his Haverhilll-Amesbury relatives.

Captain Heath's father Josiah Heath from Haverhilll had married Tristrum's cousin Mary Davis around the time of King Philip's War and his cousin Isaac married another cousin named Mary Heath. Tristrum continued the tradition by marrying Josiah Heath Jr.'s sister Mary in Maine. Mary Davises wed Heaths and Mary Heaths wed Davises. The Heaths were neighbors of the Davis clan in England. They lived in Swindon, Wiltshire and the young people either met at church, market days or festivals. In New England it was common if one went back a few generations they'd find out that families had lived close to each other across the sea, such as his cousin Robert's wife Jane Mitton-Andrews-Alger whose father's ancestor was a minister from Wales. What was different in this new land was the lack of the aristocracy. A farmer desperately needed a wife and poor Jane had been widowed repeatedly and re-wed due to the French and Indian wars. There were some wealthy farmers, and further south, wealthy plantation owners, but the average man was not a tenant on the Lord's lands. The average New England free holder was just that: a holder of land, free of bondage to the Lord of the Manor. Every settler belonged to his Godly congregation first, not first to a lord or even a king. Unlike England with rich landowners in the Commons or House of Lords, this land had representatives elected by freemen who only went to Boston occasionally and who had one year terms. (Of course many were the wealthier men and the Winthrops, Winslows, Dudleys, Phips, Bradfords, etc. often passed the positions on from father to son. Which was fine with the average farmer as he was too busy to travel to Boston, Hartford or Salem to partake in sessions of the House of Representatives.) Two of Tristrum's relatives had to serve on the juries during the infamous Witch Trials. Winifred Davis, served on an all-woman jury in Windsor, Ct. and his cousin from Salem who got ensnared in the insanity there said he could never live with himself having sentenced people to hang for behaviour that was odd but not necessarily satanic.

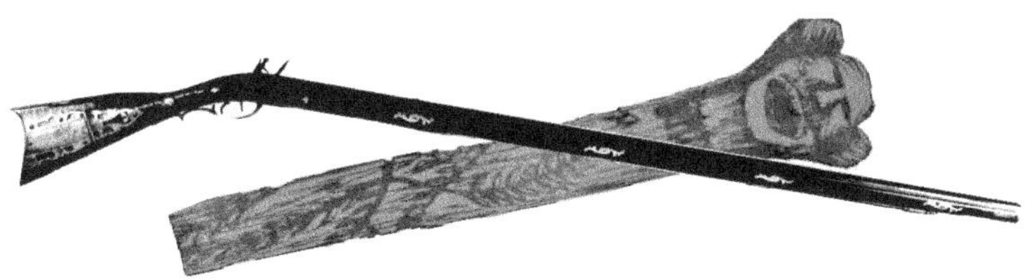

CHAPTER SEVENTY-TWO

Building a Town

1725

During the French and indian wars to the north Jonathan Lamb was in charge of transporting soldiers to Rutland in 1722-3. He met Tristrum Davis during that time and they often talked about where they would settle after the conflict.

Soldiers and their heirs from Hingham, Lynn, Reading and Beverly who fought in the 1685 uprising each received shares in various eight square-mile land grants in payment for their service. (These 'Narragansett Seven' land grants from the northern conflicts and King Philip's Narragansett Swamp Fight weren't allotted by the Massachusetts General Court until 1722-3.)

The soldiers who wanted to settle in the Brimfield area had to surmount a challenge by Wait Winthrop because he had the lead mine claim in the area but in June, 1733 Joseph and Timothy Ruggles and Ebenezer Pierpont got a six square mile grant in the area with the condition that 60 families had to settle the claim within five years. The heirs of Benjamin Church challenged it, claiming they were owed 500 acres but in November, 1733 the Massachusetts General Court accepted a plan put forward by Joshua Lamb and Joseph Wright and 66 others went with him to settle the Cold Springs area near The Elbows. By the terms of the grant each of the 63 Brimfield shareholders plus the minister, were to build a one story house 18 feet square, clear four acres and have another three for 'English grass' and to lay out three shares in the town with 1/63 part of the town for the minister, schoolhouse and meetinghouse. A typical town had a common grazing land in the center with the houses laid out around it. The first public building to be constructed was a meeting house but when the claims were being disputed a storm damaged its uncovered frame and the settlers got so angry they threatened to walk away if they weren't guaranteed their primitive homesteads if the meetinghouse weren't immediately reconstructed. Tristrum and his friends the Blodgetts preferred to settle outside the town limits as Tristrum's relatives were south of Brimfield.

Once the Eastward in Maine quieted down Tristrum and his brothers wasted no time to move inland from the Connecticut River to settle the vast stretches of valleys south of Brookfield and Worcester and east of Enfield. The river towns were nice because they gave instant access to shipping but the Davis men who went inland were farmers at heart. Their Welsh souls responded to the lushly vegetated gentle hills and valleys with their old forests. Away from the bustle of the river towns a man could truly speak to God from the top of his sloped hay field.

Tristrum and Mary settled in what was initially called Brimfield but then their area was split off into South Brimfield. The large grant of Brimfield would later be partitioned into Monson on the west, Holland on the east a new town further south was formed called Union but it was in Connecticut. Brookfield was to the northeast and the Bay Path ran from Brimfield to the Dudley/Oxford area and later through Worcester and on to Boston.

Technically, Brimfield was granted permission to settle in 1722 with Jonathan Belcher submitting the petition to the Massachusetts House of Representatives but it was another decade before all the conflicting claims were ironed out. In the meantime Tristrum stayed with his cousin, James and Cicely's son grandson John in Enfield.

A farmer bonds with his land and so it was with Tristrum. He and Mary, with the help of neighbors or family, worked on both building a proper house and outbuildings for their cows, sheep and chickens and clearing spots for her kitchen garden and crops. A well was hand-dug and lined with the large stones their plows constantly turned up in the fields. Mary was pregnant with the second child within a year of Mary's birth, the pattern of a child every two years common to the women in New England.

The second child, a son whom they named John, was born during a blizzard just before dawn in the middle of February, a cruel, cold month in New England. Winter was when the maple trees were tapped for the precious sap that they would boil into a syrup that substituted for sugar or molasses. The goal of a farmer was to provide for most of his needs, going to the stores only to trade for goods he could not provide for himself. As John let out his first cry, Tristrum said a prayer of thanks to God for a son as a farmer needed many sons to help him with all the daily tasks. Mary had said a similar prayer when Mary was born as a farmer's wife also needed extra hands to help with her tasks. Farming was a hard job but more so in the wilderness where nothing was ready made. But, as Tristrum and Mary sat looking out over their fields at the end of the day, they smiled and held hands, pleased at what in just two years they had accomplished. Here, inland, away from the rivers, they were mostly safe from indian raids. John Eliot had tamed the handful of indians living between the Brimfields and Brookfield and they were in a Praying Village next to the Freeman farm. The only problem that Tristrum and Mary, and other outliers had, was that the meeting house was a fair trek on the Sabbath. Settlers closer to the Big Pond, later called Lake George after the king, were talking about building a meeting house at its northern edge. This would make the Sabbath easier for the outliers as there was a prayer meeting, the almost all day Sabbath, to which they brought a picnic lunch, and then fast days as declared by the governor to ask for the Lord's forgiveness for their many sins.

Tristrum's first house was a one room affair with a straw filled mattress on the rope-frame bed in one corner, the fireplace and chimney along the opposite wall with a home made wooden table and chairs in front of its hearth and a rocking chair and cradle plus a chest that Mary kept her precious linens in. Tristrum had built crude shelves and an even cruder basin stand for the pitcher and basin but next to their little 'hut 'he and his relatives were already digging out the foundation for a proper four-and-four two story clapboard sided home that would have real slate roof shingles as a slate deposit had been found nearby.

Homesteading was hard work but the pioneers were up to the task. The men grew harder and tougher and stronger but the women tended to grow weaker as constant childbearing and nursing took its toll. In 1732 they'd had a daughter, named Mary. Two years later, in November, near the annual Thanksgiving Day in remembrance of the early pilgrims first harvest in Plymouth, a son, named John, was born. His birth was followed almost to the day four years later by another son, this one named Joseph in 1740 and Benjamin in 1742. In between was Elizabeth.

The basic farm house had been built by then so Mary had a proper bedroom in which to bring the squalling infant into the world. Helped by Dolor's grandsons who lived nearby in the Worcester-Dudley area, the house had two large fireplaces with the parlor on the right, a sitting room behind it, the kitchen on the left with a dining room behind it with a central staircase running up the middle on the left of the entry hallway. Beneath the stairs was a pantry and the door to the cellar. The upstairs had two large rooms with small storage rooms set off behind them and a nice attic ran the whole length of the house. It was a fine house. Nothing as grand as the old English and Welsh homes his ancestors had lived in, but for New England in its first century of English occupation, this house with its deep, earthy cellar and large, attic with a window at each end, was as fine a house as could be found anywhere nearby.

Just south of South Brimfield was the town of Union, settled primarily by Scots-Irish. These were Scottish Puritans that fled the religious persecutions and went to northern Ireland but were now being forced out by failed harvests or deportations. Scotland was at war with King George and those allied with the clans in Northern Scotland fighting the King were wise to flee to New England in case they were persecuted by association. The Stuarts had been Scots and King George I detested anything Scottish, especially anyone who had also had ties to the French whose king kept backing the Stuarts' claim to the English throne.

Unlike Union, Brimfield was mostly old English or Welsh families such as the Needhams, Moultons, Meachums, Hitchcocks, Sessions, Davises and others. Union had Irish surnames such as McNall, the surname of the leading family there.

The town center of Brimfield was a good hour's ride from Tristrum's farm. It had a common and a large meeting house plus intersected with the Bay Path, the main east-west route, that then ran north towards the Brookfields (where he had many relatives) and northwest to the Connecticut River towns of Halley and Northampton (where Samuel was) and others. West, it ran through Palmer (King's large land grant), through meadows and valleys, over hills to Springfield, the main city in western Massachusetts: John Pynchon's Springfield. The Pynchons owned land all over the place. John Pynchon owned a share of Brimfield and of course had an interest in the lead mine near Holland Pond. Tristrum's best friend was Joseph Blodgett who owned the farm just southeast of his. In time the larger grants would be broken up and given names honoring English gentry, such as the Warrens, Thorndykes or Belchers. Oxford was named for its English sister town although the one outside Worcester, named for the Earl of Worcester, was a crude village without any colleges. Cambridge boasted Harvard and New Haven had Yale and more schools of higher learning were being established as the Puritans felt everyone needed to be able to read the word of God: the Bible.

Tristrum's farm was adjacent to the Blodgett Place and the Davises and Blodgetts went back a fair way. When Tristrum brought his wife Mary to the farm he was only 30 years old – in his prime – and as the leaves were turning in their woods their first child, a daughter named Mary after her mother, was born in October, 1732. Their rough house had been knocked together by Tristrum and his brothers on a low plateau overlooking what would be pastures and crop fields. His land had a large brook on one side and a smaller brook coming down the back acreage. There were swampy spots near the brooks but two ponds on the land for watering livestock. To the side with the large brook, which came from Brimfield and beyond, there was a line of hills and low hills surrounded, but didn't smother, Tristrum's fair farmlands. An indian trail had been enlarged to follow the larger brook which was a tributary of the *Quinebaug* river. After the great pond the river flowed south towards John's lands and there were more ponds and fair pasturelands all around.

At town meetings there was always talk about who was to be constable, selectmen, town clerk and so on, all posts Tristrum avoided like the plague. A person was bound to make enemies even if he had the job of fence surveyor. Plus, although he'd never admit it, Tristrum couldn't read very well since his early education had been mostly oral and in Gaelic, the Welsh language that was supposed to be banned but was still spoken all over Wales. He even had a Gaelic Bible. However, Tristrum was very good with flintlocks and muskets so he captained the local militia which met at regular intervals to drill. This job he took very seriously as he knew from his own personal experience the savage enemy could be lurking in the shadows.

In the little towns as long as a man paid his taxes to cover the minister's expenses and others such as for a school and maintenance of the highways he was pretty much free to live as he pleased, in accordance with the morals of the Congregational church he and his family belonged to.

Most of the town squabbles were over the common lands and whether a new or second meeting house was to be built. New roads or mills would also present problems as no one wanted their water diverted or their lands crossed unless they were personally profiting from the mill, etc. but in general most of the townspeople put their shoulders to the collective plow and worked ceaselessly to clear land, plant, harvest, slaughter livestock, build stone wall fences or split rail fences to keep livestock in, build outbuildings and read their Bible at least once a day. The Sabbath was supposed to be a day of rest, and for the women it mostly was as they wouldn't cook a hot dinner, but there were chickens, horses, oxen, sheep, cows, pigs and goats to feed and water and cows to be milked and firewood to be split if a farmer didn't have enough stored. The women needed a lot of kindling and small wood for Monday, which was wash day. Then they needed more for their baking day, usually in the middle of the week. Farm chores knew no calendars. The calendar was the weather. The threat of rain would move up hay harvesting. Too much rain in May could delay planting and so on.

Even though Tristrum didn't want a town post South Brimfield did recognize and reward his skills in battle. He was a good militia captain and his men respected him. The British soldiers who passed through the town from Brookfield en route to Northampton or Halley or Springfield wore bright red coats that made them instant targets of the enemy. They marched by day in formation. Tristrum told his men to wear buff or brown in order to blend in with their surroundings and to use boulders or trees to shelter them when moving or firing. He'd take them into the woods as part of their training and have them try to ambush each other. He said there could be no hesitation whatsoever when faced with the enemy: it was kill or be killed. Until this last war the men had been a bit complacent but now even garrison soldiers were charged with dereliction of duty by their communities and the matter would be brought before the House of Representatives in Boston. But some were generously rewarded for going the extra mile, such as Sergeant John Lamb at Castle William who had been left solely in charge of the fort with no help in Boston

Harbor. However, even in time of war settlers resented having to billet garrison soldiers, forgetting how they cried for them to come when needed.

When not training the militia how to use the flintlock, Tristrum hunted with it. He was a good hunter and brought many deer home for Mary to butcher. Now that his oldest son was of an age to accompany him they would bring deer, opossums, rabbits, pheasants, wild turkeys and any other game to be found in the woods around the cleared farmstead. Once they shot a black bear and another time a mountain lion. These were for the pelts as the settlers didn't care for the rank tasting meat. Sometimes even a wolf could be shot and there was good bounty money for a wolf pelts, but the other pelts were good trading items. Once a family of beavers set up a dam on the smaller brook above his farm and Tristrum and his son killed them off one by one to bring the beaver pelts into Pynchon's trading post on the Connecticut. Unfortunately beaver hats were going out of fashion in Europe but the locals still valued the water repellant hides.

In Enfield to his south his brother Williams and cousin John were using the warehouses built on the river to store tobacco (original plants brought courtesy of his sea-going cousins Robert and James to the north) and other goods until they made a big trip once or twice a year downriver to the big trading centers on the coast or even across the waters to the city of New York. Northeast of Tristrum his cousins, mostly descendants of Dolor, in Dudley, Oxford and Worcester were trading more with Boston as the road was being improved with every passing year. This was one thing the settlers had trouble adjusting to: the lack of good, cobble stoned roads. In Britain the Romans had done two things that the people were grateful for: they had laid good, solid cobblestone roads and had taught the people how to divert waters to drain swamps or irrigate crops. He'd heard in Europe they had built a system of aqueducts to bring water to towns, and one was built through a mountain! Nice, solid stone buildings were also a Roman inheritance. Sad to say many of the castles and manors built afterwards were in decay due to poor lime mortar or poor siting or cannon fire. Even cathedrals crashed, such as the one at Salisbury that had to be rebuiLt. due to poor siting on a wetland. Of course, the Welsh said it was due to dragons fighting beneath the ground but Tristrum, good Christian that he was, discounted the Druid tales as fairy fiction. In New England roads, or highways, as they were called, were so important that once a year the townspeople gathered and collectively worked on fixing the spots that had fallen into disrepair. Indeed, a farmer was responsible for the road running in front of his house. This was hard for Tristrum as he didn't have a large family to help maintain it and the road ran along the hillside that ran further down to the fields and the main brook. There was talk of setting up toll stations on some of the major roads near the largest towns as the roads received heavy wear and tear.

He seriously considered inviting his uncle Joseph and his family in Wales to join them. He missed his brothers and missed hearing the old Welsh songs and eating some of the Welsh dishes that Jemima had learned to cook. Mary was a good cook but not very imaginative. He especially missed the turkey cooked with cherries and liver sausage. Mary attempted it once with raisins and apples – the latter grew in abundance on his farm – and the wild grapes made a type of wine, but it wasn't as good as the imported stuff. It just wasn't the same. Cranberries went well with turkey but had to be purchased from the coast as they didn't grow well inland. And they took a lot of precious sweetening to make them palatable. What seems to do best on his rock-studded farm was livestock. Every year a new crop of rocks erupted at plowing time. Whereas the stones were free fence and building material, they slowed the plowing and he suspected many a seed disappeared beneath stones, never to sprout in the sunlight.

In 1739 England declared war on Spain over a sailor named Jenkyns, whose ear was cut off in a West Indian port by the Spanish. Britain got the governor of the new state of Georgia – a rice producing, slave-heavy state north of Florida – to attack St. Augustine so Florida could become part of England's territory. Tristrum had stopped in the Barbados on his voyage to Maine from Wales and had seen what slavery was like and, despite wishing he had more hands to work his fields and woods, he detested the practice of buying a human life to abuse and treat like a dog. Since then he had sworn off sugar and he and Mary only used the sugar from their maple trees and its sap. He was thinking of swearing off tea as he heard the British used the Indians in India like slaves on their tea plantations but coffee was very expensive and it, too, was planted, harvested and shipped by slaves. Mostly he drank cider, made from his own apple trees, and good, clear well water. When having neighbors over to help he and Mary would bring out the precious port or wine they kept down in the cellar but for everyday drinking the children had curds in with the whey that wasn't fed to the chickens or hogs. Milk that wasn't converted into butter or cheese was rare and the adults drank cider, tea and water. They were fortunate that the water on his farm was clean and 'sweet'. In the cities and near Boston water was often contaminated and cholera and other diseases spread from house to house. Living as an outlier had its disadvantages but living in cramped villages could be bad for your health.

To the far north Spencer Phips, adopted son of Governor Phips, Thomas Westbrook and a man named Samuel Waldo, son of a rich Boston merchant, had bought up most of the early patents and were establishing new, fortified trading ports. The first one was called St. George. It was on the George River and had a nice, sturdy fort. There was also Fort Richmond. Many of the families from the Lincoln area that had been burned out by the savages had settled there and it was promising to do very well. Waldo was now importing a lot of Germans to settle a second trading port in Broad Bay. These were the Palatine Germans displaced by all the years of war between the countries on the Continent. Heirs of the Clarke and Lake Company were resettling Arrowsick and Robert Temple was settling people back onto the lands the indians had burned and ravaged. In New Casco (Falmouth) there was a truck house and another in Saco called Fort Mary. The indians were not happy when they had to travel distances to bring in beaver pelts that were now worth less and very unhappy that under new laws the English wouldn't sell them firewater, their name for liquor.

CHAPTER SEVENTY-THREE

The Soldiers Come for Issac

1740

In New England they were still fighting over religion. William Davis's Quaker cousins on the Cape and Long Island weren't being put to death anymore thanks to the 'Act of Tolerance' England passed but if a person weren't a member of an organized Congregational church he or she was still considered an outcast.

The basic rights of voting and freedom from having to pay the salary of another religion's minister in one's annual taxes were still being fought for. William's cousins on Long Island established a community of Quakers and the Crown had granted a territory called Pennsylvania to William Penn and others for Quakers but in New England there was still controversy over the Quakers' pacifism and their refusal to swear an oath to the king. England had moderated and allowed an alternative statement that allowed them to declare a form of allegiance without putting the King higher than God, the only authority they answered to.

In Wales Joseph Davis felt it was ironic that New England was founded by people persecuted for their religious beliefs yet the Puritan oligarchy persecuted the Hutchinsons, Wheelwrights, Williams, Gortons and anyone else who didn't subscribe to their form of worship. Sarah's ancestors had been with the Cottons and a son was baptized the same day in Boston as Seaborn Cotton but by 1740, a little over a century, many New Englanders were still being persecuted for religious differences.

The Civil War had ruined many of the old castles and estates and years of poverty, plague and famine had decimated England, Wales and Ireland and the recently vanquished Scotland. When Joseph Jr. and Sarah Colby had come back on their honeymoon they were greeted by a country eager for new workers as many had been deported as political prisoners to serve as indentured servants in the West Indies and Virginia.

The Davis family was either loved or hated, depending on whether one was in their wealthier class or had relatives slaving away on tobacco or sugar plantations. As they were a maritime family they were loved when they bought goods to resell in the colonies but spat on when they sold imported goods at a price to cover their shipping expenses. However, they, and families like theirs, provided many good jobs: carpenters, shipwrights, blacksmiths, weavers, etc. but depending on the state of the economy were either in or out of good favor with locals and even the government.

Great Britain was constantly at war. The long wars with France and Spain were draining its resources. Joseph and his family on their large, beautiful farm in Wales tried to stay out of politics. His brother, who lived with them, was more outspoken but when King George II's soldiers appeared in their red uniforms on Isaac Davis's 16th birthday in 1740 as the men were working in the fields and grabbed the youth to be sent to fight the French Joseph became a different man.

The soldiers approached on horseback, callously knocking down hay that had yet been harvested. The men who were cutting the stalks with sickles and the women who were tying them into sheaves looked up, angry at the intrusion.

"This one!' the officer in command shouted, pointing at Isaac.

The other soldiers surrounded him with their horses,

"What's this?" demanded Joseph.

"Britain's at war with Spain, or haven't ye heard?" the officer in charge barked. His woolen uniform was ringed with sweat as it was a hot day in Wales – a perfect day to cut hay so it could dry and be brought in nice and dry for winter feed, The officer in charge announced, "The King needs men."

"Take me," Joseph cried, throwing down his sickle, "I can fight. I'm strong. Isaac is just a boy,"

"Nay, look at 'im," the officer replied as Isaac was forcibly hoisted behind a soldier, "Ye have a family to support, man. He can be spared."

Isaac looked back, his face full of woe, as the soldiers galloped off to the next farm.

Joseph's son Nathaniel, who had been working in the upper field, came running.

"What happened?"

"They impressed Isaac," Joseph said over the cries of his wife and children.

"Why?"

"Why else? That lop eared pirate, 'tis why. It wasn't eno' for England to get the thirty year asiento or monopoly on the African slave trade to the West Indies sugar plantations (which I refused to be part o') and to the rice and tobacco plantations in the southern states now including Georgia and the Carolinas in the 'Treaty of Utrecht' under Queen Anne. Plus the privilege to fill up a 620 tun ship full o' Spanish loot every year in the South American ports. Nay, England had to let rouges like Jenkyns run all around the Caribbean sneaking in and out o' ports in violation o' our treaty. War with Spain means it won't be long til they be a'fightin the French over Canada again. Sir Robert Walpole, a good Norfolkshire man, kept this land free o' war, lowered the excise and land taxes and has done us much good but he's being pushed out by that Bolingbroke's clique, led by Henry Pelham, Duke of Newcastle. Pelham is in with William Pitt, who I am ashamed to say hails from our lands near Tisbury in Wiltshire."

Joseph sighed heavily, "Our Isaac might have to go back to where we escaped from to face those brutal French and their savage armies."

"'Tisn't right," said Nathaniel, who was shorter with jet black hair and blue eyes like his cousin Tristrum, unlike his father who had fair skinned Viking features. The genetic mixed bag of dark Moor, Celtic, and tall, fair Vikings was common in English families due to the invasions of the Danes, Romans and even Germanic races who raped and impregnated the natives of the isles. The Irish and Scottish had more of the red haired Danish blood but descended from Welsh royalty were shorter and darker skinned.

As the sun cast long shadows on the fields, Sarah was weeping, surrounded by the younger children.

"Just seems we can't get away from it," said Joseph as he sat down and drank from the clay switchel ring.

"I'm going back!" Nathaniel declared, "William, John and Tristrum have written to me many times saying I'd be more than welcome to come work on their farms. I'll try to find Isaac if he is sent there and see if I can protect him or, if he's captured, redeem him."

"Aye, they had a bad spell for a while with Deerfield, Brookfield and Northfield being attacked but where me brothers are is in the mid Connecticut Valley and it is quieter than up to the north."

"Cornelius has a lot of land. He's offered for ye to come, too," said Nathaniel.

Joseph sighed heavily. He was fighting back tears. The sight of his son disappearing on the back of the soldier's mount would live with him forever.

"Aye. We moved here to run away from that but there comes a time when ye have to fight. I suppose Jemima and me and the young ones will be a'goin back, too. Through her grandfather she's inherited a lot of land in Halley and Windsor so there'll be no shortage of farms to work."

"I'm going to fight, father! I'm going to drive them damned savages back to hell!" Nathaniel exclaimed, his fist hitting the side of the hay cart for emphasis, "That's our land, our blood and sweat cleared it and made roads and built homes that they burned down. But they didn't take the foundation stones and, by God – "

His father cut him off, scowling at taking the Lord's name in vain.

The father and his oldest son sat quietly, the hay untouched. In the distance they could see clouds forming over the mountains.

Joseph sighed deeply, "Well, we best be loading up the carts, 'Twill truly be a sad harvest without Isaac, but we can't let the livestock starve due to our grief."

CHAPTER SEVENTY-FOUR

A Letter from Wales

1740

A letter had come from Tristrum's uncle Joseph in Wales just before his third son was born. He told of Isaac's impressment and how Nathaniel was going to volunteer in order to find his brother and look after him. Joseph asked if Tristrum felt the place was safe now should he and Jemima decide to move back.

As Mary lay upstairs in her childbed, covered with a fine quilt she had sewn by hand and stuffed with wool from their sheep, who were housed in the cellar during the coldest time of the year, he re-read the letter in his English rocking chair.

Anticipating her delivery, Mary had set out cold beef, cheese and bread along with beer and Tristrum and the young children ate a cold supper while the wind picked up outside.

"Looks like snow's a'coming," he said to the six year old John and eight year old Mary, "Ye need to get out to the barn and make sure the cattle are well hayed and watered and, this to four year old Elizabeth, "Ye need to make sure the hen coop is well shut and they have lots of hay to bed in. I'll get the rope attached to the back door as this'll probably be just the first layer o' snow and if we get a blizzard ye'll need the rope when ye go to the outhouse or sheds."

After the tasks were done and small flecks of snow began swirling around in the moonlight, Tristrum lit a lamp and he and the children went upstairs after banking, or covering, the coals in the downstairs fireplaces. Upstairs they lit the fire in the children's bedroom over the living room and parlor and then put more logs on the fireplace in Mary and Tristrum's bedroom across a hall landing and over the kitchen and dining room.

Mary woke as Tristrum shucked off his pants and shirt and slipped into bed in his long nightshirt.

"How's the little fella doing?" he asked as he stroked its little red, black-haired head.

"Benjamin's a strong one," Mary said, almost in a whisper, exhausted from the birth. The midwife had left hours ago but Mary had hardly drank any tea or cider and had refused food.

"I got a letter from me uncle Joseph in the old country," he said into the dark.

"Joseph?" she asked, putting her own little Joseph, two years old and sleeping next to her, to her breast. He was almost weaned and only needed a suckle at bedtime. Now all the milk would go to the newest babe.

Mary and Joseph, thought Tristrum. Mother and child. Not the holy Mary the Catholics worshiped but a human woman chosen by God to bear His holy son.

"The redcoats took his Isaac to send over here to fight the French and indians."

"Oh, no!" Mary said, more of a sigh than an exclamation.

"Aye, and Nathaniel's a'goin to enlist to come over, too. Joseph is thinking of moving his family back across the sea to be closer to them."

Mary shook her head on the down-filled pillow, encased in her beautifully embroidered linen.

"Where's he thinking of settling?" she asked quietly.

"He has his choice, he says – up north near Haverhilll or even further north to the Eastward or on the Cape – anywheres here in the Valley, or even Long Island as Sarah's brother has a Quaker settlement there."

"Is he a Quaker, then?" she asked with alarm.

"Nay, I don't think so, goodwife. Ye know we Davises are a contentious lot and got involved in a lot of that dissension early on with Winthrop and the Dudleys but methinks he might settle next to Cornelius or William or John, makes the most sense. O' course the Tiltons are involved and that complicates things, them being very rich and all."

"Does he know about Deerfield and our John's family? That terrible, terrible attack and all those people taken to Canada by the indians?" she asked softly.

"Aye. He's not interested in there but his wife's family owns a lot of land in Halley."

Mary closed her eyes and in the moonlight that streamed through the panes of wavy glass Tristrum kissed her on the cheek, then kissed his youngest son.

"'Tis one reason many men are starting to talk about breaking off with Great Britain," he whispered, "they say we'll never know peace if we are tied to the war-loving King's apron strings."

The wind picked up, howling around the snug house, the snow pinging off the windows and white clapboard siding. Tristrum debated whether to close the shutters but felt so much peace in the bed next to his beloved helpmate, his Eve, he had no desire to get up and cross the plank flooring. Mary had put hand-braided rugs down in the bedroom but even with his woolen socks the floor would be cold beneath his feet.

"Joseph says there's a new campaign starting against them Frenchies," he told his sleeping wife and son, "There's coming a day when we will have to settle this whole Canada thing once and for all. When the time comes, me Mary, I will have to go to battle, too. Ye need to be strong for the children when that day comes."

The moon went behind a cloud and the room went dark. Tristrum said a prayer of Thanksgiving for his wife and children and his many blessings and then said a prayer for his nephews' safety in the King's Army.

CHAPTER SEVENTY-FIVE

Beginning of the The French and Indian War

1744

Although New Englanders weren't intimately affected by European wars they read enough to know that France, Spain, the Netherlands, the Austrian Netherlands (the prize they were really fighting over this time), Prussia, Germany, Austria, Italy and all the other countries were constantly jockeying for power and to either establish new possessions such as those in India – which made families such as the Pitts from the Davis territory in Wiltshire immensely rich – or to keep territories. And France kept harboring Stuart pretenders to the throne. Tristrum knew England lusted after Spain's South American possessions and after France's northern ones and as much as he tried to ignore it, felt New England was going to be squeezed as in a vise between the two.

Now in 1744 Tristrum had two relatives in the British Army and knew if a peace weren't reached war would corrode the peacefulness of their humble, new villages. He would serve if asked but knew with a young family he'd be one of the last called. He thanked God his sons were still too young to have to face the horrors of war with the skulking, vicious savages.

"Father, I snared a gopher!" six year old Joseph excitedly as he ran up the fields, his trophy heavily dangling from his thin arm.

"Well done, son!" Tristrum beamed although it was only good for pig feed, "One less to eat our crops!"

Then Tristrum suddenly grabbed the boy and told him to stand still. Two rattlesnakes were just beyond them, sunning themselves on rocks.

"Stand back, boy!" he commanded as he swung his shovel and got one of them. The other slithered like quicksilver into the high grass. He hoped he got the female. The pigs killed many of the snakes on the hill across the road – it was called rattlesnake hill as it was full of those vipers and adders and the ponds with water moccasins – but everyone had to be careful as this was raw land, still occupied by wildcats, snakes, foxes, wolves and every variety of wildlife.

Joseph immediately ran over to the snake, bending over it as it writhed in its death throes.

"Don't grab it, boy. 'Taint dead til it stops moving. Let it be and come back later but be careful of its fangs, they still carry poison."

Joseph, enthralled as are all young boys by snakes, couldn't wait to go get his younger brothers Benjamin and Tristrum junior and show them it but he heeded his father's warning and said he'd wait until later.

"Now, get yerself up to the house and wash for dinner," his father said sternly, "And maybe next time ye can catch one o' them pesky raccoons that been a'stealin eggs from the henhouse!"

"Yes, father," young Joseph said as he dragged his feet home. Tristrum noticed the leather on one of his soles was sprouting a hole. Shoes were one thing they had to buy. He'd repair a pair as best as he could but after time and after going through more than one child's pair of feet, leather shoes were little more than patching material for newer shoes. One of his cousins set up a shoe factory near the Merrimac River but he didn't get a family discount. He was a shrewd trader, though, and knew he'd work a deal to his advantage next time he went to Springfield. He'd been nicknamed "Cheatum" by his neighbors for his sharp dealings but Tristrum wasn't ashamed of the moniker as he felt it showed a good business sense. A New England farmer had to be religious and industrious, make use of any opportunity presented. One of his favorite sayings was "God helps them as helps themselves."

Humming an old Welsh song he hefted his shovel and hoe over his muscular shoulder and walked uphill towards the delicious scent of bread as it was Mary's baking day and the younger boys had been helping since dawn splitting and carrying kindling and the girls with the kneading of the heavy wheat, corn and rye dough.

He smiled. The sun was shining. God was in His Heaven and, for now at least, on this little farm in an area the indians had called *Quaboag*, Tristrum was at peace with the world.

****

After what had been dubbed 'Queen Anne's War and 'Dummer's War', Fort Frederick, named for King George's son Frederick, Prince of Wales, was built by the English in the area the English first settled called Sagadahoc. The French also built a Fort Frederick at Crown Point in upper New York. In 1727 Governor William Bennet of New York personally paid to have Fort Oswego built on the New York side of the Niagara River, a critical control point for river-to-sea trade. The French built Fort Niagara on the opposite side where the Niagara River entered Lake Ontario.

At Sagadahoc Col. David Dunbar led new settlement plans and was granted a patent for the area from the Kennebec to the St. Croix River as an independent state, not the property of Massachusetts. Dunbar, himself Scots-Irish, imported wave after wave of immigrants from Northern Ireland to repopulate what the French called Acadia. Massachusetts Governor Jonathan Belcher and Samuel Waldo, whose property was included in the 'new' territory, and other prominent men were incensed at Dunbar's actions and Belcher threatened to send forces to make the colony submit but it was under the protection of King George II.

Massachusetts filed a complaint with the Board of Trade which got the new patent overturned in 1731. Waldo had St. George Fort built inland in a bay on the St. George River to the northeast of the original settlement of Sagadahoc to protect the inhabitants. The old settlers felt strongly that Massachusetts hadn't done enough to protect them in the past and the new settlers were determined to defend themselves, regardless of what Massachusetts did. John Davis and his son Jedediah from the Kittery area were two of the local militia and Tristrum's cousin Nicholas had taken over the captaincy of the *Trader's Increase* which sailed from Acadia all the way down the coast to the Barbados, Jamaica, Cuba and Santa Domingo plus Virginia, the Carolinas and Georgia. As a merchantman he was open to opportunity and had seized Spanish ships in the Caribbean, sending half the booty back to King George II.

In 1744 war was officially declared by England against France. The year before King George II personally led troops in battle at Dettingen to fight on the side of Maria Theresa, who had assumed the Austrian throne four years before. Under Lord Stair the army proceeded through Germany but was trapped at Hanau by French troops in late June. Sword in hand, the Germanic-English King George II led a brave charge against the enemy and the troops were able to escape. For England the stakes were the Austrian Netherlands, a vital trading position on the continent. And also the right of the Hanoverian regency as France still supported the Scottish Stuarts's claim to the throne.

In March 1744 in North America the French didn't wait for the official declaration to reach them. In mid May 1744 Governor Dusquenil of Nova Scotia sent savages into the trading post at Annapolis Royal to spy on the English and report its weaknesses. He subsequently sent a force under Father LeLoutre and Monsieur Clermont with 600 Micmac and Machites, indians from Cape Sable and St. John, plus French soldiers to try to take the fort but the Lt. Governor of Annapolis, Paul Masacrene bravely defended the fort and with the arrival of Captain Edward Tyng in the *Province Snow* with 80 men in early July drove them off. Capt.Tyng left soldiers to rebuild the badly deteriorated fort, penned the pigs and ships roaming wild and left to alert Boston to the attack. He said the French at Annapolis thought his ship was from Ft. Lousibourg and actually sailed out to meet it, fleeing once they saw their error.

The French had previously seized a fishing village and its garrison at Canso in the northern tip of Nova Scotia. Taken by surprise and with little reserves with which to fight, the garrison surrendered. The prisoners were sent to the French fort at Louisbourg on Cape Breton.

Fort Louisbourg was in disrepair and the French were barely able to support themselves in the surrounding village, let alone a large group of English prisoners. Faced with possible revolt by their own people, the French released the prisoners, shipping them to Boston.

Massachusetts had declared the United Colonies to be on a war footing and sent reinforcements to break the sieges of the northeastern forts.

In June, 1744 New York's Gov. Clinton called the sachems of the Six Nations to Albany to try to work out a peace treaty with his representatives Thomas Hutchinson, Jacob Wendell, Thomas Berry, John Choate and John Stoddard. He invoked the famous 'covenant chain' of his predecessor to attempt to solidify an alliance. The sachems said they wouldn't be the aggressors against the French but didn't pledge their allegiance to England, either. The Western Mohawks were the only tribe that wanted to remain neutral but the Eastern bands didn't commit themselves to honoring Dummer's Treaty as they had blood relatives in many of the Eastern tribes.

That summer French ships harried English fishing and trading from Louisbourg all the way down to the West Indies. Nine fishing vessels and a large merchantman from Ireland were seized before the tide turned and the English, with the aid of privateers and Quakers from Rhode Island and Pennsylvania and the warship *Prince of Orange* ruled the seas from the Grand Banks to the gulfs of St. Lawrence Seaway and Maine.

Waldo's fort at St. George was reinforced and held 40 men and officers. Fort Richmond at the head of the Kennebec River had 29 soldiers and Ft. George at Brunswick and Fort Frederick at Pemiquid were reinforced by Massachusetts. The governor of Massachusetts, William Shirley, had asked Captain Jabez Bradbury, truck master and commander of Waldo's Fort George, to use his Penobscot contacts to ascertain the situation to the north. The indians let him know they had been warned by the French to withdraw if they didn't want to be part of the upcoming hostilities. The natives had been peacefully coexisting with the settlers for decades and had no desire to raise their war sticks but the priests in the missions had the eastern tribes worked up to a frenzy and the new Scotch-Irish settlers were in the mood to fight so the situation was tense.

CHAPTER SEVENTY-SIX

Gov. Shirley's War

1745-9

Whereas Swansea had been repeatedly threatened in King Philip's War, in the early 1700s the northern settlements of Deerfield and Northfield took the brunt of the first 'French and Indian Wars'. Almost whole towns were ambushed and the men killed with the women and children carried off to Canada. The settlements to the north in what would be called Maine and New Hampshire were likewise attacked and even northern New York, despite Gov. Clinton's efforts to seek neutrality from the Six Nations.

As with many families, the Davis clans had families in Maine, the northern towns, either in Massachusetts or New Hampshire, on Cape Cod and along the coast from Rhode Island to New Jersey. Branches moved inland such as John Davis who settled in Somers, which was part of Massachusetts at the time, and Simon and Samuel who favored Oxford and Dudley. Other Davis families settled in Northampton, Halley, Brookfield and Springfield, sometimes relocating if their garrisons and farms were burned out. The savages preferred to lie in ambush and get a husband and wife going out to milk early in the morning or young men rounding up cattle or horses from the forests in the afternoon or small groups of men taking grain to the mills or a farmer threshing grain in his barn.

Repeatedly until the end of 'Governor Shirley's War' the Forts George, Massachusetts and Fort Number Four were prime targets for major attacks of troops comprised primarily of northern indians, led by French officers and sometimes priests.

Like Clinton, Shirley was close to the Duke of Newcastle at court in England. He came over to New England in 1733. During his time as governor he lived in Boston in Province House kitty corner to that of his daughter Harriet, wife of Robert Temple (with Maine connections) ,who lived in a fine house in the middle of Boston on Milk Street. He also had his original land in Roxbury on the Dorchester boundary.

In the spring of 1744 Gov. Shirley ordered 300 troops raised to be sent to the Eastward (coast of Maine) and Capt. Edward Tyng (related by marriage or ships to most of the marine families in Maine and New England), in his ship the *Prince of Orange* had arrived at Annapolis fort in time to relieve its siege by the French. The combined French and indians were driven off but Tyng found the rubble of a fort had been so neglected that hogs and sheep roamed all over the ruins. Tyng left men to pen the livestock, reinforce and rebuild it and by December, 1744 it even had a contingent of indian rangers, or scouts in it.

After Annapolis Tyng sailed to Fort Louisbourg, which was held by the French but was the next target on Shirley's list to be taken and held for England. While Tyng was at Annapolis Capt. David Donahue and his brother with his ship the *Resolution* plus two armed war ships brought 900 soldiers from Annapolis to Louisbourg to bombard it. The ships were to bring to Louisbourg 200 pounds of four pound cannon, 50 three pound cannons, double round and partridge swivel guns plus small arms and revolvers.

On the morning of May 15th Capt. Beckert and Jones's ships plus the *Resolution* encountered a French fleet in Advocate's Harbor consisting of two sloops, two schooners and a huge number of canoes. The wind ceased and the ships were almost driven into shallow water. Two of the ships fired off all their cannon and under heavy fire finally managed to get loose but lost sight of Donahue's ship. It had become trapped out of sight in shallows and no one knew its fate until two months later when a survivor of the *Resolution* arrived in Boston and said the captain and 39 men had fired off all their cannon, then jumped into the water and made it to shore but were surrounded and fought to the death with only their pistols for defense against over 250 enemy fighters.

Commodore Peter Warren arrived at Louisbourg with a ship earlier captured from the French in the East Indies of five to six tons armed with 28 guns and 99 men to help evacuate the French from the fort. Deliberately the English didn't immediately take down the French flag and it lured more French ships into harbor laden with valuable loot.

In June the French finally surrendered Fort Louisbourg. Nine thousand cannon balls had turned it to rubble. During the two month bombardment John Davis was wounded a second time. He had received a wound at Fort George but was still in fighting form. During the siege on the western front a young farm boy William Phips, 16 miles above Fort Dummer near Narragansett #2's land grant was hoeing corn when he was attacked. He fended off his attackers and killed one with his hoe but he was then ambushed and killed then mutilated with his own hoe in retaliation for his 'hoeing' of the indian. The same band of indians shot Deacon Josiah Fiske near Keene, New Hampshire as he was driving his cows out to pasture.

However, in Boston, Governor Shirley declared a Day of Thanksgiving on July 18th for the victory at Louisbourg.

The next day Fort George was again attacked, a man and women wounded and 40 cattle killed.

Capt. Jabez Bradley sent word to Shirley and Capt. Thomas Sanders sailed with men up to Falmouth and told the Penobscot indians they had 14 days to surrender the attackers but they never returned. Other attacks occurred at Brunswick and Topsham.

Morale turned sour at Fort Louisbourg as the men felt their victory there should have brought the depredations to an end. Governor Shirley and his wife sailed to Cape Breton on August 3rd to raise the morale. Spencer Phips as Lt. Governor was in charge in Boston during Shirley's absence. He immediately declared war on the Canadian indians yet attacks continued at Fort George, Sheepscott and Great Meadow where throughout the fall many captains were killed and many men taken to Canada as prisoners of war. The only thing that brought relief was the coming of deep snow to the north, forcing the indians to retreat to their winter villages. Morale under Phips in Boston was so low that when Gov. Shirley was sighted on Tyng's ship in Boston harbor on the 8th of December the residents sent up a loud cheer.

The missionaries and Clinton kept up hope that they could eke out a peace but they were outnumbered by the Catholic priests and their burning hatred of Protestants.

In October, 1744 Governor Shirley declared war on the Cape Sable and St. John indians as they had violated Dummer's Treaty. The indians had met with Pepperell at Ft. George in early July and promised to send 40 warriors to fight with them but due to their ties with the Penobscot they had reneged and sent word in mid-January 1745 that they would not comply. This was taken as a hostile act. To stress that he meant business the Massachusetts General Court offered a reward, good for six months, if the war lasted that long, of 100 pounds sterling for each scalp of a male over the age of 12 and 105 pounds for a captured live male and 50 pounds for the scalp of women or children and 55 pounds for any captured women or children.

In November 1744 Col. William Pepperell left Kittery to meet with sachems of the Penobscot villages at Ft. George to tell them of the official war declaration and to remind them that, through their signing of Dummer's Treaty, they were obligated to support the English. He told them that if they didn't send warriors within 40 days Massachusetts would declare war on their tribe. His position was overruled by Gov. Shirley who told Jabez to watch and learn as they prepared for an assault on Ft. Louisbourg. The prisoners of war who had returned, especially John Bradstreet, who had been assigned to Canso garrison, had given Massachusetts militiary leaders good information about how the fort was crumbling, low on provisions and ordnance and how the villagers outside it had low morale.

Gov. Shirley went before the General Court in January 1745 to propose an expedition to retake the fort. Governor Benning Wentworth of New Hampshire (the entire state was basically owned by the Wentworths) and Bradstreet were in communication with Capt. Ryl, a Prisoner of War (POW) from a British ship seized in the harbor of Louisbourg but who had extensive experience sailing the waters in that area about leading a fleet to retake the fort. In on the plan with Ryl was William Vaughn, a wealthy merchant-mariner from Damariscotta. Shirley asked for a force of 2,000 men but the General Court turned him down. The Davis mariners/traders as well as other wealthy Maine men such as their peers the Phips and Shapleighs worked on the members of the court and their petition to mount the expedition was finally approved in late January, 1745. Massachusetts sent requests to the other states and all agreed to contribute money, men, munitions or a variety of these to retake the port as its position was vital to north coast trading interests. Maine was the major supplier of timber for England and the West Indies and pelts for industries requiring leather or beaver skins for hats.

William Pepperell was chosen as the general leader as Massachusetts was contributing most to the campaign. Samuel Waldo was commissioned as brigadier general. England at the time was fighting on the continent and in Scotland where 'Bonnie Prince Charlie' was attempting to take the throne from George II but Henry Pelham, the Duke of Newcastle, Secretary of State to the Colonies and one of the wealthiest and most powerful men in England, sent notice to Commodore Peter Warren in Antigua to send three British warships north. En route to Canso Warren commandeered the escort ship the *Eltham* and was in position by late March with the warships the *Mermaid*, *Supurbe* and *Launceston*. Over a hundred colonial ships with 13 supply escort ships and an army of 4,000 men left Boothbay for Canso on March 24, 1745 as the cannons finally arrived from New York and the ice had finally broken in the harbors of Nova Scotia. In a lifting fog the colonial fleet weighed anchor and joined the British war ships at Canso.

The combined colonial and British fleet, under Commodore Warren, arrived near Fort Louisbourg on March 30th. South of the main force, Pepperell landed his troops in Gabarus Bay. The French retreated into the fort proper. Vaughn and his men took to its 'Grand Battery' leaving cannon and shot behind in their haste. Vaughn and his men, some former prisoners behind the fort's thick walls, began their bombardment of the fort.

Before the attack on Canso, Governor Shirley ordered the levying of 300 troops to the Eastward and 200 to the upper Connecticut Valley. Castle William in Boston harbor was reinforced with new 42 pound cannon, mortars and shells, mortar beds, carriages and shot for the 13 inch cannon. Shirley had ordered a line of forts be built from the Connecticut River to the New York line and sent 96 barrels of gunpowder for the garrisons to use in their defense.

In March, 1745 New York Governor George Clinton wrote to the Duke of Newcastle with information about the strength of the combined French and Indian forces. Frustrated with his colony's representatives' lack of action, he dissolved the

New York assembly in May, castigating the men for not protecting the English in the frontier lands.

Nathaniel Davis was with Commodore Peter Warren in the West Indies, captaining the *Trader's Increase* when the latest war broke out. Robert Davis was also running ships from Maine down the coast, to New York, Virginia, the Carolinas and on to the West Indies. Peter Warren was related to Spencer Phips through marriage. (And Phips had been in with the Davises to salvage the French vessel off the coast of Barbados.) In the Barbados the ships would fill with sugar and rum and some molasses and sail across the Atlantic to Great Britain, unload their cargo, fill up with English manufactured goods and fine textiles from India and then sail back to Nova Scotia, run down the coast selling English wares and fish and lumber then restock the most valuable cargoes: sugar and tobacco, in the West Indies. Tea drinking had taken hold in England and on the Continent but it was bitter and needed lots of nice sugar to sweeten it. And, with the tea the people like to eat scones or little cakes, again sweetened with sugar. The poorer folks and slaves settled for molasses or maple syrup to sweeten their cakes and tea. Slaves were being brought from Africa to South America but the people who captained or built ships knew it would only be a matter of time before the West Indies began importing them in large numbers.

When Governor Shirley's war call went out John Davis and his half brother Jedediah from Barnstable were among the men who volunteered to help their beleaguered relatives to the north. They were sent to Fort George and then later to Fort Louisbourg.

The Hull and Warren families were close friends of the Davis families and were already involved in shipbuilding in Newburyport and other Maine sites plus at Swanzey and across the Neponist River close to where the Baptists were. In 1656 Dolor Davis's wife Margery had died and within two years he had remarried Joanna, daughter of the Rev. Joseph Hull, an un-ordained unconventional preacher who had been kicked out of Barnstable and went north to the Isle of Shoals to preach. Joanna was the widow of John Bursely of Kittery and Barnstable. It was in Kittery that Dolor met Joanna and, after marrying her they returned to Barnstable, where, feeling a little like John the Baptist, her father ended up after the rigors of preaching in the Maine wilderness.

In 1665 John and Mary (Tilton) Nichols (the Titltons were from Tisbury) and

11 others got a patent from Gov. Nicholls of New Jersey to found a settlement near Monmouth. James Nichols got eight square miles of land in south central Massachusetts in 1685 and Robert Nichols got five square miles in Casco Bay in 1680. In Swanzey the Welsh Rev. John Myles brought a Baptist congregation from just north of the Davis stronghold in Carmarthen, south Wales to Swanzey. Eventually the Baptists outnumbered the Congregationalists in that town. (Western New Jersey was bought from John Bulkeley by the Quakers in 1674.) Samuel Davis and Sarah Eastman had been involved in the New Jersey deal as Joseph Davis Sr. was married to Jemima, granddaughter of the rich Northampton Tilton.

Dolor's great-grandson John had settled in Somers, Connecticut, having received a large land grant for his father Cornelius's service at the Great Narragansett Swamp fight in King Philip's War.

Dolor himself tried to stay out of religious controversy but his sons and grandsons and their children often found themselves in opposition to the "state" church. For the Baptists the main sticking point was infant baptism. The Congregationalists insisted upon it but the Baptists believed it should not be done until the person to be baptized was of an age to understand the commitment they were making to Christ. There were other religions such as the Quakers, who the Barnstable and Cape Cod branch of the Davises belonged to, going so far as to establish a colony of Quakers on the most southwestern part of Long Island in a town named Gravesend led by Nicolas's, John Davis's son.

Quakers had problems with war and also with taking an oath to an earthly being. And of course there had been the Hutchinsons, Williams, Wheelwrights and Gordonites since the settling of New England who didn't agree in totality with the Puritan oligarchy and were banished. Dolor's son John had been a Wheelwright supporter and had moved north to the Merrimac River area where James and his kin had settled in and around Amesbury and Newbury. The minister Roger Williams' people were settled across the river from Swanzey and it had taken an act from King Charles II to stop the persecution of them and to grant them their little corner of New England to be called Rhode Island. Maryland, New Jersey and the Welsh Pennsylvania were also founded so people who didn't want to follow the dictates of the clergy in Boston and Hartford were allowed to worship Christ the way they pleased and not be forced to pay for the house and wages of a Congregational minister and be fined if they didn't attend services.

In a sense the wars in New England with France was about religion, too, as the French soldiers were being incited by Catholic priests and the indians they had converted in Canada comprised a large percentage of their troops. The English who weren't shot, hacked to death by tomahawks, clubbed and scalped were taken to Canada. Like the English the French offered bounties for dead adult male English men and women and children and paid for scalps brought in. The indians found war and the loot they got from the English homes and barns to be more profitable than raising their own corn and trading in wampum at the trading posts where they felt cheated when the pelts they brought in were exchanged for knives, needles, cloth and iron cooking pots but they couldn't buy rum or alcoholic beverages from the English. However, when they raided English villages they were able to sack the houses before burning them and take whatever they wanted, including hard cider, rum and wines. They would kill the livestock, sometimes butchering cattle in the field to carry meat home to their villages. After a raid a garrison and village was nothing but cellar holes with burned out timbers on top. The settlers who escaped and weren't carried off on the long, arduous journey to Canada and on to Quebec faced ruin. After repeated raids in the late 1600s Samuel and Sarah and their son Joseph Davis had gone back to Wales. Joseph's wife Jemima was the granddaughter of the rich Halley settler Tilton who died in 1699. By English law she didn't inherit but instead her brother – who was declared to be an idiot, or mentally incompetent, inherited. Jemima and Joseph were so disgusted and so in need of an infusion of money to rebuild after the indian depredations that they had gone back to Wales but they returned after Jemima came into the inheritance. However, instead of trying to rebuild on the northern border they went where it was safter, to the lower Connecticut River Valley where John had been granted land on one of the "Narragansett Seven" land grants the Massachusetts General Court finally awarded to survivors of the great Narragansett Swamp Fight (of which only a few were still living) or their descendants. Many of the new frontier towns in Massachusetts (which included Maine and New Hampshire and northern Connecticut at the time) were thus begun with eight square miles of land to which each claimant received about 100 acres, usually to include some upland, some meadow.

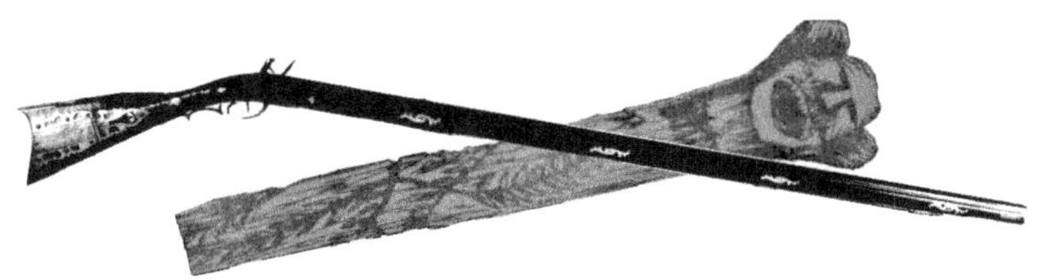

CHAPTER SEVENTY-SEVEN

The Northern War Continues

1746

In April, 1746 the attacks began anew, this time in Gorham township, Maine where the Briant men and their garrison guards Jacob Read, Ed Clouton and Robert Dunbar were ambushed while plowing a field. Dunbar managed to escape but Read was injured and with others carried off into captivity. Around the same time Fort Number Four was attacked again and they got three men going to a mill with their team of oxen. The indians killed the oxen and ate their tongues, raw and bleeding.

Isaac Davis was enlisted by then and joined a snowshoe expedition overland to Fort Louisbourg. In Boston the 1,000 men each received a pair of lined moccasins and snowshoes before embarking north.

Deerfield, Northfield, the garrison at New Hopkinton, Upper Ashelot (Keene), and Fort Number Four were attacked that April with many casualties and captives taken.

In early May Seth Putnam was killed as he left #4 in the early morning, Major Joseph Willard, related to Dolor through his deceased wife Margery, ran out to drive off the indians and with two more soldiers assisting him they drove them off before they could take the fort.

In Upper Ashelot the indians were fended off when a soldier shot through a door and killed the one on the other side. In Falltown (Bernardston) John Burke fended off an attack by having the women reload the flintlocks and give him a fresh one as soon as he shot. At Schenectady, Fort Massachusetts (Ft. Adams) John Myles and Sgt John Hawks were fired on as they rode outside. Their horses died but both soldiers survived. Ten miles north of Deerfield in Coltrain Matthew Clark and his wife and daughter were attacked as they traveled from the garrison to Clark's house. Matthew was killed but with the help of garrison soldiers his wife and daughter made it to the safety of the garrison. In Albany six settlers were killed, in Saratoga three men and a settler were attacked while fishing. A settler and one soldier escaped, one settler was killed and another captured.

It was at St. George Fort that John Davis, serving under Capt. Bradbury, received his last wound and he was captured and along with 12 men taken to Canada. Fort #4, Sheepscott, Ft. Dummer were also attacked in May with many casualties and captives. In June Rev. John Serjeant, a missionary to the indians in Housatonic who settled Sheffield, wrote to Gov. Shirley that the English needed to go on the offensive and take the fight to the indians.

On June 3rd the Massachusetts General Council voted to levy 207 men to be added to the 470 already posted, 20 to scout for Stockbridge, of which 16 would be friendly indians, 61 to Middleton county, Worcester and the Merrimac River, ten to Sheffield, ten each to Forts #1 and 2 and 50 to range the woods with large dogs.

The dogs were a major decision. Although they'd been used in King Philip's War the English were uncomfortable with the use of dogs to track down indians like animals but it was argued that with their keen hearing they could warn of ambushes and of troops gathering outside forts.

****

Tristrum was working on the lower pasture, clearing where weeds had started to clog the stream that his cattle depended on when his son John, who had taken the team of oxen and a cart up to the town center of Brimfield to buy supplies, hailed him from the road.

"Father! There's a letter for you!" John yelled, waving it over his head.

The day was extremely hot and humid. Tristrum had shed all but his long nightshirt and trousers, both soaking with sweat. His hole-ridden leather shoes were wet and the cotton stockings had been shed long ago. He pulled his soaked handkerchief out of his trouser pocket and wiped his face. He almost didn't have the energy to walk uphill to where the cart was but it was getting close to dinner time and he gathered his wet clothes and hoe and trudged up through the deep grass to meet his son. A letter usually meant bad news and they had received their share from their relatives in Northfield, Deerfield, Northhampton, Halley and Maine the past year.

"Aye, what ye have there – ?"

"'Tis a letter from Aunt Jane in Kittery," said John.

"I'll read it after I clean up," he said, wearily throwing his clothes and hoe on the back of the cart and climbing up beside John. His oldest son was growing up to be a strong lad. At 12 he was already almost as tall as Tristrum and he had his mother's fairer features.

Mary met them in the dooryard, her face showing worry as she wiped her hands on her coarse apron. She'd heard her son and saw him wave the letter and knew in all probability there was bad news.

Outside the farmhouse was a crude table with a tin pan and tin pitcher of water and a rag for the men to use before they entered the house. Mary was a meticulous housekeeper and didn't allow dirty boots or dirt on anyone or any clothes to enter into her domain.

"Ye'll have to shuck yer trousers," she told her husband, "and look at the state of those stockings! I don't think I'll ever get them white again!"

Tristrum grumbled but complied. The unspoken rule of the land was that the men ruled outside the house and the women ruled inside. A farmer couldn't take care of both a house and children and his fields and animals and the women knew how important their role was. There were no shortages of men needing a wife to replace one who died in childbirth or from epidemics or accidents and no shortage of widows likewise needing a husband to replace the one she had just buried. Even men like Dolor, now in his old age, had remarried an old woman as a man needed a helpmate, an Eve, as the ministers called them. Old men who married women of childbearing age often had up to 20 offspring from several wives. The oldest would usually get their own farms or take up a trade but the youngest would inherit the farm with one third going to the widow.

The family sat down in the dining room around a table laid with starched, embroidered linen tablecloth on which red clay pot of beans with salt pork sat on a trivet and redware bowls held mashed potatoes, turnips, salted beef cut into chunks and redware plates held loaves of fresh three-grain bread (corn, wheat and rye) and slabs of fresh butter. A large redware jug held hard cider and the redware glasses were all filled before Tristrum led the family in prayer. For everyday use the local potter's red clay utensils and tinware were used but the hutch held Mary's precious Blue Willow china for company. She had a set of leaded glasses to go with the redware mugs, which were easy to replace when little hands dropped a plate or something got knocked off and landed on the hard wood plank floor. In the parlor they had a woven rug from the rug weaving mill in Stafford Springs on the river to the south but the parlor was only used for company with the family using the room behind as a sitting room on the Sabbath and at the end of the day's work when they gathered to read from the Bible

As Mary looked across the table at Tristrum she saw he was going bald on the very top of his head. His hair was still slicked with sweat but the mud had been washed off.

The meal was quickly eaten and each napkin laid beside the plate after the last piece of berry pie had been licked off the wide knives they used along with tablespoons for implements. A pointed three-tined implement called a fork had recently been introduced but most common people still used the wide, flat knife or even their fingers, although Mary didn't allow that at her table.

Tristrum cleared his throat and looked around at his family.

"'Tisn't from Jane," he said, "'Tis from Hannah, one o' our Warner relations who had been in Brookfield before the big attack in me father's time. He was close to old Captain James's family. He had an uncle named Henry who was a brewer in Dover," he looked at John,"'tis why it has that northern postmark. Old Henry Warner's kin were close to the Owens, both having been in Brookfield. James Owen was killed just a short time ago by the murderin' savages near St. John's Fort with Capt. Rouse. Shot down and scalped after our men surrendered! But he had learned our cousin John was taken prisoner at Louisbourg and is on one of Father Rale's prison ships. He's in a real bad way from his wound and our friend says we should try to get him released."

"How?" asked John.

"I don't know, son. We aren't rich and it takes money to get someone out of Canada. I can try writing to our Willard relations and James up in Newbury but our family doesn't have the influence it once had. All the original men of influence have passed on except Spencer. Maybe I can write to Nick and see if he can get Phips to arrange a hostage exchange. Hannah doesn't say what ship or exactly where he is, though. And I haven't heard from Isaac or Jedediah in a while."

A collective sigh was heard around the table.

Mary got up and brought the Bible over.

"I think we need to read the '*Psalms*'," she said, handing the Bible to Tristrum, "and to pray that the Lord will be with our men as they walk through the Valley of the Shadow of Death."

"Aye," Tristrum sighed as he opened the worn Bible, "but, dammit! I should be up there fightin', hackin' indian heads, not a hackin' at earth!"

Mary shot him a look of disapproval, both for his swearing and also because they had had this conversation many times in the past year. Mary insisted his duty was to his family first and that the younger men without families were the best to go off to war.

"I don't like this one bit," he exclaimed, "I'm a trained soldier, dammit! I could be fightin' and drive the bastards all the way back to France!" He pushed his chair back so hard it banged against the chair rail and Mary jumped, startled at his temper. The July heat and drought had made everyone cross and her youngest, Tristrum, had been naughty and had to be punished as Mary, Elizabeth and her Little Mary were making dinner. Mary was very pregnant again and cross.

John joined in, saying he wanted to go, too, but his mother shooed everyone out and told them to go soak their hot heads in the pond and that there'd be no one going off and leaving her to try to run the farm by herself.

****

In August outside Fort #4 John Proctor's son Samuel (John Proctor had been hanged as a witch in Salem) was killed with some relatives but only one child was killed, the rest taken to Canada. The Proctors had moved to Portsmouth in 1718 to start anew without the stain of witchcraft accusations.

At Fort #4 itself the dogs gave warning and the attack was limited to only one casualty.

In Winchester six men including Rev. Rawson's grandson were attacked. Ironically only Rawson's grandson was killed. Rawson had been a minister to the indians and no one thought his family would be harmed. Then a young man in Northfield was ambushed bringing in the cows and there was a failed ambush of the Allen farm in Dover. An attack on Shattuck's fort was avoided when the English failed to fall for the ruse of a white flag of truce.

The forts were usually built of heavy logs, sometimes two deep, and had pointed logs facing outward in the ground beyond the corners (abatis), which held square lookout towers. Unfortunately, being constructed of wood, they were vulnerable to fires, either from flaming arrows or carts loaded with flammable materials set afire and rolled to a wall of the fort. Most of the men attacked were either traveling between forts or were out cutting wood or tending fields or rounding up horses or cattle. Inside the fort with their strong doors the soldiers could usually fend off an attack unless it went on so long they ran out of ammunition and food.

But on August 20th Fort Massachusetts was attacked by the French General Rigaud de Vadrevil with almost 800 troops. Only eight of the soldiers in the fort were healthy enough to fight as the other 14 were sick from measles. Sgt. John Hawks held out as long as he could but they were down to just three pounds of powder and lead so he was forced to surrender. The French said they would be unmolested but once on the trail to Canada indians ambushed and killed five of the captives including Thomas Knowles and Josiah Read, the latter having relatives in the Somers-Brimfield area. The first night en route John Perry's wife delivered a girl they named Captivity. Amongst the settlers was David Warren, who had relatives in Brookfield. Nathaniel Hitchcock, related to the lower Connecticut Valley Hitchcocks, and others joined them in October as they were marched to a prison in Quebec. He'd been in Deerfield when the attack happened and was one of the four captured when they went to relieve Fort Massachusetts. By late August most settlers on the western frontier had fled to the safety of the garrisons in Deerfield, Boston or Orange (Albany) as their farms were burned out. Even the outliers near

Northampton were attacked. Constant Bliss, a garrison soldier who had relatives in Colchester, was killed between Colrain and Deerfield, which was attacked again on August 30th as men in the south meadow were harvesting corn. Adonijah Gillett, also of Colchester, provided covering fire so the men could escape but he was shot on the Connecticut River bank. Capts. Hopkins and Cleeson rounded up a party to pursue the indians but they had escaped as the sound of gunfire was so common due to hunting that they weren't aware of the attack until the men straggled in from the field.

At Pemaquid John McFarland and his son were wounded as they were rounding up cattle. The cattle were all killed and McFarland's plantation burned out. Albany and Saratoga were also attacked at the time and a band of indians arrived at Crown Point on the last day of August with six scalps, including that of Constant Bliss.

Governor Shirley sent swivel guns to the forts and lent the same to the colonial garrisons.

Just as morale was at a low point word was received that a huge French fleet was heading for Boston Harbor. Six thousand men mustered on the Boston Common to meet the threat but in a twist of fate, in what the colonists felt was Divine Intervention, bad weather forced the fleet back, as it had done to the Spanish Armada under Queen Elizabeth's reign.

On November 7th Governor Shirley declared a Day of Thanksgiving to God for protecting His colonies.

However, in New York Saratoga was threatened and Gov. Shirley sent 500 men under Brigadier General Joseph Dwight to spread around the forts in the western frontier. But provisions were so low that 50 dogs had to be put down due to lack of food. At that time it was decided, amid much controversy, to enlist friendly indians to help as scouts, to be supervised by English captains, under John Stoddard.

The weather turned cold and the indians retreated and the English stayed indoors, or close to their dwellings as 1746 neared its bloody end. J

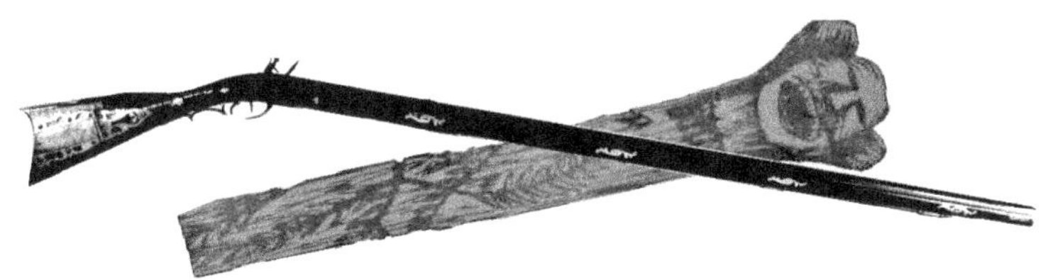

CHAPTER SEVENTY-EIGHT

The End of the Second French and Indian War

1747

While Boston was celebrating a Day of Thanksgiving Tristrum and his relatives were mourning the loss of John who they learned had died of his wounds onboard a French prison ship.

In early January Gov. Shirley sent approximately 700 men to Nova Scotia under Col. Arthur Noble. The French learned of the expedition and intercepted it. Four officers and 70 soldiers were killed and 630 men marched off to Canada. It was the worst disaster the English had suffered but instead of demoralizing the colonists it just made them mad and more determined than ever to rid New England of the French and indians.

In March men traveling between Shattuck's Fort and Hinsdale's were attacked. Daniel Shattuck owned the fort, having moved from Worcester to Northfield and then further north near Ft. Dummer. He valiantly fought off the indians so the settlers could get to safety across the river as half the fort was torched. Capt. Eleazer Melvin set out from Northfield to relieve the fort but by the time they arrived it was deserted. He ordered his men to burn the rest of it so the indians and French couldn't use it.

On April 1st a petition was sent to Gov. Shirley begging for help for the Northfield area, asking to have garrisons built every four miles and each blockhouse to be protected by 20 soldiers and swivel guns. Shirley responded and the entire territory was heavily reinforced.

Around the same time the English decided to take Rev. John Sergeant's advice and go on the offensive. Gov. Clinton sent Mohawks to Crown Point under Col. Johnston. Lt. Walter Butler led a war party that surprised and ambushed French soldiers outside the fort as they were dressing touchwood.

Fort #4 which had been abandoned was re-occupied by English under Capt. Phineas Stevens and 30 soldiers who dug trenches along the outside walls so men could bring buckets of water and put out fires during an attack. When the indians and French attacked they couldn't burn down the fort and retreated. Commodore Sir Charles Knowles was so pleased with Steven's innovative tactic he gave him a silver hilted sword and the fort was renamed Fort Charlestown.

At Fort Saratoga Capt. Trent, Lt. Proctor, Cpt. William Livingston and Capt. Bradt fended off an attack around the same time.

But victory was short lived as men near Kinderhook and in Maine were ambushed, killed or carried off into captivity and a little after sunset on April 15th as they were bringing cows into the fort. Ashahel Burt and Nathaniel Dickenson were ambushed, killed and scalped. (In 1640 Henry Burt followed William Pynchon from Roxbury to Springfield and he served as clerk of the writs in Springfield for years. Burt daughters married Blisses and Stebbinses in Springfield and Henry of Northampton's widow married Deborah Stebbins, who had been married to Benjamin Alvord. Daniel Burt of Brimfield was to be a captain with Tristrum later on. Like his relative David Burt of Deerfield who had been captured in 1669 and taken to Canada but never returned he was a soldier at heart. There were Burts in Windsor, Connecticut also. As was a pattern in New England, families had branches in Massachusetts, Maine and Connecticut at this time.)

A number of settlers at Saco, Falmouth and Darmariscotta and Wells were attacked, killed or carried off in May. There was an ambush of a canoe with settlers in it near Topsham and on May 21st two men returning from a grist mill between Amouskeag and Suncook were ambushed and at Pemequid Falls. Capts. John and Joshua Cox lost their lives defending the men who were attacked as they gathered alewives by the river. Benjamin Cox, son of Joseph and Ezekiel Webb were amongst the men carried off to Canada.

Four days later men rebuilding Ft. Massachusetts were ambushed as they were bringing supplies to the garrison at Stockbridge. The indian sachem *Konkapot* was killed by the soldiers, and their indian scouts triumphantly scalped him.

In mid-June Saratoga was attacked by 3,000 French and indians. Sixty English soldiers were killed but Col. John Schuler arrived to relieve the fort and the indians were driven off. However, Lt. Chew's expedition from New York was ambushed and 102 men were taken prisoner and sent to Crown Point.

In late June the Mohawk war chief Hendricks ambushed indians on the Isle St. Zauvre, killing nine indians but losing four of his men.

In mid-July Eleikim Sheldon, who had relatives in the lower Connecticut Valley, was shot in his field as he was hoeing corn outside Fall Town. He managed to make it into the fort but died the next day from his wounds.

A week later a party of settlers, mostly women and children were ambushed near Burnet's field and later in July Pennacock and Mt. Swag suffered ambuscades with several Hilton men killed.

Towards the end of August French ships with 271 POWs arrived in Boston Harbor for the English to redeem. The captives said there were 100 left in Canada and 30 were too sick to travel and another 30 had died in captivity.

In late August Elijah Clark was killed as he threshed grain in his barn at Northampton. Pemaquid also suffered an ambush that killed two men in the field. On Sept. 2nd Fort St. George was attacked again. Four soldiers were killed but the indians and French were driven off.

In early October Peter Boovee was captured while hunting near Fort Massachusetts. Two days later there was a prisoner exchange at Isle de Baswue south of Quebec and 63 French were exchanged for 16 English.

The missionary David Brainerd of Northampton died and a week later Mr. Josiah Willard, Dolor's cousin, and Capt. Alexander and troops were attacked traveling between Ashelot and Northfield.

Again, with the coming of winter, the hostilities ceased but in February, 1748 Sgt. John Hawks was returned in a POW exchange. In the fort Samuel Allen and Nathan Blake were returned to the English and officer Pierre RaimbauLt. wounded by Capt. Alexander a few months prior, was returned to the French.

Across the sea the French and English duked it out in the English Channel. Although England had twice as many ships the English lost 520 sailors in the battle.

In March Fort #4 was again attacked, eight soldiers ambushed while outside getting firewood. The fort had no snowshoes so a pursuit wasn't ordered.

About two weeks later, in late March, between Ft. Dummer and Colrain three soldiers were attacked. The men in the fort were sick with measles and had no snowshoes so the attackers weren't pursued.

In Maine John Boynton was killed but his son shot through a loophole in the door and killed the indian outside, driving off the party. There was an attack in *Poquoig* (Athol), outside Fort St. George and at the mouth of the Merrimac and Suncook Rivers. Nine men who were cutting wood were captured and the cattle killed. The indians stripped the cattle of meat and the starving indians ate the raw tongues on the site. In May about ten miles northwest of Dover Mr. and Mrs, Hodgedon were attacked as they went to milk their cows. Only Mr. Hodgdon made it to safety. Also in May, Brunswick was attacked and Capt. Burnet killed. North Yarmouth was attacked and Eaton and Lake carried off. Near Southampton Noah Pixley was ambushed. He was the son of William Pixley, one of Westfield's early settlers. And again Ft. Massachusetts was attacked but the indians were repelled.

On May 25th Capt. Melvin, who had served with Capt. Lovewell many years before in the massacre to the Eastward, with his men attacked indians in a canoe near Crown Point. They thought they had gotten clear but the indians' fellow warriors followed them as far west as the West River near Ft. Dummer where they were ambushed and six men killed. There were several ambushes between Col. Hinsdale's garrison and Ft. Dummer at the time.

Towards the end of June Capt. Humphrey Hobbs left Fort #4 with 40 men headed into Canada to recapture prisoners. Twelve miles out they stopped for a noon meal and drink and were ambushed. In a four hour long battle Capt. Hobbs shot their leader but lost three and had three wounded. The party then went on to Northfield.

On July 2, 1748 peace talks began between France and England but New England didn't receive word until months later (although the French knew and pursued the war anyway).

On July 5th Fitch's garrison north of Lunenburg was attacked. There were supposed to be four soldiers on duty but two were too sick to hold scout. John Fitch and a Blodgett, who had relatives in the Brimfield area, and Sgt. Isaac Jennings were surprised outside. Fitch and his wife and family were carried off to Canada.

Again Upper Ashulot was ambushed and Sgt. Thomas Taylor and 17 men ambushed between Hinsdale and Dummer. Capt. Stevens and his men found the corpses of Hobb's ambush and buried the men.

On July 18th three miles from Schenectady there was a big battle between Lt. Darling and his Connecticut troops and the enemy that ended in hand-to-hand combat. Dutch settlers killed and captured but the indians were driven off.

On July 22nd Gov. Clinton called for an assembly of the Six Nations in Albany. A huge number of indians attended and, with the help of money and gifts, agreed to help the English.

The next day Northfield was attacked again at dawn with one person killed and on August 2nd Ft. Massachusetts was to be attacked but the dogs inside alerted the soldiers. There would have been no casualties but several men, disobeying orders from the fort's commander, Capt. Williams, went out after the indians. Williams and a party had to go out and rescue the men. They were surrounded and almost perished but managed to make it back into the safety of the fort.

On August 4th three friendly indians brought word to Gov. Shirley about the peace talks but the French refused to stop fighting. However, they did send a ship with 175 captives under flag of truce to Boston two weeks later. Two English had died en route and the POWs reported 173 had died in captivity in Canada.

Sheepscot was ambushed around the same time, two killed and one captured.

On October 7th the *Britannia* sailed into Boston harbor with a large number of English captives that the French had taken off English ships.

On October 7, 1748 the' Treaty of Aix la Chapelle' was officially signed in France but news of it didn't arrive until six months later in New England.

But the New Englanders were once again reclaiming the seas of New England., Capt. Jedediah Prebble and Capt. Tristrum Coffin of Newbury sailed from Annapolis Royal to the St. John's river and Capt, John Gorham with 30 men followed on the *Anson.* On October 18th Capt. Nathaniel Davis sailed the *Warren,* a new ship built in the shipyard in Rhode Island across the river from Swanzey, up to join them and with five oarsmen paddled up to the western side of the harbor but saw few indians. They did capture a chief's son and took two other prisoners of war.

In May, 1749 the Governor of Massachusetts declared a 'Proclamation of Peace' but skirmishes continued until late October when the last of the indian tribes signed the treaty.

It wasn't until the summer of 1750 when all the remaining POWs were returned under militiary escort. Some refused to return to English ways, much like Eunice Rowlandson from Lancaster who earlier had married an indian and adopted indian ways. Some of the men married indian wives during their captivities or young boys forgot their English customs and chose to live in a more wild manner with their captors. Some of the captives never recovered from the trauma or loss of everything they owned and were insane yet some said the indians had treated them well.

Capt. James Merrick, the son of a Welshman from St. David's who had settled in Springfield, with his sons Gideon and Aaron, returned to their 100 acre farm in Brookfield; Ichabod Bliss, married to Methible Stebbins returned to his big farm on Tower Hill, Brimfield; Corp. Daniel Graves returned to Brimfield; Samuel Kilborn returned to Litchfield but died in mid-December 1748; Nathaniel Clark from Haverhilll returned to Woodstock; Humphrey Gorden, one of the Scots-Irish deported to New England, returned to Hampden; Charles Hoar and Daniel Morgan from Wales returned; Henry Burt returned to Springfield; Dr. John Nelson returned to Suffield but moved to Vermont, Joseph Billings from Hatfield and his son Joseph Jr. went to New Hampshire where the Gov. Benny Wentworth had received a huge 28,040 acre land grant on the border of Lake Champlain; Nathaniel Munger also returned to Brimfield. The whereabouts of Corp. Medad Hitchcock from Brimfield and Mark Ferry from Springfield were never known.

Tristrum's brother, the Welsh born Isaac Davis found a spot on a lake in New Hampshire (Branford) that he fell in love with and he settled there after being released from His Majesty's Royal Army. Nathaniel was a British Naval soldier.

For the Davis men whose sons or grandsons had fought or, like Tristrum been forced to remain behind, or who had been in Virginia or Pennsylvania or the West Indies while relatives fought and died for England the peace treaty was a relief.

But it was only a reprieve. More war was to come.

CHAPTER SEVENTY-NINE

After the Second French and Indian War

1749

During Governor Shirley's War Simon and Samuel Davis were in touch with the Stevens family, or what was left of them. In the summer of 1723 their farm had been attacked and the sons Phineas, 17, and Isaac, only four years old were carried off into captivity. Their father Deacon Stevens worked ceaselessly to gain their release. Phineas came out first but Isaac had been adopted by a different tribe and had taken up indian ways so his release was more complicated but he arrived in Worcester County in 1724, later married and had a farm of his own in Rutland. His older brother was a captain during Gov. Shirley's War and with his knowledge of the language and ways of the savages he was a chief negotiator for the release of the captives in 1749, making several trips for the Massachusetts governor to redeem as many as possible, even if he had to pay in horses.

Deacon Stevens had a 200 acre land grant (in what is now Princeton) and in his old age sold it to Benjamin Houghton for a half-pound per acre. Capt. Phineas moved north to New Hampshire.

Deep anger and disgust spread throughout New England after they learned that the treaty of 'Aix la Chapelle'. In October, 1748 had returned the blood-and-sweat soaked Fort Louisbourg and Cape Breton to the French. A bitterness began to take root towards the mother country that had so disregarded the sacrifice so many men had made to conquer and hold those areas. England justified the concession as it was losing the European Continental war but it felt like a betrayal to the American Continental troops and their families.

No sooner was the ink dry on the October 16, 1749 'Treaty of Falmouth' in which the chief sagamores of the Penobscot, Norridgewock, St. Francis and Beconcour tribes basically renewed their pledges taken earlier with Gov. Dummer, than an incident occurred near Kittery, north of Sheepscot where a branch of the Davis clan lived.

In February Tristrum went northeast into Oxford with a load of hogs to sell and met up with a cousin who lived in Sheepscot, near other relatives in the Kittery and Damiscotta area of Wicasset, just south where their cousin's farm had been attacked

He told him a band consisting of the sachem Hegan and two sub-chiefs called Andrew and Capt. Job were returning from the long treaty meeting at a nearby fort to their lands and camped overnight outside Wicasset on December 2nd. Some English settlers ambushed them in their sleep, killing Hegan and critically wounding the two other sachems. As revenge killings were specifically banned in the 'Treaty of Falmouth' that reiterated that an injured party had to seek justice from an English 'Court of Remedy and Redress' the survivors of the ambush immediately escaped by canoe and paddled up to Parkers Island to seek redress. Daniel Davis was no longer constable in Kittery but Major Samuel Denny, the chief magistrate and judge, or justice of the peace, for the area heard the complaint filed by Hegan's widow and another indian female. The band had familial links to all of the critical tribes who had signed the 'Treaty of Falmouth'. Denny and Deputy Sheriff Samuel Harnden had no choice but to issue a warrant for the arrest of the settlers responsible for the murder.

The main suspect was Obadiah Albee, Jr. who immediately jumped aboard a schooner headed for Boston. Denny and Harnden arrested Samuel Ball, Benjamin Ledite, Benjamin and Richard Holbook and Richard and Unity Brown, all from Wicasset and who had lost relatives in the early morning attack on Wicasset in February, 1692 in which half the town was killed and over 100 either wounded or carried off to Canada. The town had previously been attacked in July, 1747 when the Hiltons and John Boynton were killed and Benjamin Hilton taken captive. Wicasset and York County had no sympathy for Hegan's widow or the other indians. In Boston Albee was arrested as the captain of the ship that brought him south turned him in at Marblehead for the bounty money. He was held for trial in Boston. The Holbrooks (posting bond) and Browns were released on condition that they would testify at Ledite and Ball's trial. The two men accused of the murder escaped while being transported to the York County jail as, en route to the jail, during an overnight stay a mob broke into John Thom's house in Portland and released them. For three weeks, despite a reward of 50 pounds per person the two men managed to elude apprehension and capture but Capt. Jonathan Bean of the Saco garrison finally caught them and brought them to the York County jail. A guard of nine men was set up to prevent another mob from freeing the men, who the Maine residents felt had every right to avenge the deaths of all the families and soldiers brutally killed or forced to march to Canada in high snows or with summer fevers. Phineas told how he saved his little brother's life on the trek by carrying him on his back as the indians would usually split the head open on any captive who couldn't keep up on the march. Many a mother had to watch as her toddler was killed and the horrors of the forced marches broke the minds of some of the captives to where they lost the will to live and perished in captivity.

The commander of St. George's Fort, Capt. Jabez Bradbury was warning New England that if the murderers weren't tried and hanged immediately the indians would take matters into their own hands,

After hearing all this it was with an lighter ox cart but heavy hearts that Tristrum and John returned to South Brimfield. Just when the settlers thought the threat of war had ceased they learned the tribes were seeking justice and that the English courts were not eager to try and hang men who killed savages in an act of anger and frustration.

"They are standing around with their thumbs up their arses," Tristrum said to John as they plodded homeward, fancy textiles and household items for Mary in back. Mary liked fine things and one of the items was a beautifully carved silver hair comb for her thick, blond hair, now streaked with grey. Tristrum hoped she liked it.

"Aye, father," John said, working the team around a mushy spot in the frozen road, "But how can ye hang them for killing people they thought killed their kin?"

Tristrum sighed.

"'Tis a complicated thing, son, this eye for an eye business. Why d'ye think England and France keep a'fightin? They sign a piece o' paper and kiss and make up but the resentments keep on a'simmeren like a pot on the hearth over hot coals. All it takes is a fresh injury blown on the coals an' the whole pot gets to biling again. And them indians never, ever forget an injury or insult. Never. They can hold a grudge for years and years until it erupts and they kill to avenge it. 'Tis a serious defect in their race, son. Not that we English or the French or others are much better but we usually honor a treaty until something serious happens to nullify it."

John harumphed and scratched his head.

"Looks like snow, father," he proclaimed, seeing the darkening sky."

"Giddap Alpha and Omega!" shouted Tristrum, flicking the switch at the ponderous oxen. team

They were so close to their farm he thought he could smell the pot of beans on the hearth and the fresh bread coming out of the bake oven and his stomach growled. The extra hogs had been a nice bonus this winter and he had a cart full of new implements he couldn't find locally.

****

In June, Boston finally tried Albee and found him not guilty. Knowing how angry the tribes were William Lithgow, commander of Fort Richmond, Bradbury and Denny took in the indian survivors of the attack for the winter, and in July Lt. Gov. Spencer Phips sent invitations to sachems to meet with him in Boston. While he was gifting and feasting the leaders to appease them he received word from Thomas Fletcher, second in command at Fort St. George to tell the 70 indians threatening his fort that the Penobscot leaders were in Boston seeking peace and to hold off attacking. Bradbury was then notified but by then two families – the Widdons and Nobles – living on Swan Island in the Kennebec River had been attacked and family members carried off to Canada. The following day in Sheepscot, north of Wicasset, William Ross and his son were taken and then farms in Topsham and Brunswick were attacked. In a panic the settlers sent an urgent letter to Gov.

Phips. He responded by authorizing the levy of 150 soldiers to reinforce the garrisons from Saco up to St. George. In the meantime Bradbury wrote to Phips that two Penobscots came to him and Lithgow and said it was finished – the indians had gotten their revenge but told them they would not release the 17 captives bound for Canada where they were to be sold as slaves to wealthy French families.

It wasn't until July of the following year when York acted on the murders. Ball had escaped from prison in March and rumor had it he'd escaped west to the Ohio River Valley where English settlements peopled from Pennsylvania and Virginia were sprouting up, met by French forts the new Canadian governor was erecting along the valuable trade riverways.

As the trial for Ledite neared the tribes to the north began raids to show their impatience with English justice. Ledite was charged with murder but he wasn't executed. He had a rope placed around his neck beneath the gallows, was whipped 20 stripes and ordered to pay 100 pounds in fines and had to take an oath to keep the peace for three years. His public humiliation plus the gifts English had given to placate the tribes managed to keep things quiet on the northern front for a few years as the French shifted their attentions to locking in their hold on the Ohio River Valley.

CHAPTER EIGHTY

The last French and Indian War, early years

1750

In 1750 to the north the French and English established a boundary line with the northernmost part of Merrymeeting Bay going to the Norridgewocks and French. The returning of Louisbourg and Cape Breton to the French was a bitter pill for the provincial soldiers to swallow but life went on.

To the south a new boundary survey in 1747 gave Woodstock, Somers, Enfield and Suffield to Connecticut. (An official survey in 1713 had put them within Massachusetts territory.) Fifty families who had settled the area were now separated by an invisible line.

Shubel Dimmick moved to South Brimfield (still called Brimfield) and built a store and mill across from the a pond in town. The first settlers such as the Baptist minister Ebenezer Moulton had set their homes on the larger of the two ponds on the path that led south to Stafford. There was a second trail further south that went into Union. The Needhams, Mungers and Moultons had come from Salem and Anthony Needham, one of the first settlers of South Brimfield, was married to Molly Moulton, whose four brothers settled in the western part of the town.

Tristrum's brother Joseph Davis had come from Wales and settled to the south, near Stafford and owned land on the road and up to the hill on the other side of the road that led to Union. From Union came Bill Felton, an Irishman with an over-fondness for liquor (which got him into trouble with the authorities). Tristrum felt a kinship to Felton, especially when he spoke Gaelic. They both loved singing the old songs from the places of their birth.

Daniel Burt was in Brimfield and the Stebbinses and Allens (they were everywhere it seemed) and Bliss family were there, just to name a few. Tristrum's brother William who had settled in Somers died but his son Samuel remained there, marrying Martha Wood. Their relative Nathaniel had brought tobacco plants from Thomas and James's Virginia plantations and some of the farmers were experimenting with its cultivation in the rich soil near Somers.

In South Brimfield Reuben Townsley married Sarah Blodgett, daughter of Tristrum's closest neighbor. Reuben was Tristrum's best friend and was often a guest in the Davis sitting room, much to Mary's discomfiture. Reuben loved to hunt and usually showed up with a bloody animal dangling from his hand, dripping on Mary's painted canvas entry rug.

Another settler Daniel Burt, had been a captain in Gov. Shirley's War, or King George's War as it was referred to by the colonists. There had been King William's War, Queen Anne's War and King George's but a new one was looming on the horizon. Both the Blodgetts and Burts were related to the Stebbinses through marriages. Burt was related to the Chapins and had relatives who had been captured or killed in Deerfield. John Stebbins''s family in Deerfield had been carried off to Canada and many hadn't returned. For generations the specter of indian raids had hung over their heads and they hoped by settling further south they would be spared surprise attacks from the indians and French from Canada.

To the north the Wentworth family had obtained most of New Hampshire, selling off parcels but keeping the finest lands for themselves. New York was claimed by a few high-ranking men such as Sir William Johnson, a wealthy Irish landlord, and the De Lancey's. The Crown had declared South Carolina a Royal Colony after a handful of wealthy proprietors got greedy and tried to claim all the land the settlers had fought the indians for as their own. It was producing a lot of rice and indigo but was using African slaves, as were most of the plantations since the British prisoners of war did not thrive in the tropical climate and a good negro slave was purchased for life, not just for five to seven years with a settlement of land, goods and cash at the end of their indenture. Coarse cloth was given to the slaves and they were each encouraged to hoe and plant a small vegetable garden near their shacks to supplement the corn and beans the proprietors fed them. Occasionally they would get some pork or they might trap small game to add to the pot. In Pennsylvania the Penn family owned a huge grant including a half-million acres north of the Lehigh River. Lord John Berkeley and Sir George Carteret, Earl Grenville now, had New Jersey. Delaware and Maryland were awash with conflicting land claims. Maine had reverted to the Massachusetts Bay Colony in 1652, affecting the patents claimed by Gorges and Mason. After the southern settlements in Maine were incorporated into Massachusetts the Allens got so greedy to the north that the settlers complained to the court.

Quitrents of two shillings a year were usually paid to the patent holders in addition to local taxes to cover the meeting house, minister's house, school house, repair of roads and upkeep of the minister and teacher via a small salary.

To men such as Rev. Moulton in South Brimfield the supporting of a different congregation was an insult and he petitioned for the right to build a Baptist church on the main road. Its original location was too swampy, though, so the church had to be taken down and built in another spot at the northern part of the big pond. It was a shared meetinghouse and each denomination had a certain number of Sabbaths depending on the size of their congregations. The women sat in the west end and there was no center aisle. The deacon and minister's seats were high-backed and none had cushions. John Wesley, who had been in Georgia, had started a denomination called the Methodists so the Congregationalists weren't the only religion now, unlike in 1630. Had Roger Williams or the Wheelwrights or Hutchinsons emigrated in 1730 instead of a century earlier they probably wouldn't have been persecuted and driven off but by doing so the colony had inadvertently expanded English influence further south and north. As New England was mellowing, to the north the French were rabidly Catholic and priests were busy converting tribes to their form of religion and stirring up in them a hatred of the Protestant English.

On Nova Scotia the French Catholic priests ran a proxy war against the settlers via the Micmacs and other tribes. After handing Louisbourg and Cape Breton island at the entrance to the St. Lawrence seaway back to the French the English set about constructing a new settlement and fort on Nova Scotia in the Bay of Chebucto. They imported a large number of settlers and founded a town called Halifax on its southern coast. It was thriving by 1749 and was governed by Edward Cornwallis. Another fort, to be called Fort Lawrence, was built on the inland bay at Beaubasin. The French used the hill there called Beasejour to spy on the English and the building of an English fort at the edge of the marsh was challenged as a violation of the treaties that gave Acadia to the English. What exactly constituted the area called 'Acadia' was never really resolved: the French claimed a large territory when it was theirs and then claimed Acadia was smaller in size when the English occupied it. The English seized a French ship at the mouth of the St, John River claiming it was carrying arms and powder and shot to supply the indians and the Acadians who refused to take the oath of loyalty to King George II as required by Governor Cornwallis. It originally stated that the Acadians, though free to practice their Catholicism, as British subjects were eligible to be drafted in times of war to fight on the English side. The French immediately set about, via their priests, to convince the Acadians that they shouldn't sign the Oath. Their priests and the indians they controlled actually burned settlements such as Beaumaris and harassed and harangued the settlers to pick up and move to Isle St. Jean (Prince Edward Island) or Cape Sable to be free of the English requirement of fealty and potential militiary service to the English. While this undeclared war was going on Captain John Rouse of the Royal Navy (related to a captain who had been imprisoned for a year and a half by Chief Justice Sewell in Boston for trading with the enemy in 1706), fired without provocation upon the brig *St. Francois* at the mouth of the St. John River and captured the ship, bringing it to Halifax. Capt. Rouse claimed the ship was arming the fort recently rebuilt by the French at the mouth of the river but in actuality it was only carrying supplies and no arms. The court in Halifax didn't condemn the action, raising the ire of the French. Nova Scotia was now a tinderbox just waiting for a match.

The real prize in the American colonies was to the west, though. Following an exploratory expedition by the frontiersman Christopher Gist from the Atlantic coast to the Ohio River, the Ohio Company – consisting mostly of Fairfaxes, Masons, Washingtons and Lees plus other wealthy plantation owners – obtained a grant of 200,000 acres with the caveat that a fort be constructed on the Ohio River. They were to receive an additional 300,000 acres if another fort were built and manned and settlers brought in. For this purpose large numbers of land-hungry immigrants were imported and sent west.

A chain of new fort building by the French to secure the river ways from their northern boundary and down through the middle of the country to their territory of Louisiana set the stage for the actual match that set off the fourth and final French and Indian War.

Wealthy plantation owner-land grantees were always at the mercy of the inner circle, the Board of Trade, the Privy Council and men of enormous power across the sea. And enormous wealth and power in and around the courts of the French King Louis XV, the Prussian King Frederick-II, rulers in Spain, the Netherlands, Sweden and other major powers were vying to either seize colonial trading ports such as India where Robert Clive wrested it from the French and the West Indies plus the western, or gold coast, of Africa.

In the American colonies the opening salvo was fired by the French when his new governor to Canada ordered the construction of Fort Le Boeuf on the Ohio River, to be followed by more fort construction along the river. Rumors that the French were violating the treaty and building a fort at the head of the Kennebec River were forwarded to Gov. Shirley. The Earl of Holderness wrote to the colonial governors that *"in case the subjects of any foreign Prince of State should presume to make any encroachment on the limits of his Majesty's dominions, or to erect Forts on His majesty's Land, or commit any other act of hostility"* the governors were to levy forces and repel them by force. Gov. Shirley and Lt. Governor Robert Dinwiddie of Virginia were eager to repel the French advances.

After returning from the frustrating convention in Paris where the post-war boundaries had not been solidified Shirley explored the area between the St. Lawrence and Penobscot Rivers in 1753 with Thomas Johnston who drew an accurate map showing the forts, villages and settlements in the area. In 1754, in response to Capts. Jonathan Bean and James North and Lt. Thomas Fletcher's warnings about a new French fort, Shirley sent three expeditions, headed by troops from these commanders of Fts. Frederick, St. George's and the garrison at Saco to investigate but they found no new fort construction.

However, Shirley was uneasy and wanted any French in the area pushed north into Canada, After his expedition Shirley had seen the need for more forts. He asked the Massachusetts General Court in its late March, 1754 assembly to authorize the building of a fort near the head of the Kennebec between the Norridgewocks and the Canadian border. Fort Frankfort was to be built with the help of the Plymouth Company to provide defense of the northernmost territories but it took sweet talking by Capt. Lithgrow and Samuel Goodwin, like Shirley, shareholders in the Kennebec Company, to assuage the Norridgwocks in order to get the fort built above what the indians considered 'their' territory.

Shirley told the assembly that the French had recently built a fort on the St. John's River and he had learned the new governor was building a chain of forts from the Great Lakes down the Ohio River and to the west of the colonies on the eastern seaboard to terminate at the mouth of the Mississippi River in the great gulf to the west of Spanish-held Florida. The French had sent explorers all down the rivers and they claimed the territory by right of exploration but the English didn't agree as their original patent went from sea to sea. The French already had Fts. Quebec, Frontenac (across from the English fort at Oswego), Ticonderoga and Nigaria plus smaller ones downstream.

The Massachusetts Assembly had no problem authorizing a new fort, but when it came to troops it was another matter as the colonies each had to assume the cost of provisioning and paying the soldiers and armaments until England reimbursed them. It had taken time for the English to reimburse the colonies, mostly Massachusetts, for the huge costs they had incurred in the taking of Fort Louisbourg, only to see it ceded back to France. However, private individuals with vested interests came to the governor's aid and advanced monies to kit out troops and provide for 800 troops under Major General John Winslow.

Wives, friends and family waved goodbye to their men at Falmouth on an early hot July day as Maj. Gen. Winslow ordered the fleet up the Kennebec River. Shirley, working with Dinwiddie, had planned this expedition to take attention away from the real expedition in western Virginia.

In the western frontier Maj. George Washington's men had followed the Potomoc River from Williamsburg then up through Virginia and the mountains over the Ohio River and up to where it joined the Allegheny, then up it to the French River below Presque Isle on Lake Erie to deliver a demand from Gov. Robert Dinwiddie to immediately leave English land as he was "in violation of the Law of Nations and the Treaties now subsisting between two Crowns". Washington had presented the letter to Legardeur de St. Pierre Repentigny, the commander of the newly constructed Fort Le Boeuf. En route Washington mapped the area and felt the perfect site for an English fort in honor of King George II would be at the junction of the *Monongahela* and *Allegheny* Rivers just below where the French were planning to build another fort.

William Trent, a renowned fur trader in the region was told to recruit men to built the fort but when it was just above ground level the French appeared, 500 strong, led by Capt. Pierre de Contrcoeur. The French drove out the English and finished constructing the fort, which they named Ft. Duquesne. On the way back from Le Bouef, Washington's troops routed French troops near Great Meadows because Half Chief, the English-friendly chief sachem in the area with his village at Venangdo below Le Bouef informed him a party had been sent out looking for Washington to kill him, the indians with him and his guide. After the brief battle 21 French POWs were taken. Washington and Gist, the explorer who had mapped the area from the coast to the Ohio River, walked almost non-stop back to Williamsburg with Gist suffering from frostbite. Washington reported to Dinwiddie, who went to the Assembly with the news of the new French fort. They authorized Washington with 200 men and the trader Trent as his lieutenant to build a fort, which they named Ft. Necessity. The going was rough and it took Washington's men 14 days to cut a rough road through 20 miles of heavily forested mountains.

To the north, as Winslow's troops were about to sail from Falmouth, 700 French soldiers and 350 indians left Ft. Duquense to attack Fort Necessity, now a crude log-palisaded garrison in a meadow to the southwest of Duquense, situated with a gully in front. Washington had been trained in the European way of battle where one army met another on the field and he felt the gully would give his troops protection. However, the French and indians used the indian-style of guerilla warfare and came up on Washington's troops from behind trees on two sides from the forest. Vastly outnumbered, the English under Washington fought valiantly but after losing 31 soldiers Washington accepted French terms of surrender under which the English would be allowed to leave unmolested as France and England were not formally at war. On the road back to Williamsburg Washington and his men rebuilt Fort Cumberland at Wills Creek.

On the Kennebec Winslow's men rested at Fort Richmond before proceeding further north to Augusta where the Plymouth Patent Kennebec Proprietors had built Fort Western at their own expense to be the storehouse for Ft. Halifax, 17 miles north at the confluence of the Penobscot tribe's primary trade route, the Sebasticook and Kennebec Rivers. After the troops built Ft. Halifax the men were decommissioned and sent home by the end of August leaving only Capt. Lithgrow and 120 men to man the northernmost inland outpost on the English-French frontier.

The French were incensed over the killing of an officer from Ft. Duquense in what they felt was the encroachment of the English into French territory with Ft. Halifax.

Upon his return to Williamsburg Washington was severely criticized for his failure to hold Fort Necessity and he resigned his commission at the beginning of November.

To the north, during that winter the French sent a hatchet to the chief of the Penobscots and told them to use it against the English. Fletcher relayed to Lithgrow information from his friendly Penobscots that a huge gathering of indians was being planned to be held on the Kennebec in the spring. As the warning arrived, so did the attacks on settlers to the east in Nova Scotia.

When he became Prime Minister in England Pitt had begun a shipbuilding program to create a strong, new Navy. As news of the defeat at Ft. Necessity reached London news was also received that France was sending a fleet with a large number of troops to Canada. The Parliament, urged on by the news, voted to expand the Regular British Army and Navy and send troops under Major General Edward Braddock, an Irish landowner, to Virginia to meet the threat.

Braddock had little respect for the volunteer, or provincial, army yet Washington blamed the defeat at Ft. Necessity on the sluggish response of the King's Army which was ill provisioned and moved ponderously, laden with women and children, poor discipline and rotten gunpowder. Braddock arrived with two Irish regiments at Alexandria in mid-April where Govs. William Shirley, Robert Dinwiddie, Arthur Dobbs of North Carolina, Robert Morris of Pennsylvania, Sharpe of Maryland and James De Lancey of New York convened a council of war. Shirley and Gov. Lawrence were planning an attack on the French at Beausejour and were planning to take Fort Crown Point at the head of Lake Champlain, then moving in and up and routing the French all the way down the St. Lawrence seaway and into the Atlantic.

Braddock liked the enthusiasm of the old soldier but he came up with his own plan. It involved simultaneous attacks at four points: Ft. Duquense; Crown Point; Beausejour and Niagara. Braddock was to lead the attack on Ft. Duquense; Shirley and Pepperell to lead their (now Regular) regiments against Ft. Niagara and provincial solders from New York and New Jersey were to take Crown Point with another provincial force to take Beausejour.

To the French the English fort at Oswego was a thorn in their side. Its location was an impediment to total French control of the inland valley down to Louisiana – a territory both the French and English claimed from past treaties.

CHAPTER EIGHTY-ONE

Tristrum Goes Off to War

1755

Governor Shirley of Massachusetts was one of the first to beat the war drums. He knew from reports the new governor of Canada and France's plan to build forts from the Atlantic Ocean all the way down the western frontier (western Virginia and western Pennsylvania) to the great gulf west of Spanish Florida. He and other governors had met with the newly arrived Major General Braddock and his two Irish regiments in mid-April 1775 in a new camp at Alexandria, Virginia. Gov. Shirley's son William became Secretary to Braddock and Gov. Shirley learned through him the English general made no secret of his disdain for the abilities of colonial, or provincial, soldiers.

In a council of war Govs. Dinwiddie of Virginia, Morris of Pennsylvania, Sharpe of Maryland, De Lancey of New York and Lawrence of Nova Scotia drew up a plan of attack against the French.

Commander-in-Chief Braddock wanted a four pronged attack, all to happen simultaneously to draw the French in different directions. To the northeast British General Monckton would lead troops to take Ft. Beausejour and then drive the French out of Acadia; Shirley and Pepperell would take two forces – Shirley's 50th

Regiment (to be clad in the English scarlet coats and regalia) to take Fort Niagara and Oswego – and Pepperell's 51st (likewise attired and treated as British Regulars) to take Crown Point and Braddock would lead a regiment of British, colonials and indians to take Ft. Duquense on the Ohio River with (now) Col. George Washington as an aide de camp along with Capt. Roger Morris. Commodore Augustus Keppel would gather a navy to help to the East and to coordinate troop transport and supplies. Col. Johnson, nephew of Admiral Peter Warren but of Irish birth (and related to Lt. Gov James De Lancey), was to act as intermediary with the Five Nations to seek their support.

Shirley rushed back to Massachusetts and immediately got the Assembly to authorize the levying of money and men for three expeditions for the campaign.

****

Hearing this in South Brimfield Tristrum Davis told Mary he was joining up.

"Mary, me love, 'tis time I do me duty. Aye, I helped a bit with scouting in King George's War to the Eastward but that wasn't real soldiering. This time I'm enlisting as a foot soldier. Seth Pomeroy from Northampton has recruited Daniel Burt to lead a company and Joseph Dwight further south is recruiting for his company. I will not sit by this time, Mary!"

Tristrum's wife was still very ill. She'd never fully recovered from the birth of their youngest, Sarah, born the previous August. Tristrum hadn't asked her to perform her wifely duties, knowing this last child almost killed the pale, thin woman he loved. She'd borne him ten children. He saw enlisting as an opportunity to go away and not be tempted to bed her in her fragile state.

He continued, "Ye have our John and his family to help ye," he told her, gently rubbing his thumb over her worried brow. "'Tis only an hour's walk from his place to ours."

"But won't he be enlisting, too?" she asked, removing the little baby girl from her breast and modestly covering up.

"Nay, they don't take two of the main providers from one family," he said, but added, his voice a little husky, "but young Joseph wants to go and he being of adult age, I can't stop him."

Mary sighed deeply.

"How many times are we to be a'fighting the French, then? How many families will be slaughtered or led off like cattle on ropes to Canada, their farms all burnt to ashes?"

"Mary, me dear, this, I vow, will be the last war we fight with the bloody bastards!"

Mary admonished him for his swearing and slowly rose to go out to the privy. Since Sarah she hadn't stopped bleeding but hadn't told Tristrum. He knew, though, for the smell of blood wafted up when he sat on one of the two holes in it. He quickly added, "John will send Sarah, Mary, little John and Edward over from time to time to help you and Elizabeth will come over from the Fenton Place to help ye as she can. And John's Allen relations will be a'helpin with the farm, Ye've got Benjamin – a strong boy for his fifteen years – and little Tris, plus Sibbie. Sam and Willie are getting bigger, too, so I think the farm will be well taken care of."

"What if we get attacked?" Mary asked, walking slowly out the back door to the privy that sat on the edge of a stone wall that dropped to a lower field.

Tristrum laughed, "Ach, me love, we seem to have been guided by God to pick a peaceful place for our farm. Me poor relations to the North and East are under constant threat, and them in the outlying Virginia and Pennsylvania settlements are now seeming to get the brunt of this Popish-spurred French and indian wrath."

In her heart Mary knew Tristrum needed to go. He was 51 and had felt the coward during King George's War. And she knew if he stayed she'd end up with child again. Her neighbor and midwife Sarah Blodgett had told her one more child would kill her. Plus Tristrum was getting angry a lot and she felt he would be better off venting his anger against the enemy than his family. What he'd said was true – there was a good support network of family and friends now and the lower Connecticut Valley had been living in peace with the Eliot Praying Village indians to the northeast of Quaboag pond. Poor Deerfield and Northfield kept getting attacked but they were closer to Canada and the New York tribes.

So it was that Ensign Tristrum signed up at the end of March, 1755 and marched off with Joseph Davis, Tom Blodgett, Gideon Dimock and many of their neighbors and friends' husbands and sons along with Capt. Ebenezer Moulton's larger company from Brimfield to Springfield to join Capts. Dwight, Pomeroy, Hitchcock,

Stebbins, Pynchon and many other men from the families that had settled the area after King Philip's War. All across New England grandsons marched off to once more defend what their ancestors had claimed with their sacrifices, blood, sweat and tears over the past century.

Those left behind, like Mary, wondered if there would ever come a day when the men weren't marching off to war. It seemed to her that history was just one long battle that never seemed to end: war an insatiable monster that fed on fresh blood every generation.

At least she knew she'd sent them off with well sewn, clean clothes and some good food in their packs. The shoes, blankets and other needs the army would supply.

As the sound of the marching feet receded down the road the needs of her hungry children took over. Life on the farm would go on. What her husband and son would experience she had no control over. Getting the cows milked and the eggs collected and the pigs slopped and then the fields planted and harvested, the kitchen garden planted and weeded – all these matters were left in her hands now and, like a soldier taking up his musket she and her army marched on, their battleground the fields and the main enemies drought, deer and crows.

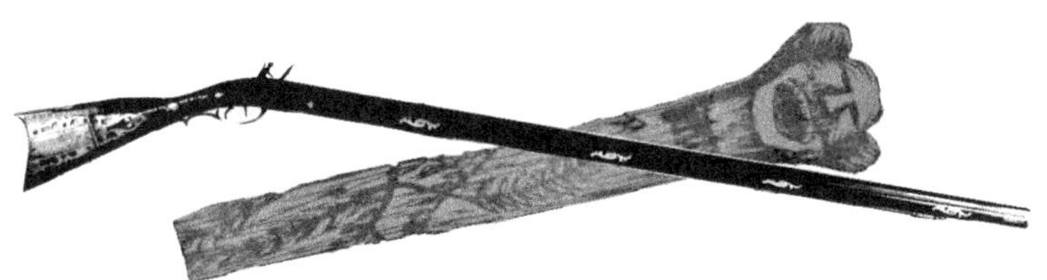

CHAPTER EIGHTY-TWO

The First Battle

1755

Tristrum and Joseph marched out at the end of March when there was snow on the ground. All the Massachusetts troops, one Regiment under William Pepperell and the other under Shirley, rendezvoused in Albany, New York. For the men it meant a miserable march over the Berkshire Mountains in knee-deep snow and nights spent freezing in cold tents. In Albany the two leaders divided for a two-pronged attack with Shirley heading further west to Fort Oswego in order to take Fort Niagara and Pepperell's men went southwest to build Fort Lyman, later renamed Fort Edward on the Hudson River.

To the East the men were under General Monckton in Halifax, having arrived via ship from Boston and other harbors along the east coast.

General Edward Braddock's Irish British Regulars and provincials should have taken a river route to their destination but instead went north and then blazed a trail through the woods and mountains towards Ft. Duquenese on the Ohio River. This wasted valuable time. Braddock and Washington marched 1,500 men to the head of the Ohio River. As they were heading to Ft. Duquesne in the woods near Turtle Creek the columns of soldiers led by Lt. Col Thomas Gage were ambushed and the expedition lost 900 men including Braddock.

Brigadier Robert Monckton's force in Acadia was the only one to succeed that spring. His ships sailed into the harbor below Ft. Beausejoir and it readily surrendered. They then went on to take Ft. St. John and the French retreated into Canada with their Micmacs and priests. The rest of the summer Monckton's men spent rounding up the French Acadians and shipping them out, then burning their farms so the French couldn't reoccupy the land. Under Monckton Robert and John Davis's relatives didn't take part in the forced evacuation of people who had refused to take the oath of allegiance to King George II. The French had been told by their priests that to do so would banish them into a long purgatory in the afterlife since the Protestant English to them represented the AntiChrist. It was hard duty for the colonials who had to serve in Nova Scotia and St. John Island as many of those they forcibly deported had been neighbors and friends. Many felt deep shame and refused to talk about their service but John and Robert's relatives serving under Shirley's Lt. Col. John Williams and his captains never felt that way as they were busy scouting and pursuing the French and indians who terrorized the Maine countryside that summer in a brutal series of sneak attacks. No mercy was shown to any French or indians they found who were slaughtering, scalping and capturing friends and family and burning with abandon their homes. That the Acadians had been forced to side with the French was of little account to the men in Maine. They would gladly have driven them all out as they knew there would never be peace until they were gone, root and branch.

James and Thomas Davis's kin were busy that summer sailing up and down the coast to supply the troops. A big problem was that many of the goods were either delayed in getting to the provisioners or were siphoned off. The situation was so bad in Virginia that the wealthy Benjamin Franklin had to step in and set up an organized system of supply. Even Shirley and Pepperell's troops were wanting for basics and the men became sick from eating spoiled food or wormy game and the sanitation in the camps and forts was very bad. With summer the flies and mosquitoes swarmed around the cess pits and animal slops and manure. Germs were unknown to the people at the time but anyone who observed flies landing on manure, human or animal, then landing on food on the table had to know they carried filth on their legs. Smallpox and cholera decimated almost entire companies as they waited for the supplies they needed in order to push forward to their destinations.

Braddock's delays cost the campaign dearly. Had he followed the trader Gist's path and taken the river route to Ft. Duquense he would have arrived earlier and the French wouldn't have had time to reinforce the fort. As it was, they didn't reach the vicinity of the fort until June 7, 1755. A little later Braddock made a fatal error and insisted his men march in formation, continental-style, against the French and Indians who hid behind trees and boulders.

On the Lac St. Sacrament, which Sir William Johnson later renamed Lake George for his king, a war council was held to determine the best path to the sturdy fort. There was an overland route and a route that would use the waterways. Johnson sent half the regiment overland along a path that was through thick woods. They took no cannon as they didn't anticipate meeting the enemy until the cannon had been brought in later. They were ambushed in the woods by a huge party of the enemy and Capt. Elisha Hawley and Capt. Ephraim Williams were massacred along with over 200 men. Near Lake George outside Ft. Edward Tristrum, under Capt. Daniel Burt, and Joseph plus Thomas Blodgett and his relative Samuel, who was a sutler, heard the shots from the woods and took positions behind the felled trees they had placed as breastworks to confront the French troops heading their way. All the men took the full brunt of the French and indians charging out of the woods. For four hours the fighting went on. As the powder and shot began to run out Tristrum and his fellow soldiers leapt over the barricades and began fighting hand-to-hand with the enemy.

Tristrum's musket ran out of ammunition so he began using it first as a spear with the bayonet, then as a club. One of the indians grabbed him by his hair, which was a prelude to scalping and with a strength he didn't know he possessed, he twisted around and grabbed the upraised arm, forcing the knife into the indian's belly instead of into his scalp. He then grabbed the indian's war club with its hideous bloody screaming mouth and Devil horns and began swinging it, smashing anyone who came close.

As the French began to run away in retreat he was still swinging the club, his eyes wild, his breathing coming in great gulps as he screamed Welsh curses.

It took Joseph to settle him down and lead him back to camp. Dead men were everywhere including some of their friends and neighbors, others oil and ochre painted indians in breechcloths and French in white, now red-stained, uniforms.

The captains gathered up the remnants of their companies and parties were assigned to dig mass graves for the English fallen and others to take the French and indians and dump their bodies in the lake.

Tristrum had never been so tired in his life but he performed the duties assigned to him, as did Joseph. After the dead had been buried the men gathered for ham with beans and bread plus camp tea, afterwards raising their exhausted voices in prayer to God for their deliverance.

Some of the men in the woods weren't found until later and their mutilated corpses, minus the tops of their heads and hair, were a sad sight but a sight familiar to the men from the northern settlements.

The battle took place on November 8th but the men weren't released until the 27th as many were ill. They learned about the massacre of Braddock's troops while waiting for further orders.

Shirley, on Lake Ontario, who had also had supply problems, learned that the French had reinforced Ft. Niagara and with winter approaching had to make the painful decision to send his men home. He set the shipwrights to work at Ft. Oswego to build a fleet for a spring campaign.

****

It was mid-December by the time a foot sore Tristrum and Joseph finally walked down the dirt road to their farm in South Brimfield.

Mary and Rebecca were shocked at how their men looked. They were thin, haggard and their clothes torn and filthy.

Mary immediately got the children gathering wood and water so she could fill the tin bath in front of the fire and get Tristrum bathed. Joseph and his young wife Lois (nee Warriner) left for her parents' farm and his own long, hot soak.

It was late and the snow blowing outside by the time Tristrum was bathed, shaved, clothed in a clean nightshirt and stuffed with Mary's fine beef stew and hot bread. The children had been sent off to bed and it was just Tristrum, Mary and the baby in the sitting room in front of a blazing fire.

"I prayed for you and Joseph every day, many times during the day and the minister always gave long prayers in the services for our men and boys to return," she told her husband as he smoked his well-worn pipe. It was made from a cherry tree knot for the bowl and a carved piece of ivory for the stem with a silver top and chain and had been a gift from one of his mariner relations years ago. The sailors were expert carvers, using ivory or any material to whittle little figurines or objects during long slow times on deck.

"I felt yer prayers, goodwife," he said, smiling over at her in the shadowy room. A gust of wind outside sprayed the window with sleet and a draft blew down the fireplace, "I prayed for ye, also."

"God was merciful," she said, "as not many of our men were killed. I've heard–"

"Nay!" he said suddenly, "they'll be no more talk of what happened, do ye hear? Joseph and I talked and talked about it all the way home and we decided what happened on the battlefields needs to stay on the battlefields. Men turn into something other than humans when blood is all around them, Mary. We do things we don't want to remember. A lot like if a bear is charging ye, you just shoot and don't care if it's a mother defending her wee cubs. The bad feelings come later. Joseph and I will have them in our brains for the rest o' our lives. We don't want to talk about them. I just wish I could put the picture of all our men in that mass gave out o' me mind. They each deserved a decent funeral with their loved ones a'mournin at the grave."

"If ye want to put it out o' yer mind, why did ye bring that hideous thing home with ye?" Mary asked, pointing at the blood-stained war club sticking out of Tristrum's battered, torn pack.

Tristrum blushed,

"'Tis my conscience made me do it, Mary. Everytime I look at it I am reminded that for all me Bible reading and all my praying and good Christian-like living, I am a sinner."

Mary shook her head.

"Well, ye can't hang it over the mantle and I never want the boys to touch it. It might be a sin but I just feel it has the devil in it and don't want its evil to be touched by anyone else."

Tristrum laughed.

"Aye, wife. 'Twill do as ye say. I'll do you one better and stuff it into the foundation stones. It'll be there where I know it is but no one else will know. Will that satisfy thee?"

"Oh, Tristrum, I've missed ye so!" Mary exclaimed, going over and kneeling in front of him in the wing back chair.

He bent down and kissed the top of her white and grey head.

"I've missed ye, too, Mary me love."

As they walked across the hall to their downstairs bedroom (the former dining room), he stopped and turned to her, searching her face, "Is it safe? I mean...?"

Mary chuckled, "Aye, husband. Me monthlies are gone now so there will be no more a'child bearin!"

She took his hard, calloused hand in hers and led him gently to the thick down filled mattress on top of the rope framed bed.

Winter raged outside and pent up love met its fury in the little bedroom on the plateau while a panther screamed in the woods and the cattle shuffled restlessly in the barn outside.

Tristrum didn't tell Mary but the war wasn't over. He knew Shirley and the other commanders were going to spend their winter planning the next offensive – and he knew he'd be a captain in the next battle and he'd be leading neighbors, sons and friends into the fray in order to drive the French and indians out so their children and grandchildren could finally live in peace and not be afraid of hearing war whoops in the woods.

And he knew despite his Christian upbringing he had Welsh paganism in his blood and that carved root ball club with its open, screaming mouth was in a sense a protective charm he was leaving with his family to keep the devils away.

CHAPTER EIGHTY-THREE

Captain Tristrum

1756

In November 1755 Massachusetts Deputy Governor Spencer Phips declared war on the Penobscots. The settlements all up and down the coast and inland up and down the rivers were then subjected to constant indian ambush attacks. Houses, barns, docks, sheds were all set to the torch and fields were littered with dead cattle, sheep and goats. Settlers who weren't massacred or carried off to Canada fled to the safety of the forts and garrison houses.

The British were slow to respond. Gov. Shirley was chomping at the bit to get a head start on the spring campaign to drive the French from Lake Ontario and the western riverway but the man London chose to replace the massacred Gen. Braddock didn't even leave England until June whereas in April France sent a new General Louis Joseph Marquise Montcalm-Gozen de Vern, shortened to Montcalm, to take charge in Quebec. While Shirley and Pepperell's troops were assembling at Albany he was sailing with 1,200 French Regulars to Quebec to take Forts Ticonderoga and Niagara.

Tristrum was now a Captain with his own company of volunteers including his oldest son John and his best friend Reuben Townsley plus the usual collection of men from the Moultons, Allens, Needhams and other Brimfield families with Israel Walker as his sergeant and John Mighill as his clerk and Ephrain White as his corporal. He had told Seth Pomeroy after the last campaign that he'd only reenlist if he had an officer rank with a voice. The British officers were very harsh with the provincials, who were given fatigue duty (tree cutting for roads and the forts, carrying supplies that the ox carts couldn't take or portaging over places where the shallow boats couldn't manage). Some, such as the Blodgetts, were sutlers, or provisioners in charge of keeping the supply lines flowing. Others were scouts. The army needed cooks, surgeons, chaplains and all sorts of tradesmen as well.

On May 18, 1756 England declared war on France. The next day France declared war on England. The war came about partly because Frederick the Great of Prussia had seized Silesia from Princess Maria Theresa (and her son King Louis LXV as the French King Charles had died without a male heir). England, Frederick II's ally, and the Hanoverian and Protestant nations on the Continent went with war against France, Austria and Russia. France's Army was brought up to 100,000 men but its Navy was weak, having been destroyed by England earlier. Fighting a war without a strong navy didn't bother Montcalm as he knew he had innumerable canoes to help them ferry supplies through the St. Lawrence seaway and down through the great lakes to the forts on the great rivers.

Govs. Shirley and Canada's Vadreuil didn't wait for the formal declaration of war (or the arrival of Montcalm) to prepare for war. Shirley sent his troops to Fort Williams on the Mohawk River and Fort Bull on the banks of Wood Creek, the great carrying place, to stock the storehouses with ammunition and barrels of pork, bags of flour, beans, peas, blankets, rum and other provisions his volunteers would need for their attack on Forts Frontenac and Niagara.

In February Vadreuil's force of almost 400 French, Canadian provincials and indians attacked Fort Bull, which only had 30 garrison soldiers at the time. The gates were closed barely in time and the men held out bravely, firing muskets and throwing hand grenades over the palisade but the French succeeded in smashing in the log gates and they slaughtered the men inside. John Davis had been one of the soldiers. He'd arrived with a load of supplies and was about to return to Ft. Williams when the attack occurred. He received a bullet in his side but was able to bury himself under sacks of flour until the French finished pillaging and plundering and scalping and left with as much as they could carry.

He and two other men struggled through the deep snow to Half Moon, the carrying place, and were able to hire a farmer to take them by horseback down to Albany where a doctor removed the bullet, stitched up the flesh wound and put fresh dressings on it daily for two weeks until he was sure there was no infection, then John was released back to his father's company.

Capt. Tristrum hugged his son but pulled back when he saw him wince.

"Ye sure you want to continue on?" he asked, his blue eyes searching the face of his tall, brown eyed, light brown haired son. Tristrum was shorter with jet black hair, now shot with silver. He had the darker Welsh complexion whereas most of his children took after their mother with fairer skin and lighter hair.

"After seeing what those sons of the Devil did to the men at Ft. Bull I am more determined than ever to go out and kill each and every one of them!" John exclaimed, clenching his fist.

Tristrum knew his fury well. It had saved his life at Crown Point. It and the indian war club that he secretly felt was his lucky charm and had left with Mary and his family to protect them.

Gov. Shirley appointed John Winslow for his field Commander-in-Chief and was collecting a large army at Albany of Massachusetts provincials under Pepperell; the remnants of Braddock's battalions; the Jersey Blues and companies from North Carolina. There were four companies of British Regulars who had been billeted in New York City, also. London sent word that the deceased Braddock's replacement, General Abercromby, would be arriving and he was preceded by Col, Daniel Webb, both experienced in Continental warfare. Gov. Shirley and Gov. Vaudreuil were both getting shoved aside as the professional officers sent from England and France were taking over. While awaiting Webb and Abercromby Shirley set the Massachusetts men to rebuilding Fort Bull and set up garrison posts along the route to Ft. Oswego, which he knew the French would be attacking since it held a critical post at the opening of Lake Ontario, which led down to the Ohio River Valley. He had 5,000 men camped at Half Moon, whose rapids were so swollen that men had severe difficulty portaging goods across the river to the forts along the way. The English were building small forts or garrisons beginning at the Hudson and continuing past Albany and Schenectady, then west on the Mohawk River, following it west to the William Johnson garrison, which had Fort Hunter opposite, then to German Flats, Fort Herkimer, Forts (just palisaded storehouses) Bull and Williams at Half Moon, then on to Lake Oneida to Fort Brewerton on its west then down the Oneida River then the Oswego River up to Ft. Ontario on the east side of the lake and Ft. Oswego on the west.

Winslow made Half Moon his headquarters as it was at an intersection. From there provisions coming from the east were taken off the boats and put on ox carts and driven several miles past the Upper (Hudson) Falls, then down to the lakes or portaged and sent west to Fts. Oswego and Ontario.

The southern approach followed the Hudson from Albany to Ft. Edward, the falls and a portage place over to Lake George's Ft. William Henry. Lake George then connected north to Lake Champlain but the French had a fort named Carillon guarding the fork opposite the newly built stone fort called Ft. Ticonderoga.

On the southern route reached by land from Albany was Ft. Edward, built by Ct. Col. Lyman the year before, below the Hudson River where the great falls were. Supplies could then be portaged past the falls up to Lake George to Ft. William Henry. There, the troops massed for an attack on Ticonderoga on Lk. Champlain. Ticonderoga looked out over the waterways and was a prime target for English occupation. Between Half Moon and Ft. Edward in the elbow of the Hudson Shirley had small garrisons at every branch of the Hudson River.

****

Every soldier fights his own war. They see the war through the lens of their battles, their movements, their postings. It is for the generals to see the overview, to plan the battles. Soldiers are given orders and their job is to follow the orders to the best of their abilities. Tristrum's company was stationed under Col. Jonathan Bagley at Fort William Henry at the southern part of what the English called Lake George. Tristrum and most of his men were put to work cutting wood for the sloops and hundreds of whaleboats (the small Nantucket sleigh riders) in order to take the army up the lakes to Fort Ticonderoga so they could attack Fort Frontenac and then move on to Oswego for an attack on Ft, Niagara. Gov. Shirley enlisted hundreds of whalemen and put Col. John Bradstreet in charge. During May Bradstreet's sailors convoyed tons of supplies to Ft. Oswego. With empty boats they began the return to Ft. William Henry, which also was supplied via Ft. Edward and Albany. The French attacked the men in the empty boats and were held off by Bradstreet and Capt. Schuyler's men who fired back from an island in the river. Hearing of the battle Capt. Patten brought 200 grenadiers from Shirley's regiment on the *Onadonga* River to help the whalers but they arrived after the battle.

The next day, the Sabbath, summer rain fell without stop and Bradstreet decided against trying to pursue the French through the pine swamps, instead he brought the remnants of his companies back with him down the rivers and lakes then overland to Albany with whatever loot they were able to scavenge from the French and indians plus some prisoners of war. About 70 men were either killed, wounded or captured but the English considered it a victory since the French were driven off and didn't take Ft. Oswego and its shipyards.

Dr. Kirkland, worn out with fatigue, recruited some of Tristrum's men to help carry the wounded on carts to Ft. Edward where the hospital was set up. This was where John would have gone in March but the fort was barely staffed and no doctor was present at the time.

Shirley's 50th Regiment had been in bad shape from starvation and diseases and across the river Pepperell's 51st Regiment fared little better. In order to proceed with their plans the English needed a strong fighting force. In late June Gen. James Abercromby and Col. Daniel Webb made it to Albany with 900 British Regulars and a company of Scottish Highlanders playing bagpipes and wearing the kiLt. which had been outlawed by the English after Scotland surrendered. The old kilt that was little more than a plaid blanket wrapped around the waist and hanging almost to the ground had been replaced by a shorter pleated and belted one that allowed freedom of movement. A fur covered pouch called a sporran hung in front in which the men could carry powder and shot. When Major General Shirley was forced to give over his commission he was ordered to go to the settlement on Manhattan called New York city to brief the Scottish Earl Lord Louden.

After reaching Albany Louden sent Lt. Col. Burton to inspect the provincial troops. Winslow had continued to reinforce Ft. Oswego with half the troops waiting at Ft. William Henry to advance and Gen. Phineas Lyman's Connecticut men plus Tristrum and his provincials were sent back to Ft. Edward or the other forts along the route.

Tristrum had faced his first challenge as a captain at Fort William Henry. He was roused from his cot by a sergeant and two soldiers holding Reuben Townsley between them.

Tristrum's first thought was that Reuben, raised half wild by parents or grandparents who had been captives in Canada from Deerfield, had gone native and went off hunting. He was known to disappear for weeks on end, leaving his family clueless until he returned with a deer or other game.

"This man was caught sleeping on duty!" one of the soldiers said, shoving Reuben roughly.

Tristrum sat up. He had enlisted as an officer in order to be able to look after his son and his friends and neighbors, not to punish them. But sleeping on watch was a very serious offense. The men were half-starved, living on peas and bacon and had to stand twelve hour shifts, sometimes as many as nine times in a row.

Sitting up and pulling on his trousers and coat Capt. Tristrum Davis ordered the men to the main room of the fort where the officers had tables for paperwork.

This was a moral dilemma. Reuben was his closest friend, more a brother than his own kin, yet he couldn't show preference.

Tristrum sat behind the "desk" and asked,

"Private Townsley, is it true that ye were found sleeping when ye should have been keepin' watch?"

Reuben mumbled, "Yes, sir."

"Ye know Ye'll be given the cat for your dereliction of duty," Tristrum said, sternly facing the crumpled man in front of him, "And ye should be glad they brought ye to me and not to a British officer but I cannot overlook so serious an offense."

He and the other provincial officers routinely got the charges reduced so their men could be punished at the provincial regimental level and not by the British Regular officers.

One of the soldiers holding up Reuben said,

"It's not unusual, sir. I've often found my watch asleep when I reported to duty."

"And ye didn't report it?" Tristrum thundered, rising and scowling deeply.

"Sir, we only reported this fellow because a British Regular spotted him first."

Tristrum came out from behind his table. Everything in the fort was rough-hewn, raw wood. It was dark and dank inside. A rat scurried across the floor as he moved in closer to Reuben.

Reuben fainted. Tristrum caught him.

"This man is out of his head with fever!" he exclaimed, feeling the hot, sweaty forehead of Reuben, "He didn't fall asleep, he passed out from sickness. Take him to the hospital immediately."

As he watched them carry Reuben to the tents where 500 men were lying sick in cots he worried that his friend would be in the five to eight graves the soldiers had to dig every day for those who died from dysentery and fevers. Exhaustion weakened their constitutions, usually robust and healthy on their open air farms, and they couldn't fight off the diseases that spread like fire amongst the tightly-packed troops. He called for Chaplain Graham who lived south of Brimfield in Suffield to go and see what he could do for Reuben then sought out Lyman to explain that the man was exempt from punishment as he didn't willfully sleep but rather passed out.

A month later the French under Montcalm attacked Ft. Oswego. They attacked Ft. Ontario first. Pepperell only had about 370 men in the star-shaped log fort on a plateau above the river. It was built to repel attack by soldiers with muskets but its eight small cannon and one mortar were no real defense against a huge French force of Regulars. Across the river Col. Mercer sent word that the men should abandon the fort and join him at New Oswego as the combined forces would do better facing the French. The men were ferried in boats the 500 yards across the river, allowing Montcalm's men to claim the higher ground of Ft. Ontario, from which they proceeded to pound Oswego with artillery. The 51st had thrown ammunition into the well and spiked the cannon before they abandoned the fort but the French sent round after round of grape shot from field cannons and cannon balls, shattering the fort's walls. Although Ft. Oswego had cannon it wasn't portable and had been positioned to face attack from the west, assuming Ft. Ontario would protect its eastern flank. All day the men, many sick and many so newly recruited they had hardly fired muskets, fought valiantly. When the wall went they stacked pork barrels three high and three deep and sent returning fire from their badly exposed position. Col. Mercer stood up to direct fire and a cannon ball cut him in two, spewing his blood over men already shell shocked. Around this time some French sneaked into their midst and the senior officers conferred and ordered a white flag of surrender to be raised. The French took 1,600 English prisoners, including shipwrights, women and many young, untrained soldiers.

By August most of the men at Ft. Edward, including Tristrum himself, were in the hospital with dehydrating diarrhea. After Oswego was lost the men were ordered to the English Ft. Ticonderoga where they cleared the forest for a mile inland, leaving the trees strewn to create a barrier to French and indian troops. Others hauled stones or mixed lime mortar to help complete the new thick stone fortress. While there Tristrum met Robert Rogers and his companies of Rangers, or scouts. They'd had some small successes against the French and Tristrum longed to be included on one of their escapades and spy missions but he was an old man and Rogers needed young, strong fast men for his rough camping and canoeing missions. He asked if Robert were related to the many Rogers in Brimfield and the surrounding area and the tall, big boned and big nosed fellow laughed as he replied,

"Aye, like ye Davis men, we dropped kin all over. Me parents bought land from the Allens and they from the Wentworths. So, probably through the Allen clan we are related to the Brimpsfield clan. Ye said your eldest son married a Rebecca Allen?"

"Aye," Tristrum replied, envying the soldiering Rogers Rangers were doing. While he and his men were digging ditches, cutting down trees and doing all the grunt work men like Rogers were in the thick of it, facing the French and actually inflicting damages.

In December Tristrum's company put on a brave, cheerful face as they marched homewards down the road from Springfield to Brimfield but the men were demoralized. They felt beaten, defeated and then further let down when they learned that Gen. Shirley had been ordered back to England in disgrace.

The following year Tristrum and the Brimfield men weren't called to service as the British Regulars under Mag. William Eyre and other men were at Fts. Edward and William Henry plus Lord Louden had gathered a huge number of ships and men to retake Ft. Louisbourg. The French attacked Ft. William Henry in July. Major General Daniel Webb took men and fled to Ft. Edward leaving Lt. Col. George Munro with 1,400 regulars plus Highlanders. Col John Stanwix had 1,900 provincials encamped near Ft. Edward but the French, after taking Fort William Henry retreated, sparing their lives. Rogers Rangers reported that the French had retreated to their winter quarters leaving only 350 men at Fort William Henry and 150 at Crown Point, making both targets easy for the English to retake.

Why the British generals didn't proceed against Louisbourg or the forts on Lakes George and Champlain was a mystery to the colonial militiary leaders. True, once the snow began to fall the going became harder in the north – but also easier – as sledges could be hauled by horse over frozen rivers (and Rogers' Rangers intercepted many French supply trains on the ice this way). The main problem with winter fighting was that the colonial troops died from frostbite and pneumonia and respiratory diseases as they often had to sleep on the frozen ground with just a thin woolen blanket around them. The men refused to serve in the winter and the British knew that other than scouts who wore ice skates or snowshoes, the provincial forces weren't equipped to fight in the north during winter.

It had been 86 years since the colonial forces marched out in the snow into the Narragansett swamp but the horrors of that campaign were still retold around the fireplaces. For their sacrifice and service seven grants of land had been given to their descendants in New England, the grants named the 'Narragansett Seven'. Cornelius and John Davis had been a beneficiaries in the Somers-Stafford area, which was part of Massachusetts at the time, and other Davis men got land in Maine (at the time part of Massachusetts), and in New Hampshire. But the men didn't want to fight anymore as winter approached. They resented the way the British officers treated them like dogs and couldn't comprehend why their men were so cruelly punished for the smallest offenses, sometimes receiving so many lashes of the cat (cat o' nine tails) that they died; some having to ride the 'wooden horse' and some were even hanged.

The following year Tristrum and his sons didn't join Capt. Daniel Burt's company but Reuben Townsley, his relative Ebenezer Stebbins, Moultons, Needhams, Blisses, Blodgetts, Hitchcocks, Kings and Elijah Mighill's younger brother Nathaniel went out to meet the French under command of Gen. James Abercromby on the lakes or under General Jeffrey Amherst on the eastern front.

In Maine Davis mariners joined the expedition against Louisbourg as part of the Navy, either carrying troops or supplies to the cold Atlantic waters off the coast of Maine.

CHAPTER EIGHTY-FOUR

The Home Front

1758

Tristrum's Brookfield kin (there were many now that it had been resettled) Ebenezer had enlisted in 1757 and served under Capt. Jabez Upham at Crown Point. Dr. Isaac Davis, from Somers, had been cleared of desertion charges as he had left his fort to attend to a medical emergency of a British officer in Albany and there had been no time to draft proper papers. He never enlisted again but pursued his private medical practice in Somers and was married to Rachel Sheldon whose relatives lived in South Brimfield.

Isaac Davis started a new religion that he called 'Davisonism' but he had few followers. As far back as Anne Hutchinson, John Wheelwright, Roger Williams and the Quakers there were always some Davises who didn't want to conform to the state religion. In South Brimfield the AnaBaptists were tolerated and a new sect named Methodists were also gaining members. The Puritans, who had themselves come to the New Land in order to practice their version of Protestantism, had lost a lot of their influence after Judge Sewell and the witchcraft hysteria. However, every provincial regiment had a chaplain and prayers were held before battles and hymns were sung after the drums and patriotic music played on the fifes, or in the case of the regiments with Scottish highlanders, the bag pipes. The chaplains gave rousing sermons to inspire the men to be as brave as the Israelites and the followers of Jesus and commanders used many Bible passages when raising enthusiasm for battle.

Joseph Davis married Mary, sister of Joseph Browning of Brimfield and moved north to that town center. The larger grant of Brimfield was now being referred to unofficially as South Brimfield, Brimfield, Western (or Warren) and Monson. To its south the line between Massachusetts and Connecticut had a new survey and the towns of Union, Stafford, Somers, etc. went to Connecticut. By now Tristrum and Joseph because of their accents were being lumped in with the Scots-Irish that had settled Union but the brothers just referred to themselves as from "the old country".

In 1758 there were no Davises from South Brimfield in the army but the farmers worked extra hard as they not only had to grow crops for their families and raise livestock for their own smoke sheds, curing crocks, woolen looms and hide tanneries but were expected to sell supplies for the troops. It was more profitable for a farmer to stay home and sell goods to the government than to work as a provincial soldier for very small wages. Where it helped was when a family had a surplus of teenaged sons who weren't necessarily needed on the farm but who could be fed by the army.

Tristrum was a Royalist. He loved his King and his British Country. Having spent his youth in Wales he felt more British than New England colonist so he never questioned his duty to help England fight her enemies. His sons weren't as convinced, especially after Gov. Major General Shirley had been disrespected by the crown.

But it was in 1758 that the worm began to turn and the British troops started winning against France in North America.

After the aborted Ft. Louisbourg mission Lord Loudoun was called back to England and replaced by Major General Abercromby with Col. Lord George Howe as his second in command. Unlike the other British officers Col. Edward Howe respected the abilities of the provincials and he had Robert Rogers promoted from captain to major. Maj. Rogers had seven companies under him. His first mission in early March was to spy on Ft. Ticonderoga and report back the French strength. However, his men encountered almost 700 French and indians before reaching the fort and he lost 100 rangers, or scouts. Acting without the aid of Rogers' Rangers' intelligence Abercromby led 1,400 men to attack Ticonderoga. In June they were assembled at Ft. William Henry with Howe having command of seven regiments of British Regular soldiers and Lt Col. Thomas Gage leading the light infantry and Rogers leading the scouts. An army of men in boats followed the larger ships that set sail up Lake George, through the Narrows that led to the long Lake Champlain that branched out to Wood Creek.

At the same time on the eastern front Gen. Jeffrey Amherst had arrived in Halifax from England with a fleet and 11,000 regulars. As Abercromby's force began its northward trip to Ticonderoga. Amherst was leading a fleet from Halifax to Cape Breton. Amherst was backed by Admiral Edward Boscawen and Brigadier Generals James Wolfe, Edward Whitmore and Charles Lawrence. The English vastly outnumbered the French at Ft. Louisbourg but it took 49 days of heavy cannon bombardment to effect the surrender of the fort. The English had under 200 casualties but the French lost over 350 men and over 5,000 French were taken prisoner. The French fleet had been diverted to Cape Breton but by the end of the month-and-a-half battle it was decimated. The English swept up the area and finally gained control of the entrance to the St. Lawrence seaway and the north coast of Maine.

Abercromby's men were not so fortunate. He had chosen to attack the fort on its one landward side. Rogers and Howe led the troops but they were almost immediately met by heavy French and indian resistance. The English gained sawmills and garrisons but Abercromby halted the advance as he waited for the main body of his troops under Sir William Johnson to catch up. While Abercromby waited Montcalm brought in reinforcements from Ft. Frederick via Lk. Champlain. The English general grew restless and decided to attack before his heavy artillery arrived. He felt his men could scale the stone breastworks but the result was a slaughter and the English were forced to retreat, losing almost 2,000 men. The main force was then diverted to the Great Carrying Place and construction of Ft. Stanwick was begun. Gen. Bradstreet was sent with 3,000 regulars to attack Ft. Frontenac on Lake Ontario. The army traveled by water down the Oneida, then Onondaga River and over to Lake Ontario.

The French commander of Ft. Frontenac only had about 100 men. Knowing he was greatly outnumbered he surrendered the fort, which was the main storehouse for supplies and ammunition for Fts. Niagara and Duquenese. To the south the British under Brigadier John Forbes used this to their advantage and recaptured Ft. Duquense, which they renamed Ft. Pitt in honor of Prime Minister William Pitt.

The English then captured what was left of the French fleet on Lake Ontario. The summer of 1758 was one of great victories for the English and New England as they now controlled the Atlantic coast to the St. Lawrence seaway; Lake Ontario and the French supply lines down to Pennsylvania and Ft. Duquense plus Ft. Louisbourg and all of the area formerly called Acadia.

A new fort on the Ohio River, called Ft. Bradford, was built but Brig. Gen. John Forbes succumbed to one of the camp diseases and died. He was succeeded by Gen. Amherst as Commander-in-Chief, who was knighted in honor of his Louisbourg victory, and Col. General George Washington, replacing Gen. Shirley, was in charge of the provincial soldiers. Col. Archibald Montgomery was in charge of the Highlanders as 1758 came to a close.

CHAPTER EIGHTY-FIVE

The Fall of Quebec

1759

The year opened with a battle between France and England in the Caribbean. To finance the war the New England and English sugar barons needed to sell sugar, rice, tobacco and indigo. France was intercepting their cargo ships in the West Indies, using the harbors of Guadeloupe with ships anchored at Forts Louis and Royal. Pitt's shipbuilding program had already paid off with the huge victory at Ft. Louisbourg so in January he sent a fleet under Major General Barrington to take out the French at two small islands north of the Barbados, which were the first stop of the slave ships from Africa. Thus, by taking Guadeloupe they deprived the French of new slaves and lessened production (and money) from its colonies. The British went for the head of the snake, taking out the life source for Canada on several fronts: Louisbourg, Frontenac and then Guadeloupe. However, the real prize would be Quebec. Until England took it the French were still in control of the St. Lawrence seaway all the way to the west and down the Mississippi River to Louisiana.

The Davis men sailing cargo ships up and down from Nova Scotia to the West Indies had been affected by French attacks at sea but when the English got

Guadeloupe it was a big victory as the lucrative slave trade for the French was interrupted. It was a brilliant move, one unexpected by the French.

The English had victories off the coasts of India and a fleet under Frederic of Brunswick sailed to the Philippines to take territories of strategic value from the French while on the Continent King George II continued to support Frederick the Great of Prussia who had a victory in Minden, France.

In Virginia Major General Sir Jeffrey Amherst took over as Commander-in-Chief of the New England war against New France. The chief goal was to take Ft. Ticonderoga and Crown Point as they held the Champlain waterway that led down to Fts. William Henry and Edward. In order to seize the territory from the east to Lake Champlain, Amherst put Major General James Wolfe in charge of the British fleet to the east. To the south the goal was to take Ft. Niagara and all the forts above Ft. Pitt, cutting off the French as far north as Lake Erie. This would give the English the western St. Lawrence, Lakes Ontario and Erie and Onadonga so they would have nowhere to attack the Colonies other than from offshore. The British Navy had decimated the French Navy in the English Channel. Pitt had followed the example of Queen Elizabeth and knew England's greatest strength lay in her navy.

Amherst wasted no time in going for Ft. Ticonderoga. He amassed an army of Regulars and provincials on the shore of Lk. George, had extra blockhouses built there then moved his army up the lake to Champlain where the saw mills were. From there they proceeded to bombard Ticonderoga with cannon and in five days the French deserted the fort. Within a month the French had abandoned Ft. Crown Point and Amherst's forces occupied it, rebuilding and re-fortifying where the stone had been ruptured. Both forts were sturdy stone and mortar and had thick redoubts where large 32 pound cannon could be placed plus cannons decreasing in size to the portable field cannon. Each large cannon required six men to load pounds of powder into the touchhole, load a bag of grape shot or a heavy cannon ball into the shaft and then one man to light the fuse. The cannon moved, sometimes even jumping, when fired, and men were injured or killed if they weren't paying attention or the cannon traveled an irregular path in its recoil. The sound of cannon was deafening and more than one soldier ended up with bleeding ears and permanent hearing damage from duty on the earth-packed cannon wall.

Amherst was fortunate that his early to mid-summer campaign had cost very few lives this year. However, because the French had four heavily armed men o' war on Lake Ontario he couldn't proceed upriver to Montreal. Amherst set his men to rebuilding Crown Point and also had Capt. Loring at Ft. Oswego build ships so the troops could fight off the French and sail east to help Gen. Wolfe.

To the west Gen. Sir William Johnson led his forces, which included James and Nathaniel Davis from Connecticut, on boats from St. Stanwix, down Wood Creek and then Lake Oneida and Onondaga to Fort Oswego (which the French had destroyed then abandoned). They continued down the Ohio and laid siege to Fort Niagara. During the siege the French General Prideaux was mortally wounded. His replacement fought until he realized no reinforcements would be arriving and then surrendered. Johnson and his troops then took the fort and the English continued until they held all the forts including Venango, Le Bouef and Presque Isle ,and Col. Frederick Halimand repelled the French at Ft. Oswego. They had driven the French all the way back to Detroit and their indian allies crept back into the woods.

Thomas Pownall was appointed to replace Governor Shirley in January 1759 and he immediately got support from Secretary of State/Prime Minister William Pitt in London to construct a fort at the mouth of the Penobscot River. Holding that point the English would control all river traffic into the interior and deprive the French and indians of an important trading route.

Pitt and Amherst backed Pownall's plan and the Massachusetts General Assembly authorized him to lead an expedition and raise troops from Maine to build a fort under the direction of Gershom Flagg, the man who had designed Ft. Western earlier:. Ebenezer Davis was now a corporal, having served with honor under his brother Israel Davis in 1755 and 1756. After promotion he served in Maine under Capt. Sylvanus Walkins. When the troops first landed in May Pownall sent a communication to the Penobscots telling them the English were going to build a fort there and if they didn't like it they could come out and fight. They didn't. While Pownall and his engineer and escorts went out reconnoitering to find the most suitable spot for the fort, they discovered a pleasant waterfall on the river. While admiring the view, Pownall's second in command, Samuel Waldo dropped dead on the spot. In spite of the loss of a prime Maine financier, Pownall and the men managed to build a four pointed 'star-shaped' fort by July of 1759, thus securing the north of Maine below St. John's and Nova Scotia.

The main action occurred further north that spring through fall as the young James Wolfe, son of Gen. Edward Wolfe, renown for his militiary prowess on the Continent was appointed Major General in charge of the British forces in North America. Because he was only 33 (but had seen a lot of action on the battlefields of Europe and in Scotland) the older officers resented Pitt's appointment but Admirals Saunders Holmes and Durell, Brigadiers Monckton, George Townshend and James Murray and the Highlanders under Capt. Alexander Montgomery eagerly accepted it and knew tall, pale, thin, frail Commander-in-Chief Wolfe was a brave man. On the 22nd of February the fleet left Spitwell with a very seasick Wolfe on the *Neptune*. In all there were 22 "of the line" British fighting ships, frigates, sloops of war and a variety of ships carrying goods and troops in the fleet. After they docked at Louisbourg they were joined by Durell who brought some provincials from New York and Nova Scotia. In all, Wolfe had over 12,000 soldiers plus sailors as he set sail for the St. Lawrence to bring the fight to the French at Quebec.

Wolfe, in spite of his sickness, had a reputation as a dogged fighter. He sailed up the St. Lawrence with the aid of French pilots he had captured by trickery as at a particularly perilous section of river where ships would stop and take on the pilots (he raised the French flag and the pilots rowed out to meet the ships, which they thought were French troops to reinforce Montcalm and Gov. Vaudreuil at Quebec). After capturing the pilots the English then lowered the French flag and raised England's white and red one and sailed without impediment through the tricky section of the river. His fleet of 60 ships then audaciously kept sailing until his fleet reached Isle of Orleans, just three miles east of Quebec. He sent 40 New England Rangers onto the island and, meeting a little resistance, they found it deserted the following morning, allowing the British to land their troops and set up camp within view of the fortress-like Quebec that sat on steep hills surrounded by the St. Lawrence and Charles Rivers on three sides. Montcalm had heavily fortified the city and fort and the forts further downstream. He didn't send troops out to meet Wolfe, intending to hold them off until November when the Canadian winter would lock their ships into ice unless they left.

Wolfe had other ideas. He gained a plateau across from Quebec (Levi Point) and fired on the lower parts of the city, then ran ships up past Quebec and forded the Montmorency River and landed troops at L' Anse de Foulon to gain ground on its western side. For three months Wolfe worked at pulling the French out of their fortifications and he finally found a weak spot that led up to what the locals called "the Heights of Abraham", a grassy plateau that overlooked Quebec's weakest side.

In late August he'd received word from Amherst that his ships wouldn't be ready in time for his troops to get to Montreal in time to help Wolfe. Undeterred, two weeks later Wolfe sneaked in about 100 volunteers during the night to Abraham's Heights and they overtook the small unit guarding it. New England's Rogers' Rangers were to the English what the indians soldiers were to the French: bush fighters who knew the terrain, knew how to rough it in the wild, were quick to think on their feet and excellent at disappearing into the woods. In addition, Wolfe had sharp shooters capable of taking out targets from behind rocks or trees with amazing accuracy.

After Wolfe got the main body of his army onto the plains they stood three-deep for almost a mile facing Quebec. His right flank didn't reach the cliff face so on that side he had his men deployed in a perpendicular pattern so the French couldn't outflank him. For all his frailty Wolfe was a militiary genius – and he was lucky as his other troops were stretched thin and too far apart to come to the aid of the other if attacked. The French had grown complacent. They felt come winter the English would leave. They always had before.

On the morning of September 13, 1759 Montcalm and Vaudreuil woke to the British challenge above the city stronghold. Unlike the indians and French who screamed and made a lot of noise when attacking, Wolfe had his redcoats stand in rows in complete silence as they looked down on Quebec. Silent, menacing. The message: Come out and Fight.

Montcalm ordered men and field cannon to be marched over a ridge in between the English and his city-fort but Wolfe told his men to wait to fire until the French came in close and then they fired a volley in unison, aiming for the French Regulars in the middle while sharp shooters picked off Canadians and indians on the sides. He had his men lie down on the ground when the cannons fired grape shot across the field and then they rose and fired in unison again while the bagpipes skirled and the drums kept up a steady battle beat in the distance.

It was over quickly. Both Montcalm and Wolfe were mortally wounded. Wolfe's second in command Monckton was wounded so Capt. Townshend took over as the

French fled. The British held their ground and within two days Gen. Ramesey, who had been given command when Vadrieul retreated to Montreal, surrendered Quebec to the English.

Most of the fleet was withdrawn as winter moved in. The fort had been so destroyed by the constant bombardment from Levi Point across the river that there was little shelter to be found. Men were assigned to only one hour watches and even then many got frostbite. Besides the cold the men got scurvy, dysentery and other camp diseases but England and New England held onto Quebec.

The French, however, were not finished.

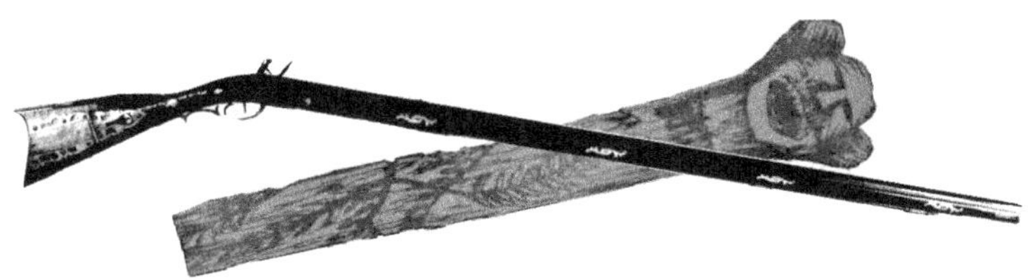

CHAPTER EIGHTY-SIX

The Final Battles and Capitulation of France

1760

During the end of the Quebec campaign Capt. Tristrum and three of his sons were called up to serve on the western front. In early 1760 Quebec was held by mostly British Regulars, the volunteers having been sent home except for the Rangers who lived off base and in the woods. The Scottish regiment in short kilts suffered greatly from the bitter cold and the Catholic nuns in the hospital knitted long underwear for the men to wear under their 'skirts'.

As soon as Gen. Duc de Francois Levi and Gov. Pierre Vaudreuil got to Montreal they began combing the countryside to conscript Canadians at the point of a musket. The indians in the fort at Point Levi bragged that they would soon be giving the British haircuts. Brig. Gen. James Murray reinforced St. Foy and Old Lorette and when he heard the French had bragged they would eat Christmas dinner inside the walls of Quebec he'd had enough and sent Major Dalling with light infantry and some Highlanders across the frozen St. Lawrence to rout the French from Point Levi.

Next he sent Capt. Donald MacDonald and 500 regulars to LeCalviare near St. Augustine to drive the French away, even though the fort was two days march from Quebec. Over 100 men returned with frostbite but the English only had six wounded in a brief but fierce fight. Eighty French soldiers were marched back as prisoners of war. At Ft. Lorette the Rangers heard the French were planning a major offensive and Rogers left Capt. Hazen with 14 men to guard the fort while he and his Rangers went to Quebec for reinforcements. They were ambushed en route but drove the French attackers off. In late February the Rangers reported the French were amassing an army of 11,000 men to retake Quebec. But no assault happened. As soon as the weather turned warmer and the ice began to break up on the river Murray told the French inside the city they had three days to leave as he knew Vadriel had spies inside and some Quebec patriots were stealing English supplies and smuggling them to Montreal where they were being processed into articles for warfare.

On April 20, 1760 Vanquelin and troops of the line, or French Regulars, Canadians, colonials including a battalion of artillery and indians set sail with two frigates, two sloops of war and numerous smaller vessels to sail upriver and retake Quebec. Along the way they forced Canadians to join their ranks so by the time they got to Cap Rouge they had between almost 9,000 in their ranks. The French built a portable bridge and crossed the river, easily overtaking Old Lorette, which was hastily abandoned, the men having orders to retreat to St. Foy. In a raging sleet, rain and thunderstorm with lighting striking all around, the French pursued the English soldiers but the boggy thawing ground finally made them stop. Their pause allowed the British to reinforce the ridge between the plateau and Quebec but then Murray made a big mistake and sent troops to chase off the French. They also became bogged in the slush but the ground was not yet soft enough to drive logs in deep enough for a palisade. Murray knew the walls of the fort would not withstand cannon fire but his men fought the elements as they tried to drive the French away so they couldn't entrench cannon on the side of the hill facing the city. Despite the slogging, the wounded Hazen and Col. Frazer with his 78th Highlanders retreated in formation to the city gates and MacDonald, mortally wounded, was carried inside. The wounded and dead on the field were brutally scalped during the night. Murray lost about 1,000 soldiers, a big loss as he only had about 3,000 fit to serve. He put the invalids to work filling sandbags to reinforce the walls and the men in the hospital made wadding for the cannon. The walls were reinforced and field cannon dragged up so the English could fire down on the French as they tried to build a place for their cannon to be positioned.

Murray had sent word to England on the frigate *Racehorse* bound for Halifax that Quebec was under siege and the English and French both watched the river for signs of ships bringing reinforcements, cannon, ammunition and supplies. Unbeknownst to Levi the English Navy had captured the resupply convoy from France. On May 9th a ship of war was spotted and neither side knew whose it was until the Lowestaffe's red English flag was seen flying from her mast. It anchored below Quebec and was followed by the *Diana* and *Vanguard*. The ships then went down the St. Lawrence and attacked the French fleet beyond Quebec. Its admiral,Vaquin, was taken prisoner but the French fought until the end. However, Vaquin refused to strike the white French flag from his mast. The French across from the city knew they were in trouble and immediately evacuated the hillside. They left behind in their fleet 34 cannon, six mortars and all their tools and even muskets in their hasty retreat. They also left their sick and wounded.

One the same day Lord Holderness in England received news of defeat, then news of victory almost simultaneously while eating peaches grown in a new invention, the Dutch oven or hothouse.

As the fighting season approached Gen. Amherst planned a three-pronged offensive against Montreal. He, with the main body of troops would go overland then through Lake Ontario and on to St. Louis to block the French from escaping west to Detroit. Murray was to move his troops to St. Louis and Brigadier Haviland to come up Lake Champlain. The plan called for all three forces to meet at the same time at Montreal.

Murray had sent the invalids to the Isle of Orleans to recuperate so by the second of July he was ready to start with 32 fighting ships and many smaller bateaux. He had been reinforced with the troops from Louisbourg under Lord Rollo, per the order of King George II, as it was critical that the English control the interior waterways. The French hoped to delay the fleet at Three Rivers but Murray audaciously sailed past. He had sent word out that any Canadian who surrendered his arms and declared neutrality would not be harmed and his property would be spared. The Canadians were demoralized because they knew what the English could do to them as Wolfe had run a scorched earth campaign the year before to get the countryside to submit or flee. The French sent out word that any soldier who submitted would be hanged without a court martial but the number of deserters grew by the day.

Rogers and his Rangers kept up a steady supply of information about the progress of the troops. Haviland with his Regulars, Highlanders and provincials left Crown Point and Amherst put his troops into whale longboats and ships from Oswego onto Lake Ontario by the 10th of August. To clear the way Rogers' Rangers swam with tomahawks in hand out to the French fleet of three ships and gunboats on backside of the Isle de Noives, silently boarding and killing the sailors. The other ships saw what happened and surrendered, leaving the coast clear for the English to continue down the St. Lawrence.

Amherst's fleet encountered the French armed brig *Ottawa* on Lk. Ontario and overtook it then spent three days firing cannon into Fort Levis. The wooden fort was a pile of splinters before its commander, Gen. Pouchet surrendered. The 700 indian troops under Sir William Johnson were eager to go in and scalp the French but he ordered them to stand down. Most of them left the English Army there, angry that they had been deprived of their scalps, and scalp money. The indians had figured out a way to take one scalp and cut it into three so they could claim more money and their longhouses were full of dried English scalps hanging from the rafters.

The only danger between Amherst and the French at Montreal was a series of brutal rapids. He lost 46 whale boats, 18 others were damaged and he lost 84 men in the rapids before he was able to get his fleet to the quiet waters of Lake St. Louis.

On September 9, 1760 his troops sailed for La Chine, nine miles away from Montreal. There the troops disembarked for the march to join Hazen and Murray. Two days before Murray's troops had camped below Montreal and Amherst set camp above them with Hazen on the opposite shore. The English with the provincials and a small number of indians totaled about 17,000 men and cannon were being brought up behind Amherst.

The French commanders in the town of Montreal, little more than a long street with little defense, saw the army surrounding them and held a council of war. The following morning Gen. Bouganville personally rode into Amherst's camp under a flag of truce and presented 55 Articles of Capitulation. Under its terms all the French lands in Canada and its possessions were to be surrendered to the English.

Most of the Articles were agreeable to Amherst but he refused to let the French soldiers keep their arms and cannon as they marched out in formation with the promise they would go back to France and not take any more part in the present war. The officers were enraged about the disarmament. This was an insult. This went against convention. But Amherst held his ground stating that the French didn't deserve convention as they had committed the "most horrid and unheard of barbarities in the whole progress of the war".

On September 8, 1760 the French accepted the terms and the soldiers and officers plus any Canadian citizen who so desired were allowed to leave Canada by ship and return to France unmolested. From the start Amherst had followed Wolfe's example and had told his troops not to kill women or children and to leave unmolested any who stayed neutral. The exception had occurred the year before when Rogers' Rangers were allowed a revenge killing massacre of the village of St. Francis after a betrayal by its indians.

At this time Capt. Tristrum Davis's company was in active duty under Col. Haviland and included his sons Joseph, John and Tristrum Jr. as well as Samuel Blodgett and others plus Reuben Townsley. In one of the battles as the troops moved upriver towards Montreal Reuben was captured by the indians. Tristrum sent out men to look for him but wasn't entirely sure he'd been taken against his will. With a crucial deadline to join with the other two forces, he was forced to leave off the search but his blue eyes searched all along the riverbank for signs of his dear friend as they sailed into battle. James Davis, Tristrum's relative from over the border in Connecticut was taken into Sir William Johnson's Ninth Company as soldier of the Royal Army. Johnson had been made a Baronet and Major General of British forces in North America. Ebenezer and Nathaniel Davis, both of Connecticut, were also under Johnson and Col. Nathan Whiting. Ebenezer, who had served at Ft. Ticonderoga and Ft, Duqeunse was wounded in the final battles of 1760 and finished his enlistment in His Majesty's hospital in Albany. He died in November. Timothy Davison likewise was in the Eighth Co., Fourth Regiment under Johnson and Col. Eleazer Fitch and Col. Israel Putnam.

After the capitulation the provincial volunteers were discharged to return home by the third week in November.

Tristrum had met Cyrus Houghton at Crown Point and learned his Irish relations were in Union, Connecticut. The two men had a lot in common and after the war promised to keep in touch. The Houghtons, like the Davises and many other families now living on land grants for service, had owned large estates in England, Ireland, Scotland and Wales and often reminisced about how they came from royalty in the distant past. But of the many now in New England only Humphrey Davis's line held a title in England, the rest having been displaced by kings or queens or Cromwell in the centuries between King Edward I and King George III, the new Hanover prince who had taken the throne upon the death of his father.

As 1760 came to a close this new king sat on the English throne with a new philosophy about foreign relations.

Tristrum and his sons and relatives who had served were ebullient about the surrender of Canada and all of New England celebrated for months with the new Gov. Sir Francis Bernard of Massachusetts declaring a day of Thanksgiving.

Though not often in the front lines, the volunteers had suffered. Many carried home lingering wounds from frostbite or infected splinters or accidents and almost all were infested with lice as the men had to sleep in their clothes, not knowing when the alarm would sound.

Upon the return of her men the first thing Mary did was burn their clothing and then they soaked in tin tubs of hot water and scrubbed with bars of hard, strong lye clothes-washing soap. Many had lost teeth to scurvy. Tristrum suffered from constant cramps and attacks of diarrhea but for years after his service his deepest wound was the loss of his close friend Reuben. After the surrender Tristrum was given permission to go with some Rangers to try to find him but no one had seen the long haired blond, big Englishman who liked to dress like the Rangers and indians in buckskin sand moccasins.

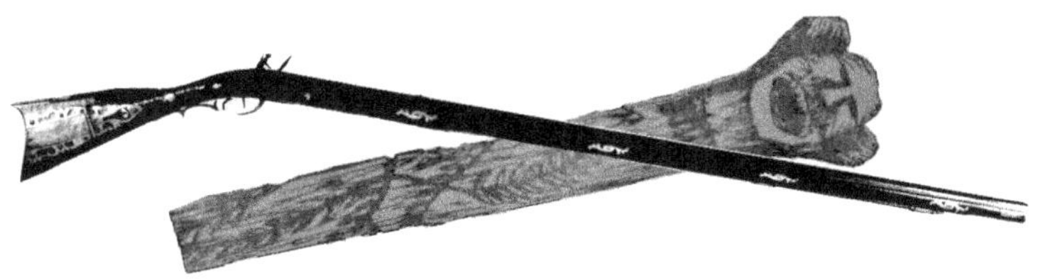

CHAPTER EIGHTY-SEVEN

The lull Between Wars

1763

In England power had passed from the Duke of Newcastle and his brother, Henry Pelham, to William Pitt, from Old Sarum near Tisbury, Wiltshire, but then swung back to a Pitt-Newcastle coalition government but Pitt "the great commoner" (until he became Earl of Chatham) refused to serve with Newcastle, who resigned. His Whig friend William Cavendish, later was dismissed as lord chamberlain after he refused to support the King's favorite, John Stuart, third Earl of Bute. The average farmer or tradesman in the colonies wasn't directly involved in the London power struggles but while William Cavendish, Baron of Cavendish of Harwick and fourth Duke of Devonshire – and a major backer of the Virginia and Bermuda colonies – was titular head of the Whig ministry, William Pitt was actually calling all the shots behind the scenes. The decline of Newcastle in West Riding didn't affect his relative to the east, the Earl of Holdernesse Robert Darcy, of East Riding near the critical port of Hull. Holdernesse, related to the Percy's, was now Secretary of State for the Southern Department and as such he was highly influential in the

New England colonies.

The fighting between England and France and their allies continued on the Continent after France capitulated in New France. The new king, George II's grandson George III wanted peace. Pitt and England wanted more war. Austria, Prussia and France were at the end of their resources. The king of Spain died and Carlos III took his place. In Russia the czarina Elizabeth died. She was an avowed enemy of Frederic of Prussia along with the King of France's mistress, Madame de Pompadour whom everyone knew actually ran France and Austria's Maria Theresa. As royal chess pieces were replaced in Russia Czar Peter III took the throne and he became an ally of Frederic.

During 1762 France formed a secret treaty with Spain and English ships sailed into the West Indies to take more sugar islands including Cuba and more Indonesian ports as well as all of France's Indian and African ports.

After Pitt and Newcastle were gone the King's men John Stuart Bute and Charles Townsend took over his foreign policy and began peace negotiations with France. George Grenville became the British Foreign Minister in 1764.

The French tried one more rally in Canada and sent four ships with 1,500 troops to the Bay of Bulls in Newfoundland where they took the fort there without opposition in mid September 1762. In response, Sir Jeffrey Amherst sent his brother Lt. Col. William Amherst with Vice Admiral Lord Colville north and within days Newfoundland was recaptured after only one day's bombardment of St. John's fort.

In western Virginia and western Pennsylvania the indians under chief Pontiac retook Fts. Le Bouef, Venango, Presque Isle and others. Amherst sent Capt. James Dalyell with reinforcement to Niagara and Detroit. The indians tried to take Detroit but Major Henry Gladwin held the fort and when the indians couldn't take the supply ship *Huron* in its harbor they surrendered in late October 1763.

For these campaigns Amherst, just before resigning his commission to Brig. Gen.Thomas Gage, requested 1,400 men from New York and 600 from New Jersey but their Assemblies only agreed on the condition that a matching number be raised from the other New England states and Pennsylvania. The New England states weren't keen for more war but supplied the men. Pennsylvania, which benefitted the most from the troops, had been a poor supplier of men from its eastern areas to defend the western frontier but the men of the Susquehena Valley were ready fighters. The pacifist Quakers in eastern Pennsylvania felt the settlers had provoked the indians because they had invaded their territory so they had brought the war on their frontier settlements upon themselves. The Pennsylvanians' unhelpful attitude was especially seen in their apathy when a settlement from Connecticut including the Hopkins family from Hartford set up in Susquehena territory and was brutally massacred by the indians, with only one former Connecticut man escaping.

The 'Treaty of Paris' was signed on February 10, 1763 and returned to France none of the Canadian but most of the French possessions in the West Indies and took Florida from Spain, who was given the Louisiana territory by the French since Spain had been its ally in the war. Pitt had wanted France brought to its knees, unable to ever wage war against England again but King George III was more lenient.

Benjamin Franklin from Philadelphia was in France during the peace talks and assured the English that if the French threat were gone the colonies wouldn't turn on England as they were too fractured and uncooperative to unite and fight for independence.

The French were allowed fishing rights off the upper coast and islands of Canada but all of its land to the north and down the Ohio River Valley were ceded to the English.

As Johnson worked on getting treaties signed with the Ohio River Valley indians and New York and Maine indians, prisoner exchanges were happening and the final exchanges took place in late November, 1764, four years after the French had surrendered.

In the years after the war Tristrum and Cyril Houghton became fast friends and Tristrum's youngest daughter Sibyl met and fell in love with Houghton's son Asa in Union, Connecticut. (Timothy Houghton was a captain with Tristrum and both had sons serving under them.)

The Houghtons had an estate and castle in Lancaster across from Donhegn Ireland. No longer royalty, in Union Asa's father and brother Thomas were content to buy Lawson's shingle sawmill. Asa was friends of Daniel Parker and he met Sibyl while selling hay to Col. William Blanchard in Wilmington.

Asa's father had been granted land in Union and had relatives in the Plantation of Lancaster, Massachusetts. The earliest Houghton settler to New England was a butcher in Boston who had moved to Connecticut. He and Dolor met when he was building his brother's house in Concord.

Tristrum also served with Jonathan and Abiather Houghton at Crown Point and Levi Houghton under Willard and with Ralph Houghton. Ralph's father was drowned when Port Royal in Jamaica sank in 1692.

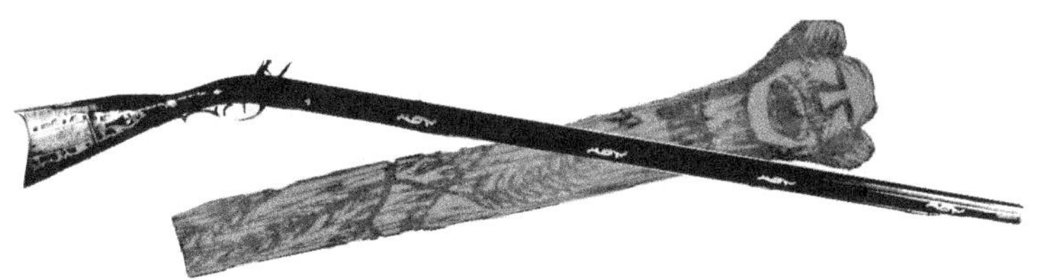

CHAPTER EIGHTY-EIGHT

The Tyranny of King George III

1763

When King George II died suddenly on October 25, 1760 his 22-year old grandson George III took the throne. (George II's heir Frederick, Prince of Wales, had died in 1751.) Although a Hanoverian by birth this King George had been raised in England and didn't identify with Germany.

But George III wasn't a benign monarch. Almost immediately he showed his true colors. He wanted to restore the monarchy as it was under the first King Charles who claimed the Divine Rights of Kings. England in the meantime had beheaded King Charles I and after a brutal civil war made Parliament more powerful than the king. Reluctantly Charles II was restored but his powers were greatly hampered by giving Parliament, i.e., the House of Lords and the House of Commons, the true powers to legislate and tax.

From the start George III, who disliked Pitt, worked to force his resignation, likewise Newcastle. He wanted to rule via a strong royal clique of his hand-picked ministers and didn't want to answer to the Whigs in Parliament. He brazenly bought seats and votes in the House and ruled with imperial arrogance. His Scottish Tory favorite Lord John Stuart, Third Earl of Bute, became Prime Minister and he answered only to the King, not to Parliament. However, public opinion was against Bute as he was seen as the architect of the 'Treaty of Paris' which didn't crush France and almost seemed to reward her by giving it back the lucrative, profitable sugar islands in the Caribbean and certain other posts that the British had taken during the Seven Years' War. In Parliament the Whigs, who had been all-powerful under Pitt/Newcastle, were now divided with a pro-Pitt group under the Marquis of Rockingham and an anti-Pitt faction under George Grenville and the Duke of Bedford.

Prime Minister Grenville brought the wrath of the colonies against the government in 1763 when he managed to pass the frontier "proclamation line" legislation against the colonies to stop the settlement of the English past the Alleghenies in the Ohio River Valley. The 'Proclamation Line' was devastating to the colonists as it ran along Maine's western boundary, down along the northern boundaries of Vermont and north and western New York and south, excluding all of the Great Lakes and Ohio River from English settlement. Grenville's reasons were twofold: to appease the indians who felt they were being invaded and to send a message to the colonies that England wasn't going to supply free troops to look after their ever-expanding frontier. The Virginia and Pennsylvania settlers were outraged as many had fought to obtain land in which to spread westward or, like George Washington, to speculate in land sales. Additionally, the British Parliament also wanted the colonies to pay for a standing army of 10,000 troops, one fourth of which would be in the West Indies.

A dispute arose at this time in Virginia when the tobacco farmers passed a 'Two Penny Act' which paid the Church of England ministers two cents for each pound of tobacco sold. As the colonial paper currency was practically useless and the southern farmers used tobacco to pay for their debts, two pennies per pound added up and those who weren't C of E members resented paying for a minister who didn't lead their congregation. A young lawyer named Patrick Henry represented the wealthy farmers against the clergy and won by claiming England in the person of the Church had no right to tax American colonists. He stopped just short of calling King George III a tyrant who should not be obeyed if his orders went against the English constitution that gave every free Englishman personal and property rights. The sentiment that colonists should only tax themselves and not have taxes imposed by a

Parliament across the sea struck a chord and rang throughout the thirteen colonies.

To the north in Boston a maltster named Samuel Adams began to get a following in his protests against English soldiers in their midst, to be funded by a Stamp Tax on legal papers and publications, and then in March 1764 the Sugar Act, a bill Charles Townsend, Chancellor of the Exchequer, had brought to Parliament. Under this Act the duty on molasses was decreased but the duties on Madeira wine and sugar increased. For years the colonists been smuggling in molasses from the West Indies and converting it into rum which they traded for furs and slaves. Under the 'Currency Act of 1764' England wouldn't let the colonies have their own paper currency so rum and molasses had been used in lieu of the scarce pieces of English sterling and gold. The Act was not enforceable as the colonists backed by James Otis and Rev. Jonathan Mayhew openly defied the Crown by hanging in effigy Boston's Royal Tax Collector Andrew Oliver and abused royal tax collectors and the Royal Governor, Francis Bernard until it was eventually repealed. Via a profusion of printed pamphlets that found themselves passed from ship to ship or tavern to tavern, the people began to shout, "No Taxation without Representation!" and "Power to Tax is Power to Destroy!" up and down the New England states and as far south as Georgia.

In Farmington, Connecticut the Assembly declared, all in bold print, "NO LAW CAN BE MADE OR ABROGATED WITHOUT THE CONSENT OF THE PEOPLE BY THEIR REPRESENTATIVES". They went on to state the legislators in Britain were nothing but "pips and parasites". The colonists felt that a duty was one type of tax but a tax levied by Parliament to pay England's bills was a different sort and that their own assemblies with men they had elected and who were answerable to their constituents had the sole power to levy domestic taxes on them.

In London, instead of repealing the tax Parliament then passed the 'Stamp Act' in 1765 which taxed legal papers, playing cards, publications, marriage licenses and other items. The Act was passed in March and seven months later, in October, representatives from nine colonies held a Stamp Act Congress in New York City. This was the first time the colonies had acted in unison since the war. They sent petitions to London reiterating their stance that only representatives elected by their own townspeople could tax colonists. They refused to comply with it and were hostile to tax collectors, most of whom resigned.

Parliament repealed the Act a year later but on the same day, March 18, 1765 they passed a 'Declaratory Act' stating Parliament had supreme power to tax the colonists and any of their laws superseded anything the colonial governments passed. And then they passed the 'Currency Act 'on April 19th which prohibited importation to the colonies of English silver or gold currency but outlawed the printing of colonial paper money. The Parliament then passed the 'Quartering Act' a month later forcing colonists to provide room and board for British troops. New York was the only colony to raise money to pay for the troops but its Assembly, after being coerced by the New York 'Suspending Act' two years later, openly said the Parliament had no right to tax them in that fashion. According to Parliament, Royal Government laws nullified individual state, or colony laws: the issue was Parliamentary Sovereignty (Federal versus State rights). Right after the repeal of the latest tax, Parliament passed the 'Townshend Revenue Act' with increased import duties on imported items and the 'American Board of Customs Act' to create a board of commissioners to collect taxes in the colonies under the supervision of a royal supervisor, Alexander Oliver. The colonists responded by boycotting tea, glass, lead, paper, paint and other items and wives began spinning flax and wool at home for household cloth. Mint tea replaced imported tea on many tea tables. The voices and words of John Locke's devotees, John and Samuel Adams, James Otis, John Hancock, Patrick Henry, a devotee of the 'New Light' religion from Virginia who had heard Rev. Samuel Davies, (a relative of the New York Davises who had earlier formed their own cult on Long Island), preach to New Lights that in the spirit of Jonathan Edwards from Northampton and Whitefield – the main preachers of the 'Great Awakening' – a man's moral character was more important than his material wealth or social status and he should answer to God and not other men.

Quoting from John Locke's *Two Treaties of Government* pamphlets circulated, promoting the idea of inalienable rights given to man by God, freedom to pursue one's happiness on one's land free from governmental interference such as General Warrants or taxes unless raised by the colonies for the colonists. It was a 'By the people and For the people' dogma.

In London Col. Isaac Barre, who had fought alongside the colonial volunteers in the last war with the French and indians, defended the effigy hanging and sacking of royal tax collector Alexander Oliver's house in Boston and referred to the rioters as “Sons of Liberty”. The name caught on and came to be used in the next decade in secret meetings in taverns such as the Green Dragon and the Bunch of Grapes in Boston harbor and on docks and rope galleries up and down the Atlantic seaboard. *‘The Boston Gazette’* openly criticized England and its agents. In Boston Thomas Hutchinson, great grandson of Anne Hutchinson, was Lieutenant Governor, and President of the inner governing circle, the Council. Governor Bernard additionally appointed him Chief Justice, and that set off a firestorm about separation of powers, fanned by the fiery oration of James Otis in the House of Representatives.

King George III didn’t like to be criticized and the general population wasn’t happy with his treaty with France. In England there was unrest and an unhappiness with King George III.

In England, MP John Wilkes began publishing a newspaper entitled the *‘North Briton’* in which he repeatedly excoriated the king and his “friends” for the treaty. George III had his secretary of state issue a General Warrant to arrest Wilkes and anyone connected to his paper. Wilkes said the General Warrant was illegal as it didn’t specify charges – which under English law could only be issued for treason, felony or breach of the peace against a member of the House of Commons.

In 1765 King George III’s Chief Justice, First Earl of Camden, Downton, Charles Pratt, sided with Wilkes and decreed general warrants were illegal. Wilkes won his case and collected a large sum in damages. However, the House of Commons, controlled by the king’s men, voted that Wilkes’s position wasn’t exempt from the charge of writing and publishing seditious articles and the majority had the last issue of the paper publically burned by the royal hangman and expelled Wilkes from the House. They said even though Wilkes didn’t openly call for it, Wilkes’s writings were exciting the public to traitorous insurrection against King George III and the Court of King’s Bench charged him with libel.

Wilkes was challenged to a duel and wounded then left England for France. In absentia he was declared an outlaw.

King George III had no compunctions against using the State for his own personal vendetta but the English people saw in his actions the footprint of the tyrant. The English had the right of freedom of speech and George’s dictatorial attitude created sentiment against him. They clamored for Pitt to return. Reluctantly he did in 1766 but the old lion had been bearded and he resigned after bills he presented were either used to criticize him or not passed by the bought-and-paid-for House. He was replaced by Augustus Henry Fitzroy, third Duke of Grafton as PM. A movement arose calling for "Wilkes and Liberty!" and Wilkes returned to England and ran for Parliament twice and won his seat but the House refused to seat him.

The men in the American colonies who had fought for their freedom from the French and indians were in an ugly mood in the years following the peace. They hadn't fought to have their liberties and freedoms taken away by tyrannical legislators in London.

In 1770 Prime Minister Grafton resigned, replaced by Lord Frederick North, second Earl of Guilford. North was a yes-man and whatever King George III wanted, he delivered.

But the biggest problem for the colonies was the 'Quebec Act' passed in 1774. In this Act King George III restored lands to France in Canada down to the Ohio River Valley, where the English had been excluded. This was a major insult to all the colonists who had fought and suffered or lost loved ones fighting to free the area from the French. It was a major slap in the face and the colonists called a 'First Continental Congress' in Philadelphia to decide how they could deal with King George III and his lackeys. Especially egregious was the billeting of 4,000 British soldiers in Boston and the revocation of the right of citizens to freely assemble in that city.

Earlier Boston had been the scene of civil disobedience as Sons of Liberty, dressed and painted to look like indians, under the cover of night boarded English East India Company ships in Boston Harbor and dumped into the sea almost 400 chests of the tea England was trying to force them to buy via the 'Tea Act' in 1773 in which King George III's government planned to use colonial tax money to bail out the East India Company. Patriotic Boston merchants had stored the despised tea in damp cellars or let it rot. The merchants of the colonies had previously bought tea in England and then resold it to their fellow colonists. This forced purchase of the 'state' tea robbed them of any profit and gave a monopoly to the East India Co. The granting of Royal monopolies were an old and hated royal practice and one the English Civil War had brought to an end. In retaliation King George III had suspended Massachusetts's charter and closed the port of Boston.

By April, 1774 the Sons of Liberty were taking up the call for freedom from the arbitrary, punitive rule of King George III.

In South Brimfield Sybil Davis married Asa Houghton and he moved from Union to the farmhouse her father had built 40 years before.

Over the years Tristrum had become friends with Judge Abijah Willard, a relative in the Worcester/Dudley area and several times a year he made the journey northeast to spend a few days playing chess and debating with him over the role of the colonies in relation to Great Britain. Tristrum was a Tory, or Royalist, as he still believed that the colonies owed everything to the mother country but Judge Willard and he both knew from talking to younger men that America had become like the teen-aged son who was about to throw a punch at his father as he asserted his independence.

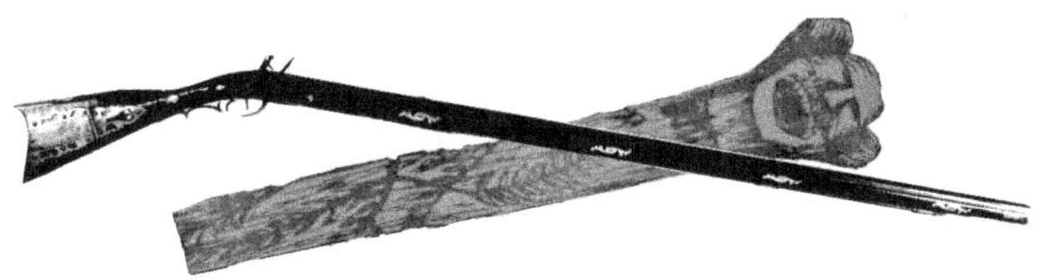

CHAPTER EIGHTY-NINE

The Punch is Thrown

1774

Reuben Townsley appeared one spring day at Tristrum's house. Most had given him up for dead. His sudden appearance both shocked and pleased Tristrum who was busy mucking out the dirt floor in the root cellar where the sheep had been kept during the winter.

"Reub!" Tristrum exclaimed, hugging the scrawny ghost-like figure in the dark cellar. Reuben's hair was long and hung in greasy strands. He had a long, unkempt beard and was clothed in buckskin from head to toe with a coon skin cap on his head. When he embraced his long lost friend he noticed he smelled like the indians and was sorely in need of a good bath.

"When did you get released?" Tristrum asked, then added, "Has Sarah seen you yet?"

Tristrum noted Reuben's front teeth were missing and the rest badly stained as he smiled. His voice was rough, as if he hadn't used it in a long time.

"Nay. I only just a'came into town. I've been living up ta' Rattlesnake Hill near the small pond."

Tristrum frowned. His wife had commented that she thought she smelled a campfire in that direction and Tristrum was going to walk up the hill to investigate after the ground dried out from the melting snow. Mary was always afraid of indians camping nearby.

"Well, my friend, let's get you upstairs and Mary can draw you a bath and I've some old clothes you can change into. We'll send word to your family – "

Reuben cut him off, "I don't want to see 'em."

Tristrum shook his head, "Whyever not, Reub? We've all been a'missin' you for ten years but Sarah has been faithful. She never gave up hope one day ye'd return and Praise the Lord, ye have!"

Sarah was a daughter of Tristrum's neighbor Capt. Joseph Blodgett. Her mother was Sarah Stone. Relatives on Reuben's side included Stebbinses and Williams. He was related to Rev. Williams of Deerfield who had been captured by the indians and to the Thompsons, who helped settle Connecticut and minister in Springfield and be missionaries to the Pequots, and the Allens with ties to Kittery

Reuben was edgy. He couldn't stay still. He kept moving around the cellar, his dirty, caked hands rubbing the huge, rough granite foundation stones.

"Did they hurt you?" Tristrum asked quietly.

"Aye. I had to run the gauntlet, 'twas beaten something fierce but then they pretty much left me alone. I went out hunting with them and they gave me a squaw to take care of our wetu. I learned a lot of their language and ways and all about the animals and plants and learnt some French, too."

"Did ye try to escape?" Tristrum asked cautiously. The fellow in front of him was as skittish as a wild animal. One wrong move and he'd flee.

"At first and then I just gave up, I suppose. The livin' was pretty good and after England got Canada back the fighting stopped. Of course they always go a'fightin' with other tribes. It's their way of proving their manhood, to count coup in battle."

"What does that mean, count coup?"

"They take their war club and touch the enemy but don't bash his brains in."

Just then Reuben's hands found the edge of cloth in which Tristrum's war trophy had been wrapped. He tugged on it and the club came out into his hands.

"Where did ye get this?" Reuben angrily demanded, holding up like he was going to strike Tristrum, who had moved back against the stones where a large grey spider dropped onto his shoulder. Reuben was like a loaded cannon whose touchhole was just waiting for a match so Tristrum didn't dare move to brush the spider off as it crawled over his neck.

"Ye remember, don't ye?" he asked, his voice quavering, ''Twas when we were at Fort Edward with Johnson and they swarmed our defenses."

Reuben growled, swinging the club. Then he began to howl and the howl turned into great, wracking sobs. His whole body shook and he keened and sat down in the dirt, rocking back and forth.

The noise had brought Mary and Sybil to the doorway of the cellar and Tristrum warned them to stay away.

For what seemed like hours Reuben sobbed, muttering, sometimes in an indian dialect, sometimes in broken French, the stained war club clutched to his dirty, greasy chest.

Tristrum sat next to him, helplessly trying to calm him down. Mary handed down a pot of hot ribwort tea and two cups (they didn't dare drink India black tea as neighbors were spying on those who did and calling them traitors to American Liberty). Reuben finally stopped his wailing and suddenly stood up, flinging the club into the dirt. Without a word he rushed up the narrow wooden stairs, almost knocking Mary and Sybil over in his haste to run out of the house. Tristrum rushed after him, calling to him as he ran up into the woods.

Mary was standing in the dooryard, her eyes wide, her hands wringing her apron as Tristrum came back.

"We must notify his family," she said, "or the constable."

"Nay, wife. I've seen it before. Me cousins in Deerfield – remember? They are wild when they come back, and some like that minister's daughter from Lancaster don't want to come back 'tall. Reub's got to have time to reintegrate, gradual-like. Ye remember that cat we had who took off one day and we didn't see him for two years?"

Mary smiled. He'd been her favorite. A big grey and black striped tom that would let her pet him when she put a saucer of milk in the barn and as he drank he'd vibrate with a deep, loud purr. He was the biggest cat she'd ever seen with long legs and Tristrum said he might have lynx in him. But he was a big, gentle baby around her. He'd disappeared one day and they called and called but old Tiger never came back so they felt he'd been killed by a fox or wolf as sometimes a small pack of very skinny wolves appeared on the hill across from the farmhouse. After two years Tiger suddenly appeared one day but he seemed to have forgotten that Mary was his friend. He was skittish and never let her pet him again. One of his ears was half-torn off but healed and he had some scars but nothing to explain his sudden feralness. He'd been raised as a kitten by the children and wasn't people-shy but wasn't one hundred percent tame, either, which they preferred for a barn cat as they were only there to mouse out the barns and sheds.

"Tiger? Ye mean Reuben's become like Tiger? Not tame yet not totally wild, either?"

"Aye, love."

"Is he dangerous, Tris?"

"Nay, but don't let the young 'uns go up there. I figure in his own time and his own way he'll make it back to his farm and settle in. But ye know he always used to take off without notice to go a deer huntin' in the fall, always did and always will."

They both sighed. The wars had changed them all. And now their once orderly world was changing due to the new king and the hostility he had stirred up, especially in Boston and Virginia.

"I told ye to get rid o' that thing!' Mary sternly chided as they went back to the house.

Tristrum said he'd take care of it but just found a deeper crevice to stuff it into. It was their lucky charm but he couldn't tell any of them that he was superstitious as it wasn't a proper Christian thing. And with the Great Awakening everyone was suddenly more religious than ever, always wanting to know if one had a personal relationship with Christ. He longed for the old days when religion was more formal and dignified. He longed for the old days when England, now Great Britain, and the colonies were allies, not enemies. He wanted the two countries to kiss and make up but with every day the mood grew uglier and more rebellious around him and King George III seemed to like to provoke them, for what reason Tristrum couldn't fathom.

****

During the final French and Indian War Tristrum had made two friends that were to have major consequences in his life.

The first was meeting Levi Houghton at Ft. Edward during the Crown Point expedition where Levi initially served under Maj. Willard and through him Tristrum's daughter Sibyl met Asa Houghton, whom she married in Union and proceeded to have children with. Sibbie, as he still called her, was his favorite, maybe because she'd always reminded him of himself with her black hair and blue eyes.

The second was Abijah Willard, a distant relation through the original Simon Willard and his sister Margery who married Dolor Davis in the early 1600s. Abijah lived in Lancaster but often traveled between Worcester and Springfield for business. Whenever he came to South Brimfield he stopped for a day or two at Tristrum's house and they spent many hours reliving their experiences in the forts of Lake George and Lake Champlain and Abijah had served in the final war in Nova Scotia rounding up the Acadians to send back to France or to New France (Louisiana). The Willards and Learneds (like the Houghtons from Lancastershire) pretty much owned or controlled most of the Worcester area and Abijah had moved up the ranks from Captain under his father Samuel Willard in the 4th Massachusetts Regiment, then under Gov. Shirley and later under Lt. Col. Robert Monckton to the rank of Colonel. He then commanded a regiment under Gen. Timothy Ruggles of Harwick at Fort Edward and served under William Haviland there.

After the 'Treaty of Paris' in 1763 he returned to Lancaster and became Ruggles's neighbor and good friend. In accordance with the Royal decision to only have judges appointed by the King , Gov. Thomas Hutchinson appointed Abijah, who was by then fifty years old, a "mandamus councillor" in 1774. As part of the 'Punitive Acts' King George III wanted to try anyone who disagreed with him for sedition and he went over the heads of the Massachusetts Assembly by appointing Loyalist judges instead of the ones the representatives had elected. This was a very controversial action in colonies that had been basically self-governing.

In contrast to the slender, wiry, darker complexioned Welsh Tristrum with his blue eyes and now, at seventy-three with mostly white hair, Abijah had a pale yet florid complexion. He was a large man, tall and rounded with a magisterial air and had been a lawyer in the Worcester area even before his royal appointment.

Throughout the colonies associations were now being formed to refuse the importation or use of British goods. Every town had a committee and, although they were elected by the populace, they were not legal bodies of government. They felt they were. They claimed the right to govern themselves and the issue of local sovereignty versus rule by England's Parliament came to a head when 3,000 pounds in value of East India tea was dumped into Boston harbour where it had been sitting on ships because no one dared to unload it. The Association publically shamed and shunned anyone who was using British goods, especially the tea

Following what jokingly was called 'The Boston Tea Party' King George III was furious and his Parliament passed the 'Punitive' or 'Coercive Acts' – or as the colonists called them 'the Intolerable Acts' – in which he dissolved the Massachusetts legislature and appointed officials himself. Most local Loyalist lawyers or men of wealth were appointed, including Abijah Willard.

Amongst other things the colonists felt had infringed their liberties was the closing of the harbor in Boston until the money for the tea was paid to the Crown (that is, to the English East India Company). To enforce this, the King sent General Gage in with troops to Boston and took away the right for the colonists to assemble except for a town meeting once a year.

King George III poked a stick at a hornet's nest. Many New Englanders who had been hoping for a peaceful resolution to the taxation without representation and billeting of soldiers without consent went over the edge and gathered to speak around their town's 'Liberty Pole', a pot of tar at its base to tar and feather anyone who spoke up for these Acts that ran against the very fabric of American liberty.

In July Abijah was sworn into office. In August he was in Union to conduct business and members of the Association saw him and began calling for patriots to come and arrest him. By nightfall there was a mob of about 4,000 people and they marched him north to Brimfield where he had recently purchased a farmstead.

Tristrum was sitting in the back room slowly reading a newspaper when his middle son, 24- year old Benjamin burst in.

"Father! Come quick! They've got Abijah and they are marching him to jail!"

Tristrum dropped the paper and grabbed his coat. Whatever could Abijah have done? he wondered as they ran down the road towards the main road into Brimfield.

Torches lit the mob that overflowed the road as shouts, cheers and taunts rang out.

Tristrum and Benjamin were crushed and couldn't get to the front of the long line of people until they got to the town common in Brimfield. Tristrum's sons Samuel and William and their cousin, the blacksmith Abijah Davis were in the crowd but remained out of sight.

Tristrum and Benjamin forced their way through to where Judge Abijah Willard was being restrained next to the Liberty Pole.

The Celtic temper came out in Tristrum. He rushed forward and demanded to know what the townspeople were doing to a man he knew as fair and honest.

"He's a traitor!" one yelled.

"He's a bloody Tory!" yelled another.

"Abijah, what crime are you guilty of?" Tristrum asked, the seething hate of the crowd burning his back. A fire had been started and the tar pot was put on it next to a bag of feathers. The crowd was jeering, shouting, full of blood lust.

"All I did was take the oath of office as a Mandamus Councillor," Abijah explained, his face wet with sweat. He was a man who never left his house without proper attire but in the madness of the mob his coat, hat and vest were missing and his long undershirt was loose from his trousers in several spots, hanging loosely under his round belly.

Tristrum turned and faced the mob. His face was red with fury and his blue eyes blazed as he called for silence.

"Who do ye think ye are, ye old geet?" yelled someone in the mob. A crab apple whizzed by Tristrum's ear. Benjamin pulled a chair off a porch and Tristrum stood on it.

"Who do I think I am?" Tristrum thundered, sticking out his lower jaw, "I'm one of the men who almost died fighting for ye! I am one of the men who lived on stinking peas and rancid bacon while ye sat on yer comfortable arses in yer own parlors! I helped start this town in the wilderness, cutting trees to make pasture, digging a well, building a house wit' me own two hands and then paying taxes for the privilege of living on me own place!"

Another apple whizzed by. Tristrum stood up even higher as one yelled, "Piss off ye old cheater!"

That voice Tristrum knew as he had been sued by the farmer who claimed he sold him a dried up heifer. Abijah had been in Union consulting with the lawyer who had defended Tristrum in that suit.

"Who am I? Me and my sons volunteered when the call to arms went out. I paid for powder and shot for some of you in my company just a few years back as we went up against the French and indians! Me wife is home right now cowering in the cellar because she thought the indians were attacking when she saw all yer torches a'blazin all along the road! Ye wouldn't be free if not for me, my boys and men like this fine man Abijah Willard! From the time of the Puritans a'fightin' the indians every army has had Davises and Willards in it! Abijah's ancestors fought in France for English kings long a'fore this colony was formed! How dare you ask who I think I am? I'm a freeborn, loyal American colonist – loyal to England who freed us from the French and indians! Have ye forgotten so soon the terror ye lived in, not knowin' if the indians would creep out o' the woods and burn ye out then scalp, kill or capture any who ran through the fire? Who am I? I might've been born in Wales but I'm a native son of America!"

The crowd had been quiet but now began to stir and Tristrum could smell hot tar.

"I'm a son of America but a loyal son of Great Britain, too! We fought along the British Regulars to drive out the French and them bastard indians!"

A loud "boo!" sounded as he swore.

"I'm a loyal American but also a loyal British subject! Don't ye see, ye pack o' bloody stupid fools? The two aren't exclusive. Ye can be both – "

An apple hit him right in the face and he almost fell off the chair.

"Ye just don' get it, ye old geet! *We* cleared these fields!"

Another one in he crowd shouted and was joined by others,

"*We* planted the corn!"

"*We* lost farms and family to the indians the French!"

"*We* built these homes!"

"*We* made these towns!"

And, loudest of all, " *We the People* do not owe a thing to Bloody Old King George!"

The crowd was roaring now,

"There'll not be liberty with the tyrant Georgie wearing the crown!" one yelled, followed by, "They want our taxes but take away our representation. They replaced them" he pointed to Willard, "with men like your precious Abijah!"

Abijah had stood silent, judging them. He was proud and dignified even when they tried to disgrace him.

"Go back to Wales, then, ye love yer English King so much!" another yelled as the crowd moved in closer.

"We will work it out! Have ye no faith in diplomats and negotiations? Ye are actin' like a bitch that ate from a hand when starvin' then turned around and bit the hand that fed it!"

"No more talking! Their redcoats massacred our men on the Boston common, have ye forgotten that, ye old git?"

Suddenly Tristrum was in the dirt as the chair was upturned. Before he knew what was happening his clothes were stripped off and then he felt hot tar being brushed all over him –in his hair, his eyes, his face, all over his body as Abijah and Benjamin were held back from trying to rescue him. The bag of feathers was then dumped all over him and he couldn't see, his eyelids were clotted with hot, sticky tar and puffs of feathers. He kept his mouth shut so none would go down his throat but his nose was getting clogged and just as he felt he was going to have to open it his mouth they tied him to a rough rail, or fence post, and carried him as if he were on horseback to the edge of town and dumped him in the road.

Benjamin finally freed himself and ran after his father, untying the tarry ropes and sitting him up. He took his handkerchief and wiped at the tar on his father's face but all it did was smear.

"Don't ye be cryin!" Tristrum ordered him. As he looked up he saw Asa Houghton come up the road from Union on horseback. He dismounted and put the stinking, sticky mess that was Tristrum on his fine leather saddle and walked the horse back down the seven or so miles to the Davis homestead.

No one spoke. A handful of Tristrum's friends walked alongside. In the distance they heard the cheers and laughter of the rowdy mob.

Finally Tristrum spoke, puffing away feathers near his lips, "What do ye think they'll do to poor Abijah?"

Asa replied in the dark, "I heard they are making the men who took the oath of office as sheriffs, councillors and other appointees either recant and apologize or be sent to Newgate prison in Simsbury."

Another added, "They locked them out of the court in Springfield."

Tristrum was fuming.

"How dare they do these things and call themselves lovers of liberty? Locking up legally appointed judges! Don't they see their own rioting actions run counter to their claims they can run an orderly government?"

Asa replied, "We are getting a Continental Congress together in Philadelphia that will do things the proper, legal and correct way. These hooligans are lawless and their actions will be punished when order is restored."

Mary was hysterical when she saw Tristrum in the moonlight in their front yard. But she also had to hold herself back from laughing at the bird-like figure that stood there so pathetically, a patchwork of black and white feathers.

She grabbed a tub of lard and began to try to rub the tar off with it but it had hardened and just smeared. As the sun came up Tristrum was sitting in a hot tub in the front yard but even with vigorous scrubbing with a brush and lye soap the tar wasn't coming off. Most of the feathers were gone but brown, smeared tar covered almost every inch of the old man.

"Ye're making it worse," he told Mary, grabbing the hand with the brush, "I'm rubbed raw, woman. Just get me something to wear and let me sleep."

Mary laid old horse blankets on their bed in the back room and gently helped lay her poor, battered husband down onto it.

"Why'd ye do it, Tris? Why'd ye open yer big mouth?" she asked, covering him with the oldest, shabbiest sheet she could find.

Surrounded by the black and brown tar Tristrum's eyes were even bluer as he looked into hers.

"Someone has to try to stop this insanity, Mary. Ye should o' seen them – a pack of bloodthirsty wolves they looked like!"

Asa stood in the doorway and coughed.

"Did ye ever think, sir, that maybe they've a right to be angry?"

"Not you, too!" Tristrum croaked.

"I think there is a war with Great Britain on the horizon, sir, whether you or I want it or not. King George wants it, that is clear. They defeated France and we grew strong and now he is afraid we are growing so strong we will demand our independence since we don't have to fear the French any longer. Benjamin Franklin told them we wouldn't – unless we were faced with intolerable tyranny. King George is determined to bring that tyranny on us, it seems."

Benjamin spoke up then, "I, for one, will not join any army that treats an old veteran the way they did my father!"

"Well, then, you might want to go to Boston and sign up with General Gage," Asa replied sarcastically.

"Aye, I will do!" Benjamin said angrily but his father put a tarry, greasy hand on his arm.

"Jesus forgave the crowd and men who crucified Him, remember that, my son before you go off half-cocked. I'm mad as hell at what people who pretended to be my friends did to me but you and your brothers need to learn all you can about what is really true before ye act rashly. War is no triflin' thing, boy. I've killed men and I've almost been killed and I've seen me close friends be a'killed and then when it's all over the kings get together and divide the spoils like they did with Canada and the citizens be damned."

He added, "'Tis like a royal game o'chess to them and we be the pawns."

Benjamin began to rebut him but Tristrum cut him off,

"I've fearfully tired, boy. This is the only battle I'm fighting in this war. 'Tis up to your generation to sort it out. I'm staying out of this one and all I'll be doin' is pickin' tar from me ears and hair instead of firing a musket or flintlock. I'm done fighting. I don't care who wants to tax me anymore; I just want to be left in peace."

He turned away and shut his tar-smeared eyelids, not sure if he'd be able to open them when he woke.

Abijah was forced to resign his commission six miles out of town and recant his loyalty to the crown and then about a month later all the Worcester County officials who had been sworn into the mandamus government were forced to resign and recant.

In Pennsylvania the Continental Congress met and a Committee of Correspondence was set up as the colonies united to stand up to Great Britain. Each state set up its own Provincial Congress with men it elected, not men chosen by the king.

Abijah went to Boston and joined the Association fighting the Acts.

Benjamin went to New York and signed up there to fight for the British. In the years to come in a civil war families such as Tristrum's were divided into two camps: those on the side of Great Britain and enemies of the colonists and those who called themselves Patriots and fought against their brethren for the rights they believed only God was empowered to grant.

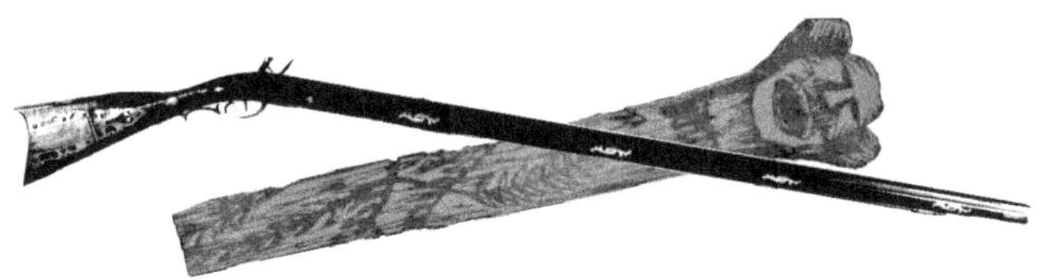

CHAPTER NINETY

The Revolution Begins

1775

Abijah Willard dominated any space in which he stood, much like the General George Washington of Virginia that the Continenal Congress had commissioned Commander-in-Chief of the United American Colony's troops a month after General Gage and his British regulars marched to Lexington and Concord to seize a powder cache rumored to be there. Finding no powder house they were marching in formation on the road back to Boston but were fired upon by a militiaman in the woods. In the ensuing battle militiamen from surrounding towns swarmed to the area and the British soldiers' orderly retreat turned into a rout with colonists figth-ing indian-style at the stiff, red-coated British soldiers. Willard had enlisted to help Gen. Gage after the events of the previous spring.

There were other Americans who joined the British ranks, though, men from families such as the Wentworths, Rogers from New Hampshire and New York who had formed bonds with British officers during the last French and Indian War. However, Willard wasn't with the troops that marched to Concord and Lexington. He was on a ship bound for Halifax to recruit more troops for the fortifications of Castle William and the area around Boston.

From April 19, 1775 Boston was under siege by the colonists. The British troops were surrounded by Patriot militias who had taken the high grounds. Connecticut sent troops under Gen. Israel Putnam; Rhode Island's troops were led by Gen. Nathaniel Greene, both men already in the Boston area when 'The Revolution' began. Within a short time 16,000 troops from the New England colonies had come to Boston in response to the Committee of Safety's calling out of the militia.

Brigadier General Timothy Danielson brought troops from South Brimfield including Tristrum's youngest sons Samuel and William, plus many members of families who had sent men to fight the French and indians including the Blisses, Blodgetts, Hitchcocks, Mighills, Shermans, Stebbinses and Reuben Townsley (as a scout) and his sons. Brimfield Selectman Capt. Daniel Winchester was a delegate to the Provincial Congress in Salem that summer. The Provincial Congress sent a committee to Lexington and Concord to interview witnesses and then sent a full report to London making it very clear that it wasn't only the militia or minutemen of those two towns that had risen up: it was all of New England.

For two months the British troops remained on the peninsula (Boston Neck) and there was little trouble between the two armies. The Committees of Safety met to arrange for provisions and arms. Brig. Gen. William Heath was in charge of the troops for a day until Gen. Artemas Ward took over and held a council of war. Col. William Prescott (ironically brother-in-law to Abijah Willard) was in command of placing guards around the city and local mariners were being commissioned to keep English ships from getting to Boston.

On the sixteenth of June rumors began that the English were going to attempt to take Bunker's Hill in Charlestown in order to set cannon against the patriot entrenchments around the city. Patriot officer Col. Prescott took men with six small field cannon to fortify Breed's Hill which he mistook for Bunker's Hill, but the British had moved troops over the Mystic River to Charleston and they set out from the Navy Yard to march up the hill and take the cannon through a formal linear frontal attack while Gen. Howe kept up a cannon bombardment on the hill from the ships in the river. The ground was muddy and the British soldiers didn't make much progress up the slope on the first two attempts as patriots had entrenchments and fired at close range to save musket balls and powder. The British were using the Brown Bess musket, a heavy gun that had to be loaded by 'seconds'. On the third try the British broke out the bayonets and, in single file charged up the hill and the colonial army took heavy losses as it retreated in a disorganized rout. The British army did, too. In the battle the much beloved and respected Dr. Joseph Warren was killed.

At the same time in Virginia Gen. George Washington was promoted to Commander-in-Chief of the United Provinces of North America's Army and, after he officially addressed his troops, he set sail for New England, arriving in Springfield on July third then proceeding overland to Boston where he introduced order into the ragtag assemblies of troops. He appointed Gen. Artemus Ward to oversee the troops in Roxbury on their right wing; Gen. Israel Putnam over Cambridge and Gen. Charles Lee to oversee Brig. Gen. Nathaniel Greene on Prospect Hill and Brigadier General John Sullivan on Winter Hill.

Gen. Gage had told London he felt Boston was indefensible and the troops would have a better chance of mounting a proper resistance against the colonists in New York. He was replaced by Gen. William Howe, although he had seconded his assessment.

Gen. Washington organized a navy under John Glover of Marblehead and a fleet of armed ships patrolled the coast, capturing many English supply and troop transports that summer including a fully loaded and cannoned brigantine named *Nancy.*

One thing Gen. Washington lacked was cannon and Ethan Allen took men to Fort Ticonderoga, removed the cannon from the fort and sledded 50 cannon, mortars and munitions over the White Mountains to Boston in February . In Dorchester Heights the Patriots entrenched during the night, repeating their June surprise for the British by daylight of March 4th, 1776.

Gen. Washington ordered the men to fill barrels with small rocks and stones to roll down on the British if they tried to advance up the hill.

The British troops, now feeling the stress of the almost year-long siege, did attempt to take the hill under Lord Hugh Percy but with 10,000 determined patriots against them, he retreated and sued for terms of surrender on March 8th. On March 17th the orderly evacuation of Boston began. British soldiers and officers were loaded onto ships, which were scarce. One of the ships en route to Boston was the armed sloop Margaretta, captained by James Moore. When it arrived in

Machias, Maine on June 2, 1775 the townspeople there protested by sending out Jeremiah O'Brien and Benjamin Foster in sloops to capture the vessel and arrest its crews. After the victory the Patriots gathered at the Burnham Tavern in Machias to celebrate. The inn with a low attic and windows at is gables had been a Sons of Liberty gathering place for some time. Others evacuees were sent out to Cape Cod to await ships and in these ranks were thousands of Tory families who had fled the city with whatever possessions they could cart, some going to Nova Scotia or New Brunswick.

After the British militiary and the supporters of King George III left, the Patriot mob wanted to ransack and loot their residences and even occupy them. The Provincial Congress passed a law making it illegal to touch the houses or animals but later had to relent as the animals needed to be taken care of. They allowed the sale of livestock and later allowed prominent Patriots to lease the mansions with all rental income to be held in trust for the families who went to Canada or England.

The men who returned to Brimfield and South Brimfield and Union and all the surrounding towns in the summer of 1775 were jubilant. The British with the strongest army in the world had been driven off American soil.

In his neat, two-story white farmhouse on its little plateau overlooking pastures and stone walled fields Tristrum had become withdrawn. After the townspeople had turned on him he became bitter. He gave Benjamin his blessing when he went to New York but hardly spoke to Capt. Asa Houghton or Samuel or William when they came back from Boston. His oldest son John had refused to participate and he and his wife moved in with Tristrum and Mary who only had their youngest, unwed daughter Sarah left in the large house. Now a widower, his brother Joseph had moved in, too. Like Tristrum Joseph was a Loyalist but in secret, giving only lip service to the Revolution. Joseph's oldest son John had taken over his farm on the road to Union and his youngest son Edward and his two young daughters filled the gap left by Tristrum and Mary's sons and daughters who had married and left home. The previous summer the men of fighting age enlisted for a one year term of service but as the war continued the Provincial Congress and Continental Congress began competing with each other to offer bounties of money and land to any who would sign up for the duration. Tristrum and Joseph both knew how long the last French and Indian war had gone on and shook their heads at the foolishness of signing up for an indefinite term. They'd seen how at Ft. Edward and Crown Point men often refused to serve when their terms had expired but were forced to stay on at the barrel of a musket.

Gen. Washington and the Continental Army suffered defeats in Manhattan that fall and had retreated across the Delaware River. Britain held New York City and was planning an advance down from Canada to take the forts along the Ohio River.

The future was uncertain. Tristrum's health was failing and he was wracked with painful arthritis. He had sores that wouldn't heal caused from tar burning his skin. The country he had fought for against the French had now turned on him. He didn't recognize the younger men who read Thomas Paine's *Common Sense* pamphlet out loud in the town squares and ripped off tavern and shop signs with any royal wording such as the 'Kings Arms' and burned them in bonfires on town commons. He felt he had outlived his times, much as his relatives felt when driven out of Wales or later out of England, Ireland, Wales or Scotland because of their religion or loyalties to the crown.

Tristrum was shaken in May, 1776 when the constable came riding up the road with his deputies and banged on the sturdy wooden farmhouse door.

Mary answered, wiping her hands on her apron. Tristrum was out back chopping wood even though pain shot up his legs with each thunk of the axe. She brought the constable Daniel Thompson around.

"Mr. Davis," Thompson said, pulling out a rolled paper from his saddlebag, "I have here the Test ye must swear to in accordance with law passed by our Provincial Congress."

Tristrum put the axe down and leaned on its sturdy ash handle.

"Aye? I heard nothing o' this. 'Twernt so long ago we were forced to take an oath of loyalty to the king!"

Thompson handed the paper across.

"It says here if ye don't sign and swear allegiance to the United Colonies ye will be considered an enemy of our country."

Tristrum spat on the ground.

"Ye ride up on me land like ye own it and shove this piece of shit in my face?" he spouted, his face red with rage, "I was a respected Captain o' troops in wars to fight for this country! My country! And now ye say I'm an enemy o' the so-called State – and it's not even a legitimate state at that Ye've some nerve,!"

His son, Tristrum Jr. was with the constable. In his forties and considered a bit feeble minded he wasn't the first choice of the draft board so he was still at home. Seeing him with Daniel almost gave Tristrum a stroke,

"Ye, too, Trus?"

"Father, ye have two weeks in which to sign this – " he hesitated, looking around anxiously, "but for the sake of mother and John I suggest ye swallow your almighty pride and just sign the bloody thing! John already signed it in town."

With a hand shaking with rage Tristrum signed it on the chopping block, stained with many a chicken's blood.

"Mr. Davis – " Thompson began and Tristrum cut him off, "Don't ye get all formal on me, Danny boy! I've a known ye since ye were a wee one sucking on yer mother's tit. Ye and yer young friends are all puffed up a'thinkin' ye are the governors or lords and we, who fought for the king and love Great Britain are now yer lowly serfs."

He angrily continued chopping, venting his anger on the logs.

Mary invited the constable inside, apologizing and trying to soothe things over by giving her son and the young man tea and gingerbread.

"You must forgive him," she said, pouring the fragrant mint tea brew into her china cups in the parlor," he's been in constant pain since that traumatic event," referring to the tar and feathering. The men looked down at the rug, ashamed at how mean it had been.

"Mother," Trustrum said, reaching out and putting a hard, calloused hand on her arm, "father needs to accept that things will never go back to how they were. We are determined to fight to the last man to assert our freedom and our right to govern ourselves and not be subject to a tyrannical monarch. If you can't accept it you and father need to keep quiet or you'll be drummed out and sent up to Halifax. Did you sacrifice so much to carve this beautiful farm out of the wilderness just to have to abandon it?"

Mary replied, "Well, even if we are sent packing they can't take our farm!"

Which the town almost did when the next taxes came due and the people were forced to use the paper currency the state printed. Tristrum had always paid in silver coins but silver and gold were scarce so the people had to use almost worthless Continental script backed by questionable reserves.

Tristrum went into a deep depression and felt shame when Asa Houghton paid his taxes for him. He'd argued with Asa but Sibyl had finally persuaded him to take it as a loan, not charity.

****

In July 1776 the Continental Congress issued a formal 'Declaration of Independence' that was sent to King George III and throughout the colonies. The king declared the colonies in formal rebellion in August.

His daughter Sibyl, even though she was married to a Patriot captain, often rode up from Union where she was helping her husband's parents in his absence, to spend time with her father, bringing the young grandchildren to play at their grandfather's feet. They would sit in the sun (which helped Tristrum's sores) and speak of the old days. He'd tell her about Wales and the tales of King Arthur and his Roundtable and knights and the quest for the Holy Grail and of the large circles of monoliths in Great Britain, erected by Merlin's magic. He no longer sang the old songs as his voice was feeble. He'd used up the last of his strength when he stood up for Abijah, who was an officer of the American Association and now settling his family on the five hundred acres the English granted him in New Brunswick. Tristrum noticed Sibyl was always knitting or sewing for the soldiers but he didn't mention that the new Union of 13 States had ordered every town to supply a certain amount of cloth or clothing articles for the Continental Army. Mary had told him the women in South Brimfield were meeting weekly at the Baptist parsonage to weave flax or cotton but she stayed away, a hermit now like Tristrum on their outlying farm. She, too, only wanted peace and quiet in her old age. They had felt all the fighting was finished in 1763 and never thought they'd see a civil war come to the lands near the great pond, now named Lake George, land the English had purchased with their blood from indians who, like the wolves, were now rarely seen on the lands they once dominated.

CHAPTER NINETY-ONE

Of Death and Birth

1777

News arrived almost daily during 1776 and into 1777 about new laws passed by the Provincial or Continental Congress and new Committees of Safety or other committees that were set up. Each colony was establishing its own constitution and one after another Tristrum's three youngest sons entered into the Massachusetts regiments to fight for the Continental Army under General Washington.

Samuel and William were sent west to New York to hold back a rumored push from the north down the Ohio by the British. Trustrum was also enlisted but he was sent to the north. Along with his brothers and Asa he wrote to Sibyl, who was now staying in the farmhouse with two daughters and three sons. They occupied the large upper room over the parlors and John and his family lived in the large room over the kitchen and dining room. Mary and Tristrum had converted the sitting room into their bedroom and the household used the formal front parlor as their sitting room. A loom took up one corner and in the kitchen/dining room there was a large walking wheel for the spinning of wool. The women worked non-stop to card, spin and weave, then sew or knit items for the soldiers.

Sibyl would read her husband and brothers' letters aloud to the people in the sitting room in the evenings while every female hand worked loom, spindle or needle. Tristrum and Mary could hear her through the fireplace that opened into both rooms.

"*We now have a Navy!*" Trustrum wrote, saying the Continental Congress had authorized the building of five ships," *and we are flying the flag of freedom: it is beautiful, sister. It has 13 red and white stripes – one for each colony or state as they are being called – and in the corner has the St. Andrew cross mixed with St. George's but I'm told a new one is being made that will have thirteen stars on a field of blue. I'm one of the sailors aboard the Andrea Doria and it's a beautiful armed brig. Our fleet has been meeting the British all up and down the coast and even to the northernmost West Indies. We took lots of British cannon and armaments in our battles but our ship took damage and is now in the shipyard of its birthplace, Gloucester, New Jersey. Our cousins to the north in Newbury and Rhode Island are busy building more ships and many of our cousin's ships in Maine have been commissioned to serve in our own Navy. Our Continental Congress has authorized us to take any British ships found off our shores but we have to impress men to serve onboard as they are afraid if the British capture them they will be hanged as pirates. Myself, I don't care, for if I can't live in a country that is free of tyranny I choose not to live at all! I've found a love of the sea that I never knew I would have – growing up on a farm and never even seeing the sea – but my cousins from the Cape who are also part of our Navy said sailing is in the blood of the Davis men. I wish I could talk to father about his ancestors as I've heard we had a very famous navigator in our past but I know from what you've written that he is bitter and refuses to talk much now. I'm truly sorry about that awful thing that they did to him but please let him know he's always in my thoughts. Please give my love to him and mother when you can.*

Your loving brother,

Trus"

In the back parlor Tristrum grumbled to Mary, "Aye a pitiful little Continental Navy against the mighty English Navy? They be fools, Mary. They cannot hope to win this war."

What no one but the inner circle of men in Philadelphia and Paris knew was that a secret treaty was being forged between France – which not only had a navy but many, many troops – and the new government. Had he known, Tristrum wouldn't have approved as he'd fought the French and couldn't conceive of them as allies.

****

In April, 1777 Tristrum came down with a high fever and was put in bed, out of his mind with delirium. His cousin, Dr. Isaac Davis of Somers and Enfield was immediately summoned.

The elderly Dr. Davis entered the bedroom and knew from the stench that there was probably gangrene in the sores that hadn't properly healed in Tristrum's legs since the tar and feathering.

Tristrum's eyes fluttered as Dr. Davis pulled back the quilt and started unwrapping the bandages from his lower legs.

"How long has he had these?" he asked Sibyl, who was helping him.

"They never went away these two years," she replied as they looked at the deep festering ulcers on his calves.

"These sores are badly infected," Isaac said as he noted there was no gangrene yet faint red lines indicating blood poisoning were streaking upwards. "The infection is spreading to his blood. I must apply the leeches and let some of the poisoned blood out of him. Are you squeamish?"

"No, I've nursed plenty of my children and men's wounds from accidents and burns," Sibyl replied, her expression firm, "I'm no stranger to the sickbed or blood."

As each leech was taken out of the jar and placed on Tristrum's sores they dug in and began feeding. By the next day they were engorged with dark blood. Dr. Davis had spent the night in order to monitor his patient. If the streaks worsened there would be nothing he could do.

Sibyl held the plain candles holder close as Dr. Davis inspected. He took long tweezers and removed each leech, putting it in an empty jar. The streaks had retreated. He then put fresh leeches on the sores and left a jar with more for Sibyl to apply every day until the pus receded.

Then Dr. Davis sat with Mary alone in the front room.

"He's out of danger for the moment, Mary, but if the sores don't heal soon his blood is going to become septic. You must give him lots of feverfew tea and put this ointment" he held up a jar of the juice from the boiled bark of willow tree and lard "on his sores and cover with clean cloth every day. The sores must be scraped clean every day and it will cause him a great deal of pain. Does he like brandy?"

Mary suppressed a laugh. Asa and her men all liked to drink. Were perhaps overfond of it.

"Aye, but it takes a fearful lot to get him unconscious."

Dr. Davis pulled a blue bottle out of his leather medical bag.

"I wouldn't normally offer this as it is imported and illegal, but this solution of laudanum made from poppies might help ease his pain. Give him a tablespoon a short while before you scrape and he might not be in as much pain. It will put him to sleep so his body can heal."

Mary looked at the bottle of white liquid. She didn't care if it were illegal as the whole boycott of British goods was illegal as far as she and Tristrum were concerned.

Dr. Davis then cleared his throat, "Does he have a will, Mary?"

Mary's eyes widened. A will meant death was near. She stammered, "Nay, doctor. His family are known for livin' hearty and hale into their nineties, even siring young in old age. We never thought – "

"I don't mean to alarm you," the doctor said as he latched his case and rose, "but for your own protection and that of your family, I suggest you get a lawyer in here and have him dictate his will."

Mary sent John to fetch a lawyer, telling him not to get the ones from Union that Tristrum had used in the past and had recommended to Abijah in his defense of his Mandamus Councillor appointment. They had turned on Abijah and had been responsible for the mob that marched him to Brimfield. She said Daniel Winchester in Brimfield, if he wasn't off with the troops, could be trusted.

A will was drawn up and, with the help of the leeches and the ointment, Tristrum's sores became less inflamed but were still deep and raw. He didn't leave his bed. His days were full of pain and even the slightest weight on his lower legs gave him pain. Many bottles of the white liquid came into the house via Dr. Davis over that summer and into the fall.

By early October the new general in charge in Quebec, Gen. John Burgoyne had gathered over 8,000 British Regulars, Hessians (Germans paid to be soldiers for the British), Brunswick Germans, Tories and Canadians and 400 Iroquois warriors at St. Johns and they went to Montreal, intending to move south and take the forts along the Ohio. To the south Gen. Howe was to advance north from Delaware but he led his fleet up and down the coast in an attempt to confuse Gen. Washington and didn't meet up with Burgoyne in time to deliver a pincher movement against the Continental Army.

The Northern, or New England Army was under the command of Gen. Philip Schuyler. Schuyler was an aristocratic Dutchman and he wasn't liked. There were constant desertions as the soldiers refused to be abused by his method of soldiering. When Gen. Burgoyne appeared with his troops outside Ticonderoga, having taken over the deserted Crown Point fort to use as a supply station and hospital, Schuyler led a retreat, sending the wounded and sick by boat down Wood Creek to Saratoga.

The British under Brig. Gen. Simon Fraser had pursued Schuyler's Army but Col. Seth Warner's company at the rear fought them off for hours before retreating to join Schuyler's hasty retreat that left Ft. Anne and even Ft. Edward deserted in its wake. The British would have overtaken them but Gen. Burgoyne halted to await arrival of his train with his wife, daughters and supplies.

He then kept marching south to Stillwater and the mouth of the Mohawk River towards Albany.

Gen. Washington had promoted Horatio Gates Brigadier General earlier in the year but the Continental Congress backed Schuyler as the commander of the northern army. In August Schuyler received word he had been replaced by Gates and the morale of the troops instantly improved. Gates was one of them: born to a servant on a tobacco plantation he had risen to own his own plantation in Virginia and had been elected as a representative of the people. He had served under Gen. Braddock in the last French and Indian war and was respected by the men.

In September Brigadier General John Stark's Continental troops surrounded the English troops near Bennington and had them at bay on the eastern side of the Hudson where they proceeded to hold them under siege.

In early October Burgoyne, not receiving aid from Howe, finally had to move. In the dark he moved his troops to the western shore of the Hudson and began advancing south again.

The troops under Gates had set up a line of defense at Bemis Heights next to the river. With the hill and steep riverbank they felt they could hold off the British from moving south. New York's British General Henry Clinton sent 7,000 men to take the forts to the south but Gates didn't retreat. His men were taking a stand above Freeman's Farm. In these troops were Samuel and William Davis, under regimental commander Brigadier General Ebenezer Learned from the Worcester area.

On October fourth Samuel received a letter from his mother telling him he and his brother must come right away as their father was close to death. It was with a heavy heart the two left their regiments to make the journey down river and overland to arrive in South Brimfield on October 7th.

Tristrum was passing in and out of consciousness, his blood filled with sepsis. He shook and sweated, hot and cold from fever.

"Has Trus been notified?" Samuel asked, shucking his crossed straps to let his pack fall in the hallway. Both men were in buff leather breeches with buff linen tops. Their calves were wrapped in canvas and both wore regimental medals in front of their hats. Their sisters and wives had sent clothing and stockings to them and even regimental great coats for the winter but they had traveled light for their seven day leave of absence.

"Nay, he is at sea," said Sibyl, "but Joseph is arriving soon. Sibyl sent word to Asa but it's harder for officers to get leave and he isn't a blood relative. Joseph's brother-in-law Capt. Joe Browning has gotten away and he's in with him."

The sons went into the darkened sitting room turned sickroom and knelt by the side of their father's bed. The stench from his infected sores was stifling in the Indian summer heat.

The house was quiet except for the ticking of the grandfather's clock in the parlor. Benjamin had almost immediately reverted to the Continental Army and been forgiven for his youthful brashness in thinking he would join the British in New York. He was between service, having come home with others to help with the harvests on their farms. He arrived with his wife Mary, a Rutherford. His sister Elizabeth was there but her husband Fenton was away in service.

Benjamin put his face close to his father's wet one and whispered, "I'm so sorry, father. That night I should have fought them off – "

Samuel pulled him back.

"You aren't the only one sorry for that terrible thing, my brother. Not a day goes by but Will and I remember with shame that mob and what they did to our father." He stopped suddenly as he'd almost admitted the secret shame they were in the mob and hadn't come to their father's defense.

Tristrum's neighbor Reuben Townsley suddenly came into the bedroom. He and Sarah had built a small farmhouse on the road that lead to Holland, uphill and adjacent to the Davis farm.

"Am I too late?" the scruffy-bearded wild ape-like form croaked.

"Nay. He's rattling, though," said William, referring to the final breathing of the dying.

Reuben was crying. He grabbed Tristrum's hand and squeezed.

Tristrum opened his eyes, no longer a nice bright blue but a cloudy, whitish blue.

"Is that you, Reub?"

"Aye, my friend."

Tristrum saw Mary and she took his other hand.

"I'm sorry … been … burden to ye," he said softly, his breath faint.

Mary smoothed back his hair and kissed his forehead, burning with fever.

"Ye did yer best, Trus, which is all we can do in this life. Ye gave livin' yer all. In spite of your crustiness we all love ye."

Tristrum's lips were cracked. They bled when he tried to smile.

He closed his eyes and soon his breath, and the clock's hand in the parlor were stopped.

****

Samuel and William returned to New York and were there when Gen. Burgoyne surrendered in Saratoga. The Continental Congress refused to return the almost 6,000 British POWs by ship to England but instead sent them south to sit out the war in a concentration camp in Virginia as they felt they would just be re-deployed against the Continental Army after reaching England.

In Pennsylvania Gen. Washington's men fought bravely at Brandywine Creek and Germantown but were forced to retreat across the Delaware to spend a cold, miserable winter at Valley Forge as the British officers partied in Philadelphia. It was the dark before the dawn and in the following year the Continental Army with the help of the French had victory after victory and drove the English out of the United Colonies of America.

As Tristrum lay dying a new country was being born.

Within four years the British had formally surrendered and a new Constitution and Bill of Rights were being drafted and circulated to govern the new country. The soldiers returned to the ponds and peace once again settled over the forests and fields that had been fertilized with so much human blood over the years as tribe fought tribe, then tribes fought the English settlers and the settlers fought France then Great Britain to call these lands their own.

Above the Great Pond, now called Lake George, the sun rose and set, the birds flew, the seasons came and went. Only the two leggeds who lived around it knew the land around it changed from a Nipmuck name to English names then finally was called Wales.*

Tristrum would have liked that.

THE END

**Not after the country of Wales but after Oliver Wales who gave the town a lot of money in the 1800s. Tristrum's section was called Shawville and the town named Clinton after it changed from South Brimfield. The story of the New England mill heyday and Civil War will be told in another book, probably by another author.*

BIBLIOGRAPHY

This book was researched and written over a period of many, many years and I might have left out a couple of sources but the following list is an approximate listing of books I found helpful in part or whole in my research:

A History of Wales, John Davies

Story of the Irish Race, Seamus MacManus

The History of Scotland, Plantagenet and Fiona Somerset Fry

Scottish Highlanders, Charles MacKinnon

The Secret Country, Janet and Colin Bord

The Welsh Learner's Dictionary, Heini Gruffudd

Scottish Clans and Tartans, Ian Grimble

The Quest for Arthur's Britain, Geoffrey Ashe

The Discovery of King Arthur, Geoffrey Ashe

An Etymological Dictionary of Family and Christian Names, William Arthur

Le Morte d'Arthur, Sir Thomas Malory

From Columbus to Castro, Eric Williams

A Brief History of the Caribbean, Jan Rogozinaki

A Topographicall Description and Admeasurement of Yland of Barbados in the West Indies, R. Ligon

The Thirty Years War, C.V. Wedgwood

The Making of England: to 1399, Hollister, Stacey, Stacey

This Realm of England 1399-1688, Lacey Baldwin Smith

The Plantagenets, Dan Jones

The Awakening of Europe, M.B. Synge

Westward Ho!, Charles Kingsley

The Century of Revolution 1603-1714, Christopher Hill

The Age of Revolution, Winston S. Churchill

The Age of Absolutism 1660-1815, Max Beloff

The Lives of the Kings and Queens of England, Antonia Fraser, editor

Royal Panoply, Carolly Erickson

Queen Elizabeth I, J. E. Neale
Charles II, Ronald Hutton
The Age of George III, R. J. White
Albion's Seed, David Hackett Fischer
Cromwell, Antonia Fraser
Debrett's Peerage of England, Scotland and Ireland, John Debrett
A History of England, Goldwin Smith
Palaces, Masterpieces of Architecture, Laura Brooks
Village Walks in Britain,Ordnance Survey
Abbeys of Europe, I. Richards
Village England, Peter Crookston, Editor
A History of Lincolnshire, Steward Bennett
A History of Somerset, R. W. Dunning
Wiltshire, Ralph Whitlock
Britain and Her People, Antony Kamm
Europe, Norman Davies
Treasures of Britain, W.W. Norton
Oxford Dictionary of British History, John Cannon, editor
A Shortened History of England, G. M; Trevelyan
The Dictionary of World History, Chambers
Encyclopedia of World History, 6th Edition, Peter N. Stearns, editor
The Timetables of History , Bernard Grun
The Rise of the West, William H. McNeill
Wonders of the World, Godhill, Rabb, Glancy
Handicrafts of the Sea, Steven Bailes
The Map Thief, Michael Blanding
Exploring Britain, Fodor's
Encyclopedia of American History, Richard B. Morris
The Oxford History of the American People, Samuel Eliot Morison
The European Discovery of America, Southern Voyages 1492-1616, Samuel Eliot Morison
The European Discovery of America, The Northern Voyages, Samuel Eliot Morison

The Story of Mt. Desert Island, Samuel Eliot Morison

Life, Liberty and the Pursuit of Land, Daniel M. Friedenberg

British Committees, Commissions Councils of Trade and Plantations, 1622-1675, Charles M. Andrews

Ship Passenger Lists National and New England 1600-1825, Carl Boyer 3rd

The Story of the Old Colony of New Plymouth, Samuel Eliot Morison

Mayflower, Nathaniel Philbrick

Dorset Pilgrims, Frank Thistlewiaite

Fire From Heaven, David Underdown

The Pilgrim Story, William Atwood

New England Bound, Wendy Warren

Founding the American Colonies, 1583-1660

Winthrop Fleet of 1630, Charles Edward Banks

The Journal of John Winthrop 1630-1649, Dunn and Yendle, editors

Puritans, Indians and Manifest Destiny, Charles M. Segal and David C. Stineback

The Puritan Oligarchy, Thomas Jefferson Wertenbaker

The American Colonies 1492-1750, Marcus Wilson Jernegan

The Mary and John, the Founding of Dorchester, Maude Pinnry Kuhn

Mayflower and Jamestown (several articles), National Geographic Magazine

Builders of the Bay, Samuel Eliot Morison

From Puritan to Yankee, Richard L. Bushman

A New England Town, the First Hundred Years,Kenneth A. Lockridge

The First Frontier, Life in Colonial America, John C. Miller

The Bay Path and Along the Way, Levi Chase

King Philip's War, George Madison Budge,

Flintlock and Tomahawk, New England in King Philip's War, Douglas Edward Leach

Everyday Life in Early America, David Freeman Hawke

Changes in the Land, William Crondon

Everyday Dress 1675-1800, Elizabeth Ewing

The Keyes of the Kingdom of Heaven, and the

Power Thereof, According to the Word of God, Mr. John Cotton

Peaceable Kingdoms, New England Towns in the Eighteenth Century, Michael Zuckerman

The Founding of New England, James Truslow Adams

Puritans and Pragmatists, Paul K. Conklin

Mysticism, Bruno Borchert

Book of the Witches, Samuel Drake

The Pilgrim's Progress, John Bunyan

Narratives of the New England Witchcraft Cases, George Lincoln Burr, editor

Soul Liberty, the Baptists' Struggle in New England 1650-1833, William G. McLoughin

Jonathan Edwards, Pastor, Patricia J. Tracy

The Challenge of Change, Three Centuries of Enfield, Ct., Ruth Bridge, editor

Massachusetts, A Federal Writer's Project, 1937, Houghton Mifflin

A Survey of Maine, Moses Greenleaf

Maine Beautiful, Wallace Nuting

The History of Maine from the Earliest Discovery of the Region by

the Northmen Until the Present Time, John C. Abbott, 1805-77

Possessing Albany 1630-1710, Donna Merwick

Early American Inns and Taverns, Elise Lathrop

Old Boston in Colonial Days, Mary Caroline Crawford

Coaching Roads of Old New England, George Francis Marlowe

A Genealogical Dictionary of the First Settlers of New England, (4 Volumes), James Savage

A Compendium of the History, Genealogy and Biography of the Town of Wales

And its principal Families and individual Inhabitants, Absalom Gardiner

Commonwealth History of Massachusetts (Vol-1-5), Abert Bushnell Hart, editor

Journals of House of Representatives, (Vol 4) 1722-23, Mass. Historical Society

Springfield 1636-1986, Michael E. King, editor

Invasion of America, Indians, Colonialism and the Cant of Conquest, Francis Jennings

The Conspiracy of Pontiac, Frances Parkman

The Ambiguous Iroquois Empire, Francis Jennings

Samuel de Champlain, Father of New France, Samuel Eliot Morison

Nova Scotia, Lesley Choyce

True Stories of New England Captives, C. Alice Barker

Quaboag Plantation alias Brookfield, Louis E. Roy, M.D.

The Unredeemed Captive,, John Demos

One Told Tales of Worcester County, Albert Southwick

The French and Indian War 1754-1763, Seymour I. Schwartz

Five Years French and Indian War, Samuel G. Drake

Biography and History of the Indians of North America, Samuel Drake

Dawnland Encounters, Colin G. Calloway

French and Indian Wars in Maine, Michael Dekker

A People's Army, Massachusetts Soldiers and Society in the Seven Years War, Fred Anderson

Massachusetts Officers and Soldiers in the French and Indian Wars 1755-1756

K. David Goss and David Zarowin, editors

Montcalm and Wolfe the French and Indian War, Francis Parkman

Of the People to 1877, Oxford History Series

The Glorious Cause, Robert Middlekauff

Almost a Miracle, The American Victory in the War of Indpendence, John Ferling

A People's History of the American Revolution, Ray Ralphael

Patriots, A. J. Langguth

Wages of War, Richard Severo and Lewis Milford

The Last American Freeman, Robert M. Weir

Ethan Allen, Willard Stern Randall

Fabric of Freedom 1763-1800, Esmond Wright

The Birth of the United States, Jim Bishop

The Old United Empire Loyalists List, 1885 Rose Publishing

Founding Father, Richard Brookhiser
The First Salute, Barbara W. Tuchman

Internet sources:
Ancestry.com
Geni.com
Wikipedia.com
Davis Family history, Somers, Ct.
Old Kittery, her Families

From Archive.org: or JSTOR:
A History of Rehobeth
Annals of Witchcraft
History of Barnstable
History of Hadley
History of Haverhll
Historoy of Ipswich
History of Newbury
History of Northampton
History of Rowley
History of Roxbury
History of Woburn
History of Enfield, Ct

ABOUT THE AUTHOR

Kelly Savage grew up in the town of Wales, Massachusetts in the farmhouse Capt. Tristrum Davis built. She currently lives in the desert in Arizona in a house she built herself. She has published a series of five 'Emerald' books and *The Pond Dwellers.*

Contact: DesertLion@Duck.com

www.ingramcontent.com/pod-product-compliance
Lightning Source LLC
Chambersburg PA
CBHW060526310726
48982CB00002B/447
9798988688822